BLACK COAST

First published 2021 by Solaris
an imprint of Rebellion Publishing Ltd,
Riverside House, Osney Mead,
Oxford, OX2 0ES, UK

www.solarisbooks.com

ISBN: 978 1 78108 824 1

A CIP catalogue record for this book is available
from the British Library.

Map by Gemma Sheldrake/Rebellion Publishing
Cover art by Head Design
Designed & typeset by Rebellion Publishing

Printed in the US

THE
BLACK
COAST

MIKE BROOKS

SOLARIS

KIBU
THE

SUNDAI
RIVER
○ 19

CATSEYE
MOUNTAINS

○ 18

THE
HUDANAR

○ 17

○ 21

LAKE
WOUSOULD
○ 16

○ 20

GREEN
ISLAND

GREAT
BOW RIVER

13   14

○ 15

10   ○ 9
RIVER
12 ■   IDRA
8

CROWN
ISLAND

7

6
4   5
3
2
1

MOUNTAIN   ○ SETTLEMENT   ～ MARSH   BROADLEAVED   RAINFOREST
                                      FOREST

～ HILLS   ■ CAPITAL   PINE   MANGROVE
                       FOREST

1. BLACK KEEP
2. IRONHEAD
3. SMOKING VALLEY
4. DARKSPUR
5. TAINMAR
6. BRIGHTWATER
7. WAYMEET
8. IDRAMAR

9. NORTHBANK
10. GREENBROOK
11. TORGALLEN
12. TORGALLEN PASS
    (TO MORLITH)
13. GODSPIRE
14. SACRED
    MONASTERY

15. BOWMAR
16. WOUSOULD
    HASTE
17. HIGHBRIDGE
18. WHITTING MOOR
19. NORTH MARCH
20. NEW BAYCLIFFE
21. EMERALD BAY

22. EAST HARBOUR
23. WEST HARBOUR
24. KOSZAL
25. TORAKUDO

I don't know exactly who this book is for,
but whoever it is, I hope they find it.

PROLOGUE: TILA

THE SUN PALACE, atop its mighty sandstone plateau, was the jewel of the city of Idramar. It blended beauty with fearsome defensive architecture, and had stood as the symbol of Narida's unquestioned power since the God-King Nari rose from obscurity to conquer the lands between the Catseye Mountains and the ocean. From the mighty Eight Winds Tower of the central stronghouse the current God-King could look east across the waves that lapped at his city's shore, follow the great River Idra west towards the Catseyes, hundreds of miles distant, or gaze north or south across the wide floodplain and its fertile fields.

Unfortunately the current God-King was doing no such thing, and Tila could feel one of her headaches coming on.

"Where is he?" she demanded. The servant, a scar-faced pox survivor, bowed and began to stammer a reply. Tila slapped him, and grabbed his tunic to haul him in front of her black veil.

"Let this princess make something clear," she growled. "She knows His Divine Majesty likes to disappear and keep his *advisors*"—the word got mangled as it passed her teeth—"unaware of his whereabouts, but she will find him eventually. You can either tell her where he went, or she can put you through that window and do this the hard way. *Where is he?*"

"The Oak Avenue, Your Highness!"

"A thinker." Tila snorted. "How remarkable. Congratulations on choosing to see another meal." She released the servant, wiping her hand on her dress and ignoring his miserable bow. She never exactly set out to mistreat the staff, but she always had so much to do—or at least, there was always much *that needed doing*—and they inevitably slowed things down.

She did indeed find Natan, God-King of Narida, on a bench catching the winter sun slipping through the bare branches of the oaks lining one of the private avenues within the Sun Palace. He was enjoying a goblet of wine from his northern vineyards, and he was not alone.

Tila didn't know his companion's name, but the youth was a dragon groom; a strapping fellow, whose clothes did little to disguise his well-formed limbs. Such vigour was hardly surprising, since a groom had to be both strong and quick on his feet. Even the most amiable beast could accidentally crush a man too slow to dodge a swinging tail.

Any other member of the Inner Council might have awkwardly cleared their throat, or made some other discreet announcement of their presence. Tila didn't bother with such niceties: she marched up to the groom and tapped him on the shoulder, causing him to hurriedly disengage his mouth from that of the God-King.

"You," Tila snapped, clicking her fingers. "Leave. Now." She eyed his half-unfastened tunic. Idramar had mild winters, but even so... "And cover yourself."

The poor youth glanced desperately at the God-King, back at her, and hared off through the trees, presumably towards his duties. Tila folded her arms and shook her head at her monarch.

"Are you happy?"

"His Divine Majesty *was* happy," her older brother replied sourly. "We need to talk about your propensity to interrupt his intimate moments."

"Do not take that form of address with your sister," Tila snapped. "And kissing a groom *here* is not 'intimate'."

Natan looked around ostentatiously. The royal guard stood in pairs some distance away, to intercept anyone intruding on their ruler… so long as that intruder wasn't Princess Tila Narida, since they weren't fools. Otherwise, there was no one to be seen.

"Besides, that is not the point," Tila continued. "It is unseemly for you to consort with such a lowborn man."

"And what do you know of his parentage?" Natan demanded, sipping his wine.

"It is clearly low enough for the stables!" Tila snapped.

"Your brother fails to see how it matters," Natan said, running a hand through his hair, which was starting to thin very slightly on top. Not from stress, Tila doubted. Natan Narida would reach forty summers this year, and she could count the number of difficult decisions he'd made on both hands with digits to spare. "We are Nari's blood. *Everyone* is lowborn, compared to us. It is just a matter of scale." He looked at her, eyes suddenly sharp. "This is presumably some prelude to trying to make your brother court a woman, is it not?"

"No," Tila said tiredly. She sat down next to him, in defiance of all convention that one should wait for the Light of Heaven's permission. "Or at least, not a specific woman. Quite frankly, anyone would do."

"You would be happy for the God-King to court a lowborn *woman*, then?" Natan asked in mock surprise.

"You need an heir," Tila said bluntly.

"Oh Nari's teeth, not *this* again."

"You *need* an *heir*," Tila repeated, even more firmly. "Preferably more than one, as well you know."

"Your brother does keep fucking the men, but so far they have stubbornly refused to get with child," Natan said, swirling his wine. "He supposes he will just have to try harder."

"Would it kill you to pick a highborn woman, marry her, fuck her until her belly swells, then go back to your men?" Tila asked bitterly.

11

"Tila, your brother would not have the faintest idea what to do with a woman. He understands the theory, but could never bring himself to enact it."

Tila closed her eyes and scrubbed her forehead with her hand. "Your sister cannot believe she is having this conversation with you, but Nari knows no one else will. What about if you were blindfolded? If you were only aware of the other person through touch, then—"

"Your brother is not some stud dragon for you to breed a prize calf from!" Natan snapped, hurling his goblet away. "He refuses to be held hostage to your notions of what he should be doing with his cock!"

"It's not about your cock," Tila said with a shudder, "it's about the future of the nation! An unbroken line of *male* succession, may Nari help us all. Woe betide Narida if it suffers another Splintering!"

Natan rubbed at his right eye. "Tila, you know your brother would give up the throne to you in an instant."

"Your sister knows," she replied, trying to keep frustration out of her voice now he was at least attempting to be reasonable. "Although she thinks you underestimate how different your life would be, once you were no longer God-King. But that aside, it cannot happen, so there is no point speculating. The thanes would rebel against a woman's rule in a moment."

"You cannot *know* it would lead to another Splintering," her brother said, and Tila sighed. No matter how many times they had this conversation, he never seemed to fully accept the truth.

"Yes, your sister can," she told him bluntly. "And that, incidentally, is why she came to find you. You missed another Council meeting."

"Resentful, power-hungry people your brother cannot stand, discussing things about which he has no interest," her brother muttered. "And you, of course."

Tila gritted her teeth. "So dismiss them, and choose others whom you like better, so long as they are competent. Your sister would not miss any of the current council on a personal level."

Natan waved one hand gloomily. "It would cause too much trouble."

Very briefly, Tila contemplated whether she would rather be remembered chiefly for regicide or for fratricide.

"More trouble than letting them run the country without you?" she said instead. "No, do not answer that. Your sister will just keep trying to control them in your name, and hope their respect for our bloodline wins out." She took a deep breath. "But she needs your approval for something."

"We both know you are a better ruler than your brother anyway," Natan said. "Write the decree, and he will sign it."

"No," Tila said patiently. "This will not be written down. But your sister will not do this without your approval."

Her brother's thick brows narrowed suspiciously. "Go on."

"The Council wants to move against the Splinter King again."

Natan's face hardened. "Remind your brother how many times assassins have been sent after that family, within our lifetimes?"

"Three times," Tila replied neutrally. She didn't need to. Her brother might be self-absorbed and uninterested in affairs of state, but he remembered these particular details.

"And how much success have we had?"

"The family is still there," Tila admitted. "When we were children, our agents were intercepted before they could even make the attempt. Father tried sending agents again a few years later, during a festival, but the guards stopped them."

"Alaban fighters are particularly deadly, your brother hears," Natan commented. Tila raised her eyebrows in surprise: she honestly hadn't expected him to know that.

"They can be," she acknowledged. "In single combat, at any rate."

"So you are suggesting we send sars on dragons?" Natan asked. "That is not in keeping with your usual preference for subtlety, Tila."

She snorted. "As entertaining as the notion is, no. The third time an attempt was made, shortly after Father's death, we had slightly more success. Archers killed the eldest male child, but both parents and the two younger children survived. The ruling Hierarchs take the safety of their poor foreign pets seriously, and limit opportunities for them to be seen in public."

"It all sounds impossible," Natan muttered. "Impossible, cruel and pointless."

"All the attempts so far have been made on the family when they appeared in public," Tila told him. "Yet most of the time, they are unseen. They live another life, unmasked, away from public view."

Natan frowned. "And guarded, your brother would have thought."

"Of course," Tila agreed. "But less so, to avoid attention. Day to day, their safety relies on being seen as nothing more than a wealthy family of a minor Naridan bloodline."

Natan's eyes narrowed. "You are not speaking speculatively, are you?"

Tila smiled tightly behind her veil. "Your sister is not."

"You know the family?"

"Yes." She still carried a faint shadow of the excitement she'd felt when she'd read the final pieces of the puzzle from her agents, and drawn her conclusions.

Natan rubbed his chin. "How? It is a foreign city that knows we have tried to kill them... however many times, over the last few centuries. Your brother knows you are clever, Tila, but how have you managed this when no one else has?"

"No one else asked the right questions," Tila told him simply. "They only thought of the Splinter King as a silver-masked imposter appearing in public, when he was an obvious target. They never asked where he was the rest of the time."

"It appears His Divine Majesty's low opinion of his Council is not inaccurate," Natan muttered.

"This took your sister ten years!" Tila snapped, angry at having the success of her hard work dismissed as simply due to the incompetence of others. And Nari knew, there had been incompetence, but that didn't diminish her achievements! "*Ten years*, Natan! Your sister infiltrated the City of Islands' society with her own agents and, more importantly, with locals who have no idea the people they take money from for tasks or information take *their* pay from her! She knows that city very nearly as well as she knows our own!"

"Forgive your brother," Natan said, scrubbing at his face to hide what might have been embarrassment. "He did not mean to demean your work. He had no idea... Ten years?"

Tila sighed. "Ten years. Your sister did not tell you, as she knew you would not be interested." She snorted a laugh. "And after all of it, one man was the breakthrough. A former servant with a fondness for drink, and not enough money to buy his own. His drunken speculation might have gone unremarked in a city where gossip is rife, but one of your sister's agents heard him, and provided further lubrication to his tongue. Not enough to be certain on its own merit, but when combined with what we already knew..."

Her brother actually had the decency to look impressed. "And would you make their deaths look accidental?"

"An extravagance we cannot afford," Tila said firmly. "We will get one opportunity at this. Once the Hierarchs realise we have discovered the family's identity, they will have no option but to guard their pets closely at all times, whatever the cost."

"So it is perhaps not impossible," Natan acknowledged reluctantly. "Your brother still feels it is cruel and pointless."

"The older child, the male heir," Tila said, deliberately avoiding looking at him, "has reached the age of majority. Hence the need to try again."

Natan tapped his chin with a finger. "What if your brother were to adopt?"

Tila gave him the sort of look she usually reserved for impertinent servants. "What?"

"Your shadows can place a knife in any city in the known world, given enough time," Natan pointed out. "Surely they could find a suitable candidate to become your brother's heir?"

"We are the divine blood of the God-King!" Tila hissed at him. "Our family, alone in all of Narida, *must* continue by blood inheritance! The people will accept nothing less!"

"Your brother is the divine blood of the God-King, and we both know he is not a good ruler," Natan argued. "The people would not know if any heir of your brother's was *truly* his blood, in any case. They'd know what they were told. Find a young, sensible, intelligent man. Say, sixteen years or so; of an age where we could claim he was your brother's bastard, fathered by laying with a woman in the depths of his low mood following Father's death. An orphan would be ideal. Your brother can adopt and legitimise him, and you can teach him to run this country well. Once he is ready, your brother can abdicate, and you can worry less."

"We cannot risk it," Tila told him. "There are rumours that Nari Himself has been reborn. The foolish mutterings of country folk, undoubtedly, but even so—"

"If Nari Himself *has* been reborn, as prophesied, your brother's rule is invalid anyway, doubly so the Splinter King," Natan said lazily. "Not to mention that we'll have bigger problems: the sun going out, dragons ravaging the land, and the ocean rising to swallow us all."

"This is no laughing matter!" Tila hissed.

"Who's laughing?" Natan responded, more sharply than she'd expected. "Tila, you have raged since we were children against the rules that bind us. *Let us break them.* Who is to say your brother's blood-son would be any better at ruling than he is? You won't live to guide Narida forever. Choose a competent heir, and we need not worry about the scions of our great-great-great-great-uncle, thousands of miles away in Kiburu ce Alaba."

Her brother was actually making sense, which was enough to

make Tila consider his words carefully. She also couldn't deny the transgressive appeal of subverting the system that had held her back all her life. Even so, she'd always been cautious.

Well, apart from that one time. But she'd been wallowing in self-destructive grief, and it hadn't turned out too badly. In the end.

"It could be done," she said slowly. "But some nobles may suspect the ruse, and view the Splinter King as a viable alternative. Narida's future is still at risk while that family lives."

"They must be almost pure Alaban by now," Natan objected.

"Even so."

Natan slumped back on the bench. "This, then, is the choice you are giving your brother? Your king? Marry a woman and father children, or send assassins after distant relatives, despite all previous attempts having failed?"

"Your sister would prefer you did both," Tila admitted. "But, yes."

"Fine." The God-King buried his head in his hands. "Go find your knife-men."

PART ONE

SOME MAY QUESTION *whether Narida is indeed the centre of civilisation, as our scholars claimed in the days of Divine Nari. Arguments rage over whether the great buildings in Kiburu ce Alaba, the City of Islands, are more impressive structurally than the Sun Palace; or if the Morlithians' ability to channel and harness their limited water to green the desert and grow crops makes them somehow more capable than our own farmers.*

These arguments, while of interest to the scholars of those disciplines, are of no great importance. What truly sets Narida above foreign lands is our sense of self and, critically, our society.

Traders or diplomats who communicate in other tongues are always struck by their shocking looseness and laziness, in comparison to Naridan. Other languages refer to the self with no information about the speaker's societal position, or how they perceive themselves in relation to the listener! A Naridan abroad, speaking a foreign tongue, finds himself unable to easily indicate his social standing, or have any idea whether the person to whom he talks addresses him as equal, superior, or inferior.

This lack of morality is not limited to rank. In Alaba, for example, even the simplest social structures are ignored. Alabans claim that concepts of 'man' and 'woman' do not apply, and insist they have either five or six genders, depending on how they are counted, between which these heathens will move depending on their whims. As a tonal language, the same sound with different inflections carries different meanings, so a Naridan must be very careful to avoid misrepresenting himself: for example, '*mè*' is '*high masculine*', used by those in whom the fire of manhood burns strongly, while '*mê*' is '*low masculine*', for in Alaban society it is no great shame for a man to admit to womanly character. The largely uninflected '*me*' is the gender-neutral formal, but '*mé*' is '*low feminine*', favoured by women who lack the qualities appropriate for their gender, and '*mē*' is '*high feminine*', the only appropriate usage for any Naridan lady of decency. Even stranger is '*më*', used only by those who insist they have no gender, even in the most informal settings. Such immorality is hardly unsurprising in a land that has provided succour to exiled pretenders since the Splintering.

Needless to say, Naridans should resist these pernicious local customs and only use the '*high*' forms for themselves when visiting this land, lest they cause themselves considerable embarrassment.

As for the wild Raiders from across the sea, we know nothing of their society—aside from the fact that both their men and women fall upon our coast each year, bringing death and misery...

Extract from '*On The Self*' by Yaro of Idramar, written in the six-hundred-and-seventy-fourth year of the God-King

DAIMON

"RAIDERS! RAIDERS!"

The cry jumped from throat to throat, spreading like one of the devastating Upwoods fires that swept through the pine forests in late summer. The bronze bell in Nari's shrine was tolling a warning even before the first panicking fishermen were seen steering their skiffs back upriver, chased from the sea by their ancestral enemies.

"How many?" Daimon Blackcreek shouted, hurrying up the stone steps that led to the narrow rampart of the castle walls. He was already doing the numbers of battle in his head, and finding them unfavourable. It was still winter! The Festival of Life wasn't for another two weeks! Besides, the Raiders hadn't bothered attacking Black Keep for a decade, always going further north along the Black Coast for richer targets, so his father Asrel had neglected to hire any Brotherhood mercenaries for the last three years. But the accursed demon-worshippers never raided this early...

Daimon had trained with weapons since he'd been five summers old, but he was only two-and-twenty, and the Raiders had never struck since he'd been of an age to face them in battle. He'd hoped that should the day come, he would be filled with the courage and martial vigour that would befit a sar of Narida.

Based on how his stomach was churning and the cold sweat that was prickling beneath his clothes, it seemed unlikely that was going to be the case.

"How many?" he demanded again, reaching the top. Two worried faces looked around at him; Rotel and Ganalel, members of his father's household guard, but not men he'd ever have considered soldiers.

"L-Lord?" Ganalel stammered nervously. He was an older man, with grey strands liberally sprinkled through his dark hair, and his teeth stained brown from the leaf the lowborn chewed.

"Tell me, boy," Daimon's father's voice instructed, and Daimon turned to see Lord Asrel Blackcreek climbing the steps to join him. His law-father was shorter than him, as indeed was his older brother Darel, and the hair forming their warrior's braids was an almost pure black. Daimon's height and the reddish tinge of his own hair marked him as the adopted law-son that he was.

"How many ships?" Asrel snapped, shoving him aside to get a better view. It wouldn't benefit him much: Lord Asrel's eyes had never been the keenest, and now he was past his fortieth year they seemed to struggle with distances more and more. Daimon turned to the ocean to see for himself and save his father the shame of admitting in front of his own men that he couldn't make out the details.

What he saw dotting the waves of the ocean turned his bowels to water.

"Seventeen," he croaked, barely managing to prevent his voice from failing and unmanning him.

"*Seventeen?*" His law-father's shock was understandable. The Raiders' strange, double-hulled ships usually came in twos or threes, or sometimes as just one. Daimon had heard of a four-boat raid further up the coast once, nigh on a hundred screaming milk-faces descending with fire and their crude yet deadly blackstone weapons, but that had been an anomaly. The numbers of battle clicking through his head came to a standstill: Black

Keep would be overwhelmed, overrun in short order. There were almost certainly more Raiders on those ships than there were people in the entirety of Black Keep town, and very few aside from Daimon, Darel and their father had any skill in battle.

"Find Malakel and open the armoury," Asrel snapped at the two guards. "Arm anyone who can carry a weapon. Go!"

The pair bolted away to do their lord's bidding, leaving the two Blackcreek men alone.

"Even the women and children, Father?" Daimon said, startled despite himself. The Code of Honour, to which his father absolutely deferred, stated that battle was a man's pursuit.

"We are not sending a levy to the Southern Marshal's forces, Daimon," Asrel said bluntly. "All we need them to do is stand on the walls and try to look like men, and hope the Raiders lack the spine to press an attack."

Daimon looked to their left, towards the town. The walls were high and strong enough around the castle Asrel's great-grandfather had built on and in a curve of the Blackcreek River, using its waters as moats. The town's walls had always been of poorer craftsmanship, however, and the last few years had not been kind to them. The ramparts had crumbled here and there, leaving the footing atop the wall unsafe, and in one place the wall had half-tumbled down, leaving that point an obvious one to attack.

"Do you think it will work?" he asked dubiously.

Asrel looked at the sun, dipping in the northern sky but still well clear of the Catseye Mountains to the west. "Your father doubts it," he admitted heavily. "Were it approaching nightfall we could bluff them, perhaps, by the time they reached us. We could give each peasant a torch and have them walk the walls, and we would seem well guarded. In daylight they'll see we've no strength here, but what other option do we have? Our war dragons still slumber, and Tavi would need time to prepare the charms of waking. The three of us alone could not hold back even one ship's worth of this vermin in the field. Our only hope is to feign strength of numbers and give the bastards pause, at least."

"Then send Darel away," Daimon urged. "Have him go north to seek aid."

Asrel snorted. "From the woodcutters? It is a week to Darkspur, and Thane Odem holds no love for us, as well you know."

"Lenby, then?" Daimon suggested desperately. He couldn't bear the thought of his brother falling to the Raiders' blackstone axes.

"Lenby is still three days away," Lord Asrel said dismissively. "Sar Elzur and his men would answer our call, yes, but not in time. Besides, the demon-worshippers will surely head north next, because they'll find little enough here. Elzur would achieve nothing other than leaving his home undefended."

"Father," Daimon tried again, "Darel is your heir."

Asrel shook his head. "You know better, Daimon. Darel is heir only by the leave of the Marshal, and any thane's son who breaks his vow to defend his people will never inherit. Your father would be sending him into a life of shame, for no purpose."

"He would be alive," Daimon replied quietly, but he had overstepped his bounds, for his law-father's eyes flashed angrily and the familiar fires of his temper rose to the surface.

"Darel understands duty as you understand swordplay," Asrel bit out. "Would that each of you were the other's match!"

Daimon lowered his head, but the rebuke lashed at him nonetheless. The plague of twenty years ago that had swept across Narida had been triggered by Heaven's upheaval at the violent death of the old God-King, according to the priests. It had taken not only Daimon's family but many others in the town, and also his law-father's wife, Lady Delil. Lord Asrel had adopted Daimon as an orphan, but it was not merely pity that had moved the Thane of Black Keep to such an action: he had wanted a second heir besides Darel, to guard against any other tragedies that might break the line of Blackcreek once and for all. Daimon had spent all of his life that he could remember trying to live up to his law-father's decision, and prove himself worthy of the honour that had been bestowed upon him, coming from peasant blood as he did. To know that Lord Asrel still found him lacking cut deeper than any injury he'd taken on the sparring ground, or in falling from a dragon.

Lord Asrel's mouth tightened as soon as the words had left his lips, and for a moment Daimon thought he caught a trace of regret, but his law-father did not take back what he'd said. After all, the Code of Honour required a sar or a thane to consider his words before speaking, and to apologise suggested that this had not been done.

"Enough," Lord Asrel said, his voice clipped and emotionless. "Haul your brother's nose out of whatever book he's studying. Osred will have heard the bells and will be readying our armour. We can make these bastards pay a price of blood, at the least. If this thane is to die on a Raider's weapon today," he declared bitterly, "then he will die dressed for war."

"Your servant obeys," Daimon replied, bowing too low and turning to leave. It was petty of him, to take the obeisance and form of address of a servant instead of a son, but his father did not call him back as he hurried down the steps to find Darel.

As he ran, he tried to puzzle out how their doom would come to them. Would the Raiders land downstream and circumnavigate the walls to attack the Road Gate, on the west side? Would they sail past the castle walls to try the River Gate, braving the arrows the defenders could send into the channel? Or would they just slog through the marsh to attack the walls from the east, trusting to weight of numbers and the defences' disrepair to carry the day?

He realised, with a leaden sense of dread, that it barely mattered. If his count was true, their enemy would have enough warriors to attempt all three at once.

SAANA

SAANA SATTISTUTAR HAD watched from the *Krayk's Teeth* as the smudge of coastline grew steadily, and she could now distinguish the black mud of the beaches from the green flats of the marsh. These turned into fields, then into the dark trees of forest to the north, and west towards the distant mountains. The coast was strange, compared to the stony shores she'd left behind: the land was more open, flatter, and far, far bigger. Even the mountains looked different, more angular and possibly even higher than the smoking peak above her home in Koszal.

No. Not her home anymore.

A headland jutted into the sea, the northern edge of moorlands that ran south towards the great ice ocean. The outcrop would have looked pitiful next to the cliffs where she'd raided nests as a child, but it loomed over the salt marsh to the north. And there, perhaps a mile back from the coast, was the settlement she'd seen once before, fifteen years ago, when she was still Unblooded. The memory was vivid: the roar of waves growing as they approached the shore, setting down her paddle as the keels hit the mud, taking up her blackstone axe in her right hand and dropping it again to hastily strap her shield onto her left arm while Black Kal roared at her for getting in the way, leaping over the side into the breakers and letting the salt water kiss her feet for luck before battle.

She registered a presence at her left shoulder, and looked around to see Otzudh. Her daughter's father was tugging at the bone spur in the lobe of his left ear, as was his habit when agitated.

"What's wrong?" she asked, facing the land again. She allowed herself a small smile in the brief pause before he spoke. Otzudh had never realised how easy he was to read, and seemed to view her perceptiveness as something not far short of witchcraft. Saana was increasingly glad she'd refused his offer of marriage. He'd been fun to lie with, and remained a dutiful father to Zhanna, but she could only ever marry someone who could match her in wits.

"Should we release the crows?" Otzudh asked, his tone deferential.

"No." She didn't look at him, instead studying the beach as though it would give up some strategic advantage if she looked hard enough.

Another pause, and she pictured his face rearranging into puzzled concern. "But—"

"No crows." Now she turned to face him. "The Flatlanders know we bring death when the crows fly. If no crows fly, perhaps they'll listen to us."

"There's never been a landing without crows," Otzudh argued, although his tone belonged to someone already resigned to the outcome.

"Just because no one alive remembers one doesn't mean it's never happened," Saana said shortly. "Pass word to the other ships: if anyone looses a crow, they go overboard."

Otzudh nodded and picked his way across the wide deck of the *Krayk's Teeth*. Saana looked at the curve of the woollen sail—a healthy wind carrying them to their new homes, surely a good omen—and then at the wooden cages lashed to the deckhouse where the crows sat, cawing from time to time.

Of old, the Tjakorshi had carried crows as a last resort in the face of the ocean's challenges, releasing the birds if navigation failed, then following them to land. No one now could remember a ship going astray, but Father Krayk's sacred birds had still been captured and taken on long voyages as good luck charms, and reminders of the need for humility in the face of the ocean. Upon reaching their destination, sailors would release the crows as thanks for safe passage, and the birds would head for shore.

Of course, when the Tjakorshi sailed to the Flatlands they raided and killed, so it was understandable that Flatlanders had come to associate the sudden appearance of crows with approaching death.

A flash of red hair caught Saana's eye. Zhanna was sitting just off one of the paddlers' positions and checking the teeth of her axe, fierce concentration on her face. Saana's stomach tightened a little at the sight of her daughter, sixteen summers old and more beautiful and fierce than Saana herself had ever been. Her hair was like fire, a far richer shade than it had any right to be given Otzudh's muddy red. Saana wished she could hold Zhanna to her and keep her back from the fighting, but she had no right.

Her daughter would stand with the Unblooded, and what was more she *wanted* to stand with them, to earn the thick stripe of black down her forehead that marked an adult. A fighter had no higher status than shipwright, fisher, or even herder, but every hale adult was expected to be Blooded, even if they never again took up a weapon in their life. Saana had been almost shamefully late to it at twenty summers, and had sworn to herself she wouldn't restrain her own daughter as Satti, now three years with the Dark Father, had done with her.

However, Saana was finding—as was so often the case—that there was a great difference between swearing something to yourself and carrying it through. She snorted in wry amusement while Zhanna exchanged good-natured jibes with Tsennan, a long-jawed lad of seventeen who'd raided through the islands already. Saana had uprooted her clan and brought them across the ocean to the Flatlands, leaving Tjakorsha behind forever.

They would disembark onto a foreign shore, not as plundering raiders but as settlers fleeing disaster, bringing everything they could carry with them, and that little enough. Their way of life was irrevocably changed, and she'd endured long hours of argument with and amongst the witches over whether Father Krayk would even recognise them as his children anymore once they'd lived on the Flatlands for a season. Would they then find the seas as hostile as the Flatlanders did?

She'd taken the most momentous decision of any chief in history with consideration, but with certainty. Yet she was still blown in the wind about her daughter bloodying her teeth.

She'd looked too long. Zhanna glanced up and caught her gaze, then carefully set her axe down and stepped across the deck towards the prow. Saana felt the urge to turn back to the approaching land, as though she were a guilty child and Zhanna her parent, but resisted the impulse. She smiled as Zhanna reached her, the clan chief greeting her daughter.

"You were looking at me," Zhanna said. Her tone was largely neutral, but held faint hints of question, and accusation. She was starting to test boundaries, and Saana was still navigating through how to relax as mother while maintaining the authority of chief.

She nodded calmly, trying to mask her doubts. "I was. Are you ready for the landing?"

Zhanna clearly thought the question idiotic. "I was *checking* my *axe*."

"Your axe's teeth can be as sharp as Father Krayk's," Saana replied, a little more harshly than she'd intended. "It won't help you if your swing is off." She sighed, and moderated her tone. "You know we don't intend to fight today, don't you?"

"You think the Flatlanders will just move aside and let us settle, with no arguments," Zhanna said. A twist to her lips indicated her opinion.

"I don't think that," Saana said, "but I hope for it." She leaned a little closer, lowering her voice. "I need you to do something for me."

"I won't stay out of the fight," Zhanna said defiantly, "I won't!"

Sanna tried to control her frustration. "I'm not—"

"You said you'd let me—"

"*Zhanna Saanastutar!*"

Her shout caught the attention of the entirety of the *Krayk's Teeth*, and probably carried across the water to several other ships as well. Zhanna's mouth snapped shut, although her eyes still blazed. Saana wanted to shout at herself for losing her temper so quickly, but she felt like she'd been dancing on coals for days now. Given everything that depended on her, it was a miracle she hadn't snapped and ordered anyone thrown overboard yet. She composed herself, straightened, and put on what she thought of as her most chiefly expression.

"If you won't listen to your mother, listen to your chief," she said flatly. "I do *not* expect the Flatlanders to step aside for us, but I won't have a battle unless there's no choice. How many Unblooded do we have?"

"Nineteen," Zhanna responded immediately, "unless the Dark Father took anyone in the crossing."

Saana nodded. She'd known the answer, but she liked to make sure her daughter was paying attention. "That's eighteen others as eager to prove themselves as you are. I want you to take command of them."

Zhanna's expression slipped from defiant to stunned. "I... What?"

"I can't ask a Blooded fighter to lead you," Saana explained, "but this is no ordinary raid. I need the Unblooded to hold until we know a fight's inevitable; you can't just charge the moment we reach the shore. You're the chief's daughter. I need you to hold them until I give the word."

Zhanna was doing a creditable impersonation of a freshly

33

landed fish, judging by the way her mouth was opening and closing. "But... but what if they don't listen to me?"

Saana snorted. "I ask myself that question every night and morning, and have done so since the witches named me chief." She turned and sat cross-legged on the deck beside the fearsome figurehead, a likeness of the black-scaled Father Krayk himself, and beckoned Zhanna down to her. After a moment her daughter joined her, staring out towards the dark shore from the other side of their god's carved neck.

"I remember what it's like to be Unblooded," Saana said, loud enough to be heard over the kiss of the waves against the hulls, but not enough to carry to the rest of the crew. "You're full of fire on the ship, but the closer you get to shore the more your stomach starts jumping, like you've swallowed a live eel."

Zhanna said nothing, but judging by the set of her mouth, she wasn't disagreeing.

"You won't be alone," Saana continued. "They'll all feel the same, near enough. Some will hide it better, and the ones who boast the loudest will probably feel it the worst, and there might be one who genuinely won't have a drop of fear in them. Normally the one you'd least expect, at that." She sighed. "What I'm saying is, when it comes down to it, there's very few who *want* to run into a fight. They all want to be Blooded, right enough, but if there was an easier way, most would take it. And that gives you what you need to know to hold them."

Zhanna looked at her, understanding dawning. "If they get *told* not to fight, it's not their fault if they don't fight?"

"Exactly," Saana replied, smiling slightly as she leaned across to look her daughter in the eyes. "Yell at them to hold. *Curse* at them to hold. Make it obvious you think they're on the verge of ignoring you and charging the Flatlanders. Use my name, and curse that name too. The louder you shout, the less their courage can be questioned, and the more you curse *me* the less yours can be."

Zhanna nodded. "And while I'm yelling and cursing, what will you be doing?"

Saana grimaced. "I'll be trying to talk to whoever I can talk to."

"And if that doesn't work?"

Saana sighed. "You'll be blooded."

They sat there together for a time, rocked by the swell and watching the land grow larger. Saana was just about to suggest they should make their final preparations when Zhanna spoke again.

"What are they like, these Flatland fighters?"

"You're better off asking one of the raiders," Saana said. "You know I only came—"

"I have asked them. Now I'm asking you." Zhanna's voice wasn't aggressive, merely firm.

"It depends," Saana admitted. "There shouldn't be many real fighters here. They'll have metal weapons, but probably won't know how to use them. There could be a couple of hunters with bows, perhaps. But the proper warriors, the *sars*..." She tasted the foreign word on her tongue and grimaced. "They're monsters wrapped in steel and sorcery.

"Even when they're not riding those dragons of theirs, they're incredibly dangerous. The one time I came here, I saw one of them fighting on foot. His beast had been brought down, but he kept going. He shrugged off javelins and axe blows as though they were nothing, then swung his sword and opened a lad up, crotch to ribcage." Her mouth twisted as images flashed up unbidden into her mind, and the salt on her lips suddenly tasted like blood instead of seawater. She'd been near the front of the charge. "They're dangerous even if their swords are sheathed, remember that. They can draw and cut in one move, and their blades are sharp enough to take your head clean off."

"But they're slow?" Zhanna asked. "In all that steel?"

"Not as slow as you'd want," Saana said grimly.

"And what about the dragons?" Zhanna asked, her voice suddenly small. "Is it true they can fly?"

Saana laughed with sudden relief. "No! Not the ones they ride, anyway. No, their dragons are huge, and terrifying, but they walk on land like us." She pointed ahead of them. "That's why we're approaching through the marsh. They won't take their dragons into the soft ground, they're too heavy. If we have to take the town by force…" She grimaced. "Dragons at close quarters are horrific, but it's more dangerous for them too, penned in between buildings. They can't turn easily, can't build up so much speed, can't cover each other's backs. You can get close and take them down, if you're brave, and lucky. No, the place you *don't* want to be against dragon riders is on firm ground, in the open. Then, you're dead."

"But—"

Saana held up a hand to forestall further questions. "Get your axe and shield. We have no more time." She put one hand on her daughter's shoulder as Zhanna turned to go and leaned close again, her stomach clenching, because no matter how long she'd known what this day would mean it was only now that she truly *understood*. "I know you'll do yourself proud. Just remember…" She hesitated, reluctant to voice the words, then pushed them out. "Remember, that doesn't have to include dying on a sar's blade, or a dragon's horn."

Zhanna just rolled her eyes and shook Saana's hand off, then returned to where her axe lay. All around, the Brown Eagle clan were readying their weapons and shields. Thankfully, the less experienced were taking their lead from seasoned raiders, and everyone was moving purposefully.

Saana caught the eye of Ristjaan the Cleaver, who was shrugging his barrel chest into his armour. He settled the shirt of sea leather in place and greeted her with his usual insouciant grin as she made her way to where he stood by the deckhouse. "Still can't keep your eyes off me, eh chief?"

"Someone needs to make sure you don't fall into the water, sheep-brain," Saana laughed. She and Ristjaan had been friends since childhood, and she thanked the winds he'd never steered wrong since she'd been chief. She wouldn't have enjoyed confronting him.

"Sheep-brain?" He wrinkled his nose at her, and the darkened scars on his lumpy, battered face pulled at his features. "I've clearly gone up in your thoughts. You called me a 'pestilent goat-fucker' before we set off."

Saana nodded gravely. "I did. I was…" She paused, trying to verbalise the sheer strain of organising the migration of an entire clan; adults, children, animals and supplies, as well as dealing with the final, desperate arguments of those who wouldn't or couldn't accept it had come to this. "Busy," she said finally.

Ristjaan's ripping laugh sounded mean and mocking, even when it wasn't. "Busy? You were trimming the sails on the greatest damned voyage the clan's ever taken! No one's done anything like this, Saana, *no one*. Not since the Great Voyage, if that even ever happened."

"Which means there's uncountable ways we can still fuck it up," Saana muttered. She slipped past him into the deckhouse where supplies were stored, and reached for her cured sealskin wrapping. The layers folded away under her hands to reveal her own sea leather jerkin, dark grey and scaled, and the precious steel sword her father had brought back from one of the great cities to the east.

"Still trusting to that dagger, eh?" Ristjaan asked from the doorway. His tone was jovial, but it held a serious note that Saana knew well. Ristjaan's huge, straight-bladed steel axe, with a cutting edge a foot and a half in length, had given him his name. Nalon had said it reminded him of the tools his Flatland kin used to butcher meat, and Ristjaan had taken that description to heart. There were a few steel weapons scattered here and there through the clan, proceeds of trade or raids, but most used more traditional tools of war. Javelins and slings did for ranged work. Up close, the trusty blackstone axe, the flat length of wood with a deep groove around its edge into which were inserted shards of blackstone, darker than night and sharper than the dawn. However, the sword was all Saana had left of her father, Uzhan.

"How I choose to fight is none of your concern," she told him, trying to match his tone, but she could hear her own defensiveness.

"How my friend fights may be her business," Ristjaan conceded, lowering his voice, "but how my *chief* fights..." He squatted down beside her as she unfolded her sea leather. "You shouldn't be fighting at all, but if you do, why use a sword? Swords are for people who know how to use them. With all the love I bear you, Saana, you are not one of those people."

She glared at him. "You of all people should know better than to tell me I can't do something."

"Saana, this crossing is *your* doing," Ristjaan said earnestly. "Every one of us is here because of you. If we reach this shore and then you fight and you die... Any clan can lose a chief, but *this* clan cannot afford to lose *you*, not now. If we lose your vision before we've settled, we'll splinter like a cheap shield."

Saana stood up, her armour in her arms. "The sars rule here, and they all use swords once they're off their dragons; they seem to think the sword is a leader's weapon." She raised her arms, letting the krayk hide slide down over her. "Since women don't rule in the Flatlands, and I have no dragon, I need *something* to make them think I speak for our clan."

"The Flatlanders are mad, Saana," Ristjaan said sadly. "Even Nalon thinks so, and he was born there."

She snorted. "Well, I never said this was going to be easy, did I?"

JEYA

THE COURT OF the Deities on Grand Mahewa was rammed with people despite the heat, and the storm clouds brewing to the south. Stone columns carved in honour of the gods looked down from four of the court's five sides, but today was sacred to just one: Jakahama of the Crossing, shē who'd lashed hēr boat together from the bones and tendons of the dead, and transported the first souls from the Grey Lands to the Garden, where the worthy could finally rest. Not everyone in Kiburu ce Alaba worshipped hēr, but enough did that the huge space was filled with a hundred hundreds, or so Jeya thought.

This many people clustered together would normally be perfect targets for theft, but Jeya knew better than to do such a thing where all the gods were watching. Hér chance would come later, when the celebrations finished and revellers streamed back homewards.

"Can yóu see, little one?" Nabanda asked. Hê used the low feminine tone to hér, which was the one shé usually preferred.

"Not really," Jeya admitted, scrutinising the wall of backs in front of hér. Shé'd always been small for hér age, and it seemed shé wouldn't be growing any taller. That came in handy for thievery, but had drawbacks, such as trying to see the temple occupying the entire fifth side of the Court.

"Up yóu get, then," Nabanda said. Hîs tone was grudging, but Jeya knew hê wouldn't have made the offer had hê not been genuine about it. Nabanda half-squatted and shé scrambled like a monkey onto hîs back, so when hê stood up again shé could see over hîs shoulder. Shé heard a murmur of discontent from behind, but ignored it. The Court of the Deities was no place to start a squabble, and it was very unwise to start a squabble with Nabanda in any place.

"Are yôu sure yôu'll be able to hold mé up?" Jeya asked, hér legs around his waist and hér arms loose around hîs neck. Shé used the low masculine tone to hîm, his usual preference, which shé knew would have confused many foreigners who came to the sea docks where Nabanda worked. A lot could understand Alaban, but not the meanings behind the words: they tended to assume a certain size or body shape—or societal position—always correlated to a particular gender. They almost always thought Nabanda was high masculine, and even addressed hîm as such without permission. But that was foreigners for you. How could they think to tell someone's gender just by looking at them?

"Yóu weigh nothing, little one," Nabanda laughed, hîs deep voice vibrating against hér chest. "Î've carried heavier loads for a mile when the ships come in."

"Yôu're strong as an ox, Nabanda," Jeya said in hîs ear.

"And twice as smart!" hê replied jovially. Jeya was about to make a joke in return, but a ripple of noise ran through the gathered crowd.

"Hush now!" shé told hîm. "They're coming!"

Sure enough, there was movement on the third level of the temple's five-tiered walls of dark stone, carved into bas-relief depictions of the deities. A bright splash of colour appeared: the High Priest of the Hundred, clad in a sky cape of shimmering feathers from the birds of the forests that cloaked the high places of the archipelago, and the mainland on either side. Following them were all seven Hierarchs, in scarlet maijhi and vivid blue karung. Jeya chewed hér lip and eyed the brilliant clothes enviously. Such colours!

And then, a respectful distance behind, came the Splinter King and hìs family.

They wore the impractical, ground-trailing robes of Naridan royalty, the tails held up by young Alabans following gracefully. Each one—the king, the queen, the adult masculine child and the younger feminine child—wore masks that caught the light even at this distance. Jeya had never seen one up close, but they were rumoured to be breathtakingly intricate silverwork inlaid with mother-of-pearl, and studded with precious stones. A few years ago shé'd hatched an idiotic plan to steal one, until Ngaiyu had pointed out the obvious flaw: no one knew who the Splinter King's family were. If they wore those masks away from the public events, no one had ever seen them. "And do yóu think yóu could take one from their faces in front of the Court of the Deities?" Ngaiyu had asked, with a throaty laugh.

There was little hope of that. Even had Jeya not been wary of offending the deities, or of thieving in front of a hundred hundred people, the Splinter King was guarded at all times by at least four of the Hierarchs' best warriors. They took up their positions now, and Jeya saw a hookbill axe, a pair of crutch blades and the glint of double crescent knives. It had been years since the last Naridan assassination attempt, but the Hierarchs still took the safety of their guests very seriously.

"Look at them," Nabanda said quietly. "Foreign beggars in fancy clothes, standing next to our leaders."

"The Naridans think the Splinter King is a god," Jeya pointed out.

"Most Naridans think hè's an imposter," Nabanda retorted. "That's why hè's hiding here, instead of ruling there." Hê used the high masculine tone for the Splinter King because, with typical foreign crudeness, the genders of the Naridan royals were common knowledge.

Someone made a shushing noise. The Priest of the Hundred was raising their arms, and the crowd did the same. Jeya didn't join in, for fear of falling backwards, but Nabanda did. It wasn't a requirement to clap, but was considered good manners. Folk at the back of the Court would be hard-pressed to even see the priest, let alone sing in time, and the prayer to Jakahama should begin as much in unison as possible.

The priest brought their hands together, and the Court of the Deities did the same, with a reverberating boom as loud as any of the storms that regularly battered the Throat of the World. The crowd lurched into motion and song, and Jeya slid off Nabanda's back to give hér friend greater freedom of movement. Hê plunged into the crowd, hîs hands coming together in another clap as the next great beat emerged. Jeya didn't follow hîm. Everyone found their own way in the prayer dance for Jakahama, so shé turned and dived into the press of bodies around hér, hér voice raised in song and hér eyes searching for the path that would open for hér through the crowd.

THE STORM WASHED Grand Mahewa with sweeps of blood-warm rain. Jeya danced under the roaring sky until the god reached out from the Garden and took hold of hér, guiding hér steps, and shé was throwing hér head back to catch great fat drops on hér tongue and letting them soak hér to the skin, plastering hér maijhi to hér body.

Shé didn't know how long it was before Jakahama released hér again, but suddenly hér calves were burning and hér voice was hoarse, and hér steps, so certain mere moments before, were clumsy and ponderous. Others kept moving and clapping and singing, either still being ridden by Jakahama or still hoping to achieve it, but Jeya knew hér dance was done. Shé wove her way to the edge of the Court on slightly unsteady legs, then out into the streets beyond.

There were plenty of people who hadn't been worshipping,

of course. Kiburu ce Alaba was the great melting pot of the world, or so Jeya had always heard it described, and more than a hundred deities had been brought here by its peoples. There were dark-skinned Morlithians from the far west beyond the Catseye Mountains, who marvelled at all the rain, and even darker-skinned Adranians from the deserts of the east who complained about it, since it washed away the colourful powders with which they painted their faces. There were the leather-skinned sailing tribes of the northern seas and the small, lithe-bodied fishing folk from the islands to the south, the kind that were highly prized as slaves by the wealthy. There were sober-faced Naridans with their coppery skin and their strange man-god, and even a few of the tall, salt-pale savages from the far south, who suffered the most when the sky was clear and the sun was fierce. People said the sea sometimes turned white, cold and hard where they came from, and the sun disappeared for days at a time, although Jeya was sure that was a spirit tale for children.

Then there were the Alaban tribes themselves, as varied as the trees in the forest. Jeya's môther had been a tribesperson and hér fàther an Adranian, although hè'd been born in the islands and so had been Alaban by any standards that mattered, including the one that said hè could never be a slave. There were tens of hundreds of people like Jeya across Kiburu ce Alaba, shé was sure; people whose parents had melted together to create something new. Even one of the Hierarchs apparently had Morlithian blood in them.

This all meant there were plenty of people in the streets with money in their pockets on this festival day, so Jeya still had a chance of getting enough together to sleep under Ngaiyu's roof tonight without dipping into hér meagre stash of coins.

Shé ignored the usual markets with their displays of fruit, vegetables, and fish, and instead tried hér luck around the stalls set up especially for the Festival of the Crossing; the puppet shows, sweetmeat vendors, sellers of sticky pastries, and fortune tellers.

The richer revellers wouldn't be buying basic foodstuffs: they had servants for that. The regular markets offered slim pickings, and the marks there knew the dangers of pickpockets and cutpurses. No, the wealthy of Grand Mahewa would be paying over the odds for a honeyed scorpion on a skewer, or chortling as puppets performed plays peppered with innuendo.

That didn't mean Jeya's task was easy. Not all rich people were careless with their money, even if they weren't used to looking after it in public. Shé lurked around a puppet show that was performing a farce and surreptitiously studied the crowd, looking for the right sort of clothes. Shé considered a tall person with a nasal laugh and the tight-twisted, bell-and-bead-decked hair of an Adranian, but decided at the last moment that they looked a little too alert, and the war-sickle at their belt a little too sharp.

A youth near them, though, looked more engrossed in the play. Jeya sidled closer, nudging people aside as though angling to get a better view of the garishly painted wooden box where the puppets squawked and tittered. Another crude joke rang out and the crowd laughed, and Jeya took the opportunity to approach right up behind the youth, slightly to their right.

Their cheeks were smooth, they were a little taller than hér, and their dark hair was pulled back in a tail under a conical straw hat that dripped with rainwater. Their maijhi and karung were dyed a deep indigo, with delicate green hem-stitching, a sure sign of wealth. Shé watched their cheeks crease and dimple as they laughed at slapstick violence. They were thoroughly engrossed: good.

Shé waited for the part shé knew was coming, the call-and-answer routine where Kangkang the violent puppet was held to account for hìs actions by Nyoi of the Watch. It kept the attention of any children in the crowd, lest they persuade their parents to leave before the show concluded (when money was traditionally left), and it maybe also helped some of the cruder innuendo sail over their heads. However, watching adults would invariably join in as well, harkening back to their own simpler days.

"Oh no Ì didn't!" Kangkang squealed, in response to Nyoi's stern accusation.

"*Oh yes yòu did!*" the audience chorused joyously. Jeya joined in.

"Oh no Ì didn't!"

"*Oh yes yòu did!*"

The Kangkang puppet turned fully towards the audience, as though to menace them with hìs stick. "Oh no Ì *didn't!*"

"*Oh yes yòu* did!"

And, as the traditional trio of exchanges was completed and everyone in the close-packed crowd shouted as loud as they could, with appropriate waving of their arms, Jeya swiftly but delicately coaxed a purse out of hér mark's pocket.

Sa, god of thieves and tricksters (amongst others), must have been smiling on hér: it was a small cloth pouch, secured with a drawstring, and shé experienced a brief thrill of triumph as it came free. Triumph because the mark didn't twitch, despite their damp clothes sticking to them and making it more likely for them to feel what shé was up to. Triumph also, because the pouch was reassuringly heavy, and promised possibilities beyond just a roof and food for the night: perhaps she could even buy into a crew...

Brief, because as shé stepped casually away a hand grabbed hér arm, and shé found hérself hauled around by the Adranian shé'd decided not to target in the first place.

SAANA

The KRAYK'S TEETH cut through the low surf and hit the black mud with an undignified squelch. Saana leaped off the flat deck and onto her clan's new home before her yolgu had even stopped moving. The salt water splashed her boots, but she didn't linger in the breakers, pushing on up the beach with her alder roundshield strapped to her left forearm and sea leather helm on her head. However, her father's sword remained sheathed. Instead she carried a stick with the clan's whitest sheepskin bound at one end, to be unfurled when necessary: the white flag she hoped would open the way for parley.

Behind her she heard the rest of the Krayk's Teeth crew following her lead, and then the hulls of the other ships making landfall. There were seventeen; seven taughs, weather-beaten veterans of long fishing trips, and no less than ten mighty yolgus, the great ships in which her people crossed oceans to raid and trade. Five were on their maiden voyage, with new sails spun over the long, dark winter, and between them they'd carried the Brown Eagle clan and as many possessions and supplies as possible.

Saana looked dubiously at the marsh, still scattered with patches of snow and undoubtedly riddled with bogs and streams. The sleds would struggle over this terrain, but it would be better than hauling everything by hand. She just needed to ensure they stayed behind the shieldwall.

They'd been seen, of course; the local fishing skiffs had fled as soon as her fleet had come into view, back to the town on the shore of the wide tidal creek that cut up through the salt marsh, away towards the distant mountains. She could see the tiny shapes of defenders on the walls.

She looked over her shoulder at the semi-organised chaos, and scanned it until she found the person she wanted. "Nalon!"

The Flatlander looked up, then kissed Avlja on the cheek and made his way towards her. Saana studied him as he approached, wondering again whether this was the best course of action, whilst also knowing that it was the only one available. Behind Nalon, Avlja fixed Saana with a glare promising retribution if her husband got hurt.

Nalon was the only Brown Eagle who hadn't been born on Tjakorsha: he was from these Flatlands, which he called Narida, although considerably further north. Some twenty years previously, Iro Greybeard had chased down and boarded the Flatlander ship on which Nalon had been a passenger. Normally that would have ended badly for Nalon, but Avlja Ambastutar had been on the Greybeard's crew that day and had stepped in, somewhat smitten. Nalon had been given a choice, courtesy of Iro's very rough grasp of the Flatlander tongue and, Saana suspected, some emphatic hand gestures; go with them, or go over the side. He'd unsurprisingly chosen the former, and once Avlja had some time to work her charms on him they'd wedded, and now had two sons. The elder, Tamadh, would be in the shieldwall alongside his mother.

Nalon reached Saana and nodded respectfully. He'd taken some time to break his habit of bowing to everyone, but these days he was as relaxed as anyone from Koszal. "You needed me, chief?"

"I need to talk to the sars," Saana told him simply. "I want you there."

Nalon's face twisted. "Your language is good, they'll understand you." His speech was accented with the overdeveloped vowel sounds of the Flatlanders, which meant many people found it hard to tell his mood from his voice. However, after months of being instructed in Naridan by him Saana could read Nalon as well as anyone in the clan save his own family, and he was obviously agitated.

"I don't just need them to understand," she explained, "I need them to *believe*. You were a Flatlander; they might listen to you."

"As well reason with a mountain as with a sar in his armour," Nalon snorted, switching to the Flatlander tongue. It had the rhythm of an old saying, and didn't do much for Saana's confidence. She hoped Nalon's low opinion of the Flatlanders' ruling warriors was something idiosyncratic to the man. If they were truly as uptight, unbending, and ferociously stupid as he claimed...

Well, as she'd told Ristjaan, she'd never expected this to be easy.

"Then let's go and speak to some mountains," she told him grimly, and turned back to the disembarking clan, raising her voice. "Rist! You're with us! Tsolga, bring the fighters up, but *hold back* unless this all goes to the depths! Zhanna!" She caught sight of her daughter's red hair, and held her gaze for a second. "Keep the Unblooded in the centre!"

"Good luck with that," Ristjaan muttered, trudging up with his axe slung casually over his shoulder.

"Shut up," Saana said sharply. "I can't have this ruined by a bunch of hotheads."

"Suppose this works," Ristjaan said, as they set off towards the town while Tsolga screeched the fighters into some sort of order. "Suppose you talk the Flatlanders into letting us settle. What will the Unblooded do then? Remain Unblooded forever? Live a life of shame?"

"We've crossed an ocean, Rist," Saana said, hopping over a narrow stream trickling down to join the main creek. "Our lives

49

will change in ways you and I can't imagine. Perhaps that will be one of the lesser changes. But," she sighed, "I doubt it will come to that. They know war here, too."

"Chief, you want to wave that flag?" Nalon asked nervously. "I'm not looking to take an arrow in the eye."

"We're still out of range," Saana replied.

"Even so," Rist said, "it can't hurt to let them think on it a little longer."

Saana eyed him for a moment, wondering if it was a good idea to have brought her old friend along, instead of someone less likely to question her authority. On the other hand, should everything go to the depths there was no one she'd rather have beside her than Ristjaan the Cleaver, the most renowned Scarred warrior of the Brown Eagle clan.

"You two are as timid as my mother," she muttered, but paused a moment to fiddle with the binding that held the bleached skin in place, before shaking it loose. She passed it to Nalon. "There. You wanted it out, you can carry it."

"A fair trade," he nodded, raising it above his head. The wind that had brought them ashore caught it, and made the sheepskin flap clumsily. "I hope they respect the flag of parley here."

"Don't tell me *now* this flag may not work," Saana said, exasperated.

"Southerners are strange people," Nalon replied defensively. "You can never tell."

"But they're northerners," Rist protested.

"They're southerners to me," Nalon pointed out. "I'd never been further south than Idramar until the Greybeard took me off that ship. I heard all sorts of strange stories about southerners when I was a boy."

"What was said?" Saana asked, intrigued despite herself. There was some movement on the walls of the town ahead. Perhaps their flag had been sighted, and was causing a stir, but she would take any last information she could get about these foreigners.

"Some said they eat their own children in the winter, but we always took that as a scare tale," Nalon said. "Others said they don't follow honour, but I can't see any sar unbending enough for that, southerner or no. Mainly, people just said…"

"Yes?" Saana prompted.

"Mainly, people said they're little better than the bloody Raiders," Nalon muttered.

"Wait, is that us?" Rist asked, frowning.

"Uh…"

"That's us," Saana sighed. She'd always thought of the Flatlanders as one people, and never really considered that northern Naridans might not like the southern ones. Then again, until she'd started speaking to Nalon in detail, she'd never thought the sars might be seen as anything other than warlike protectors. Instead, Nalon had drawn on memories of his youth to paint a picture of arrogance, hubris and occasional brutality. Clearly, this land was as complex as anything they'd left behind in Tjakorsha.

"Looks like three are coming to meet us," Rist said, squinting. "Think they're sars?"

"They're on foot, but I doubt it would be anyone else," Saana replied, seeing the glint of sunlight off metal. She glanced over her shoulder and saw the reassuring mass of her warriors trailing behind, with Tsolga at their head. The old woman might lack the strength for combat now, but she still had a voice like a blackstone axe, and had been the clan's horn-sounder since before Saana had been born. Attacking or holding, Tsolga would leave no one in any doubt as to what they should be doing.

She could see the three Naridans more clearly now. The central one was slightly more advanced, presumably their chief, and stocky. The one on the left as she looked at them was of a similar build, but the one on the right was taller and slimmer. The Flatlanders tended to be short—Nalon was amongst the shortest men in the clan—but that one looked to be her height.

Each one wore a suit of the curious sar armour. It looked like a heavy cloth jacket with metal nail-heads glinting in it at regular intervals, and two chest plates polished until they shone, but her people had long known that, thanks to Flatlander sorcery, any part of it could turn an axe blow. The clan had hoped Nalon might be able to tell them more, but he'd denied knowing anything, despite having learned from a Flatland ironwitch—a 'smith', as he called it—for a few years before his capture.

The sleeves extended past the elbow, and the coat was split from the waist into panels reaching to the sars' knees, allowing them to straddle their monstrous mounts. Their shins were protected with solid metal guards, and their forearms and hands were encased in armoured gauntlets. Their plumed metal helmets had armoured panels affixed that fell to protect their necks, while allowing them to turn their heads. Each one of them carried almost a clan's wealth of steel into battle on their bodies. Even their faces were armoured; only their eyes could be seen above the snarling visages of their war masks, and those eyes were no softer than the metal.

A jolt of recognition struck Saana. She'd seen the central sar's mask before; a scaled face baring shark-like teeth. Of course, a mask could be duplicated, or passed between owners, but as they got closer she became certain.

"The one in the middle killed Njivan," she muttered to Rist.

"Njivan?"

"You don't remember?" But of course, Rist had been on any number of raids since Saana had made her one and only venture to the Flatlands, fifteen years ago. Now she thought back on it, Njivan and Rist had never been close. "He took an axe hit from Njivan, then carved him straight up the middle."

"Wouldn't surprise me," Rist nodded, then laughed grimly and patted the handle of his weapon. "Well, I've got a better axe."

"Let's hope we don't need it," Saana said. They were perhaps twenty paces away from the sars. "Stop."

Her two companions halted. She took two more steps, then planted her feet in the coarse grass, all that was keeping her from sinking into the soft ground. Behind her, she heard Tsolga yell obscenities at her shieldwall to stop them lumbering into the usual whooping, screaming charge.

The sars also halted, each with one hand on the hilt of the longer sword sheathed at their waist. Saana noted almost absently that the long scabbard of the central warrior was decorated to about half its length with carvings and artwork, while those of the two flanking him were bare, white wood.

Saana took a deep breath, made one last mental rehearsal of the words she'd practiced with Nalon so many times, then began to speak.

DAIMON

"Father," Darel asked uncertainly, as the three of them trudged across the salt marsh towards the oncoming Raiders, "why are we doing this? They don't follow the Code, so their flag of parley holds no weight."

It was a question Daimon wanted to hear answered, too. Black Keep's walls would barely serve to repel a thief in the night, let alone the advancing Raider horde, but he still felt more and more vulnerable the farther behind he left them. It would have been better had he been mounted on Silverhorn, but even had they been willing to risk their mounts in the unsteady footing of the marsh, the great longhorn dragons were still deep in their winter torpor. Tavi the stablemaster had his tricks, but he couldn't rouse them this quickly.

"Your father would learn how the savages know about the flag of parley in the first place," their father replied grimly. "Also, the leader presumably intends to treat with us somehow. This gives us an opportunity to sever the viper's head."

"You would violate a parley?" Daimon asked, surprised despite himself.

"As your brother stated, they do not follow the Code," Asrel snorted. "In fact, they likely intend the same for us. Look to your weapons, and be alert. Should they seek to take our lives then they will learn that no Raider is a match for a sar."

"Father," Daimon said, frowning. "The one with the flag... he does not look like a Raider."

"He is dressed like a savage," Asrel retorted, "but your eyes are better, boy. What do you see?"

"He is right, Father," Darel weighed in. "The man looks like one of us!"

"Curious," Asrel said. "A hostage?"

"Perhaps," Daimon agreed, but it felt wrong. The man certainly looked Naridan: he wasn't oversized, his skin was a healthy copper rather than milk-pale, and although he had whiskers they were only a shadow of the animal-like growth of hair the male Raiders sported. However, he wasn't bound, or even under a close guard, and wore skins and furs. He appeared to be accompanying the other two of his own free will. Like them, he sported a thick black line from his hairline down to the bridge of his nose. Only the big man, however, also had what looked like black-stained scars on his cheeks.

The central Raider raised a hand and the other two stopped, while beyond them the crawling battle line of fighters also came to a slightly irregular halt, to Daimon's mixed relief and surprise. His father stopped, and Daimon did too. He could easily draw his blade before any of the invaders could get to him, which was all that really mattered, although he worried that Darel was opposite the huge brute with the massive steel-bladed axe slung casually over his shoulder. Their father's earlier words had been true, if harsh: Darel was no incompetent, but he had always been less skilled in combat.

It wasn't until the central Raider started speaking that Daimon realised it wasn't a heavily built, smooth-cheeked youth under the strange, scaled leather armour and helm, but a woman. Her wargear and clothing were undecorated save for her belt, which was thick leather and adorned with cunningly engraved discs of bronze, and even gold. To his amazement, she spoke in Naridan: accented and slightly broken Naridan, but understandable nonetheless.

"This man is Saana Sattistutar, chief of Brown Eagle clan," she began, her voice strong and clear. "We want no fight."

Daimon stared at her in amazement. She was a woman, and a Raider to boot, yet she addressed his father, a thane of Narida, as though she were a man of equal rank.

"*You* are a chief?" Asrel asked in disbelief. "A woman?" Daimon half-expected his father to draw his longblade simply at the insolence of being addressed in such a manner, but he showed incredible restraint and kept his weapon sheathed.

"Yes," Sattistutar replied simply.

"If you say you don't want a fight, why bring an army?" Asrel demanded angrily.

Sattistutar shrugged, an oddly familiar gesture. "You might not agree."

"This thane is Asrel Blackcreek," Daimon's father declared, pride filling his voice, "and these lands are his. Why are you and your rabble here?"

"We are here because we wish..." The woman grimaced in apparent frustration and paused for a brief, muttered conversation with the flag-carrier, before turning back to them. "Settle. We wish to settle."

While he tried to process what he'd just heard, Daimon was shocked to realise his father had been rendered speechless. He couldn't recall that happening before.

Darel was the first to recover his voice. "*What?*"

The big man with the axe started to say something Daimon didn't understand to Sattistutar, but she hissed him into silence. Then, to Daimon's amazement, the brute looked over his chief's head and caught Daimon's gaze before rolling his eyes.

"We wish to live here," the Raider chief said, her eyes flicking from Darel's face, to their father's, and then to Daimon's. "We cannot live at old home now. We bring food and seed. We can fish." She nodded towards Black Keep. "We can help mend walls."

Daimon winced behind his war mask. The condition of Black Keep was a sore point with his father, but they no longer had the masons to keep it in good repair. He suspected he knew how Sattistutar intended the statement—that she could see their defences were poor—but such an oblique threat would only anger his father.

"You scum have harried our lands since before this thane's grandfather's day," Asrel bit out. "Why should he care if you can no longer live where you used to? Crawl back to the sea, and rot."

Daimon cared. Daimon dearly wanted to know why the Raiders had changed their habit of centuries, but he remained silent while his father spoke.

"You should care because we can help," Sattistutar said firmly. "On this man's honour as clan chief, we mean no harm. We will build, farm, fish, hunt, or fight your enemies."

"Your 'honour' means less than nothing to this thane," Daimon's father declared. "You clearly have no understanding of it, or else you would not address him as though you were a man!"

Sattistutar's face darkened, but Asrel held up one gauntlet, palm outwards. "Hold. You there; you have the look of a Naridan. What is your name?"

The man with the flag glanced at Sattistutar, who gave him an encouraging nod. He looked back at Asrel.

"Nalon." He paused for a moment longer than he should have, then added a reluctant, "Lord."

"And what is your place here, Nalon?" Daimon's father asked.

"Metal-worker to the Brown Eagle clan," the man replied. His speech held some of the odd, sing-song notes of Sattistutar's, although less pronounced. However, Daimon realised Nalon also had an accent from the north of Narida, like some of the traders that came with the summer caravans. "That, and the only person who can speak both languages properly."

"Metal-worker? You serve these savages?" Asrel asked, appalled.

"Serve? No." Nalon hawked and spat to one side. "S'man served a sar once, as a 'prentice smith up in Bowmar. Nasty piece of work. He put s'man on a ship down to Idramar to learn some new skills from another smith, but the Raiders boarded before we made port. That would have been the end of s'man, but one of their women liked what she saw and s'man didn't fancy taking a swim that far from shore." The man fixed Daimon's father with a steady gaze that would have been insolent even if he hadn't also been addressing Asrel as an equal, and in the slurred speech of a lowborn.

"Turns out the Tjakorshi"—Nalon nodded sideways at his companions—"don't really have smiths, on account of there being bugger all iron on the islands save what they've traded for or stolen. They were glad to have one who could repair and remake what bits they've got, and they pay s'man well for his work instead of taking it from him as their due."

"You speak as though you welcomed this," Asrel said, and Daimon could hear the danger in his father's voice.

"It's a hard land, and it breeds a hard people," Nalon said levelly, "but s'man has a Tjakorshi wife and son in that shieldwall, and his youngest is standing behind it. S'man has lived longer in Tjakorsha than Narida, he's seen both ways, and he's standing with the one he prefers."

"You are an insolent whelp, and a traitor," Asrel growled, placing a second hand on his sword. Nalon edged backwards, warily.

"He is our man," Sattistutar cut in, steel in her tone and her right hand now resting on the hilt of her own sword, "and you will not threaten him. What do you say, Asrel of Blackcreek? This man cannot change what happened years ago, before she was chief, but on her oath, let us settle and we will not fight you again."

Despite himself, Daimon suddenly found himself believing her. There was something about her face, foreign and sickly pale though it was; an earnest desperation to be believed that went beyond trying to trick an enemy. The big man, too, looked tense.

He doesn't know if he's going to have to fight, Daimon realised, certain he had the truth of it. *He's ready to fight, but that's not their plan. This is no trick.*

"Father," he said urgently, but his father was already speaking.

"This thane says you are sea demons, and he trusts you no more than he would a serpent in his bed," Asrel snarled. "Begone, before we throw you back into the waves!"

"This man came here once before," Sattistutar said, her voice hard and low, "fifteen years ago. There were seven of you sars then, she thinks. You killed this man's friend, you yourself. This man killed two farmers with pointed sticks who not knew which end to hold. Now there are only three of you, and this man has two hundred fourteen warriors."

Daimon swallowed nervously. His hands were sweaty inside his gauntlets as he gripped the hilt of his longblade. He didn't doubt the Raider was telling the truth: he hadn't counted the shields arrayed beyond her, but they easily outnumbered Black Keep's poor muster of defenders twice, perhaps three times over.

Neither he nor Darel had seen genuine combat before, and it seemed unfair their first experience of it would be against overwhelming odds. It was the sort of thing the heroes of song and poem had won renown for, but usually because they'd died in the process.

"We *must* live here," Sattistutar continued. "We do not wish fight but if you say no then fight we will. This man does not think your people will fight once dead you are, they will wish to live also. You sars fight well, this we know. We may lose thirty to your blades but you will still die, and we will still settle." Slowly, she let go of her sword and held her empty hand up.

"Help us both. Once warriors charge, this man may not be able to call them back. Work with her so all may live."

"Father!" Daimon said, eyeing the huge warrior on Sattistutar's left. He couldn't make Asrel believe the Raider chief, but perhaps he could appeal to a different motive. "It is our duty to protect our people! Surely we can do that better alive than dead?"

"You would allow these savages within our walls so they can murder us in our sleep?!" his father demanded incredulously.

"Look!" Sattistutar shouted, gesturing furiously behind her. "If we wish kill we have no need of tricks!"

"Nor does this lord," Asrel Blackcreek growled, and snatched his longblade from its painted scabbard as he took three quick steps forward. The master-crafted sword slid free with barely a whisper, and Daimon's father turned the motion into a slashing cut at Sattistutar's face with the ease of an expert swordsman.

The Raider chief barely got her shield up, but managed to catch Asrel's blade before his blow landed. She backed away, wrenching her own sword from its sheath: a thick-bladed, overly heavy affair so far as Daimon could see, but he knew the quality of the weapon was not so important as the skill of the fighter. The Naridan longblade was the finest sword in the known lands, but only a fool thought that alone made him invincible.

Nalon was already fleeing, but a roar drew Daimon's attention and he saw to his horror that the huge Raider had his massive axe in hand and was moving to his chief's defence. Skilled swordsman though Asrel was, Daimon doubted he could deal with the brute and Sattistutar as well.

Then Darel stepped in. Loyal, honourable Darel, more skilled with a quill than a blade, drew his weapon to protect his father against the giant.

The monster wasn't just powerful; he feinted a clumsy overhand blow, then abruptly changed to an upwards cut that could have taken Darel's arm off at the shoulder had it landed. Daimon's law-brother scrambled backwards just in time, but his counter-cut was shaky and hesitant, and easily swatted aside by the Raider's shield.

A mournful wail split the air, answered by a roar from many, many throats. The Raiders were coming, which meant Daimon, his father, and his brother would be dead in the space of a few dozen heartbeats.

Asrel was driving the Raider chief backwards with scything cuts; she was catching them on her shield but seemed unable to mount much in the way of counter-offence. Of course, the more she backed away, the closer she came to her onrushing warriors.

Daimon came to a decision.

"Father!" he shouted, charging in alongside Asrel and aiming his own slash at Sattistutar. "Help Darel!"

The massive Raider chose that exact moment to let loose another bellow and catch Darel's helm with his axe. Daimon's brother crumpled with a cry, and the sound of his blood-son's fall was enough to distract even Asrel Blackcreek. He turned and ran at his son's attacker, longblade raised, leaving Daimon facing down Saana Sattistutar.

If he pressed his attack, Daimon thought he might just have time to kill her before he was overwhelmed: his father was also an excellent swordsman but now past his prime, whereas Daimon was two-and-twenty and had a longer reach. However, Sattistutar's death wouldn't change anything other than giving the Raiders incentive to exact revenge on Black Keep.

He just had to hope he'd read her intentions right, and commend his honour to Nari.

Daimon held his longblade out behind him and raised his other hand, palm outwards. "Do you swear to treat our people fairly?" he yelled, over the noise of the onrushing horde.

Sattistutar's brow creased in confusion as she peered over the rim of her shield. "What? Yes!"

Daimon's heart was thundering and his guts were tied in knots, but he'd made his mind up. He pointed towards his father, who was unleashing a flurry of blows at the big axeman to beat him back from the groaning Darel. "Spare their lives, and this lord will help you!"

Sattistutar glanced over her shoulder, then looked back at him and shrugged helplessly, as if to say, *you've left it a bit late.*

Daimon ran towards his father and brother. The big Raider was swinging his axe at Asrel's head, but Daimon's father leaned back from the blow expertly and stabbed upwards at the Raider's chest. The big man twisted away from the thrust and reset his stance, a calculating look in his eyes as he sized up this new threat.

Daimon swept Asrel's legs out from under him, then kicked the longblade out of his father's hand.

Asrel took a gasping breath, although whether from shock or in reaction to being winded was unclear. However, Daimon had more pressing matters to attend to. He hastily sheathed his own blade, held up both hands in the face of the startled axeman and the rapidly approaching Raiders, and raised his voice.

"*Stop!*"

Most of the Raiders didn't understand the word, of course. In fact, most probably hadn't heard it. Daimon stared into the screaming, spittle-flecked faces bearing down on him and wondered if he'd made a mistake.

Well, he was certain he'd made a mistake, it was just a case of exactly how bad that mistake would prove to be.

Then Sattistutar appeared in his field of vision, her arms outstretched as she faced her fighters and screamed something at them. The charge didn't stop so much as shamble to an uncertain halt, but three breaths later Daimon found himself not being bludgeoned to the ground as he'd half-expected, but instead within a semi-circle of puffing, confused foreigners. Sattistutar was speaking loudly and quickly in the Raider tongue and, he hoped, presumably telling them how he'd agreed to help.

"*Traitor!*"

There was the whisper of steel clearing a sheath beneath him, and Daimon stepped hurriedly to one side to evade a lunging stab from his father's shortblade, the weapon a sar carried as a backup, or to pierce his own heart if honour demanded his life. Asrel Blackcreek lurched up to his feet, tears in his eyes as he advanced on Daimon, the invaders around them forgotten.

"You cowardly, lowborn rat!" his law-father spat at him. "Is this is how you repay—"

Sattistutar shouted something, and half-a-dozen Raiders grabbed Asrel; two to each arm, one around the waist from behind, and one who hovered uncertainly, apparently unable to find a body part but still determined to look useful. The shortblade was wrenched from Asrel's grasp as he was borne backwards into the crowd.

"Do not hurt him!" Daimon shouted desperately, not quite able to believe what had just happened. His father was stern, yes, and unbending, but to the point he would have killed his own son over a matter of honour?

"Will he fight too?" Sattistutar asked, pointing at Darel, who was now back up on his knees.

"This lord does not know," Daimon admitted. He raised his voice. "Darel! It is over. Lay down your weapons."

"What?" Darel looked up in confusion: his helm had prevented the big Raider's axe from cleaving his skull, but the impact of the blow had clearly knocked him woozy. However, it seemed that Sattistutar wasn't interested in waiting. She barked another command and four more fighters surged forward, taking hold of the disorientated sar and hauling him none-too-gently to his feet before he could seize his longblade, which still lay on the ground where it had spilled from his hand when he'd been struck.

"Daimon?" Darel's eyes were wide, but narrowed as they focused on him standing next to the Raider chieftain with his blades sheathed. "Daimon! What have you done?"

"What your brother had to," Daimon replied sadly. "His honour is forfeit, but your lives are not."

Darel wrenched against his captors' grip, but was held firm. Sattistutar shouted something else and all the Raiders, including the ones holding Darel, began to move at a walking pace towards Black Keep. Daimon retrieved his brother's and father's longblades and walked at their head at Sattistutar's side, promising himself he would open the Raider's throat if she proved false, while fighting the thought he should have already done that.

"This lord has no brother!" Darel Blackcreek shouted, but when Daimon turned around Darel's escort had muscled him away into the crowd, and he was lost from view.

RIKKUT

Rikkut had been looking forward to testing himself against the warriors of Saana Sattistutar's Brown Eagle clan, but it was looking like he might be too late.

Amalk Tyaszhin, warrior and sailor, and fearsomely renowned at both, had led them here to Koszal. Blunt-featured and broad-shouldered, his impressive bulk enhanced by the mantle of sea bear fur on his cloak, and his grey-streaked beard reaching his chest, the *Red Smile*'s captain's very presence inspired confidence in his followers and trepidation in his enemies, or those that might become his enemies.

He was also quite obviously very, very angry.

"Where the *fuck* are they?" he barked, kicking a rough timber door. It swung open to reveal the longhouse's interior, dug down into the cold earth so only the roof and the tops of the external walls were visible. The roof itself, pine branches and bracken over a wooden frame, started at waist height above ground and looked pleasingly flammable to Rikkut's eyes. Something told him that now was not the time, however, and not just because all the longhouses here were empty.

"The Brown Eagles have flown the nest," Olja remarked dryly, looking around at the abandoned village. She clearly didn't share Rikkut's sense of appropriate timing, because Tyaszhin whirled around and punched her in the nose. She sprawled on the ground, clutching her face and scrabbling backwards to avoid the kick the old bastard aimed at her ribs.

"Do you know what this means?" Tyaszhin growled over her as Olja picked herself up, wiping at her involuntarily streaming eyes. The first few flakes of the next storm's snow were whirling down out of the iron-grey sky: Long Night was over for another year, Father Krayk had released the sun and the quickening was approaching, but the islands of Tjakorsha would taste snow for another two short moons. "It means they're gone. *The Brown Eagle clan are gone!*" He shouted the last sentence, and as his cheeks wobbled and his spittle flew, Rikkut realised that *Red Smile*'s captain wasn't just angry.

He was scared.

The Brown Eagles hadn't been the largest clan, or the best sailors or warriors. Rikkut had never heard of them taking any torcs at Clanmoot, when the clans of Tjakorsha came together to test their skills against each other. But of course, there hadn't been a Clanmoot for two years now, and the being responsible for that had ordered Tyaszhin and his warband here, to the westernmost island in the archipelago.

"So they're gone," Olja said, wiping her eyes and glaring at Tyaszhin. "That's what it wanted, right? Just saves us the trouble of cutting their throats and dumping them in the shallows like the Stone Ghosts."

"It doesn't want them *gone*, fool," Rikkut said, weighing his blackstone axe in his hand. "It wants them swearing fealty, and it wants their chief's belt. We scuttled the Stone Ghosts because they were too fucking proud to save their own necks." He looked at Tyaszhin. "The question is, *where* have they gone? Inland?"

Tyaszhin looked north-east towards where Kainkoruuk rose. It was one of Tjakorsha's mighty Five Peaks, thrust above the waves by Father Krayk during the Creation. It was hidden from view at the moment by the lie of the ground and the tall, dark pines, but Rikkut had seen the smoking summit crowned with snow as their ships had pulled through the straits. There were meadows of rich grass farther up the mountain, where flocks of hardy Tjakorshi sheep would graze in the long days of summer, but only a fool would forsake their longhouse's shelter for a night under the stars up there, so early in the year.

"Nah," Tyaszhin said, and spat. "Not all of them. And where are the tracks? That many people would leave tracks." He gestured at the ground between the longhouses, worn bare from footfalls. "The only place they wouldn't leave a tell is on the shore."

"You think they've gone around the coast?" Olja asked, squinting back down towards the stretch of shingle where their ships were beached. Beyond them, the water was wild and rough. They'd all taken a soaking getting ashore, and they'd had neither a fight nor the Brown Eagles' cookfires to warm them afterwards. "Through the stones, to avoid leaving tracks?"

"No," Tyaszhin growled, turning on his heel. "Let's check their ships."

For a moment, Rikkut didn't see the point. Then he looked more closely at the handful of small boats hauled far up the beach to keep them safe when the southern storms screamed in, and he understood.

"There aren't enough," he said, uncertainty stirring in his gut. "Not nearly enough. And nothing larger than a fishing tsek. Where are the taughs, the yolgus?"

"They can't all be out fishing?" Olja asked dubiously. And she was right, although Rikkut was struggling to believe it.

"They've gone," he said, turning to scan the beach just in case he'd somehow missed the huge, fifty-ell vessels. He hadn't, of course. "They've taken everything, and sailed. The whole clan."

"They wouldn't have enough ships!" Olja protested. "No clan has enough yolgus to carry everyone, not with all their animals!"

"Check the forest," Tyaszhin said grimly. Some of his warband were still wandering aimlessly through Koszal, as though expecting to find the entire Brown Eagle clan hidden behind a tree, or somehow missed in a longhouse. "I reckon we'll find a bunch of cut trunks. That bitch Sattistutar must've planned this over the winter, and built some more." He kicked at the beach, sending up a clattering spray of shingle. "Fuck! I said we should have come before Long Night!"

Rikkut and Olja exchanged glances. That had sounded uncomfortably close to a criticism of their master, which wasn't something you did if you wanted to keep your blood in your veins. A draug walked Tjakorsha now, something that could see the thoughts of men and women in the flames of its fires, and which wore the skin of a man but could not be killed. Rikkut had seen scars from old wounds that should have slain it; he'd seen the draug pull the noose from which it had been hung for half a day from around its own neck and stand back up again, and that was enough to make anyone nervous, even a battle-tested warrior like Rikkut Fireheart. Rikkut would sooner face down Amalk Tyaszhin's blackstone axe while naked and armed with nothing except foul language than cross their master, and he felt no shame in that. Some things were beyond the ken of mortals.

"Let's head around the coast," Rikkut suggested. "There's still the Seal Rock clan on the north shore. Perhaps they know where the Brown Eagles went. Even if not, we still need their chief's belt, and their fealty."

"We'd best hope for all our sakes they *do* know," Tyaszhin said. "It wanted two belts and two chiefs, and the Dark Father help us all if that's not what it gets."

JEYA

IT WAS JUST hér luck to be grabbed by some over-enthusiastic bystander, but the gods had not totally abandoned Jeya: the arm the tall stranger had seized was the one holding the money pouch, leaving hér other hand free. Shé didn't bother trying to talk hér way clear. Only direct action would help now, so shé reached up and clawed at their eyes.

They reared back automatically, and their fingers loosened on hér arm enough for hér to twist hér rain-slicked skin out of their grip. Then shé was away, the money pouch in hér pocket, pushing through the crowd and screaming for help. A thief was quiet, and tried not to attract attention; everyone knew this on some instinctive level. Had shé fled silently, the crowd might have assumed hér guilt. By drawing attention to hérself shé would in turn draw attention to hér assailant, and perhaps some well-meaning fool who hadn't seen hér theft would step forward to defend hér from this aggressive, larger person. Shé only needed a small head start and then shé'd be away, no matter how long hér pursuer's legs were, unless they knew the byways of East Harbour as well as shé did...

Strong arms wrapped around hér waist and snatched hér off hér feet before shé'd even reached the edge of the crowd. Shé kicked and yelled, wondering how in the gods' names the Adranian had

71

caught up with hér, then as shé was wrenched around shé realised the Adranian was stalking towards hér with thunder in their face. Shé'd been seized by someone else! Since when had the Festival of the Crossing brought out so much public spirit?

"Where is the purse, thief?!" the Adranian demanded.

"What purse?" Jeya retorted, kicking furiously but fruitlessly against whoever held hér. "Let *go* of me!"

"What purse?" the Adranian repeated with a disdainful snort. "Pfah! Hold their arms!"

One of the arms gripping Jeya abruptly shifted position, releasing hér waist and wrapping around hér chest, pinning hér arms. Thus secured, shé could do little but snarl as the Adranian reached into first one and then the other of hér pockets, before smugly withdrawing the money pouch.

"That's mine!" Jeya declared stubbornly. Shé had no recourse now, other than to play this out.

"Indeed?" the Adranian replied with a raised eyebrow. They loosened the drawstring and upended the purse onto their palm in front of the crowd, seemingly all of whom had decided that this was far more interesting than puppet shows. Jeya expected the fat jangle of copper that emerged, but not the flash and silky tinkle of silver and even—-was that a *gold* coin?! Hér soul sank and her guts turned watery. Shé'd misjudged hér mark, very badly. That was enough money to get hér hanged.

"Hardly the purse of such a ragged thief!" the Adranian declared to the crowd, who muttered agreement. Jeya could feel their eyes, weighing and judging. They might not rush to bear hér to the magistrate, but shé'd certainly receive no help from that quarter now hér crime was laid bare. The Adranian had judged the situation well.

"Màster?" the Adranian said, looking over their shoulder. "What should we do with them?"

The youth emerged from the crowd, and Jeya felt like shé'd been punched in the same guts hér soul had just sunken into. The

Adranian, and whoever still had hold of hér from behind, were hér mark's guards! Shé'd tried to rob someone with *guards*! Not even the most merciful of deities would forgive such foolishness.

The other reason hér stomach twisted was because hè was beautiful.

Hè was a true Child of the Islands, as was the poetic way to refer to Alabans of mixed parentage, but now shé saw hìm head-on there was definitely something Naridan about hìs skin tone, hìs cheeks, and hìs eyes. That would explain why hìs guard had so casually gendered hìm in public, if hè held to the crude ways of that people… Oh, *but* those eyes! So deep and dark they drank in what light filtered down from the occluded sky, under the wide brim of hìs straw rain hat, and between the curtains of hìs long, dark hair. Shé studied hìs face, searching for a flaw, but could find nothing. Even the slight scar on hìs chin, presumably some childhood injury, merely subtly emphasised the clean line of hìs jaw.

Jeya had never felt so cheated. Shé'd always thought that if shé were to be sent to the magistrate, and the gallows, it would be by some spiteful, ugly elder who resented hér very existence. To be condemned to death—and condemned shé surely would be, when accused by someone of hìs apparent standing—by such a beautiful creature left hér not just despairing, but hollow and conflicted. Shé at least wanted to be able to hate hìm, not feel this confusing whirl of fear, lust, and envy…

"Bring them," the youth said after a moment, tilting hìs head. Jeya felt hér captor's arms loosen for a moment, but before shé could make a break for it a strong hand twisted itself through hér sodden hair, trapping hér as securely as any chain would have. Shé found hérself marched forwards, head held down so shé stared at hér own sandalled feet as shé was propelled along. Out of the corner of hér eye shé saw the Adranian shooing the crowd away, back towards the puppet show.

Shé was forced onto one of the smaller side streets. What shé'd give for Nabanda to be nearby! But even hê wouldn't intervene in this, good friend though hê was. Hê'd get hîmself sent to the gallows too, if hê laid a hand on this yòuth or hìs guards.

"Look at mè," the yòuth said, and the hand in Jeya's hair pulled back, forcing hér face upwards. Shé grunted at the sharp pain in hér scalp, and blinked when the rain fell into hér eyes as hér head was tilted too far. Shé reached up to wipe them clear, then found the rain had stopped.

Or rather, the yòuth was now holding hìs rain hat over both their faces. Which, given the hat wasn't *that* big, meant hìs face was now mere inches away. Jeya swallowed, hér mouth dry.

"Why did you try to steal from mè?" the yòuth asked. Hìs voice was smooth, barely deeper than hér own, and made hér think of the sticky honey glaze on sweetcakes... *Stop that, yóu little fool! Be ready to run if yóu can!*

"I'm hungry," shé said simply. It was true; praying to Jakahama had given hér quite the appetite. Shé tried to stare at hìm defiantly, but hér heart was pounding for a variety of reasons, and shé doubted shé looked particularly impressive.

"What will happen if Ì send you to the magistrate?" hè asked softly.

Jeya swallowed again. "They'll hang me." Shé didn't use a gendered intonation because neither hè nor hìs guards needed to know. At least hè hadn't presumed; but then, even Alabans with Naridan ancestry knew better than to do that for others, no matter how brazenly they might announce themselves.

Hè pursed hìs lips, plump and full—*Stop that!*—and shook hìs head a little. "That will never do. Not for someone whose only crime was hunger."

Jeya's soul leapt into her throat. Did hè mean...?

"Give mè your hand. Please."

Stunned, Jeya obeyed. Hè placed hìs hat back on hìs head and took hér fingers in hìs, which sent tingles dancing across the back of hér hand. Then hè wrapped her fingers around the cold, hard shapes of several coins, and stepped back.

"Please do not try to rob mè again." Hè raised hìs eyes slightly to look past hér. "Let them go."

"Màster…" the guard behind Jeya said, the word as close to a protest as they probably thought they could get away with.

"Let them *go*," the yòuth said, hìs brows lowering. Jeya felt more than heard the guard's frustrated huff, but the fingers in hér hair relaxed and withdrew; a little clumsily, because the curls shé'd inherited from hér fàther had a mind of their own sometimes, as well as soaking up the rain until hér head felt twice as heavy as usual.

Shé snatched one last look at the yòuth's face, hastily stammered hér thanks, then turned and ran before hè could change his mind. Shé was three streets away before shé stopped to look in hér hand, and shé was glad shé'd run as fast and far as shé had. Hè'd given hér three coppers and, by Jakahama's paddle, a silver!

Jeya instinctively looked around, then tucked the coins safely away. The silver was a tidefall shé could put towards buying hér way into the Shore Birds. Nabanda hadn't liked hér plan of joining a thief crew, but Jeya was sick of scraping by. Shé wasn't big, like Nabanda, and couldn't rely on hîm always being around to stand up for hér. A place in a crew would mean more danger in some respects, but at least shé wouldn't have to worry about having hér food snatched off hér, or being kicked out of a sleeping spot because someone bigger had come along. Besides, the Shore Birds were rumoured to be decent sorts, and not too closely affiliated with any of the Sharks. Working for a Shark was a good way to get rich, but it was also a good way to get dead if something went wrong, and Jeya's dreams of wealth weren't as important to hér as keeping breathing. There was a reason why "swim with the Sharks, and you end up as bait" was a saying in East Harbour.

That was the plan for the silver. The coppers, however, would do nicely to sate the hunger still gnawing at her belly…

MIKE BROOKS

* * *

NGAIYU'S PLACE WAS a squat structure of sun-bleached wood on low stilts, a few streets back from the waterfront. No one Jeya had ever spoken to knew how Ngaiyu had come by it, but its history was nowhere near as important as its function: a relatively safe place to get your head down at night. The walls might be cracked and their paint might be peeling, but the roof was sound and the floor usually dry, and there would be a steaming pot of something over the fire. Ngaiyu charged for shelter and food, but not so much the street kids couldn't afford it, unless the day had been very bad indeed. Ngaiyu never asked where the money came from, either, although that didn't mean thëy didn't know. Ngaiyu knew most things thëy needed to.

Jeya had bedded down in hér favourite corner and hér eyes were starting to close against the dull light of the cookfire when shé became aware of someone settling down beside hér. Shé pushed hérself up onto one elbow and gripped the knife on hér belt that Nabanda had given hér years ago; it was a small thing, but capable of parting flesh if needed. Most people knew better than to inconvenience another of Ngaiyu's guests, but there would sometimes be someone new, or foolish.

"Jeya?" the new arrival whispered.

The voice seemed familiar, but shé couldn't place it. "Who's that?" shé replied, keeping hér voice low. No one wanted to attract Ngaiyu's wrath for disturbing the room.

"Damau."

Jeya relaxed a little. Damau was harmless; a year or so younger, and smart in every way except those involving dealing with people. They trusted easily and unwisely, and Jeya had intervened more than once to stop bullying from becoming something more serious. Ngaiyu had told Jeya shé wasn't helping, but Jeya hadn't been able to stand aside and just let it happen.

All the same, shé was trying to sleep. Knowing Damau, they wanted someone to talk to and assumed Jeya would want to talk as well. It was how they tended to think.

"Damau, it's late."

"I saw what happened in the market."

Jeya tensed again. Had Damau seen the money? Had they followed hér and watched hér stash the silver? But why would they let on?

"So?"

"I followed them back to their house."

"You did *what?*" Jeya very nearly forgot to keep hér voice down, and the last word came out as a strangled squeak. "Why, in all the gods' names?'

"I saw them give you money, so I thought they must have quite a lot, and maybe they'd have more at their house."

Jeya swallowed hard. "Damau, tell me you weren't seen. Tell me you didn't go into hìs house!"

"Of course not! I'm not *stupid*, Jeya. But—"

Footsteps, across the wooden floor. A sudden patch of darker darkness that swept in front of the fire and plunged them into even deeper shadow. Jeya held hér breath, too startled to make a noise. By the Hundred, Damau *had* been seen, and now someone had followed them back here...

"Who's that, next to Jeya?"

Jeya breathed again. It was only Ngaiyu.

"Damau." Their voice was suddenly small—not just quiet, but actually small. Jeya had noticed Damau had a different voice for talking to people who scared them, and Ngaiyu was one of those people.

There was a rustle of cloth as Ngaiyu crouched. Jeya caught a whiff of the earthy hair oil thëy used, which brought back memories. Jeya's môther had kept Jeya's hair short when shé'd been young, since Jeya had inherited hér fàther's hair and hè'd not been around to tell either of them how best to look after it, given the ship hè'd sailed with shortly after Jeya's birth had never returned. It hadn't been until hér môther died and Jeya found her way to Ngaiyu's place that she'd learned about bone combs and hair oil.

"You're under my roof, you respect my rules," Ngaiyu whispered hoarsely. "Ï'll have you quiet, or you go back on the street tonight, and Ï keep your copper." Thëy stood up and walked back across the floor, picking thëir way to thëir rocking chair with the near-silent expertise of one who knew the location of every creaking floorboard. Bone combs and hair oil or not, Ngaiyu didn't play favourites when it came to keeping order.

Jeya lay back down and shut hér eyes.

"Jeya?"

Shé rolled over until shé was close enough to Damau to feel hér own breath reflected back off their skin. "*If you get me kicked out of here…*"

Damau still didn't stop talking, but they lowered their voice to the very faintest of whispers. "Jeya, the house is *huge.*"

Jeya cast a glance over at Ngaiyu's chair. There was more than one way to buy into a crew. You could approach with a fistful of money, but you could also tip them off to a lucrative score. It would need to be a bigger score, because it would be the crew taking the risk, but it could still set you up.

The city's large houses could seem tempting for a thief, but rumour was they weren't always as full of riches as they looked. You needed to be sure they were worth the risk. On the other hand, a yòuth that gave money away to a pickpocket probably wasn't short of it.

In hér mind's eye shé saw those eyes again, shaded beneath a rain hat. Jeya bit hér lip thoughtfully.

"Show me tomorrow."

DAIMON

"Lord?" Gador the smith called uncertainly from behind one of the less solid parts of Black Keep's walls, as Daimon and the Raiders approached. The lowborn still clutched weapons, but the steady, non-aggressive approach of the foreigners had confused them. Instead of preparing to fight, or fleeing, most of Black Keep waited to see what happened next.

Daimon unfastened his war mask and removed his helm to ensure they could all see his face, then shook his braids loose. Worried, curious eyes stared back at him. They'd drawn a wagon across the largest gap in the wall, but the grey stone was little more than eight cubits high in any case, and such makeshift barriers would do little to repel a determined assault. It was fortunate indeed Sattistutar hadn't come here to pillage.

He hoped.

"People of Black Keep!" Daimon shouted, praying silently to Nari that his appraisal of Sattistutar's intentions had been accurate. "The Raiders have come in such numbers that they could kill us all, but this is not their wish! This lord has spoken to their chief, and they wish only to settle here!"

"But Lord Daimon," someone shouted, "how do we know they won't kill us in our sleep?"

"We don't!" Daimon replied, with a sidelong glance at

Sattistutar. He realised such honestly might not encourage his people, and so hastily continued. "But when they came in this lord's youth, a far smaller force attacked our home when we were better defended, and they used no such subterfuge then! Why should they use tricks today, when they have even less need of them?"

"Where is Lord Asrel?" a mellifluous male voice spoke up. Daimon frowned, scanning the wall until he saw the speaker: Shefal, the handsome son of a disgraced sar. The young man had a small freeholding that had once been his father's, and never missed an opportunity to remind everyone Daimon had been lowborn, so long as he could do so surreptitiously. Privately, Daimon suspected Shefal had always resented not being adopted by Black Keep's lord.

"Lords Asrel and Darel felt honour compelled them to die fighting," Daimon admitted, "but no one needed to die today! Chief Sattistutar has spared their lives despite the fact Lord Asrel tried to kill her, and this lord takes that as evidence of her goodwill!"

"Those bastards killed your man's wife!" a grey-haired man screamed, apparently unable to contain himself any longer. "You'd have us live alongside them!?"

"Aye, and your woman's brother!"

"And your man's husband!"

And so it begins. Daimon raised his hands. "What this lord would have you do has no bearing here! The Raiders have decided to settle in Blackcreek lands, and there is little we can do to stop them. No family will be turned out of their home; there are empty buildings enough within our walls." He solemnly drew his shortblade. "Some may say this lord has forsaken his honour, but he swears on such honour as remains to him, and on his life itself, that he shall exact what revenge he can on these people if they prove false."

To his surprise, and no small amount of apprehension,

Sattistutar chose that moment to step forward and remove her own helm. She turned out to have hair the colour of ripe wheat, cut untidily short at the front and falling only to her shoulders at the rear.

"This man is Saana Sattistutar, Chief of Clan Brown Eagle!" she shouted, prompting no small amount of murmuring. "She give promise as chief: any Brown Eagle who hurts or steals from you will face this man!"

Daimon moved to her side and put his mouth close to her ear. "You do realise you are telling them that you are a man?"

"Nalon told this man that to say you are woman here is to say you are less than a man," Sattistutar replied with a derisive snort. "Your tongue is…" She trailed off, but Daimon got the impression it was only because she didn't know words that were sufficiently uncomplimentary. He bristled, but forced himself to remain calm. He would help no one by starting an argument over a savage mangling his language.

"They may be more inclined to believe you are peaceful if they see something other than warriors," he said instead, eyeing the wall of giants with barbaric weapons behind her.

Sattistutar nodded, and turned to shout something. There was some muttering and shuffling, but then the mass of wooden shields parted to reveal a sort of Raider the folk of Black Keep hadn't seen before. There were old folk and young children swaddled in blankets against the vicious chill of the late winter winds, and the sick and the lame. There were also able-bodied adults with no shield or weapon, carrying sacks or pulling rough wooden sledges loaded with the Raiders' supplies; the seed and food Sattistutar had spoken of, as well as tools.

"Send them in first," Daimon said, gesturing at the newcomers.

"Will they be safe?" Sattistutar demanded.

Daimon pulled his right gauntlet off, and rubbed at his eyes. "This lord has no idea, but we must start somewhere. They will be less threatening than your warriors, in any case."

"You realise that if your people attack, this man's warriors will attack also?"

Daimon looked at her, this pale-faced barbarian chieftain from across the ocean with hard, dark grey eyes like two pieces of flint, and snorted. "You didn't expect this to be easy, did you?"

To his amazement, she laughed. "No."

"Then we are in agreement." He turned back to the walls. "Open the gates! Clear a way! And stay your hands from violence, unless you want to doom us all!"

This was the test. If his people held back and refused to acknowledge him, he had no idea how long Sattistutar would be content standing outside Black Keep's modest walls like a beggar. He watched Shefal through narrowed eyes, waiting for him to say something foolish. No, not foolish; the man was no fool. Self-serving, rather.

Shefal's lips pursed, but he held his tongue. Perhaps he didn't want to draw the attention of a couple of hundred armed Raiders, especially when their chief could apparently speak and understand Naridan. Instead, with many uncertain glances at each other, some of the townsfolk began to disappear from the tumbledown ramparts.

"Come," Daimon said to Sattistutar. "The Road Gate is on the west side. Your sledges won't need to be lifted over the walls."

Sattistutar made a sweeping motion with her arm and shouted something, which was echoed with truly startling volume by a rail-thin woman with two thick, greying braids and a face like an angry hatchet, who stood in the warriors' front rank. The Brown Eagle clan milled confusedly for a few seconds, then began to shuffle towards where the north road terminated at Black Keep's hard old gates of iron-studded white maple.

"What of these?" the Raider woman asked, gesturing towards where Asrel and Darel were still held by some of her armed companions. Neither his brother nor his father would look at him, for which Daimon was both grateful and angry. Everything he'd been taught since his adoption told him he'd brought great shame upon himself and his house, and had failed his people... but as yet, the Raiders hadn't swept down on Black Keep and eviscerated the population. As yet, no one had died. Surely, *surely* that was better?

"Sar?" said the Raider woman.

He blinked, and pulled himself out of his brief lapse into self-doubt. The bones were cast, and he'd have to trust to luck, to Nari, and his ancestor spirits that they'd fall in his favour.

"Bring them, but do not harm them." He thought for a second, then decided it couldn't remain a secret for long in any case. "They are this lord's father and brother."

Sattistutar's eyebrows climbed up her face, disappearing behind her ragged fringe. "One of them tried to kill you."

"This lord's father," Daimon acknowledged, a hollow growing in his chest. He could read the confusion in her face, despite her alien features. "He felt his son had betrayed him, and abandoned honour."

Sattistutar seemed to digest that, then nodded soberly. "This man sees now why you sars are so fearsome, if you must defend from your own families."

"It's not... Never mind." Daimon sighed. "Bring them. A secure place must be found for them."

"You fear they will try to kill you again?" Sattistutar asked as they began to skirt Black Keep's wall amidst the jumble of slightly subdued-looking Raiders. Daimon supposed they weren't used to meekly filing into a foreign town's gate, and wondered for a moment if many of them would feel more confident about charging in, weapon in hand, knowing exactly what to expect.

"Perhaps," he admitted, reminding himself that Sattistutar and her barbarians would know nothing of the sar's honour code, "but they may also try to take their own lives out of shame for not dying in battle. This lord cannot allow them near a blade. The shame is this lord's, not theirs, though they will not see it as such."

"Many ways to die do not need blade," Sattistutar pointed out.

"None they would take," Daimon told her. "The only honourable death for a shamed sar is by a blade."

"You are strange people," Sattistutar said seriously. "There is much this man must learn."

Those few words gave Daimon hope. He looked again at the collection of unarmed Raiders trudging towards Black Keep's gates, and some certainty solidified in his gut. These people truly meant to settle and stay. He had not been deceived, had not betrayed his father's trust for nothing. The Raiders could overwhelm Black Keep if they chose, but could not hope to withstand a force brought against them by the other nearby thanes, let alone if Marshal Brightwater were to rally the south. To survive here they would need to keep their heads low and, as the Brown Eagles' chief had just acknowledged, learn.

He wondered if Sattistutar realised what leverage that gave him over her.

He pushed the thought from his mind. The head of the Raider column had reached Black Keep's gates, and therefore the next obstacle to reaching sundown with no blood spilled. None of the barbarians seemed too eager to approach the entrance, which was unsurprising given that the gates were not yet opened.

"Come," he said to Sattistutar, "it is time to show this lord's people why they should not fear yours." The Raider eyed him coolly, but followed as he strode up to the pale wood and thumped it with his gauntlet.

One of the double gates swung inwards, and Daimon found himself face-to-face with Gador. The smith was holding a spear, with a scabbarded sword tucked into his belt: not a longblade, but Gador was competent, and the weapons he forged were good quality.

"Lord?" the smith muttered, nervously eyeing the assembled Raiders beyond. "Should we send to Lenby for help?"

"And turn the entire town into hostages?" Daimon asked

softly. "No, Gador. If a force arrives, this peace will break and many of us will not survive: the Raiders will not give us a chance to ally our strength to our countrymen and attack them from within. Our only hope is to make this work... but that applies to them, as well." He waved a hand at a couple of fearful-looking Black Keepers. "Get that other gate open, men. And someone find Osred!"

"The steward, lord?" Gador looked confused.

"Aye," Daimon confirmed. "The Raiders have food and seed, and this lord would see it stored with our own. Osred knows best how to manage such things." He leaned closer to the smith and lowered his voice. "This lord must also press an urgent task upon you: sturdy bars to secure rooms at the keep. This lord's father and brother cannot be thrown in the cells like common criminals, but cannot be left free while their actions may endanger us all."

The smith swallowed audibly at the notion of being party to such an act, but took a deep breath and nodded. "Yes, lord. This smith has bars at the forge that should suffice."

The second door of the double gate creaked open. Daimon turned to face the Raiders who still lurked uncertainly beyond it.

"Enter then, if you truly come in peace!"

Sattistutar raised her voice, repeating what he assumed were his words in her own language, then stepped forwards. Her people followed her as though expecting a trap, but their chieftain seemed unafraid. Daimon wasn't sure what that warranted more; grudging respect, or wariness.

SAANA

Saana wasn't sure if she'd ever been so afraid.

Certainly, her one and only raiding trip, to this very town, had been full of fear. However, that had been largely blocked out by the roar of battle until only the faintest tint remained at the edges. The sheer press of combat had left no time for fear: there'd only been the strangely muted roar of voices, the thudding ache of her left arm as she'd caught blows on her shield, and the watery weakness of her right trying to swing an axe that seemed to weigh as much as a sleeping goat. Only when the sars had appeared with their deadly blades and their dragons, and the father of this Flatlander had eviscerated Njiven with the same ease she would gut a fish, had the fear rushed back. The tide was already turning by that time, and she was able to retreat towards the yolgus without having to face that particular nightmare.

Now, however, she was not one insignificant part of a screaming battle line led by Black Kal. Now she was the leader, and her people lacked the simple unity of purpose possessed by a raiding force. They'd held together on the sea voyage—they might be the children of Father Krayk, but even a fool knew the Dark Father wouldn't hesitate to take down the unwary on his domain—but these were uncharted waters for them all. Save Nalon, perhaps, and even he'd received a frosty welcome from his birthland.

But what could she do, other than grit her teeth and walk into this maze of buildings? She hadn't expected this to work so well. She'd expected to be rebuffed and attacked, forced to fight simply to find somewhere to live: that was why she'd chosen this small, isolated place. Now this Daimon Blackcreek had gone against his people's customs and was allowing them to settle. She couldn't work out if that made him a coward, or indeed whether she should care even if it did.

"Where would you have us go?" she asked Daimon hesitantly in his language, trying and failing to read his ruddy, flat features.

"First, to the town square," he replied, after a moment's thought. "We must see you, and you must see us." He turned and led the way through Black Keep's muddy streets, either not noticing or choosing to ignore the fear or hatred on the faces of most of his folk. Saana saw the expressions, however, and had no trouble reading them compared to their reserved lord. Her initial reaction was to clutch her weapons tighter and scowl back, but she curbed that instinct ferociously. She needed to convince them her clan really wasn't going to slaughter them all in their beds.

She looked at her people. Some of them looked relieved at how things were going, but most seemed as uneasy as the Flatlanders. A couple of the Unblooded looked positively sullen: they'd have to wait for another day to prove their worth in battle. Yelling at them to smile would hardly help, but...

Ristjaan passed by her, whistling tunelessly. It was about the only sign of stress the big man ever showed, and Saana swore he only did it to aggravate others so his own nerves were less apparent. However, it gave her an idea.

She grabbed Tsolga by the arm. "Start a song."

"A what?" The horn-sounder looked at her as though she'd gone mad.

"A song," Saana repeated. "Not a war chant. Something... softer. We need to show them we're people. Only people sing."

"Birds sing," Tsolga pointed out.

Saana gave her a level look, which she hoped conveyed exactly how close she was to pushing the old woman over into the mud.

"Fine," Tsolga sighed. "One of the Songs of Creation?"

"That would do nicely," Saana said. Tsolga took a deep breath and tilted her head back, but instead of a braying battle command, an ululating wail issued forth.

It certainly attracted attention, from Naridan and Tjakorshi alike. It was only usually heard in the clan's great longhouse during Long Night, when the seas raged, the gales howled, Father Krayk had swallowed the sun, and there was naught to do but keep the fires burning and huddle around them. Then the clan would pass the time with songs and tales, and oldest of all were the Songs of Creation.

Tsolga sang of the ocean, and Saana quickly joined in, despite the fact she'd never been the best singer: the ocean was chaos, after all. Others quickly took it up, a raucous chorus of voices, but then a purposeful current emerged from the noise. Saana sang a little quieter as some of the men began the part of Father Krayk, moving through the ancient oceans before time itself was born.

The swell of singing rang out through the buildings of Black Keep, and heads lifted to join in all along the line of the clan. The Songs of Creation weren't *sacred*, the word Nalon had used to describe the Flatlander buildings devoted to their God-King, but every Brown Eagle knew them, and no one wanted to hear them sung poorly.

Crack! The first land was separated from the seabed by Father Krayk and pushed towards the surface. In the longhouse, the clan would clap at once, or slap their chests. Here, many struck weapons on their shields. Saana looked around, worried the Naridans would assume this was a prelude to an attack, but to her surprise and no small amount of satisfaction, she saw no sign of it. The locals seemed transfixed and, in many cases, curious.

Good. The more they know about us, the more they may think of us as like them. Saana broke into a jog, ruefully aware it would do little harm to her singing, and made her way to the head of the line. She reached it just as the first Brown Eagles followed Daimon Blackcreek into a paved square between buildings. On the far side was a narrow strip of water—a moat, Nalon had called it, a water channel used as a defence—and beyond this, over a short and narrow stone bridge, was the wall of Black Keep's stronghouse. This, she presumed, was where the lords of Blackcreek lived. As someone who'd grown up in one end of a thatched longhouse, she had to concede the stone monstrosity was impressive.

Daimon Blackcreek looked uncertain, insofar as she could tell. She slapped one hand onto her sea leather as they reached the part where another land was born, ignoring the stinging in her palm, and walked over to him.

"What are you doing?" he asked.

"Singing of how the world was created," she replied. A thought occurred to her. "Do your people sing?"

"Do they…? Of course."

"Well," Saana said, watching her clan file into the square. "Once we came and brought death. Now we come and bring song." She looked at him. "What are we to do now?"

"This lord must speak to his people. Not all were at the wall earlier." He bit his lip as though in thought, and Saana was struck by how young he looked. She'd thought of him as a sar, first and foremost, but now she could see him as a callow youth. She would wager there were Unblooded in the Brown Eagle clan's ranks not too much younger than this man with his hair in narrow braids.

He leaned slightly closer to her as the number of Brown Eagle voices in the square swelled the noise of singing. "Do your people farm? Do you sow crops?"

"This man said we brought seed," she replied, confused. What did he think they intended to do with it? Where did he think it came from?

"Of course you did." He made a gesture with his hand she didn't quite understand, and she tried to remember to ask Nalon about it later. "This lord apologises."

Saana snorted, unable to totally strangle off a laugh. Daimon's face closed off again and he leaned back, and she realised he must be offended.

"This man is apologies as well," she said soberly, then ruined the effect by snorting again. She tried to explain before this young sar decided to draw his sword again. "Here we stand, her people in your town, and we are falling over our..." She couldn't remember the word she wanted, and fell into frustrated silence.

"Manners," Daimon finished softly. A faint quirk at the corner of his mouth suggested he understood her meaning, and why she found it amusing. "A deadlier foe than either of us."

Saana smiled in return. Perhaps not all sars were quite as harsh and humourless as Nalon had suggested. "You asked of farming."

Daimon nodded. "It is spring, and the ground is thawing. This lord's people are starting to turn the earth and plant seed. If you would settle here, you must help."

"We have no wish to starve when winter comes," Saana replied, watching the last of her clan enter the square. "We would do these things in Tjakorsha."

"Good." Black Keep folk were coming in after the clan, watching them with apprehension, but also curiosity. The song was drawing to a close, and Saana signalled Tsolga that she shouldn't move into another. The old woman nodded and let out another high-pitched wail as the melody of Father Krayk sank back into the chaos of the ocean, the lands now standing proud and tall above the waves, and the clan fell silent.

"Go stand with your folk," Daimon instructed her, turning away. Saana bristled at being given orders like she was one of his Flatlanders, but he was already several paces away and raising his voice. She contented herself with glaring at the back of his head, and did as he'd said.

"I'm impressed," Ristjaan said, as she rejoined them. "We're inside their walls and we didn't even have to kill anyone!"

"There's a reason she's chief, you big idiot," Tsolga told him sharply. "The real question is; how long will it last?"

"That's my worry," Saana admitted. "Still, this Daimon seems sensible."

"Easy on the eye, too," Tsolga cackled, pushing her fist through the fingers of her other hand.

"Tsolga!" Saana scowled at her. "He's young enough to be your grandchild!"

"And since when has that stopped me?"

"Never," Saana sighed. Zhanna appeared at her shoulder, and she turned to her daughter. "Thanks for reining in the Unblooded. I thought our hope was lost when Tsolga sounded the charge."

Zhanna looked at her sullenly. "They'll all think I'm a coward now, no matter what you said."

"I pity the first one of them who calls you that to your face," Saana replied, trying a smile. Zhanna just turned away and studied the shoulder of the clanswoman next to her, who stared straight ahead in turn rather than get involved in an argument between the chief and her daughter.

"I don't see the problem," Tsolga grinned, showing cracked and stained teeth, attempting to lighten the mood. "When the Dark Father wants me to stop chasing men, he'll take me from this world. Until then, I reason I'm owed a bit of pleasure."

"How come you've never looked my way?" Rist said, sounding hurt.

"I said 'pleasure', not 'disappointment'. You think the women in this clan don't talk to each other, boy?"

"Shut up, both of you," Saana snapped as Rist laughed his nasty, tearing laugh again. The Black Keep folk had assembled in the square, facing across from the packed mass of the clan. There was no mistaking the difference in numbers: the Naridans were outnumbered by about three to one at Saana's best guess, and most clearly didn't fancy themselves as fighters. It would have been a slaughter had it come to it, even with the nominal protection of the walls. But where were the dragons?

Someone had pushed a wagon into the square, a rough wooden thing with wisps of straw still scattered on the bed, but Daimon Blackcreek clambered up onto it nonetheless. Thus visible to all, he began to speak.

"People of Black Keep! This lord has spoken to the chief of these folk from over the sea whom we know as Raiders. Tomorrow, they will lend their efforts to yours to till the soil, to gather firewood... We know of their skill in ships to come this far, they can fish with us as well. There is one among them, a man called Nalon, who was Naridan before they took him from a ship. He has lived with them and has married, much as Amonhuhe of the Mountains did when she married Bilha. I do not deny the Raiders have wounded us in the past, but they no longer wish to take what they need by force. Perhaps we can learn to live with them."

Saana watched the people of Black Keep. There was much turning of heads and muttering with neighbours, not to mention distrustful glances across the square. However, she also saw some nods here and there, as well as what looked like a couple of disagreements. She took those as a good sign, too: if there was disagreement, hopefully not all of the Flatlanders wanted to slit her clan's throats while they slept.

"Tonight, we will break bread together," Daimon continued. "They have brought food, and this lord will have Osred open our stores." A pleased-sounding ripple ran through the assembled Naridans, but Saana didn't think that was why Daimon had stopped speaking. She was proved correct when he took a deep breath and began again.

"Some of you may think it is not this lord's place to make these decrees." He seemed to be looking for a particular face in the crowd, but Saana had no idea who. "Lord Asrel is the Thane of Blackcreek. He wished to fight, even though we would have surely died. This lord also fears that had we fought, the killing would not have stopped with the three of us." Daimon turned to look Saana in the eyes. "This lord would like his father and brother brought forth."

By the Dark Father, you might have given me some warning. Saana turned to the uncomprehending mass of her clan and raised her voice. "Bring the sars out! We've got two of their chiefs here so make it nice and easy, don't let them fall on their faces, but for the love of Kydozhar Fell-Axe, don't let them grab a weapon!"

The two were escorted through the ranks, still held by Tjakorshi captors. Both only had one Brown Eagle on each arm though, so presumably they'd worn themselves out through struggling.

The Black Keep folk reacted predictably, a mix of gasps and outraged shouts, but Daimon held his hand up for quiet. "Father! No one has died, and your son does not believe anyone will. Do you still think we should attempt to drive these people from our land?"

"You are a wretch, without honour." To Saana's surprise, the older sar's voice wasn't a snarl of anger. It was simply level and heavy, as though stating unpleasant fact. "You are a traitor to this lord's name, and to this land. He does not know what error of judgement drove him to choose you as a child, but he bitterly regrets it."

Daimon's jaw set, but Saana could see he'd been wounded by the words. "Then exile this son, if you must: he has no wish to be Thane of Blackcreek while you still live. But first swear to him, on your honour, that you will not doom your people by taking up your blade."

"This lord will swear no such thing. He knows his duty, though it may cost his life." The older man barked a hollow laugh. "You think you've saved this town? High Marshal Brightwater will hear of this, and he'll come south! He'll drive this scum into the sea, he'll take your head, and he'll probably execute half of Black Keep as an example!"

Daimon shook his head as worried mutters passed through the Black Keep folk. "You know we're unlikely to see pedlars for a while yet, Father: only Amonhuhe's folk come to trade before summer, and they won't care who lives here so long as we have fish oil and salt to barter. Should the Marshal come south, we'll have to ensure all he finds are hard-working folk, living in peace." He moved his gaze slightly to the younger sar, the man he'd described as his brother, although Saana couldn't see much of a resemblance. "Darel, are you with our father in this?"

"This lord is."

Daimon's face clouded. Saana wondered how much of that was due to the reply, and how much due to the wording. As she understood their strange, complicated language, Darel should have referred to himself as a brother. To say "lord" implied he now saw Daimon as beneath him.

"So be it," Daimon said heavily. "Your brother will arrange for quarters in the keep to be secured."

"You will not even let us take our lives in shame?" his father roared, suddenly trying to wrench free. To Saana's great relief, her clansmen's grip held true. "It is bad enough that *you* have forgotten honour, without taking it from us as well!"

"Your son hopes he can prove the wisdom of this course to you," Daimon said soberly. He turned back to face the townsfolk, who'd been watching the exchange with apprehension. "Who here wishes this lord's father and brother freed, to take up arms against the Raiders?"

There was an uncomfortable silence of shuffling feet and oblique glances. The villagers clearly felt caught between their lords, which didn't seem like an enviable position to Saana. However, no one stepped forward to cry for the immediate release of the other two Blackcreeks, so Daimon nodded with finality.

"Let it be remembered that Daimon Blackcreek takes full responsibility for this decision, and all that follows. He will face High Marshal Brightwater, the God-King, or Nari Himself should he return to us, and ask them to attribute to him any blame they may feel rests on you." He clapped his hands. "But now, we have work to do! Bring out the feasting tables, and build fires!"

"Lord Daimon!"

One of the Naridans had stepped forward, and Saana saw Daimon's face drop as though he'd just bitten into a rotten fish.

"Shefal," Daimon said, quickly restoring his blank expression. "You have something to say?"

"Lord Daimon, it may be as you say," the man called Shefal said. He was smooth-cheeked and soft-faced, and entirely too skinny in Saana's opinion. He'd never survive a harsh winter on Kainkoruuk. "Perhaps these Raiders have had a change of heart; perhaps they truly mean us no harm. But what have they shown us of that, other than not yet drawing their weapons on us?"

"You do not think that a significant change?" Daimon asked. His tone was light, but Saana could hear something lurking beneath it. There was dislike between the two of them, she could tell that much.

"What if they were willing to offer further assurance?" Shefal suggested. "A hostage, perhaps?"

Hostage. Saana didn't know the word. She looked over her shoulder, trying to spot Nalon.

"Someone of value to them?" Shefal continued. "Your man is sure your people would feel safer if the Raiders knew your blade was always ready."

That gave Saana all the context she needed. It wasn't unheard of in Tjakorsha, although rarely done. Her immediate instinct was to refuse, but how could she expect the Naridans to believe her folk wouldn't kill their entire town, if the clan wasn't willing to put just one of their own lives in harm's way?

"This warrior!"

Zhanna stepped forwards. Saana cursed and reached out desperately, but her daughter shook her hand off and twisted away, then took another three quick steps and faced Daimon.

"This warrior!" Zhanna smacked herself in the chest, then reversed her grip on her blackstone axe so it hung upside down from her fist: a gesture of peace, although Daimon wouldn't know that. "Zhanna Saanastutar, chief daughter!"

Zhanna had been there when Nalon had taught Saana the tongue of his birthland. By the wind and waves, Saana had made Zhanna *practise* it with her! She'd not considered what her daughter might do with that knowledge. Now she watched in terror as Zhanna put her neck figuratively, and perhaps literally, under the exceptionally sharp blade of the man whose home they'd just walked into, with no more thought than when she'd dived off the *Krayk's Teeth* at seven winters old to try to swim with a baby leviathan that had surfaced nearby. Saana's heart had nearly stopped then, and she'd screamed herself hoarse at her daughter to come back. The terror she felt now was no less great, but she dared not show such weakness in front of the Naridans.

Daimon's eyes flashed from Zhanna to Saana, back again, then to Shefal, then to Zhanna once more. He clearly understood what she'd said.

He nodded. "So be it. A room will be found for you." He clapped his hands once more and jumped down from the wagon. "Come! Fire and tables!"

The Naridans began to mill into life. Saana knew she should be talking to her clan, explaining to them what had just been said, but instead she stormed forwards and grabbed her daughter by the shoulder. This time she kept her grip on the sea leather as Zhanna tried to twist away, and wrenched her around.

"What in the name of the Dark Father do you think you're doing?" she growled, biting down on the end of the sentence so it didn't become a scream of terrified rage.

"I'm helping!" Zhanna protested.

"Helping?!" Saana wanted to slap her daughter across the face, or possibly envelop her in the biggest hug imaginable and drag her away from the incomprehensibly foolish decision she'd just made.

"Helping who?"

"You!" This time Zhanna did manage to get her shoulder free, and she glared at Saana with fury that she'd dragged up from somewhere. "You can't do it, the clan needs you. The Flatlanders want someone important to you, so we don't kill them. It's got to be me. No one else would do."

Saana bit her lip in anger, but Zhanna actually had a point. It wasn't even just about someone important to the clan—Tsolga might have sufficed, or one of the witches, or one of the elders— it had to be someone the Naridans would *believe* was important. The daughter of the chief would fulfil that role in a way that no one else would.

A suspicion bubbled up in her chest and slithered past her teeth before she could stop it. "Tell me you didn't do this just because you didn't get blooded today."

Zhanna's face set into the stubborn mask Saana had become more and more accustomed to. "They can't call me a coward now. They *can't*."

Daimon was walking towards them. Saana readied herself to warn him of what would happen if he harmed her daughter... but wasn't that the point? If her clan broke their word, Daimon would kill Zhanna. If Daimon harmed Zhanna, the clan would destroy Black Keep.

The sun hadn't even dropped behind the mountains, and things were already going to the depths.

TILA

TILA HAD PAID close attention to her childhood lessons, as behoved the daughter of the God-King, and so she'd learned much about the world. There was, however, a difference between knowing something and experiencing it. The City of Islands was so *warm*. And disgustingly moist.

She watched the lumps of green-swathed rock growing larger as the southerly wind swept the *Light of Fortune* towards their destination. The ship was a merchantman, packed with sail, and the fastest she'd been able to commandeer. Even so, the voyage had taken a month, hopping cautiously up the coast.

Tila shifted position uncomfortably, surreptitiously trying to unstick the fabric of her dress from her side. Kiburu ce Alaba didn't even really have a winter, as a Naridan would understand it. Perhaps it was the constant heat that had unhinged their brains when it came even to simple matters like men and women.

"High Lady," Captain Kemanyel said deferentially, stepping up alongside her. He was a bluffly handsome man, with his dark hair in one thick plait that hung to the small of his back. "Will you want your possessions taken ashore when we make port?"

"There'll be no need for that, Captain," Tila replied. "This lady shouldn't need to remain here long."

"As you wish," Kemanyel said with a half-bow, and moved

away. Perhaps he'd hoped to get his cabin back for a few nights, but he'd be disappointed. Tila had no intention of trusting herself to an Alaban boarding house. After all, she was essentially two potential assassination targets in one, although for very different reasons.

One of the reasons Tila was so feared in the Naridan court, the reason her nickname was "The Veiled Shadow", was because many suspected she was in some way ensuring that events elsewhere occurred as Narida wished, but no one understood how she managed it. The closest scrutiny of finances, had anyone attempted it, would find no money travelling out from the Sun Palace into the world that might be used to pay spies or knives. Even Tila's own money—allocated to her as, somewhat laughably, a ward of her brother, the Crown—wasn't used for such things.

Or at least, the money everyone *thought* was hers wasn't used. But Tila was, quite literally, more resourceful than even the most suspicious courtiers could imagine.

The Princess of Narida couldn't travel to Kiburu ce Alaba on a merchantman, stroll ashore and hire some local knives to kill a local family. It was a ridiculously unsafe proposition, not to mention politically disastrous. So it was just as well that, so far as anyone knew, Princess Tila Narida had taken a leave of absence from court, as she was sometimes wont to do when the spirits seized her soul and dragged it downwards. It was well known she was still keenly affected by the violent death of her father, the old God-King, at the hands of a Morlithian border patrol when she was seventeen. It was, after all, why she still wore her mourning veil everywhere outside her own chambers twenty years later. Every now and then, her old misery reared up and caused her to partition herself off from the world, leaving the courtiers to quietly edge around each other and expand their little influences until she returned to put the fear of Nari into them again.

And she would. But first she had business to attend to here, in the warm, humid north.

Tila wore no veil on the deck of the *Light of Fortune*. Captain Kemanyel was transporting Livnya the Knife, the undisputed head of Idramar's criminal underworld and the very last woman he wanted to cross, especially since he was a smuggler. Tila had been living her peculiar double life since her father had died and, so far as she knew, there was still no one who'd realised the truth of it. No one who ever saw Livnya's face was likely to get close enough to Tila to recognise her beneath the veil, neither woman had to keep hours to suit anyone else, and Tila had never needed much sleep.

It meant Livnya's considerable wealth—built up from her "inheritance" of a criminal empire from a man named Yakov, who'd eventually died with her knife in his eye socket—could be diverted to ensure the interests of Tila's country were protected through the most unofficial of backchannels. Money Livnya made from smuggling, or stole from rich merchants and nobles, paid for Tila's eyes and ears, her bribes and knives. It was an untraceable ghost tax, and all that was required for it to work as intended was for Tila to continually outwit two different social circles containing some of the most ambitious and ruthless people in all of Narida.

Easy.

Young Barach, formerly Little Barach, was lurking by the main mast with his burly arms crossed. He was twenty-two summers old and had been Livnya's bodyguard and personal enforcer since his father, Big Barach, had retired two years previously. There was a lot of his father about him in his face and build, but Young Barach struck Tila as a touch more thoughtful than his sire.

"How do people work in this?" he asked mournfully, staring at the sky in general. "Your man thought this may've been the work of sea spirits, but it's worse now we're approaching land." He was stripped down to a short-sleeved linen shirt, which stuck to his torso in damp patches, and his breeches. Most of the sailors were bare-chested in the humid air, a fact that bothered Tila not at all, but Barach seemed possessed of greater modesty. She found it almost endearing.

"The Alabans are used to it," she told him. "They're a thin-blooded people, and the heat doesn't bother them."

"It's not just the heat, it's the air," Barach muttered. "It's like trying to breathe in a river." He looked up again as thunder rumbled ominously. Heavy clouds were building, and had already obscured the sun. "Rain soon, then."

"This lady imagines so," Tila replied. "She hopes we'll make port first."

They didn't make port first.

There were long-necked water dragons darting between the wave crests outside the East Harbour of Grand Mahewa, each beast as long as the *Light of Fortune*'s twelve-person rowboat. Tila and Barach stood at the rail watching the scaled heads, little bigger than their own, appear and disappear as they came up to breathe, when the first heavy drops of rain began to fall. Tila considered getting her cloak, but any protection it offered from the rain would have been nearly outweighed by the sweating she'd have endured from wearing it. She let the rain wash her down, occasionally wiping it from her eyes.

East Harbour was in a natural bay, the mouth of which had been narrowed by twin breakwaters of mortared stone. A watchtower stood on each, tall and proud, and Tila could just make out the skeletal shapes of ballista atop them.

"Do they expect an attack?" Barach asked, eyeing the ballista somewhat nervously. The notion of being on a ship while bolts as tall as he was rained down clearly did not appeal.

"Alaba controls the Throat of the World," Tila told him absently. "Any sea trade from the lands to the north comes through the channels between these islands, and the Alabans take their tax for the privilege of using their waters. Over time, others have taken exception to that." She laughed. "Or Alabans from other islands have decided that they should be the ones reaping the rewards. Either way, East Harbour's had need to defend itself over the years. But with these," she gestured up at the watch towers, "the war fleet within, and Lesser Mahewa behind us to send ships to aid them, you'd have to be a fool, a god, or the commander of the greatest navy the world has seen to attack the city from the sea."

Captain Kemanyel was barking commands, and his crew were reefing sails, but Tila doubted it was due to the weather. Heavy though the rain was, and despite the thunder, this was no violent storm pushed by a gale; it was as though the air simply couldn't carry its moisture any longer. However, the *Light of Fortune* was definitely slowing as it passed through the harbour's mouth.

"Captain!" Tila called. "Is there a problem?"

"We must wait for a harbour guide," Kemanyel replied to her, pointing off the starboard bow. "One approaches now."

The harbour guide was a small rowboat with six Alabans working the oars and another sitting in the bow, scudding towards them across the rain-battered waters of the harbour. Tila watched it approach until it came alongside the *Light of Fortune*, whereupon Kemanyel ordered a rope ladder tied to the railings and tossed overboard. The Alaban in the bow seized it and began climbing, and only then did Tila notice only one leg protruded from the bottom of their flowing lower garment. It didn't seem to arrest their progress much: they lurched up the ladder, bracing their single foot against the rungs and pulling themselves up with their arms. When they reached the top they swung their leg over the railing and rested against it.

"Blessings be," the harbour guide said in their own tongue. Tila knew some of it, a strange mix of courtly Alaban and the rough language used by sailors and associated thugs she'd dealt with in Idramar's backstreets. As a result she could handily welcome someone to a palace, or tell them to perform a lewd act on their own mother, but her ability to conduct a more regular conversation was limited.

"Blessings be," Kemanyel replied in the same language. "*Light of Fortune*, out of Idramar."

"Cargo?"

"Naridan ale."

The harbour guide nodded. They had no beard, and the stocky figure under their clothes could have belonged to either a man or a woman. Tila knew enough about Alaban culture to make no assumptions.

"Do you know the fees?"

Kemanyel passed them a small leather pouch. The guide undid the drawstring and tipped the coins out, then nodded again in apparent satisfaction.

"Everything seems in order. Follow to your mooring, then wait for inspection." They stowed the purse somewhere in their robes, then swung back over the side and onto the ladder. Tila half-expected them to miss their footing and fall, but they descended just as nimbly as they'd ascended. The rowboat turned and made off across the harbour, and Kemanyel called his crew to take up oars and follow.

East Harbour, as it slowly became revealed through the rain, was enormous.

Idramar sat on the northern bank of the Idra estuary, the mightiest of all Narida's rivers, and its docks were both large and busy with trading traffic. However, Tila quickly realised as she looked around, it paled in comparison to East Harbour.

The bay looked as though a giant had taken a bite out of the side of the island, and must have been a mile across. It was not a truly smooth circle, but wasn't too far from that, with the breakwaters further narrowing the open side. All shores were packed with wharfs and jetties, and clustered behind them was the city itself.

"It's a fair sight, isn't it?" Captain Kemanyel offered.

"Truly," Tila agreed. She'd understood, to an extent, the level of Kiburu ce Alaba's influence, but it was a different thing entirely to see it. And this was, she reminded herself, just one of Alaba's many ports. None were so large as Grand Mahewa's East Harbour, it was true, but the sheer amount of wealth that must flow through these islands was absolutely staggering.

"We'll moor near the Naridan Quarter?" she asked the captain, who nodded.

"Aye. Slip the guide a few extra coins and they'll ensure you get berthed near your potential buyers. Stint them, and you'll end up where no one'll find you."

Tila snorted in amusement. That was good business sense.

"High Lady," Kemanyel said tentatively. "This captain wonders… so he may best assist you… what is your business in East Harbour?"

Tila smiled to herself.

"This lady needs to find a Shark."

SAANA

"WHAT IS THIS?" Daimon asked dubiously, studying the small wooden cup. It contained a measure of pale liquid, poured from a miniature cask the clan had tapped especially for the meal.

"It is shorat," Saana said. "You do not have it?"

"Not by that name," Daimon replied, sniffing it. He recoiled with a startled cough. "Not at all, this lord would wager!" He looked around the walled yard, which Saana had learned was the first of three protecting the home of the Blackcreek men, and those who served them.

Saana had struggled with the notion of serving-people. Tjakorshi who yielded in battle owed their captors service for a year and a day, as was proper, but the idea there were people who made their living serving others was hard to get her head around. There even seemed to be different importances: the high table, where she and Zhanna had been seated, was clearly the place of greatest honour, yet there were at least two servants here. A man called Osred was a steward, a chief-of-servants, with long black hair that fell past his jaw in scraggly waves, and shot through with the same grey that touched the stubble on either side of his chin. The plump, balding Kelaharel was a reeve, whose apparent role was to ensure everyone in the town behaved as they were supposed to. Also present was Aftak, a priest; large for a Naridan, and in his middle years, with ferocious eyebrows and a dark beard almost fit for a Tjakorshi.

It wasn't lost on Saana that apart from her and Zhanna, everyone seated at the high table was a man.

"Your people drink this?" Daimon asked, sniffing his drink again.

"It is good for cold nights," Saana said mildly, throwing hers back in one. She was used to the burning liquor, and her eyes watered only slightly. Daimon narrowed his eyes, but imitated her.

A moment later he was clutching at his throat and coughing uncontrollably. Saana laughed despite herself, while Zhanna emitted a sort of strangled snort, but then the steward Osred stood and pointed an accusing, bony finger.

"Poison! Poison!"

Saana stopped laughing abruptly. She and Zhanna had been seated in what was apparently the guest of honour's place to Daimon's left, but there were plenty of Black Keep folk all around them. What was more, many faces had looked up at the steward's shout. All the Naridans had a metal dagger or knife to cut their food, and suddenly the yard looked less like a feasting area and more like an under-equipped battlefield.

"Wait!" Daimon spluttered, struggling to his feet and waving a hand frantically at Osred. "Wait!" He coughed again, then wiped his streaming eyes and raised a voice slightly hoarser than before. "This lord commends his steward's vigilance, but this lord simply swallowed something the wrong way!"

There was general laughter from the Naridans, and most turned back to their meals. Saana's folk hadn't understood either the steward's shriek or Daimon's response, but most of them also seemed to realise that whatever problem had arisen was gone now. Ristjaan didn't dive back into his food, though, instead raising his eyebrows at her in an obvious query. Saana shook her head slightly at him in response, to tell him that everything was fine. He shrugged, but then turned back to the tankard of foaming brown liquid in front of him that the Naridans called ale. Saana's was only half-drunk: she'd found it unpalatably bitter.

"You did not swallow that wrong, did you?" she said in a low voice, when Daimon retook his seat.

"How do your people grow so tall, with drink of this kind?" the sar said with a grimace. "This lord's throat is on fire!"

"It takes everyone like that at first," Saana admitted. A young Naridan girl came up with the shorat cask and, at Daimon's gesture, poured another cautious measure into each of their cups. Saana sipped hers more gently this time, enjoying the slow warmth. "You get used to it."

"This lord cannot imagine why you would want to," Daimon replied, but managed another sip with only a slight splutter. "Nari's teeth, that is strong!"

"You have said that name before," Saana said, taking a bite of dark bread. "Nalon said he is your god, but also he was a man."

"Nari was the first God-King," Daimon said. "He lived many years ago." He stabbed a piece of meat with his knife. "Some say he will return to us one day, reborn into a child, but they also say that his return will herald an age of ruin, for many will resist him. This lord would not wish to see such times."

"But you have another God-King now?" Saana asked. "You spoke of one earlier. Is that a different one?"

"Nari was the first, but his lineage lives on." Saana didn't recognise the word and her incomprehension must have shown, because Daimon elaborated. "His son, and then his son's son, and then his son's son's son, and so on. Nari saved us from the Unmaker, drove her demons from the land, and founded Narida. Our current God-King is Natan Narida, the third of his name. He is named for the entire country, as this lord is named for Blackcreek, the land over which his family rules."

Saana frowned. "And a king is... a chief of chiefs?"

"You have no king?" The notion seemed to shock Daimon.

"Tjakorsha just has chiefs," Saana replied, plucking a piece of meat from the bone. "A chief may have powerful clan, may conquer another clan, but no chief is above other chiefs." *No mortal chief is, at any rate.*

"Are you sure?" Daimon's eyes were focused on her, uncomfortably scrutinising. "You seem uncertain. Is this why you could not stay?"

Saana grimaced. "There is… Nalon said your closest word was 'demon', but that he had not heard of such a thing here. We call it 'draug'. Draugs can take the body of a sick person, or a dead person if the proper rites not done are, and wear them like clothes. It has been killing chiefs, breaking the clans."

"This lord thought you worshipped demons," Daimon said, taking a small sip of his shorat. Saana stared at him.

"Why would we do that?!" She held his gaze for a moment, then dropped her eyes. "Well, this man hears some of the broken clans worship this draug, think of it as a god. They are… Their thoughts are… not right?"

"Crazy?" Daimon offered.

"Perhaps." Saana would have to ask Nalon the word later.

"What is this demon called?" Daimon asked. "Have you seen it?"

"No," Saana said vehemently, shaking her head. "We have not heard that anyone knows whose body it is, but we know the draug is terrible and fell in battle, and the witches say it cannot be killed. We know it only as The Golden."

It had seemed like a Long Night fire tale, at first. Only a few of the clan could remember the last time a draug had managed to possess someone, and that had been a weak thing that the witches had driven out. When the rumours came of this being calling itself The Golden, the clan had dismissed it as Easterner nonsense. But the rumours kept coming, and then they'd heard about how the Skua clan had seized The Golden during a raid, taken it back to their lands and hanged it like the worst of criminals. Half a day it had hung, and when its followers had arrived to cut it down, it had pulled the noose from around its neck and gotten up to open the throat of the Skua clan's chief itself. What could you do, against a being like that?

Daimon didn't seem to know what to say to that, and looked away from her out across the tables. "Did you lose many on your crossing?" he asked. There hadn't been room for everyone inside the walls, so many of the clan were eating around fires in the great square beyond the gate.

"Very few," Saana replied proudly. "The voyage took less than ten, sick and old. Lodzuuk Waveborn was kind."

"Is that your god?" Daimon asked, and Saana laughed.

"No! Lodzuuk Waveborn was a man of old, a mighty one. He split the First Child of the First Tree to make a ship, and braved the Dark Father's realm to take it upon the waves. It is from him we have our skill at sailing."

"Who is this Dark Father?" Daimon asked. "This is your god, then?"

"Father Krayk swims the seas and created the lands," Saana said. "We are his children."

"And you think he keeps you safe?" Daimon asked. Saana laughed again.

"The Dark Father keeps no one safe. But every day he has not chosen to take this man, and this man hopes his gaze falls elsewhere for many years yet."

Daimon shook his head. "He sounds a cruel god."

"Father Krayk is not cruel," Saana retorted. "The sea is not cruel. The sea just is. So is Father Krayk. A fool does not respect the sea, and a fool will die there. A fool does not respect the Dark Father, and a fool will be taken by him."

"Are you calling this lord's people fools?" Daimon asked, his tone growing slightly sharper.

"How often do your ships sail out of sight of land?" Saana asked levelly.

"This lord is no ship's captain, but he does not think it happens often."

"Your people are not fools, then," Saana replied, finishing her shorat. "To cross oceans as we do, without respecting the Dark Father... *that* would be foolish."

Between two rows of benches, a Naridan servant edged around the flickering fire while steadying a flagon of ale, with an expression of furious concentration. The footing was clearly uneven, though, since she tripped and fell. She managed to prevent the jug from smashing on the stone, but the ale itself sloshed out in a foaming brown wave...

... and hit Ristjaan the Cleaver square in the back.

All conversation around the big man abruptly ceased. Saana caught a brief glimpse of her friend's expression slipping from jovial to furious as he swung around, one huge hand reaching for the monstrous steel axe that mercifully wasn't there. The Naridan, still prostrate on the floor and clutching the jug, looked up with abrupt and abject terror.

Saana sucked in a breath to shout Rist's name, well aware it probably wouldn't do any good. Daimon was rising, along with his steward. Ristjaan drew himself up to his full height, taller than anyone else within the walls.

And then he laughed.

Saana paused as that awful, tearing laugh rang out, and in that second Rist leaned down and hoisted the serving girl back to her feet, then ruffled her hair and sent her on her way with a gentle push. The girl staggered off, eyes wide in fright, but the danger was past. Ristjaan looked over at Saana and winked.

"See, Chief?" he bellowed. "These folk can't wait for me to get my clothes off!" He suited actions to words and hauled his tunic over his head, exposing a burly and hairy torso, then held it out towards the flames as though to start drying it, while a chorus of mirth and good-natured abuse rang out from the Tjakorshi benches.

"Father Krayk bless you, you big oaf," Saana muttered under her breath in her own language. Ristjaan wasn't malicious, but he could be prickly. She'd have wagered he wouldn't have been so forgiving with a Tjakorshi. Here, though, it seemed he didn't want to risk what she'd worked so hard to achieve. She glanced sideways and saw Daimon puff his cheeks out in what seemed to be relief.

"That could have been a lot worse," the sar remarked, a sentiment Saana fervently agreed with. "Who is— Wait! You there! Stop!"

A Naridan had stood, dagger in hand, and was heading for Ristjaan. Daimon's shout attracted Rist's attention, and he turned towards Saana's table. He took in the armed Naridan approaching and his expression changed again. Saana had seen that face on him before, usually immediately before he swung an axe at someone.

"Hold him!" Daimon barked, and two other Black Keep men lunged at their townsman and grabbed him. "You, man! What are you doing?" He frowned. "What is your name?"

"Evram, lord," the man replied. He didn't struggle against the men holding him, but turned to face Daimon. He had touches of grey in his dark hair: Saana supposed him to be somewhere over forty winters, if Naridans aged like the Tjakorshi.

"What are you doing, Evram?" Daimon demanded. Beyond Evram, Ristjaan was grimly pulling his still-damp tunic on again.

"Lord, that man killed this servant's brother!"

DAIMON

OF ALL THE things Daimon had hoped to hear from Evram's mouth, that wasn't one of them. He took a deep breath, trying to calm his racing heart. "How do you know this, Evram?"

"These eyes saw him do it!" the man shouted, tears starting to well up. "When the Raiders last came here, that one cut poor Tan down with an axe near as tall as your man! And he *laughed*! Your man's heard that damned laugh in his dreams! Your man thought he recognised the bastard, but held his tongue because he couldn't be sure, it was so long ago, but when your man heard him laugh..." Evram was openly weeping now, the tears sparkling in firelight as they fell.

"This servant is a good man, lord; he works hard in your fields when it's his days to do so and he's never taken what's not his, he keeps the laws your father set, but he won't stand for this! Your man will let them live here if they must, but not *him*! Not the bastard what killed this servant's brother!"

The big Raider called out in his own language, but Sattistutar snapped something at him and he subsided. Daimon hesitated, uncertain how to proceed. How would his father have handled this? Well, his father would already be dead, having fought a doomed battle against the Raiders outside Black Keep's walls and possibly killing one if not both of the Brown Eagles who spoke a civilised language, so that thought hardly helped him.

Nonetheless, his people were expectant. He'd already denied his father and brother the right to act according to their honour, what difference did it make if he did the same for this lowborn?

The difference, he thought bitterly, was that Lord Asrel's honour had required the deaths of the entire Brown Eagle clan. Evram wanted to take the life of just one, and would undoubtedly fail.

But it was Daimon's duty as lord to protect the lives of his people. He'd taken on that responsibility when he'd ordered his father and brother imprisoned. How could he pretend to be just if he let a killer go unpunished, and how could he be anything but a coward if he let one of his people die on a foreign blade?

"Does anyone else recognise one of the Brown Eagle clan as someone who has killed one of us?" he asked, raising his voice. "Will anyone swear to Nari that they know it to be true?"

One woman stood. Daimon vaguely recognised her as an alewife. Inba, perhaps? "Lord, this woman knows the big Raider too. It's as Evram says: he killed Tan. This woman swears to Nari Himself that it's true."

No one else stood, which was something. Daimon had suffered a brief vision of the courtyard being filled with hurled accusations, and descending into violence that would inevitably spell the end for his town. However, it didn't help his current problem.

There was only one thing for it. He turned to Saana Sattistutar. "You understood what has been said?"

"Yes," she replied grimly. "And you understand Ristjaan will him kill, if you let him fight?"

"This lord does." Daimon sighed. "Which is why Evram will not be the one fighting."

Sattistutar took a moment to get his meaning, but when she did her eyes widened in shock and fear. "You? He will kill you, too!"

"We shall see," Daimon replied. In truth, he had no idea, but it could be argued that he'd only lived past the afternoon on borrowed time in any case. "Will you speak this lord's words to him in your language?"

"Nalon speaks our words better than this man speaks yours," Sattistutar replied shortly, rising to her feet and shouting the man's name. Nalon proved to be on one of the closest tables and came forward apprehensively, glancing nervously about him. Daimon heard the mutters from the Black Keep folk as they caught sight of him, dressed in Raider clothes and bearing their clan mark on his forehead, but still unmistakably a Naridan by birth.

"This lord needs you to translate to the big man for me," Daimon told him, without preamble. Nalon raised his eyebrows, but nodded.

"Fine, but s'man's staying out of arm's length of him, in case you say something foolish and he gets it into his head to go for s'man."

"Something…?" Daimon bit down on an angry response. "You'd do well to remember who you're talking to."

"You want s'man to go sit back down so you can reason with Ristjaan the Cleaver using grunts and hand signals? That's fine." Nalon shrugged. "Good luck."

Daimon reminded himself that Naridan or not, Nalon had never been a subject of Black Keep, and right now he was certainly considered part of the Brown Eagle clan. "Just translate this lord's words and you can go back to your meal, if that's your concern."

"Let's get this over with, then." Nalon turned his broad shoulders away from Daimon and strode towards the big man, who was still standing near the fire with an ominous expression on his large face. "Ristjaan!"

The big Tjakorshi grunted something, then nodded to Daimon as he approached. It was odd, Daimon reflected briefly, that the Raider seemed more respectful than the man who'd grown up in these lands. Nalon and Ristjaan exchanged a couple of sentences, presumably establishing Nalon's role, then Nalon turned to Daimon. "Go ahead."

"Tell him he's been accused of killing that man's brother, when his folk last raided here," Daimon said, gesturing towards Evram. "This lord knows the same may be true of many in the Brown Eagle clan, but he is the only one this lord's people remember for certain."

Nalon spoke with Ristjaan, whose response barely needed translating given the expressive shrug which accompanied it. "He says he may have done, but he can't be sure."

"So he has raided here before?" Daimon asked, his last hope sinking.

"Don't even need to ask him that," Nalon replied. "Heard him talking about it."

"Tell him his victim's brother has demanded his life."

Another exchange. "He says the man's welcome to try to take it, but he doesn't feel like going to see the Dark Father today." Nalon paused, glancing back at Ristjaan for a second while the big man fixed Daimon with a piercing stare. "Uh, the Dark Father is—"

"This lord got the gist," Daimon cut him off. "Sattistutar spoke of their god." He took a deep breath. "Tell him that as that man's chief, this lord will fight on his behalf."

Nalon's eyes widened. "You'll do *what*?"

Daimon curled his lip. "Just translate it."

Nalon whistled softly under his breath, but turned to Ristjaan and spoke in Tjakorshi. Daimon wasn't sure what reaction he'd been expecting—amusement perhaps, or instant aggression—but was taken aback when Ristjaan frowned at him and spoke urgently to Nalon.

"He wants to know if you think that's a good idea," Nalon said. "He's worried this will all go very wrong if he kills you."

That's putting it mildly. "Thank him for his concern," Daimon replied dryly, "but tell him that this lord doesn't feel like going to see the Dark Father today."

Nalon opened his mouth as though to protest, then shut it again. He did, however take a step back from Ristjaan before speaking again. The big Raider's brow furrowed further as Daimon's words were translated, but then he let loose another of the coarse laughs that had brought them to this pass in the first place, and spoke again.

"He says he has no..." Nalon paused, searching for a word. "Blood money, maybe? It's a Tjakorshi thing, paying to settle an honour debt. Anyway, he doesn't have any, so he can't even offer that. So if you truly want to leave your people without their chief, he'll go get his weapons and armour."

"We will fight in the square," Daimon replied. At least the Raider hadn't refused: Daimon had no idea what he would have done then.

Nalon relayed that and Ristjaan grunted, then nodded at Daimon once more and turned to walk away. Daimon put the heat of the fire to his back and crossed the flagstones to where Evram still stood.

"The man Ristjaan killed Evram's brother Tan when he last came here," he announced. "He does not deny it. He will not surrender his life as judgement, and Evram is no warrior to have a chance at taking it. This lord, however, is."

He saw a glimmer of hope in Evram's features at about the same time he caught sight of sudden despair in Osred's. The steward had fretted near to tears over the dilemma of which of his lords to support, and the notion he now might lose the one he'd stood with probably weighed heavily on him.

"Evram, this is your honour," Daimon said seriously. "This lord can take it on, but you have the right to face the man yourself, if you wish it."

"Lord," Evram replied humbly, then seemed to struggle for words. He sheathed his dagger. "May Nari go with you, lord."

"So be it." Daimon grabbed Osred by the sleeve, pulling the steward away from the others.

"Lord, you will need your armour—"

"This lord won't be wearing it," Daimon cut him off. The steward's jaw dropped.

"But lord—"

"This lord has seen him fight, Osred. One blow to the head stunned Darel even wearing his helmet, and the next one would have killed him had our father not been there. The man has a steel axe, and is so strong that armour would only slow this lord down, it would not truly protect him. This lord knows what he is doing." *He hopes.* "Then again, if it turns out that he does not, do as you see fit."

"*Lord?*"

"Lords Asrel and Darel would doom this town," Daimon said shortly, "and probably execute you for treason. All things considered, this lord recommends you don't free them."

Osred swallowed, but nodded.

"The Raiders' chief…" Daimon continued, snatching a glance at Sattistutar, who was watching him with an expression that could have hewn stone. "She seems sensible, for a woman. You know as much about running Black Keep as this lord's father. If this lord should fall, speak with Sattistutar. Make this *work*."

"*Daimon*." Osred's thin, pinched face looked more shocked than Daimon could ever remember. "This servant is not a thane! He's not even a sar!"

"You are a steward," Daimon reminded him, "and a fine one, at that. This lord knows tales where stewards took over their lord's lands after his death, until another was appointed. That's what the title *means*."

"Perhaps," Osred conceded desperately, "but never when there were two more lords locked up in the keep!"

Daimon snorted humourlessly. "Then we'd both best hope this lord lives through the night, hadn't we?"

RIKKUT

RIKKUT LED THE charge between the longhouses, his breath steaming and a grin on his face. This was where he felt alive and vital; where he could find the glory he craved, imposing The Golden's will and breaking those that resisted it. This might have been Tyaszhin's warband, but Rikkut Fireheart was already a named man at one-and-twenty, and there was still glory aplenty awaiting him.

A Seal Rock clanswoman dived into her longhouse, then emerged with blackstone axe and shield in hand, but no helm on her head, or even a sea-leather jerkin to ward her from harm. She bellowed a war cry in her mush-mouthed Kainkoruuk accent and charged, her eyes filled with hatred and no expectation of survival. Rikkut would have hated to disappoint her: he deflected the woman's axe with his shield, feeling her weapon scrape across its surface, and swung low with his own, chopping into the side of his enemy's left knee and spinning away. He wrenched his axe across her leg and the savage blackstone teeth tore through her furs, lacerated skin, sliced through sinew, grated across bone. The other warrior screamed, and sprawled into the mud, her injured leg unable to support the momentum Rikkut had neatly sidestepped.

Rikkut's next blow came up underneath her neck as she struggled to rise. It was a high tide wound, releasing the red waters within to flow freely, and that was an end to it, and to her.

Parents tried to call children to them in panic, or villagers desperately gathered what valuables they had and ran for the trees. They didn't get far, but that wasn't Rikkut's concern. He wasn't after metal, or fire gems. He pressed on, at the head of a loose dozen fighters who'd elected to follow his lead.

The clan chief here was Ludir Nekoszhin, known as Snowhair even since his youth, but his ice-blonde mane had long since faded to the pure white of age. The old man had organised his warriors around him, and let the buildings fill the gaps in the shieldwall. It wasn't a bad plan when faced with superior numbers, but Ludir had never faced Rikkut Fireheart.

There were eight shields ahead, with stern-faced and armoured warriors behind them. They were the chief's Scarred; fighters who'd taken his personal mark, scored and inked into their skin as a symbol of loyalty. They wouldn't yield while Snowhair still called for them to fight, and they would be hard to break down. Impossible to outflank, too: there were similar knots of warriors blocking the other three ways between the longhouses to where Snowhair stood, his thin voice exhorting his warriors to hold.

Well, if he couldn't go through them, Rikkut would have to go over. He scanned the faces around him and his eyes lit on two: Zheldu Stonejaw, a giantess as thick as two men and undefeated at wrist-wrestling, and Rodnjan, wiry but strong.

"You two!" he snapped, pointing. "I'll need you both, with a shield. The rest of you, get in their faces!"

They had no real reason to obey him other than he seemed to have a plan and wasn't asking them to break the shieldwall themselves, but that was enough. They advanced up between the roofs on either side of them, clashing their weapons against their shields and shouting challenges. Snowhair's Scarred held their positions, their faces grim and set. There would be no charges from them; they'd just lock their shields and hold fast, and wait for the attackers to risk trying to break them down.

Rikkut called Rodnjan and Stonejaw to him, one hand on each

of their shoulders, and quickly outlined what he needed. Stonejaw nodded once and that was that; so far as she was concerned, he was welcome to get himself killed playing the fool. Rodnjan's bushy eyebrows raised in surprise, but he made no objection, and just slung his axe in the loop on his belt before pulling his shield off his arm.

The rest of their fighters had moved up the street to almost within reach of the shieldwall, shouting, taunting, and casting crude aspersions on the parentage of those in it. Stonejaw and Rodnjan took up position right behind the others, then went down to one knee with Rodnjan's roundshield held flat between them, at roughly knee height.

Rikkut took three deep breaths, tightened his grip on his axe and started to run.

It was a terrible risk, but he didn't care. The world wasn't safe anymore. Rikkut had learned that when ships swept down on his clan one summer morning two years ago. Yngda Podastutar of the Tall Pines had refused to swear fealty or surrender the belt that marked her as chief, and Rikkut had been there when she'd burned under the stars that evening, the flames' reflections dancing in the gilt-chased mask that watched her perish. Now the clans were broken and the world was being remade. There was nothing to stay safe *for*. There was only glory, or death.

He reached the line of his warriors, jumped onto the shield and was hoisted high into the air as Stonejaw and Rodnjan rose to a standing position and heaved him upwards with twin grunts of effort.

He saw the startled, upturned faces of the men and women in the shieldwall as he cleared them before they could think to take a swing up at him. He knew their moment of distraction would be all the rest of his warriors would need to jump them, and start hacking their way through.

His time aloft lasted a mere moment, during which he caught a glimpse of white hair, and two other faces turning towards him, and then the ground was rushing up to meet him again with almost malevolent glee. He landed, his left boot slipped, and he dropped to one knee with a curse.

Death came for him.

Two of them, presumably Snowhair's best. The first was on him before he could rise, black-edged axe flashing down like the claws of a stooping fish eagle. A strong blow, but clumsy: Rikkut raised his shield to protect his head and caught it. The impact shivered the timber, but he hooked his axe behind the other warrior's leg and pulled back at the same time as he drove upwards with his shield. He felt the axe teeth bite into their calf as he bore them backwards and down into the path of the second fighter, and heard a scream of pain, but his axe was wrenched from his grasp. The second warrior, a red-bearded man, stepped aside to avoid having his companion land on his legs. That gave Rikkut a second to draw his long spearfish-bill dagger, but it wasn't going to be an even fight.

The red-bearded man swung an axe at him overhand, faster than Rikkut could get his shield up to properly defend. The teeth didn't bite his flesh, but it overshot his shield and the beard wedged in the back, and the other man wrenched his weapon to try to pull Rikkut's shield aside. It should have sent Rikkut stumbling off-balance, but he anticipated it and stepped in with the momentum to headbutt the man in the face.

His enemy staggered, and Rikkut swung the rim of his shield as hard as he could at the other man's head. The Rockman tried to raise his right arm to block and caught the blow high on his bicep, which knocked his axe from his grasp and must have numbed his arm. He tried the same thing in retaliation but Rikkut was quick enough to use his own shield to block, then kicked his opponent in the balls and drove his dagger into the red-beard's neck as he sank to his knees. Blood gouted and Rikkut pulled his hand away, leaving the dagger in place. The man was as good as dead: he still had killing to do, and he needed a dry grip for that.

He snatched the other warrior's axe up. It was slightly longer than his, with a more pronounced beard, and one of the teeth had broken off, but it would serve his purpose. Their altercation had taken but a few heartbeats. Such was the margin between life and death in the world these days.

The dull *thunk* and *clack* of blades striking shields was all around him. Tyaszhin's warriors were pressing Snowhair's Scarred hard, but the Rockfolk were holding for the moment. That left Rikkut on his own against the chief and his last defender.

She'd staggered upright and kicked his axe away from her leg to make sure he couldn't reach it. Young, probably about his age, crow-haired and missing a tooth. She spat at him and spun her own weapon expertly, a blurring circle of wood and blackstone. Nothing flashy; just enough to show him that she knew axework back-to-front.

She was trying to stall him. He'd be wary of her skill normally, but he'd already injured one of her legs, so he charged straight at her. She couldn't meet his rush head-on so she tried to catch him with an underhand swing on his way in, but he'd read it and batted it aside with his shield even as he drove into her. He didn't bother with his axe: the simple impact of his shoulder against her shield knocked her off her somewhat unsteady feet and down into the mud a second time.

Snowhair came at him with a strange, slightly curved sword in both hands—a metal sword! He'd had no idea these Westerners were so rich—and a wavering battle cry. Rikkut just stepped aside and swung the flat of his axe at the back of the old man's legs. Snowhair crumpled to the ground and Rikkut kicked the strange sword out of his hands before hauling the Seal Rock chief up in front of him, turning his axe so the blades pricked Snowhair's throat.

"*Yield!*" he bellowed, turning on the spot. "Yield, or your chief dies!"

Gap-tooth was struggling up again, but Rikkut saw her lips

twist as she took in her companion, now face down and bleeding out with Rikkut's dagger in his neck, and Rikkut himself holding an axe on her chief.

"Say the words, old man," Rikkut hissed into Snowhair's ear. "I don't fear death. My deeds today are already worthy of song, and I'm prepared to meet the Dark Father."

"I yield," Snowhair croaked, his body sagging even more in Rikkut's grip. "I yield!"

Gap-tooth heard him and nodded bitterly. She dropped her axe and raised her voice, far louder than her chief's weak lungs could manage.

"Seal Rock! We yield! We yield!"

The cry was taken up around them as, one by one, the Scarred realised what had happened. The knots of fighting quietened as warriors stepped back, dropping their weapons. Tyaszhin's fighters didn't press the advantage: to attack an enemy who had yielded was cowardice worse than not fighting at all, nearly as bad as pretending to yield in order to gain an advantage. Father Krayk had no use for cowards.

Amalk Tyaszhin shoved his way through his own warriors and the downcast Scarred of the Seal Rock, but the grim pleasure on his face soured when he saw Rikkut's axe at Snowhair's throat. If the chief had yielded through realising his position was untenable then it would have been Tyaszhin's glory as raid leader. As it was, most of the glory would be Rikkut's, especially when tales got around of his daring leap over the enemy shieldwall. He would make sure Stonejaw and Rodnjan were mentioned in the verses, and ensure they heard him calling for it. He could afford to be generous, and they would be good warriors to have at his side, hungering for more renown.

"Fireheart," Tyaszhin said grudgingly. "You can release my captive."

Rikkut deliberately held his axe in place for a couple of moments while he locked gazes with the captain of the *Red*

Smile, then lowered the weapon and shoved Snowhair away. He walked over to where the strange metal sword lay, and picked it out of the mud. The blade was thin, and surprisingly light, yet it seemed sturdy. He grinned. Snowhair was clearly not able to wield such a weapon properly. Rikkut Fireheart would be a more suitable owner.

"Captive?" the Seal Rock chief quavered, looking up at Tyaszhin. "But—"

"Captive," Tyaszhin said firmly. "All chiefs must swear fealty at Torakudo. You're going to see it, old man.

"You're going to see The Golden."

SAANA

RISTJAAN THE CLEAVER had his sea leather shirt back on and was waiting in the space between four fires in the town square, the flickering glow lighting him up as though he was bathed in flames. Benches and tables had been hurriedly cleared away, leaving a spill of ale here, a smudge of some unidentified food there. Most of those eating here had been from the clan, and they were already clustered around the edges of the rough square, although not too close to the fires. Saana estimated the space they'd left at thirty ells a side.

"Chief!" Rist bellowed when he saw her. Saana gritted her teeth and made her way over to him. Daimon hadn't appeared yet: she'd left the castle yard while he'd been talking to his chief servant, or whatever the man was, and assumed he was still getting armoured.

"I hope you're not going to ask me to let the boy take my head," Ristjaan said as she approached. His tone was jovial, but she could see uncertainty in his eyes.

"I can't make jokes about this, Rist," she said tightly. The Dark Father help her, but there were members of her clan whose deaths she could have reconciled herself to if it meant satisfying the Flatlanders' honour. Ristjaan, however, was not one. And yet, the notion of her friend killing the young lord who'd actually turned against his own family to welcome them made her stomach twist. That would surely be the death knell for any hope of settling here peacefully.

"They were bound to recognise one or other of us at some point," Rist said. He raised his huge axe and rested it on his shoulder. "And it was probably going to be me, right? I figured this might happen." He winked at her. "Don't worry, Saana. I won't hurt the lad too much."

Saana's mouth went dry. "What do you mean?"

"I'm not a *complete* fool," Ristjaan said wryly, looking down at her. "You can't afford for him to die. He's barely more than a boy, and I'd be surprised if he's lifted his sword in anger." He nodded sideways at his axe. "This thing's only got a blade on one side, and I've got my shield. I can't promise he'll be healthy, but I can knock the fight out of him well enough."

"Rist, he'll be trying to *kill* you!" Saana snapped, but her friend just smiled.

"People have tried that for twenty years, and no one's managed it yet." He looked up as Saana heard a commotion behind her, and his face took on a puzzled cast. "Well, here he is. I think he's forgotten something, though."

Saana turned around. Sure enough, Daimon Blackcreek was making his way out of the main gates of his stronghouse. However, instead of the coat of nails and war helm that she'd been expecting, he was dressed in a shorter version of the robe he'd worn for the feast: dark green with black trim, and a circular emblem picked out in black, blue and green on each breast. This only reached his knees, instead of to the ground, and his legs were clad in breeches and boots instead of the usual metal greaves. The only concession he'd made to protection were armoured gauntlets.

"Nalon!" Ristjaan roared. There was a small disturbance in the crowd and Nalon shuffled into view, albeit through nudges in the back rather than his own volition.

"Aye?" Nalon said, eyeing the Cleaver warily.

"Ask the boy if he's forgotten his armour," Ristjaan called, his voice carrying easily across the courtyard. Nalon rolled his eyes, but turned to the approaching Daimon and translated the words into Naridan.

"Tell him this lord will not need it, so long as no one watching stabs this lord in his back," Daimon called back, one hand resting on the hilt of the longer of the two blades belted at his side.

"And have people think he can't win on his own?" Nalon scoffed. "No fear of that!"

"Then shall we begin?" Daimon said, planting his feet and staring at Ristjaan with no obvious signs of fear.

Nalon switched back to Tjakorshi. "He says he's fine as he is."

"I gathered," Ristjaan replied with a frown.

"What?" Saana asked him, concerned at his sudden uncertainty.

"No armour? I'll crack him like an egg," Rist muttered to her, then blew out his moustaches in resignation. "Well, if the boy wants to meet his man-god this badly, so be it. I can't promise how he'll fare if he won't even take me seriously enough to wear armour."

Saana bit down on her lip. "Just take care, Rist."

"Will you wish me luck?" he asked, sliding his huge axe off his shoulder.

"I wish us all luck," Saana replied shortly, and walked away from him towards Daimon. She briefly caught sight of Zhanna in the crowd, which didn't help her nerves. If Ristjaan cut the Naridans' lord open in an honour duel, would they target her daughter as revenge?

She approached Daimon and stood in front of him, meeting his stare. Now she was close she could see the pulse fluttering in his throat, and the quickness of his breathing. He didn't have the calm of a seasoned warrior, and hope glimmered. Could she talk him out of it?

"We have had no killing," she said to him in his tongue. "Why must this happen?"

"We have had killing," Daimon replied levelly, lifting his gaze past her to focus on Ristjaan. "The killing was many years ago, but it happened."

Saana's hope withered and died. "But—"

"We never asked for your people to come raiding!" Daimon snapped at her. "We never did the same to you! We never marched on you in war! We lived our lives until you *chose* to come and take them!" He glanced at her and she caught a momentary glimpse of the conflict inside. He wanted to protect his people, but she'd been a fool to think he'd have made peace had he not needed to. Daimon Blackcreek would have been a child when she'd come to his walls: her people would have been the monsters in the night, and now he was old enough to lift a sword against those monsters.

"This lord's father and brother would have killed you all, if they could, for what was done many years ago by some of you," Daimon continued, his voice tight. "This lord will kill one man only, *that* man, for something he *did* do."

"This man told you, and your father," Sattistutar said, lowering her voice until only he could hear, and stepping within reach of his blade. "She killed two farmers the day she came here."

"You did," Daimon acknowledged.

"Why then you do not wish to kill her?"

"Because no one remembers you did it," Daimon said bluntly. "No one has brought an honour debt against you."

Sattistutar stared at him for a couple of seconds, then hissed through her teeth. "Your people are…" She groped for the word he'd used earlier. "Crazy. *You* are crazy."

"Move away," Daimon told her, focusing on Ristjaan once more.

"This—"

"*Move away*, unless you wish to fight for him."

For a moment, Saana considered it. She could call for her sword, shield and sea leather, and face off against Daimon Blackcreek.

Would that make him think again? No, the boy was set on his honour combat. Could she fight and lose?

She eyed the long steel sword at his side. No, not if she wished to live. She knew how sharp a sar's blade was, and had no illusions Daimon would pull his cuts. His stupid honour demanded a death, and she had no wish to see the Dark Father yet, not while Zhanna was still so young. Besides, Rist had been right, back on the *Krayk's Teeth*. Her clan needed her. She knew every one of them: some better than others, admittedly, but she knew their names, their faces, their temperaments. There were those that might make a good chief—better than her, perhaps— but right now her people needed at least one anchor of certainty and stability in the swell.

She told herself this as she turned away from Daimon Blackcreek and joined the crowd, but it didn't make her feel any less of a coward.

There was no longer anyone between the two warriors. Tjakorshi faced Naridan across flat stone slabs; one tall, broad, and dressed for battle, the other shorter, slimmer, and clad only in a simple robe. The firelight licked over both of them, and for several heartbeats neither man moved.

"Shall we begin?" Ristjaan called, presumably unaware how he was echoing Daimon's earlier words. Daimon didn't reply. He stood still, one thumb hooked over the circular hilt of his longblade, the other hand resting lightly on its grip.

"You can still back down, if you'd like," Ristjaan offered, starting to walk forward. Daimon didn't speak or move, and Ristjaan's lip twitched. "Nalon, tell him—"

"What did I tell you about sars, Cleaver?" Nalon interrupted him. "Stubborn as rocks, every one. He'll know what you're saying, and he won't give a shit. He's not leaving here until one of you gets carried out."

"Fine," Ristjaan snapped, rolling his axe shoulder. "Can't blame me for trying."

The big man began to swing his axe in looping arcs. It looked showy, but Saana knew there was a deadly purpose to it. When swinging a weapon with most of its weight at the far end, stopping a swing halfway would not only tire you quickly, but also potentially pull you off-balance, leaving you open. In the rolling brawl of the battlefield you took your cuts where you could, but in the shield circle you could concentrate on one opponent, and on your own form. The key was to have your weapon already moving for when you saw an opening, so you merely needed to redirect a swing instead of starting anew.

Of course, that tactic was normally based around an axe of wood with blackstone teeth, not a pole with a cubit of steel cutting blade on it, but Ristjaan was far from a normal warrior.

He advanced, the great circle of his shield covering his left side. Daimon watched him come, motionless save for the ever-changing shadows on his face from the flames. For a moment Saana thought that the boy had frozen in fear, or was actually going to stand there and let Rist strike him down in some bizarre, incomprehensible self-sacrifice.

Then she saw the young sar's left thumb move so it was resting against the scabbard instead of over the hilt, and knew it was an illusion.

Ristjaan's axe was long, so the loops of his guard position were by necessity long as well. It meant he was utilising the reach of his weapon to the full, but it made the motion comparatively slow. If they were to be as efficient as possible, it also made them predictable.

Rist had seen a sar's draw-cut before, of course he had. He'd raided the Naridan coast for years, after all, and he'd seen Daimon's father nearly take Saana's head off earlier that day. So although Daimon's sword cleared its sheath towards his face faster than the eye could follow, Ristjaan was already raising his shield to protect himself and bringing his axe around to trap the longblade against his shield with the beard, then wrench it out of Daimon's grip.

He was too slow. Blackcreek's first cut was a feint, and the Naridan was already slipping to Rist's left. With Ristjaan's shield raised high Daimon went low, and the edge of his longblade sliced through Rist's breeches and into the back of the bigger man's calf.

Saana bit back a cry of alarm, but Ristjaan whirled around, sweeping with his shield and clipping Blackcreek's shoulder. The Naridan stumbled away from the blow, just far enough to be able to take one further step back from Rist's follow-up axe swing. Ristjaan pulled the force of his cut back into his guard loops again to stay balanced, and took a step towards Daimon.

It was only now he realised he'd been wounded.

Saana saw her friend wince, saw his left leg give ever so slightly under him. It wasn't much, but it was enough. It was hard to tell in the firelight, but she thought she could see a dark wet stain on the fabric of Rist's breeches just above his boot, and it looked to be growing. Blackcreek's blade might not have cut that deeply, but it would undoubtedly slow Ristjaan down.

"You little rat!" Rist snarled, all his good humour evaporated. "Fine, then!" He launched into a roaring, slightly limping charge, his massive axe held high. Daimon was in a half-crouch, his sword held upright in front of him, but Saana could see immediately that he had no intention of standing and meeting the bigger warrior. Instead he sprang to his right, away from the axe and towards the leg he'd previously injured.

Which was exactly what Ristjaan had expected him to do. He veered to his left at the last moment, ignoring his axe and simply slamming his shield into the off-balance sar. Daimon flew backwards and skidded across the flagstones, one hand clawing for purchase and the other holding his longblade up to keep its cutting edge clear of the ground. Ristjaan blew his moustaches out in satisfaction.

"You'll have to be quicker than—"

Daimon rolled back up to his feet, shaking out the arm that

had taken the brunt of the impact. Rist grunted, then spun his axe once through the air and caught it again by the haft.

"Don't fuck around!" Saana found herself whispering through gritted teeth. Her friend had always been a show-off—and a braggart, she had to admit—but he had to take this seriously, he *had* to, because Daimon Blackcreek certainly was.

Rist advanced again, his grip now slightly higher up his weapon's haft, which lessened his reach slightly but made the guard swings tighter and faster. Saana could see him grit his teeth as he used his left leg, but he still seemed steady on his feet. Daimon didn't have any intention of waiting for him, though: the Naridan circled to his right, far enough back that Ristjaan couldn't catch him by surprise with a sudden rush again.

"Come on!" Ristjaan barked. "You wanted this fight, boy!" Saana wasn't sure what he hoped to achieve by the words—Blackcreek certainly couldn't understand them—but they encouraged her clan, who'd been watching in apprehensive silence until now. Some cheered Rist on, while a few voices jeered at the Naridan as he backed away. Saana dearly wanted to find those people and slap them until they learned some sense, but she couldn't tear her eyes away from the potentially deadly dance unfolding.

Rist suddenly lunged, stabbing the toe of his axe's blade at Daimon's body. The young sar was caught off-guard by the unexpected move and didn't twist away fast enough: the point scored down his ribs, tearing the robe that was all he wore. Blackcreek let out a strangled grunt of pain and slashed at Ristjaan's face, but it was deflected by the big roundshield. Rist huffed in satisfaction and stabbed again, but this time Daimon managed to sidestep the weapon and grabbed the axe just behind its head with his free hand, then cut at the outstretched fingers holding it.

Saana flinched in horror: she knew a sar's longblade was easily sharp enough to shear clean through a thumb or fingers, and probably a wrist if it struck in the right place. Ristjaan knew that too, though, and he was both fast and strong enough to tug his hand back just behind the line of the shield, throwing Blackcreek's balance off and leaving the longblade to bite into the haft of the axe. Daimon tugged his sword free and kept hold of the axe, but before he could aim another cut Ristjaan was powering into him with his shield again, dragging the Naridan around in a half-circle and forcing him to release his hold on the axe or get thrown off his feet.

Daimon stumbled away and Ristjaan followed up, but the sar recovered his balance and reversed his momentum, driving a wicked, double-handed slash upwards across the line of Rist's body. Saana remembered it well and her fists clenched involuntarily, nails digging into her palms: that was the move that opened Njiven up like a gutted fish, spilled his innards onto the ground and left his blood on her face. Ristjaan had followed in too hard and too eagerly, and there was no way for him to avoid it.

But he got his shield in the way.

The longblade struck the bottom of the roundshield, but this time the blade wasn't skittering across the broad surface. Instead, it bit deep into the edge Rist had left unrimmed for just such a purpose, and stuck fast.

Rist knew how to take advantage of this, of course. He started turning to his left to keep the blade wedged in place and bring his axe into play. Daimon, desperately holding onto the grip of his sword, would either find it plucked out of his grip or would be dragged off-balance and become an easy target for the axe now descending in a vicious diagonal cut. Ristjaan's talk of roughing the Naridan up without killing him had, fairly typically, been just talk.

But Daimon didn't get dragged off-balance. He let go of his longblade as soon as Ristjaan began spinning and ducked to *his* left, directly underneath and inside of the bigger man's swing.

Rist was off-balance and, for one critical moment, Daimon was behind him and already reaching to his belt.

Daimon Blackcreek performed a draw-cut with his shortblade.

The shortblade was a mere cubit of steel, but its edge was just as keen as its longer cousin. Saana screamed in horror as Daimon slashed it across the back of both of Ristjaan's thighs, slicing through even the thick sea leather armour and into the tendons that held the big man up. Rist's cry as he fell was the ugly, tearing sound of a man whose world had suddenly been entirely eclipsed by pain.

Ristjaan the Cleaver landed hard on his back, legs twisted under him, and screamed at the night sky as his mighty axe fell from his hand. Daimon stepped back, then put one foot on the shield still held loosely by Rist's left hand and wrenched his longblade free from it. Ristjaan didn't react: he was too busy screaming.

"*No!*" Saana shouted desperately, lunging forward. "Don't do it!"

She should have stayed back. She should have stayed back, stayed quiet, let the honour duel take its course, and wept silently after the event. She should have counted herself lucky their home in this new land could be bought at the price of just one life, even if that life was a childhood friend. She should have told herself it was better Rist than ten, twenty, thirty others. Better Rist than the clan's children. Better Rist, with his abrasive, warlike nature, than someone whose skills would serve them better here.

Better Rist than her.

But she didn't. She ran forward, yelling at Blackcreek to stop, first in her language and then, desperately and poorly formed, in his. She saw stirrings among the Naridans, saw one or two men starting forward as if to intercept her, became aware of her own folk surging forwards too...

None of it mattered. The young sar freed his blade, raised it over his head, and brought it down in one motion, dropping to one knee. There was a hideous wet crunching sound, then the scrape of steel on rock as the blade met the flagstones, and Saana's rush came to a stumbling halt.

Blackcreek didn't look at her. He wiped his blades clean on his robe in swift, sure movements, sheathed them, then bowed slightly lopsidedly to the now-headless body on the ground in front of him, wincing and clutching at his bleeding side as he did so.

An ugly murmur ran through the Brown Eagle clan.

"*Quiet yourselves!*" a voice bellowed. It was Tsolga, suddenly at Saana's elbow. "You just saw a duel! You get that, goat-brains? A *duel*! We've all seen 'em before!"

That was a lie, Saana's brain noted numbly. Some had, certainly, but there'd been relatively few disagreements either within the clan or with their neighbours severe enough to warrant such a thing, at least in recent times.

"Sometimes your fighter wins and sometimes they don't," Tsolga continued, her voice ringing out across the yard. "You have to accept that! Ristjaan didn't get any worse than he's done himself, time and again! I should know, I've been there often enough! The Dark Father waits for all of us, and tonight he came for the Cleaver! Ristjaan took that fight for his own honour, and honour's now been satisfied! You want to shit on his honour by starting the fight he gave his life to prevent?"

Another lie, sort of, but one that stabbed Saana through the heart. Ristjaan wouldn't have refused the challenge even if there'd been nothing on the line, but she knew well enough he'd also have taken a challenge if it meant fighting for something she'd worked so hard to build. She'd half-closed her eyes to try to hide her tears, but didn't blink them away. She didn't want to see what was left of her friend.

"Go sit back down," Tsolga was telling the others. She had her hand on Saana's shoulder now. "Eat. Drink. The sun'll rise tomorrow and we'll all still have to find a way to live here that doesn't involve getting anyone else killed. I'm not saying it'll be easy, but we've got to do it!"

"Thank you," Saana said to her quietly. Her cheeks were wet. "I should have said that, but I—"

"Who d'you think I was talking to, girl?" Tsolga muttered in her ear.

Saana blinked, then sighed as she realised. "Me?"

"I just shouted it out a bit so no one realised, that's all," Tsolga said, steering her away from the centre of the square. "Seems to have worked well enough for now, but the first night's the hardest: that was true for all my husbands, and I don't see it being any different here."

Saana swiped at her eyes and looked at the old woman, confused. "What?"

"Hardest? First night?" Tsolga gripped one bicep with her other hand and pumped her forearm. "No? Probably not the time for puns, I'll grant you, but my point stands. As did theirs." She shook her head. "Never mind. Cry for Ristjaan later, but for now this lot need their chief."

Saana wiped her eyes. Tsolga's off-colour and poorly formed jokes had jolted her slightly out of her initial state of numbed shock, and the old woman had the right of it. Being chief meant she had to put the clan first, even if that meant stamping on her own feelings.

She took a shaky breath, exhaled, and swiped at her eyes once more. "Is Blackcreek still there?"

"The sar?" Tsolga looked over her shoulder. "No, he's disappeared. Probably well overdue for getting a stick back up his arse."

Saana nodded. "Good. I don't think I could trust myself not to punch him." She forced her thoughts into some kind of order. "Go and find Chara. She'll need to see to…" She bit her lip. "To the body."

"Right you are, chief," Tsolga said, and slipped away to find the corpse-painter.

"Mama?"

Zhanna's arms slipped around her waist. She turned and hugged her daughter, pulled her in tight, buried her face in Zhanna's hair and whispered noises of comfort. This was the first violent death Zhanna had seen, and it was her mother's friend. Which wasn't to say Saana didn't need the comfort herself.

"Are you going to kill him?" Zhanna whispered in her ear, and Saana had a momentary, unbidden image of burying her father's sword in Daimon Blackcreek's chest.

"No," she whispered back, feeling her chest hollow out as she said it, as though she'd betrayed her clan by uttering the word. But what could she do? "No, I can't. Not if we're going to live here."

"If the clan break their word... he'll kill me, won't he?" Zhanna said. Her breath tickled Saana's ear as she spoke.

"Yes," Saana admitted. "And then I *would* kill him. But that won't help you, or me." She hugged her daughter more tightly. "Perhaps someone else can go in your place, perhaps—"

"*No!*" Zhanna pulled back, but this time she didn't look angry. She looked scared, and there were tears in her eyes, but she was still determined. "No, it has to be me. You can hold them to the course, Mama, I *know* you can."

Her daughter meant it encouragingly, Saana knew, but the weight of responsibility settled on her like never before. If Daimon Blackcreek would stand up to a warrior of Ristjaan's size and ability on a matter of honour, and kill him without fear of what the rest of the clan would do, he'd not hesitate to take the head of an Unblooded Tjakorshi girl.

"What if I can't?" she whispered, so quietly only Zhanna could hear her. She knew she should be encouraging her daughter, telling her everything would be fine, but she was tired, *so* tired, and the stoked fire that had burned in her belly throughout the long crossing had been replaced by icy water and wet shingle.

Zhanna's smile was shaky, but it was there. "Then I'll have to kill him first."

A tentative shadow in a Naridan robe approached them: Osred the steward. He bowed uncertainly. Nalon had claimed there was a whole language of bows, but also that Naridan nobility made it up as they went along so they could, whenever they chose, beat the lowborn for getting it wrong.

"Your pardon," Osred said to them, then faced Zhanna. "If you would come with me, I will show you to your quarters…?"

For a single moment, Saana considered punching him. She considered calling for the clan to pick up their weapons and subdue the town—not necessarily kill everyone, just subdue them—and make it theirs, the old-fashioned way. Then her daughter wouldn't need to live under the keen shadow of a sar's longblade.

But to do that would be to fail. Her people couldn't hold this place against the other Naridans that would surely come, isolated though this town was. She'd merely be buying some time: perhaps no more time than they could have got had they stayed in Tjakorsha, but with an end just as final and disastrous.

"All will be well, Mama," Zhanna told her.

"All will be well," Saana repeated, trying to sound firm and reassuring. Zhanna smiled, then turned to Osred. The balding Naridan backed away for a few steps until he was certain Saana's daughter was following him, then turned and led the way between the fires towards the looming stronghouse. Saana watched them go for a few heartbeats, then heaved a breath and headed towards the nearest knot of her people. She felt a bit like one of the little shellfish in the rock pools when the water retreated—a soft mess inside thin, brittle armour, clamped tight shut against the air.

She had a nasty feeling it would be some time until the tide next came in, and she could relax her shell again.

JEYA

Damau wanted to be a barge hand, ferrying goods along the canals that crisscrossed East Harbour and the low hills of Grand Mahewa. Jeya had no idea how realistic that was, but Damau got a few acknowledging nods when they led hér to the river docks in the morning, while Jeya received only cursory glances, so Damau had clearly been spending some time there.

"Why are we here?" shé asked, stepping around a pile of sacks. The river, just on the other side of the lock from the docks, was tidal this close to the sea, and the tang of the brackish water mixed with the green smell of waterweed laying in clumps on the shore. Shé could see a snake-bird out in the main channel, diving for fish. What shé certainly *couldn't* see were any large houses, such as the one shé was intending to check over; they were in entirely the wrong area of the city.

"The house's garden backs onto a branch of the Second Level," Damau said. "I know someone going that way today."

"And why aren't we walking there?" Jeya asked. Hér legs ached from praising Jakahama yesterday, but it wasn't like shé couldn't put one foot in front of the other.

"Because if anyone saw me on the street there yesterday, and then saw me again today, they might start wondering what I was doing there," Damau replied simply. "We'll be less noticeable on a barge."

It was a fair point, Jeya conceded. Neither shé nor Damau belonged on the richer streets, and there was every chance they'd be chased off. Or possibly beaten, depending on the temperament of whoever noticed them, and how fast they were on their feet.

Damau led hér to the end of the docks, past the large, dark-hulled barges loading grain or barrels in huge quantities. Jeya eyed these crews warily; they didn't seem the sort of people who'd take kindly to a know-nothing like hér tagging along, no matter what relationship Damau might have forged with them. Damau didn't stop there, however, carrying on until they reached a rather smaller vessel painted a peeling yellow. Someone in Morlithian clothes, complete with headscarf, was engaged in heated conversation with an Alaban carter on the dock.

"I have no interest in your wheel-that-is-new," the Morlithian was saying, their fingers flickering like dancing raindrops as they spoke. "We had an arrangement, hee? Morning, Damau dear. It matters not to me that you have incurred additional expense; *why* is my normal cargo not here?"

"Morning, Abbaz," Damau replied in the momentary gap before the carter replied. That was the way with Morlithians: they conducted several conversations at once and just assumed everyone else could keep up with what was being said to whom.

"I had to buy a new *wheel*," the carter said, in the long-suffering tones of someone who thought this explained everything. "Means I had less money, so I couldn't buy all your normal cargo. It's not complicated."

"Not complicated? Not acceptable, that's what it is," Abbaz sniffed. Their face was heavily wrinkled and their cheeks and chin flecked with grey hairs, but their eyes were sharp. "Who's your friend? Should I find someone new to bring my cargo from the sea docks, then?"

"This is Jeya," Damau said. Abbaz's gaze flickered sideways and Jeya got the feeling shé'd been scrutinised, measured, weighed and assessed in the time it took hér heart to beat once.

"That…" The glance the carter cast at Damau held some irritation; apparently they were being thrown by the parallel conversations. "That won't be necessary. It's not going to happen again."

"You have another wheel," Abbaz replied, casting a meaningful look at the two-wheeled handcart on the docks beside the carter. "An old wheel, a wheel presumably a similar age to the wheel-that-was-broken, hee?"

The carter's cheek twitched. "Look, do you want this stuff or not?"

Abbaz pursed their lips thoughtfully. "Eight silver."

"Eight?!" The carter folded their arms beneath their breasts. "Normal price is fifteen. There's well over half your normal cargo here."

"Eight is over half of fifteen."

The carter jutted out their jaw. "Eleven. That's fair."

"Eleven is not eight."

"You're damned right it's not."

Abbaz sighed. "I am old, as you can see. I now have to hire help to move my craft." They waved one slender-fingered hand at Damau and Jeya. "I cannot afford that with the damage to my reputation that will occur when I cannot provide my customers with what they expect from me. Not at eleven silver."

"You haven't hired them. You didn't know who they were," the carter argued, pointing accusingly at Jeya. "You had to ask."

"They're here to help with my craft, or Damau would not have brought them here at this time," Abbaz replied smoothly. "It is only polite to enquire their name."

The carter's nostrils flared, but they just about kept a hold on their temper. "Ten. That's as low as I'll go."

"A pity." Abbaz folded their fingers over their stomach and shook their head slowly. "I wish you luck in selling my cargo yourself. I must spend the day finding someone more reliable."

For a moment Jeya was convinced the carter was actually going to turn and wheel their cart away, or possibly push Abbaz into the river. However, after a strained silence the carter silently held their hand out, face thunderous. Abbaz counted out eight silvers and the carter unceremoniously unloaded half a dozen wooden crates onto the docks, then stormed off with their cart bouncing behind them.

"How did you know they wouldn't just walk away?" Damau asked curiously.

"Money, my dear," Abbaz replied with a smile. "They do not know my customers, so would not know where best to sell my goods. To do so would also take time, and I suspect they have many other jobs they need to do today, lest another employer should grow equally dissatisfied with them." They clapped their hands together. "But speaking of time, we are wasting it! Come, load my cargo, and let us be off."

Damau nudged Jeya and bent to pick up one of the crates, but as shé moved to imitate them Abbaz stepped forward and took hold of hér upper arm.

"A moment, please." Abbaz squeezed, not hard, but hard enough. "Hmph. Not the strongest, I'd wager, if wagering were not a sin in the eyes of God. But strength is not as important as skill. Have you used a pole before?"

There was no point lying. Jeya shook hér head. Abbaz's eyebrows raised. "Damau? You have brought me someone unskilled?"

"I wanted to show Jeya the rich houses on the Second Level," Damau replied. "They're so pretty!"

Jeya narrowed hér eyes at Damau, standing with a crate in their arms and smiling happily at Abbaz. It sounded an awful lot like Damau was playing up the impression they sometimes gave of being naïve, and a little simple. Shé schooled hér face as Abbaz turned back to hér.

"Damau is a good soul," Abbaz said, "and uses the pole well, but I will have no weight on my boat that is of no use. If you will ride, you must pay a fare."

That would never do. Jeya had little enough money, and knew shé looked like it. Being willing to pay just to look at rich houses would instantly draw suspicion, if Abbaz was half as sharp as Jeya thought they were.

"What if I pole for you?" shé suggested. "If Damau has learned, I can."

"You say this as though it were a favour that you do me," Abbaz sighed. "Teaching someone to pole is more work than doing it yourself! I would be giving you a skill you could use to earn money for the rest of your life, and would you be paying me anything for it?"

Jeya sighed as well. This had clearly been a foolish idea all along. Shé was about to turn and walk away when shé saw Damau waving one hand from behind Abbaz's back in a way that was probably meant to indicate 'wait', so shé held hér ground.

"And yet," Abbaz continued, when shé didn't move, "my bones are getting older, that is true. Perhaps a day of shouting at a child will be preferable to straining on a pole. I thank God for my long life, but I do sometimes question how Shē can leave me at the mercy of my body. Fine, child. Load the crates and take a pole. I shall watch you, and correct all the mistakes you make."

Jeya raised hér eyebrows at Damau, who shrugged.

"If you fall into the water, hold onto the pole," Abbaz said as Jeya reached for a crate. "At least, if you wish me to pull you out again. A good punting pole is worth several coppers. And if you damage my boat, or cause it harm through your failure, I shall push you in myself."

EVRAM

THE SHORT MOON had set, although the smaller, brilliant disc of the long moon still lurked in the sky, and the fires in the main square had dwindled and died, much like the mood in the town. The air of cautious celebration sparked by young Lord Blackcreek's opening of the stores had been quenched by the death of the Raider's champion, and the sea demons had filed off sullenly to the empty houses while one of their number in a blue robe had busied herself around the body. Evram hadn't taken any particular joy in the man's death, but he was satisfied justice had finally been done. Lord Daimon had shown he wasn't the coward some had whispered he was, when he'd allowed the Raiders to enter the town unopposed.

Of course, Evram thought as he fed another stick to his fire, it would remain to be seen whether the Raiders could truly act like a civilised people, or if their savage instincts would triumph. He was almost grateful for his poverty. At least he had very little worth being killed for.

There was a sharp knock at his door, and his hand went instinctively to his belt knife. It was past the time most folk would be in bed, but the day had been an odd one, and he doubted he'd be the only one watching a fire and musing. However, it was late to be abroad, and he knew of no one who'd come to his door at this hour.

He drew the small blade silently, and stood. "Who's there?"

"Keep your voice down, man!" the person on the other side hissed. Evram frowned: the voice wasn't one he knew.

"Who's there?" he repeated. "Answer, or s'man will start shouting."

His visitor made a wordless, strangled sound of frustration. "It's Shefal. Will you let this man in, or do you intend to keep him out here all night?"

Evram frowned in surprise. Shefal? Now he'd spoken again Evram did recognise his voice, but couldn't fathom why the freeman would be calling on him. Still, it would not do to keep such a visitor outside, even if it was late. He drew back the rough iron bolt and pulled his door open.

"Please, enter."

"Thank you." Shefal had a leather satchel slung over his shoulder and was wearing a hooded cloak, which was understandable given the bite in the night air, but something in the way he kept the hood up until Evram had closed the door suggested he had another reason for choosing that garment. Evram bowed, as was appropriate: Shefal had no claim over him, but had a freehold, while Evram had only a small plot allotted to him to grow vegetables for himself, and he owed the thane of Blackcreek many days of labour in the field every year.

"You showed great courage today," Shefal said. "Speaking up to name that brute as the killer of your brother, may Nari have mercy on him."

"It... It was merely the truth," Evram managed. Shefal was young, and good-looking, and had never before concerned himself with the deeds of the lowborn so far as Evram could remember. His father, Sar Reul, had been much the same, at least until he'd been banished by Lord Asrel for cowardice in the aftermath of the same attack that had claimed Tan's life.

"The truth is not always easy to speak," Shefal said seriously. "You must have realised, Evram, that what you said was potentially disastrous for you. Had Daimon not taken up your cause…"

"But he did," Evram said firmly, although he couldn't deny feeling a shameful spurt of terror in the moments after he'd blurted out his accusation. "Lord Daimon didn't let the killer harm s'man."

"He didn't," Shefal nodded, "and we can all give thanks to Nari for his bravery and skill. But can he protect all of us, all the time?"

Evram frowned, searching his visitor's handsome face. "What's your meaning?"

"This man's meaning is that our new lord's protection is based on the sufferance of this barbarian chief," Shefal said urgently. "She *allowed* that combat. She could have ordered them to kill us all instead. Perhaps she felt it was an acceptable sacrifice, but who's to say she'll feel that way tomorrow if one of her savages cuts one of us down in the street, or takes what's ours by force? You can't tell me they'll know to follow our laws, Evram."

"S'man had been wondering the same thing," Evram admitted, chewing his lip.

"Then you see our problem," Shefal nodded. "They won't stand for Daimon killing one after another of them in single combat. Sooner or later they'll kill him instead, and if they'll kill him, then why not us too?"

Evram grimaced. Shefal made a compelling point. "But won't they fear what the Marshal will do, if they did that?"

"They should!" Shefal hissed. "Why shouldn't they? Oh, this man doesn't doubt they're savage fighters, but the Southern Army could sweep them back into the sea without a thought! It's never numbers that make the Raiders dangerous, Evram, it's the fact they always strike where we're weakest, and move on before our forces can catch them." He smacked his right fist into his left palm. "But here they are, staying in one place! We need to capitalise. We must get word to the other thanes and the Southern Marshal, so they can wipe these vermin out once and for all!"

"But Lord Daimon said they'd probably kill us too, for not fighting," Evram pointed out. The lords of Narida had a tendency to expect the lowborn to follow their code of honour, even though it seemed easier when you'd learned it since you were a child, and were a trained warrior.

"Evram, word will get out about what's happened here soon enough," Shefal said. "There'll be pedlars on the roads soon, we might get a merchant ship calling here, perhaps the miners will come down from Ironhead earlier than expected. We can't just hold those people here forever. *Word will get out.* We can't be seen to be trying to hide the Raiders' presence here, or that truly *will* be the end of us. No, we need to send for help."

Evram rubbed his chin uneasily. "But Lord Daimon—"

"Lord Daimon is a clever man," Shefal cut him off, "and knows what he needs to say to keep the Raiders content. He couldn't just stand there and tell us someone should go and get help, could he?"

That made sense, and Evram found himself nodding.

"He's bought us some time, and we need to use it as he'd wish us to," Shefal said seriously. "Someone needs to go to Darkspur, explain the situation to Thane Odem, and tell him we need aid against these savages."

"But who?" Evram asked.

Shefal sighed. "Evram. Why do you think this man came to you?"

The crackling fire suddenly didn't seem to be giving off any heat at all. Evram bit down on his lip so hard it hurt. "*This* man? But—"

"You're brave, Evram," said Shefal, interrupting him. "You showed that today. You've got a good head on your shoulders, too, or you wouldn't see how necessary this is. This man would go, but he'd be missed. With the greatest of respect to you, you live alone. Will your neighbours notice your absence? Perhaps in normal times, but these aren't normal times. There are strangers amongst us, and they'll be foremost in everyone's thoughts." The freeman leaned closer. "This man knows you can do it, or he'd never have come to you."

"But this man's never been to Darkspur!" Evram protested desperately. "He wouldn't know—"

"Evram, the north road takes you straight there," Shefal said gently. He pulled a small purse out of his satchel and pressed it into Evram's hand. "Here. It's not much, but it's all this man can spare. If it costs this to get rid of this filth once and for all then he'll consider it a better bargain than any trade he's ever made."

Evram felt the purse. Even if the contents were all coppers, it would still be a sizeable sum for a man like him.

"And you'll need food," Shefal added, proffering his satchel. "There's bread, some cheese, dried meat, sweetsap cake, and the last of the autumn's apples. There's a waterskin in there too: you'll find plenty of streams on the way."

"But they'll miss this man in the fields," Evram managed, still looking at the purse. "Someone will—"

"The barbarian woman said her people will help in the fields," Shefal countered. "This man promises you, Evram, there'll be so much confusion over who's working where that you won't be missed. This man will see to it himself."

Evram said nothing. He felt frozen, as though he was carved of ice and a movement one way or the other would snap him irreparably.

"This is your chance to make a difference, Evram," Shefal said softly. "Not all the heroes in the old songs and tales are sars and thanes. A lowborn man in the right place, with the right heart, can change the course of an entire country."

Evram looked up at Shefal from the corners of his eyes. It felt like if he raised his head and met the man's gaze head-on, he'd be committed.

"You're sure they won't miss s'man? And you're sure this is the only way?"

"This man is sure," Shefal said, his eyes clear and steady. "You'll be saving us all."

Evram nodded again, took a deep breath and let it out slowly. "Very well. When do you think s'man should leave?"

"Now."

"*Now?*" He glanced reflexively towards the door. "But it's still night!"

"You won't make it far in the morning!" Shefal almost snapped at him. "Nari's teeth man, think! There are enough holes in the walls for you to sneak out and make for the road without being seen. It's a clear night, and even the long moon will give you enough light. Once you get to the cover of the forest you can lie up until morning, then travel by day and find a safe place to sleep when darkness falls. You'll just need to leave the road if you hear someone coming up behind you."

"There's dragons in the forest," Evram said uncertainly. He'd rarely been under its boughs other than when cutting back the trunks for a new field, and he didn't regret that fact.

"And you know they're there," Shefal pointed out. "The dangerous ones won't be this far south yet, but the old traveller's trick is to sleep in a tree. Besides, you know the pedlars that come here every summer. One of them must have seen seventy winters! If he can survive the road from Darkspur, you assuredly can."

Evram snorted in momentary amusement. He did indeed know the man Shefal spoke of, and there was something to what the freeman said. He nodded again, and straightened.

"Very well. S'man will do it."

PART TWO

IT IS, IN *truth, difficult to verify the authenticity of the works ascribed to Tolkar, popularly known among the lowborn as the Last Sorcerer. Some evidence suggests the originals of many of his writings were destroyed in the years after the death of the Divine Nari's mortal form. This may have happened at the instruction of Gemar Far Garadh, the God-King's greatest general, since surviving contemporary texts imply differences of opinion, rivalry, or even outright enmity between the two men. Perhaps this was restrained whilst Divine Nari still wore flesh, but broke out upon his departure.*

Of the writings believed to be penned by Tolkar, we mainly know only copies, or copies of copies, while General Garadh's works on military organisation and the orderings of Naridan nobility (which he viewed as not dissimilar) survive to this day in their original (and largely legible) forms. Some of Tolkar's alleged writings can be dismissed out of hand as later forgeries intended to further another's agenda—such as the heretical "Torgallen Letters", which dispute Nari's divinity. Other texts are so mundane there appears little point in ascribing them to such a historical figure were it not the case—a selection of recipes being one of the stranger examples. It is notable that Tolkar never recounts how to perform the sorcery for which he was renowned, leading scholars to argue whether it was a capacity innate to him, or he simply feared to record his methods lest they fall into the wrong hands.

However, the anomaly is the Foretellings, or Prophecies. This work, phrased erratically and with a much poorer grasp of written language than all others attributed to Tolkar, also has notably shaky handwriting. And yet, the copy present in the Royal Library at Idramar is the sole text believed to be an original, surviving example of the Last Sorcerer's own work.

In it, the author outlines events he claims will foreshadow the next ascension of the Divine Nari in His own flesh, rather than through His bloodline, and should be taken as an indication that He has been reborn. These vary from statements so vague as to be essentially meaningless (a reference to "masks falling from faces", with no indication as to whether this should be interpreted literally or as metaphor, or "death and life standing together") to the confusing (such as a mention of a period of extended darkness, which of course happens every year at midwinter in the far south, beyond even the Black Coast) to the truly alarming yet thankfully unlikely (the very earth erupting in flame, a plague of dragons, the ocean swallowing cities). Some have argued this last may have actually been fulfilled by the town of Bayecliff falling into the sea in 582GK when the cliffs upon which it was built collapsed, but a careful reading of the text shows it refers to the ocean rising, and presumably in a manner far beyond that seen even at a double moon...

Extract from 'A Study of the Life of the Last Sorcerer, the man Tolkar' by Omriel Kinnel, written in the five-hundred and ninety-eighth year of the God-King

ZHANNA

ZHANNA AWOKE TO stillness, and silence.

She'd woken to the ever-present sounds of the sea, and the motion of the *Krayk's Teeth* beneath her, ever since she'd left Koszal. Sometimes it had been the cry of a bird, or the barely audible splashing of water beneath the deck's timbers. Sometimes it had been the howl of a southern gale, and the deck beneath her tilting to spill her across the floor of the deckhouse with other sleepers and anything not lashed down. Even in the longhouse she'd shared with her mother, the whisper of waves on shingle had been near-constant, save for those rare, dead days when the wind stilled and the water rested.

In the stronghouse of Black Keep, behind high walls of stone a mile from the shore, the silence was so loud Zhanna thought for a moment that she'd gone deaf. It was only when she rolled over and heard the crackle of the bed beneath her that she realised she was simply missing something that had been virtually ever-present, and which had certainly been inescapable over the last two short moons.

She sat up, swung her feet out from under the thick woollen blankets and onto the floor. It would've been dirt in a longhouse, trodden down firm, but here it was wooden boards. They'd been fitted together with no gaps, long and straight and even, and were as smooth as polished blackstone. She'd slept in her shirt, but she pulled on her leggings, furs and sealskin boots before she padded to the northern window and unlatched the artfully carved wooden shutter.

Morning light flooded in, although most of the view was the white-painted wall of another part of the building. Zhanna turned and surveyed the room behind her, of which she'd seen little the night before.

The charcoal fire in the central pit had burned down to crumbly white ash, but she could still detect a hint of heat when she held her hand close. Otherwise the room held a desk and chair as richly carved as the chieftain's seat her mother had left back at Koszal; and the bed, which was by far the strangest thing to her eyes. In Koszal, beds were chests of stone filled with bracken, then covered with furs. Here, the bed frame was carved wood, raised off the floor on legs like a chair, and the soft part was a wrapping of fabric around a filling of... something, possibly reeds. Whatever it was, it had been comfortable.

The room's entrance was covered by a thick curtain, and when Zhanna pulled it aside she found herself in a living space. She'd walked through it the previous night, but the light the Naridan servants had been using hadn't been strong. She now realised it was larger than her mother's entire longhouse, and looked just as unused as the bedchamber.

A low table—little more than a polished block of wood, in fact—waited immediately in front of her. On it were arrayed a loaf of dark bread roughly the size of her hand, a small bowl of nuts and a wooden cup of what proved to be a watery version of the ale that had been served the previous evening.

A little while later, still chewing the last of the nuts (which tasted like they'd been dipped in honey), Zhanna ventured outside and descended the wooden steps leading down from the door of the building, and saw for the first time exactly how much space the Flatlanders had.

She was within the third walled court of the castle, she'd known that much. Now, in daylight, she could properly see the rich grass through which ran paths of gravel, a stand of trees—tall, dark pines she knew from Kainkoruuk, but also slender, silver-barked strangers—and even a small part of the river, diverted through the grounds. A stream emerged from the trees and formed a deep pool, spanned by a wooden bridge, then ran on and eventually disappeared under a small arch in the boundary wall to rejoin its parent.

Then, forming part of the wall bordering the river, was the looming monstrosity of the Black Keep itself.

It was built on a rampart of stone that alone was higher than Zhanna's head, up which ran a flight of steep steps to the only door. It looked like three buildings stacked on top of each other, each slightly smaller than the one below, and with a flared skirt of red tiles that splayed out around its lower edge. The windows on the lowest level were covered with metal bars to prevent attackers from gaining entry to them, the crest of its roof was higher than a yolgu's mast, and the whole thing had been stained dark, which presumably gave it its name.

However, of most immediate interest to Zhanna were the two massive skulls that flanked the door. Even from this distance she could tell they must have been as long as her outstretched arms, but they weren't the flat, broad shape of a krayk.

Dragons.

The sound of footsteps on gravel alerted her to company, and she turned to see the old Naridan man Osred approaching. He was trailed by a girl, little more than a child, who peered curiously and somewhat fearfully at Zhanna from behind her elder.

"Good morning," Osred said in his language, stopping a few paces away and bowing very slightly. Zhanna looked around. The sky was fairly clear, and although the day was not warm, she was nowhere near as cold as she'd been on the voyage here.

"Yes," she replied, feeling some response was required.

"Tirtza brought word you had risen," Osred said, and Zhanna narrowed her eyes. Had the girl been spying on her? For her part, Tirtza ducked slightly farther behind Osred. "Lord Daimon asked this steward to speak with you when you awoke."

Zhanna frowned. Did all Naridans tell you they were going to speak to you before they spoke to you? She didn't recall Nalon doing that.

"Yes?" she said, trying to help him along.

"You cannot leave the grounds," Osred said. "If you try, the guards are instructed to stop you. You may not enter the keep, or the Lord's chambers." He gestured behind him, and Zhanna saw for the first time that there were more buildings, beyond the stand of trees.

"Who live here?" she asked, pointing to the door she'd just walked out of.

"These are the women's quarters," Osred replied. "Lord Bla— that is, Lord Asrel's wife is no longer alive, and he had no sisters or daughters, so they have been empty for some time. Lord Daimon was gracious enough to set one suite aside for your use."

Zhanna frowned. "Women not live with men?" Truly, these Flatlanders were strange!

Osred's expression was hard to read. "Not the nobles, no. For the lowborn, yes."

Even stranger! Still, it suited her, so she changed the subject. "What this warrior do here?"

Osred frowned. "Do you mean, how will you spend your time?"

Zhanna grunted. She'd thought the question was a straightforward one.

"How would you spend your time at your home?" the steward asked.

Zhanna shrugged. What kind of a question was that? "Fish. Plant. Cook. Cut wood." She neglected to mention practicing with her weapons, since she hadn't got them here, and didn't think the Flatlanders would like to be reminded of it.

Osred seemed taken aback. Perhaps he'd assumed Zhanna and her mother lived like his Lord Blackcreek did, with people to do things for him. "You may fish in the river, of course." He looked around as if for inspiration, then brightened and seized the girl behind him by the shoulder. "This steward has tasks he must complete. Tirtza, show…" He paused, and glanced at Zhanna uncomfortably. "Your name?"

"Zhanna."

"Tirtza, show Zhanna where she can go in the stronghouse." He bowed slightly again, then walked hurriedly away with the air of a man who'd just discharged an unpleasant responsibility and had no intention of waiting around to see if he was required further.

Zhanna eyed the girl. Show her where she can go? Yes, and spy on her while doing so, she had no doubt.

Tirtza, clearly just as uncertain how to behave towards Zhanna as Osred had been, took refuge in what she knew. She bowed, smoothing her skirts over her knees, and looked up expectantly.

"What can this servant show you?"

Zhanna didn't even have to stop to think. She smiled broadly. "Dragons."

TILA

Tila had decided virtually immediately that the docks of the Naridan Quarter of East Harbour weren't much different to the docks of Idramar in any respect other than the pervasiveness of the smells. Something about the incredible humidity meant the stink of rotting seaweed, dead fish, tar, unwashed bodies and general water scum took you by the throat and settled. No wonder there were so many taverns; anyone working here must always be searching for a way to get rid of the taste.

"Your man is going to sound stupid," Barach began, as they walked along the dock front. The surface was paved with slabs of stone, which was just as well; the torrential Alaban rain would leave the ground as slick mud otherwise.

"You're wondering why this lady came ashore to find a Shark?" Tila asked with a smile. She'd bought a local contraption to keep the rain off—a cunningly-designed affair of waxed canvas—and was enjoying the relief of not having water constantly in her eyes.

"Your man is," Barach admitted.

"This lady wasn't referring to an actual shark," Tila told him gently. "The Sharks of Grand Mahewa are the gang bosses, and they'll each have their own turf or business. This lady has influence here, probably more than they realise, but these are still their waters, as they'd say. A Naridan woman trying to hire local knives won't go unnoticed. Best to do these things openly."

"You're going to... ask permission?" Barach asked, surprised.

"If an Alaban came to Idramar and arranged for a family to be killed, in her city, this lady would take offence," Tila pointed out. "She might even decide to make an example of them. She wouldn't wish to be on the other end of that." She peered past the canopy of her rain-roof and saw what she'd been searching for: a door with a quill pen painted above it, at one end of a tavern. "Ah, we're here."

"A scribe?" Barach asked, wrinkling his wet brow.

"Who better to keep this lady appraised of events in a foreign city?" Tila said. She nudged the door inwards, causing a bell above the jamb to tinkle merrily, then folded down her rain-roof and stepped inside.

A narrow staircase rose steeply, closed in on both sides by wooden walls and illuminated by the light from an unshuttered window. Tila could see another door at the top, propped open, leading to the space above the tavern.

A voice called a question in Alaban from above, an enquiry about identity.

"Is this the house of Skhetul the scribe?" Tila shouted back, in Naridan.

"... Who asks?"

"It's the right place," Tila muttered to Barach. He began to climb the stairs, the wood creaking under his weight, and Tila followed him up.

"This man says again; who asks?" the voice demanded, although with a slightly querulous tone. Tila wasn't surprised. Barach's heavy tread would surely sound ominous to a man who listened to his customers ascend and descend, and could likely judge their size accordingly.

"Someone who doesn't wish to announce herself loudly," Tila replied. "Fear not, we mean no harm."

Barach reached the top of the stairs and ducked through the door, which was quite low, since it was set on one side of the sloping roof. Tila followed him a moment later, and found herself in a long, low room with wooden skylights above, although the shutters were closed against the rain. The two other windows were open, providing a view of the tavern's vegetable garden, but it seemed the cloud-covered sky outside didn't give enough light for the room's occupant, who'd lit an oil lamp on the large desk behind which he was sat.

Skhetul was short and stocky, with hairless cheeks, and wore the hair on his head so short it must have been shaved with a wet blade. He was frozen in mid-movement, his quill halfway to the inkwell on his desk with what looked to be a bill of lading stretched out in front of him.

"Does this man know you?" he asked. Skhetul wore loose clothes in the Alaban style, and his Naridan was accented, but his features and colouring spoke of his ancestry.

"Only through our correspondence," Tila told him. "This lady is Livnya of Idramar."

Skhetul went very still for a moment, then calmly laid his quill down and bowed in his seat. "High Lady. To what does your man owe this pleasure?"

Tila felt Barach inhale beside her. She could guess what he was about to say, and cut him off with two fingers on his wrist.

"The family of which you spoke in your most recent message," she said to Skhetul. "Which of the Sharks should this lady speak to, to ensure they can be removed?"

"Re-removed?" Skhetul stuttered. "As in..."

"As in blades, and flesh, and the application of one to the other," Tila said calmly. "You write of the Sharks, so this lady knows you have at least some awareness of their names and natures."

"High Lady, many people call upon this scribe to record things for them," Skhetul said quietly. "He makes guesses and fills in blanks from what he hears, but—"

"Skhetul," Tila cut him off. "If you're willing to make bold claims when this lady is many miles distant, yet hesitant about them when she stands in front of you, she must ask herself how valuable you truly are as a source of information."

Skhetul bowed his head again. There was a faint sheen of perspiration on his brow, which Tila was certain had not been there when she'd entered the room.

"High Lady, this scribe suggests you attend the blue warehouse on Fourth Channel, three evenings hence. You'll be asked your business at the door, and should say you're there to buy Morlithian silks. Take money to gamble; it's a night of personal combat where wagers are staked by the spectators, and those who don't wager are soon removed. The Hierarchs and the Watch don't approve of it, so you must be discreet."

"And must this lady speak those code words in Alaban?" Tila asked.

"Naridan should suffice," Skhetul replied. "Once inside, this scribe believes you should seek out a person named Kurumaya. If this scribe has guessed correctly, Kurumaya is a Shark, and the one most likely to have resources in matters pertaining to violence."

Tila nodded. "Thank you, Skhetul. This lady knew her faith in you wasn't misplaced." She turned for the door.

"High Lady," Skhetul said from behind her. "If you're asked how you came to know these names... If you should mention this scribe, it's not likely he'll be able assist you further. Kurumaya is not, he thinks, someone who'd appreciate being exposed in such a manner."

"This lady understands, Skhetul," Tila told him. "Come, Barach. Let's leave our friend in peace."

They were down the stairs and out of the door, and Tila had raised her rain-roof once more, by the time Barach found his voice.

"That was a wom—"

"Skhetul is a man, Barach," Tila cut him off quickly.

"But she called hers—"

"*He* called *himself* 'he'," Tila corrected him. "We're in Alaba, and you shouldn't assume anyone is a man or a woman until they say so. Once they have, you should respect what they say, even if your eyes tell you different." She sighed. "This lady's seen knife fights between Alaban sailors where, between attempting to kill each other, they've used the foulest terms for each other their language can devise, yet not once did they refer to their opponent in such a manner. It's beyond an insult, here."

"It's confusing, is what it is," Barach muttered.

"Perhaps," Tila said. "But given where we're going three nights hence, this lady suggests you learn to guard your tongue. Lest the knives we seek end up aimed at us."

DAIMON

RISTJAAN THE CLEAVER was to be given to the waves.

Daimon hadn't seen details of the preparations, which had been done overnight. All he knew was that when he'd risen and come to pay his respects to his fallen foe, he'd found half of the man's body had been painted in whorls of blue. The apparent artist was a dour-faced woman of middle years in a hooded robe, which was also dark blue. Her fingers were stained with whatever she'd used to prepare the corpse, and Daimon realised that it was the first time he'd seen any Tjakorshi wearing the colour. He also noticed there was a discreet distance between the woman and the score or so of other Tjakorshi gathered around Ristjaan's body, laid out on a makeshift bier made from a sledge.

"That's Chara, the corpse-painter," Nalon said, when he voiced his question. Daimon hadn't wanted to face Sattistutar so soon after having killed her friend, and had sent Osred to seek the man out. "The designs are supposed to appease Father Krayk and allow Ristjaan's soul to go back into the chaos of the ocean, instead of being trapped on land."

"She does not seem to receive many thanks for her work," Daimon noted quietly.

"Her hands are stained blue," Nalon shrugged. "Blue's an unlucky colour for a living person to wear, because of the death paint. The corpse-painter is necessary, but not welcomed. S'man's never understood why someone would want to become one, but Chara's always seemed to prefer the dead to the living anyway."

Daimon grunted again as a thought occurred to him. "Sattistutar mentioned witches last night. Do the…" He prevented himself from saying "savages", remembering that Nalon had married one. "Did Tjakorsha truly have such women?"

"Not just Tjakorsha, and not just women," Nalon replied. "The clan has four witches, three women and a man. S'man should say though," he added hurriedly, perhaps in response to Daimon's expression, "the word probably isn't the right one. They use charms, read signs in the flight of birds and the like, but they're tasked with helping to guide the chief. Naridan doesn't have a word for what they are, really. S'man remembers tales of witches up in the hills from when he was young, and they're nothing like that."

"Who are they?" Daimon asked, looking around. Naridan lore told of witches; evil, malicious women, the last remnants of the Cult of the Unmaker, the demon Nari had banished before He ascended to the throne. They could be marked in different ways, but the most common was a ravaging of their features due to the nature of the ruinous powers they wielded. Daimon had certainly seen none like that in the Tjakorshi who'd filed through "Black Keep's gates.

"Why? You're not going to kill them too, are you?" Nalon asked, his face sceptical.

Daimon gritted his teeth. Nalon's time away from Narida had done his manner no favours, if he'd even been possessed of a good one to start with. He certainly didn't accord Daimon the respect he deserved, but Nalon did not seem a fool, and must have realised that as one of only two people who spoke both Naridan and Tjakorshi well, he was practically invaluable. Unfortunately he seemed to have decided that meant he could speak to Daimon as an equal.

"This lord is responsible for protecting his people," Daimon said tightly. "He would at least know who these charm-weavers are."

"You'd best ask Saana," Nalon replied, uncomfortably. "One chief doesn't approach another chief's witches without permission, and if s'man interferes he'll end up on the wrong side of his chief *and* her witches."

"This lord does not think Chief Sattistutar will be introducing him to anyone any time soon," Daimon commented. A movement on the far side of the square caught his eye, which turned out to be the woman herself. She was wearing the same furs she'd worn for the feast the previous night, and her face looked even harder now than it had when she'd been warning his father of the folly of battle.

"Well, you did kill her friend," Nalon pointed out. "She'll come around. She's not made of stone, so she'll have taken it hard, but that's part of the reason why she's such a good chief. You can't lead your people well unless you care for them."

Daimon opened his mouth to ask Nalon what he knew of leadership, but shut it again when it occurred to him that actually, the sentiment made sense. "How long until everyone else gets here?" he asked instead.

"This is about it, probably," Nalon said, looking around. "S'man wouldn't expect anyone else. Zhanna would come, perhaps, but she's in your castle."

"So few?" Daimon was confused. Less than a tenth of the Raiders had turned out for the rites to mark the passing of one of their greatest warriors.

"Well, Ristjaan wasn't best-liked, you see," Nalon confided in a low voice. "A fearsome fighter, right enough. Respected, certainly, when axes were involved. But the rest of the time he was a bit... well, loud, I suppose. Boastful. Coarse. Did as he pleased without much concern what others thought. Don't get me wrong, he could be right happy to lend a hand when needed, but he was just as likely to tell you to swallow sea water, depending on his mood. S'man didn't much care for him. To be honest, if you had to kill someone over an honour debt, he'd have been one of the better choices, other than him being the chief's friend."

"This lord does not follow," Daimon admitted, frowning down at the shorter man.

"S'man thinks most of the clan would be happy enough to trade the life of Ristjaan the Cleaver for safety here," Nalon said, a little shame-faced. "Your people get to see one of the Raiders killed for past crimes, and that kind of clears the air? Now, if you'd decided that Tsolga Hornsounder needed to die"—here he nodded towards the old woman Daimon had seen leading the singing as the Tjakorshi had walked through Black Keep—"that might have been a different matter."

Daimon studied her. The old Raider's long grey hair was woven into two large, tight braids that wound around the back of her head, and her face was lined enough that she looked weathered and worn even at this distance, but her back was still straight and her voice clear and loud as she greeted her chief. "She is popular, then?"

"If there's one person from the clan you want to get on your side, it's Tsolga," Nalon said, scratching his chin. "Not sure how well she'll take to learning Naridan at her age, mind, but she's like a grandmother to most of them. Well, a grandmother who's buried three husbands and is on the lookout for a fourth, at least."

"Ah," Daimon replied noncommittally. Lord Asrel had been very vigilant in ensuring Daimon hadn't had any opportunity to sire a bastard on any lowborn girls, but there were precious few highborn girls to court this far south, either. Nalon's casual discussion of the woman Tsolga's appetites had caused Daimon to realise that with his father and brother secured in the stronghouse, he had a certain level of freedom he'd never enjoyed before. If he was the Lord of Blackcreek sufficient to imprison his kin and allow a few hundred Tjakorshi to settle, surely he was able to set about courting a woman? He tried to push the thought aside to be dealt with at another time, but it was a persistent one.

"What happens now?" he asked Nalon.

"Now they take the bier to a yolgu and take it out to sea, sing over him a bit, then drop him in."

Daimon was slightly surprised by the lack of respect in his tone. "You haven't taken their customs to heart, then?"

"They don't expect s'man to," Nalon said. "Father Krayk is their god, not his. The voyage here was the first time s'man's been on the sea since Iro Greybeard snatched him off that ship, and he won't be going on it again while he lives, if he has any say in the matter. Whatever god takes his spirit after he dies, it won't be that black-scaled bastard."

Daimon watched Sattistutar as she stood at the side of Ristjaan's bier, hands clasped in front of her. She was weeping: not the gasping sobs of the hysterical, but the quiet, steady tears of someone in deep pain. Despite knowing the big Raider's death had been necessary for honour, it was still hard for Daimon to see the suffering it had brought to others, barbarians though they were. Ristjaan had accepted Daimon's challenge and, warrior that he had been, had accepted the consequences before the combat had even started. The mourners gathered around his body had not been able to prepare themselves in the same way.

Steeling himself, and in no way confident he was doing the right thing, Daimon stepped forward. A muffled swearword behind him indicated what Nalon thought of his decision, but Daimon wasn't overly concerned about his opinion. Sattistutar looked up as she heard footfalls on the square's flagstones, and when she saw him her expression shifted from sorrowful to murderous.

"What?" she bit out. Only the lack of a weapon at her belt and Ristjaan's body between them convinced Daimon that she didn't intend to go for his throat then and there. The other Tjakorshi muttered and stepped back slightly, but let their chief confront him.

"This lord wishes to offer his assistance," Daimon said, as neutrally as he could manage.

Sattistutar's face twisted in angry incomprehension. "Why?"

"This lord does not like leaving something unfinished," Daimon said, nodding in what he hoped was a respectful manner at Ristjaan's body. "He was an honourable man. This lord took his life; he would help return his spirit to where it needs to go."

Sattistutar regarded him blankly for a second or so, then stepped back to speak to another woman of roughly her age, although shorter and stouter. It wasn't until the second woman glared at Daimon that he recognised something about her eyes and nose.

"His sister?" he hazarded a quiet guess to Nalon.

"The same."

"What are they saying?" Both Tjakorshi were quite animated in their discussion, although they were keeping their voices low.

"If the chief wants you to know that, she'll tell you herself," Nalon harrumphed.

Sattistutar turned back to him and Daimon braced himself, uncertain what manner of reaction he would receive. To his surprise she stepped to the head of the makeshift bier and picked up the two ropes attached to the head of the sledge, then tossed one to him. He caught it more out of instinct than anything else. "What...?"

"You want to help?" Sattistutar snorted, slipping her shoulder underneath the other rope. "Pull."

Daimon was taken aback, but she was in deadly earnest. He also realised, too late, that he had no countrymen with him. If Nalon was to be believed, these barbarians were going back to their ships, and out to sea. What had seemed like a respectful gesture now struck him as foolhardy in the extreme, should one of them decide to exact revenge.

"In Narida, only family or close friends bear the dead," he said, trying to buy some time. "Why do you ask this?"

"You killed him," Sattistutar replied shortly. "This man brought him here. It is our fault he is dead. Now pull, or go back to your house."

It came down to trust. Trust that the Tjakorshi would restrain themselves. Trust that they understood Daimon was their only hope of living here successfully. He'd already wagered his people's lives and his honour on this barbarian chief's intentions, so his own life seemed a meagre thing in comparison. But what of his position as the lord of Blackcreek? Would his father have lowered himself to haul a sled like a common farmer?

No. But Daimon was certain his father would have shown respect at the death rites of an honourable foe defeated in single combat. This was a time of change in Blackcreek. Besides which, Daimon's honour would be suspect again if he reneged on his offer.

He took a firm grip on the rope. "To the sea?"

Sattistutar nodded slightly. "To the sea."

It was hard work, for Ristjaan had been a huge man, and the ground was far from even. The mud of Black Keep's streets caused both Daimon and Sattistutar to slip on occasion, although neither actually lost their footing. Once outside, the stems of the long, rough salt marsh grass bent easily beneath the sled's weight and their burden slid more smoothly than Daimon had feared, but he was nonetheless sweating before they had travelled a bowshot from the walls. He remained respectfully silent, but beside him Sattistutar kept up a running grumble in her own language which he couldn't help but feel was aimed at him.

"What are you saying?" he asked finally, and somewhat breathlessly, as they were hauling the sled up the bank of a rivulet running down to the Blackcreek river. The sled was very nearly wedged, and the rest of the funeral party were pushing to shift it.

Sattistutar didn't even look at him. "This man is asking Ristjaan why he ate so much and became so big, then let you kill him so she has to haul him back to the ocean. She is asking your mud why... *unnh*... why it grips so hard, and your ground why it is not flatter. She is asking herself why she did not beach our ships on the river next to your town instead of... *hnnrrgh*!... where it meets the sea!"

The sled finally came free and they both stumbled at the sudden give in the ropes. Daimon recovered first and reached out without thinking, snagging Sattistutar's arm and keeping her from falling. He snatched his hand back immediately, but the Raider chief simply took her rope over her shoulder once more without any acknowledgement.

"Had you brought your ships to our walls, this lord fears more than just Ristjaan may have died," Daimon offered as they began to pull again. "You were wise to seek parley as you did."

"This man does not need you to tell her that, Blackcreek," Sattistutar huffed.

The Raiders' huge ships were where they'd left them, pushed to the top of the black mud of the beach that gave the entire Black Coast its name. However, high tide was approaching, and the lapping waves were not far from their keels. Sattistutar directed their group to one of the largest, fronted by a fearsome visage of dark-painted wood protruding from the deck.

"Is that... Father Krayk?" Daimon asked.

"It is," Sattistutar confirmed.

Daimon studied it while the Tjakorshi busied themselves with working out how best to lift the sled bearing Ristjaan's body onto the ship. The monstrous, blackened head had a dragon's scales, but the head was flatter than any dragon Daimon had seen, and no dragon had Father Krayk's spiralling horns, or the sparkling red eyes with neither pupil nor iris. As he looked closer Daimon could see the eyes were made of crudely shaped gems, or something similar.

When Sattistutar said her people were the children of Father Krayk he'd imagined some sort of ancestor figure, perhaps similar in appearance to the marble statue of Nari that sat in Black Keep's shrine. When Nalon had described Krayk as a "black-scaled bastard", Daimon had thought he was using some derogatory Tjakorshi phrase.

He'd never imagined the Raiders would worship some monster of the ocean depths like this, let alone consider themselves its children.

"Blackcreek."

He surfaced from his shocked reverie to see Sattistutar looking down at him. She jerked her head at him. "Climb aboard."

"Do you not need to push it into the waves?" he asked, puzzled.

"Aye, but you are no sailor. Climb aboard, if you would see this through."

He vaulted aboard easily enough, for there were no raised sides such as there would be on a Naridan boat. The Tjakorshi disembarked as he did so, and as they bent to the task and the ship began to slip through the mud he had a momentary image of them simply pushing him out to sea, leaving him to either float away with Ristjaan's body, or take the humiliating swim to shore. They did no such thing, of course, and as the waves began to lap around the ship's timbers the mourners climbed aboard with all the ease of a sar mounting a dragon.

"What do you wish me to do?" he asked Sattistutar, as she clambered up beside him.

"Nothing," she replied shortly, directing her fellows to paddles with points and quick snaps of her fingers. "Stay low, and do not move."

Daimon was only too happy to obey, for ships were near as foreign to him as the Tjakorshi themselves. Naridans had boats, of course, but none of Black Keep's fishing skiffs were anywhere near this size. The cargo cogs that sometimes came south to trade may have been a little larger, but were notoriously slow and unreliable. His father had cautioned him against ever putting much faith in ships, for it seemed a source of constant debate whether their frequent disappearances were the result of pirates or simply poor crewing.

Daimon watched the Tjakorshi settle into place, each taking up a paddle and stroking in time with Sattistutar's shouts. Once the ship was in the open water of the Blackcreek's mouth they ran out the huge, angular sail, and even the relatively light breeze sent the ship fairly scudding across the wave tops.

He couldn't help but consider the possibilities. Naridan ships were unreliable, yes, but Tjakorshi ones? Sattistutar had said every ship survived the passage. If the sailing expertise of the Tjakorshi could be turned from piracy and pillaging to trade...

The Tjakorshi were singing again. It wasn't the boisterous melody he'd heard the day before, with raucous discords and moments of unexpected, almost beautiful harmony, but something far more workmanlike; a steady, rhythmic chant that rose and fell in time with the paddle blades, and was undoubtedly designed for that very purpose.

Daimon couldn't deny there was a thrill to pulling away from the land. It came with a certain fear, because even the Tjakorshi didn't trust the sea, no matter how skilled they were, but that was what lent excitement to the whole thing. As they passed beyond the headland to the south of the Blackcreek's mouth Daimon looked up and down the coast, and realised that this was the farthest east he had ever been.

They kept going, of course. It was the best part of half an hour by Daimon's guess before Sattistutar called a halt, by which point the coastline had diminished considerably. Without the singing there was nothing to hear except the wind, and the gentle splashing of waves against the ship's timbers. Far above, Daimon could just make out a couple of dark dots against the patchy grey clouds; seabirds, presumably. There was a strange sense of peace here, even for someone unused to the ocean.

The Tjakorshi shipped their paddles and furled the sail, and Ristjaan's sister passed a waterskin around to everyone except Daimon as they gathered around the dead warrior. Each Tjakorshi drank deeply, then once their throats and tongues were moistened they began to sing once more; in fact, Daimon was starting to wonder if there was any event in their lives that wasn't marked by song. This one was different again, low and slow and undoubtedly melancholy, with odd harmonies. He wondered briefly what would happen if someone died when none of their family or friends were good singers. Maybe there was just something about Tjakorshi?

Sattistutar grimaced as she missed a note. No, Daimon reflected, not all Tjakorshi could sing perfectly.

The song droned on, and Daimon found his attention wandering a little. He looked up at the sky again and found the two dots he'd seen previously, now spiralling down towards them. He unconsciously loosened his longblade in its scabbard, for there was always the possibility he'd misjudged distance and scale, and these were a pair of kingdrakes far afield from a nest in the Catseye Mountains. However, as they circled lower he realised his initial assumption had been correct; it was merely two gulls, coming to investigate. The birds glided by with barely a wingbeat, but when one of them gave voice to a raucous cry it had a startling effect on the Tjakorshi.

The group looked up as one. They kept singing, but as the gulls came back for another pass they began to sing faster, and more urgently. Ristjaan's sister pulled out an earthen flask and uncorked it, then handed it around. Each Tjakorshi paused in their song to take a swig. To Daimon's surprise, when Sattistutar had knocked hers back she stepped across the benches to bring it to him.

"Drink," she instructed when he didn't immediately take it. Daimon sniffed it, and recoiled involuntarily at the acrid smell of shorat.

"Why—"

"You are here, you must drink," the Tjakorshi ordered urgently, looking up at the gulls. Daimon took as small a mouthful as he thought he could get away with and handed the flask back before swallowing cautiously. The cursed stuff still burned its way down his throat, but he managed to avoid choking.

"Why the hurry?" he wheezed when his voice would obey him once more, but Sattistutar had already turned away.

There was no doubt the rites were being concluded. The song drew to a close in what appeared to Daimon to be almost unseemly haste, then Ristjaan's body was lifted off its bier in a sling of cloth. Daimon hadn't known what to expect, but he'd thought committing the dead man's body to the waves would be the most involved part of the process. Instead, it seemed the song and the shorat held the greatest importance for the Tjakorshi. Ristjaan's corpse disappeared into the water with little more ceremony than a farmer dropping a bucket into a well, after which his sister said something hurried with tears in her eyes. The rest had already returned to their places, and began the process of getting the ship moving again even before Sattistutar could give instructions.

Daimon stepped cautiously along the deck towards the rear where the Brown Eagle chief held a large steering paddle. Sattistutar barely looked at him: she seemed more concerned with the water.

"Why the hurry?" Daimon repeated himself when he was next to her. Sattistutar glanced at him, then resumed scanning their surroundings.

"The birds are an ill omen," she replied darkly. "We call on Father Krayk to take the spirit of our dead."

"And you fear he will not?" Daimon asked, when she did not elaborate further. Sattistutar tore her eyes from the waves long enough to fix him with a stare holding pity and contempt in equal measure.

"No, Daimon of Blackcreek. This man fears that he comes, and that we are not far enough away."

Daimon's eyes were drawn back to the fearsome carved figurehead. "You believe your god will come and... eat this ship?"

"Do you remember what this man said when we ate together

last night?" Sattistutar asked. Daimon frowned.

"You said many things."

"She said a fool does not respect the sea, and a fool will die there. A fool does not respect the Dark Father, and a fool will be taken by him." The ship was now fairly flying back towards the river's mouth. "This man is no fool, Daimon of Blackcreek."

Something dark and scaled rose into view behind her.

It was there for only a moment, and Daimon could make out no details, for it barely broke the surface. He couldn't even tell if it was a back, the top of a head, or something else entirely, but his knees were water nonetheless. He drew his longblade, as though it would help.

"Faster!" he urged. Sattistutar glanced over her shoulder and shouted, and the paddlers redoubled their efforts.

The massive underwater shadow sank again. Daimon envisaged a huge, horned head on a mighty neck suddenly erupting from the water, or perhaps simply a titanic jaw rising from the waves on either side of them, teeth as long as he was tall, taking the ship down to the depths with a single bite, but no such thing materialised.

Still, perhaps the ocean was not as peaceful a place as he'd imagined.

ZHANNA

She was going to see dragons.

Zhanna did her best not to giggle like an overexcited child as she followed the servant Tirtza over a narrow wooden bridge spanning a moat and into the castle's second yard, around the edges of which all manner of buildings were clustered. Smells of cooking reached Zhanna's nose, but she didn't allow them to distract her, and it took all her willpower not to push in front of Tirtza once it became clear they were heading for the long, low building occupying most of the yard's far side. Tirtza cautiously poked her head through a smaller door cut into one of the two huge wooden ones that reached up for most of the building's height.

"Tavi?"

Zhanna sniffed again. The smell from beyond this door was nowhere near as enticing. It wasn't exactly unpleasant, but it lodged in her throat, deep and full and *strange*.

The smaller door was pulled open to reveal a thick-set Naridan man, perhaps the age of Zhanna's mother, or a little older.

"What is it, girl?" He looked past Tirtza and then up at Zhanna, for he was perhaps a hands-breadth shorter than her, but unlike Osred and Tirtza he didn't show any obvious sign of discomfort upon seeing her. "You must be the hostage."

"Master Osred told this girl she must show Zhanna around the castle, and Zhanna said she wanted to see dragons," Tirtza said, as though apologising.

"He did, did he?" Tavi looked at Zhanna again. "Zhanna, is it?" He tapped himself on the chest. "Tavi, stablemaster. Come in, then, if it's dragons you want to see." He turned away. Tirtza followed him and Zhanna followed her, wrinkling her nose as she did so.

"Behold," Tavi said, sweeping an arm out grandly. "The dragons of Black Keep."

At first, Zhanna could see nothing. Then, as her eyes adjusted to the gloom, she made out a series of barred metal gates as high as her chest, enclosing walled-off pens. These ran across the entire back wall of the stables, and inside…

… were huge piles of straw. She frowned, and cautiously stepped closer. There was the faintest hint of a noise, just on the edge of hearing.

Things abruptly swam into focus. The straw was packed under, atop and around a massive form. Zhanna saw the tips of four horns, and a leg as thick as a small tree terminating in a blunt-nailed, three-toed foot wider than her chest. The faint noise ceased momentarily, before a hollow wind rose in its place as massive lungs slowly emptied themselves of air they'd just collected. The top of the straw pile began to sink as the beast exhaled, but it was nearly as tall as she was, and the beast was on its *side*…

"Not much to look at right now, are they?" Tavi chuckled. It took Zhanna a moment to realise he wasn't joking. This wasn't a sight that made the stablemaster's breath catch in his throat, or twisted his stomach into a knot.

"They sleep?" she asked, feeling foolish. She'd never really thought of dragons sleeping.

"Most of the winter," Tavi replied, leaning on the gate. "Longbrows and frillnecks like these don't winter this far south. The wild ones are in the north at the moment; they'll show up here before too long. But we have to bed these down, or they might not make it through."

Zhanna looked at the huge pile of straw in astonishment. "When will sleep stop?"

"On their own? Could be a moon or more," Tavi replied. "But we'll rouse them today. Can't be having Raiders in the town without our war dragons being awake, even if the Raiders say they're friendly now." He snorted in apparent amusement, and gave Zhanna a wry smile.

Zhanna eyed him. "You wake them? You have... magic?" She'd heard the word from Nalon: he'd said it didn't properly match up to any Tjakorshi word he knew, but roughly meant the ability to do things that couldn't normally be done.

Tavi rubbed his chin, his eyes narrowing. "Of a sort. People say we used to have magic to control the dragons, to bond with them as rider and mount, but that was before the days of the Unmaker, and she destroyed it." He heaved a sigh. "Tolkar's arts and the God-King's men couldn't put magic together again. Now people like s'man have to use what charms are left to us, and the sars need all their wit and skill to master the beasts."

Zhanna wasn't sure who anyone he'd just named was, and had more important questions. "Do they eat people?"

"Eat people?" Tavi barked a laugh. "No! They'll kill you sure enough, if you're in the wrong place, but not to eat you. Longbrows eat grass." He snapped his fingers at Tirtza. "Take Zhanna over to the kennels, if she wants to see dragons that eat meat."

"The kennels?" Tirtza repeated. She didn't look delighted at the prospect.

"Aye, the kennels," Tavi said. "You'll not be staying here. Dragon magic's not for the eyes of serving girls. Or Raiders, for that matter," he added. "Go bother Duranen."

Tirtza bowed to him, and turned to leave. Zhanna took one last look at the huge dragon slumbering in its pen, then followed her. The sheer size of it still astonished her. To think the warriors of her clan had actually fought against such beasts, with riders on their backs...

Well, perhaps she understood a little better why her mother had been so scared for her when they'd been approaching the coast.

The kennels were against the east wall, and had a similar design to the stables, if on a smaller scale. Tirtza was far more tentative here, and hesitated uncertainly when she raised her hand to knock.

A tremendous racket arose within before the girl's knuckles even made contact with the wood. It was a great rattling; the closest approximation Zhanna's mind could manage was many large shells being shaken together.

"Who's there?" a voice demanded. Tirtza didn't get a chance to answer before the door was pulled back and a tall, rail-thin Naridan glowered out at her. His age was hard for Zhanna to judge, since his head was as bald as a crow's egg but his face was still largely unlined. He wore brown leathers and a sour expression, and held a long, knotted length of dark wood in his right hand.

"What do you wa—?" the man began, then saw Zhanna and his eyes narrowed. "Nari's blood, girl, you've let the savage out?" He squared up to her, fingers curling around his cudgel as though to strike her.

"She's to see the kennels!" Tirtza blurted out, backing away hastily while bowing. "Master Osred said!"

"Osred said *what*?" the man demanded of Tirtza. "Don't tell s'man she just gets to walk around like she owns the place!"

"This warrior cannot go beyond the gate," Zhanna said, eyeing him warily. She probably outweighed him, but he'd have reach on her even without his weapon... and of course, she added hastily to herself, she wasn't looking to fight any Flatlanders.

If one of them attacked her first, though...

"Warrior? Hah!" The man laughed nastily, then spat. "By the Mountain, it speaks! Nari's truth, but s'man thought your kind had only bird whistles and beast noises for language."

Zhanna wasn't the best at reading Naridan faces, but she strongly suspected he was trying to provoke her, so she smiled. "This warrior has her language *and* yours."

The man's left eye twitched slightly, and he didn't look away from her even though his next words were to Tirtza. "She's to see the kennels, you said?"

"Yes, Huntmaster," Tirtza replied timidly. "She wishes to see dragons."

Huntmaster—was that the man's name?—nodded slowly. "Come inside then, savage, if it's dragons you want."

He disappeared into the building's interior. Zhanna followed cautiously, half-expecting the cudgel to strike her skull the moment she set foot through the door, but nothing of the sort occurred. Instead she found herself in a building not dissimilar in layout to the stables where Tavi had shown her the sleeping longbrows. The pens here were smaller, however, and the smell in the air was sourer. The strange dragon odour was there, but overlaid with the scent of rotting meat.

"We call these rattletails," Huntmaster said, from Zhanna's left. He drew back a bolt and pulled a metal gate open, standing back behind it.

Out prowled a dragon.

Zhanna's heart began hammering. This was no mountainous longbrow; it was a much smaller, leaner beast, although its shoulders were still at the height of her waist. It was covered in short, loose feathers in patterns of blotchy grey and brown, its muzzle was long and narrow, and the teeth in its slightly open jaws were pointed, like a shark's. It raised its head to sniff in her direction.

There was nothing like it on Tjakorsha. The sea was full of dangers—sharks, krayk, rogue leviathans and storms amongst them—but the land was safe, except for when storms made landfall and brought down trees, or the great mountain spirits stirred in their sleep and spat out chunks of rock, or clouds of ash. The greatest danger on Tjakorsha was other clans of Tjakorshi.

The dragon's nostrils widened as it inhaled, and its eyes—vertical slashes of black across bright gold-green irises—focused on her. Its tail came up, and she saw a cluster of long, bare quills at the end of it.

It shook its tail and the quills struck each other, producing the eerie rattling she'd heard when approaching the outer door. Her heart sped up again.

The rattling was answered, and a second dragon emerged from the same pen.

"Careful now," Huntmaster said, laughter bubbling under his voice. "They can smell fear."

The foremost of the two reared up onto its hind legs and, to Zhanna's mounting terror, took a couple more steps forward. The thing *walked like a person!* Its head was near enough on a level with hers now, and its nostrils widened again as it sniffed once more, sucking in her scent...

There was a scream, and the scuffle of small feet on the straw-covered stone floor. Tirtza clearly couldn't take the sight of the approaching predators, and had bolted.

Both dragons leapt forwards, a pair of grey-brown feathered blurs. Zhanna was forgotten: they barrelled past her, claws clattering on the stone, and out of the door.

Huntmaster shouted something angry as more rattling erupted, and heavy bodies slammed against metal gates. Zhanna had visions of the gates giving way and a dozen more rattletails bursting out, leaping on her with fang and claw. She scrambled along the wall and out of the door, just as screaming erupted outside.

Tirtza had been brought down in the middle of the yard.

The girl was thrashing, and lashing out, but the dragons were not deterred: they merely jerked back from the blows and then quested in again with muzzles or claws, trying to get a grip on her. Zhanna saw Tavi's head poke out from the stables, then disappear again. Huntmaster ran past her a moment later, wielding his cudgel.

"*Down! Down!*" he bellowed, and when the dragons ignored his words he lashed out, catching one of them on the hip. Both turned towards him, mouths open and claws raised, tails rattling furiously.

"*Down!*" Huntmaster yelled again, hefting his cudgel. For a moment Zhanna thought the dragons were going to attack, but then their heads lowered, they dropped to all fours once more, and their tails quietened.

"Duranen!"

Huntmaster's head jerked at the voice, but he kept eye contact with the dragons. "Lord?"

Daimon Blackcreek strode into the yard. Zhanna didn't need to be an expert in reading Naridan expressions to tell he was furious. One hand was gripping the handle of his longblade, too, which wasn't a good sign.

Tavi had re-emerged from the stables with a long, broad-bladed spear, and advanced cautiously towards the frozen tableau of Tirtza, Huntmaster—or was it Duranen?—and the two dragons. Other Naridans were watching warily from around the yard, but no one else had stepped forward.

"What is going on here, Duranen?" Blackcreek demanded. "Why are your beasts loose?"

"Your pardon, lord," Duranen replied. He reached into a pouch at his belt and pulled out a strip of cured meat. Both dragons fixated on it instantly and Duranen began walking backwards towards the kennels, the two rattletails following.

Zhanna was still directly in their path. She took several steps to one side, trying to move smoothly to avoid provoking the dragons into attacking her. They were still eyeing the meat in Duranen's

MIKE BROOKS

hand though, and ignored her. Duranen turned and threw it overhand, into the kennel doorway, and the dragons bounded after it. Zhanna saw Duranen glance at her as he followed them: he hadn't checked where she was before he'd thrown it.

Tavi was helping Tirtza to her feet. The girl was sobbing frantically, and Zhanna could see blood on her arms from where she'd been shielding herself from the dragons' bites.

"She needs the apothecary, lord," Tavi said, after a cursory glance.

"Send Faaz with her," Blackcreek ordered. He looked at Tirtza, and grimaced. "Did you see what happened, Tavi?"

"No lord, your man looked out when he heard Tirtza screaming, when the dragons were already on her," Tavi replied. He looked up, and met Zhanna's eyes. "The Raider girl would've. She wanted to see dragons, and your man told Tirtza to show her the kennels."

Blackcreek pursed his lips, then nodded once and began to walk towards Zhanna. She kept her eyes on his hands, which were resting on his longblade. She didn't think she was at fault, but who could know the mind of a Naridan lord?

Duranen appeared again, and Blackcreek focused on him instead. Zhanna noticed the thane's robe was spotted and splashed with mud and water, which struck her as odd. What had he been doing?

"Duranen," Blackcreek said, coming to a halt. "This lord still awaits your explanation."

"Lord, Tirtza brought the Raider to the kennels, saying she wanted to see dragons," Duranen replied with a bow.

"So Tavi said," Blackcreek said. "This doesn't explain why two rattletails came to be mauling one of this lord's serving girls *in the middle of the damned yard.*"

He delivered the last half-dozen words through his teeth, and there was no mistaking the edge to them.

"Your man misunderstood," Duranen said, glancing at

192

Zhanna. "He thought the Raider was familiar with rattletails, so he let two out to greet her. She became scared, they became agitated, and chased Tirtza when she fled."

Blackcreek looked at Zhanna. "Well?"

Zhanna was sure Duranen was lying: he'd intended the dragons to at least scare her, possibly harm her. However, she wasn't sure she wanted to directly contradict one of Blackcreek's household in front of him, so she shrugged. "Perhaps yes."

Blackcreek's eyes flicked back to Duranen, and narrowed. "Take greater care in future. The apothecary's bill will come from your pay."

Duranen's face hardened, but he bowed again. "Lord."

Blackcreek's fingers drummed three times on the bare white wood of his longblade's scabbard, then he rolled his shoulders and seemed to put the matter behind him. "How fare the hatchlings?"

"Not well, lord," Duranen replied, his manner becoming brisk and matter-of-fact. "'Tis too early in the year for a brood, in truth, and the mother has rejected them. It happens on their first clutch, from time to time."

"This lord will see them," Blackcreek said, heading for the kennel door. He looked at Zhanna. "Come. The dragons will be secure now, and the hatchlings will not bite."

Zhanna was dubious, but followed them inside. More rattling arose, but the Naridans ignored it, so she tried to as well. This time Duranen led them to the pen at the far right. Adult dragons approached their gates and sniffed, but none responded aggressively, and Zhanna began to breathe a little more easily.

"Here, lord," Duranen was saying, gesturing to a pen with a low wall and a gate of solid wood, rather than a metal lattice. "We keep them as warm as we can with a smothered charcoal pit, but it's not the same."

Zhanna peered in, and almost laughed at what she saw. Six tiny creatures, barely the height of her outstretched fingers, were huddled together on soft earth. Unlike the feathered adults, these were naked save for their scaled skin.

No, not six, there were seven. There was another, smaller one, slightly apart from the main group. She pointed at it. "Is that well?"

Duranen glanced at her dismissively. "The runt. Not able to fight for the warmth. It'll likely be dead by the morning.'

Zhanna frowned. "Do you not be mother?"

Duranen blinked. "What?"

"On Tjakorsha, have crows," Zhanna said, trying to work out how she could explain. "Sometimes child find baby crow... hatchling? Out of... home?"

"Out of the nest?" Blackcreek asked.

Zhanna shrugged. It could be. "Child will raise hatchling as mother. Hatchling grow well. This warrior did so when she a child be."

Duranen snorted. "Dragons aren't crows, girl."

Blackcreek eyed first Zhanna, then Duranen. "You say the runt will die?"

"Nine times out of ten. If not tonight, the night after, for sure."

Blackcreek nodded thoughtfully, then unbolted the gate and stepped into the pen, to Duranen's consternation.

"Lord...?"

Blackcreek walked around the huddle of rattletail hatchlings, reached down, and scooped the runt up off the earth. It squawked weakly at him as he walked back out and shut the gate behind him. He turned back to Zhanna, and in his hands, a scaled, featherless head on a wobbly neck peered up at her.

"You wanted to see dragons, and say you know crows. This lord's huntmaster says this hatchling will not live on its own. Very well; its life is yours."

He held out his hands, and dropped the tiny dragon into hers.

RIKKUT

THE WARBAND HAD scoured the shores and ridges of Kainkoruuk, but nowhere was there any sign of the Brown Eagle clan. It wasn't until the warriors were sullen and exhausted that Amalk Tyaszhin had given the order to turn back, and his fleet had set sail once more. Rikkut couldn't blame him for wanting to make sure, but his actions had gone past thorough and well into desperate. All that time, their captive Ludir Snowhair had sat on the *Red Smile*'s deck with his cloak wrapped around him, staring straight ahead, and coldly unresponsive to any questioning about where his neighbours had gone. "Take me to your chief, then," he'd said to Rikkut, folding his arms tighter and shivering. "Take me there, if that's your purpose, and stop wasting everyone's time."

"We have no chief," Rikkut had told him sternly.

"What do you have, then?" Snowhair had asked, displaying his first sign of interest as he looked up at Rikkut and cocked an eyebrow.

"The Golden," Rikkut had said simply, and a tight bubble of fear and excitement stirred in his belly as he said the name. "It needs no other title."

"Foolishness," Snowhair had snorted, fidgeting with his cloak again. Rikkut hadn't chastised him. The old man had yielded. It was down to The Golden what happened to him.

Rikkut was an Easterner from Volgalkoruuk. He'd performed the bone walk around the rim of its crater, the entrance to the netherworld, and although his head had swum and his legs had grown weak, he'd resisted the spirits of his ancestors and had returned to his clan, instead of leaving his own bones there. He felt a fierce pride in the rock of his home, but he still had to admit it was dwarfed by the sheer scale of the island known as Dvokolorstal.

Formed of two Great Peaks, Ogongkoruuk and Korakoruuk, Dvokolorstal's massive double-lobed shape towered above the waves and trailed clouds from its twin summits. In the great bay that made up much of its west coast sat Torakudo, The Town of No Chiefs, where grievances between clans held no weight. It had always been a safe place; a welcoming port in a storm, a place to find a crew or a ship, a place to take counsel from witches and plan the year ahead.

Now it was the seat of The Golden, and safety was a relative concept.

"I'd heard tales," Snowhair said hoarsely as his eyes lit upon the blackened, burned wrecks that had once been buildings, scattered through Torakudo. The Golden had been thorough when it had made landfall, and had ordered the home of anyone who resisted put to the torch. It was work that had gladdened Rikkut's heart, and had helped earn his name, Fireheart.

"Now you know them to be true," he said to Snowhair as Tyaszhin ordered the sail reefed, and guided the *Red Smile* alongside one of the long wooden jetties thrust out into the bay. Men and women jumped ashore with ropes and wrenched the yolgu to a halt, then made it fast on mooring posts. "Up you get, old man. Time for you to meet the true ruler of Tjakorsha."

Tyaszhin strode through the streets, Olja at his left shoulder and Rikkut at his right. Ludir Snowhair trailed behind, flanked by two more warriors, but his chin was held high, for he was still a clan chief so long as he drew breath. Most of the rest of the fleet dispersed into the town. Some were seeking shorat or fresh food, the embrace of a loved one, or a roll on a pallet with someone whose affection was for hire. The rest merely wanted to avoid laying eyes on The Golden.

Rikkut knew Tyaszhin wished him to be among those seeking their entertainment elsewhere, but the need to claim the glory of capturing Snowhair was almost fire-hot in its intensity. So he walked through the streets one pace behind Tyaszhin and one to the side, with Ludir Snowhair's blade sheathed at his belt in the scabbard he'd taken from the old man's longhouse. It was a strange thing, the pale wood richly decorated in a manner he'd never seen before.

The largest building in Torakudo stood at the very centre of the town. It had officially been known as the House of the Fates, but more commonly called the Witchhouse, and it was here the witches of Torakudo had lived and received callers. A clan chief would have their own witches for counsel, but a sea captain might wish for advice before a voyage, and some islanders would even consult the witches before arranging a marriage or deciding what crop to plant.

The Golden had killed all but two of the witches when it had arrived, added the pair it had spared to its retinue of advisors, and taken the Witchhouse as its own.

The great double doors were closed fast, with two of The Golden's own Scarred on guard in front of them, one man and one woman. Tyaszhin came to a halt and eyed each in turn. They stared back, their hands on their weapons but making no move either aggressive or respectful. In normal times a captain of Tyaszhin's reputation would expect some deference from his own chief's Scarred, so long as he respected the chief in turn, but these weren't normal times. The Golden had turned all structures on their head, and only one thing remained certain: the draug was at the top.

"I'm here to see The Golden," Tyaszhin said grudgingly, when neither warrior reacted to his arrival. "Got a chief who needs to swear fealty."

The woman reached out and hammered on the doors three times with her fist, and the thick wood began to creak open. Tyaszhin started walking forwards before they'd even finished opening and Rikkut shadowed him, not wanting to be late into The Golden's presence. Behind him, he heard Tyaszhin's two crewers chivvying Snowhair along, and the old man snapping at them.

The interior was dark and smoky, with open fires burning in the floor and red-lit shapes of people flitting between them. The Golden ordered that its fires should never die, and it only suffered witches to live if they could read the flames. It was rumoured to never sleep, and Rikkut could understand why, in this atmosphere of constant light. It was as though it sought to keep the Long Day alive, when the sun skimmed the horizon and never set.

"What have you done here?" Snowhair demanded, and now the old chief's voice was growing more strident. "This was a place of wisdom, not some sweat lodge! Who did this?"

"*I did this.*"

Between one moment and the next, the draug was there, looming up out of the flickering shadows like a plume of smoke emerging from Korakoruuk's summit. Rikkut immediately dropped to his knees, his heart hammering in his chest. Tyaszhin and the rest followed suit a moment later, leaving Snowhair standing alone, but Rikkut couldn't help stealing a look upwards from the corner of his eye.

The body The Golden had taken was that of a naked man, and was painted in russet and shade by the flames so even the fine blond hair on its chest and legs took on the colour of fire. It stood tall enough to look slightly down at Amalk Tyaszhin, although it was not so broad, and when it moved Rikkut could see muscles shifting beneath its skin, like sharks in the shallows. It was marked all over by scars. Some were hair-thin, and some were jagged and thick, but all had healed. The witches said The Golden could not be killed, and its body was testament to that. Ugliest of all was the thick rope-mark around its neck, but that too was healing.

Even here, naked and sweat-slicked in the heat, it still wore its mask. It was grey steel inlaid with gold whorls and spirals, and covered all its face save the eyes, mouth, and bearded chin. The blond hair on the draug's head was shorn so close its scalp was visible, leaving the leather straps securing the mask resting against the skin. Rikkut had never seen it without the mask: if any man or woman in Tjakorsha had, they wouldn't speak of it.

"I did this," The Golden repeated. The draug spoke Tjakorshi, and its voice was as cold and clear as a snowmelt stream, but there was something wrong about the way it formed the words. The intonation was slightly off, and the stresses came in the wrong places, as though the body and the being controlling it were not quite one.

The Golden tilted its head slightly to one side as it studied Snowhair with eyes of the palest green, like twin chips of ice that had settled under a man's brows, as hard and uncaring as the bitterest southern hail. "Because I could. You say this was a place of wisdom?" Now its voice started to rise. "They didn't know I was coming, or didn't know what I intended! What *wisdom* is that?"

Its head tilted back the other way, that cold stare unblinking, unflinching, and it sucked a deep breath of the smoky air in through its nose. "So you'll be Snowhair. Another weak old man claiming to be a chief, clinging to a title he doesn't understand." It held out one hand. "Give me your belt."

Snowhair tilted his head back, somehow finding a way to look down his nose at The Golden despite being the shorter of the two. "This belt belongs to the chief of the Seal Rock clan, and—"

"And I want it," The Golden cut him off. It seized Snowhair by the throat, the muscles on its arm standing out. The old man gurgled, reaching up with both hands to prise its fingers away, but couldn't free himself. Rikkut grinned, silently urging Snowhair to fight harder. That would be fun to watch.

"No one can stop me," The Golden said urgently as Snowhair struggled. "You need to understand that. You have to *know* it, in your heart. Or I'll burn you alive, then break your blackened bones into powder." It released its grip and watched Snowhair sag, wheezing desperately.

"You can give me your belt, kneel and swear fealty, and go back to what was once your clan," The Golden said simply. "Or I can kill you, and take it anyway."

He might have been old, but he wasn't foolish. Slowly, as though his hands were moving against his will, Ludir Snowhair reached behind his back and unfastened the belt of engraved bronze discs that had been around the waists of his predecessors for more generations than Rikkut could be bothered to think about. It slipped off him and dangled from his hand like a fat, bright-scaled eel as he sank to his knees and slowly handed it to The Golden.

"Put it with the others," The Golden said, taking the belt unhurriedly and holding it out without looking. A woman Rikkut didn't know appeared from the shadows, her face lowered in deference, and took the belt from the draug before disappearing towards the rear of the hall. Snowhair looked even more unwell at seeing the symbol of his clan's power disposed of so casually, but he said nothing.

"Where's the second?" The Golden asked Tyaszhin, its mask turning to the captain of the *Red Smile*. Tyaszhin swallowed, and Rikkut held his breath. He was looking forward to seeing the older man squirm, but there was no guarantee The Golden's displeasure would be tightly focused.

"The Brown Eagle clan fled before us, master," Tyaszhin said, managing to keep his voice steady. "Their hearths were cold, their beaches empty, their fields abandoned."

"Where did they go?" The Golden asked. Tyaszhin shook his head, words apparently failing him.

Rikkut saw The Golden's jaw shift for a moment, and then it drove its right knee directly into Amalk Tyaszhin's face.

There was a *crack* of crushed cartilage and Tyaszhin toppled backwards with a stunned grunt, his hands flying to his ruined nose, but the draug hadn't finished with him. It let out a growl and flowed down atop the *Red Smile*'s captain to straddle his body. Then it prised his hands away from his face, and battered him with open-handed strikes.

Tyaszhin tried first to shield himself, then to desperately crawl away. Each time, The Golden seized a wrist to wrench aside an arm or hand, and delivered another blow that bounced Tyaszhin's head off the Witchhouse's dirt floor. Rikkut watched hungrily until, after perhaps twenty such strikes, The Golden rose back to its feet and turned its back on Tyaszhin, the light of the flames glistening off the sheen of sweat on its skin, and Rikkut tore his eyes away to look at the floor again.

"*Pathetic,*" The Golden remarked, apparently to the air at large.

Amalk Tyaszhin pulled himself painfully back to his knees, nose streaming blood, lips swollen, right eye already closing. He should have stayed there with his head down and accepted his punishment, but although he'd changed his sails when The Golden's wind had risen in the east, Rikkut knew Tyaszhin had never been a believer. He still had too much of the old pride, a throwback to the days when a captain could look a chief in the eye and tell them they were a fool, if that seemed necessary.

Tyaszhin drew the spearfish-bill dagger on his belt and lurched upright, his one good eye focused on The Golden's unprotected back.

Kozh and Enga, Tyaszhin's two crewers who'd been escorting Snowhair, leaped into action before Rikkut could even move. They lunged as one, each seizing an arm to drag their captain back down again, for loyalty to a captain paled in insignificance compared to loyalty to The Golden. The draug turned back to Tyaszhin unhurriedly, its pale eyes almost mocking.

"There is some fire in you, then. A shame you couldn't use that to find the Brown Eagles."

"They'll have gone west."

Everyone's heads, including The Golden's, turned towards Ludir Snowhair. The old man smiled with one side of his mouth, exposing the old, stained teeth last seen when he'd been gasping for air.

"You said you didn't know where they'd gone!" Tyaszhin snarled, spitting blood into the dirt.

"I just ignored you and told you to take me to your chief," Ludir laughed wheezily. "I'm no friend to Saana Sattistutar and her land-stealing bastards, but I wasn't going to spill my guts to the likes of you!" He looked at The Golden, a sneer cutting across his face, and for the first time Rikkut got an impression of the arrogance Snowhair must have carried in his youth, when he'd been able to back it up.

"That goat-fucker did nothing but stomp around my longhouses like he had half an axe up his arse, and now he's led me here like he reeled me in himself," Snowhair spat, jabbing a finger at Tyaszhin. "You want my fealty, draug? Then I'll tell you the truth. *That boy there* was the one who did the deed worthy of song! Fair flew over my shieldwall, like Kydozhar Fell-Axe reborn! He killed one of my best, and put the other down long enough to get his axe at my throat."

The full, unblinking attention of The Golden's ice-green eyes fell on Rikkut. Bare feet walked over the dirt to stand in front of him, and Rikkut found himself acutely aware of the trembling in his muscles and the shallowness of his breathing as he focused on the floor just in front of The Golden's toes.

"Interesting," The Golden said. Rikkut felt fingers come to rest on his scalp, and he tensed in fear and excitement as he felt the draug's power wash through him, searching him, *knowing* him.

"Rikkut Jumadazhin."

Rikkut's gut spasmed as the draug said his name, and he had to try his voice once before it worked. "Rikkut Fireheart, master." Not even The Golden could deny him the warrior-name he'd earned.

"Look at me, Fireheart."

Rikkut's blood was fire and ice as one. His mouth was dry, and he moved his tongue around to moisten it as he hesitantly raised his eyes. The Golden was stood a mere hand's breadth from his face, and loomed over him like Ogongkoruuk itself. His gaze travelled up over the draug's belly, over its chest, and obediently met its eyes.

"West, you said?" The Golden was addressing Snowhair, but didn't look away from Rikkut's face.

"There *isn't* anything west!" Tyaszhin protested desperately, still being held in place. "Nothing but sea and sky!"

"Shows what you know, shit-for-brains," Snowhair sniggered. "Everyone knows Easterners can't sail, don't they? No, there's lands to the west if you go far enough, if you've got the guts to go head-to-head with the Dark Father in his domain."

Now The Golden did look away, and Rikkut felt the loss like a man straying from the warmth of a fire during Long Night. "You've seen them yourself?" The Golden asked the Seal Rock chief.

"Aye," Snowhair said proudly. "I sailed to the lands of the setting sun, and returned to tell of it. You want proof? It's stuck through the lad's belt."

The Golden looked back at him, and Rikkut tried to hide the thrill that hit his lower belly. He handed the strange sword up to his master without even being asked.

"Have you ever seen anything like that in Tjakorsha?" Snowhair asked softly as The Golden took the weapon in both hands and partially unsheathed it. "Have you ever seen anything like that in the Drylands to the north, or wherever it is you Easterners get your iron from? No. That's western steel, that is, finest in the world. I took that from one of their best warriors, some forty years ago. I went on that voyage as a captain and came back chief, on account of the little shit who wielded that killing Old Chorak and five of his Scarred in less time than it would take me to say their names out loud."

"And your clan never spoke of these lands?" The Golden said, its attention apparently still on the half-drawn blade.

"Why would we?" Snowhair asked. "Didn't serve us to let anyone else know. Oh, Sattistutar's lot knew—their damned iron-witch came from there, and how they grabbed him I'll never know—and I'm sure I saw a Quiet Shore ship heading that way a time or two. But you don't go singing about good fishing outside your own clan."

The Golden nodded thoughtfully, and finally drew the blade out the whole way. The steel shimmered, reflecting the firelight from all sides.

"Rikkut Fireheart."

Rikkut's heart jumped. "Master?"

"I like this blade," The Golden said calmly. "I'm going to keep it."

Rikkut fought down the sudden, biting disappointment. He'd been certain the draug was going to honour him. He'd at least hoped he'd get the sword back.

"I suggest," The Golden continued, "that you go and get another."

Rikkut frowned. "Master?"

The Golden spun and swung the western blade one-handed, and the head of Amalk Tyaszhin hit the floor with a dull thud, followed a moment later by his body. Rikkut stared in awe as blood gouted into the dirt from the dead man's neck. A steel blade could be near as sharp as blackstone, and keep its edge where blackstone would splinter or shatter, everyone knew that, but no mortal could have taken a man's head off with one swing, delivered with one hand.

"You brought me one chief," The Golden said, fixing Rikkut with that icy stare once more. "Now I want you to bring me another. Take the *Red Smile* and whoever else was answering to this dead man, and fetch me the belt of the Brown Eagle clan. Sail west, and perhaps you'll be able to get your own blade."

Rikkut felt like his chest might burst. "Yes, master! And the chief?"

The Golden's lips twitched in the ghost of a smile. "She's fled from me across an ocean most of my people think has no end. I doubt she'll come back of her own will. Bring back whoever you can, but those that won't come don't get to live. Do you understand?"

"Perfectly, master." Rikkut bared his teeth in a smile. An ocean voyage at the head of his own fleet, a new land to plunder and a desperate clan to hunt down. When he came back, the name of Rikkut Fireheart would be sung across the five Great Peaks and beyond.

"Then only one thing remains, Fireheart," The Golden said, turning away from Amalk Tyaszhin's body with the blood-slicked western blade still held loosely in its right hand. "I must mark you as my own." It raised its voice, addressing the thralls lurking in the shadows.

"Fetch my scarring blades!"

JEYA

JEYA'S HANDS WERE blistered, and hér arms and shoulders ached ferociously. Abbaz had given guidance, but shé'd learned just as much from watching Damau. Together they'd punted Abbaz's small craft to the lock that raised them onto the Second Level, the next-highest of the canals that made up the waterweb. From there they'd progressed slowly, while Abbaz had shouted their wares: honeyed lemons, peeled and dipped—sticky, sweet and sour all in one; plump dates from Morlith, somehow still good despite the journey; and tiny dried, dark blue fruits from the northern islands that exploded sweetness onto Jeya's tongue when shé snuck one behind Abbaz's back.

They'd passed through wealthy streets, with Abbaz hailing passers-by at the mooring places, or as they glided beneath the low bridges cutting back and forth across the canal. These were strange places to Jeya's eyes, and not just because of the larger buildings and cleaner streets. Alongside people bustling about their work there were also richly dressed folk with nothing to do save walking, sitting, and talking. These were Abbaz's customers; people who'd stroll down to the water to spend what seemed to Jeya like huge amounts of money on a snack.

Then they'd reached the next part of the Second Level, where the canal wound away from the yeng shops and tailors, and began to pass the gardens of the rich.

Since Jeya's môther had died, shé hadn't had any space to call hér own; not one shé could walk away from and come back to, at any rate. That was the way of the streets; you found the safest place to sleep you could, then moved on. You might sleep somewhere more than once, but you could never count on it being there for you again. If someone bigger or nastier had your favourite spot, or you didn't have the money to pay for a space on Ngaiyu's floor, you made do.

These gardens were probably bigger than all the different spaces Jeya had ever slept in, all put together. Not that shé could see many of them, since there were walls between them and the canal towpath, but shé'd seen the steeply sloping roofs of the houses, and could tell how far they were from the edge of the property. Shé caught tantalising glimpses of lush green grass; fruit trees in blossom; a smaller, secondary building, perhaps half as wide across as Ngaiyu's place. Was that garden so large the owner needed somewhere to rest while walking through it?

And there, too, people heard Abbaz's call and emerged from gates, or doors set into walls, and came down to the water to buy treats for themselves or their plump children. Sometimes the older children had come alone, clutching enough money in one hand to get them stabbed and robbed in some of the alleys Jeya knew. Shé'd rarely felt poorer, or more ragged.

Then, as they'd rounded a bend in the canal, Damau had crossed the boat muttering about swapping sides, and as Jeya had obliged they'd cast a significant glance towards a certain wall.

It was green-grey stone, and taller than hér, but the boughs of a majestic paddleleaf reached out from within and drooped low and far enough that the great leaves nearly touched the water of the canal. The wooden gate set into the wall looked rarely used, judging by the grass that had grown up outside it, and no one had come out in response to Abbaz's cry.

* * *

It was later, now. The afternoon had passed with another storm, and Abbaz had put a rain hat over their headscarf and complained about clouds covering the face of God, but the wind had carried those clouds away to leave the stars twinkling in the sky as though they too had been washed clean. Neither moon was full, but they provided enough light for Jeya to see by as shé picked hér way along the towpath.

There it was, the big paddleleaf leaning out low across the water. Jeya walked as briskly as shé dared, because you should never look like you were sneaking, even if you didn't think there was anyone watching. When shé drew level with the tree shé ducked under the first branch, then jumped up and grabbed onto the second before shé let hérself think about what shé was doing.

The branch was sturdy and wide, and already resting on the top of the wall, so it didn't even wobble. Shé kicked off the wall with hér feet to get hér legs up and over the branch, then hauled hérself up onto it. Shé'd always had good balance and the paddleleaf's bark was rough, so it was easy enough to get carefully to hér feet and walk along it like a highrope acrobat on a festival day, especially when another branch converged close enough to use as a handhold.

Shé crossed the wall but didn't drop down. Perhaps rich people put traps inside their garden walls, just in case thieves tried to climb over them? Besides, if shé stayed in the tree shé wouldn't risk being unable to climb back out again, and might also be able to get a good view of the house without getting so close…

The fat main trunk would have surely taken three or four people to encircle with their arms, and where the branches met it looked almost like the body of an upturned dead spider, legs in the air. Jeya settled into the hollow the branches created and squinted towards the house. Shé could see its sloping roof, angled to shed the torrential rains, but other trees blocked hér view. A couple of lights burned somewhere inside, but the distance, and interposing leaves, meant they looked like nothing more than fireflies, faint sparks in the gloom.

This was ridiculous. Shé was going to have to get a lot closer. And what did shé know about housebreaking, anyway? What had seemed like a good idea the previous night, and an exciting adventure when travelling the canals with Damau, now increasingly felt poorly thought-out.

Shé froze as a shadow moved beneath a large shrub further up the garden. It disappeared for a moment into the deeper gloom, then darted across an open patch of grass bathed in the gentle silver moonlight.

It was a person. And they looked to be heading for the bottom of the garden.

Hér first thought was that shé'd been discovered. Hér second was that there'd been no shouted challenge, and the person looked to be trying to stick to the shadows. Had shé misjudged this? Had someone already robbed the house, and was even now making off with the valuables?

Hér third thought, as the shadowy figure continued to approach at a cautious run, was that shé was sitting directly on the most obvious route out of the garden, apart from the gate that didn't seem to open often.

This was bad. Jeya wasn't sure if shé dared move, as that would certainly give hér away. On the other hand, a thief who found their escape route blocked was likely to lash out in fear and alarm. Jeya hesitated, stomach knotting with tension, and in that moment the figure changed direction to head directly for the tree shé was sitting in.

Jeya tried to scramble away, but it took hér a moment to sort hér feet out and turn, and before she could do so there was a huff of breath and a scrabbling as the other person hauled themselves up the trunk. Shé groped for hér small knife, felt the smooth bone handle under hér fingers, and pulled the blade clear of the wooden sheath just as a hooded head made of shadow appeared.

"*Nari's teeth!*"

Still torn halfway between fight and flight, Jeya hesitated. That was a Naridan oath…

"You!" The figure had swayed backwards for a moment, nearly losing their grip on the trunk, but now clutched at it more firmly. "Why are you in my tree?"

The voice was urgent but hushed, yet Jeya recognised it despite the difference from its calm, confident delivery in the marketplace the day before. Sure enough, shé'd been discovered by the worst person imaginable; someone who had not only identified hér, but could still call for hér to be sent to the magistrates.

And yet, there was a hot, tight spark in hér centre that flared up in excitement.

"Why are yòu in yòur tree?" shé found herself demanding.

"Why…? It's *my tree!* This is *my* garden!"

Jeya crouched back down onto hér heels, studying hìs hooded head. "So why were yòu sneaking across the grass, and why aren't yòu calling for the guards?" Shé wasn't at all afraid, shé realised with some surprise. Shé knew very well what someone trying to avoid attention looked like, and everything about the manner of the person currently hanging off the side of the tree screamed of it.

There was a frustrated hiss from inside the hood. "Are you going to stab mè if Ì climb up there?"

It was a clumsy dodge of hér question, but hè raised an important point. Jeya narrowed hér eyes. "Are yòu going to give me reason to?"

"No!"

"Make sure yòu don't." Shé sheathed hér knife and, on impulse, offered a hand. Hè still hesitated, and shé tutted. "The knife's away. Come on."

Hè reached out and clasped hér hand, and shé pulled hìm up onto the mighty tree's bole. Hè weighed a little less than shé'd expected, and seemed slightly smaller than shé remembered now hè was crouched directly in front of hér.

Shé realised after a moment that shé still had hold of hìs hand and hastily let go, no matter what the spark in hér belly was telling hér to do. Shé could just make out the faint curves and shadows of hìs face under hìs hood, and shé swallowed. It had become quite hard to think.

"Thank you," hè muttered, with the air of someone acknowledging a debt to clear it. "Now, *why* are you in this tree?"

Jeya hesitated. *I wanted to see if yòur house had anything worth stealing* wasn't a good answer and, if shé was actually properly honest with hérself for the first time today, wasn't a particularly truthful one either. *Yòu're beautiful and I wanted to look at yòu again* was, now shé thought about it, rather more truthful, but also far more terrifying. Shé tried to moisten her dry mouth, and went for a compromise.

"Someone I know saw what happened in the market and followed yòu here, then told me which house it was. Any other rich person would have sent me to the magistrates. Yòu didn't. I wanted to know why."

Hè shifted uneasily, and Jeya got the impression it wasn't just because hìs legs were twisted uncomfortably under hìm. "It should not be remarkable to not want someone hanged for being hungry."

"It shouldn't be, but it is," Jeya replied. "So, why?"

"How did you expect to find this out by climbing into my garden?" hè demanded. Which was a fair question, but Jeya had a fair answer.

"Look at me. I'd be chased away from yòur door as a beggar. This was the best idea I had. Also," shé added suspiciously, "yòu're dodging my question."

"It is a stupid reason," hè muttered, "and not honourable." Hè looked back over hìs shoulder in the direction of the house as hè spoke, and the moonlight glinted on hìs cheekbones as hìs hood pulled back a little from his face.

"No reason that prevents me getting hanged is stupid," Jeya said firmly. "I'm pretty definite about that. And I don't give a moons' kiss about honour."

Hè turned back to face hér, pools of shadow once more obscuring hìs features. "Very well." Hè paused for a moment, and Jeya thought hè'd decided against speaking, but then hè found his voice again, stumbling and hesitant though it was.

"Ì... thought you were very fair to look on."

Oh.

Half of Jeya's mind was laughing at hìs fanciful choice of words, while the other half was sitting in stunned silence. Shé made a small noise that held no meaning, although hè didn't seem to notice.

"It is not honourable, as Ì said." Hè lowered hìs head a little as he continued. "Justice should be based on the law, not on... appearance. Ì am ashamed to say that had you looked different, Ì may have sent to you the magistrates. Truthfully, Ì do not know what Ì would have done. But—"

"Are yòu saying this just because yòu're in a tree with me, and I've got a knife?" Jeya demanded, coaxing hér tongue into action again.

"No!" Hè bit down on the end of the word, as though it had come out louder than hè'd intended. "By my ancestors and Nari Hìmself, no."

"Right, then." Jeya wondered if there was a God of Bad Decisions amongst the myriad of pantheons worshipped across Alaba. If so, shé probably owed them a few prayers. Shé leaned forwards.

"What—?"

Hè had time for one word before Jeya's lips closed on hìs. Shé felt hìm tense and start to pull away, and hér heart sank, but then hè relaxed and melted into the kiss. Hér heart was thundering in hér ears. Shé reached out and wrapped hér arm around the small of hìs back, pulling them closer together. Shé felt hìs hand slide up, brushing over hér collarbone, and then hìs fingers were tangling in the hair at the back of hér neck, holding hér in place. Shé didn't mind, and leaned in further; shé could stay here forever, drowning in this kiss, drowning in hìm...

Hè twisted suddenly, making a noise in the back of hìs throat. Jeya pulled back in alarm, then nearly yelped as hè grabbed at hér arm. Shé didn't understand what was going on, what had happened, until hè braced hìmself against a branch and extricated one of hìs legs from underneath hìm, where it had become caught and twisted. Jeya felt heat burn into hér cheeks.

"Oh by all the gods, I'm so sorry—"

"Please, no, do not... Ì am the clumsiest fool in all the Islands." Hè massaged hìs leg briefly, then punched it as though blaming it for causing hìm pain.

Jeya swallowed. "I... probably shouldn't have done that." It was very hard to form the words, not least because shé really didn't want to admit it.

Hè looked up at her, startled. "Ì disagree."

"Oh. Well. That's good." Shé hesitated, torn by indecision. Shé really, really wanted to kiss hìm again, but it felt like the moment had gone and hè had made no move to try to kiss *hér*...

Hè cleared hìs throat softly. "Might... might Ì ask your name?"

Jeya couldn't help but smile. Had shé transgressed some rich person tradition by kissing hìm before they knew each other's names? "Ì'm Jeya."

"Jeya." Hè nodded, and shé could tell hè'd caught the difference in intonation now shé'd gendered hérself. "My name is Galem."

Galem. Jeya got to hér feet on an impulse and, wobbling slightly on the uneven footing, made a little bow such as shé'd seen Naridan folk make. "Pleased to meet yòu, Galem."

There was a snort from inside hìs hood that was almost certainly a muffled laugh. "And Ì yóu, Jeya. But might we continue this conversation on the other side of that wall? You see, my family's guards are zealous, and Ì am not supposed to be out of the house..."

EVRAM

THE FOREST WAS damp and cold, and Evram had never before
thought so wistfully of his hut in Black Keep. It was small, to
be sure, with barely enough room for his cookfire and his pallet,
but it had kept the rain off and the wind out. He'd also had
somewhere dry to store firewood, which was more than the
Downwoods could offer. He had no axe, and the green twigs
he'd managed to snap off with his hands didn't burn well. A
fire at night depended on finding dead sticks dry enough to use
as kindling, which he hadn't always managed. When he didn't,
he would wake up chilled to the bone. Even when he did find
enough for a fire, most of its heat seemed to be sucked into the
empty darkness above.

All in all, he didn't think he'd ever been so miserable.

There were small settlements here and there along the road,
with strings of brightly coloured flags to keep away evil spirits,
and often a fence of sharpened, outward-pointing stakes for the
more physical threat of roaming dragons, but never more than a
few houses clustered together. Evram had looked towards their
walls with longing, but had put his head down and powered on.
What if pursuit came from behind, as Shefal had warned? If he
was outside, cold and miserable though he might be, he could
hear someone coming. Warming himself by someone's hearth, he

might know nothing until the door was knocked in. Could he be certain these woodcutters and charcoal burners wouldn't betray him if threatened with a blackstone axe? For that matter, could he know they wouldn't promise him a dry space to sleep, then slit his throat for his coin?

No, he told himself glumly, best not to trust the safety of his skin and his task to anyone else. So he pushed on, his feet growing increasingly sore with every mile. Each day he rose with the sun and had to find somewhere out of sight to make his camp in the evenings, which still closed in all too quickly at this time of year. Trying to make his way in the deep dark of the Downwoods at night was a sure recipe for a twisted ankle at best, no matter how good the road surface.

It was the fifth night. His feet were rubbed sore by boots never intended for this much constant walking, his provisions had all but run out, and his stomach was growling as he slouched against a thick whitewood trunk, starting to nod and doing his best to soak up the warmth from the pitiful fire in front of him. He'd have to find someone to buy food from tomorrow, even though that would mean being seen. He was no good at lying, but perhaps he could come up with a simple, believable story why a peasant from Black Keep was walking the North Road this early in the year.

The next growl he heard wasn't from his stomach.

Had Evram been a hero from song he would have stood up and faced into the dark, one hand drawing his belt knife and the other braving the fire's heat to grip the unburned end of a dead branch. He would have stridden forwards to see what manner of beast had dared approach and either driven it off or slain it, then probably used its hide as a cloak after some unmentioned period of tanning or curing, the practical elements of which the songs so rarely covered.

Evram had far more common sense than such heroes, however, which is why he immediately scrambled to his feet and leapt for the gnarled, knotted and, above all, easily climbable trunk of the whitewood behind him. Blistered feet, aching joints and suddenly-banished drowsiness notwithstanding, he was more than twice his own height above the ground within a few moments, albeit moments in which he'd been expecting to feel the searing pain of claws in his back, or teeth around his ankle.

Here the whitewood's trunk divided into the first of its main branches, each one at least as thick around as his own waist, and he looked down at the ground from a position of some stability. He could see nothing at first in the flickering shadows cast by his fire save for the surrounding undergrowth, and wondered whether he'd jumped like a child at a figment of his own imagination.

Then he saw the eyes.

Golden and glimmering, reflecting the firelight like a pair of tiny lanterns, the eyes bobbed and swayed as their owner moved its head to view his fire from different angles. He could see the vague shadow of the body, but it was too far back from the light to make out any detail. It had to be a wild dragon, probably a predator. Evram's bladder swelled inside him as he realised how close he'd been to falling victim to it.

A low, whickering call came from the right, and Evram realised in horror that there was more than one. He craned his neck to see and, sure enough, another pair of golden lights glinted and flashed as the creature slunk through the bushes with barely a rustle to mark its passing over the pop and snap of burning wood. At least two, calling to each other: pack hunters. Rattletails perhaps, or razorclaws.

Evram hoped they weren't razorclaws.

As suddenly as they'd appeared, the eyes were gone. Evram strained his own eyes peering into the darkness and held his breath listening, but could get no clue where the dragons were. It didn't matter: he wouldn't be climbing down this tree until the morning, not unless his fire burned out of control and the whitewood caught.

Evram wrapped his cloak around himself and pulled his hood forward as far as it would go. Then he settled back as best he could, where two of the branches left the trunk close enough together that there was no risk of him falling between them, and resigned himself to a night even more miserable than the ones he'd already endured.

SAANA

IT WAS FIVE days after they'd given Ristjaan to the waves, and Saana had done her best to avoid Daimon Blackcreek since.

It hadn't been completely possible, of course. She could see Zhanna at sundown, when her daughter was allowed to walk the front wall of the castle and wave down to Saana to prove she was still well. They'd shouted back and forth in Naridan, so as not to arouse the suspicions of the guards accompanying her. Blackcreek was there on the second evening, but not since, for which Saana was glad.

Then there was the fact she needed to organise her folk as best she could to work in this new land, because Blackcreek had the right of it: the clan's only hope of survival lay in showing the Naridan's war leader—the Marshal, as Blackcreek referred to him—they were more valuable than they were a threat, whenever he might appear. This meant finding out which Naridans did which jobs, and negotiating who would join them. Saana used Nalon's assistance as much as possible, but some Flatlanders clearly thought him a traitor, and he wasn't the most ingratiating of men in any case. Sometimes Daimon's authority had been needed, and then there'd been nothing for it but to seek him out.

Of course, sometimes there were other problems.

She'd come to the castle and had been escorted through it by

Ganalel and Ita, two of the guards. Ita was young and somewhat overawed; Ganalel was old and sour, and had passed more than one comment Saana felt sure was intended to provoke her to violence. She'd resisted, but not by much.

It turned out that the Black Keep itself, the roof of which Saana had seen rising above the fortress's walls, was apparently simply a defensive structure in which the nobles would take refuge if their home came under serious attack. Their day-to-day quarters were a series of one-storey buildings on the typical Naridan wooden stilts, arranged around courtyards of planted shrubs and washed gravel. They were bedecked with strings of small, colourful flags that presumably held some significance, and many of the beams and plaster walls were painted with frescos of glorious colour.

And everywhere, dragons.

Not the real thing, but depicted over and over again in artwork. It took Saana's eyes a few moments to work out the shapes, but then they sprang out at her. There were small, lean ones and large, bulky ones; on two legs and on four, with horns and with claws, some with mouths open to display sharp teeth and one with what looked like a club for a tail; long necks and short; ones that flew on broad wings, and one emerging from a cave or burrow in a hillside. She could see the ones she knew, but there were many others besides. And there were some, she reflected as she eyed one with what looked to be particularly long claws, she definitely didn't want to meet.

Osred the steward emerged from the main door, frowning. He hadn't accused Saana of trying to poison his lord again in the days since her arrival, but she could tell this chief servant had no love for her, which wasn't surprising. He gave one of the little bows of his people, echoing the deeper ones made to him by Ita and Ganalel, but didn't take his eyes from her.

"Chief Saana," he said, a little warily.

"Steward," she replied, without bowing. Nalon had tried to explain the subtleties to her but she still hadn't understood it, and was hesitant to try the custom unless she knew she could get it right. "This man wishes to see Lord Daimon."

"This way, please," Osred said, straightening and turning. Ita and Ganalel didn't enter the house, so Saana climbed the stairs alone.

She found herself in a hallway that ran down the centre of the building yet was strangely light. Pale walls on either side of her were decorated with artwork depicting plants, birds, and more dragons, but they weren't stone, or wood. She thought they were glowing at first, but as she took another step she realised there were windows behind the walls, and the light from them was shining through somehow. She stopped and reached out a finger in wordless curiosity: the surface bent slightly at her touch.

"What is this?" she asked, unable to disguise her wonder.

"Paper," Osred replied, although the word meant nothing to Saana. "You do not know paper?"

Saana shook her head. "Where does it come from?"

"Trees."

Saana narrowed her eyes, trying to work out if he was making fun of her, but she could detect no mockery. Distaste, perhaps, but not mockery. She withdrew her finger and tucked her thumb into her belt, then gestured at him to continue walking. The strange paper walls didn't seem to have any role in holding the ceiling up: that was done by thick wooden pillars of planed tree trunks standing at even intervals. Indeed, as Saana looked closer at the paper surfaces she could see tiny gaps at the edges and realised what she'd thought of as walls might in fact be moveable screens, so the large space could be rearranged as needed.

Osred paused at an opening, and cleared his throat. "Chief Saana to see you, Lord."

Saana didn't hear the reply, but Osred beckoned her and she obliged. The steward stood aside to allow her in, and she found herself in the chamber of the Lord of Blackcreek.

It was bright and airy, and warmed by a crackling fire burning in a metal grate. Daimon's blades, one long and one short, rested in their white wooden scabbards on pegs on the external wall. The main feature of the room was a large wooden desk, and sitting behind it on a heavily carved, high-backed chair, wearing a thick black and green robe, was Daimon Blackcreek.

The man who'd killed Ristjaan the Cleaver, and had taken her daughter hostage.

Saana thought she'd been prepared for it but, as with every time so far, she was wrong. The memory of that first night rose up from the depths like a krayk scenting blood in the water, and with about as much mercy. She felt her heart quicken, and had to make a conscious effort to prevent her hand straying to the sheathed dagger on her belt.

"Chief Sattistutar," Blackcreek said, inclining his head slightly. "*Greetings.*"

It took Saana a moment to realise he'd spoken the last word in Tjakorshi. His accent was strange, but it was definitely a formal greeting, such as might be made from one clan chief to another. The surprise of it blunted her anger for a moment, and she stumbled over her Naridan words. "This… yes. Greetings." She nodded her head in imitation of him, determined not to let this man outdo her.

"Please, will you sit?" Blackcreek asked, gesturing to another chair on her side of the desk. It was smaller and less ornate than his own, but Saana had already gathered that chairs were common among the nobles of Narida. In Tjakorsha, chairs were only used when a chief was passing judgement; otherwise, most everyone sat on the floor, or on low stools or benches. So she sat, forcing herself to remember he was not offering her insult by treating her as a criminal but, from what she'd gathered, was showing her courtesy.

"What is that?" she asked, pointing to the rectangular object on the desk. It seemed made of wood and was perhaps as long as her forearm, slightly less across, and as thick as both of her hands laid on top of each other.

"This?" Blackcreek looked down at it. "The Blackcreek ledger. This lord has been trying to come to terms with the records of our lands." He smiled, although Saana didn't think there was much mirth in it. "He must confess his brother always had the better of these matters, just as this lord, in his turn, is more skilled with a blade. Osred has assisted this lord greatly, but Father oversaw our affairs, and so this lord feels he should do the same." He opened it, and Saana saw only the edges were made of wood: the inside was countless thin, pale leaves, many of which had markings on.

"Is that... paper?" she asked, glancing sideways at Osred. The leaves were much thinner than the screens, but it was the only possibility she could think of.

"Of course," Blackcreek replied with a frown. "Do you not have paper?"

Saana just shook her head. "What is this for?"

"To keep records," Blackcreek repeated, clearly confused. "How do you know who owns what?"

Saana snorted. "If a person cannot remember what they own, they probably do not need it. This man has goats and chickens, and she knows how many of each. Although she cannot remember the numbers in your tongue," she admitted.

Blackcreek rubbed at his chin. "And do your people... pay taxes to you?"

Saana shook her head, confused. "This man does not understand that word."

"Do they have to give you money, or grain, or animals?" Blackcreek persisted. "In payment for living on your land?"

"They do not live on this man's land," Saana said, wondering what in the depths the boy was talking about. "Not now, of course, but not before either. Zhanna and this man lived on our land. There was land enough for all, so long as the Seal Rock clan stayed their side of the ridge."

Blackcreek didn't say anything for a few moments, just looked at her with his dark eyes while one finger tapped out a rhythm on his desk.

"Things may be more different between us than this lord thought." He gestured behind him and to his right, which Saana realised must be in the direction of the keep. "Everything you can see from our stronghouse is Blackcreek land. It belongs to this lord's family."

It was Saana's turn to say nothing, while she tried to comprehend what he'd just said. The Black Keep was tall, and she'd be able to see a long way from it. Over the river to the south, where the moors began to rise. The strip of salt marsh to the east, where Naridan and Tjakorshi shepherds were grazing their flocks. To the west and north, fields being ploughed and sown, then forest, and then, far to the west, mountains.

"All this land is yours," she repeated.

"Yes," Blackcreek said. He closed his ledger again with a rustle of paper. "And everyone who lives here does so at this lord's sufferance. Many have bought their own land from his family. Some live on his land, and in return they work it for him." He steepled his fingers and rested his chin on them. "One of the things that this lord... that *we* will need to decide, is what will happen with your people."

Saana frowned. "What do you mean?"

"Your people cannot just *live* here," Blackcreek said soberly. "This lord must account to the Marshal's inspectors for his lands. Do the Brown Eagle clan work on Blackcreek land in return for somewhere to live? If so, the inspectors will expect yields to be higher. Does this lord permit you to clear an area of the forest and grant you your own lands? Your people will be expected to pay tax, not to mention the unrest that this would cause in the lowborn who have been granted no such privilege."

"But why do you need all this land?" Saana asked him, perplexed. "Why do you prevent your people using it for themselves? *How* do you prevent them? They are many, and you have only few guards." She bit down on her tongue, suddenly aware the lord and his steward might think she was intending to get Blackcreek's "lowborn", as he called them, to rise up against him.

"The Blackcreek family's title was granted by the God-King," Blackcreek said. "We have bequeathed some small freeholdings on others, but only those who have shown themselves worthy of such favour. It is our duty to ensure the land remains prosperous, and so we must be careful who is allowed to own it."

"But what gives you that right?"

Blackcreek's dark eyes flashed suddenly. "What gave your clan the right to raid our shores, kill our people and take our possessions?"

Saana gritted her teeth. "We have not done so since this man became chief."

Blackcreek held her gaze for a long moment, then exhaled audibly through his nose and nodded very slightly. His manner was still brittle, though, and Saana could feel the tension in the air.

"This lord suspects you came here for something other than to quarrel about the ownership of land," Blackcreek said shortly, tapping one finger on his ledger and looking down at it instead of meeting her eyes. "What was it?"

Saana grimaced. This was always going to have been a difficult conversation; she suspected it would be doubly so now. "There was a fight earlier, in the street. This man had to stop it. One of your men and one of the clan, who had been set to work together. The Brown Eagle was Timmun, yours was..." She paused for a moment, trying to recall. "Nahel."

Blackcreek still wasn't looking at her, but she saw the skin at the side of his eyes wrinkle as he frowned. He looked up at Osred, still standing by the door. Saana noticed the steward had a disapproving expression as he looked at her.

"Osred, do you know the name? It sounds familiar, but this

lord cannot place him." He looked back at the ledger. "He will be in here, somewhere..."

"A labourer, lord. This servant believes the reeve held him in the cells for two days, a year or so ago," Osred replied.

"What caused the fight?" Blackcreek asked Saana. He still wasn't looking at her.

Saana took a deep breath. "Timmun was too much drinking, and he is not always good man, but Nahel seems a..." She searched for an appropriate Naridan word. "He is wrong. He desires men."

Blackcreek straightened up in his seat, apparently expecting her to continue. "And?"

Saana tried to keep a grip on her temper. Was the man being deliberately obtuse? "He kissed Timmun!"

"And Timmun did not want him to?" Blackcreek asked.

"Of course not!"

"Lord," Osred interjected, "Nahel has been guilty of such behaviour, when in drink. He seems somewhat misguided as to who would want his advances."

Blackcreek opened his mouth, but Saana spoke first. "Who would want? The man is made wrong! You must see?"

"His actions are wrong," Blackcreek agreed guardedly, "but to say the man himself—"

A horrible suspicion began to creep over Saana. "Do you mean men lie with men in your land?"

"Lie with...?" Blackcreek's face didn't show revulsion, merely confusion. "What do—"

"Fuck!" Saana shouted at him. Nalon had taught her all manner of words, but she'd not thought to have to use it in this context. "Do men *fuck* men here?!"

Blackcreek's face closed down into something every bit as hard and dangerous as the war mask he'd worn on the salt marsh. He'd finally grasped her meaning. "Of course."

Of course? Saana was astounded. How could the man just

stand there and admit such a thing? Father Krayk placed few demands on his people, but the primary one was for them to survive: how could they do that unless men paired with women?

"And your women?" she asked, barely daring to hear the answer. What peril had she left her daughter in? "They will lie with other women?"

"Lie with, marry, adopt children with," Blackcreek snapped. "Why does it matter?"

"Is this why your town half-empty is?" Saana demanded, hearing her own voice rise to a shout as she threw a hand towards the window. Where had she led her clan? "Are your men too busy fucking men and your women—"

"There was plague twenty years ago!" Blackcreek thundered, slamming his fist into his desk and standing up. Saana rose with him and met his dark, burning gaze with her own as they ended up nearly nose-to-nose.

"The sickness took this lord's parents, and his law-father's wife!" the young Naridan yelled into her face. "Along with half the town! *That* is why we have so many empty houses!" His jabbing finger stopped just short of her chest, which was just as well, but the new Lord of Blackcreek wasn't done yet.

"And what do you do to men of yours who love other men?" he demanded.

Saana rose up on her toes, outraged. "No one would do such thing!"

"Really?" Blackcreek demanded. "Then how do you know about it, and why are you so scared of it?"

"Is not *scared* to hate unnatural!" Saana yelled at him. "Someone start fly like bird, you cheer? Or you kill them for being..." She tailed off momentarily, then remembered what Nalon had said about the Naridans' superstitions. "For being *witch?*"

"You *consort* with witches!" Blackcreek bellowed at her.

"Is wrong word!" Saana shouted back. "Your language not

have right word, and you think any woman who know things must evil be!"

"Get out of this house," Blackcreek snapped, stepping back from her and pointing towards the door. "Get out, before this lord forgets his manners and does something to doom both our people!"

Furious though she was, Saana would not shame herself by staying in another chief's home when she was no longer welcome. She turned and strode towards the fearful-looking Osred, but couldn't hold her tongue. "You try to doom this man's people by giving us houses of sickness!"

"That was twenty years ago!" Blackcreek yelled from behind her.

"Why you not burn them?" Saana demanded, turning around as she reached the doorway. On Tjakorsha they knew the difference between a sickness from within, such as the slow decline that might mark the end of life for an elder, and a sickness that could be passed to others. If a person had died from the latter in their longhouse then it would be burned, and them with it. This 'plague' must have been a sickness that could be passed, judging by the Naridan's words, and yet the houses still stood.

"But... why would we burn houses *in the middle of a town*?" Blackcreek demanded incredulously, throwing his arms up. "The flames would catch, and we would lose everything!"

"And this maybe why half your town die!" Saana snapped. "Everything too close!" She didn't wait for his reply, but stormed past Osred. She needed to find Zhanna. Part of her hoped a guard would try to get in her way so she could put her fist through his face, and the Dark Father take the consequences.

Coming here had been a mistake. Right now, she wasn't sure whether she meant the castle itself, or Narida in general.

TILA

TILA HAD EXPECTED Fourth Channel to be a canal running through East Harbour, and in some respects it was, but not dug by the hands of people. Instead it was one of a network of fissures in the north-eastern side of Grand Mahewa through which the sea ran, and which essentially broke that part of the island into smaller islets. The Alabans called this area 'the Narrows', and the channels were spanned by bridges varying hugely in size and integrity.

The blue-doored warehouse had been fairly easy to find, once Tila had worked out the Alaban method of numbering the channels. The door guards looked slightly surprised when she'd spoken the code words, but had allowed her and Barach entry nonetheless.

Certainly, Tila was the only obviously Naridan woman inside, at least in terms of her clothes, which might have explained the guards' reactions. The other spectators were mainly Alaban, although there was one small, rat-faced Naridan man, a couple Tila were fairly sure were Morlithians, and one or two others she couldn't place at all. All were crowded around a fenced-off oval in the middle, within which the action took place on blood-stained dust.

The first few fights were empty-handed affairs, contested until one party went limp or yielded. Tila had brought most of her money with her, wagered generously based on her gut instinct from looking the fighters over when their names were called, and after three fights had won back more than she'd staked. However, when the next bout was announced and she was once more handing over coins to the youth working her side of the oval, the question changed.

"First blood?" the youth asked in Alaban. Tila frowned, and looked back at the oval. Each fighter was being handed a pair of long knives. It looked as though not all the blood on the floor came from broken noses or ripped ears.

"That one," she replied in the youth's language, pointing at a dark-skinned fighter she'd have assumed was a woman, had she not been concentrating on keeping an Alaban mindset. They looked quicker than their opponent, and while Tila might not have backed them had the fight been to the death, that was not the question she'd been asked. This fighter, like most announced so far, had a showy assumed name: something to do with an ocean predator, Tila believed.

The youth nodded, and Tila dropped her numbered wooden token into the proffered leather bag. She kept the matching other half, to show when it was time for winnings to be paid out, and turned to watch the fight.

It didn't last long. Tila's fighter was indeed quick, but also unlucky. After a couple of nimble, slashing advances, they happened to slip at the wrong moment. Their opponent lunged in just long enough to jab their shoulder with a blade, then danced away out of range, triumphantly displaying their bloodied knife. The winning fighter received a purse of coin, with the wincing loser relying on what the crowd wished to contribute, which didn't appear to be much.

"Evening," a voice said at her shoulder, and Tila turned to find herself looking at the rat-faced little Naridan she'd seen earlier. He was a finger's breadth or so shorter than her, and had chosen to emphasise the already impressive length of his chin with a tuft of beard ranging from dark brown to gingery. He smiled, showing teeth of uncommon evenness, then flinched slightly as Barach took a looming step towards him. "Easy there, s'man means no harm!'

Tila reflected how she'd used a similar phrase to Skhetul, and wondered whether she'd sounded any more convincing. "What do you want?"

"Merely company," he assured her hastily. "S'man likes these folk well enough, but it'd do his ears good to hear his own tongue. He gets nervous, you see, especially on a night such as this."

"Why, what night is this?" Tila asked him. He seemed nervous, certainly; his words were coming too fast, and he was looking everywhere except at her. She definitely wasn't going to take her eyes off him.

"Well, in a moment s'man's husband will walk out and fight three people to the death," the little man said, with an embarrassed laugh. "It makes his heart race, no matter how many times he's seen it."

"To the death?" No wonder the magistrates were so unhappy about these events. Tila had wondered why a bit of fist-fighting was such a crime. "A four-way fight, you mean?"

"More of a three-on-one."

Tila looked back at him, shocked. "With weapons?"

"Oh yes," he nodded. "He wouldn't stand much of a chance, without." He bowed slightly. "Apologies, s'man's manners are absent. He is Marin of Idramar."

Idramar. Nari curse it. "A pleasure," Tila replied, with a perfunctory bow of her own. Livnya was well-known enough in the city that if Marin moved in the right circles, or indeed the wrong ones, he could have heard of her. There were many Livnyas in Narida, of course—Tila's old nursemaid, for one—but she didn't want to give him either of her names. Marin smiled expectantly at her, but took the hint after a few moments.

"Ah, here they come," he said, changing the subject. Tila turned her head and, sure enough, three Alabans walked out. They looked unremarkable sorts, and took their weapons—an axe, a short sword, and a spear—with no great sense of familiarity. The cryer announced their names, which seemed to just be names so far as she could tell.

Then, however, the cryer shouted two words in Naridan.

"Sar Blacksword!"

He was of an age with Tila, or perhaps her brother. His weather-beaten face was hidden beneath a very un-Naridan dark beard, but his hair was certainly braided like a sar's. He was considerably taller and broader than his husband, although not so large as Barach, and like the other fighters, he wore simple Alaban garments: a long-sleeved maijhi, and loose-fitting karung gathered at the ankles. A longblade and a shortblade rode on his left hip, and the scabbards of both were stained black.

A blacksword. A sar shamed so badly that any noble deeds he'd performed, no matter how great, had been expunged from memory, and the pictorial records of them on his scabbards destroyed. It would make sense for such a man to be earning a living fighting in a foreign land; he'd find work in Narida as a mercenary, judging by the Brotherhood tattoo she could see on his hand, but most shamed sars didn't like being surrounded by reminders of their fallen status.

He carried himself like a fighter, at any rate. Tila eyed him, then the three opponents. "What are the odds against him?"

"The odds are in his favour," Marin replied.

Tila blinked. "You're shitting."

"May Nari blind s'man," Marin declared, holding up one hand. "The house has put the odds in his favour. They hope everyone will bet heavily against, thinking they'll win big."

There was certainly an eager rush to place bets, and most tokens were going into one bag. Tila scratched her chin, thinking. "The house must be confident."

"They've good reason," Marin shrugged. "Laz is the finest s'man has seen with a blade, and s'man doesn't say that just because he loves him."

Tila studied the man announced as Sar Blacksword, and whom Marin had just named as Laz. He appeared almost bored. Either he was a superb actor, or he was truly unconcerned by what faced him. It could just be foolhardiness, of course, but he looked to have done this before.

She came to a decision, and dug a chunk of coins out of her purse. "Barach, place the bet."

Barach took the wager and her token, and joined the press of bodies. Tila glanced around to make sure no one was close enough to overhear, and leant in a little closer to Marin.

"You know the people who organise these fights?" she asked.

"We've talked with them, of course," Marin replied.

"Do you know someone named Kurumaya?" Tila had planned to ask about once she'd bet on a few fights, but this seemed a better opportunity.

Marin flashed his teeth again in a smile that was all twitch and no mirth. "Aha! Yes, um, well." He nodded somewhat sheepishly towards the oval. "You would need to talk to the cryer. After this fight, perhaps?"

Tila shrugged. "Very well." The cryer was a small-statured Alaban with hair worn loose down past their waist, and a shrill, but very loud voice. They'd now exited the oval and were watching with their back to Tila, past where Barach was placing the wager.

The bustle of betting subsided, and the two youths signalled that everyone had made their wagers. The cryer barked an instruction, and the three Alabans in the oval raised their weapons.

Sar Blacksword strode forward to the middle and stopped, slightly hunched forwards, with one hand on the grip of his longblade and the other on its scabbard.

The Alabans looked at each, then spread out. They were taken off-guard by his confidence, Tila could see that at once. The spear-wielder started to edge around behind him, while the one with the shortsword went to his left and the one with the axe to his right.

Sar Blacksword simply stood there, his eyes flickering from one to another.

It wasn't as unfair as it looked, Tila knew, as the three Alabans edged inwards. The longblade had a greater reach than either the shortsword or the axe, for one thing. The three fighters still stood a chance of outmatching Sar Blackwood if they knew how to handle their weapons, or were skilled at working together in such a situation. If not...

The axe fighter moved first. They didn't shout a battle cry; they just waited until the Naridan had glanced away from them, then lunged in with nothing more than a grunt of effort as they swung their axe up.

It never came down in the way they intended. Sar Blacksword sidestepped towards them into a classic drawcut, sweeping his longblade out and ripping it across his attacker's midsection before the axe could fall. He completed the move with a spin that ended with him facing his two remaining opponents, while the axe fighter stumbled past him, then fell onto their knees. Blood began to leak out at about the same time as the Alaban began screaming.

Sar Blacksword flicked out his longblade, sending droplets of blood spattering across the oval's floor, then raised it to guard position in front of his face. His expression hadn't changed.

The other two Alabans stared in shock for a moment, then moved in past their fallen comrade.

The spear fighter began jabbing, clearly hoping to drive his opponent up against the crude fence surrounding the oval, and limit his movement. The sword fighter closed in as well, seeking to close the trap from their side.

Sar Blacksword took two steps backwards, then as the spear

jabbed in towards his ribs again he twisted aside and caught it behind the head with his left hand, slashing at the wielder with his longblade. The Alaban panicked and let go, stumbling backwards as the Naridan's deadly blade swept through where he'd been standing a moment before.

Sar Blacksword tossed the spear up, caught it again with his left hand halfway down the shaft, then threw it at the sword fighter.

It was a clumsy throw—he was clearly right-handed—but the distraction was good enough. The sword fighter sidestepped the spear well enough, but their stance was lost. Sar Blacksword had charged the moment the spear left his hand, and his longblade flashed out. The short sword managed to deflect it once, twice, but the second parry pulled the Alaban off-balance and Sar Blacksword's blade bit into the side of their neck before they could block it the third time. The fighter grimly clamped one hand over the wound, despite the fact that blood immediately spurted out between their fingers, and lunged clumsily.

Sar Blacksword took their sword hand off at the wrist, then set his shoulders and swung his blade at neck height. The legendary edge of a Naridan longblade did its work, and head left shoulders.

He swung around as the decapitated body behind him slumped to the ground, and those spectators nearby scurried backwards to avoid getting blood on their clothes. The former spear fighter, shuffling warily towards the axe that still lay on the ground in front of its wailing original wielder, froze in their tracks.

Sar Blacksword gestured to them encouragingly, motioning for them to pick the axe up.

The Alaban turned and ran, hurdling the wooden barrier and crashing into the crowd not far from the cryer, to a hail of boos and jeers. Tila couldn't see what happened to them, but they weren't thrown back into the oval. Sar Blacksword shrugged and pulled out a rag to wipe down his sword, then stopped. Tila saw his face twist into a grimace for a moment, before he stepped forwards and leant down to speak into the ear of the wounded

Alaban still trying to hold their guts in.

He pulled them up into a kneeling position which the Alaban held while quivering with effort, teeth clenched and tears streaming down their face. Sar Blacksword swung his blade once more, and another Alaban's head left their shoulders. Only then, with an act of relative mercy administered, did he clean his sword and sheath it.

"Oh, blessed Nari!" Marin exclaimed with relief. "It never gets any easier, watching him fight…"

"Thank you for your advice," Tila told him, then began to push her way through the crowd towards the cryer. She could see Barach already providing her token to prove he'd placed a successful bet, so her winnings should be secure.

Sar Blacksword took a fat purse for winning his fight, Tila saw as she nudged and elbowed her way to the cryer's side. They turned towards her as they became aware of her presence, and Tila registered wide, deep brown eyes, a delicate mouth, and cheeks that dimpled when they smiled.

"Your pardon," she said in Alaban. "I wish to speak to Kurumaya." By all her ancestors, but it felt strange to throw that untethered sentence out, identifying herself with no indication as to her status. At least she'd remembered to use the formal neutral intonation.

"No," the cryer said, their smile widening.

Tila frowned. "Your pardon?"

"You *are* speaking to Kurumaya."

EVRAM

HE'D FOUND A barn not far from the road, and bedded down in the hayloft. Despite the tickling, scratchy tips of the hay stems, their overall softness was as close to a blissful experience as Evram could imagine, compared to the hard ground or knotted tree bark that was all he'd had to rest upon for the last week. He'd woken in the morning chill as daylight began to leak in through the rough pine slats of the roof, and had to force himself to get up and move. On the preceding days he'd started walking as soon as he'd had a piss, even chewing his meagre breakfast as he trudged, trying to warm himself with the action. Cold though it was in the barn, it was still warmer than he'd been any morning since he'd left home.

He couldn't stay there, though. There were few vagabonds on Blackcreek land, since no one had reason to go that far south, but any discovered would be treated harshly. He doubted it would be different here. Evram didn't want to catch a beating, and couldn't afford to be dragged to the local reeve and his men, so he'd hurried back to the road before anyone found him. If his message was to be heard then he'd need to present himself to the thane, not be thrown into the Darkspur lock-up with the drunks and petty thieves.

Darkspur.

He'd seen it from the moment he'd left the forest late the

previous afternoon, when to push on towards it would have meant arriving at night when the gates would almost certainly be locked, no matter how urgent he claimed his news to be. Now it rose above him, a mighty outcrop of dark rock many, many times the height of a man, that looked to have been thrust out of the earth like a monstrous, blunt dagger. The steepest side formed a formidable wall, and on the other three it was surrounded by the town of the same name and the lower, man-made walls guarding that. Atop it sat the stronghouse of Lord Darkspur, thane and protector of these lands to the north of Blackcreek, which was flying his banners: a mighty white kingdrake soaring against a green background, and the crowned sunburst of Narida, signifying his family's fealty to the God-King.

The blisters on Evram's feet had deteriorated from early-morning sharpness into the rubbing pain of background agony by the time he limped to the town gates. The guards watched him approach with a mixture of wariness and curiosity.

"Ho, traveller," one of them called as Evram drew closer. "You've come on the south road?"

Evram opened his mouth to say that no, he'd come on the north road, then realised that would mean something different to them. "Aye," he managed instead, trying not to wince as his right foot made its discomfort known again.

"What's your business at Darkspur?" the other called. He bore the scars of the pox, and eyed Evram dubiously. Travel-stained and limping as he was, Evram was hardly surprised.

"S'man brings news of Raiders at Black Keep," he said, halting in front of them. "He needs to—"

"Raiders?" The guard on the left looked at his colleague. "That's the business of the thane of Blackcreek, surely?"

"Raiders don't come this early," Pox-face said. "And they haven't been as far south as Black Keep in years."

"Must've worked out there's nothing there except fish," the first one sniggered.

"Besides," Pox-face continued, looking at Evram again, "even if there *were* Raiders there, they'll have been long gone by the time you were halfway here." He lowered his spear a little and his eyes narrowed. "So what's your business?"

Evram gritted his teeth. "They haven't gone. They've taken the town."

Pox-face's brow furrowed. "What do you mean, 'taken'? They've burned it?"

Evram really wanted to reach out and throttle the man, but that would just see him stuck with a spear. "They've *taken* it. They're living there!"

The unscarred guard snorted. "Raiders don't do that, they—"

"They do now!" Evram shouted. "There are hundreds of them! They brought their old, their children, their... their fucking *chickens*! Lord Asrel tried to fight them, Lord Daimon turned on him and surrendered the town to the Raiders, then killed one of their champions in single combat, but—"

Suddenly Pox-face's spearpoint was at his throat. He swallowed and fell silent.

"Right," Pox-face said. "S'guard has had about enough of your shit, old man."

"It's all true," Evram said, as the metal pricked his skin. "Nari preserve s'man, it's all true. Every word."

"You want us to throw you into the lock-up?" Pox-face demanded. "It's that, or you piss off."

"Why would s'man lie about this?" Evram pleaded.

"No idea." Pox-face shrugged. "We had some old bastard here a year or so ago who kept telling everyone he was Tolkar the Last Sorcerer. Never worked out why he was so insistent about it; didn't much care either." He nudged the spear forward slightly, forcing Evram to take a step back. "Now, off you go."

"Wait." It was the other guard. Evram felt a flicker of hope as he saw the man's expression.

"Nari's teeth, Mer." Pox-face looked sideways at his companion, frustration clear on his face. "The man's clearly either touched, or a liar."

"You said Lord Daimon betrayed his father, and surrendered the town to the Raiders?" the man called Mer asked.

Evram nodded, wary of the spearpoint. "Yes. He said it was the only way to avoid them killing all of us. S'man believes Lord Daimon had to lock his father and brother up in the stronghouse."

Mer chewed his lip. Pox-face looked from Mer to Evram, then back again. "Don't tell me you believe him?"

"S'man thinks we should make this someone else's problem," Mer said. "He'll go and get the captain. You stay here and watch this one. Try not to prick him too badly."

"Fine," Pox-face muttered. "On your head be it."

It wasn't long before Mer returned with his captain, a hard-faced man called Gavrel with a white scar down his left cheek, who looked at Evram as though he'd like nothing better than to knife him and leave him in a ditch. However, when Evram told his tale Gavrel rubbed his chin thoughtfully, gave a small nod to Mer, and told Evram to follow him. And so, for the first time in his life, Evram entered a town other than Black Keep.

Truth to tell, it wasn't that different. It was a little bigger, perhaps, with a few more people in the streets—although that was maybe no longer true, now the Raiders were in Black Keep—and the ground rose a little as they approached the great rock itself. Black Keep was flat, built as it was next to the river, whereas Darkspur was not only farther north but also farther west, closer to the Catseye Mountains.

The main street was wide, if not straight, and Gavrel led the way at a pace Evram's blisters complained about bitterly. The man led him to a squat guardhouse with narrow window slits sitting at the base of the winding track that was the only way of ascending the rock, save for climbing its sides. The arched gateway within was high enough to admit a man mounted on dragonback, and wide enough for a wagon, but the gates were stout and firm. At present they were open, however, and as Evram approached them he saw a couple of the guards peering out curiously.

"Is that him, then?" one man asked, pushing his helm back to scratch his forehead. "Is that—?"

"The man Mer spoke of, yes," Gavrel replied shortly. "Where's the steward?"

"Up on the Rock," the same man answered.

"Good. Come with this captain," Gavrel instructed Evram, walking on through the guardhouse. Evram hurried after him, despite the complaints from his feet, and didn't look around at the guards or the guardhouse as he did so. He didn't want to be accused of spying for Black Creek. Evram was no noble, but he knew not all the thanes of Narida saw eye to eye. Some of the greatest songs, in fact, were tales of warriors fighting not the Raiders, the Morlithians, or the Alabans, but a treacherous neighbouring thane intent on stealing land.

His feet and legs protested as the road started to climb, but Gavrel was striding ahead with the vim and determination of a younger man, so Evram gritted his teeth and forced himself to follow at the same pace. The road was at least a decent surface; a light sandy soil very different to the rich, dark earth Evram was used to tilling. It didn't stop his breath from starting to wheeze in his chest, however. He wasn't as young as he had been.

No sooner had the road finished the main part of its climb then the way was obstructed by yet another guardhouse, this one set into a wall running the width of the rock's upper surface. Here Gavrel tersely instructed Evram to wait, so he sat gingerly and looked around him. It was quite a view: he didn't think he'd ever been so high, not even in his youth when he'd climbed trees in search of birds' nests. He could see the Darkspur lands laid out below him, a patchwork of fields and pasture. Beyond was the Downwoods, dark green conifers and the sullen, bare brown limbs of the trees that shed their leaves, with just the faintest flash of light green here and there as the earliest of them began to push forward new ones.

"You. Black Keep man."

Gavrel had returned. Evram heaved himself to his feet, then noticed the man following the guard captain. He was perhaps of an age with Evram himself, although somewhat plumper. He wore a simple brown robe edged with gold, reaching to mid-forearm and mid-shin, had a longblade and a shortblade sheathed at his side, and his hair tied into warrior's braids.

Evram bowed. The man waited for him to straighten again before he spoke.

"This sar is Omet, Steward of Darkspur and cousin of the Thane. Tell him of these Raiders."

ZHANNA

LIFE AS A hostage was hard to adapt to, mainly because there was nothing to *do*. Or more accurately, nothing which needed Zhanna to do it. Her food was provided without her needing to catch it, hunt for it, pull it out of the ground, or even cook it. Since she wasn't doing anything strenuous, her clothes didn't need repairing. As a result, she'd ended up spending a lot of time interacting with the strange beast Daimon Blackcreek had so casually handed to her: the dragon runt.

It was a truly odd thing, this little rattletail, and all the stranger for being familiar in some ways. Its purply skin lacked the feathers of the adults at first, but these were now pushing through. She could almost have believed it were a bird, but it had jaws with tiny teeth, not a beak, and its forelegs were certainly not bent into the useless wings of a chick; they were definitely legs, with claws. And yet they weren't legs like the forelegs of a goat, mere props to support the weight of a body above them (although Zhanna knew well enough a goat's legs could get it all manner of precarious places). The little creature could grasp, and once it had got a bit more coordination and strength in its limbs, was able to climb all over her. When it reached her exposed flesh, or burrowed beneath her clothes to find it, the tiny claws scratched at her skin. And so, in partial defiance of her mother's insistence that she never give names to the crow chicks she'd rescued as a child, she'd privately called the baby dragon Thorn.

Zhanna was giving Thorn a meal, a few scraps of dried meat from the previous night that she'd chewed to moisten for it, when she heard her mother's voice calling her.

Her immediate, irrational reaction was that she'd done something wrong, because her mother sounded angry, and that this was somehow related to Thorn. Her second reaction was to wonder what in the deeps her mother was doing inside the castle, and she hurried to the window with Thorn still held in her cupped hands.

Her first worry—that everything had gone wrong, and her clan's warriors had stormed the castle in a way somehow silent until now—was dispelled the moment she saw the small retinue approaching. Her mother was in the lead, with a face on her like Father Krayk's own gale, but she carried no weapons and was followed by Osred the steward, as well as Ita and Sourface Ganalel. Of the three Naridans only Ita matched Zhanna's mother in height, and Saana probably weighed half as much again as he did, so the impression was almost one of an adult being tailed by three children, albeit two with grey in their hair.

A very unhappy adult, Zhanna noted with some apprehension. It was rare that Saana Sattistutar properly lost her temper with people that weren't her own daughter, but when she did so she made sure to share it out equally amongst all those around.

Still, Zhanna was as sure as she could be that whatever had set her mother off, it surely couldn't be her fault this time. She tucked Thorn into her jacket's deep hood and hurried to the front door of the women's quarters, just in case her mother got it into her head to try to kick it down, and opened it as Saana was striding over the last few ells of gravel path leading to the steps.

"Mama?"

Saana's face relaxed a little, which Zhanna took as a good sign, but her eyes were still tense and her jaw was tight enough to chew through a yolgu's deck. She didn't slow down, either, but came straight up the wooden steps. Zhanna saw the hug coming just before she was about to get alarmed, and relaxed a little: angry concern still required careful manoeuvring, but was a lot easier to deal with than anger in its purest form. She had a moment of anxiety as her mother wrapped her arms around her, but both ended up underneath Zhanna's hood and the baby dragon within.

"Are you well?" her mother demanded into her ear. She was speaking Tjakorshi: a change from the halting, shouted exchanges in Naridan that were all they'd been able to do so far.

"Of course I'm well," Zhanna replied, honestly enough. "They feed me, they largely leave me to myself. I can walk inside the walls, so long as I don't try to leave, and I'm not to go into the keep."

"And this building?" Saana asked, not letting go. "This is where you sleep?"

"Yes," Zhanna replied. "The women's house." She put some derision into her tone, to show what she thought of the strange Naridan arrangement, and was totally unprepared for her mother to draw back with a look of horror and anger on her face.

"Are there other women here? Naridan women?"

"No, just me," Zhanna assured her. What was going on? "This is for the noblewomen, and there are none. Mama, are *you* well? You seem—"

"These people are unnatural," Saana said in a low voice, as though any of the three uncomfortable Naridans standing at the base of the steps could have understood what she was saying. "They pair man with man and woman with woman!"

Zhanna blinked in surprise. "As in… they marry?"

"And the rest," her mother said darkly. "Zhanna, tell me true. Has any Naridan woman propositioned you?"

Zhanna shook her head. "No, Mama. I've barely spoken to one, to be honest. There's Tirtza, but she's a child, and she'd run should I so much as scowl at her. The cooks are women, I think, but the guards, the stablemaster, the huntmaster, they're all men." She threw the Naridan words casually off her tongue, half-hoping to impress, but her mother didn't seem to notice.

"Good," Saana muttered, and Zhanna couldn't help but laugh.

"Mama, you hear I'm surrounded by men and you're *glad*? You threatened to beat Longjaw bloody when you thought he'd tried to kiss me!" She realised too late that this was unlikely to ease her mother's temper, and raised her hands in an attempt to calm. "Mama, please. Most of them seem scared of me, and they all know the clan would come for them should I be harmed."

Although I'm sure Duranen intended his rattletails to do worse than scare me. But Mama doesn't need to know about that.

It was at this point that Thorn, who'd been clambering around amiably enough in the depths of her hood, decided to see what was going on. He clawed his way up and onto Zhanna's shoulder, and her mother's eyes fair popped out of her skull.

"What in Father Krayk's name—"

There was nothing for it. "This is my dragon," Zhanna said quickly, and mentally gritted her teeth.

"Your dragon," Saana repeated.

"Yes," Zhanna confirmed, waiting to see if more information was going to be welcome or unwelcome.

Her mother's jaw worked, but if her expression didn't exactly clear, it didn't grow worse. "Why do you have a dragon?"

"It's a baby," Zhanna said, eyeing her mother for warning signs. "It's a rattletail; they take them hunting, apparently. It wasn't doing well and I asked why they didn't look after it themselves, like we do with crow chicks. Daimon gave it to me to look after, so that's what I'm doing."

"Daimon? Daimon Blackcreek?"

Zhanna nodded. She wasn't sure if she was supposed to have used his first name, but what else should she have called him?

Saana looked over her shoulder in the general direction of the lord's quarters, where she'd presumably come from, then back at Zhanna. "What happens if it doesn't live?"

Zhanna drew herself up, annoyed. "It *will* live. I never let a crow chick die!"

"Dragons aren't crows," her mother pointed out.

"That's exactly what the huntmaster said," Zhanna snorted. "Only he said it in Naridan."

Saana's left eye twitched. Then, almost unwillingly, she smiled slightly. "So you'll be looking to prove us both wrong, then?"

"If raising a dragon was hard, a Naridan couldn't do it," Zhanna said firmly, although she wasn't sure that was true. She certainly had no dragon magic like Tavi did. She'd tried to loiter near the stables after the incident with the rattletails, but she'd only heard some indistinct chanting and smelled some form of smoke. However, it had worked well enough: the huge longbrows were now up and about, and munching their way through a stupendous amount of hay every day.

Her mother was frowning again, so Zhanna smiled at her as she reached up to tickle Thorn's jaw. The baby dragon hissed faintly, apparently enjoying the sensation. "Mama, you want them to accept us, don't you? What if I show them a Tjakorshi can raise a dragon? That would help, wouldn't it?"

"It would." Saana looked over her shoulder again, towards the unseen Daimon. "He's clever, I'll give him that. But…" She shook her head.

"Mama, all will be well," Zhanna told her, as firmly as she thought she could get away with. "Truly, it will. But I think either those three all want your hand, or they want you to go with them."

Saana looked down at Osred, Ganalel and Ita, all of whom were shifting uneasily, and laughed. "You're right." She turned back to Zhanna once more, her eyes searching. "Are you sure you're well? And that you will be well?"

"Mama, go and take care of everyone else," Zhanna said, trying to keep her patience.

"Very well," Saana said, and stepped forward to give her another hug.

"Be careful of my dragon!"

"I'll be careful of your dragon," her mother muttered, then sniffed. Her face was conflicted as she pulled back again. "You don't smell like you any more."

Zhanna frowned. "I don't?"

"You've not been out fishing with Jelema since we got here. You barely smell of the sea now."

That hit Zhanna harder than she expected. She managed a smile. "Perhaps I'll soon smell of dragon instead."

Saana nodded, but didn't smile back. "I love you," she muttered as she turned away and began to descend the wooden steps again.

"I love you too," Zhanna called after her, as Osred said something hesitant to her mother in Naridan, and the two guards fell in uncertainly on either side. She watched the mismatched foursome walk away, while Thorn patrolled back and forth across her shoulders.

DAIMON

THE INCARCERATION OF his father and brother had been a problem for Daimon, in more ways than one. As both had greater claim to the title of Lord of Blackcreek than he, leaving them free would be a recipe for disaster and confusion. He'd had Gador fit two rooms in the keep with strong bars on the outside of the doors, and had ordered a hole knocked in the thick wood of each door to allow food and water to be passed through without risk of either Asrel or Darel being able to attack a guard and steal their weapon. Although the Code had caused him much grief, Daimon was not ungrateful for it: he suspected his father would have refused food and even water on principle, but it was dishonourable for a sar to allow himself to become weak or infirm, even if imprisoned.

"Stew again?" Darel asked from the other side of his door. It was midday, not long after Sattistutar had stormed out of Daimon's chambers, and Daimon was sitting cross-legged outside his law-brother's room.

"You cannot take your own life with a spoon, brother," Daimon replied. In truth he suspected Darel could find a way, but he'd spoken the truth to Sattistutar: the only honourable death for a shamed sar was by blade. He supposed Darel could keep the spoon and sharpen the handle to a point capable of piercing his own heart, but even that probably wouldn't qualify.

MIKE BROOKS

"How goes your peace-making with the savages?" Darel asked. He had still not addressed Daimon either by name or as his brother since the Tjakorshi had arrived, but at least he would speak. Only empty bowls, full chamber pots, and stony silences came back through Lord Asrel's door.

"Your brother is surprised you have an interest," Daimon admitted.

"For some reason, scrolls and books fail to hold this lord's attention at present," Darel replied dryly.

"Your brother shall see if he can procure new ones when the spring traders come," Daimon offered.

"This lord would appreciate that," Darel replied, after a pause. "However, you haven't answered his question."

"Have you looked from your window of late?" Daimon asked him. He'd placed Darel into a room on the north side of the keep, while their father was on the south side. Bars fixed into the stone around the windows were intended as a defence against the most determined attackers, but they served equally well to keep problematic sars locked in.

"Yes," Darel admitted.

"And have you seen two peoples working the fields as they prepare to plant seed? Or driving sheep to graze the salt marsh?"

"Yes," Darel said again.

"Then perhaps you have answered your own question," Daimon said gently. "There have been problems, it is true. Tempers have flared, misunderstandings have occurred. But if our own people were perfect we would have no need of the reeve and his men."

Darel coughed gently, as he always did just before he volunteered some telling argument.

"And the shouting this lord heard a while back? He could not make out all the words, but that sounded like you arguing with the Raider chief."

Daimon sighed. "You are as perceptive as ever, brother."

"You brought her into our *home*?"

"You would have me speak with her in the street as though we were lowborn?" Daimon asked. "She—"

"She *is* lowborn!" Darel exclaimed. "She's *worse* than lowborn, she's a Raider!"

"But your brother is *not* lowborn!" Daimon snapped, although something inside gnawed at him—the thought that he had been, he was now, and he always would be. "He received her in his study, as we might with a visiting lord."

"But she is not—"

Daimon cut him off wearily. "Your brother knows she is no lord, but what would you have him do? There is no etiquette for the situation he finds himself in."

"What caused your argument?" Darel asked.

"It appears the Tjakorshi are... considerably opposed... to the concept of men that love men." Daimon paused, feeling the tension in his stomach. Daimon had never yet seen a man he had desired, but his brother was quite the opposite.

"And when you say 'considerably opposed', you mean...?'

"She responded with utter revulsion." Daimon stared gloomily at the floor. "It probably was not helped by circumstances—that idiot Nahel apparently made a drunken pass at one of them—but even so, your brother despairs. He thought they were more civilised than this, despite all appearances."

Darel said nothing. Daimon understood. It must be hard to hear that someone hated you, not for what you'd done but simply for *who you were*, something over which you had no control.

"You know, that might actually make sense."

Daimon blinked in surprise. "Your brother does not follow," he admitted.

"There aren't that many of them, are there?" Darel said thoughtfully.

"There are more of them than there are of us," Daimon pointed out. "That is why your brother did what he did."

"That depends what you mean by 'us'," Darel mused. There was the faint scraping noise of cloth on wood as he shifted position on the other side of the door. "In the town, yes. She said she had two hundred and fourteen?"

Daimon smiled. His brother's attention to detail was something he'd always admired. "Two hundred and fourteen warriors, she said. Two hundred and thirteen, since your brother killed Ristjaan the Cleaver. But there are more than that: she was only counting those who would fight, although admittedly that is most. There are old people and children too, though."

"By the by," Darel said dismissively. "If all the people on the Blackcreek lands were gathered together, we would outnumber them. Against the population of a large city they would be one sheep in a flock. Against Narida as a whole, a drop in the ocean."

"True," Daimon acknowledged. That was both comfort and source of fear to him. The Southern Army could annihilate the Brown Eagle clan with no problem, now they were settled in one place instead of striking and then retreating to their ships: the issue so far as Daimon was concerned was that they'd probably also slaughter the inhabitants of Black Keep for consorting with the enemy.

"When the Raiders speak of themselves as a group, do you get the impression they also refer to the other clans, left behind on their islands?" Darel asked. "Or do they only mean themselves?"

"Your brother had not considered it," Daimon admitted. He pondered briefly. "He believes it would be the latter. They all lived on the same land and believe they share the same origin, but Sattistutar has never expressed any form of kinship with the other clans."

"Hah!" Darel sounded pleased for the first time in a week. "The continuation of the clan must be their primary concern, then, and stuck on an island and surrounded by people they feel no kinship with, they've always had a limited amount of people to do it. Your brother imagines cross-clan marriages occur rarely." He paused briefly. "And probably with a considerable amount of either ceremony, or potential for violence. Or both."

"But that doesn't explain the extreme nature of her reaction," Daimon said.

"Oh, they probably do not think about it in those terms," Darel said dismissively. "Perhaps some chief made an issue of it years ago, and over time it passed into superstition. Do they even have a written language?"

Daimon was starting to feel like he had in his early years, being tested on his letters and coming up short again and again. "Your brother does not know. Sattistutar seemed unfamiliar with paper, though."

"Probably not much of one then, if at all," Darel mused. "Oral history can lead to a huge distortion in events. Do you know, some of the Morlithian tribes on the other side of the Torgallen Pass—"

It was like Darel had been saving up all his words, and now they spilled forth in an uncontrollable flood. The Torgallen Pass was hundreds of miles away, where the mighty River Idra cut clean through the Catseye Mountains separating Narida from the Morlithian Empire beyond. Neither of them had ever been anywhere near it, or probably ever would. Daimon chuckled and shook his head, amused once more at how Darel's mind jumped around.

"Darel, your brother would love for you to educate him further," Daimon said honestly, "but he has duties to attend to. He must put the fear of Nari Himself into Nahel, for starters, and come up with some suitable threat for what will happen if he lays his lips on anyone again without first being completely sure he has their consent, be they Naridan or Tjakorshi."

"You might want to speak to Samul and Menas," Darel offered. "And Bilha, and Amonhuhe. They should be warned about the Raiders' attitudes."

"They do not need to be warned of any such thing," Daimon

replied sternly. "Your brother will not have our people feeling we need to hide our way of life. He allowed the Tjakorshi to settle here, not dictate how we can live." He got to his feet, surreptitiously rubbing his backside.

"Daimon," his brother called.

"Yes?"

"Thinking of Amonhuhe... the Smoking Valley people have not appeared yet?"

"Not yet," Daimon replied. "They should be here any day: the Festival of Life is in a week." The mountain folk would appear every spring to trade pelts for salt and fish oil, always at about the same time, despite their apparent disdain for any form of official calendar or date-keeping. They were theoretically Naridans, but only insofar as Nari had laid claim to the mountains and everything in them: they were a different people who'd been living in the high places long before even the time of the first God-King, and no lord Daimon knew of counted them amongst his common folk, or tried to tax them. Indeed, many were openly hostile to lowlanders. The Smoking Valley people were something of an exception, to the point that many of them learned Naridan, and a woman called Amonhuhe had stayed in Black Keep one year and ended up taking a woman called Bilha as her wife.

"See if you can convince Sattistutar to stand with you in welcome," Darel suggested. "And bring news of what happens. Your brother would like to know how they take to each other."

Daimon nodded, even though Darel couldn't see him. "Your brother will. Be well, Darel."

He headed for the stairs, a faint smile tugging at his lips. The despair and anger he'd felt earlier had lifted from his chest somewhat, and in its place was something he could only define as hope. Not about the situation with Sattistutar and her people—that hadn't changed in any way—but something more important, more personal.

Darel had, intentionally or otherwise, referred to himself as

Daimon's brother today. Even more critically, Darel's incessant curiosity had won out over his misgivings and he'd started asking questions. Once he started worrying at a problem he wouldn't let go until he'd solved it, and you couldn't solve a problem without understanding it. Daimon had dreamed of being a legendary warrior, but Darel had always wanted to be known as a man of learning. What greater prize than being the first Naridan to truly understand the Raiders?

Daimon held out hope his father might one day see beyond his honour to what was possible, but he wouldn't stake money on it. Darel, on the other hand... let him think of the Brown Eagle clan as a puzzle rather than an enemy and, so long as they behaved themselves, he'd probably forget any notion of trying to drive them back into the sea. What Daimon wouldn't give to have his brother back by his side (and, for preference, taking care of the ledgers).

"This might," Daimon muttered to himself as he reached the ground floor, "*might* just work..."

SAANA

"I'M NOT SURE this is going to work."

Saana had called a meeting of the clan's council, and they were sitting in the strange, raised house she'd taken as her own. Saana had to hand it to the Naridans, they knew their woodwork: the planks of which it was built were so well-fitted, barely any draught got in except at the shuttered windows, and the soil in the fire pit didn't fall out onto the ground beneath.

It was just a shame they were so tolerant of disgusting behaviours.

"He didn't understand it's wrong?" Esser asked incredulously. She was a sturdy woman, older than Saana, with darting dark eyes equally adept at spotting wandering sheep or misbehaving clansfolk. She wasn't the leader of the witches as such, but she was the one most of the clan would least like to cross, and that amounted to more or less the same thing. "I thought you said the boy was intelligent!"

"He's bright enough," Saana replied gloomily, staring into the dancing flames that warmed the room. "That's what's so frustrating. He *seems* intelligent, then throws out dangerous talk like this!"

"We should expect no better from a godless people," Ekham said sadly. He was a shipwright who often worked with Otzudh, and he read his signs in the growth of the forest trees. He'd already expressed concerns about how well he'd manage in this strange land, with its trees he didn't know, and whether Father Krayk would still recognise the clan as his children or whether they'd become godless in turn.

"They're not godless," Tsolga Hornsounder cut in. The old woman wasn't a witch, but she had a place on the council partly through respect for her age, partly through respect for the sheer amount of fights she'd lived through, and partly because there was every chance she'd just interrupt them anyway. She shifted uncomfortably and hissed, presumably at some complaining joint or muscle. "They've got at least one."

"A man," Ekham argued, tugging at his beard in annoyance. "A dead man they've raised up and treat as a god. You can't tell me that's right."

"Perhaps it's right for them," Kerrti interjected. She was the youngest witch, and the one Saana harboured the most fears for. She doubted many Flatlanders would suspect that Esser the shepherdess or Ekham the shipwright were witches—she got the impression their roles would be thought too practical—but Kerrti knew herbs and charms to heal the sick. As Saana understood it, that could be enough to cast suspicion on the young woman, despite the fact Tjakorsha had plenty of healers who weren't witches. She wondered whether dark-bearded Ekham would be feared by the Naridans if he was the one who knew how to heal people, or whether he'd be accorded some form of respect. She suspected it would be the latter, because he was male.

"It can't be right for them if it leads to this sort of thinking," Ada countered. The last of the clan's witches had been out with the fishing crews all day, and the smell of salt was still strong on her, as it used to be with Zhanna. "Who's to say this practice of theirs wasn't what caused the sickness you spoke of?" She folded her hefty arms, and sat back. "It's unnatural, and there's an end to it."

"No one's arguing it isn't," Saana replied. She cast a glance at Kerrti, just in case, but the young healer didn't say anything. "The question is: what are we going to do about it?"

"Is Blackcreek dealing with this man of his, at least?" Esser asked.

"Yes," Saana replied, "but we can't trust him to protect our people from his *before* they act, he's made that clear enough."

"So we must protect ourselves," Ekham said firmly. "Will he tell us who these men are, at least?"

Saana didn't even bother trying to play out in her head how that conversation would go. "No."

"Then we must warn our own," Ekham said with a resigned nod. "We can't afford to assume any Flatlander is innocent."

"Is it just men?" Kerrti asked. "Or do their women do this as well?"

"Why?" Tsolga leered. "Got your eye on one?"

"That's not funny!" Saana snapped, and for a wonder the old woman subsided. "He was quite clear they do," she added, addressing Kerrti, who was now glaring at the Hornsounder. "Apparently they'll even take in parentless children, and raise them with another woman."

"This country is cursed," Ekham declared flatly.

"I won't be having that," Esser said sternly. "Don't you dare go spreading that sort of talk, Ekham! This land may be strange, its people may be stranger, and they may be powerful wrong about what they do, but they're not cursed. Any fool who listened to half the tales Tsolga tells would know that." She turned to the Hornsounder, who was picking at one of her remaining teeth with a ragged fingernail. "You've raided many of their towns, haven't you?"

"Sure have," Tsolga agreed around her own finger.

"Are they a cursed people? Are they fading from this world?"

"Fuck no," Tsolga snorted, removing her finger from her mouth and inspecting the end of it with considerable interest. "There's hordes of the bastards. I saw one of their big settlements once, from out at sea, when the Greybeard decided to swing in close and hit them when we were already on our way back home. There were enough of them that they actually put to sea to come chase us off! They couldn't catch a drenching in a gale, of course, but that's beside the point. There were two whole hillsides covered with their buildings. *Covered.* If I had to guess, I'd say there were more of them in that one place, just that one place mind you, than there are in all of the clans of Tjakorsha, and that's no lie." The old woman shook her head. "That was the time we picked up Nalon, actually."

"Speaking of Nalon," Ada said, frowning, "how is it he's never made any mention of this?"

"I've sent for him," Saana said darkly, running a finger over the engraved plates of the belt encircling her waist. The belt of the Brown Eagle clan chief was older than any living member of the clan, and a constant reminder of the responsibility weighing on Saana's shoulders. She'd never felt it more keenly than over the last year, when The Golden's breaking of the clans had forced her to choose between her people's destruction, or the uncertainty of life across the ocean. She thought she'd been as prepared for the challenge as she could be, yet there were many things she'd never considered.

"How's the fishing going?" she asked Ada, who snorted.

"Fish are fish, here and everywhere. It goes well enough, and will doubtless go better once we've learned the tricks of these shores."

"Can't you follow the locals?" Ekham asked.

"Sure, but who's to say these grassbloods know where the fish are to be found?" Ada said. "They make their catches, that's true enough, but I'd trust Esser's instincts over theirs, and all she knows is sheep."

"Thank you," Esser murmured, not looking at her fellow witch.

THE BLACK COAST

"Besides," Ada continued, either not noticing the comment or choosing to ignore it, "they pretty much shit themselves should we haul near them. Probably think we're going to steal their fish, or just board them and cut their throats!" She drew a finger across her neck with a grin. Back when she'd sailed the seas around Tjakorsha not all of Ada's prey had been under the waves, and not all of the silver she'd returned with had been fish.

There was a brief knock at the door, but the latch lifted and it was pushed inwards before Saana could get up. The firelight illuminated the dour features of Nalon, who pulled up short as he scanned the faces of those already in the stilt-house.

"Ah shit," he said glumly, then dropped down into a cross-legged position between Ekham and Ada with an air of resignation. "What am I in trouble for?" His tone was that of a man hoping that if he jokes about his fears then they will prove unfounded.

He was to be disappointed.

"You and I had a lot of conversations about this land," Saana said sternly, "and not *once* did you mention that men fuck men and women fuck women."

Nalon blew out his moustaches. "Oh. That."

"Yes," Ada said sternly, "*that*. How many years have you lived with us now? Why did you hide your people's deviancy from us?"

"Maybe to hide his own shame?" Ekham suggested, his eyebrows lowering.

"Hey, no! No," Nalon said firmly, raising his finger. "I don't have any interest in men. Never have. It's not like everyone does here, far from it. It's just that some people do."

"And you never mentioned it?" Ada demanded.

"Well of course not!" Nalon snorted. "Why would I? First off, *like I said*, I have no interest in men, so I'd no reason to bring it up. Second, by the time I'd learned enough of your language to talk about things, I'd already worked out what you thought

261

about it. I reckoned that if I mentioned how other people acted in Narida you'd get all suspicious about me, *like you're doing right now*." He folded his arms and glowered at her. "Don't think I ever forgot the Greybeard would have sent me over the side too, no matter what Avlja had said, if it weren't for the fact he worked out I knew iron-witching. I didn't know how far that would help me if one of you got it into your heads I was looking at a man the wrong way."

"One of *us*?" Saana echoed him in disbelief. "You married into our clan, have fathered children with one of our women, and you still think of us that way?"

"Hey, *she* just said the Naridans are *my* people," Nalon protested, pointing at Ada. "So you tell me, chief: am I part of the clan or not?"

Saana shot a glance at Ada, who'd jutted our her jaw pugnaciously in response to Nalon's retort. The trouble was, it was an entirely fair and just retort, and Saana was somewhat ashamed she hadn't caught what Ada had said.

"Of course you're part of our clan," she said firmly, looking back at Nalon. "And I'm sorry if you've been made to feel otherwise." Ada pursed her lips, but said nothing. "But I hope you can understand, Nalon, it would've been better if you told us about this before we came here."

"No disrespect, Chief, but that's easy for you to say," Nalon replied, albeit without heat. "I had Avlja and the boys to think about. If someone cast suspicions at me, what would've happened to them? For that matter, what would they have thought of me?" He shook his head. "Sorry, but no. You've got precious little to fear from the Naridans on that front. I'd be more worried about some fool getting drunk and pulling a knife, if I were you."

"One of them kissed Timmun today," Saana said coldly.

"Timmun's not innocent," Nalon sneered. "He got it into his head that Inkeru wanted him, and she broke his nose when he did the same—"

"*Yes*," Saana cut him off before he could finish his sentence. "That doesn't make it right."

"Well of course it doesn't, but... Look, you get Timmuns everywhere," Nalon said, waving a hand. "Arseholes, every one of them."

"You're saying that we should consider this to be normal?" Esser asked, her lips twisting in disgust as she spoke. "That we should just *forget* about it?"

"I'm saying I lived, what, nineteen years in this land before the Greybeard took me," Nalon said flatly, "and I knew more than one man with a taste for men in that time, and none of them ever harmed me." He paused. "Well, one tended to cheat at dice, but you get my point. Shit, there was a stablegirl up at Bowmar who was more predatory than any man-fucking man I've ever met." His gaze unfocused slightly and his lips quirked slightly upwards beneath his moustaches. "Good times, they were."

"This is a serious matter, Nalon," Ekham snapped.

"No," Nalon said, getting to his feet, "it isn't. You just think it is. Don't get me wrong, I like the way the clan lives far more than I like the 'because Nari said so' shit on this side of the water, but you've really got more important things to be worried about than who fucks who, like *learning the fucking language*." He dusted his arse off and snorted. "I need to make nice with Gador, because becoming his assistant is the best I can hope for here, and I can't make nice with him if I spend all day every day translating for you. Besides, I doubt the folk of Black Keep are going to spend much effort learning Tjakorshan."

"One moment," Saana said, raising her hand. Nalon scowled, but halted in the middle of turning for the door. "Speaking of that: did you teach Blackcreek how to greet me in our language?"

Nalon frowned in puzzlement. "Not me. Maybe Zhanna did."

It was certainly possible, Saana had to admit, but perhaps Blackcreek had merely heard someone else say it and imitated them: she wouldn't have put it past him. She'd been so caught up in rage and worry she hadn't asked her daughter how much contact she'd had with Daimon past the gifting of a baby dragon. Blackcreek had a member of the clan who could speak at least some of his tongue within his walls. Would he have the sense to learn from her? Would he have the humility to?

"Very well. Thank you for coming, Nalon."

"My pleasure," Nalon grunted, heading for the door. Saana could hear the lie in his voice, but didn't call him on it. Sadly, she suspected she was going to be reliant on his help to bridge the gap between the two peoples for some time yet.

"I think he forgets himself," Ada said darkly after the door had closed behind Nalon again.

"I think he remembers himself all too well," Saana countered. "You heard what he said. Nalon's always felt his presence with us was down to his usefulness, and that's doubled now. He knows we'd struggle to do this without him. Besides," she added, "he may say he prefers our way of life, but I suspect he could fit back in with the Naridans if he needed to. We're no longer his only option."

"And endanger his family?" Ekham scoffed. "The Flatlanders would never tolerate them."

"Maybe, maybe not," Kerrti said quietly. "Iron-witches are valuable people here. If it came to it, I feel he'd take that chance."

"We're getting dragged away from the point at hand," Ada said, clapping her hands together. "What are we to do, now we know about the Flatlanders' deviant ways?"

Saana rubbed her hand over her face. She was incredibly tired, and didn't think that was going to change any time soon. "We can't force them to live like us. Daimon Blackcreek may have gone against his family to allow us to settle here unopposed, but he's no coward." His willingness to fight Ristjaan over the honour of a farmer had been proof enough of that. "He'll hold firm to what he believes when it comes to his people, and damn the consequences. We must look out for—"

She was interrupted by a thunder of knocking at the door. She sprang to her feet, heart in her mouth and her hand on the grip of her dagger as a succession of unpleasant scenarios ran through her head. What if Blackcreek had set someone to watch her? What if Blackcreek had decided he now knew who the witches were, and had sent men to kill them out of fear? The clan would rise up, and Black Keep would burn: Blackcreek would know that, but wouldn't he do it anyway, if he thought it the right thing to do?

All that flashed through her mind in a moment, so by the time she'd reached the door and pulled it back she was almost startled to find it was only Tsennan Longjaw.

"What is it?" she demanded, angry at being disturbed. Then she saw his wide eyes and heaving chest, and tension gripped her bowels again. Something was very wrong.

"Kerrti!" Tsennan puffed, gasping for air as he looked past her. "Is Kerrti here?"

"I'm here," Kerrti's calm voice replied. Saana heard the swish of her skirts as she rose to her feet.

"Come quickly!" Tsennan pleaded. "It's Brida! She's taken ill!"

The tension in Saana's bowels turned to ice, and she looked up and around at the walls and ceiling. A house where someone had died of sickness, and it had been left to stand instead of being burned as was right and proper.

A house just like the one where Brida, her husband, and her children now slept.

DAIMON

THE SOUND OF wood striking wood caught Daimon's attention as he set foot upon the bridge across the fishpond, and brought him to a puzzled halt. He couldn't fathom why any of his household would be making such a noise in his family's private copse. He set off again, crossing the bridge and turning towards the sound.

What he found, shortly afterwards, was the sight of a Raider engaged in combat with a tree.

Zhanna had a sturdy length of dead branch, as long as her own arm, and was practicing cuts with it. Daimon watched her for a while, fascinated. She was engrossed in her work, and was not without skill. Her blows had considerable force, and she was consistent in her aim; they all landed in more or less the same spot on the trunk, no matter which angle she struck from, and the bark was starting to look worse for wear. As he watched, Daimon saw echoes of the swings of Ristjaan the Cleaver, and his hand went involuntarily to his ribs. The tip of the big man's axe had done little more than graze him. Tevyel the apothecary had washed and bound the wound and Aftak the priest had prayed to Nari for good health and swift healing, but it was still tender.

"Is it dead?" he asked as Zhanna struck the tree what looked to be a final blow, judging by the way she doubled over panting afterwards. The girl was straight-backed again in a moment and whirled around to level her branch at him, face flushed red and eyes wide. Had he been a little closer, Daimon might have feared she was going to attack him. As it was, he was well out of range of her makeshift weapon, and recognition dawned in her eyes a moment later.

"You watch long?" she asked, eyes narrowing as she lowered the branch.

"A little while only," Daimon admitted. He felt uncomfortable, now, about not having announced his presence, despite this being his land. He changed the subject. "How is your dragon?"

"Good. Eats well."

Daimon nodded. He didn't have much more to ask on that front, since he'd never paid close attention to the raising of rattletails. He was glad to hear the dragon lived, though; he'd hoped the gesture might go some way towards bridging the gap between Naridan and Tjakorshi.

The silence stretched out, started to become awkward. "You are a warrior?" That was how the girl had been referring to herself, at any rate.

Zhanna's lip twisted, and she shook her head. "No warrior." She touched her forehead, where her mother—and virtually every other adult Tjakorshi Daimon had seen, come to think of it—had a dark stripe running from their hairline to the bridge of their nose. "No fight yet."

So the stripe marked a person who'd been in battle? It must be a rite of passage, given how many of them bore it. "This lord does not envy your opponent, should that come to pass," Daimon said politely.

Zhanna gave him the sort of blank look Daimon knew he'd given Osred as a boy, when the steward had tried to teach him numbers.

"You look to fight well," he tried again, and a fierce grin lit up her face.

"Thank you."

Daimon snorted in surprise. "You know how to say 'thank you'?"

"Is important," Zhanna replied with a shrug. "Nalon say so." She eyed him in what Daimon felt was an appraising manner. "You are warrior."

It wasn't a question, and yet Daimon suddenly felt uncertain about his response. He'd had one fight in earnest, an honour duel where he'd been terrified nearly out of his wits, and he'd only been saved by the relentless and none-too-gentle training his father had insisted on. He didn't consider himself a warrior in the grand traditions of Narida; a mighty sar who rode into battle with keen blade and clear head, or who single-handedly fought and bested twisted monsters of the mountains.

"Yes," he said firmly. His self-doubt was just one more measure of his unworthiness, and there was no point revealing it to his hostage. How he wished he could talk more freely with his brother!

"How do fight?" Zhanna asked, pointing at the longblade at his belt. She mimed a two-handed cut with her branch.

"This lord has trained with the longblade since he was five summers old," Daimon informed her. It hadn't been with a full-sized weapon at first of course—that would have been ridiculous—but Lord Asrel had insisted he take up an adult's practice blade by his tenth naming day. Daimon could still remember the soreness of his arms and shoulders.

Zhanna nodded as though this was nothing unusual. "Show this warrior?"

Daimon wanted to reply that she'd already said she *wasn't* a warrior. *You can't just say you're something you're not,* he thought, *even if that's what you want be. That's... wrong.* Except, he had to remind himself, her mother went around calling herself "this man", so perhaps she shouldn't be expected to understand civilized language.

"You want to learn the longblade?" he finally managed, his

voice edged with disbelief.

Zhanna spread her arms. "No hunt. No fish. No dig. No cook. What to do when dragon hungry not? Must hit tree."

Daimon sucked his teeth thoughtfully, stopped himself out of habit before his father slapped him for doing something so common, then reflected he could suck his teeth all he wanted at the moment. To teach the longblade to a Raider... Well, it was unheard of. And probably against the Code of Honour. But he'd broken the Code of Honour so many ways now that once more wasn't going to make much difference.

"If this lord were to teach you the longblade," he said slowly, "he would need something from you in exchange."

Zhanna's eyebrows raised. "'Something'?"

Daimon wasn't completely sure what she'd thought he'd meant, but it was enough to send his emerging train of thought headfirst into a tree. He grappled for a moment with how to explain the complicated and very specific passages from the Code of Honour about the correct treatment of hostages to someone who not only had no concept of the Code but had only basic Naridan. Then he stumbled mentally over the fact that since he'd broken the Code so many times, even if she *did* know it she'd have no reason to believe he'd hold to that part of it anyway, and finally gave up.

"This lord meant," he said carefully after a couple of moments, "that if he teaches you the longblade, he wishes you to teach him your clan's language."

"Hnh." The grunt seemed to be a noise of consideration, as Zhanna followed it with a nod and another toothy grin. "Yes."

TILA

"We don't get many Naridans like you here," Kurumaya commented, swigging from a small leather skin. Tila detected the sharp scent of qang. The shorefront labourers in Idramar knew it as "island water", because it was clear and came from the City of Islands, or "fool's water", because of how ill you got if you assumed that because it was clear, it wasn't potent.

"Women?" Tila asked. She used the Naridan word, since there was no Alaban equivalent: merely "person", with the appropriate inflection for one of the two female genders, and she refused to define herself as such. Everyone could just address her formally.

Kurumaya mouth-shrugged, the Alaban grimace that indicated indifference. "As you say. You wanted to speak to me, foreigner. What is your reason?"

They'd stepped into one of the corners of the warehouse, where dusty canvases covered some of the few goods the building currently held. Barach was a discreet distance away, as were three large local toughs.

Tila mustered her best Alaban. "I need someone to die."

She'd expected evasion or mockery, at least at first. Possibly to be interrogated about why she thought Kurumaya could assist her, or what she thought Kurumaya's identity was; the standard power games of someone who wanted to emphasise their dominance. Instead, Kurumaya nodded as though this was a request they received regularly. Perhaps it was.

"Who, and why?"

"This family." Tila produced a piece of parchment, which she unfolded to show a family crest in the Naridan style, a copy of the one Skhetul had sent her in his most recent letter. The crest was a very complicated affair, which, had it been genuine, would have showed how minor the family was. Tila had an extensive knowledge of Naridan crests, however, and was almost certain the entire thing was a fiction, camouflage from Alaban eyes that wouldn't know what they were seeing. "I believe they live up the hill. Not high." She tried not to show how frustrated she was by her limited Alaban.

"The whole family?" Kurumaya asked, studying the parchment.

"Yes."

"Servants and slaves as well?"

"No need," Tila shook her head. "Only blood."

Kurumaya nodded in apparent satisfaction. Slavery was not universally approved of in the City of Islands, Tila knew, but it was approved of by those in power: at least, by those in official seats of power. Kurumaya's sympathies might lie elsewhere, and besides, Tila had no quarrel with slaves.

"And the reason?" Kurumaya asked.

"Does it matter?"

"Since I am asking, you may assume it matters," Kurumaya said, and bared their teeth in what may have politely been called a grin.

Tila nodded in turn, as though there'd been no edge in the words. "A personal insult, from this family to mine." It was true enough, yet vague enough, assuming Kurumaya didn't demand specifics and proof.

"An insult that requires children to die?" Kurumaya asked. "I assume there are children."

"I wish this to end it," Tila said simply, watching Kurumaya's face. Did the Alaban know who this family really were? Would they guess at the reason for Tila's insistence that everyone who shared the same blood died?

Kurumaya mouth-shrugged again. "I don't recognise this design, so this family are not important to me. Let us discuss price." They snapped their fingers, and a tough approached to hand Kurumaya a small leather pouch, which they in turn passed to Tila. It was empty.

"Fill that with gold coin," Kurumaya instructed casually. "Return when you're ready."

Tila felt her eyebrows raise. She could get a man killed for a couple of silvers in Idramar. "Is life so expensive in Alaba?"

"Life is cheap everywhere," Kurumaya smiled. "You're buying the consent of a Shark for knives to be bloodied on your behalf in their waters, and the certainty your money won't be wasted." Their eyes narrowed a little, and the smile sharpened slightly. "What streets do you walk, Naridan, that you speak so casually of death? Have you many such enemies? Or is this one just more personal than most?"

"I will answer with gold," Tila replied sweetly, which was an Alaban phrase for requesting someone else to mind their own business so long as you paid them. It occurred to her as she spoke that it was more commonly used towards an over-curious inferior, but Kurumaya's snort of laughter suggested they'd been amused rather than offended by her use of an Alaban colloquialism. Nonetheless, she wasted no time in beckoning Barach to her and sorting through her winnings to fill the pouch appropriately.

"You've had good fortune this evening?" Kurumaya asked from behind her.

"Good judgement, also," Tila replied. She passed the pouch back, now a lot heavier and clinking richly. Kurumaya weighed it in their hand, then smiled again.

"Good judgement indeed." Kurumaya passed pouch and parchment to the same tough, then flicked their fingers to shoo them away. They turned back to Tila, and made a passable bow. "Fare you well, Naridan."

"Fare you well," Tila replied, with her own bow. That was it, then. She had to hope Kurumaya was all they claimed to be, and trustworthy to boot, but it seemed a fair wager. Tila had never called Kurumaya a Shark, yet that was how the Alaban had named themselves, and it was not a title to claim lightly. As for trustworthy, reputation would be as important here as it was in the backstreets and smoke parlours of Idramar. If you took money to end lives, but didn't follow through, you quickly made enemies. What was more, those enemies would now assume you posed no threat to them.

Nothing keeps a man genuine like the threat of death. Those were the words of Yakov, her predecessor, that he used to utter in a voice so dry it sounded like sticks crackling in a fire. He'd never smiled when he'd said it, because he hadn't been joking. Tila didn't know if Kurumaya considered themselves a man, even by Alaban standards, but the sentiment held true.

She wasn't sure why she'd thought of Yakov just then. Perhaps it was the sensation of once more stepping into the murky waters of an unfamiliar criminal underworld. Looking back, she couldn't quite believe she'd ever been reckless enough to do it in Idramar, let alone here.

Still, she'd achieved what she'd come to do. Short of taking a knife to the Splinter King and his family herself—and she'd considered it, briefly—she'd was as sure as she could be that the imposters would die. Then, perhaps, she could turn her attention to Natan's surprisingly sensible idea of adoption.

"Time to go," she told Barach, and turned towards the doors.

"Wait," he said, taking her shoulder.

No one laid their hands on Princess Tila Narida without her express permission. No one did it more than once with Livnya the Knife. She froze, because Barach must have very, *very* good reason.

"Listen," the young man said. Tila could only hear the babble of chatter inside the warehouse. Then Barach's advice became somewhat redundant, as the doors crashed inwards and the two guards stationed there scrambled inside, hotly pursued by a press of the East Harbour Watch.

"Oh, Nari's teeth!" Tila swore. "Run!"

"To where?" Barach asked, as Tila hauled on his arm.

"There!" she shouted, pointing at the retreating figure of Kurumaya and their thugs. "Follow them!" If anyone had a way out, surely it would be the person running the show? She lifted her dress and hurried after the Shark.

Kurumaya did indeed have an escape route: a hatch set in the floor behind more bales of what were probably cloth. It was being pulled shut just as Tila came into view of it, and by the time she'd reached it and wrenched at the iron ring set into it someone had clearly shot a bolt on the other side, because it didn't budge.

"Let your man try," Barach offered desperately, but even his substantially greater strength was no use, and he could only rattle it in frustration.

"Kurumaya!" Tila shouted, stamping on the hatch. "Go eat your mother's entrails, you fish-fucking snake! And you'd better kill that family!" she added, her stock of Alaban sailor's insults briefly exhausted.

"Oh, Tolkar's *arse*!"

This curse was in Naridan, and Tila spun around to find Marin of Idramar and his husband clattering to a halt behind her.

"Kurumaya's bolted it?" Marin asked in panic.

"Yes!" Tila snapped, pushing past him to shoot a look at what was going on in the rest of the warehouse. It was a large building, and the Watch were struggling with punters and fighters unwilling to come quietly, but it wouldn't be long before the four of them were spotted skulking in the shadows.

"S'man doesn't want to see the inside of an East Harbour cell again!" Marin whined, clutching at his husband's arm.

Again? It wasn't the time to enquire how Marin had run afoul of the Watch before, so Tila held her tongue. "The other door?" she asked, knowing it must be a foolish question.

"See for yourself," Sar Blacksword said grimly as the labourer's door in the far wall burst inwards to admit more torch-bearing Watch. The warehouse occupants who'd fled to it backed off in a panic, and for a moment, total confusion reigned.

"Big man," Sar Blacksword said, looking at Barach. "Can you use that cutter?"

"Well enough," Barach replied, laying a hand on his long-bladed knife.

"The only way out is through," Blacksword declared. He pointed to the gaping expanse of the warehouse's main door. "There, now. Before they get control."

"You intend to kill the Watch to get away?" Tila demanded. He turned dark eyes on her, pits of deep shadow in the flickering light, and she felt a momentary rush of... recognition?

"This man intends to get away," Blacksword said simply. "If they die, they die."

"So long as we understand each other," Tila said. She reached into her sleeves for the throwing knives in light leather braces strapped around her forearms, and pulled one out in each hand. "Lead on, Sar Blacksword."

Blacksword's eyes widened in surprise, but only for a moment. He slapped Barach on the arm. "Don't draw until the last moment."

Barach nodded, and they burst into a run. Marin was burbling a just-audible prayer to Nari as he scampered alongside Tila, and she tried to block it out. She always felt vaguely responsible when people started doing that.

There were five Watch still in the doorway, making sure no one slipped out past their companions. They saw the Naridans bearing down on them at a dead run, and levelled spears, shouting demands to halt.

It had been a while since Tila had needed to land a knife in someone's neck while running, but she'd put enough practice in over the years to more or less perfect what had already been a naturally good eye. Running, jumping, turning, even hanging upside down...

The first knife left her right hand and tumbled through the air to bury itself in the throat of the middle Watchperson, who staggered backwards. Their companions had just registered Tila was a threat when Sar Blacksword and Barach drew blades, and they were forced to hastily reorder their priorities.

Sar Blacksword charged into the gap, ducked under a spear thrust, and lashed out with his longblade. It easily pierced the leather cuirass, opening its wearer up along their ribs. Tila put her second knife into the neck of a Watchperson about to stab Barach, and the suddenly unstable Alaban stumbled into the path of a companion's spear thrust. Barach kicked out, driving them further onto the weapon and knocking both Watchpeople backwards, then reached around to bury his knife in the ribs of the rearmost. Tila slipped past him, heading for the open door.

The first person she'd hit with a knife reached out to claw weakly at her knees. She shoved them away and wrenched her knife loose, turning the trickle of blood from their neck into a flood, then threw the blade at the last Watchperson. The blood made it slip in her hand and her target was struck in the cheek by the pommel rather than the blade, but it threw their balance off. It wasn't much, but it was enough for Blacksword to step in and drive the pommel of his longblade into their temple. They dropped, loose-limbed, and the four Naridans bolted out into the night.

"This way!" Tila snapped, turning right, only to find another group of four Watch directly ahead of them down the wharf, watching the warehouse. Tila looked over her shoulder, but there was yet another, larger grouping at the far end.

"Shit!" Blacksword spat.

"Charge them," Tila told her companions flatly, pulling two more knives clear of her wrist sheaths. The Watchpeople in front of them started forward with shouts, but she dropped one before they'd made two steps, and another before they'd managed two steps more.

Barach and Blacksword broke into a run, silent and menacing.

The remaining two Watchpeople, suddenly aware their fellows were no longer alongside them, took one look at the two big Naridans approaching at speed and decided discretion was the better part of valour. They fell over each other to jump into the channel, leaving the wharf clear except for the wounded. Tila drew one more knife and ran after Barach and Blacksword, with Marin tailing her.

"How many knives do you *have?*" Blacksword asked shortly, as she drew alongside him.

"Always one more," Tila replied. She actually had six left, including the one in her hand, and the shouts behind her suggested it might not be enough: the other group of Watch were already in pursuit. "Do you have a plan?"

"Running isn't a plan?" Marin demanded. Running certainly seemed about all he was built for; he hadn't even drawn a weapon yet.

"We need somewhere to lay low!" Tila snapped. Was she the only one with any intelligence? She couldn't outrun the East Harbour Watch for long, dressed as she was.

"'We'?" Blacksword snorted, hurdling a puddle. "We got each other out of there; now we part ways, unless you have a way off this island up your sleeve along with those knives!"

"We have a ship!" Barach butted in, and Marin practically squeaked.

"A ship! Laz, a ship!"

"You seriously have a ship?" Blacksword demanded, slowing his pace slightly. They were coming up on a bridge across a side channel, and Tila dearly wished to get over it as soon as possible.

However, she also knew she couldn't just run back to the *Light of Fortune* with the Watch in tow, even assuming she could stay ahead of them for that long.

It was time to gamble.

"Yes!" she told the disgraced sar. "Tied up in the Naridan Quarter! If we can get these dragon-shits off our backs long enough to get there, you can have passage!"

"You've got a deal, knife-lady," Blacksword replied, without hesitation. "This way!"

He sheathed his longblade and cut right, down the narrow path running next to the side channel. Tila swore, but followed him.

"This is taking us away from the docks!" she shouted at his back.

"You let this sar worry about his side of the bargain!" Blacksword retorted, without turning. Tila tried to keep up with him, but the stone underfoot was slippery with moisture and slime, and with only the light of the two moons to guide her feet it was hard enough simply making sure she didn't topple into the channel. Behind her, she heard both Marin and Barach slipping and swearing. And behind *them*...

"They're still coming!" Marin called anxiously.

"Trust your husband, Mar!" Blacksword said from ahead. The channel they'd been following met another at an angle, forming a corner to the islet, on which the Alabans had built a narrow wharf. Blacksword slipped around the edge of the last building and disappeared. Tila clawed her way around it, then nearly ran into him.

"What—?"

"Into the water," Blacksword said, pointing. A few yards beyond him, and out of sight until now, was yet another of the Narrows' many bridges. This one was stone, wide enough for a wagon, and spanned the water to the next islet in two arches, with a central pillar sunk into the channel. On the far shore the street split into several different thoroughfares branching off at angles: an obvious place to lose pursuers.

Tila grabbed him by the front of his tunic. "What in Nari's name—"

Even in the dim light, she saw Blacksword's expression sour from determined to malignant.

"*Get in*. Under the bridge, and keep quiet!"

Tila had two choices. She could obey him, or keep running into an unfamiliar city, hope the Watch got tied up with him, and that no one found her before she made it back to the *Light of Fortune*.

"Under the bridge!" Blacksword hissed over her shoulder, and Tila noted with some annoyance that Barach didn't hesitate. Her bodyguard took three steps to the edge of the wharf and slipped into the water feet-first with a surprising lack of noise. Marin, following after, clearly realised what his husband was planning and took a running dive in, arms outstretched, parting the water with barely a splash. Blacksword pulled both his weapons from his belt to hold them above the water as he skidded on his backside and dropped in, bracing himself with one hand on the wharf at the last moment to muffle his entry.

"Fine," Tila muttered, and followed him. She ducked down behind the arch of the bridge, placed both hands on the stone of the wharf and hopped into the channel, just as she heard the clatter of feet signalling the arrival of the Watch.

She stifled a squeak as the water soaked her up to the chest. It was warm—far warmer than the sea in the docks at Idramar, even at the height of summer—but that didn't stop her panicking momentarily. She could already feel the water pulling at her dress, trying to drag her down. She held onto the shore grimly, and shuffled along to join her companions in the deeper darkness beneath the arch. Blacksword reached out and grabbed her shoulder with his free hand, pulling her into his side.

Shouts in Alaban rang out, questioning where the foreigners had gone, then an authoritative voice ordered the rest onwards. Tila heard the *slap-slap-slap* of running, sandaled feet going over the bridge above them, then fading into the distance. She opened her mouth to speak, but Blacksword put his finger to his lips in an urgent motion for silence. Tila held her tongue, but it was becoming increasingly hard to keep herself above water with only her arms.

Something bumped against her leg. She managed to clamp down on her immediate reaction so only the barest hint of a strangled grunt emerged, but she saw Blacksword's eyebrows quirk questioningly.

"There's something in the water," Tila whispered, as quietly as she could.

Blacksword's cheek twitched. "Sharks. Attracted to the blood on our clothes. Everyone out, slow and quiet."

It wasn't easy. Tila managed to pull herself to the edge of the bridge, but the sheer weight of her waterlogged dress made it hard to lever herself out without any purchase for her feet. It wasn't until Blacksword wrapped his left arm around her legs and gave her a boost, bracing himself against the edge of the wharf with his other arm, that she cleared the water properly. Even then, shedding water like a raised wreck and with a dress clinging to her that felt like it weighed a hundredweight, it was a very good job there weren't any of the Watch lurking. She wasn't sure she'd have been able to properly lift an arm to ward them off, let alone thrown a knife with accuracy.

"What now?" she demanded of Blacksword, keeping her voice down. "We're all wet through, we must look even more suspicious than we did before, and now this lady can't even run!" She gestured at her sopping dress, still shedding water in rivulets.

Blacksword blinked noticeably when she said "lady". Certainly, she didn't look like a member of the nobility. Nor did she particularly feel like one right at that moment, but that was hardly the point. She didn't want this sell-sword to think she viewed him as her superior.

"We need a boat," Blacksword said. "The Watch are looking for us on the streets. We get a rowboat and take the channels to the harbour, then reach your ship from the water. Assuming you actually have a ship," he added.

"The *Light of Fortune*, out of Idramar," Tila snapped.

"Idramar?" Marin piped up.

"You never did share your names," Blacksword added, looking from her to Barach.

"Ship first, introductions later," Tila told him sternly. "We don't have time. And where do you intend to get a rowboat from, and how do you intend to steer it? This lady knows enough about boats and the sea to know fools with no experience regret combining the two!"

"Ah," Marin said. "This is, perhaps, where s'man can help…"

SAANA

BRIDA DIED TWO days later.

It hadn't been pretty. The woman had writhed on her pallet of blankets and clutched at her stomach, in so much agony she could barely speak. The draughts Kerrti mixed barely touched the pain, which Brida described as akin to having swallowed a hot coal, in one of the times she'd managed to muster words. Kerrti did her best, as always, but there was no denying the Dark Father when he'd set his eyes on someone. In the end the healer had given the only help she could and mixed the Last Draught with the blessing of Brida and her husband Oll, and Brida had slipped away holding Oll's hand while he wept.

The one good thing, Saana had reflected bitterly as she'd watched Chara paint the designs entreating Father Krayk to let his daughter's spirit return to the oceans, was that Kerrti had been clear Brida's illness had been from within, not without. It wasn't that Saana was happy with how their houses had come to be empty, but no one seemed to have sickened from them yet, and Kerrti wasn't sure sickness could linger for that many years.

Even so, Saana thought, as the yolgu that had given Brida to the waves came to a squelching halt under her on the black mud of the shore, perhaps it would be best for them to build new homes. Dug down into the ground, as they had been at Koszal.

Wooden beams and stone walls, with the gaps filled with mud and moss. She jumped down and turned to assist Oll, his eyes red and raw from crying. The sky was the grey of steel, and light drizzle spotted into her eyes as she helped him down. Yes, new homes, that might be the best thing. But where?

They'd have to tear buildings down to make room inside the town walls, and that wouldn't sit well with the Naridans. But where else could they go? The salt marsh was fine for grazing sheep, but too damp for houses. Further inland was farmland, even now being ploughed and planted, so there was no way that could be used, at least not this year.

What about clearing some of the forest? Saana squinted over at the dark mass in the distance. Blackcreek would have to approve it, and even if he did, she didn't fancy the idea of digging out so many longhouses through the mess of tree roots they'd undoubtedly find. On the other hand, tree stumps could probably be moved much more easily if they could borrow dragons to heave them out...

Her thoughts ran on and on in this way, turning over the possibilities as the funeral party trudged around the town wall towards the large hole in it, through which they could easily climb now they were no longer burdened with Brida's bier. Saana wasn't sure whether the sight of a group of Tjakorshi clambering through the town's erstwhile defences would be welcomed by the folk of Black Keep, but she also wasn't sure that she cared that much. She didn't see any reason why they should have to take the long way around to the gate when there was a much more convenient alternative.

"Chief!"

The shout had come from above. She looked up to see Nalon hurrying down the top of the wall towards her, his dark hair plastered to his head. He'd clearly been out in the weather without a hood for a little while.

"What?" she demanded, halting to look up at him. She'd

learned better than to try walking on the ground around the town without keeping an eye on where she was putting her feet, and the last thing she needed was to be hopping to Kerrti with a twisted ankle.

"It's Chara!" the smith shouted down, wiping his wet hair back from his eyes. "She's gone into the forest on her own!"

Saana frowned. "So?"

"So, there's *wild dragons* out there!" Nalon shouted, waving one arm wildly towards the north. "I heard it from the shepherds— one of the local sheep wandered and was nothing but fleece and bones by the time it was found, and that was only yesterday!"

Saana snorted. "Chara's not a sheep, Nalon."

"She'll be as dead as that fucking sheep if a pack of razorclaws find her!" Nalon yelled. "You were pissed off the other day because I didn't tell you something? Well, now I'm telling you something! You need to go find Blackcreek and get him to send a party out looking for her, or we'll need a new corpse-painter!"

Saana grimaced. Nalon could be a pain in the arse, but he seemed in deadly earnest. "Chara isn't one of Blackcreek's, there's no reason for him to care. We'll get a party together and—"

"No," Nalon cut her off. "Sorry Chief, but you need Naridans for this, ones who know the local dragons. You think the sars' war dragons are scary? They're just the ones that can be tamed. Wild razorclaws are like... they're like the krayks of the land. That's how bad they are."

Saana cursed under her breath. The rest of the funeral party had kept moving, and she picked up her own pace once again. "Why haven't you gone to Blackcreek about this?" she shouted to him, not looking up from the ground. "Why wait for me?"

"I tried!" Nalon replied. "Honest, Chief, I tried! But his guards wouldn't let me in, and just laughed at me when I said one of ours was in danger. But he'll see you whenever, right?"

Before, perhaps, Saana thought bitterly. *But that worked out so well for both of us last time.* "Fine! But start rounding up whoever you can, just in case he doesn't listen!" She was nearly at the gap in the wall now, and risked a glance up at him. "And that includes you! You're the only one who'll know what we're dealing with!"

"It's been twenty years—"

"No arguments, Nalon!" Saana shouted. She scrambled over the fallen stones, managing to keep her footing despite one shifting underneath her. "Whoever you can find!"

The streets of Black Keep turned to mud in the rain, and while the current drizzle wasn't heavy, it had been falling since the previous day. Only the main square and the road from the gate were paved in stone, and Saana slogged past rows of houses on stilts, like giant insects, until she reached the flagstones and managed to set a better pace. All the same, she was breathing hard by the time she reached the stronghouse.

"This man needs to see Lord Blackcreek," she shouted up at the gate tower, and cursed inwardly when Ganalel's face appeared, the guard with whom she'd nearly come to blows on her last visit.

"Who's there?"

"Who do you think is here?" Saana demanded, pulling her hood back to reveal her face and hair. "What other woman would demand entry?"

Ganalel sneered down at her. "His Lordship is busy."

Saana could almost smell the lie as he disappeared from her view again. She'd have been surprised if Ganalel even knew exactly where his lord was, let alone whether or not he'd be prepared to receive her. She supposed she could plead with him, but had a nasty feeling that would make no difference.

Well, this was no time for a half-sail.

"Ganalel of Black Keep!" she thundered, raising her voice as loud as she could without losing control of its pitch. "This man names you liar! You have no honour!"

There weren't many people in and around the main square, but they were definitely paying attention. She took another breath and continued. "You are craven and coward! You are too scared of this man to do your duty and open this gate!"

People were starting to laugh. Now Ganalel's face reappeared, scowling instead of sneering. "Listen here, Raider scum—"

Saana changed tactics. "You fuck goats!"

Ganalel's eyes widened to the point of bulging. He disappeared, and Saana thought for a moment or two that he'd just left to let her shout at an empty guard tower, but then there was a rattling of chains and the drawbridge began to lower. Saana stood back as it gained momentum and crashed down at her feet to reveal Ganalel, spear in his hands, trying to shake off the restraining grip of Sagel, another guard.

"—fucking kill her..."

Saana stepped forward onto the drawbridge without waiting for the Naridans to sort themselves out. She needed to speak to Daimon Blackcreek, and the first obstacle to her doing so had been navigated.

Ganalel stamped on Sagel's foot, causing the other man to release him with a cry of pain and stumble away, and came at Saana with his spear lowered and a murderous light in his eyes.

The problem was, he didn't know how to fight. So few of the Flatlanders did. Saana had dodged the spears of untrained, frightened farmers fifteen years ago, and while she wasn't a warrior by trade she still trained with her weapons against those who were. So when Ganalel jabbed his spear at her midriff with an angry yell he was slow and clumsy, and when she sidestepped it and grabbed the haft his reactions were far too slow for him to muster anything more than a momentary look of surprise before she closed the remaining distance between them and slammed her fist into his face.

Ganalel wasn't large even by Naridan standards, and although some people seemed to get tougher with age, he apparently wasn't one. Her punch knocked a spray of brown spittle loose from his mouth and the man himself to the wooden boards of the drawbridge, leaving his spear in her grip. Ganalel landed on his hands and knees and Saana buried a kick into his ribs that blasted the breath out of him and left him collapsed on his side, curled up and keening miserably.

"*What is the meaning of this?!*"

Saana looked up to see Daimon Blackcreek, who'd appeared in the entrance. The Naridan lord's eyes flashed dangerously in his hood as he advanced on her with one hand on the hilt of his longblade and the other resting on its pure white scabbard.

"Nalon told this man that one of her people is in danger in the forest," Saana said simply. "He said we need your help."

"And so this lord hears shouting, and comes to find you attacking one of *his* people?" Blackcreek demanded angrily. Saana realised she was still holding Ganalel's spear, and dropped it.

"He would not let this man see you. And he opened your gate because this man called him bad names."

Blackcreek's jaw worked for a moment, and the glance he cast at the wheezing Ganalel was not a friendly one. "Who is in danger?"

"A woman called Chara," Saana told him, not expecting it to mean anything.

"Your corpse-painter?"

Saana didn't bother to mask her surprise. "The same."

"Nalon told this lord of her," Blackcreek muttered, by way of explanation.

"Nalon says go find her we must," Saana said, "but he also says he heard from shepherds that things called razorclaws have killed sheep and may hunt her, so we will need you."

"Razorclaws? This far south, so early? That is a bad omen." Blackcreek cast a look up at the sky, as though checking whether his perception of time was accurate, then looked back at her and seemed to come to a decision. "Follow."

"Lord…" Ganalel groaned from where he lay on the

drawbridge, but Blackcreek had already started to turn away and head back into his stronghouse.

"If you are still there when this lord returns, he will ride over you!" he shouted over his shoulder. Saana hurried after him, past the shocked-looking Sagel and into the first courtyard, its flagstones now slick with rain.

"Have you ever ridden a dragon before?" Blackcreek asked. His pace was brisk but Saana's legs were just as long, and she settled into stride next to him.

"Ridden a..." Saana's mind boggled at the concept. "We have no dragons on Tjakorsha."

"Have you ever ridden *anything*?" Blackcreek asked, as they passed over the bridge into the second courtyard.

"No animals," Saana admitted. "Only ships."

Blackcreek's eyebrows raised for a moment, and the hint of a smile quirked the corner of his mouth nearest to her. "Well, this will be interesting."

Saana tried to keep her voice level. "You intend this man to ride a *dragon*?"

"This lord intends you to sit behind him on a dragon and try not to fall off," Blackcreek corrected her, heading for the stables. "We will need a mount to get to your corpse-painter quickly, and to help us drive away any razorclaws that may have found her. You will need this lord for that. He will need you to speak to your corpse-painter and explain to her that he means no harm."

"This sounds wise," Saana said, swallowing. He wanted her to ride on a *dragon*? This was not the help she had anticipated, had she even anticipated any help at all. She wanted to suggest that perhaps she could just run alongside, but she'd no idea if she could keep pace with one of the monstrous Naridan mounts. Besides which, her pride would not let her show fear in front of this man.

"Tavi!" Blackcreek shouted. The huge wooden stable doors were closed: they were easily twice Saana's height and looked hard to move, but the smaller door set within them was ajar. Blackcreek didn't slow as he pushed it inwards. "Tavi!"

"Lord?" a voice answered as Saana followed him in. She looked up to see who had spoken and—

By the Dark Father, the smell.

Saana almost gagged. It wasn't that the dragon stink was *bad*, so much as it was simply overpowering. It was thick and sour and grabbed at her throat like she was trying to swallow sand. She coughed, trying to clear her airways, and looked around.

The dragon house was dark, which was unavoidable given the thickness of the walls and sparseness of the windows. Directly in front of her was a Naridan man bowing to Blackcreek, and beyond him...

... were the dragon stalls.

A dark lump shifted in the gloom beyond Blackcreek and his man. There was a hissing roar that sounded like one of the great leviathans of the southern waters expelling its lungs into the air, and a huge shadow got to what proved to be its feet, then lumbered forwards. Even with a thick metal gate between her and it, even with the two Naridans closer to it than she was, the sight of a war dragon nearly loosened Saana's bladder.

It at least superficially resembled the frillnecks she'd seen pulling carts and ploughing fields, but this creature was to that as Ristjaan's favoured weapon had been to a child's stick-sword. The dragon's eyes were nearly on a level with hers, and the top of its back reached above her head, but quite the most terrifying thing about it was its skull. Instead of the comparatively small, rounded frill of its kin in the town, this creature's frill reached up and back, and was tipped with six spikes. More alarming still were the four long horns that curved outwards from its brow, two upwards and two downwards, and reached forward almost to the end of its muzzle.

It huffed out another great breath and a new cloud of dragon-stink enveloped her, tinged with notes of rotting vegetation.

"Saddle up Bastion," Blackcreek ordered his man. He looked over his shoulder at her. "And find armour for Chief Sattistutar."

"Bastion will be restless, Lord," Tavi replied, rising from his bow. "He has not been exercised recently." Saana had seen him watching when she'd nearly punched Ganalel, and Zhanna had mentioned him in passing, although she hadn't realised they were the same man. He had deep-set, serious eyes and the first streaks of grey in his dark hair, but only the faintest of lines on his brow and at the corners of his eyes. He was half a head shorter than Saana and Blackcreek, but his short-sleeved jerkin was tight across his chest and showed arms corded with muscle. That didn't surprise Saana: everything in the stable seemed of a scale to match its occupants, and Tavi would need to be strong to move much of it around.

"Yes," Blackcreek nodded in response to Tavi's words, "but he is the least likely to balk at the scent of razorclaws."

"Razorclaws? So early?" Tavi grimaced and spat on the floor. "Nari save us." He raised his voice. "Faaz! Abbatane! Saddle Bastion for His Lordship!"

There was a scuffling further down the stable and two youths appeared, one male and one female, vaulting over the gate of another stall. They paused momentarily to sketch a hasty bow to Blackcreek, then scuttled off to a wooden frame nearly as tall as them atop which sat a construction of polished leather. A dragon saddle, Saana decided uneasily, eyeing the straps for the riders' feet and the alarmingly small pommels she assumed were for holding onto.

"As for armour…" Tavi continued, rubbing his chin as he studied Saana. His eyes travelled up and down her, then he looked back to his lord. Something about it struck her as odd. "It will have to be yours, Lord. She's too tall for your father's, or your brother's."

"So be it," Blackcreek said, heading towards another rack where the strange Naridan armour hung. "She can have this lord's old suit."

That was the difference, Saana realised. The stablemaster

hadn't looked at her like Naridan looking at a Raider. He'd simply looked at her as a person for whom he'd been told to find armour. So far as Tavi was concerned, Saana could have been anyone. It was refreshing, yet also slightly disappointing.

She followed them to the far end of the stable and hauled off her fur outer tunic. Blackcreek echoed her movements, but when he unbelted his thick robe and allowed it to fall away he was wearing nothing beneath it save his leggings. He reached for a tunic hanging over a wooden beam and Saana saw the muscles shifting beneath his skin: Daimon Blackcreek might not have the same bulk as Tavi, but there was little spare flesh on him.

"Lord, you dishonour yourself!" Tavi protested, and for a moment Saana thought the groom was shocked at Blackcreek's disrobing in front of her. She was about to stifle a snicker—she had a daughter, it wasn't like she hadn't seen a man's chest before—but then saw Tavi's concern appeared to be for the robe itself, which he snatched up off the stable's dirty floor.

"This lord has no time to stand on honour," Blackcreek replied. "The robe can be washed, Tavi." He reached up to pull the tunic on over his head, an action that set the muscles of his stomach rippling. "See to Sattistutar."

The groom turned to Saana with a grunt, then eyed her once more. "Huh. S'man was mistaken. His Lordship's old armour would be too small for you. It wouldn't fasten properly across the chest."

Saana looked down at herself, then over at Blackcreek. It wasn't like she had Ada's figure, but it was fair to say she was more heavily built than her Naridan counterpart.

"You'll have to take Lord Darel's hunting armour instead," Tavi continued, pulling a coat of nails off the rack. It didn't have the same brilliantly worked designs as the one Blackcreek's law-brother had worn on the salt marsh, being green and brown with the nail heads themselves apparently blackened, presumably to be less noticeable. "It'll be too short on your legs, but it'll save you being opened across the belly."

"These creatures sound fearsome," Saana said, trying to sound composed.

"Fearsome? Hah!" Tavi spat into the straw again. "If s'man didn't know that Lord Nari had driven the demons out of this land, he'd suspect the razorclaws of being them. Foul beasts, they are. Do your people have nightmares, Raider?" He saw the confusion on her face. "When you sleep? You wake up, scared of things you saw when you slept?"

"Oh." Saana nodded. "Yes." What a strange question. Didn't everyone have those?

"Think of the most terrifying thing you saw in a dream," Tavi advised her. "Be prepared for it, because that's what a razorclaw is." He gestured with his finger. "Arms out."

"This man can put this on herself," Saana told him, taking the coat and plunging one arm into a sleeve. It was heavy, but not as heavy as she'd feared.

"Suit yourself," Tavi replied, crouching down. As Saana reached behind her and found the other sleeve she felt a pressure on her leg and looked down to see the groom buckling a greave around her shin.

"What are you—"

"His Lordship wants you armoured," Tavi replied, reaching around her. His face was very close to her crotch, but he seemed intent on his task. "There's no point giving you Lord Darel's coat if you're going to lose a leg."

Saana pulled the coat closed and fiddled with the front. It overlapped, with hooks on one side that fastened into eyelets on the other to leave no part of her upper body uncovered. However, she realised the armoured panels intended to protect her thighs did indeed look too short, stopping a way above her knees.

"A word of advice," Tavi said in a low voice, finishing with the second greave and straightening up to pick up a large gauntlet from the rack. "If you hurt Bastion in any way, or cause him to come to harm, you'll be wishing you'd given yourself to the razorclaws instead of returning."

Saana blinked in surprise as he slipped the gauntlet on her unresisting right hand. "This man would have expected you to warn her against harming your lord."

"Lord Daimon is not s'man's responsibility," Tavi replied soberly, tugging the gauntlet into place. "His father's war-dragon is." He picked up the left-handed one. "Arm out, please."

Saana obeyed, uncertain whether to laugh. She quickly decided against it, since Tavi seemed completely serious. He pulled the second gauntlet into place and she flexed her fingers experimentally. They were thick, and somewhat clumsy, but were much thinner on the palm and the insides of the fingers, presumably to make gripping a weapon easier. Certainly, the sars never seemed to have any trouble wielding their longblades when similarly protected.

"Put this on," Blackcreek said, tossing a helmet at her without looking. She caught it awkwardly, and fumbled it around. It lacked the impressive dragon plumes of a sar's war armour, but otherwise looked to be in good condition. "This lord's brother's will likely be too small for your head."

Saana placed her head in it and let it settle over her. The armoured panels reached to her shoulders, and the weight of it was far greater than her own helm, but at least it felt reassuringly solid if she was to go into a forest containing creatures from bad dreams.

"This man cannot understand how you sars can fight wearing this," she said to Blackcreek as Tavi stepped in to tighten the helmet's strap. "And yet you still move so fast!"

"It is not so much about moving fast as moving well," Blackcreek said. He'd armoured himself with quick, expert motions and now turned towards her, his own helmet in place and his gauntlets held in one hand. Whatever he'd been about to say died on his lips. and he simply looked at her for a few moments, his expression unreadable.

"Lord?" Tavi said quietly, as the silence got awkward.

"A strange sight indeed," Blackcreek muttered, looking away from her. "Tavi, is Bastion saddled?"

"Your servant will have their hides if he's not," Tavi replied. He strode towards the stall into which the two youths had disappeared, making clucking noises with his tongue that could have been to do with dragon handling, or might have been impatience or displeasure.

"We will need weapons," Blackcreek said, pointing past Saana. "Spears are best."

Saana turned and studied the selection of edged implements. "You do not favour your sword?"

"Against dragons?" Blackcreek stepped up beside her. "Not as first choice. This lord's longblade is sharp, but he prefers something with more weight." He reached past her and selected two broad-bladed spears. "Or something to keep them at a distance. If this lord can reach a razorclaw with his longblade, it can nearly reach him."

Saana took two spears of her own, then, after a moment's consideration, an axe as well. She gave it a couple of swings, testing the weight and balance. It wasn't blackstone, but it felt comfortable in her hand, and the edge looked wicked. She nodded in satisfaction and tucked it into her belt.

"Do you know how to use that?" Blackcreek asked her.

"It will be the only thing this man is familiar with," Saana told him dryly, biting back a more acerbic response. Something of her impulse must have leaked through, however, since Blackcreek pursed his lips slightly.

"This lord meant no disrespect. You had a sword on the day you arrived."

"The sword was this man's father's," Saana told him flatly. "She took it then only because she knew Flatlander lords favoured swords. She hoped it would make you more likely to think a woman could be a chief."

Blackcreek didn't say anything to that. They stood in silence for another moment, then he turned away. "Tavi?"

"Ready, lord."

The gate of Bastion's stall began to swing open with a clank of metal, pushed by the stable boy. Saana's heart sped up as another thunderous snort sounded, and Tavi backed into view with a thick leather strap in his hand.

On the other end of the leather, and clearly not being led by anything other than his own will, was Bastion the war-dragon.

He seemed even bigger out of his stall, as though he'd expanded now no longer enclosed. Each of his titanic legs must surely have weighed as much as a large man, and Saana's outstretched arms wouldn't have reached around half of his dun-feathered body. The final thirds of his mighty horns were now sheathed in metal, and even his tail was armed with four bony spurs.

All in all, Bastion was the most terrifying sight she'd ever seen. And she was expected to ride him.

"Down!" Tavi raised his hand, palm out. Bastion gave another mighty snort, but to Saana's amazement he slowly sank to his knees.

"Give this lord those spears," Blackcreek instructed her, holding his hand out. Saana passed them to him and the sar approached the war-dragon confidently, then slotted the weapons into long, apparently hollow cylindrical lengths of pale wood attached to the side of the saddle. He then patted the dragon on the neck while speaking in a low, calming tone, put one foot into a stirrup, and vaulted easily up into the frontmost of the two seats.

It almost looked easy, until Bastion let out a tectonic rumble and lurched up to his feet.

"Whoah!" Tavi barked, holding out his hand again. "Down! *Down!*"

Bastion had other ideas. The huge war-dragon shook his massive head and began to shuffle in a circle to his right until he was facing Saana. His nostrils flared as he inhaled, and he took a step forward.

Saana's mind whirled. Did she smell different from Naridans? Did the dragon know the scent of the people against whom he'd been ridden into war, time and again? Did he immediately consider her an enemy?

"Open the stable doors!" Blackcreek shouted at Tavi.

"Lord?"

"Just *do* it, man!" Blackcreek barked. Tavi had thrown him the leather strap connected to a bit in the dragon's mouth, but the sar's attempts to haul Bastion around by his head obviously weren't working, and he'd now produced a short pole with a hook on the end. Tavi and his youths threw themselves at the huge wooden doors that were all that stood between Bastion and the outside world.

"You've got one shot at this, Saana!" Blackcreek yelled. The doors began to creak open, and he hooked his pole into the left side of Bastion's mouth and pulled.

It looked like it should be incredibly painful, but the dragon just grunted. He did, however, swing his head to the left to lessen the pressure in his mouth, which not only got his horns pointing away from Saana but directed his eyes and nose towards the door. The dragon took another deep breath, sampling the fresh air now flooding in, and gave an excited rumble.

"Now!" Blackcreek shouted at her. Bastion was heading for the doors. For a couple of moments he was presenting his flank to her instead of his horned head or his spiked tail. If she waited at all he would be outside, and who knew if Blackcreek would be able to rein him in? It was now or never.

It's just like jumping onto a ship sliding into the water, Saana told herself as she ran forwards, not quite able to believe what she was doing. *Just a large, scaly ship that could kill me...*

She leapt at the saddle.

"Fuck!"

Hitting Bastion with her ribs was like diving belly-first into the sea, and nearly knocked the breath clean out of her. She'd managed to grab the pommel and cantle, but her foot had missed the stirrup and she was hanging off the dragon's flank, her legs kicking wildly as she tried to find it. Bastion was lurching forwards, and she didn't dare put her foot down in case it dragged or caught on something and wrenched her clean off. She was sure she was going to lose her grip any moment and fall off to be trampled to death, but the main thought flashing incongruously through her head was a desperate hope that Zhanna wasn't watching from somewhere...

Someone grabbed her leg, placed one hand on her arse and shoved her upwards. It wasn't much of a boost, but it was just enough for her to lever herself up with her arms and swing one leg over the dragon's broad back to settle into place behind Blackcreek. She looked over her shoulder and saw Tavi stumbling to a halt just past the stable doorway, having thrown himself off-balance helping her. She gave him a grateful wave, then faced forward again.

Bastion thundered under her, letting out a cry that throbbed through his massive body, and set off at a run.

"Are you on?" Blackcreek shouted back to her.

"Yes!" Saana replied through gritted teeth, trying to make sure she was telling the truth. She gripped the pommel with both hands to prevent herself being thrown off by the dragon's lurching gait, but she'd quickly wear her arms out if that was all she had. She took a quick look at how Blackcreek had arranged his legs and tried to copy him: Bastion's body was too wide to just let her legs hang down on either side of him, so she had to tuck them up into a half-kneeling position, resting her boots on pegs sticking out of the side of the saddle. It wasn't exactly comfortable, and she still needed to hold on with her hands, but it was manageable.

What didn't seem to be manageable, on the other hand, was Bastion's headlong charge.

"Is this normal?" she shouted in Blackcreek's ear as the gate and bridge between the castle's second and first courtyards rapidly approached.

"No!" the Naridan called back to her, doing something ineffective with the reins. "It is as Tavi said, he is restless after his winter sleep!"

The gate loomed up. Bastion had far too much sense to run into a wall, at least, and the mighty dragon thundered over the bridge that spanned the internal moat. Saana caught a brief glimpse of water stretching away in both directions, and then they were through into the first courtyard.

"Lower the bridge!" Blackcreek bellowed. "Now!" Sagel scrambled into the guard tower, leaving the gate wide open behind him. Blackcreek hauled back on the reins and Bastion began to slow: Saana suspected the dragon remembered what came next, since he trotted into the guard tower and turned towards the main gate with little guidance from his rider. The portcullis was still clanking into the ceiling and the wooden drawbridge had just hit the stone beneath it as Bastion accelerated again, thundering out into the town.

It was the fastest Saana had ever moved. It was hard to tell exactly how fast a ship could go, out on the ocean with nothing solid to mark its passage against, but surely even a ship under full sail and a strong following wind couldn't match this. It was certainly faster than she could run, and the tales she'd heard of warriors ridden down by mounted sars abruptly took on a new level of horror.

A strange sound came to her on the wind, over the thunder and spatter of Bastion's footfalls on the flagstones and through the puddles. It wasn't loud, and it took her a few moments to realise what it was. Blackcreek was laughing, the pure, joyous laugh of a young man who'd almost forgotten how much he enjoyed doing something.

It was infectious. And, as Bastion turned his mighty head towards the main gate of the town and the road that led out towards the mighty forest to the north, Saana realised that despite her discomfort and residual fear, she'd started laughing too.

RIKKUT

The Dark Father heard their challenge, and sent one of his storms screaming out of the south to collect their souls.

It was a rolling wall of stone-dark thunderheads riding on the backs of great wind-spirits that snapped at the sails to taunt the crews, and gathered up the salt water to spit it at them. That was just the beginning: sweeping closer over the ocean, darkening the very air as it came, was a curtain of rain that would not just spit, it would drench them to the bone. From the safety of land, it was a storm to send the wise running for cover. Out amongst the waves, farther west than any of them had been before, it was a sight to chill the heart.

Rikkut thought it the most beautiful thing he'd ever seen, and he'd been roused from rutting with Kovra the Fair beneath furs in the *Red Smile*'s deckhouse when it had first been sighted.

"We must turn north!" Sarika bellowed over the rising wind. "We've got to run before this! We can't face it down!"

"We're not turning anywhere," Rikkut laughed. He faced into the wind, letting the salt spray dash over the new scarring on his cheeks. "We've been given our task, Sarika."

"The task's all well and good, Fireheart," Sarika replied, "but if we try to sail through this we won't be finding the Brown Eagle clan anywhere, unless the Dark Father's already taken them to the depths!"

Rikkut licked his lips, tasting the spray on them. "I never took you for a craven."

"You might be raid-chief, but you're no captain," Sarika spat at him, pushing her hair back from her face, "and you're certainly no Lodzuuk Waveborn. The sea isn't a shieldwall you can break if you're brave enough, Fireheart! *We need to run north.*"

Rikkut shook his head. "The Flatlands lie west."

"The fucking Flatlands! There's probably no such place!" Sarika actually spat this time, hawking a gob of phlegm into the air and letting the winds take it where they would. "They're probably just some story Snowbeard put together to make himself feel important!"

"The Golden believed him," Rikkut said firmly. "And if the Golden believes him, so do I. I've seen a Flatlander sword, Sarika; held it in my hands. It's real, and the Brown Eagle clan have fled there." He turned to face her directly. She stared back at him, high cheekbones and one milky eye, her straw-coloured hair whipping around her head like the tentacles of some frenzied beast pulled up from the depths on a longline.

"I gave you this ship, Sarika. The Golden picked me, and I picked you to be my raid's First Captain. So pass the word: we stay heading west."

Sarika shook her head sadly. "You're touched by the Dark Father, Fireheart. You may be fell in battle, but you're worse than useless on the sea. A thirst for glory gets everyone killed out here, and the Dark Father sings no songs for you. Go back to fucking Kovra; she's better with a blade than a sail as well." She turned away from him, drawing in breath to bellow at the crew, ready to tell them to twist the great steering oar in the water and turn north.

Rikkut's swordfish-bill dagger took her through the throat, a high tide wound. She staggered, clawing for her own weapon even though she must have known her life was already over, but

Rikkut ripped his dagger out, grabbed her by the hair and ran her to the deck's edge. The yolgu was already starting to yaw as the waves grew, but he kept his feet well enough to dump her into the sea. The dark waters swallowed her body with no sign she'd even existed.

"Pass the word!" he roared at the rest of them. "We hold course! We're heading west, and fuck the storm! Juhadzh! You're captain now! If any of the raid breaks off, I'll hunt them down myself once we've finished with the Brown Eagle clan! So *pass the damn word*!"

There was a moment's hesitation, but only a moment. Ship crews didn't have time for lengthy deliberations: they reacted fast, or they died. Sarika had been the *Red Smile*'s captain, but Sarika was gone, without even corpse-paint to speed her soul to Father Krayk. Rikkut was raid-chief, and appointed by The Golden.

Someone grabbed a pair of signal sticks and began waving them, passing the word to the raid stretched out behind them. *Hold western course. Death to those that stray.* It was the greatest raid Rikkut had ever heard tell of, some said the greatest raid ever assembled, and it was his. The responsibility might have overwhelmed a lesser man. It would have overwhelmed Rikkut, were it not for one thing.

He had been given this purpose by The Golden, and he could feel the draug's eyes on him, even across the ocean.

SAANA

IT WAS THE first time Saana had been into the Naridan forest, and it would have been a strange experience even if she hadn't been mounted on a dragon.

Many of the trees were familiar, but here and there were scattered groupings of ones she didn't know. She knew Narida was flat, of course—there was a reason her people knew it as the Flatlands—but up until this point she'd always been able to seen the Catseyes, rising into the sky in the west. Here in the forest, however, she could see nothing but tree trunks disappearing into the distance, sparse undergrowth here and there, and the thick green moss that carpeted the ground. No matter where she looked, and it seemed no matter how far they went, she could see no rise in the ground worth the mention, whereas on any of Tjakorsha's islands you could barely walk a longhouse's length without seeing a slope. Here there was just the subtly changing forest, the apparently endless road of packed earth, and the dragon's steady, rolling tread beneath her. They were barely inside and already it felt as though they were a hundred leagues from another person.

It was like riding through a dream.

"Do you know why your corpse-painter came into the forest?" Blackcreek asked suddenly. He hadn't spoken since Bastion had slowed from his initial gallop into a trot, and then to a walk that was still deceptively fast, given the length of the dragon's stride.

"No," Saana replied, shaking herself from her reverie. "Nalon did not say. This man does not think he knew."

"It occurs to this lord that we do not know if she will be following the road," Blackcreek said. "Why would she come this way? Surely she cannot be seeking another town? They would more than likely kill her on sight."

Saana winced at the thought of Chara happening across wandering Naridans who weren't from Black Keep, and what might happen to her. As Blackcreek had said, she'd surely be killed.

"We should call for her," she said. "It is our best hope."

Blackcreek looked around at her. "You wish for this lord to ride through his forest on his father's war-dragon, calling the name of your clan's corpse-painter as though he is some alewife calling her child in after dark?"

"Do as you please, Lord of Blackcreek," Saana said stiffly. "You have done this much: this man would not wish for you to further dishonour yourself." She took a deep breath. "*Chara!*"

Blackcreek winced, although to Saana's relief Bastion appeared to pay her shout no mind. It would have been inconvenient in the extreme had the dragon decided to bolt. She filled her lungs and tried again. "*Chara!*"

In front of her, Blackcreek shook his head and muttered something too quietly for her to make out. Then, to her surprise, he too raised his voice. "*Chara!*"

They rode on like that, alternately shouting the corpse-painter's name and listening for a reply. They must have shouted a score of times each as Bastion strode on along the road, but every time the sound died quickly in the damp, still air, muffled by the surrounding tree trunks, the moss, and the faint hiss of thousands of tiny droplets of falling water striking the forest's near-infinite surfaces.

A larger drop fell from the brim of Saana's borrowed helmet to splash onto the tip of her nose, and she rubbed it away irritably. Where was the blasted woman, and why had she decided to venture into this place?

Bastion abruptly came to a halt and made a rumbling sound deep in his enormous chest. The war-dragon sucked in a great sniff of air, and his massive horned head began to track from side to side.

"What is it?" Saana asked Blackcreek.

"He smells something," the sar replied, patting the huge beast's neck.

"This man guessed that," Saana said, a trifle testily. "But what?"

"This lord is no witch, to converse with the beasts," Blackcreek snapped. "It could be your corpse-painter, it could be razorclaws or a thundertooth, it could be a female of his kind for all this lord knows." He reached out and took one of the hunting spears from the rack at his side. "It is something he was not expecting, to be sure. A dragon of Bastion's size is not overly concerned by most things."

Saana followed the Naridan's lead, plucking one of her own spears and holding it across her chest. The dreamlike forest had taken on a more threatening air, and she couldn't be certain it was only her imagination.

A faint sound reached her ears, high and thin. Bastion's head lifted for a moment: the dragon had heard it too.

"Was that—"

"A voice," Blackcreek confirmed before she could finish her question. "But this lord cannot tell…" He raised himself up in his saddle slightly. "*Hallo?*"

"*Chara?*" Saana yelled again, just in case.

They both froze, unwilling to lose any sound in the creak of leather or the faint grinding clinks of the metal in their armour, and were rewarded when the voice called again.

MIKE BROOKS

"There!" Blackcreek said decisively, pointing through the trees to their right. He slapped Bastion's left flank with his spear haft and tugged on the reins to direct his huge mount off the road. The war-dragon rumbled in response, and set off at a steady trot that was still faster than Saana suspected she could have run through such terrain. Bastion was huge, but undoubtedly sure-footed, and he picked his way over dead branches and around fallen tree trunks with ease.

"*Chara!*" Saana shouted again. She didn't yet know if the voice they'd heard was her corpse-painter, but who else would be out in this forest so far from the town? The Naridans would surely know of the dangers, and there were apparently no other settlements of any size nearby.

"*Help!*"

Now she could make out the answering shout, and while she never would have recognised Chara's voice, she could just understand the word.

"It is a Tjakorshi," she told Blackcreek. "It must be her!"

"What does she say?" Blackcreek asked.

"She calls for help," Saana told him grimly.

"This lord hopes she has not encountered some of his countrymen from farther north," Blackcreek muttered, "else this is going to get very complicated."

A stream appeared ahead of them, a sudden dark dip in the forest's green ground. Saana felt Bastion accelerate and realised the dragon was going to jump, so she wrapped her free arm around the largest solid thing she could, and held on desperately.

There was a jolt, a brief moment of weightlessness, and then a second, larger jolt as Bastion touched down again and thundered on. Saana guiltily released her hold on Blackcreek's torso as the sar twisted around in his seat to look at her with shocked eyes.

"What are you—?"

"This man would have fallen!" Saana protested, feeling her cheeks heat, then pointed as she saw a flash of blue in a tree.

"Look! There!"

The mighty pines largely lacked branches on their lower trunks, so climbing them would not have been easy, but Chara had found an entirely different sort of tree. Its trunk was wider than any Saana had seen before, and although its uppermost twigs reached up nearly as tall as the surrounding conifers, that trunk forked into a multitude of mighty branches only an arm's length or so above head height. Chara hadn't stopped there, though: she'd climbed on into the thinner boughs, some twenty cubits up.

"Chara!" Saana shouted up to her, blinking drizzle from her eyes. "What in the name of the Dark Father are you doing?"

"Saana?" The corpse-painter's face was only a small, pale oval at that height, but Saana thought she saw Chara's eyes widen in shock. She supposed she must look very strange, in sar's armour and mounted on a war-dragon.

"Chara, it's dangerous out here," Saana called, painfully aware that it looked like Chara had just climbed the tree and got stuck. "I don't know why you're up there, but—"

"Saana, look out, they're coming back!" Chara interrupted her, pointing desperately.

Bastion was already moving. The war-dragon spun without any touch from Blackcreek, frighteningly nimble for a beast of his immense size, and let out a bellowing challenge at the creature charging at his rear. He reared up and one of his steel-clad horns met the onrushing predator head-on, sinking deep into its body.

All of which would have been far more reassuring to Saana had she not been thrown entirely clear of Bastion by his abrupt movement, and if the attacking creature had been alone.

She scrambled up, her borrowed spear clutched in two sweaty hands, and bolted towards the thick trunk of the tree as multiple sets of footsteps approached and she saw shapes closing on her in her peripheral vision. She set her back against the dark, gnarled bark and turned to face this new threat.

Razorclaws.

Tavi's warning hadn't done them justice.

There were three of them, nearly as tall as she was. They moved swiftly, almost delicately on two taloned feet, but their bodies were held nearly upright in grotesque parody of a person's gait, and balanced by a tail held out rigidly behind them. They were mostly covered in fur-like tawny feathers with darker markings, but their heads and necks were bare, red-scaled skin above a black ruff. Their eyes were golden discs with hairline black slits, their muzzles were long, narrow and topped with bony ridges, with larger equivalents atop their skulls, and their teeth were plentiful and sharp.

However, the features that had named them were tucked up against their chests. Both of their long, well-muscled forelimbs were tipped with three talons as large as those on their hind feet, but the middle claw was hideously enlarged to the size of a dagger, and curved like a sickle. Saana had little doubt one slash could open someone up as effectively as a sar's longblade, given the ferocious power apparent in the dragons' limbs.

"Blackcreek!" Saana yelled desperately, not daring to look around, but Bastion was bellowing so loudly as he attacked the other dragon, she had no idea if the sar could hear her. The three razorclaws in front of her hissed angrily, but didn't retreat. The one on her left crouched slightly, and Saana aimed her spear at it.

The one on her right leaped for her.

Saana screamed, a feral, wordless shout of fear and anger as she stabbed at the beast while scrambling to her left. Her swing came up short and the metal skittered off the tree bark as the dragon landed where she'd been standing a second ago. It swayed its head back from the leaf-shaped blade jabbing at its face, but Saana had to snatch the weapon back around to menace the other one as it made a testing rush towards her. By the Dark Father, the things were fast! The second razorclaw pulled up just out of reach of her weapon and swatted at the spear blade with one of its forelimbs.

Saana pulled the spear back desperately: she couldn't afford for it to be knocked from her grasp, not when the only other weapon she had was the axe tucked in her belt. She might get the chance to bury that blade into one of their skulls, but the other one would surely have her—

Wait. The other *one*?

"*Behind you!*" Chara screamed from above. Saana tried to turn, but she was too late to avoid the third razorclaw, which had circled the tree to pounce on her from behind.

The impact bore her face-first to the floor and knocked the spear from her grasp. There was moss and leaves and dirt in her mouth and a huge, heavy weight on her back keeping her from rising. Her axe was trapped under her. Something clamped down on the back of her helmet and hot, fetid breath gusted around her. She smelled the rancid stink of rotten meat as her face was pushed further into the dirt and then there was a wrenching, a tugging on her back, and she felt the layers of cloth in her coat of nails rip and tear and give as the razorclaw started to dig down towards her spine. She could see the feet of the other dragons coming closer. At any moment one would find a part of her unprotected by armour—like her face or the backs of her legs—or the one on top of her would manage to rip the metal plates aside, and then—

What little breath she had left was driven out of her as something crushed her from above. What had it done? The beast was gurgling now, almost as though it were in pain…

"*Fuck!* Chief, get up, get up, I think I've broken my fucking leg and this thing's not dead yet!"

Saana managed to roll out from under the weight on top of her, literally wrenching her helmet free of the jaws gripping it—only they weren't really gripping it now, and the dragon that had been trying to kill her was laying on its side and twitching, *with Chara draped right across it with her leg twisted under her because she'd just jumped out of the fucking tree onto it.*

Still two razorclaws left. They'd backed off momentarily, startled by Chara's unexpected arrival, but were closing in again. Survive.

Saana dived for the spear, clawed it up out of the moss and dead leaves as one of the dragons ran at her snarling, and jabbed desperately with it. Survive.

That razorclaw backed off, but the other one came in immediately and Saana had to switch her focus to it. Survive.

She couldn't keep this up. Sooner or later she'd slip or be too slow. She had to change the game. She had to trust the Naridans knew what they were talking about.

She batted back the first razorclaw with the spear again, then hurled the weapon at the second. She didn't wait to see if it hit, she didn't have time: she pulled her axe from her belt and swung for the first one, already coming for her now she was distracted.

One of those murderous sickle claws swept down across her breastbone as the dragon lunged at her, raking downwards.

The outer cloth layers gave, but the metal plates in the coat of nails held. The razorclaw's feathered, scaled hide—struck by an axe of Naridan steel powered by all the strength in the right arm of the chief of the Brown Eagle clan—did not.

Her blow took the beast in the ribs and the axe head sank to the shaft into its flank. The dragon screamed and wrenched itself away from her and her weapon, spilling a gout of dark blood onto the forest floor. It lashed out at her again, but weakly, its only concern now to escape.

Something blurred at Saana from her left. She whirled towards it, raising her axe even though she knew in that moment that she'd be too slow, wondering if this would be when her armour gave way before the ferocious power of these beasts.

Bastion's horns caught the predator and tossed it to the ground, whereupon the mighty war-dragon reared up and stomped down on it. There was a very final crunching noise, and the huge horned head turned back to face her.

Saana whirled again, but the razorclaw she'd wounded had decided not to tangle with her, her axe or Bastion any further. She caught a glimpse of it slipping away between the tree trunks, and hoped fervently it would bleed out and die from its injury. There was the slapping sound of a man's hand on a dragon's neck, then a muffled thud as Blackcreek dismounted.

"You are well?" the Naridan asked, approaching her. He had one of his spears in his hand, the end slick with dragon blood, and he was aiming it towards the downed beast Chara had landed on. The corpse-painter had managed to get up to one leg and was holding herself up against the tree, her face drawn with pain and white as fresh-washed wool. Saana was grateful the beast she'd wounded hadn't lashed out as it fled, because Chara wouldn't have been able to escape it.

"I nearly fucking *died*," Saana snapped at him. "Where in Father Krayk's name—"

She cut herself off. She was speaking in Tjakorshi. Blackcreek's expression showed he didn't understand the words, but had a pretty good idea of the content.

She switched back to Naridan, trying to pull the unfamiliar language back into her head while she calmed her heart. "This man is not badly hurt."

"This lord regrets he could not help more," Blackcreek said seriously. To her amazement he actually bowed, a proper bow, not just the nod of a lord. "Bastion is wilful, and likes to charge razorclaws. When one is already pierced on a horn it is still in front of him, so he sees no reason to stop quickly."

Saana looked over at the huge war-dragon, who'd decided the threat was over and wandered off a few paces to chew some moss.

"You saved this man," she said. "And," she added, running her finger down the deep slash across her chest, "this armour saved her twice." Would her sea leather have done the same job? Probably not. Besides, her own helm wouldn't have protected her. The razorclaw's jaws would have closed around the back of her neck, and that would have been it for Saana Sattistutar.

She bowed in return to Blackcreek as she'd seen others do, her hands on her thighs to support her as much as anything else. By the Dark Father, but she ached! "You have this man's thanks."

Blackcreek didn't seem to know how to take that. He looked over at the last of the razorclaws. "And that one?"

"Chara jumped on it," Saana said simply. "She has hurt her leg."

"She jumped on it," Blackcreek repeated.

"Yes."

"From the tree."

"Yes," Saana said again. Was it that hard to understand?

Blackcreek walked over to the wheezing razorclaw, looked at it for a moment, then stabbed his spear into its neck. The beast twitched again, but otherwise made no move. Blackcreek shook his head, then looked up at Chara. "You jumped on this creature from the tree, with no weapons?"

Chara looked at Saana, who translated. Then the corpse-painter looked back at Blackcreek and nodded.

"Why?" the Naridan asked, apparently completely confused. "You must have broken its back, but you could not know that would happen. Were you so eager for death?"

Saana translated that as well, then parsed Chara's words into Naridan for Blackcreek's benefit. "She says it was trying to kill her chief. Which it was," she added.

Blackcreek seemed to digest that for a moment or two. Then he wiped his spear blade off on a handful of moss and gave a whistle. Bastion trudged over in response: now he'd had the exercise of a trot into the forest, and had gored and trampled a couple of razorclaws, he seemed far more docile.

"Come," Blackcreek said, gesturing to Saana, "help your woman up onto him. She can barely stand, let alone walk. She will have to ride."

"You are letting our corpse-painter ride your father's war-dragon?" Saana asked him, unable to believe her ears. Blackcreek actually laughed in response.

"Saana Sattistutar, this lord saw the wound you dealt that razorclaw with the axe he lent you. It won't survive long. Of all of us," he slapped Bastion's flank fondly, "this lord is the only one who has not killed a dragon today.

"You will both be riding. This lord will walk."

DAIMON

DAIMON WAS STARTING to regret his decision by the time they'd reached the edge of the Downwoods. In truth, the woman Chara had to ride: it would not only have been ignoble but also thoroughly impractical to suggest otherwise. Saana, however...

Daimon trudged along, tugged in different directions by his honour. The Tjakorshi chief had faced down razorclaws instead of running away screaming, which was more than could be said for many a Naridan, and had actually dealt one a mortal blow. She lacked neither courage nor ability, that was clear. Daimon had merely ridden Bastion, and while the mighty war dragon had killed two razorclaws and undoubtedly saved them all, Daimon couldn't help but feel his own contribution had been lacking. Bearing that in mind, it made perfect sense for him to offer Bastion's back to Sattistutar. He would have done the same for any other warrior whose deeds were worthy of respect.

And yet, she was Tjakorshi, the ancient enemy of his people: far more so here in the South than the Morlithians, for all that they'd killed the old God-King, or the meddling Alabans in the far north. Those were distant foes skirmishing along faraway borders he'd probably never see. The Tjakorshi were the blight of the spring and summer all along the south-eastern coast. How many stories had he heard of villages raided, settlements burned and harvests pillaged, leaving the lowborn dead or starving and even thanes forced to tighten their belts?

Should he really be walking alongside Bastion like a lowly bodyservant to this woman? And yet, would it not be more dishonourable to take his seat back now? It would not only make a mockery of his earlier gesture, but show him to care more for appearances than deeds.

This man has made his decision, and he will hold to it. It is far from the most momentous choice he has made recently.

"Has she told you why she went into the forest?" Daimon asked Saana, as they emerged from under the last boughs.

"She needed more of the flowers she uses for corpse-paint," Saana replied.

Daimon looked around at her in disbelief. "And she thought she would simply walk into the Downwoods to get some more?"

"No, Blackcreek," Saana said, her voice stern. "She says she showed some of your people the flowers and tried to ask if they knew them. She says one man pointed many times towards the trees."

"That is ridiculous," Daimon muttered. "Any child knows the Downwoods are dangerous."

"One of *your* children, perhaps!" Saana snapped. "We have not such beasts in Tjakorsha!" She composed herself a little, although her tone didn't lose any steel. "But yes, your people know of danger. Nalon heard your shepherds talk of razorclaws being near. This man has seen how your people look at Nalon; they do not trust or like him, even though he was born on these shores. If he has heard such talk, then surely all your people have. The man Chara spoke to knew of danger, and must have suspected Chara did not."

Daimon grimaced. "You think one of this lord's people sent your corpse-painter into the Downwoods in the hope she would be attacked?"

"Yes, Blackcreek, this man does."

"We shall have to see to that," Daimon said. "But first, do you have amongst your number someone who knows how to set bones?"

"Do you truly take us to be such savages?" Saana retorted. "Of course we do! Why, do you not?"

Daimon fought down a surge of irritation. Did the woman take his people for fools? "We do, our apothecary. We shall go to his house when we get to the town."

"You do not think our healer will have the skill?" Saana demanded.

"This lord does not know," Daimon replied tightly. "However, perhaps they can each learn from the other, and Chara may benefit as a result. This lord also intended this as some recompense if one of his people was at fault." He realised as he spoke that he wasn't sure if Saana would understand "recompense", but hoped the context would make it clear.

Saana grunted a syllable Daimon didn't recognise, perhaps some sort of utterance in her own language. "This man understands now, and is sorry for her sharp words."

"This lord accepts your apology," Daimon replied. He hesitated, the sour taste of an unspoken apology in his own mouth. "And he… is sorry for suggesting your folk may not have a healer." *Even if they may indeed prove to know nothing of use.* A notion struck him. "Is it one of your witches?"

"Nalon should never have spoken to you of them," Saana muttered. "It was not his place."

"It occurs to this lord that Nalon is rarely mindful of his place," Daimon observed.

Saana sighed. "He is not a bad man. This man thinks Nalon now believes both our peoples view him as being the other, and so he speaks harshly out of worry." She paused. "But, he is an arse."

Daimon managed to choke back an undignified snort of laughter.

They attracted attention along the north road from those working the fields. Few Naridans looked up for long: Daimon supposed they didn't want him to see them not hard at work. The Tjakorshi, however, showed no such reluctance, and several downed their tools or hoisted them onto their shoulders to walk down to the road and shout to Saana in their language. Her responses frequently provoked laughter, and on one occasion raucous cheers.

"What are you saying?" Daimon asked her eventually.

"They ask whether Chara and this man are now sars," Saana replied. "This man has told them that Chara broke her leg jumping out of a tree onto a monster that was going to kill this man, and you have allowed us to ride your dragon as neither of us can be trusted to walk."

"You allow them to speak to you in such a way?" Daimon asked, appalled. "And demean yourself in reply?"

"This man's father was not chief," Saana said, "and her daughter will not be chief after her unless she proves herself worthy. There is no difference between our blood and theirs. Besides," she added, "if this man cannot joke, she does not have the temper to be chief."

Daimon bit his tongue and didn't respond. He supposed it was true enough, at that: the notion of noble blood was laughable when applied to the Tjakorshi, so there was no reason for them to show their chiefs the respect even the most minor Naridan noble would expect.

The rain was coming down hard again by the time they reached Black Keep's gates. Bastion's great head was swinging low by now as he trudged doggedly on, his massive feet leaving depressions that instantly filled up to make new, regularly-shaped puddles on the road. Daimon patted the dragon encouragingly on his sodden flank and guided him to the apothecary's cottage, just within the town's walls, since Tevyel also made regular trips to the forest to gather the plants and herbs he needed for his remedies.

"Tevyel!" Daimon shouted, hammering on the closed door with his gauntleted fist. "Open up, man!"

The door was pulled open not by the apothecary but his daughter Henya, whose eyes widened when she saw Daimon, and widened further when Bastion snorted behind him. She dropped into a deep bow.

"Lord!"

"Henya, this lord has need of your father," Daimon said briskly. He'd seen the girl a few times, including when Tevyel had come to the stronghouse once at the insistence of Daimon's father to dose Darel for an ague he was suffering. She was a little younger than him, perhaps nineteen summers, and "pretty for a lowborn", as Daimon's father had casually commented to him. Daimon had precious little grounds for comparison, since the only noble girl he'd ever met had been Yarmina Darkspur, many years ago when they'd both been children, and before Lord Asrel had fallen out with her father. Still, Daimon could not deny that Henya was attractive. He might have even risked his father's wrath and pursued her quietly, but he'd never seen any sign she was interested in men.

"Who is it, Hen?" a voice shouted from within, and a moment later Tevyel himself appeared. He was somewhat portly, with grey flecks in his dark hair, and moved with a slight limp that even his own craft was apparently unable to cure. He had much the same reaction to seeing Daimon, right down to the deep bow.

"Tevyel, we think this woman has broken her leg," Daimon said, gesturing behind him. "She needs your help."

"This servant shall be pleased to assist, lord," Tevyel replied, visibly swelling with pride. "Go, girl, clear the table and fetch splints, we shall need..."

He tailed off as Saana Sattistutar slid ungracefully off Bastion's back and helped Chara down after her. The corpse-painter gave a hissing gasp of agony as she landed, despite trying to take it on her good leg.

"Lord, you surely cannot mean this servant to treat a savage?" Tevyel said hoarsely, staring at the two Tjakorshi women.

"This savage can speak your tongue, healer," Saana snapped, throwing Chara's arm over her shoulder. Tevyel flinched.

"See to her as you would any of our folk," Daimon ordered him. "This lord has not rescued her from razorclaws to see her crippled."

"Razorclaws?" Tevyel swallowed. He stepped back. "Of course, lord. Please, bring her in."

Chara muttered something to Saana that didn't sound happy. Saana looked at Daimon. "She says she wants this man to stay with her. She does not trust your healer."

Daimon nodded. "Very well. What is your healer's name, and which house has he taken?"

"Our healer is Kerrti," Saana replied. "*She* has taken house with green door, three houses towards the gate."

Daimon accepted the correction wordlessly. A female Tjakorshi healer surely had to be one of their witches? He would watch her closely.

"Tevyel," he said as Saana helped Chara up the steps towards the door, "Chief Sattistutar will stay to translate. This lord will fetch the Tjakorshi healer to assist you." He'd leave Saana to sort that particular mess out.

Tevyel's face creased further. "But Lord Daimon—"

"Try not to antagonise her, Tevyel," Daimon told the man. "She has already dealt a razorclaw its deathblow today." The apothecary backed away open-mouthed, and Saana helped Chara into his house, with the girl Henya moving to support the corpse-painter on the other side.

Daimon prepared to remount Bastion, rather than leave the dragon to wander while he slogged off to find Kerrti on foot, but a small group of townsfolk were gathering. They were a mix of Tjakorshi and Naridan, and Daimon noticed a face he recognised.

"Nalon!"

"Oh, here we bloody go…" Nalon muttered, none too quietly. "Yes, Lord Blackcreek?"

He'd at least given Daimon an honorific this time. "Your chief needs the woman Kerrti to come to this house, and this lord lacks the language."

For once, Nalon made no complaint or mockery, merely nodding and hurrying off towards the gate. Daimon addressed the rest of them, conscious not all would understand his words. "A pack of razorclaws set upon one of the Tjakorshi when she ventured into the forest. We killed them"—a small lie about the stature of his deeds, but probably a necessary one—"yet there may be more, even so early in the year. Pass the word."

The Naridans hissed or muttered, and made the sign of the Mountain in front of their chests. The Tjakorshi were, to a one, staring at Bastion.

"Lord!"

Daimon turned to see Aftak the priest, staff in his right hand and a grim expression on what could be seen of his face above his beard. His left hand was plunged deep into the pocket of his robe.

"Aftak?" Daimon asked, feeling apprehension pluck at him. The priest of Nari was neither a shy nor retiring character, but neither was he one to accost his lord so openly in public. "What is it?"

"Shoo!" Aftak called to the assembled townsfolk, waving his staff. "Go, back to your tasks!" The Naridans obeyed him and the Tjakorshi, after a few exchanged glances, appeared to conclude it would be impolite to linger, and followed suit.

"Your priest apologises, lord," Aftak said, standing close to Daimon so their bodies would block the view of anyone still watching. "This could not wait."

He pulled his left hand out and opened it to reveal a dark, flat stone, into which had been scratched a series of lines making small, angular shapes. Daimon frowned.

"What is this lord looking at?"

"Old runes," Aftak replied. "Your, uh…" He coughed into his fist, and for a moment looked more uncomfortable than Daimon ever remembered seeing him. Aftak was usually the source of discomfort in others. "Your brother might be able to tell us more. He has a goodly knowledge of such history."

"As this lord's brother is not here," Daimon said, "please explain why this stone concerns you."

"So far as this priest is aware, the old runes are only used now by those seeking to keep alive the rites of the Unmaker," Aftak said soberly. "This priest found the stone buried on the south side of the plot taken by the Raider woman who recently died."

Daimon's stomach clenched. South was where the Unmaker had fled, according to legend, and from where she still sent her stinging storms, despite having been banished by Nari from the lands of men. Of all directions, it was the most ill-omened. "You think this is a curse?"

Aftak nodded. "This priest fears so."

Daimon glanced sideways. Nalon was hurrying back towards Tevyel's house, accompanied by a young Tjakorshi woman carrying a leather satchel. That would presumably be Kerrti, their healer.

"Speak of this to no one," he instructed Aftak. "Find Kelarahel and tell him to come to the stronghouse. And give this lord the stone," he added, holding out his hand.

"Would it not be better to smash it, to break whatever curse it holds?" Aftak asked, although he dropped the stone into Daimon's hand.

"It will be done," Daimon assured him. "But first, this lord must seek his brother's counsel."

PART THREE

How, then, should this land be ordered?

The first concern must always be the defence of Narida. Though the Divine One hast scourged this land of demons from mountain to sea, the foul creatures may seek to return, and must be met with shining blade.

So too, must our land be guarded against those to whom the Divine One could not bring His wisdom. The sun-worshippers of the empty lands beyond the Pass of Torgallen and the marsh-peoples of the north languish in shadows of ignorance. True sons of Narida must ever be vigilant against their threat.

So too, must we watch for petty kings, such as the Divine One brought down before He turned to His greatest work. The lust for power that runs deep in man's heart may resurface, and any who stray from knowing the Divine One's blood as their Lord must be treated as harshly as any demon.

It is to men of war we must entrust our future: and men it must be, for the Unmaker was a she-demon of great power, and her most powerful adherents were the witches, and so we may judge that women will ever be weaker and more corrupted than men.

Before His departure from this world the Divine One disclosed to this general His wishes: that there be appointed four war-leaders, the Marshals, one for each of the Great Winds: the

Northern, or Sun Marshal; the Western, or Mountain Marshal; the Southern, or Ice Marshal; and the Eastern, or Sea Marshal. Each shall govern an area of this land in the name of the God-King. He shall appoint beneath him thanes, each with his own area of land, and these thanes shall rule over the lowborn...

... The Marshals shall each command an armed body of men, the Great Army of their realm, who shall remain always ready. In times of great war, the thanes shall raise further levies from their lands, and shall lead them under the guidance of their Marshal...

... The Sea Marshal shall have his seat in the holy city of Idramar, and hold overall command of all the armies of Narida, save only if the God-King Himself sees fit to take on such a role. However, the Marshal should take all measures to ensure that this is not necessary...

... It is this general's duty and honour, in accordance with the wishes of the Divine One, Nari, First And Only of His Name, stated to this general immediately prior to the Divine One's passing from this world, that this general should henceforth assume the title of Eastern Marshal of Narida and take on the weighty responsibility of ensuring the safety and security of this land...

Extracts from a proclamation authored by Eastern Marshal Gemar Far Garadh in the eighteenth year of the God-King, immediately following the passing of the Divine Nari.

DAIMON

DAREL HAD SUCKED in his breath when Daimon had passed him the stone, and confirmed Aftak's suspicions: the runes were in the old style, from before the days of Nari.

"Only demon-worshippers use them now," he'd said warningly. "To think such a person lives in the town...!"

"Then how do you know of them?" Daimon had asked.

"Your brother reads, Daimon," Darel had replied, not without a touch of his old aloofness. "Father has an old scroll detailing what a vigilant thane should look for. If we let knowledge of these foul practices fade from our memories, how can we know what to guard against?"

Kelarahel had answered Daimon's summons, but the reeve hadn't seemed as concerned as Daimon would have hoped. He'd scratched his nose as he looked at the rock, then shrugged.

"If enough Raiders sicken, maybe they'll leave. 'Twouldn't be a bad thing, surely?"

"This lord will not have such practices in his town," Daimon had said, shocked. "No matter the target of them!"

"It is a great affront to Divine Nari, and his victory at Godspire," Aftak had added ominously. Kelarahel had looked from one to the other of them and nodded, albeit slightly reluctantly.

"As you wish, lord. What are the reevesmen to look for?"

And there, Daimon had faltered, because he didn't know. The Unmaker's most powerful followers had always been women, but Daimon knew every Naridan in Black Keep by sight at least, even the women, and none carried the marks he'd always heard were associated with worship of the Queen of Demons. Many of the older folk bore pox scars, but that sickness had swept through all of Narida, more or less. It had claimed Daimon's blood-parents, and none who'd sickened but survived had done so easily: if the pox had been the work of the Unmaker, as some claimed, those who bore its scars had surely suffered at her hand rather than worshipped her.

Kelarahel had left with vague instructions about seeking witches, and rather more specific ones to find out who'd directed the Tjakorshi's corpse-painter to go into the forest, and Daimon had been left with many misgivings. He'd borrowed one of Gador's hammers to smash the stone, then given the shards to Aftak to pray over and dispose of, but even that act hadn't settled his mind. He'd walked back into the third yard of the stronghouse in a dark mood.

When the serving girl Tirtza appeared on the path before him, running and wide-eyed, Daimon's longblade had left his sheath before he was even aware of laying his hand upon it. It was a shameful reaction, for a sar only drew his blade in necessity, not out of fear or alarm, but what was done was done.

"What is it?" he demanded.

"The Raider woman and her beast!" Tirtza sobbed as she reached him, pointing towards the women's quarters. "She's a witch!"

"Witch?" Daimon repeated, his chest tightening, but Tirtza was running again. He considered ordering her back to explain further, but the words died in his throat. Tirtza's wounds from Duranen's rattletails had only just healed enough for her to resume her duties, and she was still skittish: he'd be wasting his breath.

"Witch," he muttered again, hurrying towards the women's quarters, his mind in a whirl. It seemed like too much of a coincidence, but Zhanna surely wouldn't know the runes of the Unmaker, or cause illness to her own people? She hadn't even been able to leave the stronghouse!

Then again, Daimon only knew the Unmaker's history in Narida. Witches in Narida worked evil magics against their countrymen, why should Tjakorshi witches be any different? And if Zhanna was a witch, perhaps she had ways of escaping the stronghouse. Nalon and Saana might claim Tjakorshi witches weren't hostile, but perhaps they simply didn't know the true witches lurking in their midst? By the Mountain, Saana was convinced there wasn't a single person in her clan with eyes for their own gender, and Daimon would eat his left hand if that were true. Perhaps she was less perceptive than she might appear.

But still, for her own daughter to be a witch, and her not to know... That was hard to believe.

Unless Saana was one herself.

Daimon tried to push the thought to the back of his mind as he approached the women's quarters, forcing himself to concentrate. He debated remaining quiet instead of calling out to announce himself, but decided against it. He was a lord of Narida in his own home, and he would not sneak up on a woman like an assassin.

"Zhanna!" he shouted, facing the building openly. "Are you there?"

There was no reply. Daimon waited, shifting his fingers slightly on the cord-wrapped grip of his longblade. In the birch tree above him a tiny wind drake sang a warning song at a rival, all rasping notes and belligerence.

"Zhanna?"

The door opened, and Zhanna Saanastutar frowned down at him from the porch. She didn't look like a witch, Daimon had to admit. She noticed the naked blade in his hand, and her frown deepened.

"You want spar?"

He'd taught her that word, since it was better than "fight-not-fight", which she'd been using before. In return, so far, he'd learned how to introduce himself. That had taken more time than he'd expected, due mainly to the bizarre Tjakorshi concept of self, which had taken a lot of understanding. No wonder their society was so disordered: it was like each person was a piling to support a bridge, without the actual bridge to give structure and purpose.

He shook his head. "Where is your dragon?"

Zhanna looked perplexed, but clucked her tongue.

There was a scrabbling noise of claws on wood, and the rattletail runt bounded out of the door. It was significantly larger than when Daimon had handed it over to Zhanna, but it wasn't the beast's size that caused Daimon's grip to tighten on his longblade: rattletails grew fast if fed well. It was the fact it wound itself between her legs and rubbed against her with every sign of affection.

Rattletails were ferocious pack predators who had to be cowed into submission from a young age, and even then would take your fingers off to get to food. Duranen was both huntmaster and kennelmaster because only he could truly control his beasts, especially once they'd brought down prey—which was what made them worth having in the first place—and even he walked a fine line. Daimon could remember a handful of times when Duranen had looked on the verge of disappearing under a pile of his own charges, before he'd reasserted dominance with his cudgel and some well-placed kicks.

Rattletails didn't wind up against you like a child trying to get its mother's attention, and they didn't come when called unless you had meat for them. Such unnatural behaviour matched the tales he'd heard of familiars, where a witch would use her dark arts to increase the intelligence of a beast so it could do her bidding.

A witch, in this family's stronghouse, brought here by this lord's own hand. Nari forgive me. Though it may bring ruin upon us, she cannot be allowed to live.

ZHANNA

DAIMON WAS MOVING differently. He'd lost his usual stiffness and had settled into the balanced, fluid grace with which he'd fought Mama's friend Rist, or when he and Zhanna sparred. It sat far better on him: at first Zhanna hadn't understood why he masked it so often, but she was coming to the conclusion he was only himself with a blade in his hand, and the rest of the time his focus on being Naridan simply got in the way.

Which didn't explain why he was acting so differently.

"What is problem?" she asked, gathering Thorn up. It was an instinctive action, but Daimon focused on the little dragon as it scrabbled around until it was perched on her shoulder.

"What witchcraft is this, that you can bend a dragon to your will?" Daimon demanded. He seemed more concerned than angry... but then again, Naridans were hard to read.

"What are words?" she asked. How useful it would be if he could actually speak a proper language!

"The dragon!" Daimon said, more sharply than usual. He was at the foot of the stairs up to her door now, and placed one foot on the lowest step. "How do you make it do what you want?'

"Am be mother," Zhanna explained. It was a poor way of putting it, since she didn't think she was incredibly overbearing in one breath yet unreasonably demanding with the next like her own mother, but such were the limitations of language. "Give food, give love." Did the Naridans not take such care of their animals?

Daimon opened his mouth, but was interrupted by angry shouting from behind him. A group of his servants ran into view: Rotel and Menaken, the guards, with their spears; Gador the smith, holding one of his huge hammers; Duranen with his cudgel; and, bringing up the rear, Tavi, with the same broad-bladed spear he'd seized when the rattletails had attacked Tirtza.

They were all armed, all heading straight for her at speed, and at least some of these Naridans weren't hard to read at all.

"There she is!" Duranen bellowed. The huntmaster's eyes were fixed on her, and his lips drawn back from his teeth. "Don't let her speak, lord! Kill the savage now!"

Kill me?! If Zhanna had her axe and shield to hand she'd have given Duranen a quick and painful lesson, but she was unarmed, and unprepared for such aggression. She shot a glance at the back of Daimon's head, willing him to order his servant to stand down, but it was Gador the smith who grabbed hold of Duranen's shoulder and dragged him to a halt just short of where Daimon stood.

"Unhand s'man, coward!" the huntmaster yelled, trying to shake himself free.

"Are you mad?" Gador shouted back. "If we kill the girl, the Raiders kill us all!"

Why is that the only reason not to kill me? Zhanna thought fervently. *But yes, listen to him!*

"She's a witch!" Rotel protested.

"Tirtza saying so doesn't make it true!" Tavi argued.

"Duranen!" Daimon said loudly, and his group of servants quietened somewhat. "The young rattletail comes at the girl's command and sits happily upon her shoulder. Is this natural?"

"Not in any way, lord," Duranen replied instantly. "They're beasts, no two ways about it."

"Or perhaps," Tavi said, slowly and deliberately, "you don't know as much about rattletails as you think."

Gador, Rotel, and Menaken all went very quiet, and surreptitiously moved apart so that none of them stood between huntmaster and stablemaster. Zhanna had thought the two men didn't like each other, and this certainly had the feeling of an old enmity abruptly voiced.

"Stick to your grass-eaters, Tavi," Duranen sneered, staring Father Krayk's own hail up at Zhanna. "Lord, the girl must be a witch. Your man should have known it when his rattletails ignored her, and went after Tirtza!"

"You told us you let them out because you thought the girl was familiar with them!" Tavi said, dragging his counterpart around to face him. "S'man took you for a fool, but he sees now that you're a liar as well!"

Duranen shoved the shorter man away and hefted his cudgel, which Zhanna thought was foolish when facing someone with a spear. "Go kiss the Mountain, Tavi! Why do you love the savage so much, anyway? Have you been sneaking her into your bed at night?"

Tavi punched him in the face.

Duranen went down hard, but scrambled back to his feet and would likely have launched himself at Tavi had Rotel and Menaken not seized him to hold him back, while Gador put a meaty arm across the chest of Tavi to prevent the stablemaster following up on his first blow.

"Enough of this!" Daimon bellowed. "Duranen! You loosed the rattletails to hurt her? You lied to your lord?!"

Zhanna tried not to smirk. She'd suspected Duranen's bad intentions, and it was immensely gratifying to see him confronted by his chief over it. Besides which, hadn't he realised that she and Daimon had been becoming... well, not friends, perhaps, but sort of pre-friends?

"She's a witch, lord!" Duranen protested, but Daimon raised his tip of his blade to the huntmaster's throat.

"A witch, based on the fears of a serving girl terrified of

rattletails as a result of your malice, and on the word of a man who lies to his lord!" Daimon spat. "How can this lord trust what you say? Perhaps Tavi has the truth of it; perhaps the girl is no witch, and you simply do not understand the beasts this lord's father entrusted you with!" He pressed harder with his blade, until Zhanna could see Duranen's skin dimpling under the pressure.

"Perhaps this lord should test your knowledge by locking you in a pen with your rattletails, without your cudgel," Daimon bit out. "Would that be fitting?"

Duranen said nothing, but his eyes were wide. Rotel and Menaken looked distinctly uncomfortable as well, but they didn't let go of him.

"Find Kelarahel," Daimon instructed the guards, after a few more tense moments. "Duranen goes into the cells until this lord says otherwise."

"She's a witch, lord," Duranen warned, with a venomous glance at Zhanna as Daimon sheathed his blade. "Beware she doesn't enchant you!"

"Take him!" Daimon spat, and Rotel and Menaken hauled Duranen away. Zhanna was almost disappointed: she'd have dearly loved to punch him herself before that happened.

"Lord," Tavi spoke up. "Perhaps your man can help."

Daimon glanced at Zhanna, as if to make sure she was still there, then looked at the stablemaster. "How?"

"Perhaps the girl has hit on something by accident," Tavi said. "Your man knows dragons, at least the grass-eaters. There's tricks to them, no doubt. If he talks to her, and can manage what she's done with a different rattletail hatchling… well, it can't be witchcraft then, can it?"

That was the second time someone had used that word about her. "What is witchcraft?" she demanded, as Thorn prowled from her right shoulder to her left.

A grimace crossed Daimon's face. "Do you know what we mean by magic?"

"Maybe." She looked at Tavi. "You have dragon magic, yes?"

"Of a sort," Tavi grunted.

"Witchcraft is magic used to do things that should not be done," Daimon said. "The penalty for it is death." Zhanna wanted to ask by whose reckoning something shouldn't be done, but held her tongue. In this land, at this time, it would undoubtedly be Daimon's. She also knew that if he truly felt she needed to die then he would kill her, and take the consequences. Happily, he wasn't swayed by the foolish notions of a hateful servant.

"Happy dragon, friendly dragon," she said instead. "Why should not be done?"

Daimon looked between her and Tavi, then sighed. "Very well, Tavi. But she doesn't see the hatchling you raise. You do that yourself. If you can do as she has, with her having had no opportunity to enchant the beast, then yes, she is no witch."

Tavi bowed. "It shall be done, lord.'

"And to make sure she does not enchant you," Daimon added, casting one more glance at Zhanna. "... this lord will join you."

TILA

MARIN OF IDRAMAR was, it turned out, a petty thief, although he insisted he was in fact an exceptional one. Tila had her doubts, given his previous remark of having spent time inside East Harbour's cells, since surely an exceptional thief wouldn't have been caught. She never voiced them, however, because he not only managed to procure a rowboat by dint of quickly picking a crude lock on a boathouse, but also turned out to be a fair hand with oars. As a result, after quite a tense time hiding under a tarred canvas in the bow to avoid notice, Tila felt a stronger swell beneath the hull suggesting they'd reached the harbour itself. It was reassuring in one way, but alarming in another.

"Are you sure he knows what he's doing?" she hissed at Blacksword. It was pitch dark beneath the canvas and she couldn't see the disgraced sar, despite him being merely the width of Barach's chest away.

"Marin can handle a boat, and knows what a three-masted Naridan merchantman looks like," Blacksword said reassuringly. "He was born and raised around the Idramar docks. He'll find your ship, have no worries."

Tila had been told many times not to worry, usually by men, and it rarely achieved the desired effect. However, as they drifted through the noises of a harbour where activity never truly ceased, even at night, she heard Marin raise his thin voice in a hoarse hail.

"Ho, *Light of Fortune*!"

Tila winced, imagining heads turning along the wharf. What if the Watch was there even now, looking for Naridans? She just had to hope Marin was being cautious.

A voice called from above. "Who're you?"

"S'man has a couple of your passengers," Marin replied. "Would you care to drop a rope?"

"No, s'man bloody wouldn't! Piss off!"

Tila sighed and fought her way out from under the canvas, then stood up cautiously. Marin had brought them up close astern of the *Light of Fortune*, and a sailor was leaning over the rail above with lantern held high. She blinked up into its light.

"Do you recognise this lady?"

"Lady Livnya," the sailor said, his tone immediately more respectful. "Should s'man rouse others to set down the gangplank?"

"No need," Tila told him. She didn't want to set foot on the dock again, just in case the Watch were lurking. "Drop a rope. We will climb."

"Aye, lady." The sailor disappeared, along with his light.

"Did he call you Livnya?" Marin asked.

"Mar," Blacksword said warningly, as he too pushed the canvas aside. "She said introductions could wait."

"But s'man's heard of a—"

"*Mar!*"

Tila grimaced. Of course an Idramese thief would have heard of Livnya the Knife. She simply hoped she hadn't made an example of one of his friends or relatives at some point.

"Heads up, in the boat!"

A rope ladder unrolled from above, splashing into the waves. Livnya eased past Barach and Blacksword, and began to climb. Her dress was still wet, and fearsomely heavy, but she wasn't willing to remain in the rowboat for a moment longer than she had to. At least the cloying warmth of Grand Mahewa meant her skin was merely clammy, instead of being chilled to the bone as would have happened if she'd taken the same soaking in Idramar.

"Lady," the sailor said quietly, helping her over the ship's rail. "The other two in the boat. Are you intending them to board?"

Tila hesitated. Barach was climbing next. It would be easy to prevent Marin and Blacksword from coming aboard, and thereby neatly end any form of association with them. She doubted Captain Kemanyel would be overly fond of two more landsmen aboard his ship, for all that he'd almost certainly do as she ordered.

On the other hand, it would have been much harder to evade the Watch without the pair's help, unorthodox though that had been. Tila had also built Livnya's reputation through rewarding loyalty and punishing treachery, so it went against the grain to break a deal.

Finally, and perhaps most compelling, Marin and Blacksword might subsequently get picked up by the Watch while the *Light of Fortune* was still in port. They'd almost certainly try to buy some clemency by offering her whereabouts, and would also have a strong suspicion as to her real identity... or one of them, at least.

"Yes," she replied to the sailor, as Barach began to climb. "This lady will speak to the captain."

Captain Kemanyel was out of his bunk not long after, and scowled at the two newcomers with all the menace of a southern gale as he regarded them by lantern light in the ship's mess.

"You caused trouble with the Watch?" he growled.

"The Watch caused the trouble," Tila told him. "These two helped us get away."

Kemanyel looked at her. "Was there fighting involved?"

"If you could call it that," Blacksword sniffed.

The captain rounded on him with a snarl. "Tits of the Sea Dragon, boy! The Watch don't take kindly to anyone drawing blades on them, let alone foreigners!"

"Which is why we're all below decks, so we aren't seen," Tila cut in, before Blacksword could object too strenuously to being called "boy" by a man only a few years his senior. A captain was the lord of his own ship, but a sar, even a disgraced sar, tended to have a low tolerance for being spoken down to by anyone save the nobility.

Kemanyel glowered at her in turn. "Lady, this captain does you every honour, but you may've brought great trouble down on all our heads. This captain has yet to take on a cargo, for he didn't know when he'd be sailing, yet now every moment we stay tied up risks the Watch deciding to search ships!"

"Put to sea as soon as you can," Tila told him. "Take a cargo at the next port, or the one after. This lady will see you fairly compensated for any loss."

Kemanyel scratched at his cheek. "See, that's the thing, lady. It wasn't a good cargo we brought here, merely the best we could find at short notice when you said you needed to travel to East Harbour. This captain's already down on money. And he honours and respects you," he added, with a glance at Barach, "but that only goes so far. To put to sea now, with no cargo... the crew won't like it. A captain only has the respect of his crew so long as they can see a benefit in what he's doing."

"You're saying they'll mutiny?" Tila asked, alarmed.

"Unlikely," Kemanyel said, matter-of-factly. "More likely they'd just leave, to a ship that offered better prospects. Then we'd have no crew, and my *Light of Fortune* would be of no use to you."

Tila recognised a negotiation when she heard one, and was in no mood for it. She wanted to get back to her cabin—technically the captain's cabin, but she'd piss on her ancestors before she gave it up—get dry, and get changed.

"A bonus, then," she said. "Two silvers for every crew member and a gold piece for the captain, bosun and first mate, when we reach the next port. From this lady's pocket."

Kemanyel raised his eyebrows, but nodded. "Aye, that'd do it. Little wins a sailor's respect like coin in their hand."

"Then we're done here," Tila said with finality. By the spirits, but she was tired! "Put to sea when the tide allows."

"One thing more, lady," Kemanyel said. "These two men, who tangle with the East Harbour Watch: who are they? It's a foolish captain who takes on passengers without knowing their names."

Tila folded her arms and looked around. "Well?"

"S'man is Marin of Idramar," Marin said, bowing to Kemanyel. "Perhaps you know his arse of a cousin, Sarvon, who works on the Idramar docks?"

"The Wine-Nose?" Kemanyel snorted. "Aye, this captain knows him, more's the pity."

"Which is why s'man always states his opinion of his cousin before naming him, especially to sailors," Marin replied with a smile. "He takes no pleasure in sharing blood with Sarvon, but that's who he is."

Kemanyel grunted, and turned his attention to Blacksword. "And you?"

"This sar is Marin's husband, and a member of the Brotherhood," Blacksword said, holding up his right hand so the mercenary tattoo on the back was clearly visible. "He was Alazar of White Hill, but these days goes by Alazar Blade, or Alazar Blacksword."

Tila's mouth went dry. "This lady will leave you to your discussions," she said, leaving the mess for her cabin. Once inside she shut the door and sat on the bunk in the dark, heedless for the moment of the wet clothes still sticking to her skin.

Alazar of White Hill. She'd thought "Sar Blacksword" had looked vaguely familiar, but she'd no idea he was still alive. Most of twenty years and an obscuring beard had combined to throw her recollection, and they'd never been close friends. Besides, there were plenty of disgraced sars around, making a living as best they could.

Alazar of White Hill. Her brother's first, and perhaps last, proper love.

The man whose cowardice had been responsible for her father's death.

SAANA

Tevyel had been as pompous and rude as Saana had feared, and she'd been able to tell that only his thane's orders and her own presence—which he clearly found quite intimidating—had kept him from turning Chara out of his house. This had worsened when Kerrti arrived, obviously Tjakorshi and obviously female. Had it not been for Henya, the whole thing might have gone to the depths. As it was, the girl had asked her father's permission to set Chara's leg. That allowed Tevyel to feel important by giving her instructions without actually lowering himself, as he saw it, to touching Chara.

Thankfully Henya seemed knowledgeable, and her discussions with Kerrti, through Saana, had shown similar understandings of how best to set broken bones. It hadn't been comfortable for Chara—by the Dark Father, that woman could scream—but Saana was confident her corpse-painter would be able to use her leg again in time.

As it turned out, bone-setting wasn't the only thing Naridans did well.

"Metal tools!" Ekham the shipwright said, with the air of a man who'd found a new god. "Metal tools, Saana! They may not be as sharp as blackstone, but by Father Krayk, they're durable. And the things the Flatlanders can do with them!"

He and Otzudh were working on the first fishing tsek of the new land. The old boats hadn't been big enough to make the ocean crossing and so had been left behind, to the distress of their owners. At the moment the clan fished from taughs and yolgus, which caused its own problems, since often two or more old fishing crews were forced to sail together, and didn't always see eye-to-eye.

"You've done fast work," Saana commented, looking at the wooden bones of the craft on the riverbank. "Clean lines, too."

"Metal tools," Ekham repeated. "We felled and split the wood in half the time. No stopping to change axes, no splintered blades." He gestured to the Naridan working alongside Otzudh. "Samul knows what he's about, no question. If I hadn't seen him work the wood myself, I wouldn't have believed one man could do it so fast."

Saana nodded. She'd seen the Naridan in the town, but hadn't yet spoken to him. He was currently chiselling the end of a length of wood into a rounded shape.

"Thank you for working with them," she said in his language. "Our ships mean a lot to us."

"S'man likes a new challenge," Samul replied, looking up with a smile. "And he likes the look of what they offered for his work." He reached into the pouch on his belt and pulled out a couple of small, red-orange stones that almost seemed to glow.

"Fire gems," Saana said, nodding. They were beautiful, rare on Tjakorsha and, so far as the traders could tell, not found anywhere else at all. Some places viewed them merely as pretty curios, while in other lands they were highly prized. Naridans seemed to haul closer to the latter, judging by her clan's bartering so far.

"A question," Samul said, as he cut away more wood. "With gems like this, you could trade well. Why come and take what we had by force?"

There was a sour taste in Saana's mouth. Samul made the final strike with his hammer and the segment of wood dropped away. He looked up at her.

She sighed, and squatted down to bring her eyes onto a level with his.

"This man does not know," she said honestly, and saw the flicker of surprise in his expression. "When this man's father's father's father came here, they did not trade. They attacked. After they did that, why would you trade with them? But why did they attack the first time? This man does not know. And so we have done since, because it is what we have always done." She reached up and touched the dark line on her forehead. "This man came here when she was a child. She fought, and so she was a child no more. But why fight here? Because that is what the chief said."

"And now... you are chief?" Samul asked. He was holding his chisel ready, but did not strike it.

"Yes," Saana agreed. "And now the chief says different."

Samul held her gaze for a moment, then nodded. "S'man is glad."

He turned his attention back to the wood, and the tension in Saana's chest eased a little. Black Kal had been a strong chief, but violent. His hair had been darker than Father Krayk's own storm clouds, and he'd taken such pleasure in destruction that he'd seemed kin to them. The clan had mourned his passing, a hero's death in battle against the Quiet Shore, but most had mourned the loss of his reputation, and the fear his name had struck in others' hearts, rather than the man himself. The time had seemed ripe for a change of tack, although many had been astonished when the witches named Saana Sattistutar as the next chief.

It was still hard to believe her clan had agreed to uproot themselves at her command and come over the sea, but the threat of The Golden had been enough to convince most that she had the right of it. Saana might have got a warmer welcome for her people in a different land, but her clan didn't know those routes so well. Most importantly, the eastern clans The Golden had conquered first didn't know about Narida.

Besides, sailing anywhere other than west would have meant taking her entire clan into seas now controlled by the draug and its vassals, just after Long Night when the Tjakorshi were starting to put to sea again. The thought of The Golden's war fleet hunting them down sent shivers right through her, even now.

"Chief?"

Ekham caught at her sleeve, and she turned and saw a squabble at the town wall, where the largest gap was. Naridan and Tjakorshi voices shouted angrily, and Saana cursed under her breath.

"My daughter's locked up in someone else's house, and still I have to look after children," she growled. She set off through the knee-high tussock grass as fast as she could, with both shipwrights and Samul behind her.

As fast as she could wasn't fast enough: she was still twenty ells away when the first punch was thrown. It was Nasjuk Jelemaszhin, one of the Hornsounder's grandsons, and his blow sent the Naridan facing him sprawling into the grass and mud.

The small knot of Naridans and Tjakorshi who'd been working to repair the town wall exploded into action as soon as Nasjuk's punch landed. Some Naridans grabbed their tools as weapons, others attempted to restrain them. Some Tjakorshi moved up alongside Nasjuk, one or two tried to hold the others back.

Saana arrived full pelt into the middle, just as the man Nasjuk had struck was scrambling back to his feet.

"What in the name of the Dark Father are you doing?!" she bellowed at Nasjuk. He was big, near as big as Tsennan Longjaw, and a few years older. Behind him as always lurked Andal the Clubfoot, nicknamed "Nasjuk's Shadow" for how close he always stuck to his older brother.

"These storm-cursed Flatlanders think they can talk down to us!" Nasjuk spat, pointing over her shoulder at the Naridans. "They need to be reminded who we are!"

"Talk down to you?" Saana laughed in his face. "You can't even speak their tongue, and they can't speak ours!"

"I don't need to understand a man's words to hear his voice and see his eyes!" Nasjuk retorted. "We never should have stowed our axes!"

There was a rumble of agreement, and Saana's gut tightened. "Are you so eager to die?" she demanded scornfully. "You could have stayed in Koszal to welcome The Golden, if that was your wish."

A flicker of fear passed over Nasjuk's face, but it smoothed out within a moment. "The Flatlanders aren't draugs," he said. "We're here, why shouldn't we live like Father Krayk's chosen, instead of licking the feet of these arrogant little shits?"

Father Krayk's chosen. Those were Black Kal's words. Which wasn't surprising, given Black Kal had been Nasjuk's uncle, having married Khanda, another of Tsolga Hornsounder's daughters.

"Your uncle got a lot of good people killed trying to prove we were Father Krayk's chosen," Saana said warningly. She spread her arms, encompassing them all. "The Dark Father doesn't protect anyone, Nasjuk."

"My uncle was a better chief than you'll ever be," Nasjuk sneered. "And what are you going to do about that, now Ristjaan's not here to back you up?"

Fire flashed up in Saana's chest, hot and quick, but Nasjuk seemed to either not notice or not care how her face had shifted, or that his fellows on either side had pulled back half a step at his words. Instead, he stepped forward and shoved her hard in the chest.

Under normal circumstances, Saana would have stood back and let others deal with him, but these weren't normal circumstances. She was angry, she was frustrated, Nasjuk's callous words had relit the fire of her grief over Ristjaan, and right at that moment she wasn't totally sure anyone else *would* deal with him. She snarled and shoved him back, nearly sending him into his brother.

Nasjuk swung a punch at her head.

Saana had only ever gone raiding once, but that didn't mean she didn't know how to fight. Uzhan had never taught her much about using his sword, but he'd done well at the Clanmoot wrestling for a couple of years. Saana blocked Nasjuk's punch with her left arm, then held onto him, stepped into him and shifted her hips to dump him over her shoulder and onto his back. He landed hard enough to knock the wind from his lungs, and Saana put one boot on his throat, none too lightly. He grabbed at her foot with his left hand, but she was holding onto his other arm with both hands, and he couldn't shift her off him.

"Be glad I'm not your uncle," she spat down at him. "He'd have opened your throat for that." She cast a glance over her shoulder to check on Andal, but Nasjuk's Shadow hadn't moved, his dark eyes fixed on her, yet showing no sign of coming to his brother's aid.

"If anyone wants to talk to me about the decisions I make as chief, my door is open," she declared loudly. "But if you swing for me, I'll put you on your fucking back. Is that understood?" There was a general mutter of assent from faces turned aside or downwards, not looking at her directly, and certainly not looking at Nasjuk.

She was about to get off his throat and speak with the angry-looking Black Keep folk, who had at least not piled in on Nasjuk when he was down, when a voice barked an instruction in Naridan and they shifted aside to let four men through. All were carrying heavy staves, and Saana recognised Kelarahel.

"Reeve," she greeted him, as she'd heard Daimon do.

Kelarahel gave her a stiff nod in reply, but didn't speak a greeting. Saana wasn't sure if that was because he actively disliked her, or simply wasn't certain how to address her.

"We heard shouting," the reeve said, looking down at Nasjuk, then at the faces around him. "Is all well?"

"Nasjuk here struck that man," Saana replied in Naridan, gesturing to the Black Keep labourer whose face was already starting to darken and swell. She'd have preferred to handle this herself, but perhaps that wasn't the best way. "You keep your lord's laws. What is the penalty?"

"He struck first?" Kelarahel asked.

"This man saw him," Saana replied.

The reeve worked his jaw, then spat. "A night in the cells, with no food."

Saana fixed him with a stare. "And would it be the same for Naridan who struck Brown Eagle?"

"As the thane commands," Kelarahel replied, which wasn't exactly the response Saana had hoped for, but possibly better than she was expecting. She finally took her foot off Nasjuk's throat and hauled him, wheezing, to his feet.

"Get walking," she told him in Tjakorshi, shoving him in the direction of the reevesmen. "You take a house and land in these people's town, then punch one of them in the face? You sleep in one of their cages tonight."

"You'll make us into the Flatlander's slaves," Nasjuk rasped. He glared at her as he rubbed his throat, but didn't swing for her again. "You shame the whole clan!"

"You want to talk about shame?" Saana snapped at him. "Once you're in their cage, I'm going to go get your grandmother, so she can come and talk to you about that."

Nasjuk visibly paled. He didn't have to ask which one: both his grandmothers were still living, but only Tsolga Hornsounder would be used as a threat. Saana might be chief of the Brown Eagles, but her authority over the clan was as nothing compared to Tsolga's over her relations, whether by blood or marriage.

"Let's go," Saana told him, pointing. She eyed Kelarahel and his men. "I'll come with you. Just to make sure they don't think they need to use their sticks." The last thing anyone needed was for four Naridans to start beating one of her clan, no matter who would have been at fault.

The cells were in the centre of the town, between the stand of pine trees the Naridans tapped for resin, and the sweetleafs from which they collected sugary sap. Nasjuk did his best to swagger there, as though the reeve and his men were his own Scarred, but he was fooling no one. He cast a dark glance at Saana when they reached the cells but clearly had no taste for risking the reevemen's staves, for he slouched inside readily enough.

"Well," a voice said from the next cell. "If it isn't the witch's mother."

Saana looked around to see a Naridan peering out at her through the barred metal door. The top of his head was shiny and bald, but the sides and back were covered with dark, grey-shot stubble of the same length as that dusting his cheeks and chin. She recognised him, after a moment: one of Daimon's servants. What was he doing in here? And more to the point...

"This man's daughter is no witch," Saana told him coldly, which was true either by her definition or his. The Naridan just snorted.

"If she *is* a witch," Saana continued, putting her hands on her hips, "why isn't she in there instead of you?"

"Your time will come, savage," the Naridan retorted. "And so will hers."

"Threaten this man's daughter, and you'd best hope Lord Blackcreek always keeps a metal door between you and her," Saana told him, as calmly as she could manage. She looked him up and down, and sneered deliberately. "Not that her daughter would need any help with you."

"That's enough out of you, Duranen!" Kelarahel barked when the bald man opened his mouth to respond. Duranen eyed the reeve balefully, but turned and slunk to the back of his cell.

"Why does he speak of this man's daughter so?" Saana asked Kelarahel in a low voice, turning away from Duranen. The reeve's face smoothed into typical Naridan inscrutability.

"You'd have to ask His Lordship about that."

JEYA

JEYA HAD GONE back to the mansion by the canal many times, always under the cover of darkness. The big paddleleaf allowed hér access into Galem's back garden, and there shé'd wait. Hè couldn't always leave the house, but when hè got away they'd sneak over the garden wall and away down the towpath, giggling conspiratorially. They would share kisses next to the water, and eat dates Jeya had bought from Abbaz or sweetmeats Galem brought with hìm, and they would talk.

It was a window onto another world for both of them.

Galem's family had money. Hè didn't know how much money, exactly, but this was because he didn't have to pay attention to details. To someone who had to count coppers from day to day, and some days simply had none to count, it was a bizarre notion. Jeya supposed that shé'd known, but until now hadn't properly understood, that some people simply *had* money. It wasn't in a transient state for them, it wasn't that they'd done something to get a lot which they then gradually spent. Such movement of money happened, of course, as they bought food and so forth, but they still had money afterwards.

Galem gave hér money to get dates from Abbaz. It was on the understanding that shé'd share them with hìm, but there was nothing to stop hér just taking the money and never going back. Jeya had taken it as a staggering gesture of trust until shé'd realised that to hìm, it would be the equivalent of losing one fish from a bulging net; hè literally wasn't concerned by it.

Galem had been at first intrigued, and then horrified, by hér stories of life on the streets. Hè'd been appalled to learn shé had no home of hér own, and had winced at hér descriptions of the fates that befell some of the other children shé'd known when younger. Hè'd also laughed at hér tales of outwitting the merchants on the market to steal food, and gasped at the desperate flights from the Watch that sometimes followed.

"And yòu?" shé asked. "What's it like, being rich?"

Hè thought a while before answering. "Lonely."

"Lonely?" Jeya drew hér knees up under hér chin, squeezing the grass between hér toes. "Í thought rich people did nothing except go to balls, and..." Shé paused, wracking hér mind for other possibilities, but shé had nothing to go on except children's tales. "And things like that," shé finished weakly.

"My family has few close friends," Galem said, looking down at the ground. "My parents keep themselves to themselves. They don't like mè spending too much time with others my own age. Or anyone, for that matter. Ì have tutors and instructors they've picked. The Festival of the Crossing was one of the few times in the year Ì was allowed to wander as Ì pleased."

Jeya frowned. "Wait, 'was'?"

Galem's lips quirked in the moonlight. "Well, the last time Ì went, a beautiful thief got close enough to steal my purse. My guards told my parents, and my mōther was furious. My guards received three lashes each. Ì don't think Ì'll have such freedoms again for some time."

Jeya's cheeks heated at "beautiful", but the rest of hìs words stole the quiver of delight from hér chest. Shé put hér hand over hér mouth, aghast. "By the Hundred! Galem, Í'm so sorry!"

Hè shrugged. "Ì feel for my guards. The fact Ì was safe meant nothing to my mōther, it was that had yóu carried a weapon, yóu *could* have hurt mè. As though my guards should have cleared a space around mè, letting no one enter." Hè snorted, then turned hìs face towards her, hìs eyes sparkling in the silver light from above, and a smile on his lìps. "Ì hope yóu do not mean mè harm?"

Jeya grinned at hìm. "Ì'm sorry, noble Galem, but Ì lured yòu to this canal with malice in my heart."

"Then Ì must defend myself!" Galem whispered, and leaned forward. Jeya laughed as shé kissed hìm, felt hìs lips move into a smile as they met hérs, and then hè was gently bearing hér backwards to the ground. Hìs hair hung down like dark curtains on either side of hér face, blocking out the sky, the stars, the moons and the trees, until there was nothing in the world but the heat of hìs breath, the play of hìs mouth on hérs, and the tingles where their bodies touched through their clothes. Shé reached up and around hìm, felt the lean muscles of hìs shoulder beneath hér fingers as shé pulled hìm closer in towards hér, then drew hér hand down towards hìs waist. Shé found the hem of hìs maijhi and slid hér fingers under it, encountering the warm skin of hìs waist, then began to trail hér fingers back up again, over hìs ribs and—

Galem pulled away, breathing heavily. Jeya withdrew hér hand instantly, anxiety tightening hér chest. Had shé gone too far? In truth, shé'd barely gone anywhere, but Galem's life had been very different to hér own, and perhaps the rich did such things differently...

"Ì... must not spend too long out here," Galem said, hìs voice suddenly thick. "If it's discovered Ì'm not in my room then there'll be no possibility of being able to meet yòu like this again. And believe me, Jeya, Ì dearly wish to go on meeting yóu."

Jeya sat up and ran fingers through hér hair, in case shé'd got leaves in it. Hér own breath was coming rather quickly. "Well," she managed after a moment. "Ì suppose that makes sense..." In fact, shé wanted nothing more than to tackle Galem to the ground and carry on kissing hìm, but hè clearly wasn't comfortable with that, at least not now.

Hè reached out to hér, and pulled them both up to their feet.

"May Í walk back with yòu?" shé asked. Shé held hér breath. Had hè suddenly decided hè wanted nothing more to do with hér?

"Of course," Galem said with a smile, and took hér arm.

"Galem," Jeya said, as they hurried back along the towpath, "does yòur family honour Jakahama, if yòu were allowed out for the Festival of the Crossing?"

"Not as such," Galem said. "But it's an important festival. Ì suppose we honour hēr, but do not *worship* hēr."

"So yòu worship Nari?" Jeya asked. Nari had hìs place at the Court of the Deities, as one of the great gods of the world, and hìs devotees had set up shrines to hìm throughout the Islands. Jeya had never quite understood Nari, since the Naridans seemed quite certain that although hè was a god hè had also definitely been mortal, born of mortal parents, but shé'd long ago decided that was their business.

Galem grimaced. "In a manner of speaking. It's more complicated than—"

Jeya clapped hér hand over Galem's mouth to silence hìm in mid-sentence. Further along the gentle curve of the towpath was a group of half-a-dozen figures dressed in dark, hooded clothes. Few people trod this path at night, and Jeya immediately recognised this group had no right to be here. They didn't walk openly, talking and laughing amongst themselves, easy and relaxed. They slunk like alley dogs, quiet, low, and purposeful. Shé knew that way of moving; shé'd used it hérself a time or two.

"*We go back,*" shé breathed into Galem's ear. The low branches of the paddleleaf lay between them and the approaching group, but the others would reach it first, in fact nearly had already. Galem's garden could offer no refuge. This group might have no interest in two young people out for a walk in the moonlight, but Jeya hadn't lived this long by taking such chances.

Galem nodded, hìs body stiff, and Jeya realised this might be the first time in his life hé'd had even a notion hé might be in danger. Shé almost laughed. They were still far enough away from the other group to have a comfortable lead if they needed to run; this barely even counted as danger, to hér.

Then, to her surprise and mounting horror, the group jumped up and grabbed the low branches of the paddleleaf one after another, swinging themselves over the wall and into the garden. Within a few moments, all six had disappeared from view.

"What the—no!" Galem muttered beside hér, and then hè was running down the path, *towards* the paddleleaf. Jeya swore under hér breath and took off after hìm, wondering what in the name of the Hundred was going on. Was this Damau's doing? Had they told someone else about Jeya's rich mark; someone who'd put a crew together to rob the place? Shé focused on Galem's back, trying to catch up. Hìs house had guards, after all, who would undoubtedly stop these thieves—

And then they'll realise hè was out on the towpath when these people were prowling, and yóu'll never see hìm again. Hìs parents will lock hìm away out of fear.

Jeya cursed louder and ran faster. Perhaps shé might know one or two of them! If shé got to them in time, explained there were guards, begged them not to go ahead with it...

It was a futile hope. Shé and Galem had always been too far away. What would have kept them safe meant there was no way for hér to reach the would-be thieves in time. Nevertheless, shé and Galem jumped for the paddleleaf's branches and pulled themselves up into the tree.

The six were already halfway to the house, running low and fast. Something was wrong: they weren't going in slow and cautious, checking for guards or likely entry points. They were moving too quickly and carelessly to be bothered if they were seen or not.

A variety of blades emerged, glinting in the moonlight.

DAIMON

"You thought this man's daughter was a *what?*"

"A witch," Daimon told Sattistutar levelly. "She appeared to have an unnatural bond with her animal."

"The dragon you gave her?" Saana demanded. They were in Daimon's study, and if their conversation was not quite as hostile as the last one in this place, it still was not a convivial affair.

"The same," Daimon said, nodding. Saana folded her hefty arms and glowered at him.

"What did you do?"

This lord drew his blade on your unarmed daughter, ready to cut her down. Daimon swallowed his honesty and tried something more diplomatic. "This lord believed Zhanna and her dragon had terrorised his serving girl. It turned out the girl was terrified, but mainly because she was still scared after being attacked by adult rattletails. When she saw Zhanna's dragon acting unnaturally, the fear consumed her. This lord will admit, it was a strange sight. Rattletails are hunting beasts, responding only to dominance."

"Zhanna always did have a way with crow chicks," Saana muttered, although in Naridan, so Daimon presumed he was supposed to hear and understand. "You now think she is not a witch?"

"Let this lord show you something," Daimon told her. He bent down, and lifted the lid off a wooden box sitting next to the grate. Saana had looked at it curiously when she'd entered, but hadn't commented on it. Now she watched him reach into the straw inside, and lift out his own rattletail hatchling.

The little dragon was younger than Zhanna's—another early clutch, but not so early—but it looked up at him when he made the strange, throbbing, cooing noise that Zhanna had taught Tavi and him. It had been a surreal experience, but Zhanna insisted it was the noise she made to crow chicks and her own rattletail. Sure enough, a few days of cooing and delicately feeding the rattletail meat morsels, and both his and Tavi's hatchlings were quite docile and biddable.

"If this is witchcraft," Daimon said softly, stroking the rattletail's head with his forefinger, "this lord cannot see the harm. Tavi says it is similar to the charms he uses with his charges. Certain noises, certain gestures, certain incantations... perhaps, with your daughter's help, we have rediscovered a piece of the old dragon lore that once bound us to these beasts." He laughed, amused once again at the unlikeliness of it. "Tavi is teaching her what he knows of dragons, since after all, dragons are not the same as crows. It is a strange partnership, to be sure."

Saana snorted. "So it is witch until you can see the use for it?"

Daimon exhaled, his good mood departing with the breath. He replaced the rattletail in its makeshift nest and closed the lid again, then rose back to his feet to face Saana. He'd debated with himself whether to tell her this at all, but could no longer see an option.

"The woman who died," he began. "She whose death meant Chara went into the forest, as she'd used up her supply of blue flowers."

"Brida," Saana supplied, frowning.

Daimon took a deep breath. "This lord believes she was cursed."

Saana's frown deepened. "Cursed?"

"Magic," Daimon explained. "Witchcraft."

Saana's face set into something dangerous. "Why do you say this?"

"Our priest, Aftak, found a stone buried on the south side of Brida's house," Daimon explained heavily. "It was carved with what he and Darel agreed were symbols of witchcraft. Darel would not lie. Not on such a thing as this."

"Why did you not speak of this sooner?" Saana demanded, colour starting to rise into her pale cheeks.

"This lord hoped to find the witch and execute her before she even knew we were looking for her," Daimon explained. He had to admit that in Sattistutar's place, he wasn't sure he'd be happy with that explanation. "If all of your people started digging on the south side of their houses in case she had cursed them too, she would surely realise." He spread his hands, fighting the burning sense of frustration and powerlessness in his gut. "Kelarahel has found nothing. But what can this lord do? If his people learned a witch had caused one of your clan to sicken and die, would they seek out the witch? Or would they shelter her?"

Saana looked like she'd been slapped. "This man thought your people hated witches."

"We do hate witches," Daimon said glumly. "But we also hate Raiders, and Raiders are here. Some of this lord's people do not resent your presence, but some still mutter against you. If they saw a way to be rid of you, without having to take up arms themselves..." He shook his head. It felt like a betrayal of his people to utter such words, but if all lowborn could be trusted to behave honourably there would be no need for sars in the first place.

"This man's people are not all good-behaved, either," Saana admitted heavily. "Today Nasjuk struck one of yours. He believes we should not be peaceful, we should take as we want." She sighed. "He is a fool, and now in your cells, but Tjakorshi have a saying: what one fool says, ten others are thinking."

"That is a wise saying," Daimon agreed. "This man Nasjuk: you think the cells will make him wiser?"

"No," Saana snorted. "The Hornsounder yelling at him may. She is his grandmother," she elaborated, and Daimon winced. The old woman struck him as formidable, despite only having seen her in passing. While he sometimes lay awake at night dearly wishing he had an older relative to seek guidance from, he had to admit there was something gloriously freeing about not having someone looking over his shoulder, correcting him at every turn.

"We cannot rely on the Hornsounder to convince all your people," he told Saana. "And although Aftak seeks to ease the concerns of this lord's folk, not all will listen. Working together in the fields or on the wall can lead to as much ill feeling as good, this lord suspects. We need something else, something to bring our peoples together, so those who harbour such thoughts begin to lose them."

"This man agrees," Saana said slowly. "Do you know what?"

Daimon was struck once more by her size. She was of a height with him, and he was tall, but while he was slender Saana was broad, with a thick waist and wide hips. It wasn't just the bulk of her furs, either: he was sure that even out of them, she'd have the same aura of solid strength.

"Blackcreek?" Saana said, and he realised he'd stared a little too long without speaking.

"As it happens," he said, embarrassment giving way to inspiration, "this lord would speak to his steward first, but he may have had an idea."

SAANA

"CHARA STILL CANNOT recall what the man who directed her to the forest looked like?" Blackcreek asked. They were standing at the stronghouse gates, looking at the main square, where a crudely man-shaped effigy of branches and olds reeds was being raised. It was at least twice as tall as Saana, with two hornlike branches protruding from its head.

"She cannot," Saana replied. "It was raining, and she was so glad to receive an answer that she hurried on her way. Besides," she added, "she says you all look the same."

Blackcreek turned her towards her, brows lowered and mouth open to protest, and Saana bit down on her smile. "This man apologises. That was a poor joke." To change the subject, she gestured towards the preparations in the square. "What is this?"

"The Festival of Life," Blackcreek replied, after a pause that left Saana in little doubt he was not at all certain she'd been joking. "When we celebrate the life to come, and our hopes for a good growing season. The lowborn burn the Wooden Man"—he pointed at the shape of branches—"we eat and drink, there is the Great Game, and..." He trailed off, looking thoughtful.

"And?" Saana prompted him.

"And usually, we trade with the mountain folk," Daimon finished. "They bring pelts, and we trade them salt and fish oil.

But they have not come this year."

"Do they come every year?" Saana asked.

"Every year this lord has been alive," Daimon replied, nodding. "And before, too. This lord has asked: no one can remember a year when they did not come. It is troubling." He nodded towards a woman raising a length of wood into place. Saana had seen her before; she had different features to most other inhabitants of Black Keep, and wore distinctive jewellery of wooden beads. "Amonhuhe was once of their people, and she has spoken of her concern."

Saana digested this. What would have happened if these mountain folk had come to Black Keep and found the Brown Eagle clan? Would they have allied with the Naridans and taken up arms? Would they have had sufficient numbers to drive her people out? Had Blackcreek hoped for this? No, surely not, else why tell her now? They could just be late, after all.

"And what of this 'Great Game'?" she asked instead.

"Another amusement of the lowborn. Our hale menfolk divide into two teams, selected by a leader, and each team has three balls of cloth. They start at either end of the town, then compete to get all three balls into a barrel where the other team started from." He shook his head. "It would seem to favour the brutish, but the quick can be just as effective."

Saana looked at him in surprise. "Favour the brutish? They..." She didn't know the Naridan word for "wrestle", if they even had one, but it was the closest she could come. "They fight, but as friends?"

"Sometimes not so friendly," Daimon admitted. "They are not supposed to actually fight, but there are few rules as to how the ball can or cannot end up in the barrel. No weapons are allowed, of course, and if one man injures another to the point he cannot work a field then the man who caused the injury must do the work instead." He looked back at her. "Do you not have any such tradition?"

"We fight as friends, one against one," Saana told him. "Try to throw or trip. We have foot races. We see who can sail fastest." She looked at the square, trying to envisage all the men of Black Keep engaged in one mass brawl, and winced inwardly at the thought. And they called her people savages! "Nothing like… that."

Daimon nodded slowly.

"This lord spoke yesterday of an idea he'd had."

Saana eyed him with disbelief as understanding dawned. "You would pit our peoples against each other?"

"Against each other?" Daimon smiled and looked back at the square. "No. No, not at all."

IT WAS PAST midday, and the square was full. The Thane of Black Keep announced the leaders of the teams, and Daimon had called forth Yaro the fisherman, father of Faaz the stable boy, and Gador the smith. Saana appraised them. Yaro was leather-skinned and wiry, whereas Gador's shoulders and arms boasted hulking power. She knew which she'd back in a wrestling contest, but was equally sure which would win a foot race.

Daimon flipped a piece of wood charred at one end, which was the end that landed pointing at Yaro. The fisherman nodded and turned to the assembled crowd of Black Keep men.

"Samul!"

There was a general cheer, and Samul the carpenter pushed forward. He was near as tall as Daimon, and more heavily set. He stood next to Yaro, and the fisherman turned to Gador to invite him to make his pick.

Gador scratched his chin, as though thinking. Then he raised his voice into a bellow.

"*Tsennan!*"

There was a moment's shocked silence. Then Tsennan Jelemaszhin, known as Longjaw, seventeen summers old and probably the biggest of the Brown Eagle clan since the death of Ristjaan the Cleaver, walked to stand at Gador's side.

Shouting filled the air, and continued even when Daimon Blackcreek raised both his hands for silence. It wasn't until his expression darkened and he placed one hand on the grip of his longblade that the townsfolk quietened.

"Yaro," Blackcreek said, "you wish to object?"

"He's a Raider, lord!" the fisherman stammered. He sounded so outraged he could barely get his words out.

"Aye, he is." Gador looked up at Longjaw, who towered above him. "He's also the biggest here, and he's on s'man's team now!"

Yaro and Samul turned to Blackcreek, their expressions beseeching. Daimon shrugged.

"You may pick any of the Brown Eagle clan who will play for you, Yaro."

"Lord," Yaro bowed low. "With respect, you never said the Raiders were playing."

"You never asked," Daimon replied. "Gador did. Of course, this lord understands if you do not wish to pick them, and he will not make you do so."

Saana saw the fisherman's eyes flicker back and forth between his fellow countrymen and the clan. It didn't take a witch to work out that a team consisting only of Naridans would be significantly smaller than one containing Tjakorshi, both physically and in terms of sheer numbers. Which was, of course, exactly what Blackcreek had counted on. Saana had to give the boy his due, he knew his people. It seemed that winning Black Keep's "Great Game" was something to brag about all the way to the next festival, and the Naridans would use practically any trick they could get away with.

Yaro hurried over to her, with Samul in tow.

"You speak our tongue, yes?"

She nodded. "This man does."

Yaro licked his lips uncertainly. "If s'man picks your men, will you tell them what he needs them to do?"

Saana shrugged. "Your thane explained the rules to this man, and she has told her clan. They already know."

Yaro shook his head in irritation. "Yes, but s'man's going to need to tell his team what to do, *how* we're going to win. Will you tell them that?"

"No."

Yaro opened his mouth angrily.

"Unless you pick *this* man," Saana added, jabbing herself in the chest with her thumb. "Then your team is her team."

"Women can't play!" Samul objected from behind Yaro.

Saana drew herself up to her full height and looked him in the eye. "If enemies attack this town, Samul of Black Keep, this man will pick up her axe and fight them alongside you. She thinks she can put a ball in a barrel with you."

Samul and Yaro looked at each other, then turned away. She caught fragments of their muttered words to each other:

"... fucking Raiders..." ,

"... unnatural big, though..."

"... can't trust..."

"... been working with two of them, they seem sound..."

They appeared to come to a consensus. Yaro turned back to her and, with an expression of extreme apprehension, raised his hand to point at her.

"Chief Saana!"

Saana smiled as she walked with them to the centre of the square, and didn't bother to hide it from Daimon Blackcreek's disapproving expression. He wasn't the only one who'd had a plan for how this would go.

EVRAM

THE CALL OF silver trumpets sent Evram scrambling to his small window. After a lengthy interrogation by Sar Omet he'd been ensconced in an empty servant's chamber, where he'd been effectively held prisoner, albeit with adequate food, water, firewood, and fresh bedding. However, Evram had spent most of his life outdoors, and the sunshine from the narrow window had been just enough to remind him what he was no longer experiencing, somewhat akin to a drowning man trying to breathe through a half-blocked reed. The days had run past, almost blurring into one, and Evram had got used to the rhythm and sounds of Darkspur.

The trumpets were new.

He couldn't see much over the roofs, but could hear commotion and see townsfolk running out of their homes and into the street. Was something happening at the town gate? He stayed at the window, transfixed despite the awkward angle he had to crane at to see out properly, for the window was high, and Evram was not tall.

Time passed. The tendons in the backs of his legs began to burn, but Evram stayed where he was. He could see some sort of movement between the houses, but couldn't make out what was going on. There did seem to be a lot of people, though...

Then the first dragon stomped into view, and Evram's breath caught in his throat.

It was a huge beast, easily as large as the biggest of Lord Blackcreek's stable, its great brow horns banded with gold. Its plumage was a blue so deep it was nearly black, save where it caught the afternoon sun, and on its longer, brighter neck quills. The townsfolk scattered in front of it and bowed deeply as it approached: not the neck-and-shoulders bow of a lowborn to a sar, nor the waist-deep bow of a servant to their thane, but on one knee in the mud with their heads lowered. Evram didn't need to understand the language of the trumpets carried by the two heralds that trotted alongside the dragon, or be able to hear the words they shouted between their blasts of music. The bows told him everything.

The armoured man sitting atop the huge dragon, his face obscured by helmet and war mask, was High Marshal Kaldur Brightwater, Southern Marshal of Narida: the most powerful man south of the River Idra and, along with his fellow High Marshals, second only to the God-King Himself.

Brightwater's retinue was strung out behind him; perhaps twenty sars on dragons, and then rank upon rank of armsmen tramping in their wake. Evram watched the column approach the guardhouse at the base of the rock until the narrow window hid them from his vision. He had no idea how many men a High Marshal would usually travel with, but this was surely a small army.

A scraping noise behind him alerted him to the bar across the outside of his door being drawn back, and the door swung open to reveal two guards in Darkspur livery. The taller, who'd most often been the one bringing Evram his meals, jerked his head.

"His Lordship wants to see you."

Evram nodded, and hobbled across the stone floor. His blisters had healed, more or less, but there was a twinge in his left hip that hadn't existed before his journey here. His body was getting old, he reflected ruefully.

"You said His Lordship wants to see this man," he said as they walked down the windowless, torch-lit passage towards stone steps leading upwards into the main body of the stronghouse. "That would be Lord Darkspur?" The Thane of Darkspur had never summoned Evram; Evram presumed Sar Omet had passed on their conversation, but he'd expected to give an account to Lord Darkspur too.

"Lord Darkspur, and the High Marshal," the taller guard said, and Evram's stomach tightened. Him, appear in front of one of the most powerful men in the kingdom? There was a hint of tension in the guards' faces, too. It seemed the appearance of such a large fighting force on their doorstep had unnerved them.

"Do yourself a favour, Blackcreeker," the shorter guard told him. "Make sure you sound convincing if His Lordship tells you to repeat to the High Marshal what you told Sar Omet."

"This man can only speak the truth," Evram replied. His apprehension twisted his words, and they came out rather snappier than he'd have chosen to address two armed men flanking him.

"Best hope the truth's good enough, then," the taller one commented. "If the High Marshal thinks His Lordship's wasted his time then he won't be pleased, and if Lord Darkspur thinks you've made him look a fool, you won't be going home."

Evram's stomach tightened even more. Should he change his story? But in what way? If Marshal Brightwater was here because of a message Thane Darkspur had sent, presumably he believed Raiders had taken Black Keep. Should Evram claim there were more Raiders, to make the threat sound greater? But what if they rode to Black Keep and found that he'd lied? No, he'd stick to the truth, and hope it served him well. Marshal Brightwater had been appointed by the God-King, so although he was only a man he had been raised to his office by divinity. That surely reflected well on his wisdom and judgement.

The stairs up from the servants' quarters were steep and winding, and Evram's hip was hurting by the time they reached an age-darkened wooden door. The taller guard pushed it open and ushered him through, and he found himself standing in the largest roofed space he'd ever set foot in.

The Grand Hall of Darkspur was a single chamber that had to have been as large, and nearly as high, as the entire Black Keep. The great flagstones beneath Evram's feet had been polished smooth from decades if not centuries of wear, and the walls were hung with vast sheets of paper taller than him, covered with intricately detailed paintings of battle scenes, or events from myth and legend. The ceiling was supported by four huge tree trunks rising up from the floor, hung with various shields and weapons, perhaps of defeated foes. Servants were bustling about, hastily lighting torches, scattering fresh petals over mats of woven rushes, and performing other menial tasks.

"You!"

At the sound of the voice, he instinctively imitated the guards beside him as they bowed deeply. When he straightened again, he saw the person who'd spoken—the Thane of Darkspur.

Odem Darkspur was a big man, nearly a head taller than Evram and broad of shoulder, with a wide face and deep-set eyes, and prominent streaks of grey in his long, dark hair. He was wearing a thane's robe in brown and gold, the sleeves double-pleated and falling to his wrist, and its heavily embroidered hemline brushing the tops of his boots. His face was creased with laugh lines, but his current expression suggested a readiness to chew through oak. Sar Omet stood at his cousin's left shoulder. At first glance, Evram wouldn't have placed them as related had he not known, although there was a certain similarity around the jaw and chin now he looked more closely.

"You are the Blackcreek man?" Thane Odem demanded. His gaze rested only briefly on Evram before it darted off again, distracted.

"Yes, lord," Evram replied, ducking his head. You couldn't be too careful with thanes.

"Stand with Sar Omet," the thane ordered Evram, pointing to

the far end of the hall where a somewhat oversized, impressively decorated wooden chair sat on a dais. "Step forward and speak only when this lord commands it, do you understand?"

"Yes, lord," Evram replied again, but the thane had already moved on, shouting instructions. It seemed the High Marshal's arrival had caught Darkspur unprepared.

"Back to your duties," Sar Omet ordered the two guards, who hurried away. The steward took Evram by the arm and propelled him across the floor, taking up station on the dais at the left side of the thane's chair. A shout from the other end of the hall sent everyone scurrying: guards took up position at the edge of the hall, servants disappeared, and Thane Odem himself hurried back towards his chair. He'd only just reached it and sat down when the main doors began to creak open, casting daylight across the floor, into which loomed the long shadows of the new arrivals. The two heralds Evram had seen earlier were first across the threshold. They raised their trumpets, blew a repeating five-note refrain, and shouted as one:

"*Marshal Kaldur Brightwater, Southern Marshal of Narida and Hand of Heaven, Trusted of the Divine God-King Natan Narida, Third of His name!*"

Thane Odem rose from his chair, as though he hadn't sat down on it scant moments before, and descended to the floor to greet the figure now entering his hall.

Kaldur Brightwater was as tall as Odem Darkspur, though not as broad; nor as old, Evram saw, when the High Marshal removed his helmet. He looked between thirty and forty summers, by Evram's estimate, and had a handsomeness very much at odds with Odem's bluff features.

"High Marshal," the thane greeted him, bowing at the waist. "You do this thane great honour—"

"This marshal did not ride here to be greeted with words of honour, Darkspur," Brightwater said, cutting him off. Evram felt Sar Omet stiffen.

MIKE BROOKS

"Your messenger brought grave tidings of Raiders who have not only landed on our shores, but *settled*," Brightwater continued, as Thane Odem straightened. "This marshal gathered what force he could and rode south, and he finds you sitting in your hall, in your best robes?"

There was an uncomfortable silence. The fact the High Marshal was armoured at all was a subtle slight to the thane of Darkspur, since it implied his lands were unsafe. There were songs of blood rivalries that had started thanks to such insults. Thane Odem would have to swallow such unvoiced criticism from his commander, of course, but Brightwater had dressed in a way even the lowborn could interpret.

"This thane's messenger must have made better time than anticipated," the thane said, slightly hesitantly. "He assures you, lord, he is ready to ride with you."

"This marshal does not understand why he is to ride *with* you at all," Brightwater stated baldly. "He does not understand why you have not already dealt with this threat. This marshal anticipated he would arrive to evaluate your results, or provide assistance if the Raiders proved more numerous or ferocious than anticipated. Do you not have the numbers to engage them yourself?"

"Lord, if we may speak privately…" Thane Odem began.

"No, Darkspur," Brightwater snapped, "we may not."

Everyone surrounding them—the High Marshal's sars, his household warriors and associated retainers, the Darkspur guards and servants—were all suddenly looking anywhere but directly at the two lords standing in the middle of the great hall.

"High Marshal," Thane Odem said carefully. "It is true this thane currently has fewer fighting men at his disposal than usual—we have been responding to the mountain savages raiding farms in the foothills. However…"

He paused, eyeing the sars behind the High Marshal, then sighed. "However, this thane also wished to wait for you because the fugitive suggests the people of Black Keep have willingly accepted the Raiders, and that Daimon Blackcreek has betrayed his own people and His Divine Majesty. Since the bad blood between Darkspur and Blackcreek is well known…"

"You wished to ensure your actions were seen to be honourable, rather than risk fulfilling honour, then be accused of bias," Brightwater finished bluntly. He waved a hand irritably. "Very well, we shall work with what we have. This marshal's men should have a day to rest before they march again; he presumes that gives you sufficient time to make your own preparations."

"Ample time, lord," Thane Odem said, bowing. Both his words and his bow were stiff with repressed anger, but Brightwater either didn't notice, or ignored it. "Darkspur's steward has already made the arrangements. Did you wish to speak to the fugitive?"

"You have him here?" Brightwater replied, looking around. Sar Omet took that as his cue and tugged Evram out into the middle of the great hall. Evram wondered if a large part of the eagerness to present him was to change the subject and give the High Marshal less opportunity to criticise the thane of Darkspur in front of his own people, but that line of speculation didn't help his nerves any.

This man is about to be presented to one of the five most powerful men in the country. His legs nearly gave way, but he managed to get close enough that his collapse onto one knee looked like an appropriate show of respect.

"Rise," the High Marshal said. His voice had lost the sharp edge with which he'd spoken to Thane Odem, but Evram kept his eyes lowered as he stood.

"You are from Black Keep? The town itself?" Brightwater asked.

"Yes, lord," Evram managed, husking out his response at the second try.

"You were there when the Raiders landed?"

"Yes lord, on the walls. Seventeen ships, there were." He licked his dry lips nervously and kept his eyes fixed on the hem of the High Marshal's robe.

"Look at this marshal, man."

Evram looked up, cautiously, and Kaldur Brightwater's sharp, dark eyes met his own. The High Marshal had clearly not neglected himself while on the march, as his cheeks and chin showed only the faintest hint of stubble. Evram was painfully aware of his own unkempt appearance when standing in front of this beautiful, gleaming warrior.

"Lord Darkspur says Daimon Blackcreek turned traitor," Brightwater said calmly. "You saw this?"

"It... It was hard to see, lord," Evram stammered. "They were a ways off, and it all happened so fast. Three Raiders came ahead with a flag of parley, and Lord Asrel and his sons went out to meet them. They must have spoken, since they stood close to each other for a time, then the Raiders drew weapons and attacked. It..." He swallowed. "It looked as though Lord Darel, that's Lord Asrel's older son—"

"His blood-son, yes?" the High Marshal interrupted, and Evram nodded.

"Even so, lord. He was struck down, and when Lord Asrel went to his aid, Lord Daimon seemed to strike his father from behind—"

"He struck him?" Brightwater pressed. "With a blade?"

"This servant can't truly say, lord," Evram said miserably. "But Lord Asrel fell. The rest of the Raiders charged, but with the other two lords down their chief called them off, and then they came to the walls with Lord Daimon. Lord Daimon bade us open the gates and said he'd allow the Raiders to settle in Black Keep, since otherwise they'd only kill us all anyway. The Raiders' chief, she said—"

"*She?*" Brightwater interrupted. "These savages are led by a woman?"

"Yes lord," Evram confirmed. "Speaks our tongue too, for there's a Naridan in their number who must have taught it her."

The High Marshal blinked in confusion. "She speaks... There is a Raider who speaks *Naridan*? And who was this poor wretch? Some manner of slave?"

"Not from what this servant could tell, lord," Evram admitted. "He seemed to have maybe wed one of their women."

Brightwater's eyebrows shot up. "This is beyond anything this lord had imagined. But what happened to Lord Asrel and his son? Were they slain?"

"No lord," Evram shook his head. "They still lived, but were held by the Raiders. Lord Daimon called upon his father to relent and to allow the Raiders to settle, but Lord Asrel refused. So Lord Daimon commanded his father and brother be confined to the stronghouse, or so this servant believes."

"Nari's teeth," the High Marshal breathed, rubbing a hand over his jaw. "The boy's lost his mind. And his honour." He shook his head sadly. "Such cowardice. It cannot be borne."

Evram closed his eyes for a moment, commended his soul to the God-King for the impertinence he was about to show, then grabbed his courage before it fled.

"Lord, this servant begs you, let him say one more thing."

Evram had thought the hall quiet already, but the aching silence echoing after his words demonstrated how wrong he'd been. He winced, expecting a longblade to clear its scabbard and strike him down for his temerity.

High Marshal Brightwater merely raised an eyebrow. "Speak then, man."

"Lord, this servant is no judge of such things," Evram hedged hastily, "but he doesn't believe Lord Daimon has wholly abandoned his honour, for he challenged and struck down the Raiders' most fearsome warrior on this servant's behalf."

There were some startled, albeit muted mutterings from Brightwater's retinue, and the High Marshal himself frowned.

"Indeed? How came this about?"

"A huge savage he was, lord. This servant remembered him, from many years ago, when he slew Tan, this servant's brother." Evram squeezed his eyes shut again. He wasn't sure what was more painful, these days: the memory of his brother's death, or the fact he could no longer clearly recall Tan's face. "This servant was going to challenge the man: he'd surely die, but this servant couldn't stand to see him within our walls. But Lord Daimon stopped this servant, and told him he would take this honour debt on himself. Lord Daimon challenged the man, who accepted, and they fought, and..."

Evram puffed out his cheeks. It was a strange thing to be able to say, after a decade or more.

"And Lord Daimon killed him."

The mutterings were louder now:

"... ridiculous notion..."

"... they have some sort of honour?"

"... boy may not be—"

Kaldur Brightwater held up one hand, and the chatter died away. He pursed his lips, and if anything the scrutiny of those sharp eyes got even more intense.

"How did the Raiders respond to the death of this man, their champion?"

"They weren't happy, lord," Evram admitted. "They wailed and cried, their chief most terribly, and we thought for a moment they were going to attack. But one of their old women shouted something and they calmed back down, of a sort. 'Twas that night this servant left, though, so he can't speak for what may've occurred since."

"There is more here we should discuss," Brightwater stated briskly to Thane Odem. "In addition, there is... other news from the north, of which you may not be aware." He glanced sideways at Evram for a moment, his expression thoughtful. "This lord will be retiring to the chambers you will have prepared for him."

He looked at Sar Omet, studying the man properly for the first time. "You are the steward here?"

"This thane's cousin, lord," Thane Odem said. "Sar Omet Darkspur."

The High Marshal received this information with a slight nod that suggested he had no great interest in that detail. He pointed at Evram. "Have this man bathed, shaved and fed, then brought to this lord's chambers."

If Sar Omet was at all surprised by these orders, he didn't show it. He snapped his fingers at two nearby servants, who hurried forward to lead Evram away.

As Evram stumbled, mind whirling, after his new guides, he caught sight of High Marshal Kaldur following Sar Omet towards another door at the rear of the great hall, while Odem Darkspur stood alone in the middle of the floor, his expression unreadable.

SAANA

NOT ALL THE Naridans played the Great Game, not even all the men: the old, young, and physically weak sat it out. Not all the Brown Eagle clan wanted to take part either, for the same reasons, or simply because they saw no point to it. Despite that, the teams drawn up at opposite ends of the town were larger than any present said they could remember since before the great plague.

Yaro had split his team, marked by red strips of cloth tied around the left arm, into two roughly equal halves: one half would guard the barrel, while the others were further subdivided into five groups, three with a ball and two to act as decoys. Saana was in a group with a ball, along with Otim, one of her fishers; Inkeru, captain of the *South Wind*; and, the Waveborn help her, Timmun, he who'd started the brawl that had set her and Blackcreek at each other's throats. Of the Naridans with them she recognised Menaken, one of Daimon's guards, and Young Elio, a fisherman, and son of Old Elio, also a fisherman and picked for the opposite team. Ganalel the guard was with them too, chewing his leaf and stabbing foul glances in her direction when he thought she wasn't looking. Nalon had been picked by Gador, although Saana suspected that had been less about solidarity between iron-witches and more about Nalon being the only other person apart from herself who could translate instructions.

Something soared into the air from the direction of the main square: a blunted arrow, with strips of fluttering red and green cloth tied to it. The signal to start the game.

"Go!" Yaro yelled. He was in a different red group with a ball, and led them off at a run. Saana's group followed, led by Menaken, but split off to hug the town wall as Yaro headed for the bakery. Yaro had sent one of the decoy groups, the largest of all, straight through the middle of the town, hollering and whooping as they went. It was an obvious distraction, but one the green team wouldn't be able to ignore. Saana was quite surprised by the level of thought Yaro had given to his tactics, and wondered if Gador had been as thorough. This wasn't quite the senseless mass brawl she'd anticipated, although of course they hadn't made contact with the other team yet.

And suddenly, there they were. A mismatched group of Naridans and Tjakorshi blocked her way, with strips of green cloth tied around their arms. She recognised Evruk and Zalika, and someone further back who could have been Voraksh. A couple of the Naridans looked familiar, too: there was Ita, his expression warring between nervous and excited, and the stablemaster Tavi. There was no sign any of them had a ball; a blocking team, then.

The rules of the game were simple, but clear: grabbing, holding, trips, or throws were fine; punches, kicks, or headbutts were not; any use of something as a weapon would result in a flogging. The game was only to take place in the streets, anyone hurdling a fence to take a shortcut across a house's land would be forced to pay the owner for damage, and the town wall was out of bounds. Since most of Black Keep's streets weren't wide, speed and positioning were critical, to avoid getting caught in a choke point where a few strong bodies could block the way.

"Straight through!" Menaken shouted, putting his head down and surging forwards. Saana didn't like the look of their chances, but picked up her pace to match him. He had the ball, after all.

It was a bizarre sensation, to be charging bodily at a group of people when no one was armed. She felt oddly naked, even though she had no desire to hurt anyone lined up against her.

Well, perhaps Zalika, a little bit. They'd never liked each other much.

Menaken veered right, as close to the town wall as he could. He had the ball, and the main body of the group ranged against them shifted to meet him. The man was clearly a fool; he was simply giving himself less room to manoeuvre. Then, at the last moment, he threw the ball to his left.

Straight at Saana.

She caught it before it hit her face, more on instinct than anything else. Menaken collided with the waiting pile of opponents, now trying to distract as many as possible. Saana saw an opening and dived for it with a fierce grin. She dodged the grabbing fingers of one Naridan, shoved Zalika aside with her free hand and dumped the other woman onto her arse, bucked off someone unseen who tried to wrap their arms around her from the side…

… and was hit in the ribs by someone's shoulder as they drove into her from the front, knocking the breath from her lungs and killing her momentum. She caught sight of a flash of red to her right and weakly tossed the ball. Timmun, of all people, snatched it out of the air, and was through and away with someone haring off in pursuit, but the rest of both groups remained locked in a struggle.

The man who'd stopped her was trying to drag her down to the ground, so Saana grabbed him around the waist and hoisted. She got his feet off the ground, but only briefly, and when he touched back down he locked his arms behind her knees and tugged. Now she fell backwards, losing what air she'd managed to claw back into her chest since he'd first hit her, and he ended up on top of her.

It was Tavi. The stablemaster flashed a triumphant smile at her, the first real expression she remembered seeing on his face, but then a shout went up that the ball had gone. He pushed himself up and away from her, ready to head off after Timmun.

Well, she wasn't having that. Saana stretched out a leg and hooked her foot around his shin, tripping him as he turned, then scrambled up and threw herself on his back. Now their roles were reversed: her group needed to slow and delay their opponents as much as possible, to give Timmun the best chance of getting away.

Tavi twisted under her like a fresh-caught blue-fin in a net, all lean muscle and power. *Looking after dragons all day must keep him strong,* Saana thought briefly. He threw her partly off, but she grabbed his arm as he did so and pulled him onto his back, taking his legs out from under him, then jumped atop him once more and straddled him to hold him down. She cast a quick glance to her right to see how the rest of her group were doing and—

"Look out!"

It was Tavi who shouted: she felt it as well as heard it. Never mind that he was on the opposing team, the man's alarm sounded genuine enough for instinct to take over. She threw herself to her right, away from the shape looming in her peripheral vision, and rolled up to her feet to find Ganalel stumbling forwards, the knife in his hand cutting through where her shoulders had been a moment before.

Saana went cold. She should have seen this coming ever since the incident on the drawbridge.

Tavi surged up off the ground behind Ganalel and slammed his arm up between his fellow Naridan's legs, and Ganalel's eyes bulged in agony. Saana caught the wrist of his knife hand and punched him in the face as hard as she could, dropping him.

"Raider scum! He's on our team!"

Young Elio slammed into her, knocking her away from Ganalel, and swung for her head with his fist. Saana blocked it, trying to remember the Naridan for "knife". Had he not seen Ganalel's attack? Did he not care?

Zalika ran over Elio from behind, introducing her forearm to the back of his head. She grinned at Saana, then got punched in the stomach by a different Naridan, who started to kick at her as she folded. Menaken tried to haul the man responsible away, got shoved back by him, then punched in the face by Otim.

"Stop it!" Saana yelled, trying to grab Otim. Everything was devolving into a straight-up brawl between Naridans and Tjakorshi, the teams of the Great Game forgotten. She managed to wrap her arms around Otim from behind, but he apparently took her for an enemy because he buried his elbow in her ribs hard enough to knock the breath out of her, then lashed backwards with the same arm and caught her in the temple. Saana staggered, losing her grip on him as her head swam, and then someone piled into her from the side. She landed hard in the mud and lashed out, panicking that whoever had brought her down might also have a knife. A boot trod on her left hand and she screamed as the bones ground together, then used her other hand to punch the culprit in the back of their knee to get them off her.

Someone kicked her in the ribs, a stab of pain that knocked half the breath from her. Saana turned towards the impact and grabbed the leg, then rose up to her feet with a roar, bearing her attacker into the air. She stumbled forwards, bouncing off at least one other person, then lunged forwards and drove her burden back-first into the wooden fence encircling the nearest house's smallholding. It gave way with a splintering crack and they both landed in the dirt, with her opponent letting out a cry of agony. Saana punched him in the jaw and he went still, so she forced herself back up and turned back to the rest of them.

"Stop it!" she yelled, her stomach sinking. "Stop fighting!"

They paid her no heed.

DAIMON

SHOUTING AND GENERAL commotion was always part of the Great Game, and Nari knew there was enough of it going on, but Daimon's fingers tightened on his longblade's grip when one knot of noise in particular began to rise above the others. He glanced sideways at Kelaharel, but the reeve didn't seem overly concerned, and simply continued to lean on his long stave. Tsolga Hornsounder, however, looked up from where she was sitting on a tree stump stool and caught Daimon's eye.

"Bad," she said in Naridan, and got to her feet. She punched one hand into the other, then nodded in the direction of the noise. "Bad."

Daimon nodded, already questioning whether he'd made a critical mistake by introducing the Brown Eagle clan to the emotional cauldron that was the Great Game. Still, Black Keep had a traditional solution for that problem. "Reeve, your men are required."

"Are you sure, lord?" Kelaharel asked, raising his eyebrows. "It could just be high spirits."

He would never have queried Daimon's father: Daimon tapped two fingers meaningfully on his longblade's scabbard and the reeve ducked his head. "As you say."

"This lord will come with you," Daimon told him, ignoring

the flash of consternation on Kelaharel's face as he spoke. Tsolga Hornsounder fell in beside him, her face grim and her fingers twitching as though searching for a weapon to grip. The old woman clearly thought trouble was afoot, and Daimon trusted her instincts with regards to her own people, at least.

"Come!" Daimon barked, and set off at the best pace he could manage through Black Keep's muddy side streets. The reevesmen kept pace with him, which he wasn't surprised at; what he hadn't expected was for Tsolga to manage it as well, but the old woman seemed hale, at least.

The disturbance wasn't hard to find.

It was a struggling ruck of people up near the boundary wall, shouting and swearing and laying about themselves, but one glance told Daimon that what he'd feared most had come to pass: Naridan and Tjakorshi were at each others' throats, in some cases literally.

"Into them!" Kelarahel barked, and he and his reevesmen waded in, staves lashing out. That was how the reevesmen worked: they broke up fights by laying about them until no one wanted to fight any longer, which was a decent enough method when dealing with Naridan lowborn who knew the reeve's authority ultimately came from their lord. The Tjakorshi, however, for whom the reevesmen might be nothing more than Flatlanders with weapons... Daimon opened his mouth to call them back, but what other option did he have? Let the fight escalate?

Shouting from behind alerted him to a half-dozen Tjakorshi approaching from the direction of the square; members of the Brown Eagle clan who'd decided not to participate. His momentary hope that they'd come to help break things up evaporated when they drew the strange, thin daggers of their people, that were neither bone nor horn but similar to both. They were here to fight, and to kill.

His heart racing, and well aware he was clad in nothing but the thick cloth of his robes, Daimon drew his longblade. He tried to tell himself that perhaps the threat of a sar's naked steel would stem their charge, but he knew before the weapon had cleared its scabbard that the hope was a desperate one. His grand dreams for a united Black Keep, one where Naridan and Tjakorshi could live alongside each other, would die today. Along with him.

An eerie, sonorous wail rang out from beside him, louder even than the noise of the fight, and Daimon's bones were suddenly ice. He was a child again, hearing that sound echoing through the streets of his home and knowing death was at the walls. The charge of the Tjakorshi faltered as well, rage replaced by uncertainty.

Tsolga blew her huge shell horn until her knees shook, then refilled her old lungs and blew again. Black Keep spirit tales held that the Raiders made their horns from the skulls of the demons they worshipped, but seeing the truth in action didn't change the effect on Daimon's soul. It was a primal fear, one that surged out of his childhood and gripped him by the throat.

Between one heartbeat and the next, the fighting stopped.

Naridans were looking around in alarm, Tjakorshi in confusion. And then, bawling in her own language and forcing her way through the middle of the press, Saana Sattistutar appeared.

She looked a mess. She was covered in mud, one of her sleeves was hanging off at the shoulder and she had a cut on her forehead that was dribbling blood down her face, but she was grabbing Tjakorshi and hauling them away from whichever Naridan they happened to have their hands on at that moment. A rough split appeared down the middle, as the two sides began to separate.

Daimon drew his shortblade and walked into that gap, one weapon in each hand, forcing the two groups to part in front of him until he stood face to face with Saana. The look she threw at him made it clear she wasn't sure whether he'd come to help her or kill her, and was beyond caring either way.

"What happened?" he asked, praying to Nari there was a good explanation.

"She punched Ganalel!" someone shouted.

"The man Ganalel," Saana snarled, half at Daimon and half in the direction of whoever had shouted, "had knife. Tried to stab."

"Stab you?" Daimon asked in alarm, and to his horror Saana nodded.

"Yes. This man hit him, but others did not see knife. They hit her, then Brown Eagles hit them. This man could not stop them all."

Daimon ground his teeth in fury. Nari's blood, but Ganalel was one of his guards! The shame on his house!

Never mind the shame, you fool! If he'd succeeded, you'd be looking at a dead chief and a clan of Tjakorshi who would burn Black Keep to the ground, and kill everyone in it.

"Did anyone else see this?" he demanded, turning in a slow circle. If an accuser had two witnesses then a claim was held to be true, unless the thane had grave doubts about their truthfulness. The Naridans shuffled their feet and looked at each other uncertainly. The Tjakorshi obviously couldn't understand him. Saana drew in breath to translate his words, and Daimon braced himself for the inevitable outpouring of loyalty to their chief, whether or not they'd actually seen anything...

"Aye, Lord!"

Tavi. The stablemaster forced his way through the ranks of his fellow countrymen, dragging Ganalel with him, one arm under each of the little man's armpits and his hands clasped behind Ganalel's head.

"Your man saw it, clear as he sees your face now," Tavi declared, his own face flat with rage. "Tried to stab the chief in the back, then ran for it when the fight started. S'man wasn't going to let him get away."

An ugly ripple ran through the assembled Naridans, and several spat in Ganalel's direction. More than one was nursing bruises or cuts, and Young Elio looked barely able to stand straight. Black Keep held the Great Game in high regard, and someone using it as cover to settle a personal dispute with a knife would be reviled in any case, let alone if that had started a fight leading to injuries.

"It's a lie!" Ganalel bawled, struggling uselessly against the stablemaster's thick arms. "You've seen him lord, always closeted with the Raider girl! No wonder he takes the side of the witch's mother!"

Daimon found the tip of his longblade at the man's throat almost before he realised what he was doing, and fought to get control of himself.

"This lord is of the opinion that Chief Saana's daughter is no witch," he bit out. "As you are well aware, Ganalel! Do you truly dispute your lord's judgement in this matter?"

Ganalel froze, his eyes cast down towards the steel pricking his skin. "No, lord."

"This lord hears your words, Tavi," Daimon told the stablemaster. He lowered his blade from Ganalel's throat, but didn't take his eyes from the guard's face. "Did anyone else see what Tavi describes?"

There was a shuffling in the Naridan ranks and Ita stepped forwards, swallowing nervously.

"Aye, lord. Your man saw it, but couldn't make the others hear him—"

Ganalel's eyes widened and he tried to round on his fellow guardsman, so abruptly that for a moment it looked as though Tavi wouldn't be able to hold him.

"You treacherous little worm!" Ganalel raged, struggling to free himself. "S'man shits on your ancestors, you milkface-loving whoreson!"

"The witnesses are noted," Daimon said, raising his voice to make himself heard above Ganalel's rantings. He'd seen his father do this before and had never liked it, but it was necessary. "Tavi, take Ganalel to the pillory."

"Lord," Tavi nodded, and set about dragging his captive towards the square, apparently having no problem manhandling

Ganalel by himself. Working in the stables must have given the man sinews like steel bars.

"Ita, run and tell Tevyel to prepare the resin," Daimon instructed the tall guard, who bowed and set off, quickly overtaking Tavi and Ganalel. The people of the Blackcreek lands had used pine resin for many purposes for as long as anyone could remember, from throat medicine to an adhesive for fletching arrows. Tevyel would need a greater quantity than usual for what was coming, however. Daimon turned back to the rest of his folk.

"Heed your wounds!" he told them as forcefully as he could. "Feel them and remember them, and remember you took them in defence of a coward who cared not if he destroyed us all!" He sheathed his blade. The lowborn muttered, and there were still one or two dark looks cast at the Brown Eagles, whom Saana was speaking to in what sounded like similar tones, but there were many more nods, and many cursings of Ganalel's name.

"What now happens?" Saana demanded, turning back to him. She still looked to be in a furious temper, which Daimon thought quite understandable. He bowed to her, the bow of a man with shame to expunge.

"This lord apologises to you, that his man should have acted in such a way."

"Apologise?" Saana said, her eyes flashing. "Nasjuk went into your cages for punching a man. This needs more than your manners, thane!"

"And will get it," Daimon told her firmly, straightening. "Ganalel will be held in the pillory. We will wait for the game to end, as this lord will need Gador to heat a blade in his forge."

"And then?"

"The law is clear," Daimon said, meeting her eyes. "Ganalel will lose the hand in which he held the knife."

IT DIDN'T TAKE long for the game to end. Members of the red team triumphantly carried their opponent's barrel back to the square with their three balls inside it, and placed it in front of Daimon. It seemed the Tjakorshi called Timmun had been the one to snatch the win with the red team's third ball: Daimon wasn't the best at reading the foreigners' reactions, but he got the impression this was surprising to a lot of them. Most of the red team were now in a jubilant mood that crossed over the boundaries between Naridan and Tjakorshi.

Of course, there was one glaring issue left to resolve.

"People of Black Keep!" Daimon shouted, raising his hands. The crowd quietened. Beside him, Nalon gave a piercing whistle that seemed to focus the Tjakorshi's attention. Daimon and Saana had agreed it would be better for Nalon to translate in this case, and Nalon had only complained about it slightly.

"It is this lord's pleasure as Thane of Blackcreek to announce the winners of the great spring game as the red team of Yaro the fisher!"

A great roar went up from the half of the square in which those wearing red were concentrated. The other half, the defeated green team, were less enthusiastic.

"However, an issue arose during the game that this lord cannot ignore," Daimon continued, while Nalon called out the Tjakorshi equivalent. "One of our town took to the field carrying a knife, and used the game as cover to attack a member of his own team over a grudge!"

Outrage. Shouts of anger and derision from all sides. Furious looks were cast at the pillory where Ganalel was held by his arms. Daimon didn't know how much word had spread of the incident before this point, but if anyone had wondered why one of his guards was on display in the town square, they now knew.

"Ganalel attempted to stab Chief Saana of the Brown Eagle clan," he declared. "In doing so he not only violated his own honour, but this lord's honour as well. More importantly," he said, raking the crowd with his gaze, trying to drive home the seriousness of the situation, "he endangered us all. Seeing only a fight, and not knowing the cause, most went to aid their own people. Had it not been for the quick thinking of the woman Tsolga"—he pointed, drawing a look of some confusion from her which only seemed to increase as Nalon translated—"this could have engulfed us all. Death could have come for many in Black Keep, over the actions of one man. Remember, our only enemies in this town are those who are opposed to peace, be they Naridan or Tjakorshi!"

His words didn't exactly draw cheers, but neither were they jeered, or even greeted with a stony silence. Instead there was a general nodding, and a low buzz of conversation. The harsh reality of what would happen if a genuine battle broke out was surely clear to his folk, and he couldn't imagine any of them wished to die.

"What of Ganalel, lord?" Shefal shouted. Of course it was Shefal. Well, he was going to be disappointed if he expected Daimon to shirk his responsibilities.

"Witnesses confirmed the accusation," Daimon said. "This lord has, in accordance with our laws, sentenced Ganalel to lose the hand that so treacherously wielded the weapon. This lord now calls his town to bear witness to the punishment."

He turned towards the pillory, and the crowd shuffled and shifted to follow. Gador emerged from the forge, holding a long, thick blade glowing dull red with heat. One of the reasons the pillory was so near the forge was to ensure the blade used for such punishments cooled as little as possible before it was needed. It was no sar's longblade, and the heating would have started to blunt its edge, but it was sharp and heavy enough for what needed to be done. Daimon took it, feeling the waves of heat coming off it. Ganalel had started to wail.

"Ita!" Daimon snapped. "The log!"

Ita rolled an upright log into position. Its length was such that it rested just below the hole in the pillory where a prisoner's hands were held, and its upper surface was scarred with old, blackened blade marks.

Daimon felt his stomach roil, but there was no turning back. It was a very different feeling to facing down Ristjaan, when he'd been overwhelmed by a nervous energy accentuating everything. This was just a sick regret. But he couldn't allow his people to just stab each other in the back, even if some of them were Raiders. He needed everyone to understand they were all under the same law.

"Ganalel of Black Keep," he pronounced, holding the blade in front of him. "You are guilty of cowardly violence, and this lord, Daimon Blackcreek, thane of these lands, will take from you the hand used to do the deed."

"Lord, your man begs you!" Ganalel wheedled. The sun was setting, but the light caught the tears on his cheeks. "His family! How will your man feed them with only one hand?"

Daimon shook his head. "Lay your hand on the log, Ganalel, and keep it still."

"But Lord—"

"Your hand, Ganalel!" Daimon shouted. "This lord gives his word he will strike true, but he can only do that if you keep still. Should you move, this lord may need to strike more than once."

Gador pulled a small sack from his belt and pulled it down over Ganalel's head, hiding his face. "There, Lord. It may help if he can't see the blow coming."

Daimon nodded, and raised the blade. In truth, it helped him not to see the man's pleading eyes, although the low, wordless wail emerging from the sack wasn't helping his nerves. He positioned his feet carefully, focused on Ganalel's wrist, and swung.

There was a *thunk* as the blade sliced through flesh and sinew to bury itself a finger's breadth into the log, immediately followed by a piercing scream from Ganalel that only increased as Gador grabbed his shoulder and pushed it forwards, forcing the severed end of the man's forearm into contact with the glowing blade. After a moment or two of obscene sizzling Gador relaxed his grip, and he and Ita hastily undid the clasps holding the pillory shut. Tevyel stepped forwards with a small cauldron giving off the sharp smell of liquid resin, a clean scent that cut through even the stench of burned flesh beginning to fill the air, and Gador plunged Ganalel's arm into the cauldron so the warm resin could bind the wound closed.

Daimon breathed out, trying to hide the shakiness that had overtaken him, and fight down his nausea. The crowd had erupted into shouts of angry jubilation or abuse of Ganalel, so Daimon turned to them.

"The sentence is done!" he shouted. "Ganalel has paid for his crime! He is still of this town, and shall be treated as such!" He waved his hands at them. "Now go! We must prepare for the Feast of Life!"

RIKKUT

THE STORM HAD finally blown itself out. The *Sea Spite* had foundered a day earlier, its deck deluged by one too many huge waves, and the sail left too full for too long. A screaming, malicious gust from the wind spirits had pulled the mighty vessel over, sending bodies spilling into the water. Most had been recovered even from those treacherous seas by neighbouring ships swinging in close to help, but some were lost. The Dark Father always took his price, sooner or later.

That had been yesterday, though. The last angry clouds had finally scudded off north, taking their drenching, bone-chilling rain with them, and there was nothing left but the blue swell of the ocean under the clear blue of the sky, both of which gradually turned gold as the sun sank in the north-west, on the start of her journey to the depths. Rikkut stood in front of the deckhouse and stared her down, letting her light fill him. She was growing stronger, and Father Krayk was swallowing her for less and less time every night. Rikkut felt much the same, but unlike her, when he reached his Long Day he wouldn't fade away again.

A shell-horn sounded behind him, then another one. It shouldn't have been possible for shell-horns to sound scared, but the soundings were tremulous, shaky, as though panic had nearly prevented the sounders from getting their lips into the right place. Rikkut turned, blinking away the pale after-image of the sun's disc.

"What?" he shouted. He could make out other crews gesticulating as their vessels began to veer away. What was the problem? The Brown Eagle clan could be the only others abroad on the oceans with anything like enough ships to threaten his raid, and they would have the old, young, and infirm amongst their number, whereas his raid was fully crewed by warriors and sailors, no dead weight. It would be a slaughter, and besides, Sattistutar would be coming from the west if she was coming from anywhere, and he'd been facing west, he'd have seen them...

A sudden incongruous swell astern was the only warning the *Red Smile* had before the water erupted and a monstrous head, half as long again as Rikkut was tall, clamped its jaws around the yolgu's flat deck with a jolt that shook half the crew off their feet.

"*Krayk!*" Juhadzh Kaivaszhin shouted, as though someone could have fucking missed it. "*Krayk!*"

Had the krayk been attracted by the blood from Sarika's corpse, and followed them from there? Or had the Dark Father sent it after them as a new challenge? Every Tjakorshi, even the ones who didn't sail much, knew what would call a krayk. You didn't clean your catch out on the sea as you sailed, lest you leave a trail of fish guts the Dark Father's trueborn children could follow back to you. You bound and stitched wounds as soon as you could. If you ran down another vessel and boarded it, you didn't linger over your prize: you took what you wanted and left again on your own, hopefully less bloody ship. Far too soon, dark shapes would gather in the water, drawn by blood dripping through cracks in the deck and leaking from bodies drifting downwards. Sharks were bad, but sharks fled from the krayk.

Everything fled from the krayk.

It was the first time Rikkut had seen a full-grown adult. Its hide was the familiar dark, pebbled grey scales of the sea-leather armour the clans turned it into when they got the chance. Its teeth were as long as his hand. Its eyes were surprisingly large, and were as dark and featureless as a cloudy sky during Long Night, yet somehow seemed to fix on him. Rikkut felt the unfamiliar swell of fear in his stomach as the boards of the *Red Smile* began to creak under the immense pressure of jaws wide enough to swallow a man whole.

He'd charge or leap over a shieldwall, or take on an enemy champion in single combat without a second thought. He'd face down a storm and laugh at it, dare the wind spirits to do their worst, because life was short and he was nothing more to a storm than an insect was to him. If the Dark Father decided it was time for a storm to claim him then the storm would claim him, and nothing he could do would change that.

To see one of Father Krayk's trueborn children, though... There was a difference between accepting the spirits of wind and wave might take you, and seeing a full-grown krayk coming for you. That made it *personal*.

Besides, Rikkut was no sailor to understand the dance of wind and wave, paddles and sail, but he knew blades and death. This was something he could fight back against. Just because the Tjakorshi feared and respected the krayk didn't mean they never hunted them. Sea leather was sea leather, after all, the best armour, unless you stole or traded for metal with the Drylands to the east.

Rikkut staggered across the tilting deck to the outer wall of the deckhouse and lifted a harpoon from the rack of three there. It was a foolish yolgu captain who set sail without something to deter a krayk, even if they weren't setting out to hunt the beasts. The harpoon must have been six cubits long, a shaft of spruce with a long, jagged head of laboriously sharpened bone taken from a leviathan, or another krayk. Rikkut didn't know which and didn't much care, either: so far as he was concerned, it was a weapon.

As suddenly as it had appeared, the krayk vanished. It opened its jaws, releasing the *Red Smile*'s deck, and the yolgu jerked forwards again as the stiff breeze was no longer counteracted by the monster's weight. The krayk slipped back below the waves, out of sight, the water closing smoothly over its huge head like a lover's embrace. Rikkut checked his stride, harpoon held ready, his eyes fixed on the splintered deck the creature had been savaging a moment before.

"You must have scared it off!" Juhadzh said, slapping Rikkut on the shoulder, too loud and too jovially to be anything other trying to hide his own fear. The man was a loose sail in a storm, lots of noise to no purpose, but behind the bluster he was actually a superb sailor. He'd been the natural choice as captain after Sarika's death, for all that he made Rikkut's teeth itch.

The krayk breached to the yolgu's south.

Rikkut had a momentary glimpse of the beast outlined against the darkening sky, its huge head connected by a short, thick neck to an even more massive body, two front flippers like the ocean's largest paddles. Then it crashed down on the deck, half in and half out of the water, and its immense bulk began to push the *Red Smile* under.

Rikkut was thrown sprawling. Men and women screamed as they tripped, slid and fell into the waves. He scrabbled desperately at the deck with his left hand, felt splinters from the wood digging under his nails, stabbed out with the harpoon, drove the point in, wrenched himself to a halt. The deck was tilting further and icy water lapped at his boots, but he wasn't in the monster's domain yet.

The krayk convulsed and lunged, shaking the ship again, and its jaws closed around the body of a paddler who'd been thrown off-balance. The woman screamed, and lashed out with her paddle, but she might as well have flailed at a cliff face. The krayk thrashed its head back and forth, and her shrieks cut off as her neck snapped. The beast's jaws closed further and another shake of its head tore the upper part of her body free, in a welter of blood and bone. The grisly remnants flopped obscenely into the water by the krayk's head, starting to stain it pink, and the monster gulped down her lower torso and legs, then turned in search of more prey.

It was facing away from Rikkut for a moment, and he saw his chance.

He didn't have time to set himself properly; the deck was too unstable for that. He simply rose from his sprawl and took two quick steps, trusting to speed over balance to keep him upright, the harpoon gripped firm in both hands. Plunging the weapon downwards, he hit the krayk where the beast's neck met what passed for its shoulders, with all his momentum and weight behind it.

The grey-scaled hide parted before the sharpened bone tip, and Rikkut felt a brief thrill of triumph as his weapon sank into its flesh. However, the strength of sea leather lay not in any curing process, but in its own formidable toughness. His blow didn't penetrate deeply, and no sooner had he felt the judder of contact then the krayk whirled, clumsily but oh-so-fast for something that size half-hauled out onto a yolgu, its huge jaws snapping and gusting fetid air as it searched for its attacker. The *Red Smile* lurched still further and Rikkut lost his balance, lost his grip on the harpoon shaft, stumbled on the sloping deck, fell into the sea.

Cold. Icy, flesh-chilling, bone-numbing cold. His lungs contracted involuntarily and he had to fight to keep his mouth shut to prevent a gasp from escaping him, and the ocean flooding down his throat in exchange. He fought upwards, struggling against the swirling mass of his furs, trying to get back to the surface before they became truly waterlogged and dragged him down.

There was a surge of pressure in the water next to him. His head broke the surface and he once more heard the screams and shouts of men and women, the splintering of wood and, closest of all, the stentorian rumblings of the beast. He shook the water from his eyes, reaching out a hand blindly. His fingers met a familiar, rough surface that shifted under his touch. It felt like sea leather.

He'd surfaced right next to the damned krayk.

He was on its right flank, between the front and back flippers. His first instinct was to turn and swim away, furs be damned, try to make it to open water where one of the other ships might dare to come in and pick him up. The *Red Smile* was foundering, unable to stay afloat under the weight of the monster as it lunged to and fro, trying to catch more prey. The harpoon was still stuck in the krayk's shoulder, but didn't appear to be troubling it at all. Most of the crew were already in the water, either involuntarily, or having jumped in on the far side of the yolgu to escape the beast's jaws. The few that remained on board were clinging to the deckhouse to avoid being tipped downwards towards the thing destroying their vessel, but the ship itself was clearly doomed. They'd be in the water before long, whatever they did.

Rikkut felt rage, shame, and fear rising inside him. The *Red Smile* had been *his* ship, gifted to him by The Golden for this voyage so Rikkut could enact its will. To lose it would be the worst of omens. The other captains might haul him from the water, sodden and shivering, but they'd never respect him again. They'd claim the Dark Father had marked him, that to follow him further would see them all go to the depths.

He'd have failed.

Rikkut snarled, drew his spearfish-bill dagger and dug it into the krayk's flank. The tip didn't even penetrate the thick hide, but it gave him just enough purchase to lever himself up onto the beast's back. The scaled skin was chill to the touch, seemingly no warmer than the water he'd just clambered out of. Krayk were truly the children of the ice-cold deeps.

The krayk shifted beneath him, becoming aware of his presence on its back, but then someone in the knot of remaining crew hurled another harpoon at it. The throw was weak, and the weapon bounced harmlessly from the side of the monster's snout, but it distracted it for a moment and brought its head whipping back around. Once more, Rikkut saw his chance. Once more, he took it.

He scrambled to his feet, ran forward a few steps along the ridged plates of the krayk's back armour, and threw himself down at the back of the beast's neck before he lost his footing and was dumped into the water once more, where it could turn its jaws on him, or swat him with a powerful foreflipper. The krayk hissed an exhalation so loud it was nearly a roar and started to thrash, but Rikkut managed to straddle its neck and hold himself in place well enough to start stabbing at it with his dagger. The point skittered harmlessly off its hide once, twice, as the huge beast's head jerked from side to side.

Then the point found an eye.

The spearfish bill sank deep into the socket, and the krayk went berserk. Rikkut lost his grip on his weapon as he grabbed at the beast's neck, cold wet hands trying to find purchase on cold wet scales, lest he fall back in and be crushed by its flailing. The krayk floundered to its left, towards the side it could still see on, further destroying the *Red Smile* as it did so. Then, with Rikkut still clinging to it, it dived.

The water rushed up, forcing its way into his nose and mouth as he instinctively tried to take a breath, pulling him loose from the back of the creature and leaving him stranded just below the waves. He kicked upwards again, broke the surface for a second time and shook his head to clear his eyes of water. The *Red Smile* was going under. At any moment he expected to feel the water surge beneath him as the krayk came back to claim him, piercing his body with savage teeth, then shaking its half-blind head to tear him apart...

"Chief!"

A yolgu was closing on him. Rikkut tried to swim backwards as it approached, but he needn't have worried: the paddlers were experts, and they swung directly alongside without any part of the ship striking him. He reached up a hand, felt it clasped by another, was towed through the water for a few cubits, then hauled aboard.

The second soaking had done it for his furs, and the cold had leached the strength from his limbs. He struggled to rise from the deck, and couldn't tell if he was weighed down more by his waterlogged clothes, or the grim knowledge of his own failure.

The crew around him started chanting.

"Krayk-killer! Krayk-killer! Krayk-killer!"

SAANA

THE HOUR WAS late, and Saana was drunk.

It hadn't been a deliberate decision, but this feast was so unlike the last it had happened naturally. Barely two weeks ago, Tjakorshi and Naridans had been sitting in uncomfortable stillness, separated by language, culture, and deep ancestral enmity. Tonight, the air rang with laughter and music, and although most people still didn't speak each other's tongue there was at least some sort of understanding. The clan had sung one of the Songs of Creation, and despite the Naridans not knowing the words, many had joined in with the stomping or the clapping, once they'd worked out where it went. The Naridans had brought out drums and reed whistles, and set up a racing, skirling tune that some of their younger folk started dancing to. There were lots of complicated steps involved, which hadn't stopped some of the younger Tjakorshi joining in, much to everyone's amusement.

Saana laughed and clapped along with everyone else, but there was a hollow pit in her stomach every time a new peal of merriment rang out. Her ears seemed focused on what wasn't there, always straining to hear the raucous, tearing sound of Rist's laughter, the sound she'd never hear again. Its absence took her mind to dark places. Perhaps that was also why she'd drunk faster than usual.

Perhaps, too, it was connected to Zhanna. Daimon had explained quietly that he didn't yet feel his people would be happy with her no longer being his hostage, but she could join them for the festivities. Saana had been delighted at first, but in truth Zhanna hadn't spent much time with her. After all, they'd seen and spoken to each other several times since she'd been shut inside the Blackcreek castle, whereas Zhanna had had no contact with anyone else in the clan. She was currently trying the Naridan dance next to Tsennan Longjaw and a Black Keep boy called Lavit, apparently the adopted son of Samul the carpenter. Samul was on the other side of the square, sitting very close to a man named Menas, and Saana had resolved to try not to think too much about that.

It didn't help her mood much when Daimon Blackcreek joined the dance. She'd expected him to stay aloof and removed, as before, but the usually staid Naridans had loosened up for this particular festival, at least, and the normal barriers of rank and position were less rigid. That didn't make it any easier to watch him spin and wheel so close to where he'd killed Rist. She'd mainly managed to push her bitterness to the back of her mind, but this was too sharp a reminder.

She tried to think about it fairly. Daimon was trying to set an example for his people. That was what their whole scheme with the Great Game had been about. Besides, he wasn't actually much older than most of the others dancing. He'd locked his father up and abandoned his own honour to save his town, an action apparently almost incomprehensible to the Naridan way of thinking. He could be excused this time of levity.

The dance changed, and Daimon ended up next to Zhanna. Saana's daughter was clumsy next to the sure-footed young thane, and he began to guide her through the steps.

Saana muttered a curse to the Dark Father under her breath, drained her tankard of sour Naridan ale, and stepped away from the table.

She heard a rough cheer to her left, and her feet took her towards a crowd of mainly Tjakorshi backs around another table. Moving closer, she saw Inkeru wrist-wrestling with Menaken. The Naridan was holding his own quite well, his jaw clenched with effort. Inkeru, meanwhile, appeared to be trying to sap his will purely through her stare. The spectators clapped and cheered each minute gain or loss, until suddenly Inkeru let out a hiss of frustration as her arm gave way and Menaken slammed her knuckles to the wood. Menaken whooped in triumph and Inkeru shook her head ruefully, then touched two fingers to her brow in salute. Someone slid a wooden tumbler of shorat in front of Menaken, who raised it to Inkeru before throwing it back. Saana smirked, expecting a reaction as bad as Daimon's on their first night in Black Keep, but to her surprise the guard simply blinked a couple of times. The Tjakorshi roared their approval and someone slapped Menaken on the back, which inconvenienced his breathing far more than the shorat had.

"Chief!" Inkeru had risen from her seat and seen Saana. "The Flatlander is as strong as he is handsome! Do you want to show him what the Brown Eagle clan are made of?"

Saana snorted. Inkeru was a salt-hardened raider on whom you could blunt an axe, as the old saying went. If she couldn't beat Menaken then Saana didn't fancy her chances, but she shrugged and took the other woman's place. Menaken smiled and reached his hand out, and Saana clasped it as the people surrounding them cheered again and, it sounded like, made quick bets amongst themselves.

Yaro the fisher had taken on the responsibility of starting the contests. He took their joined hands in his own, squeezed three times, and released them.

Saana threw everything she had into it immediately. Menaken resisted, but not quite quickly enough, and had just enough time to look surprised before his knuckles grazed the table's surface: only for a moment before he started to fight back up, but it had been witnessed by the crowd.

"Winner!" Yaro shouted, pointing at Saana. It took her a moment to realise he'd used the Tjakorshi word, and she stared at him in surprise while the crowd around them alternately celebrated, or lambasted Menaken for his poor performance. Yaro's expression turned to one of worry.

"Is that wrong?" he asked nervously in his own tongue.

"No," Saana replied, thinking doubly hard to make sure she spoke the correct language back, "that was right. How did you know the word?"

"S'man heard people shouting it when someone won," Yaro told her. "He thought it was what you did."

"It is," Saana reassured him, and he smiled.

"S'man wasn't ready!" Menaken was protesting.

"That's your fault!" Yaro said, rounding on him. "S'man gave you the signal, Menaken! Give up your seat!"

Menaken shook his head, but got up. A tumbler of shorat appeared in front of Saana and she threw it down, since it was there.

When she righted her head again, Tavi the stablemaster was lowering himself into place opposite her.

Saana couldn't stop herself from smiling. "Did this man not leave you in the mud today? You wish to lose again?"

The corner of Tavi's mouth quirked in reply, but he simply reached out his hand and said nothing. Saana gripped it and felt the calluses on his palm and fingers where they rubbed against hers. Yaro took their hands in his, squeezed three times, and released.

Tavi wasn't slow to react. Their hands quivered as they both strained, unable to move the other. Tavi's eyebrows raised in surprise, and Saana grinned at him.

"You're strong for a woman," Tavi said, his voice tight with effort.

"You're strong for your size," Saana replied, and snorted a laugh at his resulting expression of outrage. Unfortunately the laugh weakened her and her hand slipped slightly, and Tavi pounced on the opportunity. Saana groaned and grimaced as her knuckles began to creep towards the wood of the tabletop, while the spectators shouted indiscriminate encouragement in two different languages. Some people began to pound on the table itself, which jarred Saana's elbow. She managed to halt Tavi's downward pressure with a furious effort, to a hiss of frustration from her opponent, and looked around quickly to see who was banging, to shout at them to stop.

What caught her eye instead was two faces next to each other: Kerrti and the Naridan girl Henya, the healer's daughter, who'd worked together to splint and set Chara's leg. They were pressed up close beside each other, as was everyone around the table.

They were holding hands.

Saana's eyes met Kerrti's and, Dark Father help her, the witch paled and froze. She couldn't have looked guiltier if she'd tried.

Saana barely noticed her knuckles hitting the wood as Tavi seized on her moment of inattention, barely registered the shouts of the crowd. She snatched her hand out of Tavi's and stood up so quickly and clumsily she spilled the remnants of a tankard across the boards, then pushed her way out of the immediate circle of townsfolk behind her and stormed around the table to the other side.

Kerrti and Henya were still there, although they were now facing each other, and weren't holding hands any longer. The Naridan girl looked confused and hurt, while Kerrti was talking urgently to her, but not making any headway against the language barrier. The witch looked around and saw Saana bearing down on them. For a moment it looked like she might flee, but instead she took a deep breath and turned to face her.

"What in the deeps are you doing?" Saana shouted, louder than she'd intended. She'd translated between them when they'd been helping Chara! They'd seemed to get along instantly, which Saana had put down to a shared interest in healing. She'd actually been hopeful, and had thought perhaps if more of their two peoples could be like Henya and Kerrti then they might be able to integrate after all. Now it seemed there'd been darker forces at work.

"I wasn't doing any—"

"You were holding her hand!" Saana raged.

"I didn't—"

"I saw you!" Her shouts were attracting attention, but she didn't care.

"You were holding *his* hand!" Kerrti shouted back, pointing at where Saana had been sitting.

"I was wrist-wrestling!" Saana spat. "You were holding hands as you would with a lover! Was Tsolga right about you? Has this land turned your head?"

"This land," Kerrti bit out, blinking furiously, "has done *nothing* to me!"

The unspoken assertion was there for all to hear. A coldness swelled in Saana's chest to match the chill nipping at her hands and face. She drew in breath to denounce Kerrti as an abomination, perversely grateful that she'd found an outlet for the dark mood plaguing her since she'd narrowly avoided taking a dagger between the shoulders.

"*What is the meaning of this?!*"

Daimon Blackcreek arrived, robes flapping, with several of his fellow dancers in tow. In fact, the thane's sudden movement seemed to have focused most people's attention. Saana rounded on him.

"This is none of your concern, Daimon of Blackcreek!"

"You are in this lord's castle and disrupting his people's festival," Blackcreek said sternly, glowering from beneath his reddish brows. "That makes it his concern, Chief Sattistutar."

"Then tell your healer's daughter to keep her hands off our witch!" Saana demanded angrily.

Blackcreek's face returned to the neutral, unreadable expression that the Naridans did so well. "So she *is* a witch."

Saana cursed herself.

Blackcreek turned to Henya. "Well?"

"Lord, this servant swears by Nari and all her ancestors, Kerrti came to her," the girl said miserably, her eyes brimming with tears. Even through her rage, Saana felt a sudden stab of pity for her, interrogated by her ruler in front of everyone. "She doesn't speak but a couple of our words, nor does your servant speak hers, but she was eager enough to hold this servant's hand and your servant swears to you, Lord, that's all we did! And if she's a witch, she showed naught of it when we set that woman's leg."

Daimon nodded, and stepped in close to Saana. She thrust out her jaw pugnaciously.

"Yesterday, and this morning," Blackcreek said in a low voice, so quietly she could barely hear him, "we spoke of trying to bring our peoples together." His jaw worked for a moment before he continued, as though chewing over his words. "This lord confesses this was not what he had envisaged, but perhaps it is none the worse for that. Would you so quickly cast this idea aside?"

"These things are not done in Tjakorsha," Saana told him through gritted teeth.

"You are no longer in Tjakorsha."

With tremendous effort of will, Saana prevented herself from punching him. It wouldn't be so bad if the man's face actually showed some expression! "It is against the will of Father Krayk!"

"Let *him* worry about it, then!" Blackcreek snapped. "Your people wish to live here? You wish to be protected by our law, so this lord must take the hand of his own man when that man raises his hand to you? Then this lord will also protect your people from *you*, for we have no law prohibiting two men or two women from courting!" He turned away from her, but Saana grabbed his arm.

"And what of those who not wish for this?" she demanded.

"Then do not do it!" Daimon exclaimed in frustration, tugging his arm free of her grasp. "This lord cares not who does or does not court who, so long as both are willing!" He raised his voice.

"People of Black Keep! Bring fire! It is time for the burning!"

A cheer went up, and for a moment Saana thought he'd honestly called for her to be burned, but as he strode off her eye was caught by the giant effigy of the Wooden Man, and she remembered what Daimon had told her earlier. It seemed mightily convenient that it was time to set it alight just as they'd argued, but a crowd was flooding towards the square and Blackcreek was already lost in their midst. Angry though she was, Saana wasn't going to chase after him now.

She looked about her. Kerrti and Henya had disappeared. Most of her people were following the Naridans, probably on the basis that even if they hadn't understood what Blackcreek had shouted, it certainly seemed something important was about to happen. Tavi, however, was finishing some ale and appeared in no hurry to go anywhere.

"You are not watching the burning?" Saana asked, sitting down next to him.

"No," he replied, and grimaced. "S'man is... He doesn't like fire."

Saana laughed. "You don't like *fire?*" Tavi's face became even less expressive than was the Naridan norm, and she raised her hands in apology. "But you work with dragons!'

"Dragons don't like fire either," Tavi said, his brow creasing. "At least, ours don't. The big thundertooths are a different matter, but—"

"This man means she finds dragons far scarier than fire," Saana explained.

"All dragons?" Tavi asked. He turned to face her, swinging his left leg over the bench so he was straddling it. "Even the small ones?"

Saana shook her head. "Well, no. The small ones are strange, but they don't scare this man."

"Just like this man and fire, then," Tavi said with a grin. "He can cook food and warm himself without too much worry, but *that...*" He pointed out beyond the castle's gate, and shuddered. "Dragons can be understood; can be taught to an extent, as s'man and your daughter are learning. No man alive can teach fire."

Saana laughed. "True." She looked around for something to drink, but unless she wanted someone else's dregs, everything had been taken out to the main square. Tavi must have guessed her intentions, since he gestured towards the gate with a rueful smile.

"This man understands."

"No." Saana shook her head firmly. "You saved this man from being stabbed; she should not leave you on your own just so she can find a drink. Besides," she added, "this man does not ale like."

Tavi scratched his chin. "Then perhaps s'man can offer an alternative. But he keeps it in the stables, and there's dragons there."

"This man would be with Tavi, Master of Dragons," Saana declared expansively, getting to her feet. "What would she have to fear?"

"That's the spirit," Tavi laughed. He swung his other leg over the bench and got up. Behind them, a crackling noise and a cheer from many throats suggested the Wooden Man had been set ablaze. "Let's go."

Saana took one of the reed torches down from a sconce on the courtyard wall. By its flickering light they passed through the open gate into the second yard, then over to the squat shape of the stables. Tavi heaved the small door open and ducked inside, and Saana followed.

The stable didn't stink quite so badly this time, perhaps because she was expecting it. It was also slightly warmer than outside, since the bite of the night air hadn't infiltrated past the door and shutters. Saana held her breath as a huge shadow moved in the gloom, but Bastion had simply noticed their appearance and got up in his stall to see what was going on.

"Easy there, boy," Tavi murmured. "It's just your servant and his friend."

Bastion exhaled a monstrous, sour gust of air, and slumped back down again into his straw. Saana couldn't help but smile. "His servant?"

"S'man feeds them, houses them, cleans them, attends to their needs," Tavi replied, taking the torch from her and using it to light another. "Not so different to what we do for the thanes, really."

Saana laughed out loud at that. "And have you said such thoughts to your thane?"

"Hah! S'man prefers his head on his shoulders," Tavi informed her. "He speaks his thoughts to his dragons, who'd never betray him."

"This man is no dragon," Saana pointed out, following him past the stall doors.

"True," Tavi conceded. "S'man will just have to hope you won't betray him either." He knocked one side of what turned out to be a loose wooden panel in the wall at the end of the stable, and withdrew a small brown ceramic bottle, which he unstoppered. "Perhaps this will help."

Saana sniffed the neck and coughed in surprise at the tart smell that assailed her nose. "That is certainly not ale!"

"Applejack," Tavi replied, and took a small swig. He offered it to her. "Careful now. Too much will send you to sleep."

Saana raised her eyebrows, but sipped carefully. There was a moment of intense sweetness as the liquid hit her tongue, before it tried to shrivel her mouth up. It burned on the way down, too: she wasn't sure it was as strong as shorat, but the flavour was richer, if anything.

"This man thought your people could not make a decent drink," she said, wiping her mouth and handing the bottle back. "She was wrong."

Tavi laughed. "We're full of surprises." He pushed open the door of the empty stall door next to them and wandered over to the heap of straw against the far wall. He sat down, then looked at her doubtful expression. "It's clean."

"Very well." Saana scuffed her way across the floor and threw herself down next to him. Her head was pleasantly fuzzy, and her dark mood from earlier had abated somewhat. It was good to not be chief of anything for a short while.

"So how do you become chief of a clan?" Tavi asked, and Saana groaned inwardly.

"In our clan? The old chief dies and the elders pick a new one," she told him.

Tavi took another swig from the bottle. "Only in your clan?"

"In some clans a chief can be challenged to a fight," she said. "Some clans do it like we do. Some clans, this man does not know." She took the bottle from him and sipped at the applejack again, savouring the flavour of it. "You never have female thanes?"

Tavi snorted a laugh. "No. A pity. Lady Delil, Lord Asrel's wife, was sharp as a knife, but kind too. Always had time for us, though s'man was only a stable boy when the sickness took her. S'man thinks he'd have preferred her rule to Lord Asrel's, but that would never happen. Still, she might've softened him somewhat." He took the bottle back. "As it is, Lord Asrel loved her too much to ever remarry, so the boys grew up without a mother. With their father the way he is, it's amazing Lord Daimon blackened his scabbard to save us."

"He what?" Saana frowned at him, unsure if he was being coarse.

"Hmm? Oh, it's… Well, he hasn't actually done it yet. See, a sar's longblade scabbard shows their great deeds," Tavi explained. "Painted onto the white wood. If they dishonour themselves, part of it gets stained over, to show that. If they commit a great enough crime or failing, the entire scabbard is turned black and they're a *blacksword*, because no matter what they do, nothing will erase the shame of their past save their own death." He took another swig. "Lord Daimon hasn't actually stained his scabbard yet, but he'll be a blacksword once the Southern Marshal hears about this, would be this man's guess."

Saana frowned. "But he is so young! He could yet do many great deeds!"

Tavi shrugged. "Sars, thanes, and lords don't forgive easy. It's simpler for us lowborn. We just get whipped or lose a hand, and there's an end to it."

Saana eyed him, as he stared straight ahead at the stall door. "That does not sound simple to this man."

"S'man is drunk," Tavi said, looking at her. His speech was a little loose, but his eyes were clear and focused as they met hers. "He's probably saying things he shouldn't."

Saana shifted uncomfortably. "This man did not ask Daimon to take Ganalel's hand—"

"Pffft." Tavi waved his own hand dismissively. "Ganalel was a fool and a coward. But sometimes..."

"Sometimes?" Saana prompted him when he didn't speak further. Tavi sighed, and looked past her shoulder as though checking no one had followed them into the stable.

"Sometimes s'man thinks that if the God-King truly meant for us to be ruled like this... well, perhaps he was wrong." Tavi took another swig of applejack. "There. S'man said it. His head's forfeit now."

"Daimon would take your head for saying that?" Saana asked, shocked.

"Why not?" Tavi replied. "He threw over enough tradition by imprisoning Lord Asrel. If he lets much more slide, who's to say people won't start thinking the same as s'man does?" He laughed, but there was little humour to it. "You're a threat to him too, you Raiders and your women who do everything a man does. They don't like that here."

"But you do?"

"Faaz and Abbatane help in the stable," Tavi said simply. "Faaz is a good lad, he does what s'man tells him to. Abbatane knows what to do *without* being told. She understands the dragons, in a way Faaz doesn't. If she's still here when s'man gets too old to be stablemaster, she'll be the best choice to take his place, but Faaz'll be put in charge, because he'll be a man. Same goes for the apothecary. Tevyel's good enough, but he just knows what his teacher taught him, and he thinks that's all there is to know. Henya, she knows all he knows, but she wants to learn *more*. S'man's heard her talking about it. But Tevyel's the apothecary, and if he looks to train a successor he'll probably pick a lad." Tavi shrugged. "What's true for stables and apothecaries is probably true for castles and countries. Or so it seems to s'man."

Saana's heart sank at the stablemaster's explanation. She hadn't really thought about exactly how deep-set the Naridans' beliefs about women must be. "You truly think Daimon views our women as... a threat?"

"Perhaps you can work on him," Tavi offered. "He likes you."

Saana burst out laughing. "He shows it strangely!"

"The boy's never had a woman to talk to as his equal since he was raised to nobility," Tavi pointed out, and Saana abruptly stopped laughing. "His family was lowborn. He's no highborn sister, no highborn mother, he's never courted a highborn girl because we're in the arse end of nowhere, and Lord Asrel and the nearest thane hate each other. And then there's you, as tall as he is, walking around calling yourself 'this man' and looking him straight in the eye." Tavi took another swig. "He hasn't a clue what to make of you, is s'man's guess, but he likes you. Even if he hasn't realised it yet."

Saana snatched the bottle off him and took a swig of her own. "What d'you mean?"

"S'man saw how Lord Daimon looked at you in his brother's armour," Tavi said with a wicked grin. "That'll be a young thane who's had some confusing dreams, s'man would wager." He grimaced at the bottle she was holding. "Nari's teeth, but s'man's drunk. Should not be saying this."

"No!" Saana pointed an accusing finger at him. "No no no.

No. You don't get to stop talking now you've said *that*. What in t'Dark Father's name you talking about?"

Tavi laughed. "You know what s'man's talking about, else Zhanna's birth must've come as a surprise!"

Saana gaped. "But he's only a… How old *is* he?"

"Two-and-twenty?" Tavi asked himself, wrinkling his nose up with the effort of remembering. "Two-and-twenty, yes."

Two years older than when I had Zhanna. Saana had been thinking of Daimon as a youth, but actually that wasn't really accurate. But even so… "Surely he thinks this man too old?"

"Do your people stop fucking at five-and-twenty?" Tavi asked.

Tsolga's leer swam into Saana's mind's eye. "No."

"Well then," Tavi said with a shrug. "In time, Daimon may come to his senses and realise what his cock's telling him."

Saana stopped with the bottle of applejack halfway to her mouth and a flutter in her stomach that wasn't entirely related to the alcohol. "'Come to his senses'?"

Tavi's face flattened out again, and he looked away. "S'man's drunk…"

Saana grabbed his shoulder and waved the bottle of applejack under his nose. "You don't get to blame this for everything you say, Tavi of Black Keep!"

He snatched it from her and took another swig. "Very well! S'man is drunk *and* he thinks that Saana of the Brown Eagle clan is a rare beauty." He faced her, their eyes just a hand's span apart. Saana met those dark eyes, and forced herself not to look away.

"Did you bring this man here to get her drunk and say these things, Tavi?" she asked, keeping her voice steady.

"No," he replied simply. "S'man brought you here because he hates big fires, and he thought you might like applejack." He shrugged, and Saana felt the hard muscles of his shoulder move under his rough-spun shirt. She swallowed.

"This man has two questions." She raised one finger. "Does applejack make people want to fuck more than they do normally?"

Tavi's brow wrinkled. "No more than other drink?"

She nodded, and raised a second finger. "How long before we're missed?"

"The Wooden Man takes a long time to burn," Tavi said slowly. "They'll be a while."

Saana licked her lips to moisten them. "Well, then." Her mind was throwing up memories of straddling Tavi in the mud earlier, and the strength in his limbs as he bucked under her, and when they'd wrist-wrestled, and his hand upon her backside when he'd shoved her into Bastion's saddle. And maybe he was somewhat smooth-cheeked, and none too tall, but that last part wouldn't matter if they were lying down. And perhaps he was sort of handsome, in an odd Naridan way, or at least he was in the flickering half-light of the torch burning on the wall, and after ale, and shorat, and applejack. Most importantly, perhaps, he was here, and he was warm, and it felt like he was the only person in the last two weeks who *hadn't* been asking or expecting something of her...

"Wait, third question." She held up another finger. "If this man fucks you, does she have to marry you? Is that a Naridan thing?"

Tavi shook his head. "No. Definitely not."

Saana kissed him.

He tasted of applejack, which was both pleasant and unsurprising. She grabbed the back of his head and pulled him into her, and he did the same, twining his fingers in her hair. His other hand slipped up underneath her furs, fingers cold on her back. She pressed her hand to his chest, feeling the firm plane of muscle there, and slid her right leg across him so she was straddling him as he sat on the straw. He made an appreciative sound deep in his throat, and kissed her harder.

It wasn't long before she was reaching down to peel his shirt up over his head, and as she finished tugging it clear of his arms his hands found their way to her breasts. She leaned in to kiss him some more and he rolled sideways, seeking to bring her under him, but she rolled with him and ended up sitting astride him on the straw-strewn stall floor.

"You said it was clean," she told his surprised expression, reaching back to pull at one of her boots. They didn't come off easily, but after a bit of contorting she'd thrown them into a corner of the stall and started on the ties of her breeches. Tavi reached down to wrestle with his own laces as she slid off him to shuck one leg free, then she gripped the waist of his and wrenched them downwards to his knees while he wriggled to assist her.

It turned out Naridan men were made more or less the same as Tjakorshi ones, which had been a source of some speculation amongst the women, since Avlja had never been forthcoming about Nalon's body. It also seemed they reacted in much the same way to too much alcohol, so she took him in her hand and gripped firmly, then took his hand and placed it between her legs. He quickly got the idea of what she was about, and she kissed him ferociously while their hands worked a twin rhythm. At one point he started to push himself up, perhaps thinking he was ready for something more; and he might have been, but she wasn't yet, so she released her grip and pushed him back down again. With his legs still tangled in his breeches he couldn't do much to argue, and he relented.

Saana could feel pressure building inside her now, a delicious tension in her lower stomach like a storm wave building in height, until finally she crested, and broke, and dashed herself on the shore. Tavi cried out too and she realised she'd bitten his lower lip, and her nails had drawn blood from his right shoulder. Her other hand seemed to have done its work though, and she threw her leg across him to straddle him again. It wasn't long before Tavi was huffing and blowing underneath her, then spasmed and cried out, then lay still apart from his heaving, sweat-slicked chest.

Saana leaned down, kissed him again, then rolled off him and stumbled outside to piss.

NABANDA

THEY WERE INTO the garden as easy and quick as shadows. Hê'd brought five others, all good hands, discreet and capable. They'd already agreed how they were going to do this; no lurking, just going in fast and hard to overwhelm the guards.

There were two in a pool of lamp light, in maille and half-helm, spears resting on their shoulders and talking idly. They hadn't preserved their night vision, and they hadn't been alert. By the time they realised they weren't alone, it was too late.

Perlishu whipped a wind ring off the first finger of hēr right hand. The sharpened steel disc took one guard in the throat, biting so deep it nearly took their head off. They fell, their hands flying uselessly to the red tide gushing from their throat. The other turned and gaped for a second as Nabanda charged them, then fled with a panicked scream.

Another wind ring took them between the shoulder blades. The maille held, but the impact sent them stumbling. Nabanda caught them within a few steps and slashed hîs sickle across the unarmoured back of their right leg. The guard collapsed onto their side, and Badir stepped in and brought one of hìs axes down to make a red ruin of the guard's face and instantly still their limbs.

"Only two?" Badir asked, putting one foot on the guard's

forehead to wrench hìs axe free. Hè was Morlithian by name and blood, but Alaban by birth, and Nabanda trusted hìm as much as hê did anyone else in the islands.

"There'll be more inside," Nabanda said, looking up at the house. It was too much to hope the noise had gone unnoticed. "Take Perlishu, and make sure no one escapes in the carriage."

Badir nodded and loped off towards the front of the house, with Perlishu slipping out of the shadows to follow hìm. Hēr wind rings would be less use inside a building, but ideal if someone tried to make a break for it across open ground.

"Want to give me a hand up?" Tungkung said, appearing at Nabanda's shoulder. Nabanda nodded and tucked hîs sickle and knife back into hîs belt to cup hîs hands, then boosted Tungkung upwards for thëm to grab the railing running around the balcony of the first floor. The ground floor was the carriage house and stable, with high, shuttered windows, and the main wooden doors at the front that would be barred from inside. There would be stairs in there leading up into the dwelling, but getting in that way would be time-consuming.

There were three main doors to a house like this: one at each side of the front facing, each with their own steps leading down to the ground so as not to obstruct the carriage entrance, and the shutter doors at the rear. Guelan ran for one of the front doors and Kedenta the other, while Nabanda unwound the grapnel and rope from around hîs waist, twirled it briefly, then threw to hook the barbed metal over the balcony railing. Now on the balcony itself, Tungkung already had thëir blades out; a long knife and a short sword, both of them slender and wickedly sharp, much like their owner, and single-edged.

Nabanda was halfway up the rope when the shutter doors above hîm crashed open and someone wielding twin crutch blades burst out. They immediately engaged Tungkung, parrying thëir first thrust with a downward swipe of their right arm and lashing out with the left to send Tungkung dodging backwards.

"Intruder!" the guard shouted, following up. This was no amateur with a spear, but a trained warrior. Nabanda wondered if the guards who'd just died had known they were only there for their deaths to provide warning to those inside the house.

Still, despite being better trained, this guard hadn't realised there was more than one intruder. Nabanda reached the top of hîs rope and hauled hîmself up and over as quickly as hê could, praying to all the Hundred the guard wouldn't turn and skewer hîm while hê was unable to defend hîmself. At least one god must have listened, as hê got his feet onto the decking while the guard was still engaged with Tungkung.

Hê wasn't as light on hîs feet as hê might have been, and the guard heard the noise. They turned, backing away from Tungkung as they did so, and whirled towards Nabanda with a slashing blow that hê only avoided by throwing hîmself through the shutter door and into the room beyond. Hê tripped on a rug, fell, rolled, and came back up to hîs feet clawing the sickle from hîs belt, but Tungkung had pressed forwards again, and the guard was forced onto the defensive instead of being able to follow Nabanda inside and stab him.

A flicker of movement past another shutter at the side of the house caught Nabanda's attention, and there was the strangled grunt of a body having a blade punched into it from behind. Guelan must have run along the encircling balcony from where hê was supposed to be watching one of the main doors in order to get involved.

Nabanda turned, pulling hîs knife out, and quickly took stock. There were no lamps lit in here, but hê could make out the long, low shapes of furniture. A room for rich folk to sit and entertain their guests, perhaps. For Nabanda, who'd never lived in anything larger than the one small room near the docks where hê slept on a lumpy pallet of old blankets, it was a bizarre concept.

Hê heard movement above him, frantic footsteps on wooden floors. All element of surprise had gone. Hê half-expected them to shout for help, but perhaps they didn't realise how keen hîs ears were; perhaps they still thought they could hide, or that their guards' screams and shouts would have alerted the neighbours. Possible, of course, but not that likely. Rich people liked their privacy, which was why they had these wide grounds and walls, and that cut both ways.

Literally.

The room hê was in ran the entire width of the house, and there was only one interior door. Nabanda sidled towards it, hîs blades held low and ready, waiting for any movement. A sound behind hîm caused hîm to whirl, but it was only Tungkung.

"Anyone?" thëy asked quietly, picking thëir way across the rug that had tripped Nabanda.

"Upstairs," hê replied, hîs tone just as low. "Are you hurt?"

"A cut on my arm," Tungkung said. "It can wait."

"Guelan?"

"Gone back to watch hîs door."

"Come on, then." Nabanda slid forwards with Tungkung in tow. No attack came as hê passed the threshold into the next room, floored in pale marble. This too ran the width of the house, with a corridor down to the front door on the right hand side, the one hê'd sent Guelan to guard. Directly in front of hîm, taking up the remaining width of the room, was a white-painted wall with a door in it. Nabanda checked it and found a well-appointed kitchen, with its own door to the outside; the servant's entrance. A wide staircase ran up to the next floor from the main hallway, and Nabanda could see another door, set into the side of the stairs, which would lead down to the carriage house.

"*Hsst!*"

Nabanda turned at Tungkung's hiss and brought hîs weapons up, looking for the threat; two shadows at the top of the stairs, the light glinting off their weapons. One had twin crescent blades, the other a hookbill axe, a two-handed affair with a pole as tall as the person wielding it. Nasty tools, to be sure, especially when they held the high ground across a narrow front, so they needed to be tempted from it.

"Guelan!" Nabanda shouted, hîs voice so loud that Tungkung flinched in surprise. "Kedenta! Come in through the rear! Knock if you hear me!"

There was a thump on each door, then the sound of running footsteps approaching. Now the guards at the top of the stairs knew that within a few seconds they would be outnumbered by at least two to one, possibly more, at which point high ground or no, choke point or no, their situation would be much worse.

They reacted as Nabanda hoped they would: they flowed down the stairs, looking to thin the odds against them before more enemies could arrive.

"This was your plan?" Tungkung hissed in alarm, raising thëir blades as the axe-armed guard headed for them, the vicious curved blade chopping at the air. For hîs part, Nabanda was too busy to reply, for the guard with crescent blades had elected to come at hîm.

They were dangerous indeed: two lengths of sharpened metal protruding some way above and a little way below the fabric-wrapped grips, with the top curved over into a sharpened hook, while the grips themselves were protected by crescent-shaped blades that could be used in an edged punch if necessary. They were weapons in truth, designed only for killing, quite different to the sickle and long knife Nabanda carried.

The guard attacked, blades flashing, looking to hook Nabanda's weapons aside and leave hîm open for a killing stroke. Nabanda retreated, blocking and parrying without committing, gauging hîs opponent's speed and timing. Then, just before hê was going to be pressed up against the wall, hê stepped into a block with hîs sickle instead of backing away further, and lashed out with a kick that caught the other fighter in the left shortribs.

The guard threw a cut with their right-hand weapon, but they were off-balance: Nabanda spun past it and drove the point of hîs sickle into the flesh over their shoulder blade, then reached around and cut their throat with hîs knife. The guard slumped sideways, and Nabanda turned hîs attention to the other as someone screamed.

Guelan was on the floor, arms clutched around hîs own midsection. Hê'd come running in too fast, too eager, and the hookbill axe had opened hîm across the middle. The remaining guard backed off towards the stairs, aware they were now alone, but one of Tungkung's arms hung loosely by thëir side and Kedenta held only a pair of dragon claws: straight-gripped, underslung sickle-bladed knives, deadly in corridors or alleys, but of less use in a large room against an enemy with a polearm. Nabanda hadn't expected so much space inside the house; hê'd anticipated more internal walls.

There was a crash, and the door to the carriage house flew open. Kedenta whirled towards it, dropping into a ready stance with hìs dragon claws, but it was only Badir, axes in hand. However, the guard took advantage of the momentary distraction to attack.

It wasn't a killing blow, but the hookbill blade flashed in the dim light and sliced across Kedenta's shoulder, drawing forth a cry of pain. Badir roared and charged, hìs own shorter-hafted axes raised, and the guard hastily retreated behind the thick wooden bannister of the stairs, slashing out at head height as they rose up a couple of steps. Badir ducked, and Tungkung abruptly curtailed thëir lunge as the hookbill flashed towards thëm.

Nabanda ran forwards, hurling hîs knife. Hê was no expert with thrown weapons and it wasn't balanced for it in any case, but the guard flinched involuntarily as the improvised projectile glanced hilt-first off their shoulder. Badir swung again, seeking to take advantage of the opening as hè advanced up the stairs, but the hookbill's haft knocked both hìs axes aside.

However, Tungkung, leaning low and stabbing, thrust thëir blade into the guard's groin.

The guard staggered and lashed out with the butt of their axe, catching Tungkung in thëir wounded arm and knocking thëm back down the stairs with a curse on thëir lips, but this time Badir's left-hand axe met no resistance as it bit into the side of the guard's neck. The guard pitched forwards, falling on their face down the stairs, and Kedenta jumped in to plunge one of hìs dragon claws into the back of their neck.

"They were dead already," Badir snapped, from a couple of stairs higher.

"Never assume they're dead until they stop moving," Kedenta replied. Hè turned to look at Nabanda. "Should we be expecting more?"

"Do Î look like a seer to yòu?" Nabanda snapped, retrieving hîs knife from where it had landed. "Î doubt it, but go carefully."

"What of Guelan?" Badir asked, looking over at where hê lay whimpering on the floor.

"If it looks like we can help hîm when we're done, we'll take hîm," Nabanda said. "If not, it's a larger share for the rest of us." Hê led the way up the stairs, with Badir at hîs left shoulder and Kedenta at hîs right, the injured Tungkung bringing up the rear.

The next floor up was quiet, but the quiet of people holding their breath. Nabanda cautiously pulled open the slatted doors directly facing the stairs to reveal linen closets of neatly folded fabric. No one lurked inside.

There were three other doors to what would almost certainly be bedrooms. One was to their immediate right, past the linen cupboards, opening into the same wall. There were no other doors there, suggesting the room beyond was the same size as the living room below. A master bedroom, for the family's adults? Then on either side of the stairwell, towards the front of the building, two more: rooms for children? The servants might not live here, would certainly not live on the same floor as the family. Perhaps there were small chambers in the carriage house? If so, hê could trust that Badir would have killed them on hìs way past.

Two of the doors, including the master bedroom, were open.

Nabanda cast hîs gaze from one to another, thinking. They'd heard the scream, heard the guard's shouted warning of an intruder. Perhaps heard the guard die. The adults ran from their bedroom; the feet hê'd heard overhead. A child had come out of their room, or had been fetched, warned not to make a noise. Then… what? The other child hadn't woken? The family had gone in to find them, trusting their guards would deal with the threat?

You would always close the door behind you if you thought a threat was in your house. Even if it would do nothing, you'd close the door behind you.

"Watch the stairs," hê muttered to Tungkung, then raised hîs sickle to point at the closed bedroom door. "That one."

Hê went first, circling the stairwell and watching the door carefully, but no new threat boiled out of it. Hê stopped in front of it, paused, listened.

Silence.

No, not quite. A faint snuffling breath, cut off almost immediately. A frightened child's whimper, stifled by an adult's hand.

Nabanda didn't enjoy killing children, but it paid well. Hê stepped back until the rails of the stairwell were against hîs back, checked that Badir and Kedenta were ready, then launched hîmself shoulder-first at the door.

It wasn't the thickest, but it was made of decent wood, hard and heavy. The latch, on the other hand, wasn't up to the task of stopping someone of Nabanda's bulk. It gave way with a splintering sound, spilling hîm into the room.

Someone screamed. There was a flash of motion, white in moonlight, as the shutters were pulled aside and someone scrambled for the window, but Nabanda couldn't concentrate on that because a blade was coming for hîm.

It was an aggressive, downwards blow; Nabanda side-stepped the strike's arc, hooked hîs sickle around his attacker's wrist and twisted, forcing their arm down and twisting the blade uselessly towards the floor. In the same motion hê struck the flat of the blade with the knuckles of hîs knife hand, sending it spinning away across the room, then stepped behind hîs opponent and drove hîs knife between their shoulder blades.

Badir hadn't even made it through the door by the time Nabanda's attacker—the fàther, by hîs guess—was pitching forwards. Nabanda whirled around as the other adult screamed again and threw themselves at hîm. This time Badir got there first, hìs axe taking them in the chest and spraying blood into Nabanda's eyes.

"The window!" hê spat at Kedenta. "Î think one went out the window!" Badir made sure of hìs kill with hìs other axe and Kedenta rushed past them both to the window. Nabanda followed hìm, wiping hîs face.

"Godshit!" Kedenta hissed. Nabanda came alongside hìm and looked out. Below them, climbing down a robust-looking plant clinging to the house's outer wall, was a child in a white nightshift. They looked up, eyes wide with fear, dropped the last couple of paces to the balcony below, then sprinted away.

"Move!" Nabanda snapped, shoving Kedenta aside to give hîmself more room. Hê swung hîs legs over the window's edge, judged the distance for a moment, then dropped.

Hê hit the balcony hard, and a sharp spike of pain in hîs left ankle caused hîm to curse, but hê forced hîmself after hîs fleeing victim. The child was no babe, but not yet an adult either; they might be swift, but they were barefoot, scared, and had nowhere to run except all the way around the house to the other stairs, where Perlishu would be waiting.

Or, hê realised as the child jumped over the body of the guard Guelan had stabbed in the back, they could use the grapnel hê'd left on the rear railing, that trailed a rope down to the ground below.

Nabanda spat another curse and forced hîmself to move faster, but by the time hê'd reached the corner of the house the child was already swinging themselves over the rail, grabbing at the grapnel rope as they went. There was a scream and a thud as they fell, their arms clearly unable to properly support their weight, and Nabanda had a flash of dark hope they might have broken their leg or something equally fortuitous. Then hê saw the shimmer of white moving again, heading away from the dead guards on the ground and over the clear area of grass at the rear, towards the trees and bushes that had given Nabanda and hîs crew cover on their way in.

Nabanda sheathed his sickle and threw one leg over the railing, cursing hîs luck. Hê couldn't afford another drop from this height, with hîs ankle already bad. Hê'd have to hope the child stepped on a thorn, or couldn't get over the far wall, although hê didn't relish the thought of trying to get to grips with them in the garden...

Something glittered in the moonlight, like a shooting star falling to earth, and the child's left leg was no longer attached at the knee. They fell, screaming at the top of their lungs, until Perlishu jogged across the grass and sliced another of hēr wind rings across their throat.

"Yōu got them?" Badir called. Nabanda looked up to see hìm leaning out of one of the windows at the back of the house.

"Obviously," Perlishu replied, looking up from the ground. "Are yòu going to let any more get away?"

"There's no one else here," Badir replied. Nabanda felt hîs stomach clench.

"There should be one more. A grown child."

Badir simply shrugged, a peculiarly expressive gesture when performed with an axe in each hand.

"Look again," Nabanda told hìm, pulling his sickle back out.

"We already—"

"*Look. Again.*" Hê strode back into the living room, kicking aside furniture and tipping it over, searching for a cowering, hidden figure but knowing in hîs gut hê wouldn't find one. Sure enough, the room was empty. Hê made for the foot of the stairs, wrinkling hîs nose at the stench of Guelan's guts, and found Kedenta descending. "Nothing?"

"Nothing. Checked all the rooms twice. They're not that big. Nowhere to hide we wouldn't have found."

"The other three were in their night clothes!" Nabanda raged, kicking the kitchen door so it slammed back on its hinges. "Where would an adult child be, when the rest of their family is in bed?!" He turned and shouted up the stairs. "Are the parents still alive?"

"No," Badir called back down.

"Mushuru's ashes!" Nabanda swore. Hê knelt down next to Guelan, grabbed hìs head and rammed hîs knife into hìs eye socket. Guelan stiffened for a moment, then lay still.

"So what now?" Kedenta asked. Nabanda wiped hîs knife off on Guelan's maijhi and sheathed it.

"Find anything valuable," Nabanda said, raising hîs voice for Bahir and Tungkung to hear too. "We take what we can, make this look like a theft gone wrong. Then we find the lamp oil and burn this place to the ground."

"And the other child?" Kedenta asked. "Kurumaya's job was for all the family, wasn't it?"

Nabanda rolled hîs thick neck, and grimaced. Hê hated it when jobs got complicated.

"We're going to have to find them, aren't we?"

KERRTI

It was a murky morning. The sun had probably just about hauled itself over the horizon behind the clouds that rolled in overnight, but at the moment was doing about as much work as the rest of Black Keep. Drinking and merriment had continued late into the night, and Tjakorshi and Naridan alike were showing it by dint of not showing themselves. The few souls about moved slowly and quietly, perhaps out of respect for others, perhaps due to the sorry state of their own heads.

Kerrti's fire had died down to embers overnight. The witch knelt in front of it and thrust in kindling, trying to coax a new flame. She'd left the revels as the huge Wooden Man had caught fire, unable to stomach the stares and whispers of those who called themselves her clan, and had returned to her own hearth. She'd barred her door and hadn't answered the knocks that had come, although they'd been both fewer and less aggressive than she'd feared.

Flame caught, a tiny tongue of yellow licking up the sliver of wood. She laid it down and began to build over it with other twigs and shavings, looking to nourish it.

There was a knock at the door. A little tentative, as though the knocker couldn't decide whether they wanted to be heard.

Kerrti rolled her eyes. She considered ignoring this, too, but she couldn't just pretend the outside world wasn't there. It was hard, though. She'd kept her secrets for years, tried to ignore the comments and casual, undirected hatred surrounding her. It had never been pleasant, but she'd coped. It was like a scab on a wound that never properly healed; painful, sometimes, but dull enough she could usually forget about it.

Last night, she'd dared to peel off the scab in the hope of revealing fresh skin, and Saana fucking Sattistutar had decided to plunge a knife in.

The knock came again. Kerrti sighed, and stood. "I'm coming, I'm coming." She crossed the floor, drew back the bar and opened the door.

There, hood up and looking rather the worse for wear, was Saana Sattistutar.

Kerrti froze. She had a fleeting impulse to push the other woman back down the steps that led up to her door. Then Saana opened her mouth, and Kerrti slammed the door shut in her face and barred it again. She stalked back to her fire, her skin tingling and her breath coming quickly.

"*Kerrti!*" It was a hiss rather than a shout, followed by another half-tentative knock. Kerrti whirled around.

"Are you cutting my nets?!" she yelled, heedless of the noise. Why should she care if anyone heard? "You think I want to talk to you?"

"*Kerrti...* I came to apologise."

Rage flared up, and Kerrti found herself at the door and yanking the bar back before she really knew what she was doing. Saana didn't look like she'd expected the door to be opened again, and certainly not that quickly or ferociously. She leaned back, her eyes widening.

"Really?" Kerrti snapped. "Apologise for what?"

"For what I said last night," Saana replied. She looked sideways down the street, then back at Kerrti, uncertainly. "May I come in?"

The urge to push her down the steps flared up again, stronger than before, but Kerrti fought it down. This was the sort of temper she'd seen in others, a desire to break anything that dared move, speak or generally be in the way, and despite her rage she could remember how that kind of temper ended.

She stepped back so she was no longer barring the door, and took a deep breath. "Fine. But you leave when I say so."

"You have my word." Saana stepped over the threshold and waited until Kerrti had closed the door before throwing her hood back. Kerrti had always thought of Saana as quite handsome, but now that was overlaid with the memory of the hateful twist to her features from the night before.

"Well?" she said, crossing her arms.

Saana scrubbed at her face with one hand. It looked partly like a gesture of unease, and partly an attempt to wake herself up. She looked like she'd barely slept. "I apologise for how I spoke last night."

"Why?"

Saana blinked. "What?"

"Why are you apologising?" Kerrti demanded. She could feel herself quivering, and couldn't tell if it was from fear, rage or both. The simple thing would be to accept whatever apology Saana offered and hope everyone forgot about it, but she'd seen the looks and heard the mutterings. They wouldn't forget.

"Do you know?" she asked, when Saana didn't immediately respond. "Or are you just here because you need something for a sore head, and you think I won't give it to you otherwise?" And she wouldn't, either. Let the chief nurse her hangover.

Saana struggled to hold eye contact. "I shouldn't have confronted you publicly. It wasn't fair, I—"

"But you would have confronted me in private?" Kerrti snapped. "Is that what you're doing now? Are you here to tell me I'm an abomination in the eyes of Father Krayk?"

Saana's mouth opened, but nothing came out.

"Let me tell you about Father Krayk, Saana!" Kerrti said. "I came on your voyage across the Great Ocean, the greatest voyage the clan's ever made, and for *all that time* I was on a yolgu, thinking my unclean thoughts, surrounded by his realm! And yet he didn't take me! He didn't even take anyone *near* me!" She spread her arms. "The Dark Father clearly doesn't give a shit! So why do you?"

"Have you lost your *mind*?" Saana hissed, glancing at the door as though expecting Father Krayk to burst in at any moment.

Kerrti just laughed at her. "What, you think I'm reckless to speak ill of a god who loathes me? How much worse can I make it for myself?"

Saana jerked back as though she'd been slapped, but her expression hardened. "Are you telling me you'd renounce us? Renounce Father Krayk? You prefer the Naridan way, the layers upon layers of..." She spluttered, trying to find words for concepts that didn't easily exist in Tjakorshan. "... of where people stand, of who must bow to who, and women are always at the bottom?"

"What a choice!" Kerrti snarled. "To be shat upon for who I am, or for who I love?" She shook her head, daring the chief to speak. "No, I see. I understand now a little of how Nalon felt when Avlja plucked him from that ship. The alternative isn't perfect, but it's better for me. Yes, Saana, if you and the rest of the clan were to leave tomorrow, I'd choose to stay."

Saana's mouth dropped open. "You think even that healer girl Henya will ever be respected here? They'll always choose a man over her, and you'd be an outsider on top of that!"

"At least they won't drive her out!" Kerrti shouted. "She'll still be part of their town!"

Saana blinked at her. "Is that what you're worried about? What you've *been* worried about? That we'd... we'd exile you?"

Kerrti swallowed. Her throat felt swollen. Her eyes felt swollen, come to that. "Yes." It was hard to give voice to the fear. The clanless didn't last long in Tjakorsha. There was virtually nowhere that didn't belong to one clan or another, and trespassers could expect a quick death, so exiles either needed to impress another clan, or take a boat—if they had one—and leave the islands completely. None had ever been seen again.

"Kerrti, why would we do that?" Saana asked, her voice suddenly more gentle. She gave a small laugh, gesturing around at the bunches of herbs hanging from the walls; herbs Kerrti had cut before the voyage, not knowing what she'd find on these strange shores. "What would we do without you?"

Rage surged back up like a riptide.

"I don't want to be *tolerated* because I am *useful*!" Kerrti screamed into Saana's face. The chief actually retreated a step, back against the wall, and Kerrti followed her. "I just want to *live*! It shouldn't matter if I'm as fucking useless as Timmun! You should still be *my chief*! I shouldn't need some Flatlander lord to protect me from *you*!" She wanted to put her fist through Saana's face, and judging by Saana's expression, the chief realised that.

Kerrti turned away. The tentative flames in her fire pit had gone out again; the rest of the kindling hadn't caught. It should be simple enough to relight it from the embers, even now, but she suddenly felt so very, very tired.

"Why did you come here?" she said. She didn't look at Saana. Her voice sounded flat even to her ears, like a distant shout deadened by fog.

"I said, I—"

"Let me be of use." Now she turned again. She smiled, sharp as a blackstone axe and brittle as the first ice on high streams. She smiled, because otherwise she'd throw something. "Let me be of use, since that's the only value I have. What do you need from me? Something to take the pain from your head?"

She didn't know what she expected Saana to say. Nothing, perhaps. To turn and leave, or nod sullenly, or perhaps even angrily denounce her and threaten to exile her after all. She didn't expect the chief to drop her gaze to the wooden floor.

"Something to prevent my belly swelling with a babe."

Kerrti couldn't help it. She started to laugh, and didn't stop no matter how Saana glared at her, or how red her chief's cheeks went.

"You come to me, the day after you shout at me in front of everyone for holding a woman's hand, and you ask for *this*?" Kerrti sniggered. "Oh, this is a gift from the Dark Father himself! Who was it? Otzudh? Did he finally lure you back?"

"Will you give me what I need, or not?" Saana demanded, her face flushed and angry.

"Why not carry another child, Saana?" Kerrti demanded. It was cruel, she knew, but she couldn't help herself. "You're not too old yet! I'm sure Zhanna would love a little brother or sister!"

"This isn't the first time I've asked you for this, Kerrti," Saana said, her voice low and dangerous. "Why are you doing this now?"

"Because I find it funny how I'm supposed to help you avoid the consequences of your actions, when you're so quick to make me suffer for mine!" Kerrti snapped, feeling her laughter abruptly fade. She drew herself up. "Very well. Who is he? He won't dare take issue with the chief, but if he was expecting your belly to swell then he may have words for me when it doesn't, particularly now."

"That won't be an issue," Saana said. Kerrti frowned at her, surprised at the certainty in the older woman's tone. Then a startling possibility dawned, and she covered her mouth with her hand to stifle another snigger.

"You didn't... It wasn't a *Naridan*, was it?"

Saana's deliberately blank expression and stolid silence told Kerrti as much as if the chief had nodded and given her a name.

"Oh, by all the winds..."

"Will you give me what I need, or not?" Saana asked again, this time through visibly gritted teeth.

"Was it the Blackcreek boy?"

Saana's eyes flashed so dangerously that for a moment Kerrti was certain the other woman was going to strike her. "No, it wasn't! For the last time, yes or no?"

For a moment, Kerrti wavered. There was a certain savage justice in refusing. Let the clan see their chief's belly grow, with none of their men responsible. Some fine words were being cast around about how actually some of the Flatlanders weren't too bad, but Kerrti would wager her best sheepskin those words would take on a different flavour once someone realised a Flatlander had gotten the chief with child. Let Saana feel the weight of the entire clan's disapproval—and probably the Naridan townsfolk as well, unless Kerrti badly missed her guess. Let her see how it felt.

But it wouldn't solve Kerrti's problem. Saana might turn to herblore less skilled than Kerrti's, or use other, more direct methods, either of which could end up killing her. And should the child grow, and be born without killing Saana in the process, what would come of it? Saana might come to love it, but she might not. The child could be unloved, and resented. Kerrti hadn't learned what she'd learned to let lives be ruined through spite, tempting though it had been at times.

But that didn't mean she couldn't set her price.

"I'll give you what you need," she said, scanning her walls for the correct herb. "But I'll need payment."

"How much?"

"You misunderstand." Kerrti reached up, took down a large leather pouch and loosened the drawstring that held it shut. She sniffed the contents, to make sure she had the right one. "I need a promise. Your word, to Father Krayk."

"… Go on."

Kerrti took a deep breath and plunged on. "I need your word you'll take the Naridan views when it comes to men courting men, or women courting women. That you won't persecute me, or anyone else, for courting someone who wishes to be courted."

She hesitated, but there was no point stopping now. In for a crab, in for a krayk. "And you'll hold the rest of the clan to this, too."

Saana's breath hissed through her teeth. "You ask too much!"

"I ask to be able to live and love as I choose," Kerrti replied sharply. "No more and no less." She turned back to Saana, and held the bag of herbs over the embers of the fire. "Well? Do you want your remedy, or shall I burn it? I can assure you, *I'll* have no need of it."

Saana ground her teeth, but finally she nodded. "Very well."

"Your oath, Saana."

"I swear to Father Krayk that I'll do as you ask," Saana bit out. "May he come for me should I prove false."

Kerrti nodded. Something fluttered in her chest, relief or terror, or possibly both, but she fought it down. "You're an honourable woman, Saana. I'm sure you'll prove true." She took up a much smaller pouch and measured three pinches of dried leaves into it. "Sprinkle these into a small pot of hot water and wait for the water to colour. Drink it all—"

"I've done this before, Kerrti."

When Saana had left, her hood back up and the pouch tucked away, and the door barred once more, Kerrti sat back down in front of her fire pit. There were still faintly glowing embers deep in its heart. Something she could work with, at least.

She leaned forward and blew gently, scattering flakes of ash and a few sparks, but causing the embers to glow brighter. She took up the kindling and, slowly and carefully, began to build her fire up again.

DAIMON

"LORD, THIS STEWARD…" Osred sucked his teeth, a sure sign he was nervous. He'd never normally have displayed such vulgar behaviour, even in Daimon's chambers. "This steward must ask: do you think this wise?"

"Wise?" Daimon paused in pulling on his finest robe, but he barely had to consider the answer. "Yes, Osred. No just wise, but absolutely necessary." He resumed dressing himself, although he allowed his steward to help settle the heavy cloth across his shoulders and ensure the sleeves hung perfectly. He hadn't dressed so finely even for the feast on that frantic, confusing day when the Brown Eagle clan had first appeared, when he'd betrayed his father and ended up slaying Ristjaan the Cleaver. He still felt something of a fool in the stiff, brocaded robes with the double-pleated sleeves, but some things needed to be done properly. Even if virtually no one else would recognise it.

"Necessary, lord?" Osred queried, smoothing the front. The steward's face had always been thin, and increasingly lined with care and age, but the last two weeks in particular had not been kind. Daimon wondered how much he'd been lying awake at night, wracked by his conscience. Did Osred still wonder if he'd done the correct thing in supporting Daimon over his father? Would the steward make the same choice, if he had his time again?

"Traders will appear soon, Osred, and events here cannot be hidden from them," Daimon said. "There is no way to prevent news from getting out, save by locking all the pedlars in a sheep pen."

It was a poor joke, but even so Daimon was dismayed that it raised no smile at all from Osred. If anything, the steward's concerned frown deepened. "As you say lord, but... this is a course of action from which there is no easy way back."

"This lord has had no easy way back from the moment he lifted his hand against his father," Daimon said softly. He reached out, took Osred's shoulders and looked the man in the eye. He had no need to explain himself, of course, but Daimon found he had a desperate wish for *someone* to understand why he was doing what he was about to do, and maybe even agree with him.

"This lord must be bold, Osred. This action would not be his first choice under normal circumstances, but circumstances are far from normal. This lord will not sit here and rely on prayers to the God-King to deliver him, and his people, from the wrath of the northern thanes and the Southern Marshal. They will surely come, and this lord will not be caught unready. This is the only sensible choice."

Osred's face softened, and Daimon caught a glimpse of the man who'd taught him his letters and helped ease him into the life of a noble family; so very different to what he'd left behind. Daimon's law-father had changed Daimon's life forever by adopting him, the lowborn orphan, into the Blackcreek family, and Daimon could never forget that, but Lord Asrel had not been a loving parent. At first he'd been too lost in grief for his late wife to provide affection, and then determined to bring his sons up to be hard, strong leaders, but the fact remained that Osred had been the gentle, guiding hand in Daimon's youth. Darel had at least had a few years of Lord Asrel's more gentle side, before the plague had taken it along with Lady Delil.

"This steward knows you to be a noble man," Osred said,

smiling, and if Daimon hadn't known better he could have sworn the man's voice cracked. "You have always been a noble man, whatever your birth. This steward understands why you are doing this. But he is selfish, and cannot help but wish for better for you. He cannot see you achieving happiness like this, and suspects only disgrace and death will follow."

"'Happiness is secondary to duty'," Daimon quoted. "You see, Osred, this lord does recall some of his father's lessons." His robe was as settled as it was going to be. He took his sword belt from its rack and held the longblade in his hand for a moment, examining the bare white wood of the scabbard. It spoke to the world that he was untried, untested, had performed no deeds of merit.

"This lord wishes he could record his defeat of the Tjakorshi champion," Daimon said, running a finger down the finely grained wood. "That was a deed of which he can be proud. But it seems a waste of effort, given the scabbard will undoubtedly be stained black."

"You would know it was there, lord," Osred replied.

"This lord knows it happened anyway," Daimon said with a shrug, wrapping the belt around his waist and buckling it. "And besides, it might be seen as... overly provocative."

Osred nodded. "You speak truly, lord. You are set on this course of action, then?"

"This lord is, Osred." Daimon held out his hand. "The brooches."

Osred picked up two circular brooches, finely worked gold and silver the size of his palm, fashioned into the crest of House Blackcreek. He fastened them to Daimon's breast, left and right, then stepped back. Daimon saw the other man's lower lip tremble for a moment before Osred smiled.

"Well, lord. Your steward cannot pretend he does not have misgivings, but you are truly the image of a Thane of Blackcreek." Osred bowed, deeper than required by custom, the mark of personal respect. "May Nari guide you."

"May He guide us all," Daimon muttered. He fidgeted for a moment, trying to settle the robes more comfortably, then stepped forward.

As soon as he started walking, Daimon's mind settled. He'd been sure of this course ever since the night before, but being certain of its necessity was not the same thing as being comfortable with going through with it. Now, as he descended the staircase of his adoptive family's house, he felt at ease. Darel was the one who weighed all options to a nicety, and agonised over minor details; Daimon had always thought of himself as more instinctive, willing to decide based on what his gut was telling him. Once he'd made a decision, he found it hard to settle until he'd acted upon it.

Cloud had rolled in overnight, after the clear skies of yesterday under which the Wooden Man had burned, but if rain was coming then it hadn't arrived yet. Daimon walked briskly through the gardens towards the women's quarters, hoping Zhanna was ready. He'd sent on ahead this morning, but she didn't answer to him in the same way as his own people did. By the Mountain, from what he could tell she barely answered to her own mother.

He needn't have worried. Zhanna Saanastutar was sitting on the top step of the stairs up to the women's quarters, dressed in the furs of her people and swigging what was probably water from a skin. She looked up at Daimon as he approached, her expression somewhat bleary.

"Early," she managed, by way of what seemed to be simultaneous greeting and complaint. A scratchy hiss emerged from her deep hood, immediately followed by her rattletail, which in truth barely fitted in there anymore.

"It is not so early," Daimon said. He would have gestured to the sun, but it wasn't showing its face this morning.

"Drink lot. Head hurt," Zhanna muttered at him.

Daimon nodded ruefully. He suspected there was many an aching head in Black Keep this morning, and he'd seen Zhanna consume a fair quantity of alcohol the night before. Daimon himself had behaved more moderately, as he felt befitted a thane—or at least, a thane with a few hundred ancestral enemies in his town—and so was merely rather tired, with a slight ache behind his eyes.

Zhanna took another rueful gulp of water. "Last night. Dance, fire. Do much?"

Daimon frowned. "Do you mean, do we do that often?"

Zhanna nodded, then looked like she regretted it.

"No," Daimon said. "Not like that, anyway. The Festival of Life only happens once a year."

Zhanna grunted in apparent disappointment, then frowned slightly. She looked him and his robes up and down, as though seeing him properly for the first time. Perhaps she essentially was, due to a hangover-induced fuzz.

"You look good."

"This…" Daimon was momentarily taken aback by the girl's boldness, but reminded himself that she was not only Tjakorshi, but the daughter of a particularly opinionated and forthright Tjakorshi chief. None of his own people would have passed such a comment, save perhaps a member of his own family. He decided to accept it at face value. "Thank you."

"Dance good, too," Zhanna added, taking another sip of water immediately afterwards. To Daimon's astonishment, not to mention slight embarrassment, he felt his cheeks heat.

"Thank you," he said again. He paused a moment, then added: "You danced well, also."

It was true: Zhanna and the other younger Tjakorshi hadn't exactly mastered the steps, but they'd thrown themselves into it with abandon and had certainly picked up the basics. Zhanna's eyes widened as Daimon spoke, but when she went to reply she seemed to choke on a mouthful of water, and ended up coughing and retching instead. Daimon froze, unsure of what to do as the girl spluttered, bending double, while her startled rattletail jumped off her shoulders to land on the wooden steps.

"Sorry," Zhanna wheezed, as her coughing gradually passed.

She seemed to have exerted herself tremendously in the process, judging by the flush in her cheeks.

"You are well?" Daimon asked hesitantly.

"Yes," Zhanna managed, with a surreptitious final cough. She looked at him, her eyes slightly wide and mildly watering. "Why this warrior awake early?"

"This lord must speak with your mother," Daimon told her, feeling a flutter in his stomach as he said the words. "He feels you should be there."

Zhanna wrinkled her nose. "Outside gate?"

"Yes," Daimon said, nodding. "This lord must go to her."

Zhanna looked at him very intently for a few moments, then gave a sharp nod of her own and got to her feet. As she began to descend the steps she held out one arm, and her rattletail jumped onto it and took up its usual position on her shoulders.

"It won't be able to do that for much longer," Daimon commented as she reached him. Zhanna grinned at him.

"Then should do now while can." She reached up absently to stroke the little dragon's muzzle as they began walking along the gravel path. "Your dragon?"

"It grows well," Daimon said.

"And is friend?"

"Yes." In truth, his pet had given him a slight nip that morning, but only out of eagerness to take food from his fingers.

"Not witch?" Zhanna asked, shooting him a sly, sidelong glance. Daimon saw the smile lurking at the corner of her mouth and couldn't prevent one from reaching his face as well.

"Not witch," he acknowledged, and Zhanna chuckled.

The castle yards were quieter than usual: the kitchens were cold, for there was still food from the feast to be eaten today, and the cooks had not risen as early as was their custom. The stable door was open, so at least someone was about their work there. Daimon had considered calling for a mount for this journey, but Zhanna had never ridden a dragon before and there was no telling if she would take to it as well as her mother. Besides, he was already going to draw plenty of attention, dressed in his most formal robes, and he didn't want any more than necessary.

Especially if this didn't go to plan.

If his guards were surprised to see him dressed so, no one mentioned it. Nor did they comment on the fact Zhanna was with him, her dragon still perched somewhat precariously on her shoulders. Perhaps Ganalel's punishment was fresh in their minds, and they held some false notion he was quick to anger at present. Perhaps their heads were still muddled from drink and lack of sleep. It occurred to Daimon, as the drawbridge was lowered, he should appoint a new guard to take Ganalel's place. Should he speak to Malakel about it? Osred? Should he offer suggestions, or merely instruct one or other of them to see it done, and leave them to it? What would his father have done? And in any case, was that what *he* should do?

Your mind is wandering, he thought, as they strode across the bridge and into the town square. *Focus, lest you embarrass yourself.*

The burned wreckage of the Wooden Man was still smouldering, and the tang of wood smoke lingered in the air. The ashes would be spread on the surrounding fields soon. Daimon had heard that in the north his countrymen called on Nari to turn the year and bless the crops, but that was not the way in the south. Nari had been a man, and was a god of men. The folk of the south knew it was the spirits of forest and field, river and rain that needed their honour.

It was strange, yet somehow appropriate, that the Tjakorshi had arrived just before the festival celebrating new beginnings and new life. The only question was whether they marked that new beginning, or merely the death of the old ways, and Daimon's people along with it. The newcomers were undoubtedly an omen of some sort, but knowing what type of omen was work for wiser heads than his.

He wished he could trust his brother.

The streets were virtually deserted. A couple of Naridans on the far side of the square looked over at Zhanna and him, but were too far away to be required to bow, and perhaps they didn't recognise the Tjakorshi girl. They certainly paid the pair of them no great mind, and went on about their business. One of the Brown Eagle clan saw them too, a hoe over his shoulder, and he stared openly at them. Or more accurately, Daimon realised as the man pointed and said something in his language, at Zhanna's dragon. Zhanna's reply was short and apparently to the point, and she didn't slow her pace to continue the conversation.

"What did he say?" Daimon asked.

"He want to know if this warrior now Naridan is," Zhanna said with a snort.

"And what did you say?"

Zhanna sniffed. "To go to field and work."

Despite being so sure he was set on his course, Daimon found himself almost hoping for some disturbance, some problem that would require his attention and arrest his purpose. However, the town remained quiet and they reached their destination in short order, with no pretence he could use to delay.

He took a deep breath, climbed the steps that led to Saana Sattistutar's front door, and knocked on it firmly.

There was no answer, which didn't help steady Daimon's nerves at all. The notion of going away and coming back again later appealed even less than walking here in the first place had. Then, just as he'd decided that standing here waiting for any longer would make him look like even more of a fool, he heard a voice behind him.

"What in the name of Father Krayk are you two doing here?"

Daimon and Zhanna turned, a little clumsily atop the narrow stairs. Saana Sattistutar was stood in the street, hood up and face largely in shadow, and looked little more healthy than her daughter.

Daimon opened his mouth to reply, but Zhanna blurted

something angry-sounding in Tjakorshi first. Saana snapped a few words back, then raised her hand wearily and continued in a rather more moderated tone. Daimon glanced sideways at Zhanna. The girl didn't reply, but her expression could have hewn stone.

Saana addressed her next words to Daimon. "This man should warn you, her morning so far has not been a good one. But she should have spoken less sharply, especially since you have brought Zhanna. Is she no longer required as a hostage, or is there another reason?"

"There is another reason," Daimon said, trying to keep his voice level. "May we speak inside your house?"

Saana gestured to the door, and started up the stairs towards them. "Go. This man has no guards."

Even so, Daimon had no intention of opening Saana's door himself, despite the fact the house was technically his. Zhanna showed no such compunction, however, and lifted the latch to push the door inwards. Daimon waited for Saana to brush past him, then followed them both inside and entered a Tjakorshi dwelling for the first time.

He wasn't sure what he'd expected, especially from the clan chief. Weapons and armour, perhaps, hanging from the walls. The banners of defeated opponents, possibly. Riches taken from a lifetime of plundering. He'd certainly thought the small house would have very little room left inside.

Instead, Sattistutar had few possessions. The ugly, thick-bladed sword she'd drawn when they'd first met was indeed hanging up, in its scabbard on a worn sword belt, between two Raider roundshields. There were a couple of other weapons, as well; lengths of wood edged with shards of the strange, bitterly sharp black stone that was like no rock Daimon had ever heard of in Narida. One was straight, a shape not dissimilar to the steel sword, while the other had a hooked head. Daimon eyed it distrustfully. Everyone knew the Raider's weapons were lethal against cloth and flesh, but would largely be turned by good steel armour. When in his armour his thighs were protected by the panels of his coat, and his shins by his greaves, but the back of his knees and his calves were still exposed. That weapon almost looked like it had been designed to reach around from the front and cut into his flesh.

"This warrior's axe," Zhanna said with a grin as she tapped her chest, apparently catching him looking at it. "Very sharp." On her shoulder, her rattletail hissed in apparent agreement.

Saana said something to Zhanna as she shucked her heavy fur jacket off: Daimon wasn't sure what it was, but Zhanna's face fell again and she reached up protectively towards her rattletail. Saana said something else, and this time Zhanna gestured towards Daimon before stomping off towards the back of the house. Her dragon jumped up off her shoulder onto a rafter, from which it peered down at them all.

Saana turned towards him, irritation writ large on her face. "Well, thane? This man would thank you for returning her daughter, except she doesn't know why you have done so, or for how long, and it seems being your hostage has not improved Zhanna's temper any."

Daimon suppressed a grimace. There was no circumstance under which this conversation was going to have been easy anyway. Still, he'd try to make the best of it.

"May your roof turn the storms," he said haltingly in Tjakorshi. Zhanna had taught him the traditional phrase, uttered when entering someone's house for the first time.

"And yours," Saana replied automatically in her own tongue, her expression veering towards puzzlement before swinging back to irritated. Daimon suspected that she wanted him to get to the point, so with what he understood to be the formalities out of the way, he did so.

"The year moves on. We will soon see the first traders from the north, and when we do, they will see you and your people."

"Lucky for them," Saana grunted.

"When they leave, they will carry news of your presence," Daimon said, trying to make her understand. "We may not even know they have come; they might see you from the edge of the Downwoods and turn back. Either way, news will almost certainly travel north."

"And what will happen?" Sattistutar asked. Daimon caught her glance towards the wall where her and her daughter's weapons were hanging.

"This lord cannot say for certain," Daimon replied carefully. "Even if traders report that all is well here, the thane of Darkspur and this lord's father were... not friends. This lord would not be surprised if Odem Darkspur comes south with as much strength of arms as he can muster, eager to use your presence as a pretence to take Blackcreek lands for his own."

"Then we must be ready," Sattistutar said. She took a step towards the wall, but Daimon stepped into her path.

"No! That is not the way!"

Sattistutar's eyes narrowed. "You are in this man's house, thane, and she does not take kindly to anyone putting themselves between her and her axe."

"This lord betrayed his own father and brother to prevent our people from fighting each other, and now you would seek to undo all that?" Daimon demanded tightly. "If Thane Darkspur comes, do you think this lord's people will take up arms with you against him? Or do you think they will stand aside, or turn on you, and then beg for mercy when Odem wins?"

"Who is to say that he will win?" Sattistutar snapped.

"Even if he does not, it will make no difference!" Daimon said, trying to keep his voice under control. "Word will spread, and more warriors will come with more thanes, and perhaps the Southern Marshal himself. No matter how valiant your warriors, you will be driven into the sea, or you will be killed, and most likely this lord's people will be killed along with you!"

"And your answer?" Sattistutar demanded, throwing up

her hands. "This man understands you wish not to fight other thanes, but if they seek to kill her and *her* people, would you have us wait to be killed, like fish in shallows?"

"We must show that you belong and live here," Daimon said. "It is the only way to avoid violence."

"We are trying!" Sattistutar snapped. "We work fields; we fish; we play your game, and still this man is attacked with a knife! What more would you have us do?"

Daimon took a deep breath. "We need a stronger, more visible bond. One that does not involve Zhanna being kept hostage."

Sattistutar frowned. "What are you suggesting, Blackcreek?"

Daimon closed his eyes for a moment, then let his breath out again and opened them. He reached up to his left breast, unpinned the brooch fastened there, and held it out to her.

"Saana Sattistutar, chief of the Brown Eagle clan of Tjakorsha... This lord, Daimon, Thane of Blackcreek..."

He looked into her dark grey eyes, the colour of angry clouds, and prayed for all his ancestors, both by blood and by law, to forgive what he was about to do.

"... requests your hand in marriage."

PART FOUR

WHAT CAN BE said of Godspire?

The greatest mountain in all the known world, he rises head and shoulders above his brothers. Even the boastful Morlithians, so proud of their Shining Mountains in the far west, will fall to their knees and cry out in wonder when first they catch sight of Godspire's majesty: if indeed they do so, since his head is so often shrouded in cloud.

Of old he was known as Spirithome, for the ancients knew he was the centre of the world, and the place from which the greatest spirits came. And there, of course, came the problem, because it was from Spirithome that the mightiest and most malevolent spirit emerged: the Queen of Demons, the Unmaker.

She granted ruinous power to her followers, the great witches and their lesser kin, and the petty kingdoms filling the land between the Catseyes and the ocean were overrun with evil. Babes were stolen in the dark of night; crops withered in the fields; adults and children alike lost their lives to the foul blood sacrifices of the witches. And where the darkness was greatest, where the malice was most potent, the Unmaker always lurked in a body she had stolen.

This body would be fearless in battle, immune to pain, heedless of all but the most grievous wounds. Scholars refer to that time as the Rule of Night, but in truth there was no rule, no order: merely death and suffering, and a few isolated places where good men stood together against the darkness.

It was from one of these places, in the north, that the man Nari arose and became more than man. Filled with divine fury, and at just fifteen years of age, he began his campaign to drive the Unmaker from these lands. The story of how he did so is told in many other places, in much greater (and sometimes contradictory) detail, but the crux of the matter is this:

At Spirithome, Nari and his most favoured retainers—General Gemar Far Garadh, Tolkar the Last Sorcerer, and the Band of Seven—entered the great caverns at the mountain's foot and finally defeated the Unmaker and her foul converts. And there, once the deed was done, Nari at last accepted the truth his retainers had already been preaching: that he was a god, come to save the land, and to rule it. And so Spirithome was renamed Godspire, and Nari became the Divine Nari, the God-King, and the lands he had cleansed became Narida.

The entrance to the great caverns where the Divine One finally bested his enemy were sealed, and a monastery was founded there. This was originally intended as place for pilgrims to reflect on the majesty and might of our god. However, the Divine One declared he would return to it, and yet his physical form passed from this world before he did so. When the Foretellings of Tolkar became known, declaring that Nari's spirit would be reborn in another body, it was accepted that the monastery was not just a place of pilgrimage: it was where the Divine One would announce his own return, thereby fulfilling his promise...

Excerpt from 'Myths and Legends of the Catseye Mountains: A Collection' by Elidhu of Bowbridge, written in the five-hundredth and twenty-third year of the God-King

SAANA

SAANA LOOKED DOWN at the brooch, then back up at Daimon Blackcreek. At his young, earnest face, shaved to be as free of hair as any Tjakorshi woman's. At the strong, clean line of his jaw, his snub nose, his dark eyes.

She really wanted to punch him.

There was a clatter of movement to her right, and Zhanna disappeared through the back door. It banged shut behind her, and Saana bit back a curse, and the impulse to call her daughter back. There was every possibility Zhanna wouldn't listen, and Saana was in no mood to get into a row with her right now. Not when there was a far more deserving candidate for it standing only a few feet away.

"What in the name of the Dark Father are you *thinking*?!" she demanded. She hadn't meant to shout, but by the end of the sentence she was getting very close to it.

Blackcreek's nostrils flared, but he kept his voice level. "Do you, even for one moment, think you are who this lord would *choose* to marry?"

Saana raised her eyebrows. The urge to hit him wasn't going away.

"This lord was adopted into a noble family," Blackcreek was saying bitterly. "He should have been able to marry a girl of noble Naridan blood! Failing that, any number of lowborn girls would jump at the chance to marry a noble son of Blackcreek! Now he must marry Saana Sattistutar of the Brown Eagle clan, because he cannot think of any other way the thanes of the South will *possibly* accept that the Raiders have become civilised!"

"This man led her people across the ocean to escape death, or being not free," Saana snapped. She rolled her neck and placed her hands on her hips, and as she did so her left hand encountered the pouch of leaves she'd got from Kerrti. "You think she will agree to be not free to you, as Naridan women are?"

Blackcreek hissed a breath out and flapped his hand irritably. "This lord knows a lost cause when he sees one. He would merely ask you to not contradict him in front of other thanes, lest they decide you are not civilised after all."

"That does not sound very Naridan," Saana said, warily.

"It is very Naridan to wish to keep one's head on one's shoulders!" Blackcreek replied through gritted teeth. "This lord knows you will not submit to him, as a wife should to her husband. Very well! He is already a dishonoured son and brother; what difference does it make if he is a mockery of a husband as well? Either his ancestors will smile on his efforts to keep his people alive, or they will not. This humiliation will make little difference."

"This man does not know what 'humiliation' means," Saana said slowly, "but it does not sound like you would be proud to have her as your wife."

"This lord's pride is unimportant," Blackcreek said bluntly. "This is necessary." He gestured to her. "What of your pride, Saana Sattistutar? This lord swears to you, by his ancestors and by Nari Himself, he believes this will be the only way to convince the other thanes you truly belong here, thereby saving both our peoples from their vengeance. Will you spurn this offer?"

Saana took a deep breath and rubbed her eyes. Of all the mornings Blackcreek had to choose for this...

"Is this how you do this in Narida?" she asked. "The man comes to the woman's house and demands an answer, there and then?"

"This lord has obviously never done this before," Blackcreek replied testily. He paused for a moment. "However, in most cases there would have been... courting, beforehand."

Courting. Saana's mind flashed back briefly to straddling Tavi the night before, and she forced the image away before her cheeks could colour. She looked back at Blackcreek and tried to put the stablemaster's opinions about this young man, and his thoughts about her, out of her mind as well.

"So let us say you had... courted this man," she said. "Let us say this was for love, not because it is *needed*. This man would be expected to just say yes or no?"

Blackcreek clearly had no idea what she was talking about. "It is customary to give a reply there and then, yes. Do your people leave each other waiting?"

Saana sighed. She wasn't certain she knew the meaning of the word "civilised", either, but she was starting to come to the conclusion that even if she thought she did, their definitions weren't the same.

"You do not talk about the marriage first?"

"Talk about it? In what way?"

She'd been correct. Saana walked to the water barrel and sat down beside it, then pointed at the patch of floor on the opposite side of it. "Come. Sit."

Blackcreek, to her mild surprise, did so. She took a wooden cup and passed it to him, then took one for herself and dipped it into the barrel before taking a drink. The water was cool on her tongue, and a welcome relief to the dry mouth the previous night had left behind. There was a scrabbling noise and a thump, and Zhanna's young dragon half-fell down a post and landed on the floor, then trotted across the floor towards the fire, whereupon it curled up with every sign of satisfaction. Saana eyed it warily, but it seemed to have settled, so she turned her attention back to Daimon.

"If a Tjakorshi man asked this man to marry him, and she had any interest in his offer, we would sit and talk," she began. "We would talk about what we expected from each other, how we would behave. If we agreed, we would each have a friend come and we would agree on those things in front of them. Once those things were agreed, we could marry."

Blackcreek was staring at her as though she'd grown a second head. "But *why*?"

"So we would know we were a good match!" Saana said. His lack of understanding was really quite exasperating. "Why should this man marry, if her husband expected her to obey his every word, or repair his brother's clothes, or never sail again? If he expects those things, this man would never accept his offer. If he then expects them afterwards, but did not say so before, this man could call upon the friends to say he is not doing as he should, and so the marriage would end."

"And do the friends always agree, if they are asked to recall these things?" Blackcreek asked, apparently intrigued despite himself.

Saana shrugged and took another sip of water. "Not always. It is not perfect. But to lie about a marriage vow is known to anger Father Krayk."

Blackcreek grunted. Saana wasn't sure whether this was an acknowledgement of such a threat or a dismissal of the Dark Father's power, but she didn't push it. Then he frowned.

"If you are telling this lord these things... are you not dismissing his offer of marriage?"

Saana thought about the crossing her clan had made; the short days and long nights, fighting the waves and the wind, steering by the stars and the swell. She thought about her people; the old and the young, the hale and the sick, all the faces she was responsible for. She thought of how much effort it had taken to persuade them all to leave Tjakorsha; how she'd had to convince them the Great

Ocean and the largely unknown lands on the other side of it were a better option than facing The Golden—the Blight of Tjakorsha, Clan-Breaker, Belt-Taker—and its clanless warriors. She thought of all she'd risked, and all her people meant to her.

Then she thought of how to acknowledge yourself as a woman in Naridan speech was to automatically make yourself lesser than a man, and of Ristjaan's headless body, and of Blackcreek's arrogance in confronting her over Kerrti and the Naridan healer girl the previous night.

Then she thought of what Nalon had said about how important honour was to the nobles here, and how badly Blackcreek had gone against it. She looked at him, weighing him. The Dark Father help her, she believed that *he* believed what he was saying was true—that this was the only way.

"This man is not dismissing it yet," she said, and what she could only think of as an expression of uncomfortable relief crossed his face. Yes, he felt this was necessary, yet he also didn't like it. Perhaps she had to trust he knew his countrymen.

"Very well," Blackcreek said, dipping his own cup and drinking. Saana wasn't sure if he thought this was a part of the process, or whether he was just thirsty. If he'd drunk anywhere near as much as she had last night, it was probably the latter. "We have already covered some areas. This man will not expect you to submit to his will without good reason, but he will expect you not to contradict him in front of other thanes."

Saana raised an eyebrow. "'This man'? Not 'this lord'?"

Blackcreek nodded. "If this man does not expect you to submit to him, then he is not your lord."

Saana took another drink to mask her surprise. She hadn't expected that to be so easy. "Agreed, then. This man will submit to your will where you clearly have greater knowledge. She will expect you to do the same."

Blackcreek looked startled for a moment, then nodded thoughtfully. "The sea? Your customs? That manner of thing?"

Saana nodded in her turn. "Yes. This man will not have you trying to tell her fishers how to fish."

"Agreed." Blackcreek smiled faintly. "This is not how this man thought his marriage would begin. Even this morning."

"It is not beginning yet!" Saana told him sternly. She took another drink and considered her next words. If she played this correctly…

"This man will make a vow to you," she began. "She will work as hard as she can to make it so no Tjakorshi will speak or act badly towards a man who…"—she paused for a moment, but forged on—"… a man who courts a man, or a woman who courts a woman."

Now it was Blackcreek's turn to raise his eyebrows. "This man is surprised."

You're not the only one, Saana thought. But her vow to Kerrti needed honouring, and she thought she could see a way to turn it into leverage. "However," she continued, "this man needs *your* word that you will work as hard as *you* can so no Naridan will treat a woman, Naridan *or* Tjakorshi, as not as good as a man."

Blackcreek's face went very still.

"Your word, Blackcreek," Saana pressed. "This man will not be married to you as an equal only to see other women treated poorly just for being women. That will not bind our peoples together."

"This lord is not certain you understand what you are asking," Blackcreek muttered.

"Last night, you told this man she is not in Tjakorsha any longer," Saana reminded him. "You were right. But you have told this man your family makes the laws here; you honour your God-King, but you make the laws on this land. Is this true?"

"There are some laws we could not change without censure, but as a whole… yes, it is true," Blackcreek acknowledged.

"Then you can change your laws," Saana said urgently. "You must. If this man's clan cannot live here equal under your laws, your laws are not fit for us. You and this man will not marry, and the clan will face whatever may come from the north alone, if we need to."

Blackcreek grimaced.

And then nodded. "Very well. This man cannot promise it will be easy or quick to make his people accept it, but you have his word he will do this."

Saana tried to hide her relief. She hadn't been sure he would go for it. "You may be surprised. This man suspects your women, at least, will not object."

Blackcreek's expression suggested that he had his doubts, but didn't argue further. "What else should we discuss?"

Well, there was one rather obvious thing they hadn't covered. She tried to ignore her quickening heart.

"Fucking," Saana said, and felt a stab of perverse glee as Blackcreek nearly choked on his water. She waited to see if he would speak, but he seemed to have lost all command of his own language.

"When Tjakorshi marry," Saana continued, "they mostly agree to only fuck each other."

"*Mostly?*" Blackcreek wheezed, although Saana wasn't clear whether his strangled tone was due to shock or an after-effect of his choking. She ignored it.

"Daimon of Blackcreek, have you fucked a woman before?"

He was just staring at her now, wordless and apparently terrified. It was possibly cruel, but her own nerves were soothed somewhat the more he cringed, so she sailed blithely on.

"This man needs you to be honest. It is very important for marriage vows."

Blackcreek seemed to shrink in on himself further, but finally shook his head. Saana did her best to hid her smile, then found it wiped from her face anyway as another thought occurred to her.

"Have you fucked a *man?*"

Blackcreek cleared his throat and glared at her. "In the first place, after what we have just discussed, it should not matter to you if this man had. In the second place, no, he has not. Although his brother has," he added, a challenging tone in his voice.

"This man also has," Saana said sternly. "Several. She assures you, Daimon of Blackcreek, she has no intention of stopping. So, as a man who has never fucked a woman, who suggested this marriage out of duty and not love... what can you offer?"

Blackcreek looked a bit like he'd just been punched and wasn't sure which way was up. "Do all Tjakorshi marriage discussions include this subject?"

"For most Tjakorshi marriages, fucking is not a new thing," Saana said bluntly.

"Fine," Blackcreek muttered. He drained the rest of his water and slammed the cup down on the wooden floor with a loud *clack*. "Saana Sattistutar of the Brown Eagle clan; Naridans will also lie with each other without being married, but to lie with someone to whom you are not married when you *are* married brings great shame onto both you and your spouse. This man cannot agree to you lying with anyone else, should we be married."

Saana shrugged. She'd expected as much. "This man has said what she has said. She will expect you not to disappoint her." She knew he was young and hale, at any rate. She supposed she could close her eyes, if she needed to. But perhaps not. It wasn't as if he was ugly. He was just always so *stiff*, like a child's stick doll come to life. Tavi had moved and felt like a real person, warm and solid and... She pushed the memory away again as she felt her lower belly clench.

"This man will expect the same from you," Blackcreek said. He met her gaze steadily, only the muscles in his throat giving away his nervous swallowing. "If you are going to make this man agree to that in front of two witnesses," he added, more softly, "this man will insist on parity."

Saana didn't know what "parity" meant either, but she could guess. She smiled, to try to show that she'd perhaps been teasing a little. "That may not actually need to be spoken of in front of witnesses. This man would not expect you to fuck if you did not want to. She just would like to know you would sometimes want to."

She saw Blackcreek's eyes travel over what he could see of her over the low barrel. Saana had to admit, she probably didn't look her best this morning. She certainly didn't *feel* her best.

Blackcreek nodded slowly, and found his voice on the second try. "This, ah… This man… would want to. Sometimes."

Saana nodded, as though she'd never had a doubt, and tried to calm her breathing, which had got a little fast. It might never come to it, of course. It wasn't like she hadn't taken matters into her own hands before. Still, it was good to know she might have another option, if she felt the need.

"Also," Blackcreek added, his eyes not quite meeting hers, "a marriage… that is to say, a Naridan marriage… is not considered fully valid until it is consummated."

Saana frowned. "What does that word mean?"

Blackcreek coughed slightly. "We would have to lie together before the marriage would be considered valid."

Saana raised her eyebrows. "And by 'lie together', you mean fuck?"

Blackcreek just nodded.

"And… do people *watch*? How does anyone know?"

"Nari knows," Blackcreek said, with the air of a man who had very little interest in further discussing the details. "That is what is important. Your god does not watch over your marriage bed?"

Saana shuddered. The thought of Father Krayk's cold, dead eyes watching her sweating and writhing with another person would be quite enough to put her off the notion entirely. "This man hopes not! She told you before, we do not wish to draw the Dark Father's attention." She dipped her cup again and tried to put the image from her mind. "What of Zhanna? This man cannot marry you if you are to keep her as a hostage."

"If we were to marry, Zhanna would no longer be required to be a hostage," Blackcreek replied. He cast a look towards her back door. "Although this man did not anticipate her leaving so suddenly."

Saana waved her hand to dismiss his concerns. "Being hostage was Zhanna's idea. She will return if she is needed to. So," she continued, taking another sip of water, "what else do we need to talk about?"

JEYA

"WE MUST LEAVE," Galem said, hìs voice low and shaking.

"We... what?" Jeya whispered back in confusion. Truth to tell, shé'd like nothing better than to be a long way from imminent bloodshed, but this was Galem's *family*. How could hè just want to run? Shé tried to think what shé'd fear most if shé were about to enter someone else's house uninvited, whatever hér motives. "We could... we could raise the alarm! Shout for yòur neighbours!"

"No!" Galem turned to hér, and even in the moonshadows cast by the paddleleaf's boughs, Jeya could see the pain on hìs face. "Ì can't be seen! Not if this is happening!"

"What is 'this'?" Jeya demanded. It seemed fairly obvious to hér, but had Galem expected it somehow? What had happened to the sheltered youth whose mōther whipped guards for allowing a stranger to get too close to hìm? Being rich suddenly didn't seem like such a good thing, if it meant you might find half a dozen armed intruders coming for you in the night. Jeya had needed to dodge people who'd had it in for hér before, but that was usually because shé'd been in the wrong place at the wrong time.

"This is why my parents have few friends," Galem said. Hè backed away up the paddleleaf branch as hè spoke. "Someone's betrayed us, and Ì don't know who. Anyone Ì run to could be my enemy. My family spoke about this, many times. If this happens, Ì flee."

467

"Flee? Where to?" Galem dropped down over the wall and Jeya scrambled after hìm, glad to put even its questionable protection between hér and the garden. "Where will yòu run to if yòu can't trust anyone?"

"Ì don't know!" Galem hissed. "Somewhere not here! Somewhere Ì can hide until Ì can find out if my family…"

Survive. Hè couldn't say the word, but Jeya heard it nonetheless. Shé grabbed hìs hands.

"Do yòu trust *mé?*"

Galem hesitated. Then hè nodded once, firmly.

"Yes. Yes, Ì do."

"Then come with mé." Shé turned and began to run down the towpath, and a moment later shé heard Galem's footsteps following hér.

"Where are we going?" Galem asked as they ran. Jeya gave silent thanks for the blessing of the moons' light; flat and level though the towpath was, they'd be risking a twisted or broken ankle otherwise.

"To the First Level," shé said.

"The main city?" Galem exclaimed. "That's full of people!"

"All the better to hide yòu," Jeya argued. "Besides, that's where Ì know. There are places we can sleep, safe places, where no one will know to look for yòu."

"But Jeya!" Galem protested. "Ì'm not dressed to blend in!"

Hè was right. The clothes hè wore for their night-time excursions were older, simpler ones lacking the sumptuous colours and intricate embroidery of what Jeya thought of as usual clothing for a rich person, but they were still far finer than anything shé'd ever owned. Hè might not look that out of place in the main streets, but hè'd certainly draw attention at Ngaiyu's, or anywhere near there. Shé wasn't necessarily concerned about someone tracking hìm down because of it—the city was huge, and rumours could surely only fly so far—but it might mark hìm out as a target for robbery. Which led to its own question.

"Do yòu have any money?" she asked. She looked back over her shoulder, partly to make sure hè was keeping up and partly to check that they weren't being followed. They weren't: the towpath was clear behind them, which was a mercy from the gods.

"Not with mè," Galem admitted. "Why?"

Not with me. As though there was the option to go back for it! "Yòu're right: yòu'll need different clothes. If yòu can't buy any, Í'll have to steal some for yòu."

"Steal?" Galem puffed. "But the Watch!"

Jeya managed not to laugh. "Í'm not going to steal anything while they're looking! They're always hanging around the markets, but they won't be where we're going."

They passed where they'd so recently been kissing, then cut over the first footbridge they came to, the wooden slats *thunking* hollowly beneath their feet as they crossed to the far bank. The stone walls of gardens began to give way to the timber frames of warehouses as the canal reached the Second Level wharves, and Jeya slowed hér pace. Galem seemed short of breath, and there was no risk of them being chased or followed now. Better to slow down and walk, rather than have someone remember two running youths, should anyone come asking questions.

"Who were those people?" shé said quietly, leading the way between warehouses across wheel ruts still half-full with water from the afternoon's rain. Galem followed, stepping where shé stepped, as though unwilling to trust any other part of the ground.

"I don't know," hè said finally, just when Jeya was starting to think hè hadn't heard hér. "My family has enemies, though."

"Enemies?" A chill ran through Jeya, one that had nothing to do with the warm night air. "Yòu don't mean a Shark, do yòu?" If Galem's family had run afoul of a Shark, that might change things significantly in terms of where was and wasn't safe.

"No, no, of course not," Galem replied, then stopped talking again. They'd reached the top of one of the roads that wound down the steep hillside from the Second Level to the First. There were still lights burning here and there in the city below, peeping out from behind wooden shutters under the forest of roofs washed silver by the moons' light. Farther south was the harbour itself, and to the east was the broken ground, twisting waterways and myriad bridges of the Narrows. It was Jeya's world, and shé knew it well, but that didn't mean it was safe.

"Galem," shé said, turning to hìm, trying to make hìm understand. "I know yòu're worried, I know yòu're scared..." Shé paused, suddenly remembering that Naridans didn't like to admit to such things, but Galem said nothing so shé carried on. "But yòu need to tell mé what's going on, if yòu know it. Otherwise, Í can't help keep yòu safe."

Shé'd expected hìm to shrug, or say something unhelpful. Shé'd wondered if hè'd snap at her, or turn away. Shé hadn't expected hìm to suddenly envelop hér in a hug, hìs lean arms wrapping around hér and hìs cheek pressed against hérs. Shé hugged hìm back, as tightly as shé could, as though shé could make everything bad go away for hìm if she could only hold hìm tightly long enough, even as shé thrilled again at the touch of hìs skin on hérs. Despite the circumstances, it dried hér mouth and set hér blood singing to have such a beautiful thing so close.

"Ì'm sorry," hè whispered into hér ear, hìs breath catching. "Ì'm sorry. But Ì've never told anyone about it before. Ever."

"It's okay," Jeya found hérself saying. "It's okay. Just... just tell mé what yòu can. Maybe Í can—"

"Jeya," Galem whispered. "Those people would have been sent by the Naridans. Because Ì'm the Splinter Prince."

SAANA

"So we are agreed?" Daimon asked, his voice still carrying a hint of nervousness, and a slight rasp from how long they'd been talking. Saana had built the small fire pit back up twice, an activity in which Zhanna's dragon had taken a great interest. "We marry, under Naridan law and Tjakorshi custom. We are equal. You defer to this man in front of Naridan lords, this man defers to you in front of your witches. We each expect all our people to treat one of us as they would the other."

Saana's throat fluttered. She was sailing into unknown waters. Blackcreek was proud, stubborn, and still sometimes unpredictable. She'd never really expected to enter into marriage with anyone, let alone this serious, smooth-cheeked youth from another land. If she stopped to think about it, the idea was nonsense.

But if she'd stopped to think about actually getting everyone here across the ocean, she'd likely have dismissed that as nonsense as well. *Sometimes you just need to steer into the wind, meet the wave head-on, and trust in your ship.*

"Agreed," she said, and was proud of how steady her voice was. "Daimon of Blackcreek… this man accepts. She will marry you."

She held out her hand. Daimon looked at it for a moment, apparently uncomprehendingly, then gave a small start of realisation and handed her the brooch he'd offered her earlier.

Saana inspected it, admiring the work. It was beautiful, there was no doubt of that, and had the heft of solid gold.

"What does this man do with it?"

"You fasten it to your clothing," Daimon said, pointing to the pin on the underside. "By tradition, we should each wear our brooch until we are married."

Saana slid the sharp metal through her furs, then looked up at him. "And when will that be?"

Daimon laughed, slightly shamefaced. "In truth, this man had been so focused on whether you would accept, he had not yet considered that. But there is no reason why it could not be soon. We must speak the vows in front of the shrine and ask Nari's blessing, and be witnessed doing so. This man would declare a holiday so the whole town could witness." He grimaced. "So soon after the Festival of Life, as well. We must hope the fields will not be neglected. But then," he added, with a small smile, "perhaps it will be popular with your folk. Your daughter spoke to this man and seemed most disappointed his people do not often celebrate as we did last night."

Saana frowned. Where *was* Zhanna, anyway? She still hadn't returned, and it was probably too much to hope that she'd left so abruptly simply to give her mother some privacy in a delicate moment. Saana fervently hoped Zhanna hadn't gone running to tell everyone what she'd just heard. Not that it truly mattered, since now Saana had accepted Daimon's offer everyone would have to find out anyway, but it would be best for them to hear it from her.

"This man is sure it will be welcomed," she said reassuringly. "But as you can imagine, she will need to tell her clan what we have agreed. And she will need to find a witness for our oaths. As will you."

Daimon nodded. "This man's steward, Osred, would be suitable."

Saana turned over possibilities in her mind. Tsolga? She'd have respect for tradition, but Saana wasn't too certain she wouldn't make coarse interjections. Kerrti? Saana had no idea if the young witch would be prepared to, but it would show her Saana was serious about keeping her oath if she swore it as part of her marriage agreement. She'd have asked Zhanna, but the girl was still Unblooded (and that was another problem that was going to loom, assuming they didn't have to fight the northern Naridans). Otzudh was out of the question, given how Saana had refused his marriage advances before. Inkeru, perhaps? She was sensible... Her mind flashed unbidden to Tavi, and she just managed to suppress a snort of embarrassed laughter. There was nothing to say the witness had to be a part of her clan, but she'd struggle to keep a straight face.

She realised Daimon was looking at her expectantly, and she gathered her thoughts. "This man must go and tell her clan. You will do the same?"

"This man's people will know what it means when they see him wearing one brooch, and you wearing the other," Daimon replied with a slightly rueful smile. "And he does not imagine it will take long for news to travel. But yes, he will arrange for a proclamation. Is there any reason we should not marry in, say, two days?"

Saana thought about it, then shook her head. "No. This man will need to prepare a hand binding, that is all."

Daimon nodded. "Then this man will take his leave of you." He rose to his feet, then paused. "Thank you. This man knows this is not what you would have wanted."

"This man did not expect to be able to lead her people across the Great Ocean to begin a new life without some challenges," Saana replied honestly, getting to her feet as well. "It is not as she would have wanted, it is true. But if you say this is necessary to protect our people, then it shall be done. This man believes you speak truly to her, Daimon of Blackcreek, so she will heed your words."

"Perhaps in time, it can come to be more than just 'necessary'," Daimon said with a small, slightly wry smile. "But we shall see. This man must go and instruct his steward to make preparations."

"And this man should find Zhanna," Saana replied. "She feels she should tell her daughter of her decision first, no matter who may work it out."

"Until later, then," Daimon said with a respectful nod. Saana snorted and opened the door for him, then watched him descend the steps and stride off into the street, square-shouldered and straight-spined. If she was truly to be married to him, she would have to work out a way to loosen him. Was that even possible with Naridan men? Or was this rigidity a failing unique to their nobles? Nalon certainly seemed to think so, but since he disliked Naridan nobles universally he was perhaps not the best judge. Perhaps Saana needed to talk to Avlja about it.

First things first, though: she needed to find Zhanna.

This proved easier said than done. Saana looked out into her garden, but there was no sign of Zhanna there, only the half-tilled earth (and she would need to get that finished soon, since the Naridans said it was nearly time to plant), so Saana pulled on her furs, then set out into the street.

The dull blanket of cloud overhead hadn't shifted at all, but more people were abroad now. She saw a Naridan looking curiously at the flash of gold at her breast, as though he couldn't quite work out what he was seeing. Saana didn't stop to engage him in conversation about it, but hailed Oll as he hoed his soil.

"Hai, Oll! Have you seen Zhanna?"

Oll paused for a moment as though thinking. His face had grown thinner in the days since Brida had died, and Saana made a mental note to get someone to check he and his children were eating enough.

"Aye, a while back," he replied. "Looked like she was heading for the river. Seemed in a powerful temper."

"When is she not?" Saana muttered. "Thanks, Oll."

"No problem, chief." Oll frowned, his eyes falling to her chest. "That's fine work, and pretty too. What is it?"

Saana hid a grimace. "I'll tell you later." Even if she hadn't been intending to tell Zhanna first, she had little desire to discuss her upcoming marriage with a man who'd so recently lost his wife. Oll just nodded and went back to his hoeing, although his heart didn't seem in it.

The River Gate was nowhere near the size of the Road Gate, being barely wide enough for three people to walk through abreast. That was by design of course, to prevent it from being an easy target for attackers from the river, although it was upstream of the Black Keep itself, so any foe would have to navigate past the castle's walls, and any defensive missiles. The gate opened onto a series of wooden jetties out over the water, where the Naridans moored their little fishing skiffs at night. The fishers of the Brown Eagle clan had begun to moor their taughs there too, but the larger vessels remained on the beach: there was no room for a yolgu to tie up here.

The gate was open, but the fishers had already gone to sea. Even a night of hard drinking wouldn't be enough to keep them from the waves if the weather was calm like this, although Saana suspected they'd started later than usual. The only people around were the old folk, both Naridan and Tjakorshi, mending nets in exchange for some of the catch when the fishers returned. Saana greeted them as she approached.

"Ailika," she said, catching the attention of one of her clan. Ailika was near as old as Father Krayk, or so she claimed, and her snow-white hair was starting to thin and leave her spotted scalp exposed. Her fingers were still nimble, though, and they didn't cease twisting fibres as she squinted up at Saana.

"Morning, girl," Ailika answered. Everyone was 'girl' or 'boy' to her, even Tsolga. "Looking for that daughter of yours?"

Saana frowned. "Have you seen her?"

"Seen her? Aye, she stamped through here like she was trying to kill all the worms in the world," Ailika cackled. "Minded her manners enough to talk to Jelema Eddistutar though, and ask her if she wanted another hand today." Ailika peered up at Saana, her expression suddenly sharpening. "She's not still supposed to be behind those walls, is she?"

"No," Saana said absently, trying to ignore the sudden sucking feeling in her stomach. Had Zhanna truly been that offended by the notion of a marriage between Naridan and Tjakorshi, that on her first day of freedom she'd run back to Jelema's fishing crew rather than spend time with her own mother? If so, there was little hope she wouldn't talk about it to the rest of the crew, and that meant the news would spread like the coughing sickness once the taughs returned. Especially since Jelema, Tsennan Longjaw's mother, was a sunny-tempered, open-hearted woman completely incapable of keeping any news to herself.

"What's that you've got there, girl?" Ailika asked, pointing at the Blackcreek brooch.

"I'll tell you later," Saana muttered, turning away.

TILA

TILA HAD MAINLY stayed in her cabin since they'd left East Harbour, feigning illness, entirely so she didn't have to share space with Alazar Blade. She'd come ashore in Emerald Bay, though, and sat in a tavern with Barach's looming presence discouraging any locals from joining them, while the sailors from the *Light of Fortune* kept their distance from fear of whatever sickness she'd supposedly been suffering from. And so, as was her usual custom when travelling, Tila listened to local gossip.

Emerald Bay wasn't reckoned to be Narida's most northerly town, but it was its most northerly port. It was a strange place, skulking on the southern edge of the Hudanar, the thick mangrove forests marking the coastal edge of the long, loosely defined border between Narida and Kiburu ce Alaba's mainland territory. Somewhere in the tangle of trunks, branches, roots, and mud was the main channel of the great Sundai river, the course of which was theoretically the actual border. However, given the Sundai's propensity for changing its course drastically during a single rainy season, and the difficulty in working out exactly what counted as the main channel, the Hudanar was mostly left to the thin scattering of people who'd lived in it for countless generations, and the swamp dragons.

Emerald Bay had no emeralds in it, or near it. The name was

a sarcastic one, referencing the bright green slime clinging to the wooden posts sunk into the water to support the jetties, spreading across the boards of the more treacherous walkways, collecting in patches on the surface of the more sheltered inlets and generally stinking. The entire place was a gigantic wooden framework, lashed together out of well-placed mistrust in the stability of the alleged land beneath it. Despite that, as the last Naridan port before some two hundred miles of largely uninhabited coastline to the north, it took a fair amount of trade from sailors, and sailors carried gossip far and wide.

"S'man swears it's true," one hoary old man was saying, his chair tilted back on two legs until his back met the wall behind him. "Heard it from some lads up from Bowmar. News is the God-King's been taken ill."

Tila didn't bother to try to hide her shock; such news would be of concern to anyone. She swallowed her mouthful of sour wine, trying to work out if she could get away with asking for more details.

"Is it bad?" a young sailor from the *Light of Fortune* piped up, his narrow face a picture of concern.

"Bad enough for us folk to hear of it, which means it ain't nothing," the old man said; a fair point. "Emerald Bay don't get to hear of every cough and sneeze from the Divine Court. But they didn't have no *specifics*, as you might say. Word is that He's took to His bed—"

"Took who to His bed?" someone shouted, and there was a bubble of laughter that made Tila's fist clench. Her brother's promiscuity was an open secret in court, but she'd tried her best to prevent word leaking out further. Clearly, she hadn't been up to the task.

"—*that He's took to His bed*," the first speaker continued deliberately, shooting a glare in the direction of the interruption, "and He missed the Festival of Life. And you can cease such talk, Hama; who His Majesty beds ain't our concern!"

"It is when there's no heir," Hama retorted. He was a stocky man with a touch of grey at his temples. "His Majesty might carry the blood of Nari, but that's no good to us when he don't pass it on! Can't he find a woman every now and then?"

It stung to hear her own words, or at least her own thoughts, coming so disrespectfully from the mouth of this peasant. Tila gripped her wooden cup and fought to keep her face calm. Barach would understand her showing an interest in the health of the God-King: such a thing could be critically important to Livnya. However, the crime lord of Idramar had no reason to be overly concerned with defending the God-King's honour. Tila wished for a moment she'd been more openly pious as Livnya, so such an action wouldn't be out of character, but she'd always feared others would make unwelcome connections. Besides, if she got involved in trouble in Emerald Bay as well as in East Harbour then Captain Kemanyel might just decide to cut his losses, leave her here, and take his chances with her deputies in Idramar.

The tavern door opened again, and Tila's heart sank farther as she recognised Alazar Blade and Marin. Of all the people she didn't want to see right now…

The old man who'd first spoken had settled his chair back on the floor, and was glaring across the tavern. "You need to think on how you're speaking of His Majesty, Hama! He's the Light of Heaven, what guides and protects us, and you'd do well to remember that!"

Hama drained his tankard and set it down on the table with a distinct *click*.

"Is he, though?"

The tavern went very quiet. Tila's mouth dried, and she surreptitiously reached up her left sleeve to find a knife. Barach was very attentive as well. Much as Tila wanted to put a blade into Hama herself, she was far more concerned by the potential for violence all around them. You didn't question the divinity of the God-King in the middle of a tavern and expect to walk away with no consequences.

Over by the bar, Marin's face had also taken on an expression of alarm. Alazar, in contrast, was attempting to attract the barkeep's attention, but the barkeep had other concerns.

"Hama!" he called, raising his voice somewhat unnecessarily, given the sudden drop in noise. "S'man'll not be having that sort of talk in here!"

"You've heard the talk downriver from the Catseyes, same as s'man has," Hama snapped back, undeterred.

"That's blasphemy!" the old man in the other corner barked, getting to his feet. His drinking companions reached out to grab him, but he shook them off.

"Blasphemy?" Hama repeated. "Is it blasphemy to speak the truth? The God-King has no heir, and lies abed sick, while Nari Himself has been reborn in the mountains!"

Uproar.

Most of the tavern's customers lurched to their feet, began shouting, or both. Tila expected Hama to be dragged outside but swiftly realised, to her horror, he had many supporters in the room: perhaps not quite as many as those angrily decrying him, but not far off. Claim and counter-claim of heresy flew back and forth. Fists were clenched and metal tankards were gripped, ready to be swung.

"Goodsar!" the barkeep wailed, turning to Alazar. "Goodsar, will you not defend His Divine Majesty?"

A scowl crossed Alazar Blade's face. Then he turned and drew his longblade in one swift, smooth motion, holding it out in front of him across the middle of the room. Everyone went very quiet, because it was one thing to hurl abuse at a neighbour when tensions had clearly been simmering for a while, and quite another to walk into the naked blade of a professional killer. Everyone could see the warrior's braids in his hair, and there was no mistaking the nature of his weapon.

Tila's fingers closed on a knife. Next to Alazar, she saw Marin do the same at his belt.

Alazar looked from one side of him to the other. Then, slowly and deliberately, he sheathed his longblade once more.

"The God-King has not been this sar's concern for many years," he bit out. "Settle your arguments yourselves. But do it somewhere this sar is not currently drinking." He turned back to the barkeep and pointed to a cask. The barkeep, somewhat shocked, and trying to hide an expression of disappointment, obliged.

A sullen near-silence settled over the tavern; the tense, angry quiet of words spoken that would not and could not be taken back, but which no one was willing to act upon right then. Tila drained her remaining wine in one swallow, and tapped Barach on the hand. "Come on."

Barach left the rest of his ale—which was testament to its quality, or lack thereof—and followed her across the room. Some patrons were slowly retaking their seats; others had apparently come to the same conclusion as Tila, and were finishing their drinks and moving towards the door, several of the *Light of Fortune*'s sailors amongst them. Marin made a polite half-bow to Tila, which she pretended not to see. Alazar just took a pull from his tankard and didn't even look at her. Perhaps he hadn't noticed her.

You want a peaceful mug of ale, and so you have the courage to face down an entire tavern of folk charged up with religious fury, she thought angrily at the disgraced sar as she shoved the door open and strode out onto the boardwalk that passed for a street in Emerald Bay. *Where was your courage when it mattered? Why was this princess's father, your lover's father, the God-King, less important to you than a drink?!*

"High lady," Barach murmured to her. "The God-King. Do you think it's true?"

Tila opened her mouth to reply, then hesitated. "Which part?"

"Both?" Barach said, although he sounded unsure. "His Majesty being ill, but also... could Nari have really been reborn?"

Tila wanted to snap an angry denial at him, but Livnya bit down on the words and forced them back behind her teeth. "This lady suspects it's merely rumour and exaggerations," she said, far more calmly than she felt. "Still, we may need to persuade Captain Kemanyel to make the best time possible back to Idramar. Change leads to uncertainty, and uncertainty is rarely good for business."

If the rumours have reached here, they'll have reached elsewhere. If the town's opinion is divided here, they'll be divided elsewhere. This princess takes care of one problem, and another crops up immediately.

Damn it all, Natan. How many children is your sister going to need to kill just to keep your arse on that throne?

SAANA

IT WAS DUSK when the boats came back, and Saana was staring into her cookfire when the door opened.

You didn't fall in, then. She bit back that acidic greeting, but didn't turn her head. She was angry, and wasn't going to pretend otherwise, but she also didn't want to outright start a fight. "Catch anything?" she asked instead, trying to keep her tone mild.

Half a dozen small silver fish thudded down next to her onto the floor, slipping and slithering off each other. Not bad, in all fairness. Jelema owned the boat, so she'd take the greatest share of the catch, and her fishers would each get a smaller portion, so long as they'd worked hard. Jelema might be warm-hearted, but she wouldn't reward a liability, and nor would she be swayed by Zhanna's status as the clan chief's daughter.

Zhanna's dragon woke up from its fireside slumber, sniffed the fish once, then ran out of Saana's eyeline and towards its owner with an excited hiss. Zhanna still hadn't spoken. Saana sighed, got to her feet and turned around. It would be polite to thank her daughter for the contribution to their meal, at least, before she had some words with her about disappearing without saying anything.

"Thank you for—"

"What is *that?*"

Zhanna's eyes were wide, her face had paled even in the light of the firepit, and she was pointing with a shaking finger at Saana's chest even as her dragon clambered up onto her shoulder again. Saana sighed.

"It's Daimon Blackcreek's brooch. Which I'm sure you know," she added a little more sharply, "since you saw him offer it to me before you *ran away*—"

"You said *yes?!*"

Saana took a breath. Zhanna was clearly upset, and Saana losing her temper because her daughter had interrupted her twice wasn't going to help anything.

"Yes," she said soberly, "I did. I was going to tell you—"

She didn't get to finish that sentence either, because Zhanna turned, still in her salt-crusted furs, and ran for the door. Saana was moving before she'd even really registered what she was doing and got there just ahead of her daughter, slamming into the door with her shoulder to keep it shut.

"Zhanna!"

Zhanna grabbed at the handle and pulled for a moment, but the door wouldn't budge and she spun away again with a wordless shout of rage. Her dragon hissed angrily, apparently picking up on her mood even though it presumably didn't know the source of it, which was a condition Saana could quite identify with.

"Zhanna!" she snapped again, astonishment warring with her anger. "What is *wrong* with you?"

"How could you say yes?!" Zhanna shrieked. Her hair was tousled from a day at sea, her eyes flashed fury, and in her furs she was the very image of an Unblooded come to wet the teeth of her axe. On any other day Saana might have paused, tried to calm her down, but she'd been on edge since the morning. She'd had visions of a rogue wave sweeping out of the east and besting even Jelema's skill, spilling everyone into the cold, dark waters. She'd dodged questions from clan members about the brooch, so determined had she been to give Zhanna the news first, as she deserved. And now here was her daughter, unrepentant and unapologetic, spitting hail at her for... what?

"If you'd stayed, instead of running off to sulk, you'd have found out!" she shouted back. "He is thinking of what is right for our peoples, and I must too! If Daimon says a marriage with him is our best chance to avoid the wrath of his countrymen, then *that is what I must do*! I trust he doesn't lie, and I trust he knows this country better than I do!" She grabbed a breath.

"I'd have expected this from some of the clan," she continued, trying to lower her tone a little, but only really succeeding in adding scorn. "From Ada, maybe, or Zalika, but my own daughter? Who's lived with me? Who watched me argue the clan around to come here in the first place? Who watched me *cry* as we left our home behind? You can't see I would only do this thing because it's *necessary*?" She shook her head, not bothering to hide her disdain any longer. "I thought you were an adult. Clearly, I was wrong."

Zhaana's lip was trembling now, her rage abruptly consumed by more fragile emotions. "You... you don't even love him?" she asked, her voice small.

Saana snorted a laugh. Finally, a break in the weather to steer by! "Love him? Is that what this is about? You're worried he'll replace you in my heart?" She chuckled and shook her head. "No. You'll always be the most precious thing to me. This marriage will be... bearable. I think. In truth, it's more of an alliance. Apparently that happens fairly often here—"

"He's too young for you!"

Zhanna darted for the door again, her eyes filling with tears. This time, Saana was too slow and too startled to stop her, and Zhanna fled out into the gathering dark. Saana started after her, drawing in breath for a shout, then stopped.

What in the name of the Dark Father? He's too young *for me?*
Things fell into place. Daimon knowing words of Tjakorshi

that neither Saana nor Nalon had taught him. Zhanna joining in the dance and letting herself be guided through the steps by Daimon, when usually she'd have snapped like a young krayk at anyone trying to tell her she was doing something incorrectly. Daimon's gift of the dragon, which to him had likely been nothing more than a curiosity but which Zhanna, who'd always loved raising crow chicks, would take as a gesture of great generosity and trust.

Oh, by all the winds and tides. She's in love *with him. Or thinks she is.*

Daimon wasn't unhandsome, as Saana herself had noted only that morning. He was brave, she supposed, and outwardly well-mannered in that stiff, Naridan way. Zhanna probably hadn't seen the bone-deep stubbornness in him. Perhaps she wouldn't have cared; she shared the trait, after all.

And it was true, Saana conceded wearily, Daimon *was* young. He was closer to Zhanna's age than Saana's. Was that it, then? Had Zhanna convinced herself she loved this strange, foreign lord a few years her elder? Had she convinced herself he loved her back?

Saana grimaced as her mind veered onto a new tack, but she dismissed the notion instantly. No, she could not believe Daimon Blackcreek had been intimate with her daughter, even if her daughter might have wished it otherwise. The man was simply too rigid for him to have deceived Saana in such a way. Everything Daimon had done since the clan had arrived had been a desperate balancing act as he tried to act as honourably as possible towards everyone, even his ancestral enemies, while still keeping as many people alive as he could. Fucking his newest ally's daughter behind her back while holding her hostage would not be in keeping with that at all.

No, Daimon wouldn't have known of this, else he'd have never brought Zhanna to witness this conversation. He must have been as oblivious to Zhanna's interest in him as Saana had been of

Daimon's interest in her, before Tavi had said what he'd said last night. Come to think of it, Daimon himself might not have fully come to terms with that particular interest yet, but Saana had a nagging feeling the stablemaster had been right about it. Daimon Blackcreek didn't seem the type of man who was good at lying, and he'd as good as said that he wouldn't only want to fuck her just once, to make their marriage good in the eyes of his god, or whatever that strange Naridan belief was.

Father Krayk preserve me, but Zhanna will never forgive me if I marry this man in two days and then fuck him, when she has her heart set on him.

Was that what being chief came down to, then? Not just cajoling, persuading, and in some cases downright bullying her clan to leave their ancestral homes and come across the Great Ocean? Not just arriving on a shore as a beggar where she'd once landed looking for battle? Not just casting away her freedom to marry a man she still barely knew, a man who for all that he might not be a bad man had, on the first day she'd laid eyes on him, killed her best friend in an honour duel? Not just marrying him simply in the hope it might mean his countrymen, when they finally came this far south, wouldn't kill her people when they were discovered?

She must drive away her daughter, and break her heart as well?

Saana closed the door and sank down behind it, buried her face in her arms, and didn't fight the tears when they came.

OLD ELIO

THEY SAT ABOUT the table, five true-hearted men of Black Keep, talking just loud enough to hear each other over the crackling of the flames in the fire pit.

"It's not to be borne," Nadar, one of the castle guards muttered, taking a swig of the ale his host had provided. "S'man thought his lordship would've seen sense by now."

"That idiot Ganalel has not helped," Shefal replied. "To take a coward's blow at the sea witch was bad enough, but to *miss*..."

"That was Tavi's fault," Yoon, another guard said. "Warned the witch, he did."

"Never had Tavi down as a traitor," Elio put in, cradling his own mug of ale in his old hands. They ached from handling his nets, but he'd be damned if he'd see the Raiders steal his fish. "S'man always liked him. Seemed sensible, you know?"

"'A man can understand dragons, or understand men, but not both'," Nadar quoted. "He's always been an odd sort."

"And he's been spending time with the witch's daughter, too," Yoon said. "She'll have put an enchantment on him, you mark s'man's words."

"Perhaps he has always been little better than a witch himself," Shefal mused. "Do any of us truly know what passes between him and those beasts?"

"Rotel's girl Abbatane will," Nadar pointed out. "She fair loves those dragons. Spends more time with Tavi than with her own da, or so it seems."

"S'man won't have that Abbatane's a witch," Yoon said firmly. "Spending time with Tavi or no, she's a sweet little thing. Not like that savage Lord Daimon brought within the walls."

"Speaking of witches," Kelarahel said, his first words for a while, "did you hear of the curse stone found on the south side of the house where that Raider woman died?"

Silence.

"Curse stone?" Nadar asked, his voice suddenly a little shaky. "You mean to say, a witch's curse stone?"

Elio glanced over at Shefal, and found the freeman looking back at him.

"The same," Kelaharel replied. "At least, that's what Lord Daimon and Aftak made of it. Lord Darel too, as s'man hears, for Lord Daimon asked his opinion of the thing."

"Why can't the witches curse the whole Nari-damned lot of them? That's what s'man wants to know," Yoon said, but his voice held the hollowness of a man seeking to cover his sudden uncertainty with bold words.

"Will a witch's curse even hold on these demon-worshippers?" Nadar asked.

"She died, did she not?" Shefal said baldly. "It seems the curse was potent." He took a sip of his ale. "And besides, who is to say the witch is a Naridan? The Raiders have their own squabbles."

"And their own witches," Nadar said, making the sign of the Mountain. "S'man's heard his lordship talking of them."

Elio took another sip of his ale, and said nothing.

"His lordship also still talks of finding the man who sent the Raider woman into the Downwoods," Kelaharel said, looking at Shefal, who stiffened.

"And?"

"And he'll not hear the truth of it from s'man," the reeve assured him. "He's in a powerful temper over it, though."

"His tempers will be his undoing," Shefal said darkly. "The guilt of his actions wars within him, and leads him to further outrage." He sighed, and took another drink. "When it comes to it, who will stand with us?"

"Too few, s'man fears," Elio replied heavily. "Even his own son has been talking about how p'raps these Raiders aren't as bad as we thought. If only more young men were like yourself."

"What of the thane's household?" Shefal asked. The first shook his head.

"Precious few. Duranen saw the truth, but then his lordship threw him in the cells." He looked over at the Kelaharel. "How secure are they?"

"Secure enough that Duranen won't be getting out without the key," the reeve grunted.

"That is not unachievable," Shefal pointed out.

"Achievable, yes," Kelaharel acknowledged. "But it would betray us, and for what? Duranen's one man. Give him his cudgel and his rattletails and he might be worth three in a fight, if he can make sure his dragons only go for Raider blood, which isn't certain. Duranen won't tip things in our favour if the rest of the town are too meek to stand up for themselves, though."

"There's no hope of swaying Aftak to our cause?" Shefal asked. "The word of Nari could bring many to our side."

"If the priest ever heard the God-King, he's stoppered his ears," Kelaharel said dismissively. "All he hears now is his lordship's silver. Aftak's been a contrary bastard at the best of times, and that beard of his makes him look half-Raider anyhow. He's more likely to shove his staff between your eyes than do the decent thing."

"No word from the north?" Yoon asked hopefully.

"This man is not in the habit of communing with the Thane of Darkspur," Shefal snapped. "Evram carried word, but we cannot rely on Darkspur. If he comes, we will be rewarded for our loyalty. But he may not come."

"Time is short," Elio pointed out. "Can you rally the town yourself?"

Shefal shook his head. "This man doubts it. He is not the best-loved, and many would rather bow their heads and live as traitors than risk their lives for freedom and honour." He drummed his fingers on the table, then stopped suddenly. "All are invited to the ceremony, yes?"

"Yes," Nadar said, nodding.

"We need a figurehead," Shefal said slowly. "We need someone who can rally the town, as you say." He left his words hanging, and it took a moment for Elio to catch his meaning. When he did, he saw that the others had got it as well.

"That's less achievable than springing Duranen," Kelaharel objected.

"Perhaps," Shefal conceded, "but worth far more."

"The captain has the keys," Nadar said. "He's loyal to his lordship, and by that s'man means Lord Daimon."

Shefal smiled. "Then we shall have to see if Captain Malakel can be persuaded. What say you? This man believes this our last true hope. Otherwise we condemn ourselves."

"It's a bold plan, but s'man agrees," Yoon said. "Malakel can see reason, and hopefully the town can as well."

One by one, the others nodded, Elio included. It would be risky, but the risk was worth it. He had no intention of seeing out his remaining years being forced to bow and make nice to Raiders.

"A toast, then," Shefal said, holding out his mug. The others mirrored him. "To the true-hearted men of Black Keep, and the confusion of their enemies!"

JEYA

GALEM WANTED TO leave hìs old clothes behind in exchange for the ones they'd snatched off a drying line, but Jeya had overruled hìm. It was too dangerous: the stolen maijhi and karung were unremarkable in their own right, but if the owner told their neighbours how they'd discovered richer clothes left in their place then it was always possible that could get back to Galem's pursuers, and that meant they might not only have an idea of which way hè'd fled but also, if they spoke to the owner, what hè could now be wearing.

Now they'd reached where Jeya had planned to spend the rest of the night, but shé couldn't find the way in.

"The Old Palace?" Galem asked hesitantly, eyeing where the wild hedge rose up beyond the old boundary wall. "Yóu want us to hide in there?"

"No, Í want us to jump up and down and shout to announce ourselves!" Jeya retorted, then immediately regretted hér words. They'd have been harsh on any night, let alone to someone who'd had to run from what had almost certainly been hìs family's murders. "Sorry, Í'm sorry. Yes, we should hide in here. It's the safest place Í can think of for now. There's a hole in the wall somewhere."

And yet shé couldn't find it. Even though they went up and

down the stretch of wall, the gap through which a person could wriggle remained stubbornly absent.

"Ì always heard it's haunted," Galem said. "Could that be it?"

"If it is, Í've never met a spirit in there," Jeya replied. Shé slammed a fist into the stones beside hér in frustration. Shé was tired, and not a little scared, and the longer they stayed here, the greater the risk of them being seen.

Then shé saw the god.

Sa, the god of thieves and tricksters—amongst other things—in their form as a golden-maned monkey, walking across the street as bold as brass. The moonlight bleached all the colour from their pelt, but there was no mistaking the thick ruff of fur around their neck, and the tufted tip to their tail. Any normal animal of that kind would be asleep now. Only Sa walked abroad at night, and their eyes were fixed on Jeya as they came to a halt, not ten paces away.

Jeya made a small noise of alarm in hér throat, and reached behind hér for Galem's hand. Shé'd never seen a god before.

"What?" Galem asked, as hér fingers found hìs.

Sa turned and trotted away, and Jeya knew immediately that shé was supposed to follow them. Shé started forwards, pulling Galem behind hér, as the god disappeared around the corner. When shé rounded it after them, shé just caught sight of the god's hindquarters disappearing through the wall.

This was where the hole was. Shé'd remembered wrong, and had been looking in the wrong section, but Sa had been watching over hér. Shé whispered a quick prayer to hér benefactor, then turned to Galem.

"Did yòu see them?" shé asked breathlessly.

"See who?" Galem replied, frowning past hér shoulder into the darkness.

"Sa," Jeya said. "They showed us the way!"

"Ì didn't see anything," Galem muttered uncertainly, but there was no mistaking the entrance the god had led them to. The hole was near-circular, with only the ancient mortar providing a somewhat suspect anchor for the stone blocks overhead.

"And yóu're sure it's not haunted?" Galem asked again.

"As sure as Í can be," Jeya replied, and to hìs credit, Galem began climbing through without any further questions. Jeya cursed the poor light which meant shé couldn't clearly see hìs karung drawn tight over hìs buttocks. "Besides," shé added, following hìm, "Í thought Naridans didn't fear the spirits of the dead?" It was a belief Jeya had always found astonishing. On the spirit nights, when both moons were dark, the barriers between the worlds of living and dead were at their weakest, and restless souls who'd strayed from Jakahama's light in the crossing would try to return, driven by the ravenous ache in their bellies. An Alaban would say their prayers and cast their salt, and hope the hungry dead didn't come knocking. Jeya had heard more than one argument about whether Naridans were endangering others, since they lit up their homes and called the spirits to them, or whether the hungry dead would flock to them and leave other, more sensible people alone.

"We honour the spirits of our ancestors," Galem replied. Hè looked to have found the crawlspace under the hedge of hìs own accord, and was still moving. "Other people's ancestors may not be so benign." Hè scrabbled through to the other side and got to hìs feet, then Jeya heard hìs intake of breath. "By the Mountain…"

Jeya smiled tightly as shé wriggled through, and came up beside hìm with the stolen clothes still in hér hand. The wild hedge had grown up around the Old Palace, hiding most of it from sight. Seeing the full building with your own eyes was a moment not to be quickly forgotten, even under moonlight rather than sunlight. Or perhaps especially under moonlight, shé thought, as the same old wonder stirred in hér heart.

Alaba had monarchs once, before the Hierarchs, and they'd lived here until one of them, their name now burned from history, had become too cruel. The people had risen up and overthrown them; not only killing the monarch but also their nobles, and the guards who hadn't either thrown down their weapons or joined the cause, as well as looting the palace. When the first Hierarchs had risen to power in the chaos that followed, they'd wanted a clean start to symbolise their break from the old ways, and so the New Palace had been built. The Old Palace had been abandoned, left to crumble away while the savage ghosts of those killed that night roamed its grounds, looking for vengeance on the unwary.

It had crumbled, certainly, but it still held majesty. The Old Palace had been built with a deep bank of earth on top of it, in which a garden had been planted. In the years since—decades, or maybe even centuries, Jeya wasn't exactly sure—the garden had grown out of control, and now resembled any other patch of Alaban forest.

Great trees, all that could normally be seen of the Old Palace from the street, towered skywards. Their massive roots embraced and, in some cases, punched through the very stone of the palace as they quested downwards in search of greater nourishment than the comparatively shallow soil in which they'd first sprouted. Between and around their trunks nestled thick clumps of shrubs, while the pale stone of the palace walls, silvery in the moonlight, was streaked with the dark tendrils of vines reaching down as though in imitation of their neighbours' roots.

The grounds of the palace had not gone uncolonised, either. What had once been lawns were now choked with growth as thick as that on top of the palace itself. The gravel beds and wide, paved terraces offered less opportunity for plants, but even here there were enterprising shoots and seedlings making the best of what little footing they could find.

Others spoke of the Old Palace in hushed tones, as though the spirits said to haunt it might hear the speaker and stray beyond the walls. Jeya had never felt any threat from it, not from the moment shé'd first pushed her way through the wild hedge. To hér, the Old Palace was a place of peace. Shé couldn't explain why, but shé was sure whatever spirits had once roamed its grounds must have long since found their way to rest amongst the life that had grown up here.

"It's beautiful," Galem said.

"Í know," Jeya agreed, delighted hè felt the same way. Shé looked around for Sa, but the god was nowhere to be seen. Jeya closed hér eyes and whispered a quick prayer of thanks.

"Why does no one come here?" Galem asked. "Ì mean, Ì know the stories of spirits, but…" Hè gestured at the palace.

"People do come here," Jeya told hìm, opening hér eyes again. "Í've come here many times, and so do others. Sometimes it's the only place to sleep. There'll probably be one or two in there now."

"Then why are we here?" Galem asked, suddenly apprehensive.

"Because rich people don't come here," Jeya said. "Rich people have their own roofs and beds, so they don't need to risk the spirits."

"Are yóu assuming the people hunting mè are rich?" Galem asked dubiously.

"No," Jeya told hìm, "I'm assuming they're going to try to think like a rich person would, once they realise yòu're not in yòur house. A rich person wouldn't think to hide here, and they won't know yòu're with mé."

Galem nodded slowly. "Ì'm glad Ì'm with yóu." Hè reached out and took hér hand. "And not just because yóu're helping mè. Or because yóu're beautiful. Thank yóu for… just being a friend."

Jeya found it hard to speak for a moment. Then shé tugged at hìs hand and pulled hìm after hér. "Come on. There's a place rainwater collects. We can drink, and wash our faces, and yòu can change yòur clothes."

It had been a bathing pool once, Jeya supposed: a stone-sided, rectangular hollow with steps down into it on one side, sitting midway along the raised terrace on the palace's east side. Small, dark shapes scuttled away as they approached, but Jeya was less bothered about rats than shé was people. Still, everything seemed quiet and tranquil.

Shé knelt down and cupped a few handfuls of water into hér mouth, because running had given hér a powerful thirst. Galem crouched and joined hér, and they drank together in silence.

"Should Ì change now?" Galem asked quietly.

"Yes," Jeya agreed. Better to get hìm out of his rich-person clothes before anyone saw hìm in them. Shé passed hìm the stolen maijhi and karung. "Let's get inside."

"Are yóu certain it's safe?" Galem was eyeing the crumbling palace dubiously.

"Of course it's not safe," Jeya laughed. "If it was safe, everyone would come here. But it's safer than some places, and yòu probably don't want to change yòur clothes out here, do yòu?"

Galem looked around at the garden, highlighted here and there in moon-silver but mainly drenched in impenetrable shadows, and shuddered. "No."

"Come on, then," Jeya said, taking hìs hand again.

Despite hér assertions, she still found herself creeping up to the gaping, empty doorway that led out onto the terrace where the pool sat: the wood of the doors had rotted away to nothing, and only the deeply corroded metal bracings remained, still strewn across the entrance where they'd fallen. There was something about the sheer size of the Old Palace that made you feel you didn't belong, for all that the old monarchs were long gone and the spirits of the dead, if they still lingered, had never bothered Jeya yet.

Once over the threshold, the entire building seemed to be holding its breath around them. The moonlight flooded in through windows, but did little to give an idea of the space they were in. Jeya had been here in the daytime and knew it as a wide hall, long since emptied of anything of value and punctuated by large, square pillars, but at this hour it was little more than blackness broken up by pale, slanting shafts.

"Wait," Galem said, as shé moved further into the darkness. "Ì need to see what Ì'm doing." Hè hesitated, and Jeya immediately understood why. They'd kissed many times now, with great passion on some occasions and delicate tenderness on others, but hér hands had rarely slipped under hìs clothes, and never far. Nor had hè ever disrobed in any way. Perhaps it was hìs Naridan stiffness, or perhaps it was something unique to hìm. Either way, despite the aching desire shé felt for hìm at times, shé'd never pushed further than hè was comfortable.

"Ì'll look away," shé assured hìm, and turned to regard the deep shadows of the palace's interior. Probably for the best: there might be someone else in here somewhere, and you never knew what kind of person it might be.

"Thank yóu," Galem muttered, with what sounded like a mix of gratitude and shame. Shé heard the slither of cloth as hè stripped off hìs own maijhi.

"So if yòu're the Splinter Prince," Jeya asked softly, "what does that actually mean?"

"One hundred and seventy-four years ago, the God-King of Narida died without a trueborn child," Galem said. "The divinity was known to be carried from father to father."

Jeya nodded, then realised that hè might not even be looking at hér. "So what happened?"

"A member of the Divine Court came forward claiming the God-King had lain with hēr, outside of both their marriages, and that hēr child Natan was actually the God-King's blood," Galem continued. "Perhaps it was true. A lot of court officials suddenly claimed to know of the God-King's infidelity. Others said there was no proof the child was divine, and the lady simply wanted to advance hēr own family. They pointed to the God-King's younger brother, Akab, and said the divine blood was with hìm."

Jeya frowned. "Í don't know much about gods, but it doesn't sound like they were going to agree."

Galem snorted. "They didn't. The resulting war nearly broke Narida. It became known as the Splintering. In the end, Natan's supporters won. Akab, hìs mōther and a few of their remaining followers fled here, where the Hierarchs granted shelter to their family. Natan was recognised as the true blood of the old God-King and hè became God-King of Narida in hìs own right, the first of hìs name."

Hìs voice became bitter. "My family's lived in the shadows ever since, for fear of the God-Ķing's knives. They've tried again and again to kill us, but always when we've been masked, parading around for the Hierarchs at a festival, and someone always lived." Hìs voice began to break, the tears audible in it. "Tonight they came for our house. They've never done that before. They've never known who we were!"

"Í am so sorry," Jeya said, not certain what else shé could say. Shé was fairly sure no one would particularly care if shé lived or died—except Nabanda of course, and Ngaiyu—and shé certainly couldn't imagine mattering to someone enough for them to repeatedly try to kill hér. Admittedly, that didn't sound like a good thing.

There was a sob from behind hér, and shé looked around instinctively. Galem had finished changing hìs clothes and had the old ones tucked under hìs arm, but was standing with hìs head in his hands, hìs long, straight hair covering hìs face, and hìs shoulders were shaking.

"Hey," Jeya said soothingly. Shé moved to hìm in three quick steps and enfolded hìm in hér arms. "Hey."

"It's all because of mè," Galem muttered, hìs voice bubbling with grief.

"That can't be true," Jeya told hìm, as firmly as shé thought reasonable.

"It *is*," Galem insisted miserably. "It must be. Ì've reached majority. That must be why the Naridans tried again. The Hierarchs announced it a few months ago. They were so *proud*," hè added, bitterness choking hìs voice again. "A new generation of their pet exiles to gloat about! And look what's happened!"

Jeya held hìm, and said nothing. Shé'd always assumed the Splinter King's family were strong allies of the Hierarchs, which was certainly how the relationship was portrayed to the people. Shé'd never considered the exiled Naridan royalty would feel like they were being used.

"We don't know what's happened," shé said, trying to sound reassuring. "It's not safe for us to go and find out now, but we can in the morning. Yòur family had guards, yes? Yòu told me yòu did."

"Yes," Galem admitted.

"Then perhaps the attackers didn't succeed," Jeya suggested. Shé didn't know if shé believed that, but it might be true. "Everything could still work out. But for now, yòu're safe, and we need to get some sleep so we can do whatever we need to tomorrow."

"Ì don't think Ì can sleep," Galem protested, but Jeya could feel hìm swaying slightly as shé held hìm. Hè was exhausted, and in fairness, shé wasn't doing much better.

"At least come and sit down," shé told hìm. Shé tugged at hìs sleeve, pulling hìm towards one of the pillars. "Come. Lie down here." Shé sat with her back to the pillar and brought hìm down with her, then stuffed hìs old maijhi behind hér back and placed his old karung in hér lap. She patted it. "Lay yòur head here."

Hè did so. They were in the darkness now, but hér eyes were adjusting a little and shé could see the shadows shift as hè moved hìs body around.

Jeya closed hér eyes. Shé'd slept in far less comfortable places than this. At least this was dry.

"Jeya."

"Hmm?"

"It's all a lie."

Shé opened one eye. "What is?"

"Everything. Everything anyone thinks they know about mè." Galem made a wet snorting noise, the sound of a half-strangled sob.

Í know being close to yòu is like morning sunlight, Jeya thought. *Í know Í could get lost in yòur eyes for hours. Í know Í would do anything to heal the hurt yòu have right now.* But shé didn't say any of those things, because that didn't seem to be what Galem meant.

Shé waited for hìm to continue.

All that met hér ears was the sudden, soft change in the rhythm of hìs breathing as sleep pulled hìm under.

DAREL

THE BELL OF the God-King's shrine was ringing, and Darel Blackcreek couldn't work out why.

There were no Raiders in sight. Well, there were, but only the ones already here, the ones Daimon had allowed to settle in defiance of tradition, honour and anything approaching common sense. The room in which Darel had been imprisoned for the last two weeks faced north and east, and he could see nothing on the sea to cause alarm. There was no hostile force coming down the North Road. And besides, the people he could see weren't moving in haste or panic. There was a general movement towards the square, but the gatehouse blocked his view of whatever was taking place.

He really hoped Daimon wasn't doing anything stupid.

The fields were ready to be planted; that was good. From what Darel had been able to see, it really did look like the Raiders had been pulling their weight. It was hard for him to tell from the keep's windows, but he could just about make out enough difference in clothing and general appearance to see the Raiders were in the fields, herding livestock, and sailing out to sea to fish on their strange ships. He'd spent the first few days waiting for the Raider chief to order the slaughter of his people, but it hadn't happened.

Even the Festival of Life appeared to have gone well. The Wooden Man had gone up in flames, and Darel had waited for the laughing and singing to devolve into screams as his revelling, intoxicated countrymen were betrayed and murdered, but no such thing had come to pass. Now, three days later, there was still no sign anyone had suffered anything worse than the traditional sore head.

Darel considered himself a man of learning and reason. He'd studied the works of scholars and great thinkers, such as his father had gathered. He'd read warnings against trusting too much in the power of one's own intellect, or persisting in a belief despite evidence to the contrary.

He was being forced to conclude the Raiders might not solely be the warlike savages he'd also supposed them to be. It was possible they might have some form of society, might be able to live alongside civilised people if they had appropriate examples to follow. It was a fascinating concept, and one that made him itch to get out of his chambers and study them. Except he couldn't, of course. Daimon still didn't trust him not to try to kill everyone, or possibly not to take his own life out of honour. Darel was, to his great shame, glad his law-brother had seen fit to remove anything bladed from the chamber before incarcerating him. He didn't relish the thought of piercing his own heart with an eating knife.

He was snatched from his reverie by voices outside his door. There'd been much commotion in the castle grounds over the last couple of days, but he'd been unable to ascertain what it had been in aid of. He'd heard Osred's voice giving instructions, but the steward had never responded when Darel had called his name. He probably felt less conflict to his loyalties if he pretended he couldn't hear.

There was a metallic jangling, and then a click. Someone was unlocking the door.

Darel looked around instinctively for a weapon, and found nothing save scrolls and bed linen. He snatched up a feather-filled bolster, well aware it was a poor tool, but perhaps it could buy him a moment's distraction should whoever was entering wish him harm. Daimon would have knocked and called first, probably demanded some assurance that Darel wouldn't try to kill him on sight; Darel knew this instinctively. So who could this be?

The lock clicked again and the door swung inwards, and Darel raised the bolster.

Standing in the doorway, Shefal took in Darel's stance and raised an eyebrow in surprise.

"Shefal?" Darel asked, perplexed. He lowered the bolster, but kept it in hand. Neither he nor Daimon had ever liked the arrogant young freeman, and usually Darel would have quite happily struck him for entering his chamber uninvited, and with something considerably harder than a bolster. On this day, however, curiosity stayed his hand for now.

"Lord Darel," Shefal said, bowing a shade too late and a hair too lightly. "Your man is relieved to see you are well."

Darel had no time for pleasantries. "What is the meaning of this?" he demanded, edging round to peer past Shefal. Two guards stood in the doorway, Nadar and Yoon, as well as Kelarahel the reeve, but there was no sign of Daimon. "Where is this lord's brother?"

"Lord Daimon is in the square," Shefal replied, still in his bow. Darel eyed him, suddenly dubious. That was the posture of a man with bad news to share.

"He is about to wed the Raider chief."

Darel grabbed Shefal by the throat and hauled him upright with a violence that surprised even him. Shefal's eyes bulged, and his hands flew to Darel's wrist.

"If you are lying—" Darel began, through gritted teeth.

"It's true, lord!" Nadar said urgently. "The proclamation went out two days ago!"

Darel's mind whirled. What in the name of the God-King was Daimon thinking? Had he been smitten by that straw-haired sea witch? Had he taken leave of his senses completely? Had he been threatened into this, or blackmailed?

"Did Daimon send you to bring this lord to him?" he demanded of Shefal, releasing his hold on the man's throat. Shefal rubbed his neck and eyed Darel, but passed no comment on it.

"No, lord," he said instead. "But your man could not stand by. He felt he had to free you and your lord father, to see if you could talk some sense into Lord Daimon."

Father won't talk to Daimon, he'll try to kill him, Darel thought bleakly. Perhaps he could persuade these men not to release his father, or command them to give him the keys. *He* could talk to Daimon, certainly, try to find out what his law-brother was thinking—

"Darel?"

Darel's heart sank as his father strode into view, cheeks darkened by two weeks of beard growth and eyes hard with fury. His blades were already belted to his hip, and he was carrying a white-scabbarded longblade and shortblade that he threw to Darel. Darel managed to catch them, which was just as well, since letting your blades fall to the floor was great shame for a sar. *Not that this man's shame can get much greater anyway.*

"Father," he said with a bow. "Your son is relieved to see you are well." The same words Shefal had used, and probably about as truthful. Darel wished his father health and happiness, but Asrel Blackcreek with a blade was the very last thing their family needed at that moment.

"Prepare yourself," Asrel told him, his nostrils flaring. He looked in a more ferocious temper than Darel had ever seen before. "We are going to find the traitor who assumed our name, and kill him."

Careful, now. Darel looped his sword belt around his waist. "Father, what of the Raiders? Daimon—"

"Do not speak his name!" Asrel snapped, spittle flying from his lips.

God-King have mercy, this is going to go badly. "Father, the Raiders are surely allied to… the traitor," Darel said carefully. "How will we even get near him?"

"If there is any honour remaining in his veins, he will hear this lord's challenge to single combat and respond," Asrel said. "If he does not, and he sends the savages against us, we will die as we should have done when they first befouled our shores. Either way, son, our story will likely end today, but we shall leave any who witness us in no doubt as to our honour."

He spun away, heading for the stairs. Darel finished buckling his belt, and eyed the four men around him.

"Where are the other guards?"

"In the square," Yoon replied scornfully.

"Where did you get the keys?"

"The captain," Nadar said.

Darel frowned. "Malakel? He is with you in this?"

"He's not with anyone anymore," Yoon said, his eyes flickering to Nadar for a second. "Called us fools and traitors, and was going to call for Lord Daimon. Nadar had to knife him."

Darel gritted his teeth. "Congratulations. If this lord is to believe what his brother has told him, you have just killed one more Naridan than the Raiders have in the space of the last two weeks."

"Lord?" Shefal said, his expression abruptly blank. Darel hesitated for a moment, very aware that if the man told Darel's father what he'd just said then Lord Asrel would probably try to take Darel's head too. The thane of Black Keep wouldn't mourn the death of a guard captain who'd had the means to free him but hadn't done so, and he'd already shown he wouldn't hesitate to wish death on a son he considered to have abandoned honour.

"Never mind," Darel muttered, stepping forward. "Give this lord the keys, and let us catch up with his father." *And while we do, this man need to work out exactly how he's going to prevent everyone he loves from dying.*

DAIMON

THEY'D TAKEN THEIR first vows in the Tjakorshi style, kneeling in front of each other in Saana's house. Osred had been Daimon's witness, doing his best to look solemn and composed as his thane spoke oaths of commitment and responsibility to a wild woman from across the ocean. Saana's witness had been a captain called Inkeru, hard-faced and with a fierce smile, who'd apparently taken the news her chief was wedding the thane of Black Keep with stolid equanimity.

The problem, of course, was each witness could only understand one person's vows. Daimon hadn't even considered this might have been a problem, but judging by Saana's frustration the evening before, it definitely was.

"Both witnesses must know all vows," she'd explained in Daimon's study, pacing back and forth. "Else this man's witness cannot hold you to yours, and yours cannot hold this man to hers. Of the two of us, this man alone speaks both languages. It would give this man too much power, for her to translate what you say to her witness."

"This man trusts you would not do that," Daimon had said, and found that he'd meant it.

"It would not be right," Saana had said, shaking her head. "It must be done properly, even if the outcome would be the same."

She'd cast a glance at him and smiled slightly. "It is like your god watching."

Daimon had coughed awkwardly, feeling his cheeks flush. "Perhaps your daughter?" He'd asked, eager to change the subject. "She knows at least some of this man's tongue, and—"

"No!" Saana had snapped, holding up one hand. "Zhanna... This man will talk to you later about Zhanna. But she would not do."

"If this servant might make a suggestion," Osred had put in, "the man Nalon speaks both languages."

Daimon had looked at Saana and had seen his own irritation mirrored, then turn into reluctant acceptance as they'd both realised the steward had the right of it.

"Very well," Saana had muttered, rubbing at her forehead. "Nalon will translate for both our witnesses."

Which was how Nalon of Bowmar had ended up also being present at the oath ceremony, despite the fact that no one, including himself, really wanted him to be there. His eyebrows had climbed at Daimon's assertion he would work to get his people to treat women as equal to men, and they'd risen even higher when Saana had made her corresponding oath about people courting the same gender. Inkeru had been taken aback as well, judging by her grunt of apparent surprise, but she hadn't stormed out or started shouting, so Daimon judged Saana had chosen her witness well.

"You've put the razorclaw among the sheep, s'man will say that," Nalon muttered to Daimon as they walked through the streets to the town square for the Naridan half of the wedding. The bell of the God-King's shrine was ringing, calling all to come and bear witness.

"This lord does not recall asking your opinion," Daimon replied coldly, not looking at him.

"S'man's opinion may not matter to you," Nalon said, his shoulders moving in a shrug in Daimon's peripheral vision, "but for what it's worth, he likes the sound of these oaths."

Daimon blinked in surprise. "You do? This lord thought you had little good to say about anything."

"Little, perhaps, but not none," Nalon replied firmly. "S'man's lived with both peoples, which is more than anyone else can say. He's seen good people in both places who'd have been treated badly by the other. If you and the chief can make this work, s'man thinks there'll be many a soul living happier."

"And yet you think this will be disruptive?" Daimon asked. Nalon snorted.

"For sure. People who've had it good don't tend to like it when others suddenly start having it good too, or don't have to beg and bow to get it."

"You speak as though you are a great authority on such matters," Daimon scoffed. "Have you been reading the same books as this lord's brother?"

"Nothing of the sort," Nalon replied as they reached the square. "But s'man has noticed how you don't expect the Tjakorshi to bow to you or pay you respect, yet it still irritates you that s'man doesn't, even though he was never of your town. Imagine how you'll feel if the rest of Black Keep starts speaking to you the way the Brown Eagle clan speak to Saana. Enjoy your marriage, Lord Blackcreek." He turned and disappeared into the gathering crowd.

"What was that about?" Saana asked from his other side. She'd been speaking with Inkeru, and didn't seem to have caught the conversation.

"Nothing," Daimon muttered. "Just Nalon being himself." But what if he'd been right? Daimon had imagined that over time, the Brown Eagle clan could be taught proper manners and would come to speak to him with the appropriate respect. But what if the opposite happened? What if their uncivilised, irreverent ways rubbed off onto *his* people?

"We must teach more of our people each other's language," Saana said seriously, and Daimon shunted his thoughts away for the moment. "Perhaps this man should get Nalon to do it. He will not like it, but perhaps he will see it will make it easier for him." She smiled conspiratorially. "And then we will not need to deal with him so often."

"Perhaps we should take a young person from each of our peoples as pages," Daimon suggested rubbing his chin thoughtfully.

"Pages?"

"Aye; a personal servant, of a sort. They would learn our speech from serving us."

"They would learn yours, but how would they learn this man's?"

"The same way this man will," Daimon said with a grin, "by listening to you speak it. This man should not rely on Nalon to learn his own wife's tongue." It was a strange thing to give voice to, having a wife. By Tjakorshi customs, of course, he already did; he was only still unwed by Naridan customs. *It makes no sense, to have two parts to the thing. Perhaps we could find a way to combine it somehow, in case others wish to take this step…*

They'd reached the shrine, set back from the square a little way, on the opposite side to the castle's front gate. It was a simple affair, but Daimon still thought it beautiful; a small building, with a traditional splayed roof supported by a pillar at each corner, in which was housed its bronze bell. The external walls of wood were carved to resemble the stems of a climbing rose, with small gaps between to let the sunlight in.

Aftak was waiting. He opened the slatted wooden doors and hooked them back, allowing the gathering crowd to watch and witness from outside, but only Saana and Daimon entered the shrine itself. It was dim inside, patterned with the shade cast by the sun through the walls, with a faint wobble to the shadows from the tallow candles in each corner that Aftak had undoubtedly lit not long before. Daimon knelt on the rush matting before the low, two-tier marble altar, the top level of which flowed into a carving of Nari sitting in meditative pose. The God-King's head was fully shaved, his robes were half open to reveal a muscular chest, and his longblade—a genuine, minute steel replica, fashioned to fit with the rest of the statue—was laid across his knees.

Saana dropped to her knees beside him and held out her right arm. Daimon did the same with his left and clasped his hand with hers, threading their fingers together. He felt his mouth dry slightly at the touch of her skin on his, and the pressure of her shoulder on his through their clothes. The Tjakorshi ceremony had, if anything, been more formal: an agreement between equals. The Naridan one felt more intimate.

Aftak stepped forward and handed them a thin length of leather, which Daimon wrapped around their wrists. He and Saana then took one end each in their free hands and, not without some fumbling, managed to knot it.

"The betrothed are bound to each other in flesh," Aftak intoned, speaking the words of the ceremony, "now let them be bound to each other in the sight of the God-King." He handed Daimon and Saana a beeswax candle each, and gave Daimon a lit taper. "Lord Daimon Blackcreek, Thane of Blackcreek; Saana…" He paused, and Daimon glanced up to see his mouth moving uncertainly. *Four syllables, and the man has forgotten them already.*

"Sattistutar," Saana muttered, also realising the problem.

"… Sattistutar, Chief of the Brown Eagle clan," Aftak continued, as smoothly as he could, "are you ready to take your vows?"

"We are," Daimon said.

"We are," Saana echoed him. Daimon placed the beeswax candle on the altar next to the stubs of rancid tallow that was all most of the townsfolk could afford when they made their own prayers, and lit it with the taper. He passed the flame to Saana, and she did the same.

"Lord Nari," Aftak intoned. "Guide your servants' thoughts, words, and deeds as they enter into this marriage. Give them the courage to be true, the strength to be honest, and the judgement to be wise." He raised his hands, palms outwards. "Do you, Daimon Blackcreek, swear to honour your wife, to cherish her, to protect and provide for her?"

"This man does," Daimon said, managing to keep his voice steady with an effort. There was a tiny part of his mind still yelling that this was an awful idea, that he should draw his shortblade, cut the leather and flee, but he blocked it out. The next few moments were critical, however.

"And you, Saana Sattistutar," Aftak continued, managing not to stumble over her name this time. "Do you swear to honour your husband, to cherish him, to protect and provide for him?"

He did it. They'd told Aftak to make the vows equal, as he would have for two men or two women marrying, and may Nari bless him, he'd done it.

"This man does," Saana replied, giving Daimon's fingers a squeeze as she did so. She knew what had just happened was important.

"Stand," Aftak intoned, and they did so, only slightly clumsily as they both used their bound hand to help push themselves up. "Now, follow me."

He led them back out of the shrine into the sunlight, although in truth he could have spoken from inside and it would barely have made a difference to anyone's ability to hear him, the shrine was so small. Then he knocked the butt of his staff on the flagstones three times and raised his voice.

"People of Black Keep! This man and this woman stand before you today, ready to be joined in marriage! Is there anyone here who knows of good reason why they should not wed?"

Daimon couldn't prevent himself from looking around, although he tried to do it surreptitiously. He honestly wasn't sure what objection someone *could* raise, other than the somewhat spurious argument that Saana didn't worship Nari, but he still felt some of the tension drain out of him when no one stepped forward and raised their voice. He'd half-expected Shefal, at least, to try to disrupt proceedings, but he couldn't even see the freeman anywhere.

"There are no objections," Aftak said, and his voice betrayed his own relief. "This priest declares you wed. You may now kiss."

Daimon turned to Saana, which was harder to do than he'd imagined given that their hands were still bound to each other, palm to palm. Her eyes were still scanning the crowd, but she either didn't find what she was looking for or decided it was of no immediate concern, as she turned to face him too.

She was very close, close enough for him to feel the warmth of her breath. Her eyes were swallowing the world. Daimon hesitated, the excited tension in his gut warring with rapidly melting walls of ice in his head. He *wanted* to... and he knew he *should*... but should he *actually*...?

Saana tutted once, reached her free hand up to the back of his head, and kissed him.

Daimon felt a thrill run through him as her lips touched his. When he'd been younger, and learning his letters, Osred had fed his eagerness with written tales of legendary warriors and their great deeds. Those heroes who survived their own tales would often marry beautiful women, who were also often described in great detail. Daimon distinctly remembered one whose lips had been compared to the soft smoothness of rose petals, which had occasioned an embarrassing incident when he'd been but seven or eight years old, when his father had found him in the garden pressing a rose to his mouth in an attempt to work out what kissing such a woman would be like.

Saana's lips were not rose petals. They were warm, and firm, and slightly rough, yet tantalisingly yielding. His right hand had come up automatically as Saana had grabbed his head and he caught her shoulder, then held her as he kissed her back. The crowd started to cheer, and Daimon began to wonder how long this kiss was supposed to go on for—

"*Traitor!*"

DAREL

DAREL'S FATHER SHOWED no signs of having been confined for two weeks, but Darel couldn't say the same. He'd not stretched and exercised as a sar was supposed to do even in captivity, in order to stay in fighting condition should the opportunity arise to free himself. He tried not to show the twinge in his left calf muscle as he kept pace with his father, but he had the nasty feeling Lord Asrel had already noticed the slight wince in his face. *Barely out of our rooms for the first time in two weeks, and already a disappointment again.*

"Father," he said out loud, "what will you do if you defeat Dai— uh, your son's law-brother?"

"Your father will turn his sword upon the barbarian woman, and then upon any other milk-faces he can reach until he is brought down," his father grunted as they approached the gatehouse. "What else would you have him do?"

Perhaps something that doesn't lead to our inevitable deaths? Darel held his tongue, and contented himself with a curt nod in response to his father's words. He wasn't cut out to be a sar, and was rapidly coming to terms with that fact. He'd have given his life to defend his father, his brother, and his town from the Raiders, he was still certain of that. It had been easy, in the first days after Daimon's betrayal, to imagine how he'd have fought against the onrushing horde had that monster with the axe not brought him down, even with the memory of the sudden fear and helplessness he'd felt when the giant had struck his helmet and sent his head swimming. He'd fight against an immediate threat rather than freeze and let his life be taken cheaply; he was confident of that much, at least.

But the Raiders no longer seemed an immediate threat, and attacking them didn't feel like a noble defence of his people. It felt more like when one of the field frillnecks had lost its mind a few years back and run loose, attacking and trampling three men before it could be brought down. Lord Asrel might be moving and speaking with purpose, but his proposed actions reminded Darel of a beast lashing out in pain, not the considered conduct of a warrior.

Darel would have prayed to Nari, but he didn't know if he should ask for courage to join his father, or to stop him. Courage *and* wisdom, perhaps?

They passed into the castle's first yard, and Darel caught sight of a pair of boots, just visible on the floor inside the guardhouse. That would be Malakel then, knifed and dragged out of sight. Darel tried to tell himself the man should never have done Daimon's bidding anyway, and that his life had essentially been forfeit from that moment, but the logic rang hollow in his own head. There'd been no *need* for the man's death, that was the problem: all it was going to lead to was more death.

His father stormed on, through the gatehouse and over the drawbridge into the square, heedless of whether any of them were following. They were, of course, but Darel caught the glances Nadar, Yoon and Kelarahel were giving each other. Perhaps they were having second thoughts about how close they wanted to be to this. Shefal had no such misgivings, though, or at the very least was hiding them better.

There was a sizeable crowd in the square, Naridan and Raider standing shoulder to shoulder in apparent harmony. Darel saw his father's hand drop to the pommel of his longblade, and for a moment feared Lord Asrel was simply going to begin his campaign of vengeance on whichever Raiders were nearest, but then he began to push through the crowd. People turned with grunts of irritation at their passing, grunts that turned to expressions of shock as they saw who'd just shouldered them aside.

Cheering and applause erupted, and Darel nearly jumped at the sudden noise. Were the townsfolk so glad to see his father free? Would they stand with him?

Then he found himself at the inner edge of the crowd, and saw Daimon kissing the Raider chief, this Saana that he'd spoken of, and understanding settled deep into the pit of his stomach. They'd kissed. That meant the marriage had been completed.

They were too late.

"*Traitor!*" his father screamed, drawing his longblade with a flash of steel in the sun. Daimon jerked away from the kiss and reached for his own sword, but he was still bound to the Raider chief by his other hand and she lurched awkwardly with him as he shifted his balance. Daimon looked guilty, an expression Darel remembered from when they were boys and their father had caught him doing something or being somewhere he should not. The Raider's face went flat and hard, nostrils flaring, even paler than was usual for the savages.

"Priest, this is a sham and a blasphemy!" Darel's father spat as a bubble of noise began to run through the crowd. He raised his blade to point it at Aftak. "Renounce this foolishness at once!"

A frown crossed Aftak's broad, whiskered face as he eyed Lord Asrel. "The ceremony has been completed, lord. Your son is married in the eyes of the God-King."

"You cannot truly believe this to be Nari's will!" Darel's father said, his eyes widening at the priest's effrontery, but Aftak, the insolent old thundertooth, simply leaned on his staff.

"This priest notices you didn't get here in time to interrupt the ceremony, Lord Asrel, so he feels you're perhaps mistaken."

"Father!" Daimon shouted. He'd undone the knot binding him to the Raider, Darel saw: it wasn't needed now the ceremony had been concluded.

"You will not address this lord in that manner!" Darel's father thundered, turning his blade towards Daimon. "You are no son of his! You have betrayed everything the House of Blackcreek ever stood for!"

"Really, lord?" Daimon asked. He'd dropped his left hand to the scabbard of his longblade now, but he gestured around them with his right. "Look about you. Do you see murder? Death? Suffering? Or do you see two peoples, aye, who have their differences, but who are beginning to learn to live together? Do you—"

"I see cowards and fools," Darel's father snapped. "Cowards and fools led astray by an arrogant, ambitious whelp!"

"Father," Darel began, as an ugly muttering began to rise amongst the townsfolk. "Perhaps—"

"We have enough land!" Daimon shouted, taking a step forwards. "We have enough houses! These people need those things from us, and we will *benefit* from that! This town has been half-empty for most of this man's life, since the sickness that claimed his blood-parents. Do you not want Black Keep to thrive again?"

"A corpse writhing with maggots does not *thrive*, no matter how vigorously they burrow in its flesh!" Asrel roared. "This lord tires of your craven words! He unnames you, casts you out of the House of Blackcreek, and calls upon you to answer his challenge to single combat!"

Darel squeezed his eyes shut. "Father…"

"Dishonour?" Saana the Raider chief shouted. Darel looked up again and saw that she too had taken a step forward, although she was still well out of range of a lunge from his father. "You speak of dishonour, Asrel of Blackcreek? You drew your weapon and attacked this man when she was under your own flag of truce! Your son saved your life with his actions!"

That's not going to help, you know.

"Be silent, sea-witch," Darel's father snapped. "Well, boy? Will you hide behind this wailing savage, or will you do the first truly honourable thing of your miserable life and face this lord in combat?"

"Do you not see this is foolishness?" Daimon asked sadly. "You attribute to honour what has its roots in pride."

"Honour does not change its nature based on what you wish it to be," Lord Asrel spat. "Well, boy? If you will not face this lord, he must do what he can to scour these savages from his land." He looked around him and Darel did the same, noting the fear of the Black Keep folk, and the confusion of the Raiders. It seemed none of them possessed their chief's mastery of Naridan, and although they'd probably caught the gist of what was going on, they wouldn't have registered Asrel's threat.

"They do not seem to be armed," Darel's father continued, a mocking tone entering his voice. "What say you, boy? How many do you think this lord can cut down? Five? Ten? Will they fight, do you suppose, or simply flee before—"

"*Enough!*" Daimon shouted. "You have taken leave of your senses, your honour and any shred of decency you once possessed!" The Raider chief took his arm, speaking urgently in a voice too low for Darel to hear, but Daimon shrugged her off. "This man accepts your challenge, Asrel of Blackcreek! Clear the square! Clear the square!"

The Naridans began to move backwards immediately, in a shuffle of feet and worried murmurings, retreating to the edges of the square and the mouths of the streets that opened onto it. The Raiders took a moment longer to realise what was happening, but had already started to follow by the time Saana bellowed out instructions in their tongue.

"Father," Darel said urgently, his stomach twisting. Would he really have attacked unarmed men and women? What about the children? "Father, this cannot end well."

"Your father knows, my son," Asrel said solemnly. He took Darel by the shoulder with his free hand and looked into his eyes. Darel saw nothing in his father's face but grim determination. "He knows. When either your father or the traitor fall, make your move. Kill their chief if you can, or as many of their warriors as you can reach if not. Anything we can do to weaken them for when our allies arrive will be of service to our country."

"Our allies?" Darel asked, grasping at his father's last words even as his mind veered away from the ones that had come before them. "What allies?"

"Did Shefal not tell you?" Asrel asked, glancing sideways at where the freeman had mingled with the rest of the crowd as they backed away. "He sent one of ours north to Darkspur on the night of our capture. Odem is a vainglorious fool, but he will come, and he must be close now. This lord does not relish the shame that will come with having him ride to our rescue, but better that than allowing these beasts to settle here."

Shefal. Darel felt his jaw tighten. It was in some respects a cunning ploy, and sending for aid was certainly what they would normally do in the face of a Raider attack. So why did it feel like a betrayal?

Because Shefal always felt Father should have adopted him instead of Daimon, and made no secret of it, even if he never said it outright. And so this man has always disliked him. But is he not correct? Has he not done what a true son of Blackcreek should have done? Is Daimon not the traitor?

Darel couldn't find the answer within himself, and that scared him.

SAANA

"THERE IS NO wisdom in accepting this challenge!" Saana hissed at Daimon. "He is but one man! This man could call for her warriors to arm themselves—"

"He is one man already armed, in the middle of a crowd of people who are not," Daimon replied grimly. "If he suspects treachery then he will attack, and people will die. Better that this man faces him as he demands."

"Did you not hear what you just said about pride and honour?" Saana asked bitterly. "He uses your pride to give him what he wants!"

Daimon snorted. "Perhaps. But we stand on shifting ground, and honour is Narida's foundation. If this man accepts the challenge, Black Keep's people will see he is no coward and will hopefully still follow him. If this man refuses, he will have no honour and his people may decide his father holds the right of it. If we should send other warriors against Lord Asrel instead of this man facing him..." He shook his head. "It would not be right. It would not be accepted. We could spark the very fire we seek to avoid. Besides," he added, "when last we sparred, this man could defeat his father two times out of three."

"You will not be sparring," Saana said, swallowing the bile in her throat. "And those are not odds your wife likes when her husband's life is at stake."

Daimon blinked, then smiled with genuine warmth. "Those are strange words to hear. But your husband thanks you for them."

"Your wife does not love you, Daimon of Blackcreek," Saana told him honestly. "But she does respect you, and she appreciates what you have done for her people." She reached up and cupped his face in her hand, drew her thumb along the line of his cheekbone. "She would prefer you not to die this day."

"Your husband is glad we agree on that," Daimon replied, still smiling. Then the smile slipped, and he looked sideways. "You see your husband's brother, Darel?"

Saana nodded. There was no visual resemblance to Daimon, of course, but the round-faced man with the braided hair talking urgently to Asrel Blackcreek could be no one else. She'd barely seen his face on the day her clan had arrived at Black Keep, but there was enough of Asrel in Darel's face for his identity to be obvious.

"And Shefal?" Daimon added in a low voice. "In the green tunic, just to their left as we look at them?"

Saana nodded again. She'd noticed the man around the town, and he'd already gained a reputation among her clan for being one of the most stand-offish Naridans.

"Your husband would wager his blade Shefal is responsible for their sudden freedom," Daimon said. "He has always resented your husband. Watch Shefal. And Darel. Your husband does not know what they may be planning."

Saana nodded. "Be careful, Daimon."

Daimon shrugged. "We may be beyond that, now." He leaned in and kissed her for a moment, in a much more assured fashion than his startled reaction when she'd done the same thing to him earlier, and this time Saana got the impression he might actually become good at it, given practice. Then he broke the contact and stepped away, his face falling into the blank mask she'd become used to seeing on him, and turned towards his father. The two men approached each other across the square stones, longblades drawn.

Ekham the shipwright grabbed her elbow, his dark-bearded face lined with worry and confusion. The witches had taken the news of Saana's impending marriage with astonishment, and a certain amount of indignation that she hadn't taken the witches' counsel first, as would normally have been the case when a chief sought to marry. They'd eventually accepted that she could marry whomever she pleased, even if that was a Naridan, but she'd had to do a lot of fast talking to get them to accept her oaths about allowing men to lie with men, and women with women.

Kerrti, who'd been avoiding the other witches since the Festival of Life, had merely smirked at Saana when she'd been told.

"What's happening?" Ekham asked. "Is this some Naridan marriage rite? Ritual combat? What's going on?"

Of course, most of her clan wouldn't have understood the words shouted back and forth. Saana cursed silently. "That's his father."

Ekham's eyes widened. "The one who was locked up? Who wanted to kill us all?"

"The same."

"*Shit.*"

"Yes." Saana looked back at Daimon and Asrel. They were within a few paces of each other now, their longblades held out until they nearly touched. "We don't know how he got out, but he's challenged Daimon to an honour duel."

"These Naridans are crazy," Ekham muttered.

"I think you might be right," Saana replied. She realised she was chewing her finger out of nervousness, and snatched her hand back down to her side. "But they're *all* crazy, so Daimon has to play by their rules."

There was no sign or signal she could see. The two men just stood there, stationary, with their weapons outstretched as the moments elongated and one breath ran into another. Then, just when she thought they weren't going to move at all, they both moved at once.

Steel glittered as the two longblades flashed through the air, each seeking skin and each being turned back. There was a furious clatter of blows, a dozen cuts, parries and counter-cuts in the space of two heartbeats, and then Asrel and Daimon stepped apart again. Asrel held his blade low, while Daimon's guard was vertical in front of his face.

"By the Dark Father," Ekham murmured in awe. "They're not pissing about, are they?"

This was totally different to when Daimon had fought Rist, Saana realised. That had been... awkward. Two warriors with different weapons and fighting styles, not to mention significantly differing levels of strength and speed, each trying to puzzle the other out. This was two men intimately familiar with each other's style and weapon, only now they were fighting in deadly earnest for the first time.

Asrel took a long, lunging step forward and slashed his blade upwards, but Daimon stepped back and knocked it aside. Asrel tried the same thing again, with the same result.

"He's not going to get him like that," Ekham muttered. "Why try it?"

Asrel lunged once more, and this time Daimon not only batted his blade aside but stepped past his father, bringing his blade up into the guard position again as Asrel whirled to face him.

"You've grown careless, lord," Daimon said out loud. Asrel's only response was a snort.

"He's not careless," Saana muttered, grim realisation dawning. "He's baiting you."

"What?" Ekham asked, confused.

"Daimon could have cut him on that last pass," Saana said. She was no expert on the swordsmanship of sars, but she was certain of it.

"Why would the father leave himself open?" Ekham said.

Saana shook her head as her gut twisted. Stupid Naridans and their stupid, stupid honour! "Asrel doesn't care if he dies, he just wants an opening at Daimon. Asrel thinks he's dead already. He'll let Daimon kill him if he thinks he can strike back."

"So why didn't Daimon take the cut?" Ekham asked. "Didn't he see it?"

Asrel advanced more cautiously now, then lunged from closer in. Once more the two blades flashed under the sun, steel ringing on steel, but this time Asrel pressed forward instead of allowing a break. Daimon's blade blocked, blocked, parried another cut...

"Low!" Saana shouted, as Daimon didn't take the opening his father's attacks left. "High! Oh, what are you *doing*?"

Daimon slipped aside from his father's downstroke, twisted his sword around Asrel's blade and wrenched, but Asrel rolled with the move and came back to his feet, out of range of Daimon's sword and with his own weapon still in his grasp.

"Don't try to his sword take, kill him!" Saana shouted in Naridan. "He's trying to kill *you*!"

"What?" Ekham demanded. "What are you saying?"

"Daimon's trying to win without hurting him," Saana told him bitterly in Tjakorshi. Neither combatant had given any indication they'd heard her shout. "He just attempted to disarm him, when he could have taken his hand off."

"So a man who wants them both to die is fighting a man who doesn't want either of them to die," Ekham said slowly. "Saana, this isn't going to end well."

"I *know*," Saana replied through gritted teeth.

Asrel raised his blade in both hands, and charged.

It looked reckless, but, Saana immediately realised, it wasn't. Asrel now knew Daimon was pulling his cuts, and so he had no reason to hold back. He yelled as he attacked with two-handed swings, frighteningly fast despite the power behind the blows. Daimon was forced to give ground backwards towards Saana and Ekham, grunting with effort as he batted the strikes away, but it was still a controlled retreat. Could he perhaps outlast his father, Saana wondered? Was he counting on his youth and reach to keep himself safe from harm until his father could no longer fight? Asrel surely couldn't keep this pace up for long, but he'd only have to get lucky once...

The two sars locked blades again and pivoted around each other. Daimon wrenched his father's blade sideways with his own, then span inside Asrel's guard and lashed out at his face with his elbow. Asrel just managed to get his own arm up in time to block the blow, then stepped back and to the side, and tried the sweeping upwards stroke that had killed Njivan and wedged Daimon's blade in Rist's shield. Daimon brought his sword down and blocked it, but Asrel immediately let go of his sword with his left hand and punched his law-son full in the face. Daimon staggered backwards, blood leaking from his nose, but he brought his sword up again ready to fend off his father's next attack.

Asrel turned away from Daimon and lunged for Saana, his longblade sweeping down in a diagonal cut.

She'd been so caught up in the fight she'd all but forgotten Asrel's hatred for her. She was off balance and unprepared, and could do nothing except throw her arms up desperately, knowing it would barely help her against the edge of a sar's longblade. It would sever a limb, then bite into her face...

Another blade deflected the blow, sending Asrel's sword skittering off to one side. Her rescuer's momentum sent him slamming into the thane of Blackcreek shoulder-to-shoulder, knocking Asrel staggering.

It was Darel Blackcreek.

"*Traitor!*" Asrel roared, launching a slashing cut at his blood-son's head. Darel got his blade up in time, but the weapon was knocked from his hand and sent spinning away across the stones of the square. He had no defence as Asrel drew back again.

Daimon's two-handed swing caught his father in the right side of his ribcage, and buried the longblade nearly halfway into Asrel's body.

Asrel shuddered and staggered, his knees starting to buckle. Daimon ripped the blade out in a welter of blood: a high tide wound for sure. Asrel fell to his knees, but turned his head towards Daimon, nothing but hatred and agony written on his face.

"May Nari curse both of you," he spat through gritted teeth. "Feeble-minded wretches!"

"Why did it have to come to this, Father?" Daimon asked miserably, his words coming out half-strangled. Saana could see tears welling up at the corners of his eyes, but he still held his blade in both hands, for Asrel had not yet dropped his.

"The fact... you have to ask... shows you are... no son of this lord," Asrel panted. He finally released his grip on his longblade and it clattered to the ground, but he reached for the hilt of his shortblade.

Daimon raised his own sword, tears running down his cheeks.

"Stand down... whelp," Asrel grunted. He drew the blade and set it point-first against his own chest. "This lord dies... with more honour... than you live with."

He threw himself forwards. The hilt of the blade struck the hard stones of the square and Asrel Blackcreek cried out in pain as the point of his shortblade was driven up into his chest and then, as he slid farther onto it, up out of his back. He shuddered twice, then went limp.

First Darel, then Daimon, fell to their knees and began to weep.

DAIMON

HE'D NEVER FELT such grief.

Daimon barely remembered his blood-parents dying. His memories of them were hazy; an impression of long hair and skirts for his mother, a deep voice for his father, and occasionally being picked up to sit on his shoulders. They were mysterious giants, not in his life long enough to know them as people. He could remember screaming with anger when he'd been told he wouldn't see them again, not understanding why someone would deny him that. He'd been taken to a huge, strange stone house and met another boy, and another giant who'd said *he* would be Daimon's father now. Daimon had cried and said he wanted his own father back, but he'd never got him. He could still remember the smile on Asrel's face the day that Daimon had, after some time spending his days with Darel, finally addressed the thane of Blackcreek as 'Father'.

Now Daimon's father was face down in Black Keep's square with his lifeblood pooling around him, and Daimon had been orphaned a second time, this time by his own hand. He wept bitterly, tears breaking through walls he'd never even realised he'd raised, walls formed from his image of what a sar should be, and his desire to please the stern, undemonstrative man who now lay dead in front of him. Asrel Blackcreek would never have approved of a sar weeping, let alone openly in front of others.

"Darel Blackcreek?"

It was Saana's voice. Daimon looked up through blurring tears to see her squatting in front of Darel, reaching out to touch his shoulder.

"You saved this man's life," she said softly. "Thank you."

Daimon's gut twisted, even through his grief. *Darel*. He was free as well, with his shortblade still in his belt, and Saana within easy reach of it. He'd saved Saana, that was true, but that was before Daimon had cut their father down. If Darel blamed Saana for that… "Brother?"

Darel looked up. Daimon wiped away tears to clear his vision and saw similar ones also streaking his brother's face. He dropped his longblade and scrambled over to him, heedless of his robes on the ground, and seized his brother in a hug. Darel's arms enveloped him in turn and they knelt like that, each with their face buried in the other's shoulder.

"Your brother is sorry," Daimon said, tears leaking from his eyes into Darel's robes. "He tried to disarm our father, to defeat him without hurting him, but—"

"Your brother saw," Darel interrupted him, and the grip of his arms tightened momentarily. "You did everything you could, Daimon. He'd… he'd taken leave of his senses. Your brother should have stopped him as soon as he started threatening to kill people if you wouldn't face him, but your brother lacked that courage." He made a snuffling noise that Daimon realised was a laugh of sorts, choked with tears though it was. "You always were the brave one."

"You would have died fighting the Tjakorshi," Daimon replied. The shoulder of Darel's robe was wet under his face now, but he didn't lift his head. "You were braver than your brother."

"Foolish is not the same thing as brave, Daimon," Darel said. "You saw no one had to die. You had the courage to question our father's words." He relaxed his grip and leaned back, and Daimon did the same. He looked at his brother, round-faced and earnest, with haunting notes of Asrel's features mixed with someone else; the woman Daimon had never known, Lady Delil, whose death was the reason Daimon had been adopted in the first place.

"It is good to see your face again, brother," Daimon said honestly. "Even in such circumstances."

Darel nodded. "Aye. It is. Now, there is something this man must do." He turned his face towards Saana, who was still squatting awkwardly next to them. Daimon tensed involuntarily. He wouldn't fight his brother, and if that meant just throwing himself in front of Darel's shortblade...

"Lady," Darel said, bowing his head to Saana. "This lord apologises for his father. Trying to strike you while in a duel... there was no honour in that. It was the action of a coward. This lord could not let it happen."

"And you have this man's thanks," Saana said. "Did you know he would do that? Was that why you were here?"

Darel's face twisted. "This lord's father told him to be ready to strike you down when the duel ended. He... does not know if he would have done so, had his father prevailed. And so he must apologise for that, also."

Saana shook her head. "This man will not hear an apology for something you did not do, when what you *did* do saved her life. That is foolishness."

Darel blinked in surprise.

"This man knows you are both sad," Saana continued, looking between Daimon and Darel, "but she must ask: who is thane now?"

Daimon looked at Darel, and found Darel looking back at him. Tradition said the older son would inherit, unless a liege-lord stepped in. Of course, the only reason their father hadn't still been treated as thane was because Daimon had imprisoned both him and Darel in the stronghouse, and the lowborn had gone along with it.

Darel cleared his throat. "Well... you seem to have been doing a good job, Daimon."

Daimon stared at him, unable to find words.

"Two weeks have passed, the fields are being ploughed and planted, and your brother sees two peoples standing together, now united by marriage," Darel said gesturing to Saana and Daimon. "His father was wrong. He was wrong. You are not savages. You have lived here without killing..."

He tailed off, his eyes widening.

"Darel?" Daimon asked, alarmed. "Darel, what is it?"

"Nadar, Yoon, Kelarahel, and Shefal," Darel said grimly, getting to his feet. "They freed this man and his father, and killed Malakel to get the keys!"

"Malakel?" Daimon felt a new stab of grief alongside the aching pit of his father's death. He'd liked the guard captain. However, the grief was rapidly overtaken by anger, and burning shame at his own short-sightedness. "Kelarahel? He was part of this? No wonder he never found the traitors; he was one of them!" He stood as well, scanning the crowd. The townsfolk had hung back a way, out of respect or nervousness, but curiosity had won out enough for many to have approached. Daimon couldn't see any of the men Darel had named, despite craning his neck to see over people's heads.

"Nadar! Yoon! Kelarahel! Shefal!" Darel shouted. "Where are they? Does anyone see them?"

There was a generalised turning of heads and muttering amongst the crowd, but no one shouted an affirmative. Darel grimaced and muttered a curse under his breath.

"Cowards! Cowards and fools!" Daimon spat. His anger at the betrayal of his own men might have been tempered by the possibility they'd merely been true to his father. However, the fact they'd fled spoke of their own lack of honour, and burned any remaining compassion out of him.

"We have another problem, too," Darel said distractedly, still searching the crowd.

"We do?"

"Aye, Shefal sent someone along the North Road to Darkspur to seek aid, the night the Raiders arrived," Darel said, turning to him. Daimon felt the bottom drop out of his stomach.

"The night they arrived?" He glanced north, despite the fact the road was hidden by buildings from where they stood. "If they reached Darkspur, and Odem believed them, he could be here any day!"

"Which is why the lack of the conspirators is so troubling," Darel said grimly, taking his shoulder and speaking in a low voice. "If they fled when... when father fell, they may have headed for the north road too, fearing reprisals. If the first messenger never reached Darkspur, or Odem didn't believe them, but then more arrive..."

Daimon nodded, feeling his hands clench into fists. Without their interference, Malakel and his father would still be alive! "Your brother will saddle Bastion, and ride them down, if he has to."

"Take others," Darel countered. "Bring them back. Do not let grief cloud your judgement, brother. The people should be allowed to see and understand—" He broke off, tilting his head. "Do you hear that?"

Daimon turned. There was a noise on the edge of hearing, a little like the mews of the seabirds that were forever in the air over Black Keep, but as he listened he realised that they were voices, the voices of people, albeit distant and muddled. There were many of them, and they seemed to be shouting.

"What are they saying?" he asked. "Where is it coming from?" The crowd around them had heard it too, and the murmur of conversation quietened as everyone strained their ears.

"Daimon," Darel said, his voice halting. "Daimon, look to the roofs."

Daimon looked up. There, perched on the roofline of the nearest houses, were a line of dark-feathered shapes. Even as he watched, three more flew overhead, cawing raucously. Fear gripped him, a fear that harked back to his childhood, for every child in Black Keep knew what these birds in these numbers signified.

"Crows…" he whispered. Beside him, he saw Saana's head turn as she followed his gaze.

The shouted words abruptly became clear enough to hear, like vision clearing as tears are blinked away.

"Raiders! Raiders!"

Daimon looked at Darel, then both of them looked at Saana. How could this be? The Tjakorshi were already here…

Saana's face drained of colour as she, too, heard the words and understood what they meant.

"It's found us," she whispered. Her eyes met Daimon's, and for the first time he saw true fear in their grey depths.

"It's found us. The Golden."

ZHANNA

THE SWELL WAS strong, and the south wind bitter. Zhanna's hands were nearly numb, even inside her thick gloves of sea bear skin, and her nose felt like it was going to drop off. Even so, she knew she'd rather be out on the waves with Jelema and the rest of her crew on the *Leviathan's Wake* than at Black Keep on her mother's wedding day.

It was sickening. Her mother should be ashamed of herself, and the fact she wasn't was even worse. Instead she'd blithely gone ahead with the whole thing, despite how wrong it was, despite how much older she was than Daimon, despite the fact she'd *seen* how upset it had made her daughter. Zhanna hadn't been back to her mother's house since that argument; she'd stayed with Tsennan's family instead. Jelema had a long talk with Zhanna's mother outside the house when she'd come looking for her that first night, then had come back in to say Zhanna was welcome to stay with them for now, although her mother wanted her to go back home.

Home. Zhanna snorted as she hauled on the nets. Home was back across the ocean, and nothing her mother said was going to change that. Home was the rocky shores and pine forests of Kainkoruuk, the chatter of the clear streams and the distant calls of the great sea eagles her clan took their name from. It wasn't the women's quarters of the Blackcreek castle, and it *certainly* wasn't a wooden house-on-stilts in which Zhanna had never spent a night.

Not all the Naridans were bad, mind. Some were arseholes, but others—like Tavi, or Ita, even the priest Aftak—were friendly enough. They were too quiet, most of the time, with their strange, singsong language that put words in a strange order, not to mention how clumsy it was to talk about yourself in it. And there were a few of them—like Daimon—where the weird Naridan features came together into a face that was truly arresting, something that could take your breath away. Daimon was quiet too, usually, but Zhanna didn't think that was who he was underneath. Something about him hinted at a banked fire, the bright embers barely visible but just waiting for the right opportunity to burst forth into heat and light...

"Zhanna! Come on girl, pull!"

Zhanna jerked at Jelema's shout and heaved on the nets again, and another cubit or so of the mesh was dragged aboard. It was hard work, but that was good; that meant they'd snagged a decent catch. Despite anything else she might dislike about the place, Zhanna couldn't argue with the fishing. Even the experienced sailors spoke of the richness of the waters here, as bountiful as the best fishing grounds of Tjakorsha. It was one of the things that had encouraged them that Zhanna's mother had done the right thing by bringing them here; Father Krayk had clearly blessed the waters around this land, too.

They'd come farther south today than ever before, beyond a finger of tumbledown rock stretching out into the waves that marked the limit of their previous ventures. When Zhanna saw dark specks in the water, far to the south and close to shore, she assumed for a moment that she was seeing another rock structure like that, the crumbled remnants of a headland not quite claimed by the waves. Then she saw they were rising and falling with the waves, not disappearing and reappearing, as stone would.

"Zhanna!" Jelema shouted. "Girl, I won't tell you again!"

"What are they?" Zhanna called back, pointing south. She squinted into the wind and spray, trying to see clearly.

"I don't care if you're Saana's daughter, Zhanna, when you're on my ship—"

"No, wait," Zhonda said from behind Zhanna. She was next to her on the net line, and a fisher of ten summers experience. "There's something there, Jelema!"

"Is it more important than getting the damned catch in?" Jelema demanded.

"Could be a pod of leviathans," Kurvodan said, and Zhanna could hear the apprehension in his voice. The huge beasts weren't usually aggressive, but their massive flukes could smash or capsize a taugh if it got in the way of a mating run, and it was the time of year for it. "Do you see any breath-smoke, girl?"

Zhanna wiped her eyes. "No, not that..." She broke off as the *Leviathan's Wake* rode up again on another swell, and she finally got a good view of what she was looking at. Perhaps they'd come that fraction closer, or perhaps it was simply that their respective positions in crest and trough had aligned, but she could make out just enough detail now.

"Jelema," she said, as a chill that had nothing to do with the southern wind ran through her blood, "we're the ship farthest south today, aren't we?"

"Yes," Jelema replied immediately. The other taughs hadn't ventured this far along the coast, and the Naridans never came this far south, despite these being their home waters. They were poor sailors in pitiful vessels, but at least they recognised their limitations.

"Then who are they?" Zhanna asked, pointing at the dark specks. "Those look like sails."

"Sails?" Jelema's feet thudded on wood as the captain strode down the deck to see for herself. "That's not possib—"

Jelema stopped, frowning towards the south.

"Zhanna," she said, "you've spoken with the Flatlanders. No one lives farther south, do they?"

"No," Zhanna said shaking her head. "Not that they know of, anyway."

"*Shit.*" Jelema spun away and snatched up her steering paddle. "Move! Get that sail in position, and grab your paddles! We're heading back, *now*!"

"But what about the net?" someone shouted.

"Fuck the net!" Jelema snarled. "Those are yolgus, and there's only one place they could have come from! Unless you want to say hello to The Golden, let the fish go and grab a fucking paddle!"

Her use of the draug's name broke the spell of confusion, and the crew scrambled to obey. Zhanna threw herself into position, took up her paddle and dipped it into the water as the first grunt rang out down the line. Kurvodan set the pace, as the most experienced paddler, and he set a hard one. Zhanna's arms and shoulders were soon aching, but she gritted her teeth and kept up; without even paddling on both sides the taugh would start to veer, and although Jelema could correct it to some degree, it would mean wasted effort all around.

"Keep it up!" Jelema shouted. "They've seen us!"

"How can you tell?" Zhanna called back.

"They're gaining! They must have started paddling too!"

Zhanna couldn't help herself: she broke off from one stroke to look back over her shoulder and sure enough, there past Jelema was a crowd of sails. They were still small, but larger than they had been. There were so many!

"Zhanna Saanastutar!"

Zhanna turned back to her paddling, fighting the burning in her shoulders. Ahead of her, Zhonda gave a cry and stepped away from her position, passing her paddle to another crew member and taking his role, dealing swiftly with the lines that ran from the great square sail. By rotating out exhausted paddlers in this way the taugh could maintain a sprint for longer, but there were only two of them who weren't paddling at any one time, so it wasn't viable over long distances. Besides, although the yolgus behind them were larger and heavier, they had more paddlers and larger sails, and could fly over the waves faster. The clan's taughs had struggled to keep up with the yolgus on the voyage here, and one of Zhanna's mother's tasks had been to keep the fleet from getting too strung out and losing touch with each other.

"We're coming up on the others!" someone shouted.

"Sing out!" Jelema called, and the crew launched into a rapid, high-pitched yipping wail. It was intended to carry far across the waves, and was the clan's signal that enemies were coming and it was time to run for home. Zhanna looked up and saw another taugh start to shift its own sails, and the tiny shapes of people taking up their paddles. The third and final Brown Eagle vessel out today was ahead, further in towards the shoreline: they looked to have seen what was coming, and were already making good speed northwards.

"What do we do when we reach the Flatlanders?" Zhonda asked, wincing as a gust tightened the line she was holding and wrenched her exhausted arms. "They'll never outrun yolgus!"

"They might be close enough to make it!" Jelema replied.

Zhanna's shoulders couldn't take it any longer. She crawled away from her position and handed her paddle over to Tchakma, who gave her a curt nod and took her place. Zhanna grabbed onto the line he'd been holding and looked back again.

She could see individual warriors now, and the wind carried the sound of their paddling grunts to her, like faint echoes of the ones made by her own crew. They weren't sprinting, she could tell that; just a steady stroke to assist the wind in their sails, easy to keep up for a long period of time.

"Keep going!" Jelema shouted again. She looked at Zhanna, and Zhanna could see the worry in her face.

"How long until they catch us?" Zhanna asked, aware of how small her voice sounded.

"Hard to say," Jelema replied, casting another glance over her shoulder. "If they sprint, they'll narrow the gap, and their sails will take the wind out of ours once they get close enough. We're already losing speed slightly."

Zhanna looked up at the sail. It still looked strained to its full extent to her, but she didn't have Jelema's experience at sea.

"But I think we can make it," Jelema continued, checking over her shoulder once more. "It'll be close, but if we can reach the river we have a better chance. They'll have less advantage from their sails there, and they don't know the channel. It's low tide; they'll get in each other's way if they all try to follow us."

Zhanna bent low to peer under the boom. There were pale scraps ahead: the small, triangular sails of the Flatlander skiffs. There were four of them, with only a few men in each. High-sided and unsteady-looking, they cut through the waves instead of skating over the top. They were never going to make it back to Black Keep, not ahead of the yolgus.

"We need to take them with us!" she said, pointing ahead.

Jelema narrowed her eyes, then shook her head grimly. "We can't do it."

"Jelema, I'm serious!" Zhanna urged her. "We can't leave them out here! They'll die!"

"If we slow down to take them on board, *we'll* die!" Jelema snapped. "And they'll weigh us down!"

"They could take over on the paddles!" Zhanna said. "They could help!"

"Zhanna Saanastutar!" Jelema yelled, wrenching on her steering oar. "I love you like a daughter, and my son loves you like his sister, but if you do not shut your mouth I will throw you to the waves myself! This is *my* ship, and I will not have my crew talking back to me!"

Jelema's stare challenged her to say another word, and Zhanna felt herself wilting under it. She'd never seen Jelema's temper break like this before, and it was a far cry from the smiling, gossiping woman who'd been there throughout Zhanna's life.

But she couldn't just leave the Flatlanders to be overhauled and butchered by their pursuers. She knew that was wrong; she knew it in her bones. Her mind flashed back to the first time she'd been approaching Black Keep on a ship, and what her mother had said about holding the other Unblooded from the charge, if it came to it. She couldn't challenge Jelema's authority on her own ship, that was true. Not even her mother could have done that, clan chief or not; but there might be another way.

Zhanna had seen Jelema hesitate before she'd answered the first time. She was a good-hearted soul. She wouldn't leave people to their deaths by choice, not ones who'd done her no harm. She just needed an excuse to convince her that what she wanted to do was also the right thing.

"Jelema," Zhanna began.

"Girl, I swear—"

"Jelema, they're going to be right behind us when we get to the town," Zhanna said, loud enough that all the crew could hear. "The Flatlanders aren't going to risk opening the gates for us if they can see we left their kin to die!"

"Then the rest of the clan will open the gates!" Jelema shouted.

"I'd rather they didn't fight about it!" Zhanna answered her, and saw Jelema's gaze flicker towards her. "Who's to say the Flatlanders will even be looking close enough to realise we're not The Golden's warriors, until it's too late? If we've got some of their folk on board with us, they'll know who we are, they'll have to let us in!"

Jelema paused for a moment, the steering paddle motionless in her gloved hands and strands of her hair that had escaped her hood buffeted by the wind in front of her face. Even the grunts of the paddlers broke their rhythm, and Zhanna became aware of heads turning towards her, towards Jelema, waiting for a decision.

"Fine!" Jelema snapped, abruptly wrenching on the steering paddle. "We'll set their boats adrift, see if they'll slow down these bastards behind us any! Kurvodan! Shout over to the *Sea Axe*, tell them to take the ones closest to them!"

"Thank you, Jelema," Zhanna said, soft enough for it to only reach the captain's ears. Jelema's expression didn't change, but she gave a curt nod and held one hand out.

"Give me that line and get up front then, girl!" she ordered. "You're the only one of us who speaks any words of their tongue! Tell them to be ready when we come alongside, because I won't be slowing, and I won't go back for them!"

RIKKUT

"WOULD YOU LOOK at that?!" someone gasped as the *Storm's Breath* cleared the headland. Rikkut's eyes travelled over the broad, flat green of the landscape beyond, and a wash of wonder struck him. His fleet had crossed the Great Ocean, sure enough, and had found land, but until now it had all been high, dark, jagged cliffs. There'd been nowhere the yolgus could beach, nowhere the Brown Eagle clan could have gone ashore. The crews had been close to despair, for they'd near run out of fresh water. There had been ugly whispers among them that Sattistutar's folk surely couldn't have come here, but despite this Rikkut had ordered them to turn north.

Then they'd sighted sails and a cheer had gone up, because ships surely meant there was accessible land with water nearby. The enthusiasm had died down briefly when they'd recognised Tjakorshi taughs. What if this was just the remnants of Sattistutar's clan, dying of thirst as they sailed futilely up and down this forsaken coast? They'd given chase anyway, and the taughs had fled, and before long they'd come upon different boats: barely seaworthy, in Rikkut's opinion, just lumbering scraps of wood with a sail attached. But those strange boats meant a local people, and that surely meant an end to the cliffs.

And now, here it was.

Rikkut had never seen land so vast. He'd heard tell of the Drylands, to the far north-east of Tjakorsha, where some of the eastern clans sailed to trade fire-gems for steel. The stories spoke of great, empty coasts of sand, fishing villages of clustered houses made from dark, twisted wood, and a mighty town at the mouth of a river, with buildings of stone the colour of his hair, rising high as a Tjakorshan tree. Rikkut had never been sure he'd believed those tales, but here was a land just as strange.

"They're running for the river!" Zhungaltor roared, fitting another stone to his sling. Sure enough, the three taughs they were chasing down had changed course. Rikkut had hoped to overhaul them, but it seemed desperation had lent strength to their paddlers' arms, possibly helped by the fact they'd taken on the crews of the floundering local ships. He could see them now, wielding the paddles with the knowledge their lives depended on it. Slings were of limited use at this distance, but every hit disrupted their prey's stroke, and Zhungaltor had managed a lucky shot that pitched one person into the water.

"Hold!" Rikkut barked, placing one hand on his warrior's arm. Zhungaltor tensed in response, but Rikkut pointed away inland. "Look there! That's where they're heading, I'd wager my axe on it! You'll need all your stones before long."

It was no towering Dryland town, but a wall of shaped rock nonetheless, some way up the river. It was the only built thing Rikkut could see: it must be where the local fishers were from. Had Sattistutar conquered and enslaved these people already?

"Ships! Ships on the shore!" That was Olja Tilistutar, pointing ahead up the shoreline. "Yolgus!"

Rikkut frowned, looking away from the foreign town. Yes, those were yolgus, pulled high up past the strange, black mud of this coast and resting in the thick grass that grew between the shore and the deeper green of meadows beyond. He felt his heart quicken as he counted them: ten in total, only half the amount he commanded, but throw in a few taughs and it was clear

Sattistutar had indeed brought her entire clan with her across the ocean. Rikkut felt a stab of admiration for her, despite himself, yet her great feat was driven only by fear of The Golden. Now Rikkut was here, as the chosen of The Golden and the instrument of its vengeance. Sattistutar must have holed up behind that wall; she would not be able to flee again.

"Into the river!" Rikkut roared, and felt the deck lurch beneath him as Akuto shifted the yolgu's course in response, despite nominally being captain. They all followed him now, without question. "And release the crows!"

He pulled his axe from his belt and checked it over. He'd found it floating on the surface of the sea in the aftermath of the krayk attack, had recognised it as his own from the fire-gems set into the head: fire-gems for the Fireheart, had been the thinking there. His raid called him Krayk-Killer now, though. Rikkut knew he hadn't killed the beast, merely wounded it badly enough to drive it off, but didn't tell them to stop using the name. He could almost feel their awe, and bathed in it, but not for him the pathetic life of chiefs like Snowhair. He wouldn't be hiding behind a shield-wall, leaning on his name so others fought for him. He would seek out Saana Sattistutar himself, take her life, claim her belt and bring it back to his master. Rikkut Fireheart, Rikkut Krayk-Killer, Rikkut Chief-Killer…

The sight of the Flatlander town had given the prey new hope. They were paddling faster, and now they'd swung across the wind they were out of the lee of Rikkut's fleet. They'd started shouting, words Rikkut couldn't understand but were presumably intended to warn the town of approaching danger. Rikkut grinned, and tested the blackstone edge of his axe on his thumb. Sharp as the southern winds, as always. Let these people sing their songs of fear. It wouldn't aid them.

He frowned. The taughs were pulling towards the southern bank of the river rather than following the most direct line to the town. Did they intend to land there, on the opposite shore to the most obvious place of safety for them? That would be a strange thing...

Abruptly, things fell into place. The river had wide, muddy shores, so the tide here was currently low, and there was a large patch of paler water ahead that the taughs were skirting.

"Turn!" Rikkut bellowed. "Match their course, damn you! Sandbank ahead!"

Akuto obeyed and the *Storm's Breath* shifted again, turning further into the wind. Someone grabbed a pair of signalling sticks and began to pass word back—*shallow water*—but Rikkut could already see the problems. His fleet had come into the river too eagerly, spread out across its entire width, and the sandbank lay directly in the middle of the channel. Some of the yolgus could avoid it, but others would have nowhere to turn but into their fellows. What had been a ferocious, focused pursuit was now at risk of becoming a mess.

"Sprint!" Zhungaltor shouted at the paddlers. "Never mind those idiots behind us, we can still catch them!"

"No!" Rikkut snapped, turning away from the fleeing taughs. He ducked under the boom of the sail and looked back, taking stock. He was no great sailor, but he could see his fleet losing momentum. The ships on the northern side of the channel had already been losing wind to the sails of the ships on the south, and now there was confusion as everyone steered away from the danger of running aground. Tjakorshi ships rode high, skimming over the waves, but these were unfamiliar and muddy waters, and you couldn't know for sure whether you'd clear the sandbank until you hit it. No one wanted to be stranded in the middle of the channel until the tide returned.

"Chief?" Akuto asked. She was a crow-haired captain of somewhere over thirty summers with The Golden's scar on her left cheek, and she'd served it for near as long as anyone else had.

"They know this river better than we do," Rikkut said reluctantly. "It narrows and bends ahead, where the walls are highest. If we pursue them past there, and there are defenders standing ready on the top…" He knew what he would do: rocks to crash down and break bones or smash holes in decks; perhaps a barrel of leviathan oil and a flaming torch or two. Would the Flatlanders have such things? Best not to chance it.

"And if we sprint now, the paddlers' arms will have less left to swing an axe," Akuto nodded. "What are your orders?"

Rikkut looked over at the northern shore. There were people running for the town, shepherds leaving their animals grazing and fleeing to save themselves.

"Put to shore there," he said, pointing.

"What if they have slingers?" Olja asked.

"Then sling back," Rikkut grinned at her. He raised his voice. "Take up your weapons, and be ready to fight!"

The crew of the *Storm's Breath* sprang into action. Most had a roundshield, a blackstone axe and a spear, although many had slings as well, and some across the raid had lost one item or another, particularly those who'd been on the *Sea Spite* or *Red Smile* when they'd foundered. Rikkut was one; he didn't carry a sling, since he'd never been good with one, and he'd only found his axe after the krayk's attack, not his shield as well. He didn't fear death, but he felt half-naked without his shield, especially since he'd lost his sea leather armour too. He briefly contemplated taking someone else's shield from them, but that didn't sit well.

Then his eyes lighted on the krayk harpoons on their hooks, and a smile slid across his face.

DAIMON

DAIMON GRABBED HIS blood-slicked longblade from the flagstones and ran for the town walls, shouting at the townsfolk to clear the way. Saana came with him, yelling in her own tongue, and between them they managed to get to the stone steps that led up onto the modest parapet only a matter of moments after they'd first heard the warning cries.

He came to a dead halt at the sight that met his eyes. "Nari's blood!"

Beside him, Saana spat something violent and unpleasant-sounding in Tjakorshi, and with good reason. Three of the Brown Eagles' smaller craft had been out fishing today, and they were now fleeing up the Blackcreek away from...

"Twenty ships, near enough," Daimon heard himself say through a mouth that was suddenly dry. "More ships even than the entire Brown Eagle clan had arrived on, and all as large as the biggest of those, or close to it."

Saana screamed in sudden anger. "How could it know?! We told no one! We crept away like thieves, and still the foul thing finds us!"

"Those are warriors?" Daimon asked, aghast. "*All* of them, warriors?" Part of him wanted to curse his new wife for bringing this doom down upon them all, but her haggard expression was testament to the fact she'd believed the demon far behind them. "We must make ready."

Saana simply spat over the wall. "The Dark Father calls, Daimon." Then her eyes widened and she clutched the battlement, leaning out as though it would help her to see better. "Zhanna!"

"What? Where?" Daimon scanned the ground in front of them but could only see a few herders running for the dubious safety of Black Keep's walls, none of whom looked like Saana's fire-haired daughter. Then he realised where she was looking, and cursed as he suddenly understood. "She was out fishing?"

"Your wife has not seen her today, but she thinks so," Saana said, her voice taut. "If so, she will be on the *Leviathan's Wake*... there, at the back."

Questions wheeled through Daimon's head—why hadn't Saana seen her today? Why was Zhanna out fishing on her mother's wedding day? Was this usual for Tjakorshi, or had he offended Zhanna somehow?—but he had no time to indulge them. Something like four hundred Tjakorshi warriors were coming, yet his mind had gone blank, his body frozen in place. He would fight any of these invaders one-on-one, but how could he protect an entire town from all of them?

"They look to be heading for the River Gate," Darel said at his shoulder, and Daimon started in surprise: he hadn't even heard his brother arrive. Darel was pointing at the fishing vessels. "Your daughter is with them?"

"This man thinks so," Saana said grimly.

"Then get to the River Gate with as many of your people as you can find between here and there, and whatever weapons you have," Darel told her urgently. "We'll open the armoury and get more to you, but you'll know best who approaching the walls is friend and who is foe, and you can hopefully find your daughter. Go!"

Saana nodded once and was gone, bounding down the steps with her wheat-blonde hair flying out behind her. She raised her voice as she went and Tjakorshi faces fell, but her clan members turned to follow her as she cut through the crowd. Several broke off to head for houses: to get weapons, or so Daimon sincerely hoped.

"You!" Darel snapped, grabbing a young girl of perhaps ten years who'd run up the steps to join them, heedless of her mother's shouts from below. "Go to the shrine, ring the bell, and don't stop ringing it until this lord tells you to! Now!"

The child turned and ran, dodging her mother's desperate grab for her as she passed.

"Aftak!" Darel shouted, and Daimon saw the priest's head come up. "Go to the Road Gate! Get as many of our people in from the fields as can make it, then shut it fast and hold it!"

"Aye, lord!" Aftak roared back, raising his staff in salute. "You, you and you, with this priest!" He struck three men on the shoulder with his staff and made off northwards through the streets. With his departure, Darel raised his hands and shouted down to the crowd of townsfolk who'd gathered below them.

"People of Black Keep, we are under attack! More Raiders have arrived, and the clan of this lord's brother-wife flees from them! Those of you who have weapons to hand, guard the breach!" He pointed along the line of the wall to the largest gap in it, where the wagon had stood when the Brown Eagle clan had landed. "Everyone else, to the castle! Anyone who can bear a weapon shall take them from the armoury, and we will then reinforce the walls as quickly as we may! The children and infirm will remain within the castle itself!"

Daimon darted after his brother as Darel hurried down the stairs. "Darel! The keys! You said the traitors had them!"

For answer, Darel held up the iron ring on which jangled the keys to the armoury and stronghouse. "Your brother said they killed Malakel to get them, Daimon. He wasn't going to let them hold onto them."

"You are wise," Daimon said honestly, as the bell of the shrine

MIKE BROOKS

started to toll out its frantic warning. He belatedly wiped the blood from his longblade and sheathed it, lest the drawn steel cut someone in the crowd around them. "What would you have your brother do?"

Darel glanced at him as they ran across the flagstones of the square, a flicker of uncertainty on his face. "You ask that? You are the warrior!"

"Your brother knows swordplay, but that does not make him a warrior," Daimon admitted, dropping his voice. "He froze on the walls. He had no orders to give."

Darel raised his eyebrows and puffed out his cheeks. "We should don our armour and get to the dragons. Can your wife ride?"

"Saana?" Daimon shook his head. "She rode on Bastion when we searched for their corpse-painter, but that was once, and she has never ridden a dragon alone."

"A pity," Darel muttered. "One apiece to guard the River Gate, the Road Gate and the breach would be ideal."

"Tavi!" Daimon said, inspiration dawning. "He knows the beasts better than anyone!"

"You would have the stablemaster ride one of our family's war mounts?" Darel asked incredulously.

"Put Tavi on a dragon and give him a spear, and your brother wagers he'll skewer Raiders better than either of us!" Daimon said honestly. "The man's near as strong as a dragon himself!"

"Very well," Darel replied. They'd reached the stronghouse's drawbridge at the head of a crowd of townsfolk, and Daimon was brought up short for a moment by the sight of a stocky figure in the shadows of the gatehouse.

"Lord... Lords?" Tavi said, stepping into the light and making a startled, hurried half-bow. "Your man heard the bell and came running, but Malakel! He's—"

"More Raiders, Tavi!" Daimon told him as they surged onto the drawbridge. "Saddle three dragons!"

554

"More—*Three?*" Tavi gaped, one question overtaking the first. "Your lord father—"

"Is dead," Darel cut in. They were in the gatehouse now, and the townsfolk were spilling into the first yard. Daimon's brother turned, searching the crowd as the stablemaster stared at him in horror and confusion. "Menaken! Open the armoury and arm anyone who can hold a weapon! Anyone who can shoot a bow gets one: this lord wants as many of those Raiders dead as possible before they reach the walls!"

"Aye, lord!" Menaken shouted back, catching the keys Darel threw at him. "This way!" The main press of the townsfolk followed him, and Daimon heard some screams: had they caught sight of Malakel? Where had the poor man been when he was killed?

"Lords," Tavi said uncertainly, looking from one of them to the other. "Three dragons? One for each of you, but who rides the third?"

"This lord will take Silverhorn," Daimon said. His mount was feisty, but Daimon knew him well. "Lord Darel will ride Quill." He put one hand on Tavi's shoulder and looked into the stablemaster's eyes, or tried to: Tavi seemed reluctant to look straight at him, which was unlike the man.

"You are to ride Bastion."

SAANA

"Do you see them?" Saana shouted up at the wall, fastening her chief's belt over her sea leather. She'd taken the risk of running back to her house before going to the River Gate, for she'd be little use against armed attackers with only her fists to rely on. Now she had her armour, her helm, her shield and her axe, and felt she might actually serve a purpose. Her stomach was lurching like she'd swallowed too much seawater, and she was offering down fervent wishes to Father Krayk that he'd protect her daughter, even though she knew how foolish that was. The Dark Father had gifted people with land and will, and expected them to do the rest themselves. He took their lives back as and when he chose... but still Saana implored him silently, just in case.

You took Rist from me. You took my closest friend, and I understood the need. But please, please, please let Zhanna live. Even if our enemies get into the town, even if they take my life, please let Zhanna live.

"Do you see them?" she screamed. The street down to the River Gate held a mass of Tjakorshi, men and women, some armed and armoured as she was, some who'd come with nothing. They'd only get in the way in a fight.

"I see them!" Tsennan Longjaw shouted down. It was no

surprise he was up on the wall; his mother had been out fishing, after all. "I see them! They're round the castle! Open the gate, open the gate!".

Saana's heart fluttered as a cheer went up, but he'd only given them half the story. "Tsennan! Are they being chased?"

The youth leaned out over the rampart and looked east. The stronghouse roof and the tall trees of its garden blocked his view, Saana realised; he couldn't see back down the river.

"No!" he shouted a moment later. "Not yet, anyway!"

That was a problem in and of itself, Saana realised, but one thing at a time. Zhanna was safe.

Or was she? Cold fear gripped her again. There'd been several Naridan fishing skiffs out as well, and she'd seen Naridans on the taughs as they'd fled upriver, so the crews must have been picked up by the faster ships. What if the *Leviathan's Wake* had been overfull, and Zhanna had been knocked overboard? What if a slingstone had struck her? Getting a good shot off at sea was virtually impossible, but a taugh was a big target, and if everyone on board was packed so tight they couldn't avoid a stone…

Calm, she told herself. *You'll find out in a matter of moments. You won't help anyone by panicking.*

"Clear the way!" she bellowed as the River Gate was hauled open. "Get back! Give them space to get off the boats, damn it!" She hauled someone back by his shoulder and realised it was Otzudh. He glowered at her.

"No surprise this should happen the day you betray our clan and marry a Flatlander," he sneered. "You've brought the attention of the Dark Father down on us all!"

Rage flashed through Saana, momentarily banishing her fear. "If we weren't waiting to see if our daughter was alive, I'd knock your teeth down your throat!" She pushed him away, and took a step towards the gate.

"A Tjakorshi man wasn't good enough for you, then?" Otzudh shouted from behind her.

"Obviously not!" Saana yelled without turning, to a few nervous laughs. She whirled back to face him, pointing accusingly. "Why don't you go and say the same thing to Avlja, see what she and Nalon have to say?" Otzudh scowled but didn't reply, which just showed he had at least some sense in his thick head.

"They're landing!" Tsennan shouted from the wall. Saana looked through the gate, and saw the first taugh pulling alongside a jetty. The tide was low, so the first woman ashore had to clamber upwards, but she quickly secured the taugh with lines thrown to her, and the crew began to disembark. Saana scanned the faces as they appeared, despite knowing Zhanna had been on a different boat. There was Otim, and there were the two Naridans Old Elio and Young Elio, the father and son. Evruk came off next, ashen-faced and shaking. They were ushered through the gates, the Tjakorshi finding their families and running to them, the Naridans clustering around each other and looking around nervously.

"Clear the path," Saana instructed the Naridans, well aware that she was the only person there who spoke their language. "More to come!"

The second taugh landed, and Ada's voice rang out as she hassled and hurried the others ashore. Zalika's tall frame was visible, and Saana fought down a surge of irritation. If that lanky string of piss had made it back but her daughter hadn't... She cast the cruel thought aside. More Naridans, too: Yaro, the captain of her team in the Great Game, and a Naridan whose name she thought might be Achin.

"Chief," Ada greeted her, hurrying through the gate. The witch's face was grim, and one hand still rested on the spearfish-bill dagger at her belt. "It's The Golden's warriors."

"Is it with them?" Saana asked, her breath catching. "Did you see it?"

"Not the draug itself," Ada admitted. "But I know Zheldu Stonejaw when I see her, even from distance over waves, and her clan swore to it last summer, as I heard." She spat at the ground. "It's an ill wind that blew these bastards here, that's for certain."

"And Zhanna?" Saana asked, dreading the answer.

"The last I saw, she was helping Flatlanders aboard the *Leviathan's Wake*," Ada said. "Fair screaming at them in their tongue, she was, but they moved quick enough when we came alongside. I'd have left them to the swell, but Jelema Eddistutar swore to the wind and waves that she'd cut my throat if I did, and I'll not cross her when she's got a storm face on."

Oh, Jelema. Always the big-hearted one. "Thank you," Saana said, as something in her chest loosened a little. "Now go get your weapons and armour; we need Ada the raider now, not Ada the fisher."

"I'm no Unblooded, Saana," Ada retorted, pushing past her, "I know what's coming! *Move, you grass-bloods!* Just because those goat-fuckers stopped chasing us doesn't meant they've gone away! They'll be over these walls in moments!"

Saana should have been doing the same, she knew that, but she couldn't bring herself to, not yet. She had to see if Zhanna was alive and well. The *Leviathan's Wake* was drawing in now and she could barely prevent herself from pushing through the folk still coming in thorough the gate.

Jelema Eddistutar clambered into view first, turning to grab a rope thrown to her and then kneeling down to tether her craft. Kurvodan was next, with another line, then a Naridan—Elka, perhaps?—and then...

Then a flash of bright red hair, and Saana's knees nearly buckled in relief. "*Zhanna!*"

Her daughter was pulling other people ashore, Naridan and Tjakorshi alike, and it wasn't until everyone was off the *Leviathan's Wake* that she made for the gate. Saana couldn't take her eyes off her, convinced an enemy yolgu was going to round the river bend any moment and send a punishing hail of slingstones ashore, or somehow get to the jetty and disgorge warriors before

Zhanna could flee, but none of those things came to pass.

"Mama!" Tsennan Longjaw came flying down from the wall and crashed into his mother with a hug that knocked her sideways, but he held onto her tightly enough that she didn't fall. There was more laughter, this time relieved, as Jelema scolded him to let her go, then hugged him herself as soon as he did so.

Zhanna hurried through the gate, rearmost of all, and Saana stepped forwards... then stopped herself. What if—?

Zhanna took one look at her, at the tears that were starting to blur her vision, and enveloped her in a hug.

"I'm so glad you're safe," Saana whispered into her ear, her eyes squeezed tightly shut. *And that you can stand to touch me now*, she thought but didn't add.

"I'm not safe," Zhanna muttered back.

"You're safe at this moment, and that's what matters most to me in the world," Saana said. "In the *world*, Zhanna."

"You should be proud of your daughter," Jelema Eddistutar's voice said, and Saana opened her eyes to see the fisherwoman releasing her son again. She stepped closer and lowered her voice. "I'd have never taken the Flatlanders on board, but Zhanna wouldn't hear of it. Near enough weighed us down too much, but we got away with it. It was the right thing to do, I just hadn't the courage to do it." She turned away from them, then came to an abrupt halt and the colour drained from her face. "What in the name of—"

There were screams and shouts of alarm from the Tjakorshi. Saana let go of Zhaana and placed herself in front of her and Jelema, drawing her axe and facing down the street. A huge shape lumbered into view, snorting and shaking its horned head.

Saana let out a relieved breath and laughed as her clan scuttled backwards like startled crabs. "What's the matter? Have none of you seen a dragon before?" She switched to Naridan. "Daimon? Is that you?"

The dragon's rider lifted off his helmet, and her new husband's face was revealed. Other Naridans carrying weapons edged past his enormous mount and began passing them out to the clan. Some warriors already had their own weapons, whether they were blackstone axes or stolen or traded metal, and clearly preferred to stick with them. However, others less familiar with battle clearly found some comfort in the notion of Naridan steel.

"Do they come?" Daimon asked, standing up in his stirrups in an effort to see over the wall.

"No!" Saana shouted back. "They gave up the chase. Did they not land on the seaward side?"

"Your husband does not know, he came directly here," Daimon admitted. Worry flitted across his face, and he turned to look back towards the east. "They'll surely attack the breach or the Road Gate, then, or both…"

A Naridan appeared in front of Saana. She shook her head when he offered her an axe that didn't look in particularly good repair, but the boy child that came after him held up a green strip of cloth and didn't seem in any mood to be ignored.

"Daimon, what is this?" Saana called, holding it up. It looked to be one of the strips used to mark out teams in the Naridan's Great Game.

"Darel's idea," Daimon replied. "To mark friend Tjakorshi from foe, should the foes get inside the walls!"

"Put them on!" Saana shouted at her confused clan, and began to fumble with it. She supposed she'd be hard pressed to pick out most of the Black Keep Naridans from ones she'd never seen before, if everyone had a weapon and some were trying to kill her. Daimon's brother didn't seem a fool, whatever else he might be.

Zhanna took the strip from her and secured it with a few quick motions, then held up a red one. "Tie mine."

Saana didn't argue. She took the cloth from her daughter and knotted it firmly above Zhanna's right bicep. "Now go get your axe. But remember," she added urgently, holding onto Zhanna's arm, "these aren't Flatlander farmers, these are Tjakorshi warriors. Don't be a Naridan and die for honour, Zhanna. *It's fine to hit them from behind.*"

Zhanna nodded again, and showed her teeth in a flash of nervous excitement. Then she was away and running, heading for Saana's house where her blackstone axe waited on the wall.

"Leave some people here in case they send warriors around by the river!" Daimon told her. "Your husband will send Darel and his mount. Lavit! Nadon! Stay here, but come running if the gate is attacked!"

The two Naridan boys who'd been handing out strips of cloth nodded at their lord, their eyes wide.

"Will you ride with your husband?" Daimon called down to her.

Saana eyed his dragon. She'd laughed at her own clan when they'd screamed, but there was a difference between not being alarmed by the thing appearing and actually getting on it.

"That is not Bastion," she said.

"No, this is Silverhorn," Daimon said, slapping his dragon's neck. "Your husband has ridden him for nearly ten years, now."

"Your wife does not know how to fight from a dragon," Saana admitted. "She will use her own feet today."

"Very well," Daimon said, and replaced his helm. He looked down at her, two dark, worried eyes regarding her from over the snarling metal war mask that now hid most of his face. "Take care of yourself, Saana Sattistutar."

"And you, Daimon of Blackcreek," Saana replied. He nodded once, then hauled on Silverhorn's reins and kicked its flanks. The dragon huffed and turned, lumbering in a half circle before trotting away.

As he disappeared, Saana heard the roar of a Tjakorshi charge coming from the east.

"I want a dozen of you here!" Saana shouted to the rest of her clan. "Get up on that wall, and sing out the moment you see movement on the river! Send one of the Flatlander children running for help! Tsennan, you're in charge. Everyone else, with me!"

"But how will they understand me?" Tsennan demanded, gesturing at the two Naridan boys, and the handful of Naridan men and women handing out weapons.

"Work it out!" Saana snapped, exasperated. Where was Nalon when she needed him? Then she turned and ran.

RIKKUT

THE FLATLANDER WALL was well over the height of a man and built of regularly shaped blocks of stone, much more imposing than the chest-high piles of rocks that formed defensive rings on Tjakorshi hill-forts. Rikkut thought he might just be able to grab the top of it if he jumped as high as he could, but wouldn't have made any wagers for the safety of his fingers, given the defenders atop it. His raid had no ladders, nothing else they could use to easily scale it, and the shield jump he'd tried against the Seal Rock clan would probably break his knees on the stone if he tried it here.

All in all, it would have given him quite the pause—had the wall not had entire blocks missing, and a gaping hole a short distance from the shoreline.

"Could it be a trap?" Kovra the Fair asked, settling her shield on her arm. She was as fierce as she was fair, but she had no objection to the name that had found her, as it made her enemies more likely to underestimate her. "Are they trying to lure us in?"

"That's no trap," Rikkut said, peering out from behind the deckhouse. The Flatlanders had no slingers, but were launching lengths of metal-tipped wood with great accuracy and force: arrows, according to the Stonejaw, who'd seen their like in the Drylands. Three warriors had fallen hauling the first yolgus up the black mud of the river shore to prevent the rising of the tide from sweeping the ships away, although an answering hail of stones from Rikkut's slingers had discouraged the Flatlanders from showing their faces for a few moments. Now he waited, taking cover as the last of the raid made shore.

"How can you tell?" Rodnjan of Kotuakor demanded.

"Some of the stones are a different colour," Rikkut pointed out. "They're newer. They've been trying to *repair* that gap. It's no trap, it's a weak point."

"Did Sattistutar breach that wall?" Olja asked warily. Few of the raid had heard much of the Brown Eagles' chief, and Rikkut had found to his annoyance that ugly rumours had spread of how perhaps she had the favour of Father Krayk, to have braved the Great Ocean with her entire clan. The last thing he needed now was for them to believe she was capable of knocking a wall such as this down by herself.

"Far more likely it was already damaged, she used it to get in and take the town, then has tried to repair it," he said. "We'll do the same."

"There must be an actual gate in the wall, though," Zheldu Stonejaw pointed out.

"Probably," Rikkut replied. "But we have an opening right here, and I'm going to take it." He waited for an argument, but none came. "Rodnjan, I want some slingers back here to keep the Flatlanders' heads down, and make sure no one gets around us to take our ships. Everyone else; we're going through that gap."

"Trap or no trap, that's going to be a killing ground," Akuto remarked.

"That's what the Unblooded are for," Rikkut replied with a grin. He drew himself up to his full height and slammed the butt of the krayk spear on the deck three times, then raised his voice again so all the raid could hear him.

"Chosen! I want the stones of their houses painted red! I want the Brown Eagle clan either dead, or on their knees swearing fealty to The Golden! And you leave their chief for me!"

"And the Flatlanders?" Olja asked.

Rikkut shrugged. "Kill 'em."

He stepped out of the shelter of the deckhouse with his weapons in hand, ran over the wood and leaped off, landing in the black mud. It was thick and deep, and the steps he took to reach the high tide line were laboured, but he made it before any of the Flatlanders' arrows could take him. One whistled overhead as he took his first strides through the thick grass, then another, and another. Rikkut cursed. The footing wasn't as sure as he'd hoped, and he was left with the choice of watching his step or watching for arrows.

"*The Golden!*"

Warriors charged past him; perhaps two score of Unblooded, hot with battle lust, thirst for glory, and probably a decent helping of fear. The Flatlander arrows shifted their aim, firing at the youths. Rikkut saw two fall, with several more taking the shots on their shields.

There was a simultaneous grunt of effort from behind him, and a hail of slingstones answered back. Many clattered against the wall and several more flew well over it, but at least three of the figures atop the wall fell out of sight as if struck, and most of the rest ducked down.

Rikkut laughed. Even with a wall to hide behind, these Flatlanders were soft and craven. But where were the Brown Eagle clan? No matter. He'd find them soon enough.

The rest of his warriors were with him, roaring battle cries. The defenders had tried to plug the gap in the wall with a wagon, but that wouldn't be much of a barrier. His raid was halfway there now, the Unblooded a little further ahead.

The defenders poked their heads up again, and more arrows rained down, but many flew wide. Another Unblooded fell with a wooden shaft protruding from his chest. Furs were no protection, and Rikkut had no shield. He laughed again. Perhaps this was how he should be fighting anyway, with nothing between him and the Dark Father except his own skill.

His slingers loosed, and the defenders dropped out of sight once more. Three figures jumped up into view on the wagon, and Rikkut recognised the clothes of Tjakorsha. There they were!

The Brown Eagles had slings, and they loosed at the Unblooded, but the stones clattered off shields with no damage done. The Unblooded were nearly at the wall.

Defenders rose up again with bows, and now Rikkut was close enough to make out their individual features. His eyes met those of one man as he drew back the string on his arrow-sling. He looked afraid.

The man released the string and Rikkut ducked as he ran. He heard the thrum of the arrow in flight, heard a scream behind him, then heard one more chorus of grunts and the man whose arrow he'd just ducked took a stone in the forehead and fell backwards. A warrior just in front of Rikkut was struck in the back of the head as well, and pitched forwards, but the rest of the stones had flown true, more or less. Rodnjan had timed it well: the defenders were in disarray just as Rikkut's warriors reached the wall.

The three Brown Eagles had stowed their slings and lowered their shields to protect themselves, readying their spears to strike, but Rikkut's Unblooded slammed shields-first into the wagon on which they stood. One Unblooded fell with a spear in her neck, but the force of the others' charge drove the wagon back across the ground beyond, and sent the warriors atop it staggering. Several of Rikkut's warriors slowed in the last moments of their charge to hurl their spears, eager to take the first blood of this fight. Off-balance and unsteady, two of the Brown Eagles were struck before they could get their shields up again, and the Unblooded's weapons finished them.

Rikkut hefted his harpoon and lunged at the third.

He collided with the backs of the Unblooded, crushed up against the wagon as they were, but the great length of bone-tipped wood reached over their heads and plunged into the gut of the last Brown Eagle warrior. She gasped in pain and folded up around it, reaching for the weapon's haft as though seeking to take it with her as she toppled backwards. Rikkut wrenched it out of her, and out of her grip, and heard the dull thud as her body hit the ground beyond.

The town's defences were breached.

"In! Kill them all!" Rikkut roared as the rest of his warriors poured into the gap. Other defenders were appearing now around the ends of the wagon, but they were already being pushed back. Members of his raid were scaling the tumbledown sides of the breach in the wall, looking to get onto a level with the panicking arrow-slingers. One warrior fell from the wall with an arrow through his throat, fired from a few arms' lengths away, but the woman behind him sprang forward to cut down his killer before he could take another shot.

The Unblooded flowed around the wagon like the rising tide around a rock, eager to close with their enemies, and Rikkut was able to take a quick glance at his surroundings. The Flatlanders made their houses of wood, it seemed, fenced around them with wood and wattle, and raised them up off the ground for some purpose he couldn't imagine. He clambered up onto the wagon and wet the teeth of his axe with the throats of the two Brown Eagles who still lay there bleeding, mercy killings to send them without further suffering to Father Krayk, or whatever foreign god would take their souls. Then he raised both his weapons to the sky.

"*Saana Sattistutar! Come out and fight me!*"

He was answered by a sound like nothing he'd heard before. It was as though the very ground itself had screamed, stunningly deep and shockingly loud, but still unmistakably a living voice. Rikkut whirled towards the noise, his palms suddenly sweating, searching the narrow gap between the boundary wall and the first houses. His warriors were in there, pushing back and cutting down the defenders, mainly Flatlanders.

A monster appeared.

It was huge, nearly the size of the wagon he was stood upon, and taller along its back. It stomped on four huge legs as wide as him, and great horns jutted from its brow; not curled, blunt horns like a sheep's, but long and wide and pointed, and... were they tipped with metal? And yet despite all that, the thing was covered with feathers like a bird, a mottled dun with a crest of longer blue at the neck.

He'd never seen anything near the same size walking on land.

Oh, krayks and leviathans were bigger, but they swam in the sea where Father Krayk would hold their great bulks up, as he did with even the mightiest of ships, until he decided otherwise. This thing was a walking impossibility, and by the Dark Father, *there was a Flatlander riding it.* Their face was hidden by a metal mask under a metal helm, their forearms and shins were cased in metal, and the rest of their body was covered by a thick coat that had to be some sort of armour. They bore a metal shield on one arm and gripped a broad-bladed metal-headed spear in the other hand, with two more spears held upright somehow behind them.

Rikkut glanced down at the fighting. The Flatlanders who hadn't been killed yet were turning and running, blundering through fences in their desire to get away, and in doing so leaving a clear path between the monster and Rikkut's warriors.

"Oh, *fuck*."

The rider slapped their mount's rump with the flat of their spear. The beast bellowed again, put its head down, and charged.

Terror transfixed Rikkut's warriors, and the monster ploughed into them before they could flee or jump aside. It crushed two beneath its enormous feet, speared another on its horns and tossed him into the air, only to rise up and flatten him even more thoroughly than it had his fellows as soon as he landed. Olja Tillistutar was down there: the rider's spear punched clean through her chest and out the back of her furs, then got lodged and left there as the monster thundered past. She went down clutching at her chest, dead meat that just hadn't quite realised it yet, while the rider reached behind them and pulled out another spear.

Rikkut's raid were some of the most ferocious warriors in Tjakorsha, a mix of battle-hardened raiders and eager young Unblooded. They'd followed him across the Great Ocean, they'd charged a defended wall for him and they'd not shy from battle against the Brown Eagle clan or the Flatlanders, but they couldn't stand against this. Those that found themselves in the beast's way turned to flee, only to discover their path was blocked by yet more warriors piling in through the breach in the wall.

The monster crashed into them all, lashing out with its horns and trampling them underfoot. The rider stabbed downwards with their spear, killing one, two, three. Some of Rikkut's warriors found courage in desperation and struck back with their blackstone axes, but their blows simply rebounded from both monster and rider with little noticeable effect.

The attack was about to turn into a rout, and not in the way Rikkut had hoped. How could he have planned for unkillable monsters?

Rikkut Krayk-Killer suddenly became very aware of the six cubits of harpoon he held in his right hand.

He didn't stop to think about it. He simply dropped his axe at his feet, grasped the harpoon in both hands, took a quick two-step run-up and vaulted off the side of the wagon, screaming a wordless war cry.

Blackstone axes were unquestionably sharper than a kraken harpoon, but they lacked its heft, let alone the driving force supplied by a running jump. Where axe blows had achieved little, Rikkut's thrust took the monster in its short, thick neck, just behind the fringe of blue quills, and plunged through feathers deep into flesh.

The noise of the beast's pain-roar was incredible. It turned away from him, thrashing, and Rikkut just had time to throw himself flat before the thing's spiked tail swept through where he'd just been. Someone else was hit and knocked from their feet with the cracking of bone. Rikkut scrambled back up to his feet again, lest one of the monster's enormous feet crushed him, and found himself next to Olja. He put his foot on her chest and wrenched the Flatlander's spear out of her dying body in a spray of blood, heedless of her screams.

The rider saw him, but was too busy trying to stay atop their thrashing mount to do more than make a clumsy stab with their own spear. The monster continued to turn, still dragging the harpoon from the side of its neck as blood leaked out onto the ground.

Rikkut set himself, and lunged as the thing whirled towards him.

The metal blade was far stronger and truer than the bone of the krayk harpoon, and it bit even deeper into the other side of the monster's neck. The great beast let out a thunderously deep moan, trembled, and dropped to its knees.

The rider leaped off, stabbing at Rikkut with their spear as they did so. Rikkut, the battle-fever flowing through him, saw the blow coming as slowly as a playful tap from a lover. He swayed aside from it, grabbed the spear behind the head and wrenched it out of the rider's grip, sending them sprawling into the mud.

The raid fell on them, blackstone axes rising and falling, terror turning to bloodthirsty frenzy in a moment. Rikkut saw his warriors crowding around, striking each other in their desperation to land a telling blow.

"*Enough!*" He wrenched the metal spear out of the monster's neck, releasing a pulsing river of blood. The beast let one out final sigh and collapsed sideways, nearly crushing him as it did so, but he managed to step out of its way just in time. His warriors pulled back from the downed Flatlander, revealing a prone body with its shield kicked aside. Their clothing was shredded, but that only revealed many small plates of metal beneath that were unbroken. The figure shifted, groaning in pain and misery. They had clearly taken a beating, but they didn't look to have been cut, despite the multiple axe blows.

"Sorcery!" someone hissed as the rider struggled to push themselves up.

"Not sorcery!" Rikkut snapped. "Metal!"

He raised the spear that had slain the monster and brought it down two-handed. The metal armour parted with a *snap*, and the spearhead buried itself into the rider's chest. They let out a howl of pain that tailed off into a bubbling gasp, and Rikkut pulled the blade out again. He looked the rider over as he did so, but to his disappointment could see no sign of a sword like the one he'd taken from Snowhair. Had the old man lied about that? Perhaps this warrior hadn't had time to pick theirs up? Rikkut would just have to hunt down more champions and kill them.

"The monsters *die*!" he bellowed, raising the blood-slicked spear. "The Flatlanders *die*! The Brown Eagle clan *will die*! Kill them! *Kill them all!*"

SAANA

THE INVADERS WEREN'T hard to find.

The Naridans knew what this more frantic pealing of the bell meant, and they'd either run for the castle—to beg for a weapon or shelter behind its wall—or had taken up whatever they'd had to hand that could be used to fight off the attackers. Scythes and pitchforks weren't the best tools for the job, but they were long and had metal blades or tines, which made them a match for much Tjakorshi armour. Saana, running towards the eastern wall, saw a Naridan swing a scythe double-handed and nearly take a man's head off with it, but he and his two companions were outnumbered. The attackers flooded forward, screaming for blood, and blackstone axes were more than a match for Naridan clothing, too.

"Throw them back!" she yelled, raising her axe, and her warriors broke into a sprint. The invaders looked up in alarm and tried to set themselves to receive the charge, but they were too disorganised to form a proper shieldwall. The Brown Eagle clan smashed into them, and for the first time in fifteen years, Saana found herself using a weapon in anger.

Or, more accurately, in terror.

She'd not even tried to engage with Asrel Blackcreek when he'd come at her on the salt marsh, because memories of Njivan's death had been running through her head and her warriors were already on their way to help her. She'd merely been trying to stay alive for long enough to make him someone else's problem. Now she was leading a charge, and needed to show her clan she was willing to fight for their new home.

Saana screamed and aimed an overhand, diagonal cut at her opponent's head, but he got his shield up to block it and her momentum carried her into him, shield-first. He fell backwards; she stumbled over him, turned as she passed him and stooped to catch the axe-slash aimed for her calves on her shield. The woman following Saana swung with all her might at where the man's shoulder met his neck, and her axe cleaved down to his collarbone. Blackstone might not cut metal, and it might be brittle, but there was a reason the clans of Tjakorsha used it to edge their weapons.

She spun around to face in the direction of the charge again, sweeping with her shield to knock aside anyone approaching to strike her. It was almost her undoing: a warrior with red hair nearly as bright as Zhanna's stepped back from her swing, then lunged in to try to catch Saana's exposed ribs.

Saana knocked the sword downwards just in time and tried a stab with the toe of her axe, but her opponent batted it away with her shield. She wielded a metal blade, longer and thinner than the one Saana had been left by her father. It tapered to a point from the cutting edge, and she held it with a flowing grace. She lashed out with two cuts at Saana's face, as fast as winter rain. Saana caught the first on her shield and the second skittered off her helm, then the other fighter stepped back before Saana's counter-cut could find her and smiled viciously. She was smaller than Saana and astonishingly beautiful, with a scattering of freckles across her nose and cheeks like the tiniest droplets of blood.

"You're the chief," she said, with a glance at Saana's belt, and chuckled. "Saana Sattistutar, yes?"

"What's it to you?" Saana snapped, watching for an attack.

She wasn't going to get distracted by the other woman's words, but perhaps she'd see an opening.

"I'm supposed to leave you for Rikkut," the warrior said through a shark's smile, "but he's not here. Perhaps he won't be The Golden's favourite after today."

She flicked her sword up so quickly that Saana barely saw it, even though she'd been looking for it. The point ripped into the flesh on her chin despite her backstep, and she felt the sting of its edge and the warmth of newly dripping blood. Saana's enemy was faster than her, and more experienced in battle, and had realised it.

Saana stepped forward and feinted another overhand cut, then reversed direction and swept her axe first down and then up instead, a ripping blow towards her opponent's crotch. It was a powerful swing, and had it landed then it would have unquestionably opened the other woman up the middle, but she blocked it with her shield almost contemptuously, and the blackstone teeth lodged fast in the unrimmed wood. She wrenched the shield aside, seeking to pull Saana off-balance and create an opening for her long, thin blade to puncture Saana's sea leather and slide between her ribs.

Saana let her weapon go immediately and, instead of being dragged stumbling to one side, she drove the rim of her own shield straight into the other woman's face.

There was a cracking noise that could have come from one of the Songs of Creation, when Father Krayk was lifting the lands above the waves. The other warrior staggered backwards, her nose ruined and several teeth now missing. She swiped across herself with her sword, but it was a blind, panicked blow. Saana let it pass in front of her, took a step, let her enemy swipe the other way, then stepped inside her guard again. The other warrior raised her shield to defend her face, and Saana stamped sideways at her right knee.

It gave way. The other woman collapsed backwards to the

ground with a cry of agony and tried to cover herself with her shield and sword, but Saana kicked her sword loose from her hand and snatched it up. It was lighter and more comfortable in the hand than her father's, and she hacked down with it at the woman's exposed legs.

Blood, screaming, a flash of white bone as the flesh parted. Saana's enemy brought her shield down instinctively to protect her legs, and the point of Saana's new sword took her in the neck instead.

"Thank you, Daimon," Saana muttered. It had been a risk to let herself get disarmed like that, like Daimon had sacrificed his longblade against Rist, but the other woman would have cut her to shreds in a straight fight.

"*Saana Sattistutar!*"

It took Saana a moment to pick out who'd shouted her name. Was it an ally? Another enemy looking to challenge her to single combat? Then she saw him, and a new chill gripped her.

A young Tjakorshi man, barely more than a youth, was advancing towards her in the midst of a new rush of attackers. He wasn't the tallest or the widest, and his red-brown beard was scraggly rather than full, but his eyes were fixed on her, unblinking. She met them, and shivered. She'd seen expressions like that before, and it had never been a pleasant experience.

"You're a long way from home, boy," she called to him. He wore no armour, but he had good weapons; a metal-tipped spear, and even a metal shield...

A metal shield that bore the symbol of Blackcreek. And the spear was a sar's wide-bladed spear, the same as Daimon had been carrying.

"Where did you get those?" she yelled. The youth grinned at her.

"I never knew Flatlanders rode monsters. It seems they die as easily as krayks, though!"

"You expect me to believe you've killed a krayk?" she

demanded, but her throat was squeezed tight and her voice came out thin and panicked. Perhaps he'd managed to pull Daimon down somehow, had merely disarmed him? But he wasn't carrying her husband's longblade, and surely he'd have taken that...

"They call me Rikkut Krayk-Killer," he said, spreading his arms mockingly. He was ten paces away from her now. "That, or Rikkut Fireheart. You've earned no name except what your mother left you."

"Rikkut," Saana said, nodding grimly. "I just took this blade from a woman who mentioned you. Friend of yours?"

"Kovra." Rikkut's eyes strayed to the sword she now held. When he looked at her again he was no longer smiling. "I was going to offer you a quick death if you gave up your belt. Now I'm going to make this *hurt*."

He charged, crossing the distance left between them in a few quick steps and leaping into the air, jabbing at her head. Saana jerked back from the spear thrust and raised her shield to bat it away, but he'd already withdrawn the weapon and when he landed he stabbed at her ribs, forcing her to desperately knock the point down with her sword. She took a step in and cut at him but he slid away, staying out of range, the spear point wavering in small circles near her eye level.

A thrust, which she took on her shield. Another one aimed at her legs, which she stepped back hurriedly from, then a third up at her face. She got her shield up and the point scraped over it, slashed along the side of her helm. She lashed out with her sword but caught only the haft of his spear, and he laughed at her.

Saana stepped in towards him, guessed he'd go for her head and deflected the blow upwards with her shield, then stabbed upwards for his gut. He drew his own shield in and caught the point of the blade on it, jarring her arm, but he was sliding his spear over her shield at the same time and then he ripped it down and to the side as he backed away—

Saana screamed in pain. Her left ear and cheek were suddenly in agony, a searing counterpoint to the throbbing ache of her chin.

"I told you I'd make it hurt," Rikkut snarled, and came at her again. Thrust, thrust, sidestep, thrust, backstep, always quick, always staying out of reach of her blade. The spear was heavy, designed for killing thrusts with the dragon's momentum doing most of the work, but it didn't seem to sap his strength or slow him.

Then Saana stepped in once more, trying to angle the point of her sword over his shield, and the tip of his spear dipped down to find her shin. She cried out in pain as the edge sliced through her skin and ground along the bone, and her lunge became a desperate hobble to keep her balance. Rikkut circled in, like a krayk scenting blood. He made his own lunge, side-on and twisting, and suddenly his spear-point was somehow around the rim of Saana's shield and stabbing her in her right shoulder. Her sea leather took the brunt of it but the tip parted her flesh before she could knock it away with her shield. She tried to raise her sword and a flash of pain down her right arm brought her to a halt, gritting her teeth in agony.

"Your clan's dying, Saana," Rikkut sneered. Saana didn't dare take her eyes off him, but she didn't need to. She could still hear shouts and the clatter of weapons on shields, but she could see bodies with green or red rags tied around their arms on the ground amidst the corpses of their enemies. The Golden had simply sent too many warriors for her clan of fishers and farmers to fight off, even with the Naridans' help.

She felt a sudden, deep pang of sorrow that had nothing to do with the throbbing of the wounds she'd taken. She'd hoped for a new life on this side of the ocean. She'd tried so hard, *so* hard to make everything work, and all she'd achieved was to bring the vengeance of a mad draug down onto a different shore.

"Finish it, then," she spat at his arrogant smirk. "If you can."

Rikkut danced forward, light over the ground, feinted first

one way then the other, and thrust his spear full force at Saana's chest. She took it on her shield, but the sheer force of the blow knocked her staggering. Her wounded leg wouldn't take her weight properly, and it buckled beneath her. She fell to the ground and the impact sent a jarring shock up her spine. She tried to get her legs under her, tried to get back to her feet, but Rikkut was already looming over her with his spear drawn back to strike—

His eyes bulged, and he stiffened. A high-pitched whine escaped his lips, his arms suddenly drooped, and a hand's span of a sar's longblade burst into view through his chest.

New shouts filled the air: young voices, higher-pitched and shrill, but raised in battle cries rather than screams. Rikkut jerked as the sar's blade withdrew again. Blood leaked out to stain his tunic, but he began to lurch around despite his wound, surely dying but not yet dead...

Saana shuffled clumsily and lunged with her blade, crying out with pain as her arm screamed at her. It was an awkward swing, but the blade of her sword sliced through the back of Rikkut's left calf. He fell to one knee and his shield arm came down to catch himself.

The longblade flashed again, and took Rikkut Fireheart's head off his neck. There was a spurt of blood as his body lolled sideways, his heart still trying futilely to keep him alive, and then he slumped to the ground in front of Saana. She looked up, hoping against hope that it would be Daimon who stood in front of her, not his brother. *Let him be alive...*

"Mama?" Zhanna asked, lowering the bloodstained blade and looking at her with wide eyes. "Mama, you're hurt!"

"I—Behind you!" Saana shouted, as another shape charged into view. Zhanna spun on the spot and the longblade flashed through the air. An arm wielding a blackstone axe was severed at the elbow, although the momentum of the warrior to whom it had belonged still sent him crashing into Zhanna. She staggered backwards, he tried to strike at her and realised he no longer had an arm at the same time as Saana managed to stab her sword up into his crotch. He screamed and folded up around the blade, and Zhanna's next swing opened his throat. He gurgled in surprise and fell backwards with red sheeting down his chest, and Zhanna knelt down next to Saana.

"Mama?"

"Help me up," Saana said through gritted teeth. Zhanna hauled her back upright by her shield arm and Saana looked around, ready to defend herself again.

Something had changed. The invaders who'd accompanied Rikkut, who'd been cutting down her clan so mercilessly, were now being brought down in their turn. Saana gaped as she spied not only her own clan's Unblooded but also youths—both Tjakorshi and Naridan, some barely more than children—attacking the invaders from behind. Even the best of warriors would have little chance if beset from both front and back, and although the Unblooded's blades didn't always fell their targets, the distractions allowed Saana's hard-pressed fighters to land telling blows.

"Some of them were getting weapons at the stronghouse, others were hiding there," Zhanna answered her unasked question. "I told them to follow me."

"And they did? The Naridans as well?" Saana asked, amazed.

"I asked them if they were going to fight for their home with us, or sit and cry like children," Zhanna said with a shrug. "My Naridan was good enough for that."

"Our clan has many stories of how children got blooded and became adults," Saana said in wonder, and no little admiration. "I don't think anyone's done it quite like you."

Zhanna beamed at her. The tiny spots of blood on her daughter's face looked incongruously like new freckles.

Half a dozen of the invaders had been backed into a circle now, hemmed in on all sides with their shields facing outwards. Saana's clan and the Naridan youths crowded around, but none seemed to want to make the first move. The invaders might have been outnumbered and cornered, but they were still warriors.

"Move aside!" Saana snapped, limping forwards. The bodies in front of her parted obligingly and she found herself staring at grim faces, eyes wide and watchful.

"I've had enough of killing," Saana said bluntly. She could hear fighting elsewhere in Black Keep, but she needed to deal with these invaders first. "I'm chief here. Yield, and you'll live."

"The Golden doesn't forgive cowards," the man facing her replied.

"The Golden isn't here," Zhanna said, shouldering her way past Saana and holding something up.

It was the head of Rikkut Fireheart, dangling by its hair and leaking blood onto the ground.

The man who'd spoken looked at it, and Saana saw the recognition in his eyes. He took a long, deep breath, drew himself up, and dropped his shield and blackstone axe.

"I yield," he muttered.

"Tumezhkan!" the woman next to him snapped, not taking her eyes off the fighters in front of her.

"That bastard Fireheart's dead," Tumezhkan said, "and the Golden's on the other side of the Great Ocean. Fuck this, I never wanted to come here anyway."

"Fireheart's not dead!" shouted a man with his back to Tumezhkan's.

"There's a girl here holding his head, and it's not attached to his body," Tumezhkan replied. "If he's not dead, he's a fucking good actor."

The woman risked a sideways look. Saana saw her jaw clench when she saw Fireheart's head.

"It's true, Kozh." She dropped her weapons too. "I yield."

One by one, three of the other four warriors imitated her. The last one, Kozh, turned on them, his eyes flashing.

"Cowards!" he bellowed, and raised his axe, then cried out as two of Saana's clan cut him down from behind before his blow could land.

"The rest of you, on your knees facing each other!" Saana ordered. "Khotia, Evruk, watch them. If any of their friends approach, kill them and defend yourselves, but otherwise they're not to be harmed. Everyone else, with me!"

She turned away as Rikkut's warriors knelt sullenly but obediently next to Kozh's body. Zhaana stayed by her side, Rikkut's head still dangling from one hand and her longblade in the other.

"Where did you get that sword?" Saana asked her, dreading the answer.

"I—" Zhanna's answer faltered as brassy wails split the air. The warriors with them halted as well, looking around. "What's that?"

Saana's mouth dried. She'd heard that sound before, and it still haunted her dreams to this day. Here and now, though...

"It could be help," she said, trying to sound hopeful.

"*Could* be?" Zhanna asked.

Saana's face was throbbing, her right arm hurt to move and her right leg was threatening to collapse under her again if she wasn't careful. She'd seen friends die this day, people who'd counted on her to lead them true. She didn't have the energy left to lie to her daughter, especially given that Zhanna was newly Blooded.

"Those are sar warhorns," she said heavily, "and they're coming from the north. It could be death."

EVRAM

EVRAM HAD NEVER expected to meet a lord other than his own. He'd certainly never expected to meet one of the High Marshals. The moment when he'd been brought forth in the hall of Darkspur and ordered to speak had been, in its own way, as terrifying as when he'd taken hold of his knife and had set his sights on the huge Raider who'd killed Tan. Once that was over he'd expected to be dismissed. He'd hoped he might be able to tag along with the High Marshal's force back to Black Keep, but had miserable visions of being put back into his room that had been a cell in all but name, and forgotten about.

Instead, Marshal Brightwater had ordered that Evram should ride in one of the supply wagons instead of being forced to struggle along in the wake of the foot soldiers. Even more astonishing, the High Marshal had instructed Evram to attend him several times in the evenings. On those occasions, with Evram barely able to speak through his nervousness, the High Marshal had ordered him to be served wine to calm his nerves, and had asked questions about the layout of Black Keep.

"This lord must know where the gates are, and where the walls are strong or weak, in case we find them held against us," he'd told Evram seriously. "He must know how the town is laid out. No one here knows these things, Evram of Black Keep, save for you."

And so Evram had swallowed his wine, done his best to swallow his nerves, and had set about discussing his home with the most powerful man in South Narida. The High Marshal was courteous, and listened carefully when Evram described what buildings lay where as a scribe took charcoal to paper to draw a rough map, or answered as best he could about the nature and temperament of Black Keep's lords. Each time, when they'd finished, the High Marshal thanked Evram for his assistance.

They had to be close to Black Keep now, Evram knew. They'd passed the last woodcutters' cottages the day before, and he'd just seen a burned, blasted pine tree he recognised. His stomach was getting tighter and tighter. They were nearly out of the Downwoods. What then? Would Black Keep still be standing? Would the Raiders have departed, leaving him a liar in the eyes of the High Marshal?

"Evram of Black Keep!"

He jumped as the shout came back down the line. A sar was approaching, their plumed helm turning this way and that as they rode their dragon between the marching ranks of spearmen and archers. Although, Evram saw, the column's march was coming to a halt. Was he about to be ordered to explain himself?

There was nothing for it. He stood up on the driving platform of the wagon so the sar could see him. "Here!"

"Come with this sar!" the warrior commanded, guiding his dragon over. He steered the huffing animal around to present its back to Evram. "Come on, man!"

He scrambled on clumsily, but the dragon was battle-trained and took little notice of his flounderings. The sar spurred it forwards and they trotted through the ranks again until they arrived at the head of the column, where the High Marshal himself sat astride his mighty war beast.

"Evram!" the Marshal hailed him, and Nari be praised, he didn't sound angry. "This lord has need of you once again." He gestured with one armoured gauntlet. "Can you name these men?"

Evram's mount took a few more steps forwards, and as the dragons of the High Marshal's retinue parted he caught sight of four men kneeling in the dirt of the road, flanked by men Evram now knew to be the High Marshal's scouts. Two wore the livery of Black Keep, and there was no mistaking the others.

"Nadar and Yoon of Lord Blackcreek's household, Kelarahel the reeve, and Freeman Shefal," Evram said without hesitation. None of them looked up at him, for all still had their heads bowed before the High Marshal, but Evram saw a slight smile quirk the corner of Shefal's mouth.

"They claim they freed Lord Asrel, but he was slain by his own son, and the rest of the town has turned traitor and now sides with the invaders," the High Marshal said, and Evram's heart quickened in shock. Could such a thing be true?

"Your man beseeches you, lord," Shefal said. "Ride forth and liberate our home!"

"Insolent cur!" one of the scouts snapped, cuffing Shefal so hard that the freeman toppled sideways, knocking into Kelarahel and nearly sending him sprawling as well. "You do not speak to the Hand of Heaven unless he requests it!"

Evram's throat tightened, for had he not done the same thing in the great hall of Darkspur? But perhaps the High Marshal had counted that conversation as being part of his initial request; or perhaps these soldiers were simply particularly vigilant, for Lord Brightwater raised one hand to forestall any further punishment.

"Is the town defended against our coming?" he asked. No one answered, and he sighed in exasperation. "This marshal asked a question! You, reeve! Is the town defended?"

"N-no, lord," Kelarahel stammered. "Not when we left. Your coming is not known. They have gathered to celebrate the wedding of Lord Daimon to the Raider chief."

"Wedding?!" Odem Darkspur blurted out. "Has the boy lost his mind?"

"A valid question," the High Marshal said thoughtfully. "And one we should soon have the answer to. Place these men with the supply wagons; we ride to Black Keep, to see if its people still know their true master! Evram," he added more quietly, as the sars around him began calling orders to get the column moving again, "ride with this marshal."

Evram gaped. "With you, lord? But your man can barely sit on a dragon, he would impede you!"

"One of the advantages of being High Marshal, Evram," Brightwater said with a grin, "is that you rarely have to see combat yourself. This marshal would have you close at hand to identify people or landmarks, and the wagons will not keep up. Since you have no mount of your own…"

And so Evram of Black Keep found himself clambering clumsily from the back of one war dragon to another, the finest beast from all of Brightwater's stables, and perched somewhat precariously behind the most powerful man in Southern Narida. So well-trained was the dragon that the High Marshal merely had to touch his heels to its flanks and it began to walk forwards, but it seemed to Evram that almost no sooner had the column begun moving again, that they'd stopped once more.

"What is it now?" Brightwater demanded testily. Evram leaned hesitantly out to one side past his cloaked shoulder, and saw a scout hastening towards them again.

"High Marshal!" the scouts called. "We have seen the town, and it appears to be under attack!"

"From whom?"

"Raiders, lord!"

Evram couldn't see Brightwater's face, but he sounded more confused than angry at such a statement. "We were told they were inside the town, celebrating!"

The scout bowed to cover his own confusion. "These ones are definitely outside it, High Marshal, but they seek to gain entry, and those inside are resisting!"

"Does nothing make sense any more?" Brightwater muttered,

so low that Evram could barely hear him, then spurred his mount forwards. Evram hung on as best he could, until the daylight around him grew brighter as they reached the edge of the Downwoods and looked out over the last—or first—stretch of the North Road that led to the gates of Black Keep.

Sure enough, the town was under attack. Evram gaped in horror at the sight; a new host of the strange Raider ships beached on the riverbank, and what looked like the last few stragglers heading for where he knew the breach in the wall lay, on the east side. However, a sizeable number were skirting the town's northern edge and making for the Road Gate. Labourers returning from the far fields were also heading there as fast as they could, but the race would be close.

"Evram?" the High Marshal said. "Do you have any insight?"

"None, lord," Evram said wretchedly. "This is beyond your man's understanding."

"Then we shall assume these Raiders are no friends of those who may be inside, and we may be able to use that to our advantage!" Brightwater said forcefully, and Evram realised that he was addressing his retinue, who had reined in around him. "Sound the charge! Ride down these scum and drive them back to their ships! Kill any Raider you see outside the walls!"

"What of any inside, lord?" someone asked.

"We shall deal with that when we get inside," the High Marshal replied.

"Lord!" Evram said suddenly. "Beware the marsh to the east! Your mounts will founder in it!"

"Thank you, Evram," Brightwater said. "You heard him! Watch the footing! Now charge!"

War horns blared, dragons bellowed in response, and the sars of the Southern Army burst out of the treeline to thunder down the North Road towards Evram's beleaguered home. In their wake ran the columns of foot troops; not at a full sprint, but the quick pace of men who could see a hated enemy and intended to close with them while conserving strength enough to fight. The High Marshal guided his mount forward at a trot, keeping pace with his spearmen and archers.

"You see, Evram?" Brightwater said. "The savages have no stomach for battle." And indeed, already the closest group of raiders, who had clustered around the now-closed Road Gate and appeared to be about to attack a group of farmers who had not made it inside before the gate had closed, had turned in shock at the sounding of the Southern Army's war horns.

Then the Road Gate opened again and another sar on a war dragon charged out, smashing through them from behind before they realised he was there.

That was enough. The Raiders turned and fled, running for their ships, and the farmers ran forwards to dispatch those who'd been caught by the dragon's charge. Brightwater's sars angled their gallops to chase those fleeing, and the Black Keep sar joined them. The farmers, their grisly work done, merely stood and stared at the procession coming down the North Road towards them. The High Marshal's bannerman rode behind him, with the huge standard snapping in the stiff breeze coming in off the ocean, and it was plain for anyone with eyes to see who was approaching Black Keep.

As the High Marshal drew close, a Naridan with a thick beard and holding a staff stepped out of the gate and ushered the farmers inside. He then knelt, alone, in the middle of the road.

"That is Aftak, lord, our priest," Evram muttered into Brightwater's ear.

"A good man?" the High Marshal asked quietly.

"Your man has always thought so, lord."

"Priest!" Brightwater called, reining in his dragon. "You bar the Southern Marshal's way!"

"This priest begs your forgiveness, lord," Aftak answered, his eyes still downcast. "He merely wishes to inform you that not all the Raiders you will see here are your enemies."

"Those are disturbing words to hear," Brightwater said sternly.

"Yet true nonetheless," Aftak replied firmly. "It has always been this priest's duty to speak the truth as he sees it, and although he understands it may see his head separated from his shoulders on this day, still he must do it. Perhaps you were too distant to see, lord? Some of those who killed the bodies that lie here"—he gestured with one hand to the dead Raiders behind him—"were members of the Brown Eagle clan, who had been working in the Blackcreek fields alongside men of this town before these new raiders arrived."

"Even if what you say is true," Brightwater said slowly, "how should this lord's men know friend from foe?"

"Those loyal to us have cloth of red or green tied around their arms," Aftak said. "A ruse devised by Lord Darel, so we should know them from the foe."

"Lord Darel?" the High Marshal said. "He fights?"

"Aye, lord," Aftak replied. "Him, and his brother Lord Daimon."

"And where is Lord Daimon?" the High Marshal demanded.

Aftak looked up, a mischievous smile creasing the lips beneath his beard. "You just missed him, High Marshal. He went that way."

He pointed in the direction the sar on the war dragon had gone, chasing after the fleeing Raiders.

"Your orders, High Marshal?" asked the captain of the foot troops, who had halted next to Brightwater's dragon.

"Clear out the town," Brightwater commanded. "Kill any who resist. But..." he added, as the man drew in a breath.

There was a momentary pause.

"But the men are not to attack Raiders wearing coloured cloth as the priest has described, should they not prove hostile."

"Yes, lord," the captain replied. If he had questions or doubts, he didn't voice them. Instead he drew his sword and led his troops onwards. Aftak remained kneeling, for he had not yet been bidden to rise, and the troops filed past on either side of him.

"High Marshal?" Odem Darkspur asked. "It is not this thane's position to question, but—"

"No, it is not," Brightwater cut him off. "But this lord wishes to see what has truly happened here. If it turns out that the Blackcreek family are indeed traitors, and the Raiders within the walls are also our enemies..."

He spurred his mount forwards again. Now Aftak did move, for it was that or be crushed for barring the Hand of Heaven's path, and that was the greater insult.

"Well," Brightwater concluded, "if that is the case, we can deal with them later. Better to fight your enemies one at a time, after all."

DAIMON

THE RAIDERS HE'D pursued from the Road Gate were fleeing into the marsh towards their ships, along with their fellows who'd fled out of the breach, and Daimon resisted the temptation to urge Silverhorn after them. An adult longbrow would stand no chance of catching people in the mud, and might get mired completely. He reluctantly pulled his mount's head around instead.

"*Daimon!*"

Other people were emerging from the breach now, Black Keep folk and Brown Eagles with cloth around their arms. And, limping in their midst, was a familiar figure with a sheet of blood down her left cheek and what looked to be a new sword tucked into her chief's belt.

"Saana!" Daimon slid down from Silverhorn's saddle and left the dragon to graze for the moment—he wouldn't wander far, and he'd more than earned it after the work he'd put in. Daimon slipped through his folk, who were doing the grim work of dealing with the Raiders who'd been injured but not killed as they fled, and made his way to Saana's side.

"You are alive!" she exclaimed as soon as he reached her, and there looked to be genuine relief in her eyes. "The leader, Rikkut, he had a spear and shield like the ones you carried! And then your wife saw a body and a dead dragon just there, inside the wall—"

"It must be Tavi," Daimon said heavily, and Saana's face fell. "Tavi was riding Bastion. We didn't know where the Raiders would attack first; Darel went to the River Gate, your husband to the Road Gate, and Tavi to the breach. He must have fought bravely, especially for a man untrained."

"Your wife is sad," Saana said, her shoulders drooping. "She did not know him well, but... he was a good man."

"Aye," Daimon muttered, tasting sour guilt. It had been his idea to get Tavi on a dragon, and the loss of poor Bastion was nearly as keen. "We have lost many good people today. But your husband is glad you were not among them."

"*You there!*"

Daimon looked around. He'd seen other sars pursuing Raiders, and had heard the horns. Three were now approaching, and seemed none too pleased to be faced with Naridans and Tjakorshi standing side by side.

"Who are you, who wears the armour of a sar but consorts with these savages?" the foremost rider bellowed from behind his war mask. His shield bore crossed golden spears, the sigil of the Southern Marshal's personal household. Daimon pulled his own helmet off and shook his braids free.

"This lord is Daimon Blackcreek, of Black Keep!" he shouted back. "These savages, as you call them, are the Brown Eagle clan of Tjakorsha, who have fought beside us today to throw back an attack from Raiders from across the sea!"

"They are Raiders themselves, man!" the rider spluttered. "Look at them!"

Daimon folded his arms. "And yet they are not raiding. They have ploughed our fields and fished our seas, and celebrated the Festival of Life with us!"

The three riders looked at each other and mutterings passed between them, too low for Daimon to make out.

"You bear the sigil of the High Marshal!" he called. "Is he here?"

"Indeed he is," another sar responded. "He rides through your town's gate even now."

"Then perhaps this lord should speak with him," Daimon suggested, fighting down the flutter of his insides. "The High Marshal will undoubtedly wish to learn what has occurred here, and this lord would not have him hear it from another's lips."

"Too late for that, boy," laughed the third sar. "Why else do you think we rode to this Nari-forsaken spit of land in the first place?"

"This man is certain the High Marshal will indeed wish to speak with you," the first rider said, apparently ignoring his companion's comment. "In fact, if you were not to seek him out, we would be compelled to take you to him."

"There will be no need for that," Daimon replied stiffly. He whistled and slapped his thigh. Silverhorn grunted in response and began to amble over, picking his way over the bodies on the ground now he wasn't being urged to trample anyone. Daimon turned to Saana. "Will you ride with your husband?"

"Your wife is not sure these sars would approve," Saana said, looking over his shoulder at the riders.

"Your husband cares nothing for whether they approve or not," Daimon said bluntly. He wiped his longblade off on his robe and scabbarded it. "He would have you with him when he speaks to the High Marshal, but you are injured, and it would not be honourable to make you walk when he rides."

"Very well, then," Saana said, eyeing the approaching Silverhorn. "If you can get your wife onto your dragon, she will ride with you."

Her apprehension proved to be unfounded, for Silverhorn had run off any excess energy, and was now perfectly happy to kneel to let them mount, then rose to his feet and set off with nothing but a breathy chuff of effort. Daimon guided him back through the gap in the wall, then through the streets beyond to the main square. He tried not to look at the dead bodies that lay in their way, or hear the screams of those injured, or the weeping of families and friends as they discovered them. He needed to speak to the Southern Marshal of Narida as a lord of Black Keep, and honour dictated that a lord must be strong and dry-eyed.

Daimon couldn't help but feel that honour had a lot to answer for.

"You said their leader had Tavi's spear and shield," he said over his shoulder to Saana as they rode. "What happened to this... Rikkut?"

"Zhanna killed him."

"Zhanna?!" He looked back at her in shock, twisting in his seat to do so. "Your daughter?"

"Yes."

Daimon found himself momentarily at a loss for words.

"She is a remarkable young woman," he said, turning back to guide Silverhorn again.

"She is," Saana replied, and if her voice sounded a little choked, Daimon wasn't going to mention it. They rode in silence for another few moments, and then Saana spoke again.

"She... used a longblade to do it."

"A longblade?" Daimon frowned. "Where did she—?"

"Your father's was... well, after he... fell, and then the attackers came," Saana said hesitantly. "It was still with him. Zhanna saw it, and thought it better than her own weapon..." She gripped his shoulder. "Daimon, she meant no disrespect, and she saved your wife's life with it. Your wife begs you, do not treat her harshly."

Daimon wasn't angry. He felt he should be, but he wasn't. He waited a couple more dragonstrides, trying to put his thoughts into words.

"It is a weapon," he said slowly. "Nothing more. Your husband's father tried to kill your husband, his own son, with it. Its last use, before Zhanna took it up, was to try to kill you. It is not a noble thing, in and of itself. It seems fair it should be used to save you." He sighed. "Your husband will speak to Darel. We each have our own blades. Since Zhanna put our father's to such good use, perhaps she should keep it."

There was silence from behind him.

"Saana?"

"Zhanna Longblade," Saana said with a snort that sounded like half-laugh, half-sob. "Daimon, your wife thanks you. It is just... she does not wish her daughter to become a warrior. She loves her too much. But she knows she will not get to decide these things."

"Let us hope Zhanna can decide, and the choice is not taken from her, as it was today," Daimon replied. He guided Silverhorn around the last corner, saw what awaited them in the square, and took a deep breath. "And that we are all still free to make such choices by the time the sun goes down."

He felt Saana shift to look over his shoulder, and heard her mutter something under her breath in Tjakorshi. It seemed his wife shared his misgivings.

Ten dragons stood proudly around the square. Each one was a mighty war beast the equal of Silverhorn, and their sars still sat astride them with their weapons drawn. The greatest of them all, a huge creature with nearly black plumage and ridden by a man who had to be the Southern Marshal himself, was standing in front of Darel.

Daimon's brother was on one knee, with his longblade drawn and grounded point first onto the stone slabs. He was watched not only by the assembled sars and armsmen bearing the sigil of the Southern Marshal, but by the survivors of Black Keep. Naridan and Tjakorshi clustered together much as they had for Daimon's wedding, and when Daimon's father had challenged him to a duel, but the stakes here were far, far higher.

Armsmen moved aside as Silverhorn grunted at them, and Daimon rode into the square. He was conscious of everyone's eyes on them. Even Darel broke from his bow for long enough to cast a quick backward glance, although nobody seemed to notice.

"Do as we do," Daimon muttered to Saana as he guided Silverhorn alongside his brother, then tapped the dragon's neck. Silverhorn knelt obediently and Daimon slid off him, then helped Saana dismount. She winced as her right leg touched the ground, and Daimon helped her drop to one knee. When she grounded her own sword he drew his longblade in one swift motion and imitated his brother and his wife, paying homage to the Southern Marshal.

"Whom is this lord addressing?" Marshal Brightwater demanded. The question was a formal one, and required a formal answer.

"Your servant Darel Blackcreek, presumptive Thane of Black Keep," Darel said before Daimon could speak. Daimon glanced sideways at him: they'd never finished the conversation about who should inherit their father's title.

Darel mouthed one word to him, silently. *Trust*.

Daimon inclined his head a fraction in the most infinitesimal nod he could manage, then cleared his throat. "Your servant Daimon Blackcreek, law-brother of the thane."

Saana spoke next. "Your servant Saana Sattistutar, chief of the Brown Eagle clan."

She paused for a moment.

"And wife to Daimon Blackcreek."

Her voice was strong, and must have carried clearly across the square, because Daimon heard the gasps and mutters from the armsmen. Several of the sars began shouting of dishonour and shame, but their voices quickly stilled. Daimon, still looking at the ground, imagined the Marshal raising one hand for quiet prior to ordering their immediate execution. He took a firmer grip on his longblade. Should he fight? Hadn't today already seen enough fighting?

There was a slither of movement, and then the thump of two boots hitting stone. The *tap-tap-tap* of regular steps approaching.

Then they stopped, just out of range of a swordsman's lunge.

"Look up."

Daimon did so, and found himself looking at the Southern Marshal.

Marshal Kaldur Brightwater was not an old man: in fact, his braided hair was yet to show a hint of grey. His boots were soft and supple dragonskin, and his coat of nails was a vivid yellow chased with blue, with circles of embroidery running from his collar to his hem, each one displaying his sigil of crossed golden spears on blue. The pommels of his longblade and shortblade looked to have been carved from dragonhorn, and his face had the marked cheekbones and long chin characteristic of the northern Naridan nobility. Daimon felt his own low birth had never been more obvious.

"This marshal was told of this union not long ago," Kaldur said, fixing first Daimon and then Saana with a dark, steady gaze. "Four men of this town brought us the news as we were approaching."

Shefal, Yoon, Kelarahel, and Nadar. Daimon would have cursed them all had he not been on one knee in front of one of the most powerful men in Narida.

"It was a strange scene that greeted this marshal when we cleared the edge of the forest," Kaldur continued, starting to pace slowly in front of them. "Raiders, those loathsome savages from across the waves, attacking a town. Nothing so unusual there, sad to say. And yet... *and yet...*"

He paused directly in front of Darel, then began pacing again.

"A man had already brought news to Thane Odem at Darkspur that Raiders had come to Black Keep, and not to pillage, but to settle. That Thane Asrel's law-son had turned upon his father and brother, and betrayed them. Of course, Darkspur assumed the Raiders would have quickly broken any trust placed in them, and slaughtered Black Keep's rightful inhabitants. Indeed, this marshal would have thought that was what he was seeing when he rode into the town… had it not been clear that some Raiders were fighting *beside* the people of Black Keep."

He stopped again, this time in front of Daimon.

"Would anyone care to explain?"

"Lord, the Brown Eagle clan are indeed of the people we have known as Raiders," Daimon said. "Some two weeks ago they arrived here from across the ocean, seeking to settle. Their chief was clear they wished to do so peacefully. Your servant's law-father, Asrel Blackcreek, having met with the chief under a flag of parley, attempted to kill her." Daimon paused for a moment, but Brightwater's expression didn't change.

"Your servant saw that only bloodshed of his people could result from this, so he disarmed his father and made a pact with the Brown Eagles' chief, Saana Sattistutar, that the people of Black Keep would not be harmed," Daimon continued. "Your servant's law-father and law-brother could not reconcile themselves to this, so your servant had them imprisoned in his family's stronghouse where they could neither harm others nor take their lives honourably. In this matter, your servant confesses he acted from the fondness of his heart, rather than as honour would dictate."

"But your law-brother is here, Daimon Blackcreek," Brightwater pointed out. "Here, armed, and calling himself the thane presumptive."

"Your servant was freed, along with his father, by the men whom you met on the road, lord," Darel spoke up. "They hoped your servant's father would prevent the marriage. Your servant confesses that when he emerged from his captivity, he saw that nothing he had feared had come to pass. The Raiders had killed no one, despite Daimon slaying one of their champions in single combat over the honour of a lowborn man. The Brown Eagle clan had honoured their chief's promise, and had begun to live and work alongside our people. Daimon's judgement was good."

"And the battle today?" Brightwater asked. "How did it

happen? Did tempers flare? Did the savages' true nature come out? Did these people from across the ocean turn on each other?"

Daimon wasn't sure quite how to answer. Saana took the choice from him.

"They were clanless. They have abandoned all that Tjakorshi call honour, and have chosen to worship a demon. It was they we fled from to come here. Black Keep and Brown Eagle clan fought and bled together to save each other."

Brightwater said nothing, but tapped his fingers several times on the dragonhorn pommel of his longblade. Then, without turning, he raised his voice.

"Thane Darkspur!"

A figure in brown and gold stepped forwards. Daimon hadn't seen Odem Darkspur for many years, since he and Asrel Blackcreek had still been on speaking terms, but he recognised him immediately.

"High Marshal," Odem said, sinking to one knee when he was three paces from Brightwater.

"You brought this matter to this marshal, and requested his assistance with it," Brightwater said. "Your concerns were valid. It was of course unthinkable that Raiders, that scourge from across the sea, should think to settle in Narida."

Daimon's throat clenched. But they'd spoken so well! How could Kaldur not see it?

"However."

The square went very still.

"This marshal does not see Raiders in front of him," Kaldur said clearly. "He sees farmers and fishers who fled misfortune and came to Narida to live *with honour*. They made promises, and they have kept them. And their chief has now married a son of the Blackcreek house."

"Lord?" Odem asked, his face twisting in confusion.

"This... Brown Eagle clan... wish to live as Naridans? Then they shall live as Naridans!" Kaldur said forcefully. "They shall work for their lord as Naridans do, they shall contribute to his coffers as Naridans do, and he shall pay his taxes to his liege-lord on the basis of that."

Daimon stole a glance sideways at Darel and Saana, unable to keep a smile from his lips. No matter his hopes, no matter his prayers to Nari or any benevolent spirits who might have been listening, he'd struggled to believe this would ever be possible.

Yet Darel's face was drawn with tension. Daimon frowned in return. What was he missing?

"Yes, lord," Odem managed. He looked like someone had fed him dragon dung. "Your servant is grateful for your judgement in this matter."

Crawl back to your home, Daimon thought at him viciously as he rose and withdrew. *If you'd dared to come against us yourself, no one might have questioned you if you'd won. Instead you sent for help, and found the help didn't agree with you.*

"However."

Daimon blinked. Hadn't they already done this?

"There is one issue that cannot be ignored," Brightwater said, looking at Daimon. "When this marshal arrived here, his men found the body of Thane Asrel Blackcreek, apparently placed in the shrine of Nari by his steward. The thane had died with honour by falling on his shortblade, but there was another grievous wound in his side, which would have undoubtedly killed him. The men this marshal encountered on the road all swore this wound was inflicted by Daimon Blackcreek."

There was no point denying it. "It is true, lord. Your servant's law-father challenged him to an honour duel, and threatened to kill people of the town if the challenge was refused."

"A sad state of affairs," Brightwater nodded, although his eyes remained hard. "But the kinslayer is accursed, Daimon Blackcreek. It is amongst the greatest crimes in this land."

Daimon's throat dried. "Even in an honour duel?!"

"No," Brightwater said. "An honour duel, conducted in line

with the Code, is exempt from this law. But is it not true that Asrel Blackcreek had himself breached the covenant of the duel by attacking your wife? And had your brother Lord Darel not drawn his own blade and engaged your father?"

Daimon breathed out shakily. "It is true, High Marshal."

"An honour duel is a combat between two warriors," Marshal Brightwater declared. "By breaching that, your father had already lost, and in so doing also sacrificed any protection he himself would have enjoyed. Had your father then killed you, Daimon Blackcreek, this marshal would have enacted the exact same penalty upon him."

He sighed, with what sounded like genuine regret.

"Death, by beheading."

TILA

IDRAMAR. THE SEAT of the divine God-King, the capital of Narida, and the centre of civilisation.

Or at least, so Tila had always believed.

She'd lived her whole life in and around Idramar, as befitted a princess of the line of the Divine Nari. She'd learned her nation's history from her tutors and had had its inherent superiority reinforced to her again and again. She'd dealt with nobles and dignitaries from other lands, and had always imagined their awe when they'd first laid their eyes on the Sun Palace. How they must have marvelled, seeing the strength and beauty of its lines! How they must have been humbled by the might of the great Narida!

Then she'd travelled to Kiburu ce Alaba, the City of Islands, and... well, it was fair to say that she looked at her own city a little differently now, as she sailed back into the mouth of the river Idra on the deck of the *Light of Fortune*.

Idramar was still large, there was no doubting that, but East Harbour was larger. The Sun Palace might be bigger than any individual building in East Harbour, but the New Palace of the Hierarchs was not far off. As for the port, Tila had always thought of the docks at Idramar as a huge, bustling place, but East Harbour's dwarfed them. Quite apart from that, East

Harbour was only one city amongst the islands that were strung out across the Throat of the World, although it was the largest.

It was a strange experience, for a princess to come back to her home and look on it with humbled eyes.

"It's good to be back," Barach said at her shoulder.

"It's going to be hard," she replied. "This lady imagines there has been a considerable amount of jostling for position while she's been away. We might have to make some examples of people." That was true for both Idramar's backstreets and the corridors of the Sun Palace, but the backstreets were going to have to wait. Family came first. What she wouldn't give to have Barach at her side for that, but anyone knowing her secret was one person too many.

"Where are we going first?" Barach asked.

"First of all, this lady is going *home*," Tila said firmly. "She's not going to walk straight into the thundertooth's lair without knowing what awaits her. She will let the news of her return circulate for a couple of days, and see who scurries for cover." The one thing she could know for certain was that her brother had not passed away since she'd last had news. Even from this far out, she could see that no mourning flags flew on the docks, or on the ships berthed there. She'd prayed to her long-distant ancestor for her brother's survival even since Emerald Bay, and it looked as though those prayers had been answered. Tila didn't know what she could do to help him, but if there was something, she'd find it.

Barach grunted and nodded. Some of Tila's criminal underlings were overenthusiastic in their efforts to get into her good graces, but Barach not only deferred to her utterly, but was a naturally cautious man. It was a good trait in a bodyguard, and one of the reasons she trusted him.

"A fine day, is it not?"

Tila's cheek twitched involuntarily as Marin's voice greeted them from behind. She'd hoped that the thief, and most especially his husband, would have disembarked from the *Light of Fortune* much earlier, but it seemed they'd decided to travel all the way to Idramar. Tila had considered having Captain Kemanyel simply throw them off the boat, but she'd leaned hard on her influence with him already. Besides, even a group of sailors would think twice about trying to force a blacksword who bore the tattoo of a Brotherhood mercenary to leave somewhere he intended to stay, and pirates were a real danger along some stretches of the Naridan coast. Some of the crew had seemed quite pleased at the prospect of a seasoned warrior being on board.

She glanced around. Sure enough, Alazar Blade lurked behind Marin like a silent thundercloud, now clad in Naridan clothes he'd bought at the port of New Bayecliffe, instead of the Alaban ones he'd been wearing when he first came on board. Tila had done her best to avoid him for the duration of the voyage, and he still didn't seem to have made the connection between Livnya and the princess he'd known in passing twenty years before, but every moment she spent around him was another chance for him to ruin her life.

Again.

"It does a man's heart good to see his home," Marin chuntered happily, staring at the city they were approaching.

"Your husband is sure the Keepers will be delighted to see you," Alazar said, shifting his weight to lean against the rail. The Keepers were the God-King's men, charged with keeping Idramar in good order, which included catching and locking up thieves.

"It's been five years, Laz," Marin said dismissively. "They'll have forgotten."

Alazar Blade grunted sceptically and crossed his arms. He looked over at Barach and Tila, and Tila turned her head away from him as though looking back up the coast northwards.

"Your husband doesn't like coming back here," she heard Alazar say. The sentiment wasn't surprising. Tila wondered if Marin knew that his husband was the God-King's ex-lover.

"You've said."

"And he'll say it again, and often, until we leave."

"We won't need to stay for long," Marin said firmly. "Your husband just needs to talk to some people, that's all."

Tila heard Alazar inhale as though to continue the discussion, but he apparently decided against it since he said nothing more. Marin probably needed to square some old debts, or perhaps make amends with former partners. Neither of the pair had been clear as to why they'd left Narida in the first place, although it wasn't hard to guess. Alazar's Brotherhood tattoo meant he'd worked as a sword for hire in Narida, but a blacksword would be the subject of suspicion everywhere in Tila's country. He could have stopped wearing the sword, of course, but you might as well ask a sar to chop his own leg off. He'd probably be more likely to do that, in actual fact.

"It is a good day," Tila agreed to Marin's original question. *Not least because this princess will no longer need to share a ship with you.* "Come, Barach: we should ready ourselves to go ashore." She turned and made for the stairs that led to the captain's cabin.

Soon, she'd be off the sea and back into her element. And then, woe betide anyone, be they noble or criminal, who'd risked overstepping their authority while she'd been away.

DAIMON

Daimon was numb.

High Marshal Brightwater had not insisted that his punishment should be carried out immediately. Instead, Daimon had been allowed to aid his brother with organising the town, taking stock of who had been lost and who had survived. Besides Tavi, Black Keep had lost Yaro and Elka the fishermen, and Rotel the guard, father of Abbatane the stable girl. Nadon, son of Gador, had died after he'd taken up a weapon and followed Zhanna's lead to attack the Raiders who'd been on the verge of killing Saana and her fighters. There were others as well, too many others, but strangely, Daimon found that the hardest one for him to take was Ganalel. He'd been killed while trying to defend his family with the one hand Daimon had left him.

Daimon didn't know enough of the Brown Eagle clan to say for sure who had died, but he recognised at least a couple of the faces laid out in the town square, ready to be sailed out to sea once Chara had finished with them. The corpse-painter's leg was splinted up and she was in obvious pain, but she was grimly drawing her designs with the blue paint she had available to her. Daimon made a mental note to get someone to go and find some more of the blue flowers, then stopped in his tracks, sighed, and raised his voice.

"Nalon?"

Nalon's left arm was bandaged from where he'd taken a wound, but otherwise he seemed as well as anyone else. He made his way over from where he'd been yelling orders at the members of Rikkut Fireheart's raiding crew who'd surrendered. According to Saana, Tjakorshi who yielded in combat owed their captors service for a year and a day as thralls, and their honour would keep them to it unless they were mistreated. Currently they were hauling their own dead into a pile outside the gates to be burned—for they'd not get any rites to speed their soul to Father Krayk—and despite there being a lot of thralls, they'd showed no signs of trying to seize weapons or disobey instructions.

"Aye?" Nalon asked, coming to a halt in front of Daimon.

"Chara will need more of her flowers," Daimon told him. "This lord needs you to organise that, because he will not be here to do so."

Nalon looked at him for a few moments, then nodded uncomfortably and blew out his moustaches. "Right you are. Right you are. S'man will, he will..." He looked around, then spat. "Ah, he'll do it himself. At least knows what he's looking for. Do you suppose the High Marshal will lend him a couple of soldiers in case of razorclaws?"

"Find this lord's brother, and get him to ask for you," Daimon suggested. "This lord doubts the High Marshal is used to taking requests from former smith's apprentices who have married into the Tjakorshi."

"Well, today seems a good day for him to learn," Nalon replied. "No, no," he added hastily, "s'man didn't mean it. He likes his head—" He stopped speaking abruptly, and an expression of absolute mortification crossed his face. "He'll get on and do that. He'll go and do that now."

Daimon didn't trust himself to speak. He nodded, and turned away.

"Lord Daimon?"

He turned back.

"Thank you," Nalon said, somewhat wretchedly. He gestured around with his good arm. "Thank you for doing what you did, when we first came here. Otherwise this would have happened back then, and Fireheart's bastards would have wiped us out when they got here. Thank you for keeping as many of us alive as you did."

"This lord just did not want to die," Daimon replied bitterly. "And look where that got him. Executed in shame as an accursed kinslayer."

Nalon shook his head angrily. "Shamed according to Naridans, maybe. Not for us. Saving our chief, after fighting your own father to prevent him killing clansfolk? Nari's teeth, s'man has heard songs sung of clan heroes who've done less." He cursed in Tjakorshi and spat again. "See, this is why Narida is such goatshit. Good men get killed for doing the right thing. May Nari watch over you, Daimon Blackcreek."

He turned and walked away without waiting for a reply. In truth, Daimon wouldn't have known what to say.

As the sun set, Marshal Brightwater had his men bring out provisions from his supply wagons, and the food that had already been prepared for Daimon's wedding feast was brought forth. Once more, Naridan and Tjakorshi sat and ate together in the first yard of the castle, although a pall of grief for those lost hung heavy over their heads.

Daimon picked at his food. He was only barely aware of what was in front of him, even when he'd put it into his mouth. Saana sat to his left, and she was barely any less tense than he was.

"It is not right," she muttered angrily, too low to be heard by Brightwater, who sat on Daimon's right at the centre of the head table.

"It is what has to be," Daimon murmured back, although his gut twisted at the thought. "This is our honour."

"Then your honour is a foolish thing," Saana hissed.

"Perhaps." Daimon sighed. "But it is what it is. There are men and women in the town now who were trying to kill us today, yet you are confident their honour will hold them to do us no harm."

"It is true," Saana said instantly. "Even the Clanless would not do such a thing."

"And this is how it must be for us," Daimon told her. "This holds your husband. If he tries to escape it, he will still only die, and probably bring down death and ruin on you, and his brother, and anyone who tried to help him."

He looked past the High Marshal to where Darel sat at Brightwater's right hand, as befitted a thane hosting an honoured guest. Darel didn't look much better than Daimon felt, but he was eating with a sort of nervous energy, and his hands shook as he took a draught from his cup. He was also very definitely not looking at Kaldur Brightwater.

He's up to something. Daimon's stomach tightened even further. Darel had almost been late to his place at the table: if not late enough to be an insult to the High Marshal, then certainly pushing it close. Daimon didn't know what he'd been doing, either, although he'd come from within the castle. He closed his eyes and prayed to Nari. *Please do not let Darel do anything stupid. Please do not let Darel do anything stupid...*

There was the scrape of wooden stool legs on the stone floor as Marshal Brightwater rose to his feet, and conversation quickly died away. Daimon opened his eyes and sat straight, his hands in his lap, staring ahead.

"This has been a strange day," Marshal Brightwater began. "Some of those people whom we thought of as no more than mindless savages have landed on our shores, and proved themselves to be worthy of our trust. The people of Black Keep, who along with many of our southern towns have long suffered at the hands of these Raiders, saw a way forward. This marshal raises his cup to the people of Black Keep."

He suited actions to words and drank, and all those assembled mirrored him: even the Brown Eagle clan, although they looked to have worked it out by seeing what the Naridans did.

"This has been a sad day," the High Marshal continued. "Others came here today, bringing bloodshed and death. However, even though they claimed lives, they were thrown back by the bravery of those assembled against them. This marshal raises his cup to all those who fought these Raiders today, no matter from where they came." He turned in a half-circle, taking in the whole yard, making no distinction between his own men, the Naridans of Black Keep, and the Brown Eagle clan. Daimon's breath caught in his throat. He'd never imagined such a gesture.

The High Marshal drank, and so did everyone else.

"Finally," Brightwater said, "this marshal has heard a tale of heroism. Of young folk who took up weapons and ran into battle to aid their elders." He turned to look past Daimon, past Saana, to where Zhanna sat. "In fact, this marshal has heard that the leader of the Raiders who attacked today was slain by none other than the girl sitting to this marshal's left. This marshal raises his cup to all those young warriors, including her."

Everyone drank. Zhanna tilted her head back to finish her drink and slammed her cup back down again, looking somewhat shocked.

"Were you expecting that?" Saana muttered to Daimon.

"No, your husband was not," Daimon murmured in return. Beyond Darel, he could see Thane Odem, who looked just as displeased now as he had earlier. Daimon stared hard at the man, trying to imprint Odem's expression on his memory. If he had to die, then he'd take some small pleasure in the fact that Odem Darkspur had been monumentally pissed off this day.

"Now, however, this marshal faces a solemn duty that he cannot ignore," Brightwater said, with what sounded like genuine remorse. "Daimon Blackcreek slew his father, and therefore he must be executed. Lord Daimon was instrumental not only in ensuring the harmony between Black Keep and its new denizens, but also in the defence of the town today, so this marshal takes no pleasure in this act. However, the law of the land is clear: the kinslayer is accursed."

The Southern Marshal turned to Daimon, looking down at him. "Daimon Blackcreek, this marshal allowed you to assist in the immediate matters of this town, but he can grant no more clemency. As accursed, you may not take your own life: to do so only invites greater shame. Take comfort, if you can, in the fact that your work here will endure beyond you." He paused, and lowered his voice somewhat. "And also that this marshal's blade is sharp, and that when he has had to fulfil this duty, he has never required more than one stroke."

Daimon took a breath to reply.

"*High Marshal!*"

It was Darel's voice. Daimon looked over to see his law-brother had risen to his feet, in defiance of all protocol. Several of Brightwater's sars rose as well, as if to restrain Darel, and angry mutterings swept through the High Marshal's men.

"Show respect, Blackcreek!" Brightwater barked, turning towards him. "And do not let filial affection blind you to the reality of the situation!"

"High Marshal, your servant intends no disrespect, and he does not question your knowledge of the law," Darel said quickly, dropping back onto his stool. "He merely believes you are not in possession of all pertinent facts!"

Brightwater's brows lowered, but he paused. "Indeed?"

"High Marshal, you are aware Daimon was adopted by your servant's father, Asrel Blackcreek," Darel said.

"Yes."

"Prior to the duel commencing," Darel continued, shooting Daimon a quick glance, "your servant's father stated clearly to Daimon, in the presence of a number of witnesses including his heir presumptive, and a priest of Nari, that he unnamed Daimon and cast him out of the House of Blackcreek."

Brightwater looked over his shoulder at Daimon. "Is that so?"

It was indeed so, and Daimon's heart twisted again at the reminder of the rage and disdain in his father's face. Why would Darel bring this up now? Did his brother truly intend to shame him even more than he already was, before his head was struck off?

"Your servant checked through the castle's library before this meal," Darel said, his voice loud enough to carry across the yard. "What he found in the documents of law we possess appears to corroborate his initial belief. Should your servant's father have wished to disown his blood-son, he could only have done so by means of a signed, witnessed proclamation. However, unless a change has been made of which your servant is unaware, a law-son may be disowned by means of a simple statement to that effect in the presence of appropriate witnesses."

Daimon froze. He didn't even dare breathe, in case he should somehow dishonour himself in some further manner that would make his death inevitable. He could see where Darel was going with this now.

"If Daimon was no longer a member of the Blackcreek family prior to the honour duel commencing," Darel continued, his voice shaking with nerves but still strong enough to be heard, "then, High Marshal, he did not slay his own father, and therefore cannot be a kinslayer."

A low bubble of conversation welled up, but Brightwater knocked his cup on the table twice, and it died back down immediately.

"Priest!" Brightwater barked. "This marshal has seen you at this meal! Where are you?"

Aftak rose from his place on the commoner's benches, where he had sat in deference to the amount of lords and sars who needed seating on the high table. "Here, High Marshal."

"You were present during this exchange?" Brightwater demanded.

"This priest was, High Marshal."

"And Lord Asrel uttered the words Lord Darel has just described?"

Daimon saw Aftak's mouth curl into a sly smile. "He did indeed, High Marshal."

A new swell of muttering filled the yard, louder than before, but Brightwater once again banged his cup on the table. "There will be quiet! Quiet!" As the noise died down, Daimon caught a glimpse of the brown-and-gold of Darkspur in motion beyond Darel.

"Thane Odem," Brightwater said, his tone neutral. "You have something you wish to add?"

"High Marshal, that priest is a man of Blackcreek," Thane Odem began. "His loyalty is—"

"This priest's loyalty is to Nari, and Nari alone!" Aftak roared, drowning out not only Odem but also the ugly grumbling that had arisen from the men around him. "What kind of lickspittle priests do you have at Darkspur, for you to suggest such a thing?!"

"*Quiet!*" Brightwater bellowed, as three of Odem's sars rose in the places to begin shouting angrily at Aftak. "The thane of Darkspur's suggestion that a priest of Nari would lie in the service of his lord is not only an affront to the honour of the priest, but it borders on offending the God-King Himself!"

Everyone from Darkspur immediately sat down, and Daimon had to bite down on his lip not to smile.

"Or so this marshal would suspect," Brightwater added, more calmly. "He would not, of course, wish to interfere in theological matters."

"This priest does not think Nari needs to concern Himself with such yammerings," Aftak said darkly, glowering at Thane Odem from beneath his bushy brows. "This priest has spoken the truth to you, High Marshal: Lord Asrel spoke as Lord Darel claims."

"Thank you, priest," Brightwater said, as Aftak sat. "In that case, bearing in mind this new information, the law is once again clear." He removed his hand from the grip of his longblade.

"Sar Daimon is no longer of the House of Blackcreek, as of the moment of Lord Asrel's statement. As a result, he is no kinslayer: he was merely defending his unarmed wife from harm, as a sar would be expected to do."

Brightwater turned his head to look at Daimon, and Daimon was sure that he didn't imagine the slight look of satisfaction and possibly even relief on the Southern Marshal's face.

"This marshal can see no evidence that a crime has been committed. Sar Daimon lives without shame, and no execution is required."

A great cheer went up from the yard as Brightwater retook his seat; or at least those parts of it where Black Keep folk were sat. Daimon heard Saana and Zhanna whooping beside him, and the rest of the Brown Eagles joined in as Nalon hastily translated what had just occurred, but Daimon himself could barely muster the ability to continue sitting up straight, let alone shout or throw his hands in the air. In fact—

Strong arms closed around his neck and nearly dragged him off his stool, and it took him a moment to realise that they belonged to his wife.

"What are you doing?" he spluttered, trying to maintain some sort of balance and dignity.

"You not dying is good!" Saana laughed into his ear. "Your wife can hug you!"

"This is—" Daimon began, then broke off as Darel appeared from behind Marshal Brightwater. "You!"

"You are welcome," Darel said with a chuckle, and stooped to also throw his arms around Daimon's neck.

"It is not that your brother is not grateful," Daimon managed, hugging him in return. "But you could have told him earlier!"

"In all truth, your brother did not know for certain that it would work," Darel said softly, so low that only Daimon could hear him. "The High Marshal might have seen it differently, or the law could have changed. Your brother thought it best not to offer what could turn out to be false hope, save at the last moment. And he also wanted the statement to be made in front of as many witnesses as possible," he added, dropping his voice even further until it was barely a whisper.

Daimon looked over Darel's shoulder to where a fuming Odem Darkspur sat. The man had basically called for Daimon's death, albeit via questioning Aftak's testimony. Daimon didn't know if the man's enmity for him was a holdover from Odem's dispute with Lord Asrel, if it stemmed from a disgust at the notion of allying with or marrying the Tjakorshi, or something else entirely. Nor, in fairness, did Daimon particularly care.

"A good plan, brother," he replied. "It would not do for someone to claim he had no knowledge of the judgement." His mind caught up with his words, and he stiffened. "That is, lord. Not brother."

"Daimon," Darel said chidingly. "We are still brothers."

"We *cannot* be brothers," Daimon protested, although the words felt like they tore him apart as they left him. He'd been a Blackcreek for almost as long as he could remember, and the relief at his life being saved by Darel's quick thinking was somewhat numbed by the shock of losing his family in a different way. "You just saved this sar's life by pointing out how we are not brothers."

"Well, *this lord* has another plan," Darel said to him with a wink, then straightened. "High Marshal?"

"Lord Blackcreek? You have a question, now you have finished your…" Brightwater eyed Darel and Daimon somewhat disapprovingly. "Your display of affection?"

"Yes, High Marshal," Darel said, composing himself and bowing. "Your servant wishes to know, for the avoidance of doubt, whether you will be officially confirming him as the new Thane of Blackcreek."

Brightwater steepled his fingers. "This marshal can see no reason why that should not occur. Henceforth you are Darel, Thane of Blackcreek, with all the lands and duties that accompany it."

"Your servant is eternally grateful for your judgement," Darel replied, with another bow. "And he asks leave to beg a boon of you.

Brightwater raised his eyebrows. "Ask."

"Would you, as a Hand of Heaven and High Marshal of the South, give witness to your servant the Thane of Blackcreek's statement, that he wishes Sar Daimon to become his law-brother, with immediate effect?"

Daimon's insides screwed up, and he felt Saana tense on his shoulder.

"Lord Blackcreek, you have just cited legal precedent for why this man is no longer your law-brother," Marshal Brightwater pointed out mildly. "Now you wish to reverse this?"

"Yes, lord," Darel said, his voice clear and true. "Your presence excepted, Sar Daimon is the wisest man your servant has met. For all the love your servant bore his father, Lord Asrel's decision to disown Sar Daimon was one of several decisions he made in recent days that were motivated more by pride than by honour or wisdom. Your servant seeks to rectify this."

Brightwater's eyes flickered from Darel to rest on Daimon, and Daimon felt the weight of his scrutiny. Then the High Marshal returned his gaze to Darel, and pursed his lips.

"You have been confirmed as the Thane of Blackcreek, Lord Darel. Your household is your own business. Consider your statement witnessed."

Darel's face was a picture of relief. "Thank you, lord."

Brightwater nodded and made as if to turn back to his meal, then paused and moved around on his stool until he was facing them properly. His expression darkened, and the flood of relief and joy that had washed through Daimon was abruptly stemmed. What had the High Marshal just remembered that would nullify Darel's request?

"Blackcreek... this marshal knows that news sometimes struggles to find its way this far south. Have you heard the rumours?"

Darel looked blank. "Lord, your servant was imprisoned in his own stronghouse until today." He glanced at Daimon. "Do you know of what the High Marshal speaks?"

Daimon shook his head, perplexed. "Lord, we have seen no travellers since before the turn of the year. What rumours are these?"

Kaldur Brightwater, for a wonder, looked momentarily uncertain. He glanced about them, as though to check no one was too close, then leaned in a fraction and lowered his voice.

"They say Nari Himself has been reborn, in the north."

Daimon felt his mouth sag open, saw his expression mirrored on Darel's face. Saana simply looked confused, and he couldn't blame her.

"We do not know if it is true, of course," Brightwater admitted. "The Divine Rebirth was foretold, but to think of it happening in our lifetimes…" He shook his head slightly, perhaps not even aware of what he was doing.

"The wild dragons have been bolder this year," Daimon said uneasily, glancing at his brother.

"At least the sun hasn't disappeared!" Darel said, with what had to be forced cheerfulness.

"Yes it has," Saana cut in. "It disappears every year at Long Night!" All three Naridans looked at her, and she frowned in confusion. "Long Night does not happen here?"

"Whatever the truth," the High Marshal said after a moment, "discord may be inevitable. We must be strong, unified in purpose. This lord had to come and attend to the south of his realm to make sure there was no canker here that could spread if his attention is drawn northwards, as he feels it will be.

"The day may come when we need all our blades to stand as one. A second Splintering could destroy Narida, or leave it open for our enemies to divide up as they see fit. The thanedom of Blackcreek must be true. This marshal wants you to come to Idramar with him, Lord Darel."

"Your—your servant?" Darel stammered, his hand flying to his mouth. "To Idramar?"

"The world is changing," Brightwater said, and Daimon saw his eyes lingering on Saana. "Change frightens some. This marshal's word is law, but only so long as he is not overruled by the God-King. You should come to Idramar to present your case, to speak of the benefits of this new alliance, so that your succession can be ratified by the highest authority. That way, there can be no unpleasant repercussions that might divide the south."

"Your servant is honoured," Darel said in a small voice. Daimon knew that was true: Darel had always wanted to visit Idramar, although he'd never thought he'd get the opportunity. "But should he not be attending to his people?"

"This marshal was under the impression you had just re-adopted your brother," Brightwater replied sharply. "Can he not manage affairs while you are away?"

"Your servant would be happy to," Daimon broke in. It was a lie—what he wanted more than anything else in the world was firstly to sleep, and secondly to hand the running of Black Keep over to Darel—but he couldn't let Darel talk himself out of the High Marshal's good graces.

"Then it is settled," Brightwater said. "We shall depart at the earliest convenience."

"Of course, lord," Darel replied. "Might your servant be excused, to speak with his brother and law-sister?"

"You may," Brightwater said with a wave of his hand. This time he did turn back to his food, and Darel hastily backed away from the table towards the blocky shape of the guardhouse. Daimon rose and followed him, as did Saana. Zhanna, it seemed, was more interested in the remains of her meal.

As soon as Darel stopped moving Daimon enveloped him in another hug, his vision blurring with tears for the second time that day.

"Darel... you are the kindest and cleverest man your brother has ever known. He thanks you, with all his heart."

Darel smiled at him and Saana; an honest, genuine smile of pleasure. Daimon realised how much he'd missed that expression on his brother's face, even just in the last two weeks.

"Brother... law-sister... You saw past old enmities. You saw hope instead of conflict. The High Marshal is correct: the world has changed. *You* changed it."

His smile widened, and took on the faintest hint of mischief.

"However, if you think your brother is going to let you get away with standing back and leaving him to deal with the aftermath alone, you are *sorely* mistaken..."

EPILOGUE

KULLOJAN SAKTSESZHIN STOOD and sweated.

The Witchhouse was thick with the scent of woodsmoke, and thicker still with the heat from The Golden's fires, but no one complained. No one dared. They stood, awkwardly and uncomfortably, while the master of all Tjakorsha sat and stared unblinking into the flames. Kullojan couldn't say for sure how long he'd stood here, with other captains and those who had once been chiefs, but it was long enough that he'd had to surreptitiously shift his weight several times. No one wanted to move too obviously, though. No one wanted to risk breaking the draug's concentration.

The consequences for that were likely to be... unpleasant.

"There."

The Golden spoke, reaching two fingers out into the flames, seeming not to feel their heat. "There, do you see?"

The assembled captains shook their heads, Kullojan amongst them, with murmurs of "No, master." The draug drew its hand back again, and tapped one finger against its body's lips.

"Fireheart has failed me."

Kullojan glanced sideways as his fellows. It was true that no ships had returned from the Flatlands, as the Snowbeard had called them, but from what the old man had said about the distances involved, that wasn't surprising. Fireheart couldn't have long made landfall, if he'd even reached it at all. But The Golden read the world in the flames of its fires, and it had never been wrong yet. Usually it had predicted its own victory over its next enemy, and although the outcome had sometimes appeared uncertain—Kullojan eyed the thick rope scar around The Golden's neck—it had always been correct in the end.

If the flames told The Golden that Fireheart had failed, then Kullojan wasn't going to doubt it.

"No matter," The Golden continued, getting to its feet. "The world has changed since he left. Sattistutar's belt is no longer important."

Kullojan frowned in confusion, but it was Kashallo Merngustutar who spoke up. "Master? Do you not need the belt to show that your rule is complete?" She pointed to where the belts of the other chiefs had been hung from the rafters; gently swaying straps of long-dead skin and old metal in which the faith of the Tjakorshi had once been placed.

"I did not break the clans in order to rule you!" The Golden snapped, rising to its feet with an unworldly smoothness and fluidity. The assembled captains deliberately didn't take a step backwards, but Kullojan knew he wasn't the only one who'd wanted to.

"I broke the clans in order to *save* you," The Golden continued, its pale eyes sweeping up and down their line. "Do none of you understand that?"

Kullojan mumbled "No, master," along with the others. The Golden didn't like those who stayed quiet in an effort to avoid censure.

"The world is changing," The Golden said, looking up at the Witchhouse's roof as thought it could see beyond it to the stars above. Perhaps it could: Kullojan wouldn't have wagered against it. "The spirits will wake, and they will bring fire, and death, and darkness, and everything you know will be shattered. But we will escape."

It looked back at them again, the reflection of flames dancing in its mask of gilt-chased steel.

"We will give ourselves to the Dark Father, and his embrace will save us. Sattistutar may have been wiser than she knew. Give the order. Fell whatever trees are needed. Build ships, and weave sails."

"How many, master?" Kullojan asked, stunned.

"Enough to carry us all," The Golden told him, fixing him with that unblinking pale stare. "Enough to carry us *all*, Kullojan. Tjakorsha sails.

"Let the world tremble.'

ACKNOWLEDGEMENTS

In 2016 MY country held a referendum, and took a decision that made me angry enough to start writing the fantasy novel that I had not until that point dared to start writing, in case I messed up all the ideas that had been kicking around in my brain for twenty-odd years. Writing about how it is actually possible to find common ground with those different to you became more important to me than whether or not I was "ready" as a writer to tackle epic fantasy, so that's one small positive I can take. I guess only time will tell if there will be any others.

However, anger in itself is not enough to will a novel into being. First of all, I must pay tribute to my agent Rob Dinsdale, who took my story that perhaps wanders a little from the median line of fantasy, and is certainly a departure from the pulpy, no-frills, grimy space operas I was writing previously, and presented it to publishers with every assurance that I could follow through on this. And I need to give thanks to Jenni and her team at Orbit, and Michael and his team at Solaris, for deciding that this was something they were interested in, and for all the support that's come along with that.

I also need to thank those who read the manuscript at various stages and gave me their feedback on it. Jamie, Jeannette, Anna, Stewart, and those who have asked not to be named, but know who they are; your input was truly valued. Big thanks go out to Nye Redman-White, who helped me try to get some sort of unified feel to the names and words used in each culture, and to differentiate them from each other: any remaining irregularities can most certainly be laid at my door. Huge thanks to Gareth, who when I was bemoaning on Facebook the clumsiness of my attempts to denote gender in Alaba said "Why don't you use diacritics?", and thereby made those parts of the novel eminently more readable in one stroke. And thanks to Carrie, for being host and guide for a trip to the Royal Armouries in Leeds when I decided I needed to know more details about how different cultures have tried to kill each other with pointy things, and avoid being killed by said pointy things.

There are undoubtedly many other people I should thank, the details of which have been lost in the blur of time that this novel has taken: far longer than anything else I've written – given it was mainly written in the edges and spare time around other projects, which themselves were being done in the time I wasn't at work – and has been through various rewrites and restructurings. If you should have been thanked here and haven't been, then please consider yourself thanked, and my apologies for my poor memory. I'd also like to extend my gratitude to the "community" of SFF authors and fans, particularly those at conventions, who have made "being an author" in the social sense so much fun. And of course, I'd like to thank everyone who's bought my books: it means a lot (and not just 7.5% of the sale price).

Finally, I need to thank my wife Janine, for sharing with me a life so stable and contented that I have plenty of time and energy for creativity, and for her part in making and keeping it that way.

ABOUT THE AUTHOR

MIKE BROOKS IS the author of The God-King Chronicles epic fantasy series, the Keiko series of grimy space-opera novels, and various works for Games Workshop's Black Library imprint including RITES OF PASSAGE and BRUTAL KUNNIN. He was born in Ipswich, Suffolk, and moved to Nottingham to go to university when he was eighteen, where he still lives with his wife, cats, and snakes. He worked in the homelessness sector for fifteen years before going full-time as an author, plays guitar and sings in a punk band, and DJs wherever anyone will tolerate him. He is queer, and partially deaf (no, that occurred naturally, and a long time before the punk band).